Praise for DREAMING THE EAGLE
The First in a Four-Part Series

"A powerful novel, alive with the love, deceit, wisdom
and the heroics of humanity." ~Jean Auel

"A massively impressive first volume . . . It looks as
if we will have a new [series] to rival *The Lord of the Rings*
in its appeal." ~*Scotland on Sunday*

"A staggeringly imaginative invocation of Britain's secret
history. Manda Scott has created a fictional universe all
her own, but close enough to our reality for it both to
warm and break our hearts. Breathtakingly good, it
reveals the best and worst in all of us."
~Val McDermid

DREAMING THE EAGLE

Manda Scott

Seal Books

Seal Books and colophon are trademarks of
Random House of Canada Limited.

DREAMING THE EAGLE
Seal Books/published by arrangement with Alfred A. Knopf Canada
Alfred A. Knopf Canada edition published 2003
Seal Books edition published March 2004

ISBN 0-7704-2926-2

All the characters in this book are fictitious, and any resemblance
to actual persons, living or dead, is purely coincidental.

Seal Books are published by Random House of Canada Limited.
"Seal Books" and the portrayal of a seal are the property of
Random House of Canada Limited.

Visit Random House of Canada Limited's website:
www.randomhouse.ca

PRINTED AND BOUND IN THE USA

OPM   10   9   8   7   6   5   4   3   2   1

FOR
ROBIN AND ELAINE
WITH LOVE

ACKNOWLEDGEMENTS

Any work of this nature requires an extraordinary amount of background material. I would like to thank the following for their expert advice and assistance: Dr. Gilly Carr, Dr. Jon Coe, Philip Crummy, Dr. J. D. Hill, Professor Lawrence Keppie and Owen Thompson, all of whom gave freely of their time and expertise, and those members of the Brit-arch Internet mailing list who so often supplied answers to mundane questions. Most especial thanks to H. J. P. ("Douglas") Arnold, astronomer and formerly Primus Pilus in the Legio Secunda Augusta re-enactment group, who provided continual support and invaluable comments throughout. As is always the case, any technical faults are entirely mine, as is the interpretation of the facts supplied.

Thanks also to Jane Judd, my agent, and Selina Walker at Transworld for having faith from the beginning and to Kate Miciak and Nita Taublib at Bantam U. S. for their support and enthusiasm.

Particular thanks to Leo, who introduced me to the dreaming, and to Carol, Hillary, Eliot and Ken, amongst others, who showed me how to live it.

CHARACTER LIST

THE ECENI

The Eceni: a confederacy of Iron Age tribes inhabiting what is now east Anglia in southeast England. A largely agrarian community, they are famed as horsebreeders and as workers of precious metals. Ferociously anti-Roman.

Key Individuals: Eceni

Airmid of Nemain: Dreamer of the Eceni, later of Mona; friend and companion to Breaca
Bán: Breaca's half-brother; hare hunter and dreamer of the horse, son to Macha and Eburovic
Breaca: Eceni warrior, dreamer of the serpent-spear
Camma: Daughter of Sinochos, sister to Nemma
Dubornos: Son to Sinochos; a warrior
Eburovic: Breaca's father; warrior and smith of the Eceni
Efnís: Dreamer of the northern Eceni
Elder grandmother: First in rank of the elders, cared for by Airmid and then Breaca
Graine: Breaca's mother; hereditary leader of the Eceni
Hail: Bán's hound
Macha: Graine's sister; dreamer of the wren, mother to Bán
Nemma: Daughter of Sinochos, elder sister to Camma
Sinochos: Eceni hunter
Silla: Bán's younger sister by Eburovic out of Macha
'Tagos: Eceni warrior

ELDERS, DREAMERS AND WARRIORS OF
MONA (ANGLESEY)

Mona, known today as Anglesey, is the sacred island where selected dreamers and warriors from all tribes (including Eceni, Caledonii, Cornovii, Brigante, Silures and Votadini) are sent for training under the foremost dreamers in a tradition going back centuries, if not millennia. The dreamers' training takes up to twelve years, warriors somewhat less. Once trained, the apprentices return to their tribes to bring the teaching to their people.

Key Individuals: Inhabitants of Mona

Ardacos: A warrior of the Caledonii
Braint: A warrior of the northern Brigantes
Gwyddhien: A warrior of the Silures
Luain mac Calma: A singer, healer and dreamer of the elder
    council of Mona, originally from Hibernia (Ireland)
Maroc: Dreamer and elder of Mona
Talla: A warrior; the Elder of elders, first in rank
Venutios: The Warrior of Mona; leader of all Mona's
    warriors, chosen by the gods

TRINOVANTES

The Trinovante were originally led by Cunobelin, Hound of the Sun, war leader both of this tribe and the Catuvellauni. He is a warrior and diplomat and holds the sworn oath of more warriors than any other leader south of the Brigantes.

He controls the rich ports of the Thames and thus controls a large part of the trade with Rome. He keeps a difficult balance, maintaining diplomatic relationships with Rome while not offending the anti-Roman tribes, particularly his northern neighbours, the Eceni. Of Cunobelin's three sons, only Amminios (cf) is loyal to Rome.

Key Individuals: Trinovantes

Amminios: Second son of Cunobelin; born to a Gaulish woman; a friend to Rome

Caradoc: The third son of Cunobelin; born to Ellin, war leader of the Ordovices; Caradoc is an ally of the Eceni and the only warrior ever to have passed the warrior's tests of three separate tribes; ferociously anti-Roman

Cerin: The only true dreamer of the Trinovantes

Cunobelin: Of the line of Cassivellaunos; known as the Sun Hound; leader of the Trinovantes and the Catuvellauni

Cunomar: Son to Togodubnos

Heffydd: Son of Eynd, false dreamer kept by Cunobelin to pass his laws to the people

Iccius: Originally of the Belgae, now slave to Amminios

Mandubracios: Legendary traitor, a Trinovantian who betrayed Cassivellaunos to the legions of Julius Caesar during the first Roman invasion

Odras: Cunomar's mother, lover to Togodubnos

Togodubnos: The eldest of Cunobelin's sons; born to a woman of the royal line of the Trinovantes and hereditary heir to that tribe; a diplomat, his instincts are to tread the same path as his father, that of appeasement of both sides

Other Key Individuals: Various Tribes

Arosted: A trader from Dobunni

Beduoc of the Dobunni: Uncertain ally of the eastern alliance (Eceni, Trinovantes, Catuvellauni) led by Togodubnos and Caradoc in the wake of their father's death

Berikos: Leader of the Atrebates, enemy of Cunobelin and ally to Rome

Cassivellaunos: Past leader of the Catuvellauni, now dead

Cwmfen: A warrior of the Ordovices, mother of Caradoc's first child

Cygfa: Daughter to Caradoc and Cwmfen

Gunovic: Trader and traveling smith; also a warrior and horse racer; later becomes a member of the Eceni

FURTHER TRIBES

The Brigantes: Northern tribe based in the area that is now the north and east of England, either side of the Pennines; led by Cartimandua, ally to Rome

The Cantiaci: Based in Kent, focus of one wave of the Roman landings

The Catuvellauni: United with the Trinovantes under Cunobelin's leadership

The Dobunni: Southern tribe, south of the Thames, led by Beduoc, uncertain allies of the eastern confederacy

The Ordovices: The Ordovices occupy the land that is currently north Wales and that led to the sacred isle of Mona. Of all the tribes, they are bound closest to the

dreamers. After his mother's death, Caradoc is accepted
as their leader.

The Silures: Southern neighbours to the Ordovices, once
their sworn enemies but united in alliance against Rome

THE ROMANS

The events described in *Dreaming the Eagle* span the reigns of
three Roman emperors: Tiberius, Gaius (Caligula) and
Claudius. Tiberius had no interest in expansion of the
Empire and made no effort towards invasion. Caligula
instigated the buildup to the invasion of Britannia but was
assassinated before he could complete his task. Claudius
oversaw the final act of invasion and the subsequent
destruction of the Iron Age tribes.

Key Individuals: Gauls and Romans

Braxus: Overseer to Amminios' slaves in Gaul
Civilis: A native Batavian; member of Caesar's army
Claudius: Successor to Caligula; emperor from 41–54 AD
Corvus: A Roman officer rescued by the Eceni in a ship-
wreck; friend to Bán
Gaius Caesar (Caligula): Emperor of Rome: 37–41 AD
Lucius Sulpicius Galba: Governor of Germany
Milo: Roman slave and Amminios' stud manager
Theophilus: Greek physician, originally in Caligula's train,
later to the army on the Rhine
Tiberius Caesar: Emperor of Rome: 14–37 AD

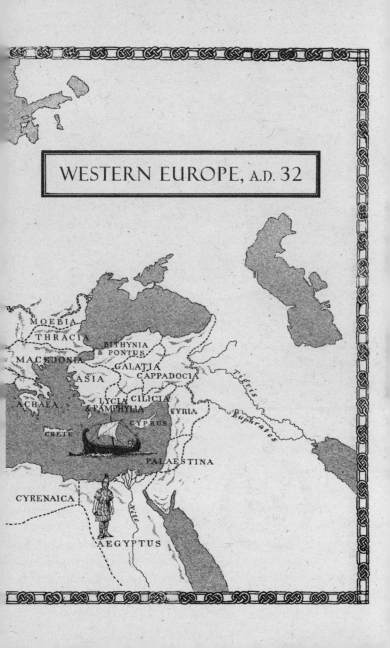

WESTERN EUROPE, A.D. 32

MOEBIA
THRACIA
BITHYNIA
& PONTUS
MACEDONIA
GALATIA
ASIA
CAPPADOCIA
ACHAEA
LYCIA CILICIA
& PAMPHYLIA
SYRIA
CYPRUS
CRETE
Tigris
Euphrates
PALAESTINA
CYRENAICA
Nile
AEGYPTUS

PROLOGUE

The attack came in the hour before dawn. The girl woke to the stench of burning thatch and the sound of her mother screaming. Outside, in the clearing beyond the hut, she heard her father's response, and the clash of iron on bronze. Another man shouted—not her father—and she was up, throwing off the hides, reaching back into the dark behind the sleeping place for her skinning knife or, better, her axe. She found neither. Her mother screamed again, differently. The girl scrabbled frantically, feeling the fire scorch her skin and the sliding ache of fear that was the threat of a sword-cut to the spine. Her fingers closed on a haft of worn wood, running down to the curve of a grip she knew from hours of oil and polish and the awe of youth; her father's boar spear. She jerked it free, turning and pulling the leather cover from the blade in one move. A wash of predawn light hit her eyes as the door-skin was ripped from its hangings and replaced as rapidly by a shadow. The bulk of a body filled the doorway. Dawn light flickered on a sword-blade. Close by, her father screamed her name. *"Breaca!"*

She heard him and stepped out of the dark. The warrior

in the doorway grinned, showing few teeth, and lunged forward. His blade caught the sunlight and twisted it, blinding them both. Without thinking, she did as she had practised, in her mind, in the safety of the lower horse paddocks, and once in the forest beyond. She lunged in return, putting the weight of her shoulders, the twist of her back and the straightening kick of both legs into the thrust of the weapon. She aimed for the one pale segment of skin she could see. The spear-blade bit and sank into the notch of his throat at the place where the tunic stopped and the helmet had not yet begun. Blood sluiced brightly downwards. The man choked and stopped. The sword that sought her life came slicing on, carried by the speed of his lunge. She wrenched sideways, too slowly, and felt the sting of it carve between her fingers. She let go of the spear. The man toppled over, angled away from her by the weight of the haft. The doorway brightened and darkened again. Her father was there.

"Breaca? Gods, Breaca—" He, too, stopped. The man on the floor pushed a hand beneath his side and tried to rise. Her father's hammer sang down and stopped him, for ever. He brought his arms up and round her, holding her close, smoothing her cheek, running his big, broad smith's fingers through her hair. "You killed him? My warrior, my best girl. You killed him. Gods, that was good. I could not bear to lose you both—"

He was rocking her back and forth, as he had when she was a small child. He smelled of blood and stomach acid. She pushed her arms down his front to make sure that he was whole and found that he was. She tried to squirm free, to look at the rest of him. He leaned in closer and his breathing changed and she felt wet warmth slide down her neck to the wing of her shoulder and from there down the flat plane of her chest. She let him hold her then, while he wept, and didn't ask him why her mother had not come in with him to find her. Her mother, who carried his child.

The stomach acid was her mother's. She lay near the doorway and she, too, carried a spear in her hand. She had used it once to good effect but they had been two against her one and the child she carried within had slowed her turn. The slice of the blade had opened her from chest-bone to hips, spilling out all that had been inside. Breaca crouched down beside her. The tentative light of the new day brought colour where before there had been none. She reached down to the small, crinkled thing lying at her mother's side and turned it over. Her father was behind her. "It would have been a boy," she said.

"I know." He let his hand rest on her shoulder. His fingers were still. His weeping had stopped. He knelt down and hugged her, fiercely. His chin pressed on her head and the burr of his voice rocked through her neck to her chest as he spoke. "What need have I of another son when I have a daughter who can face an armed warrior and live?"

His voice was warm and there was pride in the wretched grief and she had not the strength to tell him that she had acted out of instinct, not courage or a warrior's heart.

Her mother had been leader of the Eceni, firstborn of the royal line, and she was honoured in death as she had been in life. Her body was bound in fine linen and hides, closing the child back into her abdomen. A platform was built of hazel and elm and the body raised onto it, lifting her closer to the gods and out of reach of wolf and bear. The three dead warriors of the Coritani, who had broken the laws of the gods in killing a woman in childbirth, and of the elders in killing the leader of a neighbouring tribe without fair battle, were stripped and dragged to the forest to feed whatever found them first. Breaca was given the sword from the one she had killed. She didn't want it. She gave it to her father, who broke it across his forging block and said he would make her a better one, full sized, for when she was grown. In its stead, Airmid, one of the older girls, gave her a crow's feather with the quill dyed red and bound round with blue horsehair, the mark of a kill. Her father showed her how to braid her hair at the sides, as the warriors do for battle, with the feather hanging free at her temple.

In the late morning, Eburovic, warrior and smith of the Eceni, took his daughter to the river to wash her clean of the blood of battle and bind the cut on her hand and then walked her back to the roundhouse to the care of Macha, her mother's sister, the mother of Bán, his first and only living son.

I

SPRING–AUTUMN A.D. 33

CHAPTER 1

Bán had the dream for the first time when he was eight years old, in the spring after Breaca lost her mother and got a sword-cut on her hand. He woke suddenly and lay sweating under the hides, his eyes searching the dark of the roof space for comfort. A long time ago, when he was younger and afraid of the night, his father had carved the marks of horse, bear and wren on the crooked beam above his bed to keep him safe. He had spent light summer evenings tracing them in his mind, feeling the wall of their protection. Now he lay in the pressing silence, praying for light, and saw nothing. If the moon had risen, it did not shine on his side of the roundhouse. If there were stars, their light did not penetrate the thatch. Inside, the cooling embers of the fire gave off a thread of smoke but no flame. It was the blackest night he could ever remember and he might as well have been blind, or still dreaming.

He did not want to be dreaming. Blinking, he searched for other ways to anchor himself in the world of the living. Light, dry smoke tickled his nose. Each night his mother laid a tent of twigs on the embers, that the smoke of their burning might carry her family safely through the world beyond sleep. With age, he was beginning to understand the language of the smoke. He breathed in and let the different tones filter through his head, sorting them into an order that would speak to him: the acerbic touch of sun-scorched grass, the warmer, more sinuous thread of acorns roasting, the pricking of wet shale and the high, clear note of tannin, as from a hide, freshly cured. It was this last one that fixed it. An image came of a girl lying asleep under a scattering of white petals and, later, of a tree dripping red with berries the colour of dried blood that he had been told not to eat. *Hawthorn.* It would have been that.

He made his body relax. He was calmer now. His heart beat less hard. He closed his eyes and let the drifting smoke carry him back to the start of the dream. In the other world it was daytime. He was riding a strange horse, not one of his father's; a red mare with a hide the colour of a fox in winter. She was tall and very fit. He ran his hand down the length of her neck and her coat sparked like a new coin beneath his fingers. They were running fast, at dream-speed. He was naked and the mare had no saddlecloth. He could feel the bunch of her muscles gather and pull beneath his thighs. If he worked to let go of this world, he could see the steam billow back from her nostrils and hear the whistle of her breath over the splashing hammer of hooves on turf and bog. In a while, she passed out of the sunlight and entered a mist so thick he could barely see the tips of her ears. The fog swirled in banners past his eyes, making him blind. He sucked in a breath and smelled horse-sweat and stale bog-water and the mint-sour tang of myrtle crushed underfoot. Without any good reason, he lifted one hand and cupped it round his mouth and yelled a word—a name—into the dizzying white. His voice came out harshly, like a raven's, and the name itself made no shape in his head. It echoed and came back to him and still made no sense. He let it go and leaned forward instead, singing to the red mare, urging her on, promising her fame and long life and strong foals if she carried them both safely through the danger. There was certainly danger, both of them felt it; a distant malevolence kept at bay only by their speed. The mare flicked her ears back to listen and then cocked them suddenly forward. The boy felt a change in her stride and looked up. Ahead of him, a fallen yew blocked the path. The mare gathered herself and tucked her head in, shortening her stride. He wrapped the fingers of both hands tight in the snaking red of her mane, feeling the coarse cut of the hair on his palms, She jumped cleanly and he soared with her into eternity. The ground was firm on the far side. The mare stretched her forelegs to land. The boy relaxed his grip on the mane and sat upright and this time, the first time, he lost himself in the fierce joy of it, exulting in the stories he would tell Breaca and their father and later, when he had it right, his mother.

The world changed as they landed. The fog vanished and it was dusk, not daylight, and he was no longer a boy riding a mare, but a man, an armed warrior, lying flat to the neck of a war-horse compared to which the mare was a small and stringy pony. The beast was in battle fever, running its heart out, churning up clods and stones in its wake. The hammer of its passing shook the earth and ripped the trees from their roots. Bán swept a hand forward along a black, thick-pelted neck and the scarred skin of his palm came back drenched with sweat and fresh blood. He drew in a sharp breath and the stench of his own sweat flooded his nostrils, bringing with it a dread that went beyond terror.

He might have fallen then, it hit him so hard, but he felt another's arms clench tight round his waist and knew that he carried someone behind him and that the second life mattered more than his own. With sudden clarity, he understood that the danger was not for him but for the other and that there was safety ahead. He was leaning back to say this when the horse caught its foot in a hole and stumbled. It twisted violently in mid-stride, fighting to regain its footing, and the great head turned on the neck so that, for a brief, blinding moment, Bán's eyes locked with those of the beast and what he saw there froze the breath in his throat. Then a voice shouted a warning in a tone he had never heard before and, even in half-sleep, his body jerked and twitched as a blade arced down out of nowhere and severed his left hand at the wrist.

The pain of that had woken him the first time and it did so again. For a second time that night, he lay wide-eyed in the dark while the hammer of his heart made hoofbeats in his ears loud enough to shake the stars from the heavens. He was less afraid this time. He had seen a thing only the gods should see and the sheer impossibility of it pushed him through fear into the still place beyond. He breathed in and made himself feel the things around him. The hound that shared his bed had gone and he lay alone between the hides with only his younger sister to keep him warm. Silla lay on her stomach, her skin glued tight to his with the damp of their sweat so he could feel the ripple of her ribs and the angles of her hip bones pressing into his side. He concentrated on the place where the point of her knee dug into his calf and let the feel of it bring him back to himself. With that, he found that her breath whistled with the same rhythm as the mare's and then, later, that the weight of her body was crushing his left wrist, cutting off the feeling from his hand. He eased his arm out, slowly, doing his best not to wake her.

Silla was three years old and had only lately graduated to sleeping with her older brother. Bán had looked forward to that, cherishing the thought of her company with its promise of extra warmth and the novelty of sharing the hides with someone other than a hound. Reality had been more of a two-edged sword. Nine nights out of ten, she was a cheerful bundle of clinging heat who screwed up her nose and squirmed in under his armpit and listened while he whispered the stories of their father, the greatest warrior and smith the Eceni had ever known, and of their mother, who could become the wren and travel the spaces between the worlds to keep them safe. On those nights, his sister giggled and let him draw the outlines of the beasts on her skin, pressing lightly so the feeling tingled and lasted to morning. Then there was the one night in ten when some unnameable thing had upset her and all he had to do was turn over too fast in his sleep to tip her back into mewling, wailing infanthood. Without trying, she could wake half the roundhouse and experience had taught him that it was Bán, not Silla, who would wither under the weary stares in the morning.

Tonight was not one of those nights. She had listened to his story of the crow and the she-bear and had slept soundly, even when he woke with the dream. He moved himself away from her and rolled to the edge of the bed to sit up. His bladder was full and would not last the night without emptying, which was, perhaps, where the urgency in the dream had come from. He slid his hand between his thighs to check that he had not disgraced himself and then, belatedly and with care, reached under the hides to do the same for his sister. Both were dry. He stood, letting relief lever him out of the warmth into the chill of the night.

It was not as cold as he had thought. The late cloud of the evening had cleared but the wind blew warmly from the south and kept the frost from the ground. Still, he reached back in through the door-flap and dragged his cloak from the bed. It was cut down from one of his father's, scorched in places from the forge but still heavy with the smell of sheep's oil and mansweat. The important thing about it— apart from the colour, which was blue, like the sky at dusk, and marked him out as one of the Eceni—was that his mother had told him that when he wore it properly, clasped with the brooch at the right shoulder, he looked just like his father. It was not true, exactly; his father was fair, while he had the dark hair and browner skin of his mother, but the boy understood the likeness to be in the way that he bore himself, particularly around the women. He had taken care, in the time since he had heard that, to watch how his father was with his mother and to hold himself the same whenever he was with Breaca. Tonight, in the dark and with nobody watching, there was less need for formality. He left the brooch in its niche at the bedside and wrapped his cloak tight around his shoulders like a hide, draping the free ends over his elbows to keep them from trailing in the mud. Like that, he was nearly as warm as he had been in bed.

He edged quickly round the side wall of the roundhouse. He had been wrong earlier when he had thought the night completely black. The moon had long since dropped below the curve of the earth but the stars made a canopy of light from one horizon to the other, casting soft, muted shadows. High up, the Hunter stepped over the crown of a beech tree. The boy swung his fist up, giving the salute of the warrior. This, too, he could do alone in the dark when there was no-one to tell him that he was a child, not yet come to manhood and too young to make the warrior's mark.

The hounds came to join him as soon as he stepped free of the rampart. They had been at the midden and smelled of it now as they crowded round, butting him in the groin and armpit, grinning and whining in greeting. He pushed his way through them, whispering gruff threats that offered all manner of violence if they didn't let him pass. None of them feared him but they drew back anyway, showing white teeth in the starlight, leaving only the brindled dog with the white ear that shared his bed to brush up against him, rubbing shoulder to shoulder after the way of a friend. He hooked his arm across its neck and the beast leaned heavily against him as he stood upwind of the midden, holding himself straight the way his father did, to piss in an arc onto the picked-out head of a pig. The dog nudged him as he finished, pushing him off balance. He grabbed at its coat and used it to pull himself upright. The hound backed away, grinning, hauling him with it and they made it a game, tussling quietly in the dark. The dog was the tallest of the hounds, one of his mother's best stag hunters and soon to be sire to its first litter of pups. The bitch chosen as dam was well past her prime and there had been a long and heated discussion between his mother and one of the grandmothers at the time of her bleeding as to whether she was not too old to bear more young. She was the only one left of her line and she was still the only hound in the pack that had ever brought down a deer single-handed, and the old blood was a good thing, strengthening the untested fire of youth. So said his mother, and the grandmother, perhaps mollified by talk of youth leavened by age, had relented and given her blessing to the match.

That was two months ago, just before the first of the pregnant mares reached her time. Since then, he had been caught up in the foaling, watching as each one slid out and was freed from the birth-caul. On the night of the quarter-moon, he had chosen the dun filly with the sickle-shaped mark between the eyes to be his own brood mare when he was old enough to take one and she was old enough to breed. The greater part of each day had been spent at her side in the paddock, making sure that she knew the sound of his voice better than any of the others. She was three days old and already she would leave her dam and run across the paddock towards him for her lick of salt. In the stir and flurry of that, he had only vaguely taken note that the bitch, too, was close to her time. When he thought about it, he remembered that her nipples had been leaking milk for the past two nights and that when he had lain alongside her in the doorway to the roundhouse that afternoon with his hand on her belly, he had felt the press of a small, round head against his palm.

The boy felt the nudge of the sire-hound and looked round for the bitch amongst the pack. When he didn't find her there, he turned back towards the roundhouse, thinking that perhaps he had stepped over her in the doorway in his hurry to get out. She was not there. Nor, when he looked in through the door-flap, was his mother.

He let the skin fall back into place. There were a lot of reasons why his mother might be out at night and a whelping bitch was not the greatest of them. If she had gone out beyond the turf rampart, he might never find her. Besides the great roundhouse, there were only six other buildings—seven if you counted the grain-silo—within the encircling ditch, but beyond it were the paddocks and the river and then the forest, which held greater dangers than a boy of eight could handle. He was forbidden, on pain of cursing, to pass through the gate at night without adult company. If the Coritani attacked and he were about to die, or be dragged into slavery, he might flout the rule, but not otherwise.

So then, where to look? He chewed his lip and turned a slow circle, listening. The sounds of the night rang in his ears: the wet panting of the dogs, the crop and step of mares in the paddock beyond the ditch, the whicker of a nursing foal, and far out and once only the call of an owl to its young and a single high squeak in return. All he could hear of people was his father's breathing, the roll of it dulled only slightly by the wall between them.

He had decided to walk in a circle, following the path of the moon, when he heard a sound that was not of the night: the single yelping cry of a hound in pain and a cushioning murmur of voices, his mother's among them. It was what he was waiting for. He ran as fast as he could, taking care for the mess of the midden, and came up, panting, at the door to the women's place on the far western edge of the enclosure, opposite the entrance. There he stopped. When he was very small, his mother had taken him inside with her to lie in the moss, while the rise and fall of her voice kept him peaceful. Then he had passed through childhood to boyhood and the visits had slowed and ceased altogether. Twelve months more and he would be forbidden so much as to stand in front of the entrance. He stood in front of it now and heard the bitch cry out a second time; a sharp, wheedling cry of pain. The brindle dog paced at his side, whining. It was not a patient hound and had no idea that the male was not welcome inside. It clawed at the door-skin, pulling it sideways, and the boy found himself standing in an open doorway, with his eyes screwed against the sudden glare of the fire, withering under the combined stare of every woman he knew.

"Bán?" His mother's voice carried over the sucked-in breaths of the others. Her shape moved on the far side of the fire. Beside her, he saw a flash of hair the colour of a fox in autumn, bending over a single, still form on the floor. His dream came back to him, suddenly, cripplingly. He had forgotten it in the search for the bitch. Now it swamped his senses. He stumbled forward against the carved post of the doorway. The marks of the horse and the wren untwined themselves from the rest and whirled over his head.

"Bán!"

He was too near the fire. He could feel the heat of it through his shins. It was very hot. They had been burning birch, well aged, to give off the most light and the least smoke. Somewhere else, sage smoked thickly. His mother caught him and spun him round, turning him away from the fire. She was kneeling, her face close to his. He blinked through tears that were only partly the sage. "I had a dream," he said, and his voice was a child's. "I was riding a mare with hair like Breaca's."

"That's good." Her voice was gentle. Her hands were less so. "The hawthorn speaks to you. I thought that it might. Come back with me now and you can tell me your dream."

He strained to turn round. The dream had not been of a mare alone. "The hound?" he asked. "Is she well?"

"She's very tired. It's been a long night. She will be better by dawn."

"And the whelp? The black one with the white head?"

He heard the grandmothers hiss behind him. It was not a good sound. The fingers on his shoulders dug in tighter. "Home," said his mother. "Now." And then, coming back to herself, "We can talk of it there."

"Why so, Macha?" The voice was an old one, smoked dry by the years. "There is no need for haste now. The child has seen as much as he is ever going to. If the smoke has brought him, perhaps it is up to the smoke to choose when to let him go."

The grip on his shoulders relaxed. He took his chance and turned round. His father's mother's sister sat on the edge of the fire closest to the door and she was smiling at him, which was a miracle in itself. In all of his life, that one had never smiled at him. He had thought her a sow badger; slow and plodding and too readily pushed to anger. If he had heard her speak three words at once it was only to tell him to drop the door-flap and never with the depth of humour that he heard from her now. He felt his mother change her mind. With the flat of her hand, she pressed him down to sit alongside the grandmother and took her own place on the far side of the fire. She snapped her fingers. The brindle dog turned and left. Bán felt the draught of the door-skin falling into place behind it. Quite urgently, he wanted to follow. The grandmother tapped him lightly on the shoulder to hold him still. Breaca sat opposite him on the other side of the fire. Her hair was a river of living bronze, fluid in the flames, brighter now than the mare's coat had been in his dream. She smiled at him, the special smile they saved for each other in times of trouble. It was the first time he had seen it since her mother died. A wash of relief took away some of the fear. He smiled back and squared his shoulders, as his father did in the elder council.

The grandmother spoke. "There was only one whelp," she said. "He was too big and coming backwards. The bitch had not the strength to birth him herself. In the end, we had to take his hind legs and pull him out."

His heart twisted tight in his chest. "But he will live?"

"No." The grandmother shook her head. Her eyes were rimmed red with the smoke. He realized she was the one who had argued against the mating. "I'm sorry. Your mother was half right. He would have made a good hound, possibly the best, but he is too weak to live—and not well marked. The gods send these things as a sign. It is not for us to go against them."

"But then why was he sent at all?" The whelp lay in the pool of shadow cast by the fire. The boy dropped to the floor, lifting the limp form to his face. It lolled in his hands, a damp, cold, salty thing with a head too big for its body. It was not a white head, that had been a trick of the slime and the firelight, nor was the body completely black. When he looked at it carefully, he found that one ear was white with a streak like a teardrop that slid down to circle one eye and that the rest was a dark patterned brindle like all of the other hounds but with small flecks of white scattered through the coat, like hail seen on a dark night.

Hail. The word resonated inside. It was a good name for a hound. He kept it in to himself for now, cradling the thing tight to his chest. It squirmed and he felt the heart flutter under his fingers.

"Look!" He held the pup in the light. "He's not dead."

"Not yet, but he is too close for us to bring back." It was a different grandmother who spoke. She sounded tired. Around him, the others murmured assent. Underneath it, he could hear the tug and pull of other things that were not being said.

His mother had lines round her eyes that had not been there in the morning. A long string of bloody mucus crossed over one arm. She spoke to him more gently than the second grandmother had done.

"It's a hound puppy, Bán. There will be others." She reached a hand across the fire towards him. "He should have had brothers and sisters beside him in the womb but the bitch was too old and she could only make one. On his own, he grew too big and the birthing was too long. Even if we bring him back now, he won't have the strength to suckle. The bitch will run dry within hours and her son will die of hunger, having known the first breaths of life. It will be harder for him then. Better to let him go now."

Her voice rang true. She spoke as she believed. He sat where he was. "But the dream . . . the gods' horse . . ." He hadn't told her. She looked at him, squinting through the firelight. He said, "In my dream I was riding a red mare but then it wasn't a mare, it was a horse and he was black, with a white head." His own name meant "white" in the tongue of the Hibernians. He had known that since he was old enough to know the sound. He had never found the reason why.

The grandmothers linked eyes over his head. He felt the path of their stare like a sword-cut. His mother came to kneel at his side. The new lines on her face had gone. "Bán? You dreamed a horse with a white head? All white?"

"Yes. No. Not all of it. It had a black patch between the eyes, like a shield with a sword laid across it."

"And what did you see in the black?" It was the elder grandmother, the oldest of the old women, his mother's mother's half-cousin. Her hair was so thin and so white you could see the smooth scalp all the way across the top from one ear to the other. Beneath it, the skin of her face was as wrinkled and brown as bark scraped from an oak. Her eyes were watery brown with yellow at the edges and the black dot in the middle was milking over in a way that said she would soon be blind. But this evening she was not blind. Her eyes were wide and they picked up the light of the fire, shining in through his own skull to the memory of the dream. It must be so. How else could she know that he had seen something in the black sunburst on the head of the horse?

"I don't know." He frowned, trying to remember. In the dream, he had known exactly what it was. It had made sense of everything else. Now it was simply a patch in the shape of a warrior's shield that had shown him something else in reflection. He struggled and failed and saw the effort reflected in his mother's eyes. "I'm sorry," he said. "I can't remember."

His mother had picked up the hound puppy now and

was rubbing its chest absently, her gaze still on her son. One of the grandmothers rapped her shoulder and, without looking up, she handed the whelp across the smoke. Breaca took it and began to breathe for it, pressing her mouth to its muzzle and blowing deep into its chest. Someone must have taught her that, and recently; she hadn't known how to do it for the colt foal that had died by the stream. One of the other women lifted a fold of her cloak and began to rub hard over the whelp's heart. Something had changed. They were going to bring it back. He wanted to watch, to help, but his mother lifted him round to sit opposite her, with his back to the bitch and the pup. "Tell me the dream," she said.

He told her as much as he could remember. It took less time than it had taken to dream it. At the end, he could still not tell her what it was he had seen when the horse turned its head. Only the feeling of it was left with him and he had few enough words for that.

"Did you feel afraid?"

"No. The first time I did, but not the second time. I knew I had nothing to fear."

"Not even when the sword struck you?"

"No." That puzzled him. He should have been afraid of the sword. But then he had been a warrior in battle and his father had told him that, in the frenzy of fighting, some warriors passed beyond their fear. He looked down at his left arm. It was as whole as the other. "Maybe I knew it wasn't real."

"Maybe." She didn't believe it. Across the fire, something was whimpering, faintly, like the wind in a reed. The old bitch lifted her head and grumbled a greeting. The pup was rubbed one final time and placed in the fall of her teats. She licked it hard, pushing it up and in. It mewled and pawed and had no idea how to suck.

"He will have to be fed." His mother stretched forward and pressed the hindmost teat between finger and thumb. When the first bead of milk appeared, she held the pup to it, smearing its lips with white. It mumbled and sucked and, the second time, did it more strongly.

The elder grandmother spoke. Her voice was the rustle of dead leaves in winter. "The boy had the dream. The whelp is his to rear." She turned to Bán. Her eyes scored his face. "He will not live without help. Will you give it?"

"Yes." He had no doubts about that. He said, "His name is Hail."

That sealed it. To name a thing gave it life. His mother took hold of his arm. "For the first half-moon, they feed more often than not, through the night as well as the day. I will show you how. If you can do it, the whelp will live. If not, he will die. If he dies, it is the will of the gods and you are not to blame yourself. Is that clear?"

"Yes."

"Swear to me that you won't blame yourself."

He swore. He swore by Briga, the threefold Mother, and her daughter, Nemain, the moon, and by the smaller gods of childbirth and rearing. Then, because the whelp was a dog and not a bitch, he swore also by Belin god of the sun, and by Camul the war god. It was a long and complicated oath and at the end of it he remembered that he was not swearing to stay awake and keep the whelp alive but rather not to blame himself if it died. He spoke that aloud, to make it clear.

His mother was smiling when he had finished. She held out her hand and lifted him up. "Come, then, I'll show you how it is done. And then we'll find you somewhere to live with her so you don't keep us all awake through the night with your nursing."

CHAPTER 2

Eburovic woke with the moon. A dazzle of silver slid through the gap between the door-skin and the oak upright and glanced across his eyes, interrupting the dream. He lay still, listening. The night was quiet. He had been dreaming of danger and the echo of it fogged his thinking. The hushed breath of the other sleepers made a blanket of sound layered over the night's smoke to deaden his ears. He turned his head and heard the whine of a hound and the scratch and scurry of rodents. Elsewhere, in the world beyond the thatch, an owl screeched and was answered. He heard it and waited; these were the sounds with which he slept nightly and none of them had woken him. Lying still, he stopped his breathing and strained to catch the things beyond the smoke. In time, it came again, the subtle chink of iron on iron, such as a careless man might make, allowing his sword to clash on his shield hub, or his armour to grate as he climbed a rampart to attack those sleeping within. But Eburovic was not asleep. For six months, he had not truly slept, waiting for such a moment as this. Feeling something close to joy, he reached down for the sword that had been within a hand's reach day and night since the Coritani attack. His hand closed on the grip, settling in place as if born to it, and he drew the blade from the sheath. Polished iron slid on oiled bull's hide and made no more noise than the sleepers. Still, he was heard.

"Your daughter is at her work early."

He stopped. The joy left him. The whisper came from his left, from amongst the women. It was dry, like the brush of wind over stone. He peered into the gloom. The embers of last night's fire gave little light but he saw a bent shape move in the darkness and the reflected glimmer of milk-blind eyes and knew who it was. The elder grandmother was erratic and harsh with her words but he had never known her to speak without reason. Certainly she had never lied to him. He sat down on the edge of his bed and laid his naked blade flat across his knees.

"What work is that, Grandmother?" His own voice was pitched to move through the breathing, to reach her but not wake the others.

"How would I know that? You must ask her."

Her tone was scathing, but he had learned long ago to listen beyond the acid of the words to the silences that carried the real meaning. He did so now. "What work is it that must be done in darkness and alone?"

"She draws out her dream, as you should do," said the old woman. "It does not pay a man, or a child, to dream too often of violence."

He was silent for that. His dream had been the same every night since the autumn. In it, he slept with his sword in his hand, not hanging from the wall, and he did not keep apart from the women, for all that Graine was in the first throes of childbirth. He heard the warriors approach before they began the work of killing and he was there in time, standing in their path, swinging sharp and savage iron to halt their advance. In his dream none died but the Coritani. The first three fell to his hammer and his blade combined, long before they reached the women. The last, as in reality, died on his daughter's spear. He ended each night standing in a doorway facing her across the body of the fallen man, feeling the simmering ecstasy of battle ring through his head and pride fill his heart. The dawn sun sang in over his shoulder, setting fire to her hair, her smile, her shining spear-tip. She raised her weapon in salute and he thought his heart would burst with the joy of it. Then, always, he saw her eyes. In life, they were a burnished green with small threads of copper spreading out from the core, a colour all their own. Here, from the doorway of his dream, he looked into the late-summer blue of her mother's eyes and the smile that fired them was the one that had burned into his heart long before he became a father. It was the smile that made him remember his loss and brought back the crippling grief. Weeping, he watched his daughter open her mouth and knew that she spoke with the voice of her mother. He strained to hear but her words were lost in the tides of pain and always he woke before they could reach him. Now he sat in the dark and felt the ache as he had each morning, made greater this time by the understanding that Breaca, too, had dreamed of the deaths and he had not known.

"It is not a good thing for a child to dream so," he said.

"She knows it. She is working as she feels she must. It is not for you to stop her."

"No." He eased his blade back into its sheath and

stood. His tunic lay folded on his bed-skins. He slid it over his head.

"You would go to her?" The ancient voice nagged like an aching tooth and the scorn was directed entirely at him. "Would she work in the dark if she wanted you?"

"I woke early from my dream," he said, and realized that it was the first time he had done so. "Perhaps I need to see what she is doing."

"She is teaching herself patience." The grandmother dismissed it as nothing. Both of them knew it was not. "It is not before time."

"Then I will look. I will offer help only if she asks for it. I will do nothing to stop her." He stepped past the fire to the door-skin. An elderly bitch thought to follow. He pushed on her muzzle and turned her back. She padded away to his sleeping place and dug herself a bed amongst his hides. He waited until she had settled and then let himself out.

The forge stood away from the roundhouse, on the far side of the compound, with its front entrance facing south so that sparks from the fire might not, in dry weather, set fire to the thatch of the roundhouse and cause ruin. The building itself was made of wood with slatted hazel for the roof, and he wet it himself regularly so that it would not burn. The floor was beaten earth, damped and trodden and glazed by the fire until it was flat and imperviously smooth, except at the doorway where the hens had scraped a dust bowl and lay in it on occasion, basking in the heat.

There were no hens at night. They had roused themselves at dusk, pecking their way with the last of the light to the safe roost under the eaves of the granary, and he had sealed the door-skin behind them, laying a row of river stones along the skirt, so that the furnace, free of draught, might keep its heat through to the dawn. Coming on it now in the light of the moon, Eburovic saw the haze rising straight from the smoke hole and knew the fires were not sleeping. At the door-flap, he found that the stones had been laid aside, arranged in order of size more neatly than was his habit, and that the skirt had been turned inwards with a single weight holding it down from the inside. He stood for a moment with his ear pressed to the leather but heard nothing. If Breaca had been using his hammer, she was not doing so now.

He eased a hand round the edge of the skin, putting his face to the gap and bracing himself for a blast of heat that never came. He was pleased with that. It was, after all, his daughter who worked his forge and he had taught her well; she knew how to build a fire, stoking it small and hot and banking the edges so that the heat turned in on itself and was not thrown out to cook the night air. Still, it was bright inside. As his eyes adjusted to the flames, he saw she had built a fire made for casting; the banked edges were higher than he made them for forging and the charcoal at the core glowed white, falling away in white ash and small puffs of smoke. A mould stood in the heart of the fire, not one of his. Breaca crouched before it with her back to him. The backwash of light from the fire caught the deep bronze of her hair and made of it molten copper, pouring down past her shoulders. When she stood up and reached for the bellows, he saw that she wore her old tunic with the burn marks already ancient on the front of it, and covering that, the apron of boiled ox-hide he had made for her the previous summer. The apron was too small for her now, he could see that. In the six months of winter, under his gaze but without his seeing, his daughter had grown to a woman. He wondered how close she was to her first bleeding and knew, suddenly, that this was why she was here. It could not have started yet, or she would be in the care of the grandmothers, but it would be soon.

The bellows sighed as she pumped. The fire cracked and roared and the mould at its centre glowed white hot. Eburovic watched his daughter lift his longest tongs, the ones that he had made himself to let him work with the hottest iron. With care, she edged them forward, past the mould to a crucible of molten metal. He had not seen her do this before. He held his breath, watching the surface of the liquid bronze, praying that he had taught her properly— that she knew the importance of keeping her hands steady. Even if she knew, he was not sure she could do it. Her left hand was still the weaker of the two. The sword wound she had taken at her mother's death had healed poorly over the winter. The elder grandmother had spent some time on it in the dark nights of midwinter, opening the wound and probing with a newly forged silver needle until she found a fragment of bone loose inside. His daughter had sat on the bench they had laid for her, white-lipped and silent. Her green eyes had held his, still as frozen water, and he had been proud as the needle-work started that they had stayed dry. Her free hand had gripped his arm while the probing continued and he had not noticed the strength of it until later. The bruises had taken five nights to fade.

Afterwards, with poultices and care, the wound had begun to knit properly but a scar that would last a lifetime ran down the centre of her palm and a greater separation than normal showed between the first finger and the rest. More than that, the hand did not work as it used to and Breaca was not one to take incapacity lightly. She had fretted daily under the ministrations of the grandmother, trying too hard to accomplish with one hand the things she had never quite been able to do with two. When the poultice came off, she had begun work in earnest. With an aching heart, he had watched her walking the fields or the encircling rampart, flexing her fingers against a wad of old leather, biting back on the pain until it bleached the colour from her skin and brought tears to her eyes. On the one occasion when he had asked her to stop, she had rounded on him, weeping openly, and spat out that if her mother could take the pain of childbirth, she could take the lesser pain of an injured hand. At the time, he had been shocked to find her so angry. Looking back, he realized that it was the only time he had seen her weep.

In the forge, he saw her lift the crucible and then the mould to the edge of the fire. Even from the door, he could see the tremor in the last few movements. With relief, he watched her lay down the tongs and flex her fingers. She tried again and the shaking was worse. He could feel the tension growing in her spine. She shook her head crossly. He heard the hiss of her breath over the draw of the fire and the muttered curse that followed. In his mind, he saw her knock the mould at the crucial point of pouring. Molten metal flowed out across her legs, seeking out the places the apron no longer covered, making wounds that even the elder grandmother could not heal. He eased his arm through the door-flap, reaching down to lift the weight that held it, intent on going in to help. As his hand closed on the copper disc, the memory of a whispered conversation came back to him: *Would she work in the dark if she wanted you?* and his own reply, *Then I will look. I will offer help only if she asks for it. I will do nothing to stop her.*

I will do nothing to stop her. It had not been intended as an oath but words spoken in the dark to the elder grandmother were not to be discarded lightly. The gods do not look favourably on a man who breaks his word and no smith can afford to court their disfavour for the sake of it, still less one who has so recently known such loss. He withdrew his arm and let go of the door-skin, keeping only such a gap as allowed him to see. By the fire, his daughter bent her head and drew in a longer breath, letting it out slowly. With great care she put both hands to the tongs and lifted them horizontally. When it was clear that the tips were steady, she slid them forward into the fire, grasping the neck of the crucible, lifting it just high enough to broach the lip of the mould. The pour was smooth. A thin stream of liquid bronze flowed into the cavity she had made for it. Eburovic heard the hiss and sigh of the air from the side vents and the part of him that lived for his craft gave her due credit for placing them properly. The part of him that was a father stopped breathing until the crucible was empty. Then she tapped the mould three times with the hammer to knock out the air bubbles and the danger was over. It had been done neatly and well. He breathed again.

The mould cooled slowly. The time from pouring the metal to cracking the mould open had always been the hardest part for her. Of his three children, Breaca was the worst for acting on impulse. Twice as a child she had reached forward too soon and had had to be taken afterwards to the elder grandmother to have the scorched flesh bound with dock leaves and fennel root to keep it from festering. Now she stood slowly, easing the cramped muscles of her thighs, and began to tidy the tools of her working. As a man in a dream, Eburovic watched the care with which the tongs were hung back on the wall and the hammer laid in its rack by the files. His daughter, his impetuous, impatient fire-child, had never been one to care about order. Since she was old enough to come to the forge to watch him and "help," he had been mentioning, quietly, that certain things lived in certain places and it would be good, perhaps, at the end of a day's work, to put them back there. Always she had turned the great green gaze on him and grinned and promised "later" and run out to play in the paddocks or to find her mother or to attend to the dozen other things that needed her urgent attention, leaving her father to put things in order. He had persuaded himself, as he did it, that with enough nagging she might one day remember what it was to hang up a hammer. He had never thought to see it done so easily.

The piece was nearly ready. She stood over it, frowning as she watched the surface of the metal, waiting for the scum on the surface to harden. The fire, unfed, grew cooler, throwing redder light and softer shadows into the corners of the forge, drawing out the autumn tones of her hair and her eyebrows, making of the rest a silhouette. In profile, she was her mother. The high, flat brow led directly to the sweep of her hair. The nose was straight and firm, balancing the strong line of her jaw and the broad set of her cheekbones. Her skin was darker than Graine's had been. She had that from her father: the ability to darken a little in the sun, not to the bark-brown of Macha and Bán, but neither to the sun-shy red of her mother. With age, he felt, she would be grateful for that. She had his height, too. He could tell, even now, that she had taken more of that from him than either of his other children and that, when grown, she and Bán would be of a height, with Silla that little bit shorter. When she stood and reached back for his smallest hammer, he could believe, in the lines of her movement, that she was growing into her mother's grace. Then he watched her take a breath before she tapped the mould and the curve of her smile cut his heart in two. The hammer fell, splitting the mould, giving birth to the shining metal. His daughter raised her head and looked him straight in the eye, still smiling in the way she had in his dream. "You can come in now," she said. "It's finished."

He faltered. He had never been unsure entering his own forge. He was now. "How did you know I was there?" he asked.

"The fire told me." Her smile broadened. She was alive with the morning and the thing she had done. It shone from her as if she stood in full sunlight. She said, "The flames moved in the draught as you opened the flap. It had to be someone. When you waited I knew it was you. No-one else has the patience."

"You are learning it," he said. "You haven't burned your fingers."

"Not yet." She frowned again at the piece on the workbench. "But it is hard and I have to think. You have it without thinking." She raised her head. "Don't you want to see what I have made?"

"What?" He had believed it a secret. It had not occurred to him that he would be allowed to see it. "Yes. Of course."

It lay on his workbench, scorching wood already blackened by a hundred other new-cast pieces. He waited while she took the small hand-tongs and dipped it in the quenching bucket. The hiss of steam was one of the keynotes of his life. He closed his eyes and let the sound of it calm him. When he opened them again, Breaca had laid her work out on the bench and was standing by the forging block, waiting for his opinion. With some reluctance, he took his gaze from her face and directed it to his bench and the thing she had made.

Like the best pieces, it was deceptively simple. At first glance, it was a small spear-head, the length of his middle finger, with a long leaf-shaped blade and a point as sharp as any got from casting. It was a thing of fierce beauty and she had clearly modelled it on the old one he kept in his work bag, which had been made by the ancestors and passed down through her mother's line to him. He was impressed with the workmanship and the time she had taken to get the proportions right, scaling it up so that the end result was a third bigger than the original. At the same time, he knew a fleeting disappointment that she should have made something as plain as a spear-head in her first casting. He turned it over to examine the back, buying himself time.

That was when he found the first deception. It was not only a spear-head; when she laid it on the bench, she had placed it carefully so that the back was hidden and he had not seen the detail on the reverse that made it also a brooch, cast in the old style of his forefathers, with a front face that showed to the world and two holes behind for the pin to pass through and hold it in place on the cloak. It was clever, and he felt a surge of warm pride. She had learned better than he had expected from her years of watching and this was as good as anything he could have made at starting. Then, turning it round, he saw the third thing and knew she had surpassed him. Like the best of craftsmen, she had caught life in simplicity, motion in stillness, and what he saw in front of him raised the hairs on his arms. Held one way, it was still a spear, a thing made for a warrior. Held differently, the curved arcs patterning the front face resolved themselves into something quite other. He turned it on his palm to catch the light from the fire. The bronze shimmered in the heat and on the surface, moulded in place, the red kite of the Coritani fell beneath the punishing claws of the small, fierce, yellow-eyed owl that hunts by day—the one that had been the dream of her mother. All winter he had dreamed his vengeance. His daughter had cast it in bronze.

He stood for a long time in silence. The words of the elder grandmother echoed in his ears. *She draws out her dream, as you should do.* He raised his eyes. Breaca stood as she had before, her good hand still on the forging block, the other hanging loose at her side. The smile and the colour had drained from her face, leaving her grey with the morning. She would not ask; her pride would not allow it. He must give her what she needed, freely and with integrity, but it was hard to look at it critically, as he would the work of another smith. He forced his eye along the lines, matching and balancing the individual markings with the overall flow. Without thinking, he reached for his polishing sand and smoothed off a blemish on the surface. The involuntary movement of her arm brought him back to himself.

He laid the piece down again. He owed her honesty; she would expect no less. "It is close to perfect," he said.

"But. . . ?"

"But you didn't use the drawing tool. The two arcs of the eyes are not quite balanced. This one here"——his finger followed a line on the surface—"does not match the one over here."

She had known it. He could see the truth in the tilt of her head and the single vertical line of her frown. "I couldn't take the tool without you noticing," she said. "I tried to make one of my own, but it didn't work."

"But still, it is a remarkable piece. And very beautiful." He reached up to the top shelf for his workbox. The punch that lay in the centre, protected by wool, had as its end-piece the shape of a feeding she-bear, the mark of his family. He held it out to her now. "If you want to use it," he offered, "it is well worth the mark."

It was the best gift he could have given her and she had not expected as much. Her eyes shone and he realized with shock that there were tears at the corners. "Do you think it is good enough?" she asked.

"I wouldn't offer if I did not."

He passed her his middle hammer. She took the stamp from him and placed it on the front face of the brooch, on a patch of bare metal left free of ornament. The sound rang out like a bell. With the mark in place, the shape of it balanced better so that he wondered if the asymmetry had been more deliberate than she had allowed. Outside, the sun broke over the horizon. A stray shard of sunlight angled in through the doorway and fell on the bench. Eburovic moved the new piece into the path of it so that the owl shone gold. They looked at it together. He said, "Would you wear it now?"

"No." She shook her head. He saw her teeth shine white on her lower lip. In some ways she was still a child. "It is not for me."

For a moment he thought he was being offered a gift and pleasure welled within him. Then he saw the twin streaks of colour high on her cheekbones, stark against the white of her skin, and, crushingly, he understood. He stared at her in silence.

With obvious effort she said, "It is a gift for . . . the one who knew the owl."

She was rigid, her voice a drawn thread. Her injured hand was splayed flat on the edge of his workbench, her whole body shivering like a leaf under rain. The vertical line of the frown was etched into her brow, so like her mother. She took a breath to speak again and he silenced her, reaching across the gap between them before it became an impassable gulf. Carefully, because it was clear she was near to breaking and did not want to do so, he wrapped an arm round her shoulder and folded her into him, drawing her down until they sat together in the shadowy corner behind the furnace where she had spent so much time as a child. He stroked her hair, talking to her as he would a newly gentled horse that might still take flight, the rhythm meaning more than the words.

As the rising sun warmed the frost from the grass and the hens roused themselves from their roost in the granary, she became less stiff under his touch and her breathing, although stilted, felt less forced. He moved her round so her back pressed on his chest and linked his arms in front of her.

With his face close to her hair, he said, "Breaca, I am sorry. I have spent all winter nursing my own pain and had thought you free of yours. We can talk of your mother, of course we can. We *should* talk of her. It is only her name we cannot say. Her spirit is still making its way across the gods' river to the lands of the dead. It won't reach the far side until we burn her bones at the start of winter a year from her death. Until then, she is finding her path and we should do nothing that might draw her back."

"She is already drawn back." Her body had stiffened again and her voice was wooden. "I have dreamed her. I said her name in my dreams and she came. She keeps coming."

He had not expected that. Ice ran in his veins and he fought to keep himself from stiffening as she had. His mind groped for a response. "What does she say?" he asked, eventually.

"What she always said: that only the gods know the future and it is not for me to judge them; that I should not bear anger towards the Coritani, for they are not our true enemies. She said the council was right when they decided not to attack in the winter and that I should use my voice to warn against it when we meet again in the spring." She softened a little, letting her head tip back on his shoulder. "I don't want to do that."

"No. But it would be a good thing to say, and they will listen to you. You are her daughter and will one day lead in her place. And you're a warrior now. They respect you."

"I know."

She spoke with a new and unexpected gravity. In killing her attacker, his daughter had made of herself a warrior and earned a place on the council ahead of her time. It was a thing unknown in living memory but it was not unique. Once or twice in the tales of the heroes and their deeds there occurred a child who had killed young and gone on to greater things. They had no singer—her mother had been that—but there were those who knew the tales and could speak them well and it seemed each one who rose to speak in the slow nights of winter had picked a tale of a young-made hero. Eburovic, who knew the tales they chose not to tell, of those who killed young and died young and left no-one to mourn them, had listened with mixed feelings and nursed his own thoughts. Only now, looking back, he saw the shadows that had gathered around his daughter.

"Did your mother tell you to make the brooch?" he asked. "Or the elder grandmother?"

"No. It was Airmid's idea. She understands."

Airmid; the tall, silent, dark-haired girl, recently passed into womanhood and accepted as a true dreamer by the elders. In the autumn, before the Coritani attack, she had not been a special friend. That, too, had developed over the winter without his knowing. He reached up and lifted the brooch from the workbench and pressed it into her palm. "We could go this morning. If we ride now, we would reach the platform and be back before the morning is half over."

"I can't. It's dawn. I have to see to the grandmother. I'm late already."

For two years, his daughter had served as eyes and limbs to the elder grandmother, taking the hardship from the old woman's mornings and giving the strength of youth to her days. To be chosen to serve was a great honour but it was also a great constraint. He had watched with amusement, seeing his daughter settle into it as a half-broken colt settles into the harness, chafing at the ties and testing the limits. Of late, she had been more conscientious.

She began to pull herself to her feet. He felt something important slide away from him, like a fish in the river. Drawing her back into his embrace, he said, "No. Airmid was the grandmother's eyes and limbs before you. This once, could she not be so again?"

"Maybe." She turned to look up at him. Her face was wet but her smile was steady. "If she knew why."

"Will she be at the river?"

"Not yet. She's in the west house."

"I see." He did not ask how she knew. The west house was the place where the young women of childbearing age slept who had not yet taken a man. The young men of similar age slept in the south. The roundhouse in the centre was for families and the elderly. Eburovic felt another tradition sway in the storm of his family's passing; it was not expected that a man visit the west house uninvited. This morning was, he believed, a time of exceptions. He stood, releasing his daughter. "I'll go and talk to Airmid," he said. "You get the harness and catch the horses. I'll meet you at the lower paddocks."

They met as the sun touched the lower branches of the hawthorn tree in the corner of the field. Airmid had agreed to tend to the elder grandmother and the old woman had accepted the alteration to her routine. On the way through the compound, he picked up his good cloak and found Breaca had been before him, collecting her own and changing her old tunic for her new one, woven in the blue of the Eceni with a coiled pattern in a darker tone worked along the border. He fixed his sword on his back and gathered his spear and his war shield with its iron boss and the mark of the she-bear poker-burned on the bull's-hide surround. The extra weapons were not necessary but he had not travelled to the platform since it was first built and he felt a need to go in ceremony.

He walked up to the lower paddocks and found that Breaca, thinking with him, had caught the roan horse he rode to war and had spent her time cleaning the burrs and mud from its coat. Beside him, surprisingly, an iron-grey filly with a flesh mark on her muzzle and an eel stripe down the centre of her back stood bridled and ready. He looked out across the paddock at the two dozen well-handled horses, any one of which would have come readily enough to the call. Breaca flashed him a look that was both challenge and apology. "She will be good," she said. "Almost as good as the roan. She needs time before she comes to trust anyone."

He could believe it. He would have sold the filly at the autumn horse fair but she had kicked the first few who came near her and the rest had kept their distance afterwards so that he had been forced to withdraw her unsold. He had turned her away for the winter, thinking to work on her when the ground softened in spring. Someone had been there ahead of him. Smiling, his daughter said, "She hasn't tried to unman anyone recently. If you lead the roan out first, you will be safe. She will follow where he goes."

"If you say so."

They led the horses to the trackway that ran between the paddocks. Eburovic clicked the roan to a trot and ran alongside for a few paces. When the rhythm was right, he grabbed a handful of mane and made the warrior's mount onto its back. In the height of summer, with some time to practise, he could do it fully armed with his sword free in one hand and his spear in the other, knowing that if he misjudged his timing he would kill himself or maim a horse he loved. Now it was enough that his sword was in its sheath on his back and his spear hand also held his shield. He settled in the saddle, moving the shield to his arm. The blood rushed in his ears and he heard within it the sound of hoofbeats hammering the earth behind him. Spinning the roan, he saw the grey throw herself into a canter. He was reaching down for the bridle, ready to head her off, when he saw Breaca, running on the spear side, reach up for the mane. She was wrong-sided and wrong-footed—and she mounted with perfect timing. The smile she threw him then was a reflection of the morning. He found himself grinning back even as his horse matched hers at the canter. "Can you do that with a spear in your hand?" He shouted it over the drumming of hooves.

"I think so."

"Here, then." It was his war spear, slimmer and lighter than the boar spear she had killed with but with a longer reach and a blade honed to pierce metal. He tossed it across the gap, keeping the point high. She caught it one-handed and slid to the ground, ran for three paces, then, using the spear as a lever with the butt end planted briefly in the turf, vaulted back up. The grey never broke stride. Eburovic smiled and made a gesture of approval. Breaca laughed and spun the spear in the air and then, just for the show of it, she did it again on the shield side. Eburovic watched and tried to recall whether she had been able to do it like that before the winter. He believed not. Thinking back, he tried to remember if he had been able to do it on both sides at the age of twelve, the age she was now. He was almost sure that he had.

The grey was not battle-hardened. The feel of the spear whistling close to her head pushed her into a gallop. They ran free for a while, drawing the horses in the fields on either side to race with them, then curved in a circle and pulled back down the paces to a walk. It was the first ride of the spring, and it did not do to press the horses too hard. Eburovic dropped the reins and let his mount pick the way, feeling the glory of the morning. He had spent the winter existing, not living. Today, for the first time since the autumn, he felt glad to be alive. The air was bright and sharp, cold enough to crisp the hairs in his nose as he breathed in, but not so cold that it stiffened his fingers. Around him, spring was breaking the grip of winter. The first catkins hung on the willow, dusted with frost. Birch trees bore new leaves, unfurling them before the rising sun. Whitethorn flowers, tight in bud, scattered the hedges like the last remnants of snow.

The horses were losing their winter coats. The roan walked with his head up and his ears pricked, the way he walked to war. The filly nudged up beside him and did not roll her eyes when Eburovic leaned over to scratch mud from her neck. Breaca moved her on until they rode knee to knee. She was more sober now, not stiff with shock and the after-taste of dreams as she had been in the forge, but neither was she showing the wild exuberance of the early gallop. There was a sense of containment to her that was new to him. He thought of the warrior's mount she had made and the neat-ness of it. His daughter of a year ago would not have put in the hours of practise needed to get the timing right. It brought to mind the furnace she had built in the forge, with the edges banked high to turn the heat inwards. Before her mother's death, she had been a blazing hearth fire, sparking at random with a vivid, careless joy. Now, she could melt her own core if she chose to. The image nagged at him, taking the edge from the morning. He turned it over in his mind. Too often, he had seen what happened to a vessel stoked over-hot, or a mould poured without air vents. Eburovic rode in silence beside his daughter and made a silent prayer to the gods that she would find a way to let out the fire before it consumed her.

The horses nodded on. Eburovic guided the roan with his knees, remembering. The last time he had come this way he had been on foot, supporting Graine, walking at her side, fearful that the child might come before they reached the place he had made for her. She had smiled her singular smile and promised him it would not and, because it was her second, he had tried to believe her. Breaca had still been a child then; she had run on ahead, searching the paddock edges for late mushrooms, bringing them back to him in dirty hand-fuls. Graine had taken them, and later had found room in a different pouch for the strange-shaped pebble that might, from certain angles, have looked like a lizard's head and the dried casting from an owl that showed the bones of what it had eaten. Both of those had stayed with her body after-wards, making playthings for the crows.

The sun was warm on his right shoulder as they reached the ruins of the birthing hut he had made. The roofing had been taken down within days of the attack and the winter had seen to the rest. He followed his daughter as they rode past it in single file and then left the trackway, cutting right, towards the small wood that reached up the slope on the eastern side. When they reached it, they turned right again, to follow its margins.

Graine's bones lay on the platform south of the wood. She had died with a spear in her hand and the little owl had been her soul's guardian. Eburovic could imagine nothing better as a death gift than the brooch his daughter had made for her. He forced himself to think of it, imagining the shape of the mould, the carved imprint of the lines and the way it had looked when she broke the mould open; anything that meant he did not have to think about where he was going. Breaca rode on ahead of him, straight-backed, with her hair lying like a fiery cloak around her shoulders, and it was impossible to know what she was thinking.

They reached the place midway through the morning. The sun shone from behind, throwing short shadows that pooled at the horses' feet. An easterly wind blew lightly, lifting tatters of blue wool on the platform. On their arrival, a magpie and two jackdaws lifted themselves lazily and moved to a nearby branch. They made no noise. Without speaking—he could not, at that moment, have spoken—Eburovic dismounted and led his horse forward. Breaca pushed the grey to the base of a post. She was not tall enough to see on top of it. He was about to offer a hand when she reached up to the cross-piece and, with an ease that spoke of many repetitions, hoisted herself up, keeping her balance with the tip of one foot on the filly's rump. Like that, she could stretch forward and lay her brooch where she wanted. He saw her lips move but did not hear the words. He turned the roan and walked it away, feeling his gaze an intrusion. She jumped down and rode across to him shortly afterwards. He searched her face and her eyes, looking for signs that the dream had broken, that she had drawn it out as the grandmother had said she should. She smiled then and nodded and he let her be. They rode back again in silence. The wind moved round to the south and the air became heavy. In the distance, thin, grey clouds promised rain.

As they reached the fields and turned the horses out, Eburovic found his voice again.

"Are you busy?" he asked. The spring planting had started. Her days were spent in the fields. If she was not sowing seeds, she was weeding, or clearing the stones. She had washed carefully before coming or there would have been earth packed under her fingernails from the previous day. Out across the paddocks, he could see the others already at work.

Breaca had not been thinking of work. She stared at him blankly for a moment, frowning, then said, "Airmid and Macha have started planting the woad. They will need help to finish before the rain comes. I should be there now."

"Come to the forge when you're finished. I will have something to show you."

She came to him near dusk, with the hens taking the last of the evening light in the doorway. It had rained during the afternoon but the slates of the roof overhung the entrance and the scraped dust bowl was dry. A small, pale hen with a single dark spot on each feather spread her wings in the centre, fluffing her plumage and tilting her head back to catch the heat from inside. It was exceedingly hot. The fires had run all day, using up the greater part of the charcoal. Eburovic had stripped to the waist, abandoning his apron. He worked with his back to the door, hammering. Breaca sat beside the hen, watching the run of iron on iron, feeling the rhythm of it rock through her body, not quite matching the pulse of her heart. She was tired. Her injured hand ached from planting and weeding. She massaged the palm with the thumb of her other hand, letting the roll of the hammer sweep through her, carrying away the irritations of the day. She was more irritable than she had any reason to be and it worried her; she had snapped at the elder grandmother, which was pointless and only brought trouble, and had argued later with Airmid, who was her friend and did not deserve it. Even the ride to the platform had been disappointing, although she had made an effort to conceal that. She let her mind thread back over the moments, trying to find where the day had gone wrong.

"Breaca?" The hammering had stopped without her noticing. "Are you all right?"

"Yes." She smiled for him. It was not a lie. All she needed was a night's sleep and she believed that to be possible now. "I'm late," she said. "I'm sorry. Nemma is nearing childbirth and Airmid wanted to find some valerian root for afterwards. We looked for longer than we should have done."

"But you found it?"

"Of course." Her smile was real this time. "Would I be here otherwise? Airmid is not one to give up on something when she has set her mind to it." Which had been, stupidly, the source of the argument. She stood, taking care not to fluster the hen. "Am I too late for you?"

"No. Come in. I was just finishing."

The forge was much as it had been at dawn; the fire glowed orange, throwing odd, shifting shadows across the walls. The smell was of burned metal and burning charcoal and the man-sweat of her father. On impulse, she kissed his arm, tasting salt and scorched hair. He hugged her and, looking past his shoulder, she found why the fires had burned so hot for so long: Eburovic had spent the day welding. An unfinished sword lay on the bench, the blade as long as her arm and as wide as her hand, with one end narrowed to a prong that would one day take the hilt. She picked it up. The hilt end fitted well to her hand and the weight of the blade was not too great. The metal still held the bloom from the fire and the blued mackerel stripes of the woven welds that bound the nine narrow strips of raw iron into one broader blade. She swung it once, experimentally, and felt the thin thrill of almost-fear that sang through her whenever she handled her father's finished weapons. Reverentially, she laid it back on the bench.

"Well?"

"It's good," she said. She had learned from him to be careful with her praise.

"Would you test it against a real blade?"

"Can I?"

"Yes. Take it."

She did so. The feeling was more than it had been. A hollow place in the palm of her hand opened to receive it. Holding it, her joints swung more freely, as they did after riding, or practising with the spear. She swung a few times, feeling the weight of it, and then, looking up, saw that Eburovic had squared up in front of her, holding his own sword, the great blade with the feeding she-bear on the pommel that held the lives and deeds of her ancestors in her father's line. He said, "Make the back cut to the head."

The blade wanted to move. Using both hands, she swung backhanded, aiming for his temple. Iron clashed on iron. A single spark flew to the doorway.

"Good. Now on the forehand to my knee."

The air thrummed past her arms. The solid, unformed edge of her blade sang down the full length of his, riding over the notch that the white-headed champion of the Coritani had made when he fought her great-grandfather in single combat to settle the dispute of a boundary line. A storm of sparks flew high in the darkness. She let the tip of her blade bounce off the packed earth of the floor.

"And a thrust to the chest . . ."

She was more careful with this one, knowing he would catch the weight of it on the hilt. Her blade rode on his and stopped, suddenly. The shock of the impact rolled through her shoulder. The oval of red enamel on the left side of her father's cross-piece chimed out of tune with the rest but did not crack as it had done in the hands of her grandfather's grandfather as he fought Caesar's legions by the river.

"Good. Very good." He was smiling, quietly, as he did when he had a surprise for her. Taking up a chalk stone, he measured the blade against the length of her arm.

"You are young. You have two hands' more growing in you yet but it is still too long for what you will be. We will cut it, here"——he made a mark with the chalk——"at the lower third. If you want, we can use the extra iron to make the cross-piece and the pommel. Or, if you prefer it, they can be cast in bronze. If you were the one making the sword, which would you choose?"

Her eyes sprang wide. "Am I to make it?"

That would have made the day perfect. For years, she had imagined the blade she would make when he deemed her old enough to work iron.

His gift was better yet. He said, "You can help to make it if you want, but I think your own blade should be made by someone else. It is stronger like that."

Her head spun. This was more than perfect. Tentatively, she touched the unmade blade and felt the thrill of it. Her father said, "When your mother died, I promised to make you a sword. This is the one. It sings to you and you to it. And so, knowing that, would you have me make the hilt of bronze or of iron?"

Too much, too soon. She sat down with her back to the furnace and tried to let go of the song in her head. She needed to think as a smith. The quality and weight of the blade made for the length of the stroke and the power it needed to bite into flesh, but a good craftsman put the soul of the sword in the patterns on the cross-piece, the feel of the grip and the shape set on the pommel, and it was the choice of materials that made each of these unique. Iron was harder but colder. Bronze might dent but was easier to work and could carry more detail. Her father's sword hung on the wall behind him. The patterns on the hilt of the she-bear blade were ancient and complex; it would not be possible to draw the same subtlety from iron. Looking at it, Breaca found that she wanted her own blade to be as close to her father's as possible.

"The hilt and the pommel should be of bronze," she said, formally. "But we should not make them until I have had my dreaming and know what shape they need to be."

"Then it will be so. We will make the blade first and wait for your dream. Come when you can and we will make it together. I have an idea of something new we might try."

CHAPTER 3

They worked on the new blade intermittently through the remainder of the spring, snatching shared time. Foaling ended and the late planting began. Breaca spent her mornings and evenings attending to the needs of the elder grandmother and the greater part of each day in the company of every other able-bodied adult and grown child, sowing beans and peas and barley and weeding between the rising rows of winter wheat and carrying water to the high fields when the new seeds began to sprout. In the times between, there were mares to be checked for mastitis and foals to be handled and the first few steps to be taken in gentling last year's foals that had spent the winter coming to hand for their feed but had not yet known a bridle.

The sense of her mother changed. On the platform beyond the fields at the edge of the forest, the bones of the dead bleached under the sun and grew grey under the rain. For a while, as the hawthorns shed their flowers, they lay under a fall of petalled snow and took on the colour around them. She visited still, but less often, and Breaca's nights were calmer. If her mother came at all, she brought peace and good memories, not pain.

The world moved fast around them. In a birthing hut built inside the rampart, Nemma gave birth to a red-haired baby boy. Of those several youths who could have been the sire, Verulos pledged its rearing. He was lame in one foot and had failed his warrior's tests but he was a good apprentice harness-maker and it was widely agreed that he would be a suitable father. Nemma was clearly content with the outcome.

In the forge, the sword grew slowly from the dense, dark shaft to the blue iron of a forged blade. The metal worked well under the hammer. Eburovic sang over it as he had not sung all winter. Once, he asked Breaca for hair plucked from the sides of her head where it would be braided for battle, and another time for her nail parings. She gave him what he asked for and watched him build them into the start of the day's fires, still singing. He did other things as well, things that she had not seen before, and the forge became a place of new explorations that drew her back daily and sang her to sleep at night.

Elsewhere, Bán nursed his hound whelp. The small thing had become less small and found his legs. His eyes, which had been pale blue like the sky when they opened, had gone grey like her father's and then brown like Macha's and Bán's. With longer legs and better vision, he progressed from chasing snails and slugs and beetles to herding the chickens and bothering the mares. Taller still, he learned that the roasting fires were worth watching and Camma, younger sister to Nemma, who tended them, found herself daily engaged in a challenge where the winner gained at least a portion of a meal and the loser might go hungry. She did not always win.

The traders came with the change in the weather. Arosted was first; the slight, wiry salt trader who came up the tracks on the last of the snow, leading his train of splay-footed pack ponies with his son and his daughter and two of his half-cousins as helpers, haulers and guardians. He laid out his bricks of salt, still crisp and dry from the kilns, in one of the barns and the bargaining began. In previous years, he had traded for weapons. This year, because the people of the Dobunni, in whose land the salt springs rose, had made peace with their southern neighbours, he took instead brooches and belt buckles from Eburovic, two sapling hounds bred by Macha from a promising young bitch, and a pair of doeskins which had been hunted by Sinochos and prepared by Nemma, whose dream was the red doe and who could turn out their skins softer than anyone.

Besides salt, Arosted brought the first news of the outside world in the wake of winter, a service for which he was also well paid. As the flurry of trading subsided, he took Eburovic and Macha aside, conveying the news that the elders of the Coritani wished it to be known that they had cast out three of their younger warriors at the start of winter in retribution for a raid that went against the laws of gods and men. Most important, they wished it to be understood that they would never, in any circumstances, have sanctioned an attack on a woman in childbirth, particularly not a woman as honoured by the gods as was the late leader of the Eceni.

When Macha suggested politely that it was not unknown for the elders of the Coritani to lie, Arosted showed them the armband in solid gold that he had been given to ensure the message was passed speedily to the right ears. If they lied, they did not do so cheaply. Eburovic, in turn, gave him a bay horse recently broken for riding and a dagger made of hard iron with copper wire bound round the hilt. It was deemed a fair trade.

The salt trader left with the old moon. The new brought others, most notably Gunovic, horse-racer, warrior and travelling smith—and the only weapons-maker in living memory to match Eburovic in skill. He rode up from the south, bringing rods of raw iron fresh from his ovens and newly cast cakes of copper and tin from the mines and furnaces in the south and ingots of silver from the far north and red Hibernian gold. He was a big, bulky man with dark hair and skin that had weathered to brown even at the start of spring. His tunic was black, set about with brooches in gold, silver and bronze that showed off to good advantage against the dark material, and the sleeves had been cut out, the better to display the fortune he wore in bands on his bare arms. He rode through the gates on a hazy afternoon in a jingle and clash of precious metals and the trading had begun before he reached the first of the horse barns. At the roundhouse, he was given oatcakes and ale while others unpacked his baggage train for him. He sat in the doorway with Macha and the elder grandmother, exchanging news from those parts of the south not yet visited by Arosted, while his work was passed from hand to hand to get the feel of it.

In the beginning he offered the easy, decorative things: brooches, combs, dress pins, neck-pieces and armbands, all in gold and silver, copper and bronze, with or without enamel insets. This year, for the first time, there was blue enamel set alongside the red on some of the pieces; Belgic work, from the apprentice workshops on the continent. The blue was very close to the colour of the Eceni cloaks and those pieces went first, followed closely by others inset with coral or amber, or finely worked in silver and gold. Long before evening, he had traded all the pieces he intended to sell and gone on to bargain with Eburovic in the forge, exchanging, amongst other things, several cakes of raw blue enamel for a mirror in silver and a brooch cleverly made to look like a spear-head from the front but with a feeding she-bear arced across the back of it.

The place of honour in the roundhouse that evening was his. Sinochos had hunted and they feasted on jugged hare and field beans spiced with wild garlic. They asked him for a song after. Gunovic was not a singer, he had no training, but he had a good stock of stories that were common amongst the tribes and a voice to do them justice. He drank the ale and bade them stoke up the fire and, in honour of Eburovic, began with a tale for the children, of the she-bear who lived in a cave in a mountain and first brought fire to the ancestors, together with the skills to forge metal. It was a good tale, although here in the flat lands of the east, where a hill barely made a thumbprint on the horizon, he spent time building for the young ones a picture of the jagged, snow-laden mountains in which the bear lived and the great cascading waterfall, the height of nine times nine men, that tumbled down for ever in crashing torrents to fill the gods' pool below. They watched him in utter silence. Bán hugged Hail at each mention of the beast, never taking his gaze from the weaving, sensuous hands of the smith and the stream of shadow pictures they cast on the wall.

They left the bear at the gods' pool, talking to Nemain, the moon, who alone of the sacred ones showed her face twice to her people, once in the sky and again on the water, thus showing that water was the way by which one could reach the gods. The children, protesting, were gathered and wrapped and laid down, some to sleep, some to listen, some to try to listen but still to sleep. Bán was offered his old sleeping place with Silla but turned it down. Hail was old enough now not to need feeding through the night and there was no reason for Bán still to sleep in the harness hut but he liked it and was guarding the privilege fiercely. In any case, he had no intention of going to bed when he knew the best tale was yet to come. He curled in his cloak beside his mother with Hail resting on his other side and set himself to listen.

Breaca sat further round, on the right hand of the elder grandmother, ready to offer assistance should the old woman have need of it. Her scarred hand ached, deep down between the finger bones, as it did when she was tired. Absently, she rubbed the place on her knee. Gunovic leaned inwards and passed her his jug. They had raced their horses earlier and he had won, but only by a short head. He had complimented her on the grey filly afterwards and given her a brooch shaped like the small fierce owl who hunts by day. It was the only way in which he showed that he had heard of the death of her mother and it was done privately, with kindness, as was his way. Next to her father, he was the best warrior she had ever known and he had taught her some of the dirtiest moves with the sword that a man could think of. If she had killed the Coritani by skill with weapons, Gunovic was as much to thank as anyone. She accepted his jug with a nod, drank, and passed it on round the circle. The ale was warm and bitter and it cleansed the last taste of garlic from her mouth if it did nothing for the pain in her hand.

There was some shuffling and rearranging of seating as people filled the spaces closer to the fire. A piece of salt-laden driftwood as long as a man's arm was laid on the embers, sending up fierce blue sparks to dance in the roof space. The smell of it was sharp with the iron-salt tang of the sea. The flame built higher, casting long, leaping shadows to the thatch above. Carved beasts on the doorpost shimmered and came to life. Smoke layered above them, holding in the heat. A third jug was opened for Gunovic, who took it back to the singer's place on the far side of the fire. Before, he had been standing, the better to show the shadow play with his hands. Now he sat, resting his back on a hide stuffed with horsehair that leaned against the wall. When he had quiet, he addressed the elder grandmother, as tradition demanded.

"Grandmother. You have heard all tales that can be told. The choice of which to hear now is yours."

The old woman stared into the heart of the fire, her head cocked as if listening. Presently she lifted her eyes to meet those of the smith. "Give us the tale of Cassivellaunos," she said.

Other voices murmured approval. It was a classic tale of good against evil, where the colours were clear and right prevailed against the odds. Gunovic was silent for a moment, thinking. Then he lifted his head and began.

"I tell the tale of the greatest warrior, of Cassivellaunos, grandfather's father to Cunobelin, the Sun Hound, who rules over the Trinovantes and the Catuvellauni who live to the south. . . ."

His voice was new. It lost the singer's lilt and became the voice of Cassivellaunos, speaking on the eve of battle; the warrior who, alone of all the people, had the strength and foresight to unite the warring tribes at the time of Caesar's two invasions.

In her mind, Breaca saw a giant of a man with flowing copper hair seated on his roan battle horse. His great brindle war hounds gathered about him, collared in leather and iron, ready to rip the throats from the legions. Around his neck he wore the torc of leadership, cast for him in gold by a smith of the Eceni. More black feathers than could be counted hung from the end-pieces of the torc, each with its quill stained red to mark the warriors he had killed in fair battle. His shield was of bull's hide and so heavy it took two other men to lift it. His sword was of iron and when he drew it on horseback the tip reached to the ground. About his shoulders he wore a great multicoloured cloak, patched with the colours of all the tribes who came to join him: sky blue for the Eceni, white for the Ordovices, red and black striped for the Brigantes who worship only Briga, green for the Cornovii who follow the horned one, grey for the warriors and dreamers of Mona, those individuals selected from all the tribes to study on the sacred island. Only the gorse-flower yellow of the Trinovantes was missing, for it was Mandubracios, a prince of that tribe, who had betrayed the hero and his allies to the enemy.

This was close to home and had the spice of near danger; the Trinovantes held the territory immediately to the south of the Eceni homelands and the truce between the two peoples had never been easy. In the dark, Mandubracios of the Trinovantes grew before them: a venal man who coveted land and power not given him by the gods. He was a poor warrior and lacked courage but made up for it in cunning. When it was clear that he could not defeat Cassivellaunos by force of arms, he travelled to Gaul and petitioned aid from the greatest enemy of all, Julius Caesar, asking for the legions' help in defeating his enemy.

Twice, Caesar's legions invaded. The battle in the first year was the stuff of heroes but that in the second year was by far the greater. The armies met on opposing banks of the river that led to the sea and it was as if the gods themselves were fighting. The battle raged from dawn until long into the afternoon and the water of the river ran thick with the blood of both sides. Warriors died in the thousands, defending land that was not their own.

Towards evening, seeing they could not prevail, Cassivellaunos led the survivors along secret paths to his stronghold. The place was in marshland, hidden on all sides by forest, and thought safe. It gave sanctuary to the wearied warriors, allowed time to eat and rest and bind their wounds, time for the smiths to forge more spear-heads and beat out new blades, time for the dreamers to reach the gods and ask for aid.

But the stronghold was not safe. Mandubracios knew of it and he brought the enemy with him, whispering in his ear his knowledge of Cassivellaunos's only weakness. The great warrior had a war hound named Belin for the sun god and he loved it as he loved his children. In secret, men of the Trinovantes stole the hound away, luring it with fresh meat and sweet voices. It came willingly, for it was not a hateful hound unless set at the enemy in war. And so on the morning of the third day, a horn sounded from the marshland beyond the stronghold. Cassivellaunos looked from the ramparts and saw the enemy ranged about him. He lifted his spear and would have given the order to open the gates to attack, but then he saw his favourite hound crucified in front of the enemy ranks with its muzzle bound shut that it might not howl and warn its master. The dog died as Cassivellaunos watched and its head was taken off and mounted on a spear and brought forward with the demand for unconditional surrender. It was then that the great warrior's heart was broken. If the enemy could do that to a hound, which was sacred, what would he do to the people? He consulted with his dreamers and walked out of the gates of his fort and laid his great blade, which had taken many lives, at the feet of the enemy, spitting on him as he did so.

Gunovic stopped there. It was time. Breaca was not the only one weeping. All around her men and women choked and wiped their faces. At Macha's side, Bán was sobbing inconsolably. He clutched a struggling Hail to his chest and called down ghastly, graphic curses on the enemy, on all who came from Gaul, on the house of the traitor Mandubracios who wore a gorse-yellow cloak. Macha wrapped him in her own cloak and rocked him like an infant, promising him that the story became better and that the great dreamer Onomaris, whose dream was the kittiwake, had spoken with Manannan, god of the sea, calling up a storm to wreck the Roman warships so that Cassivellaunos's life was spared and Caesar's legions departed, never to return again. As was always the case, the dreamers won the battle if the warriors could not. It made no difference to Bán. The beloved hound was dead and those who did it were to be cursed for generations.

Gunovic came closer to the fire. "It may be they were cursed as you say," he said. "Julius Caesar died alone, slain by his own countrymen, and none of his line has ever been heard of since. The traitor Mandubracios died childless and it is a descendant of Cassivellaunos who now rules the Trinovantes as well as the Catuvellauni."

"Who?" Bán had moved from sobs to hiccoughs and had difficulty making long sentences. "How does he rule his enemy's people?"

"His name is Cunobelin, which means 'Hound of the Sun.' He rules two tribes because he is a very clever man who loves power, and he commands more spears than any other so that none dare stand against him."

"His sons will do so," said the elder grandmother, sourly. She alone did not show signs of weeping. "At least the firebrand, if not the others."

Bán's eyes were wide. "Who is the firebrand?"

Gunovic said, "Caradoc, third and youngest son of Cunobelin. The Sun Hound has spread his seed wide and with a purpose. Togodubnos is the first son, born to a woman of the royal line of the Trinovantes. He ensures his father's line amongst that people. He is a giant for his age, with black hair and a hooked nose. He has not yet killed in battle but he earned his warrior's tests in good faith. He is a good diplomat. He would make a fine leader did his father permit it. The second son, Amminios—he is a redhead, pale, with sallow skin and eyes that water—is out of a high-born Gaulish woman. He has been reared half in Gaul and has become so Roman that he wears the toga when he eats and plucks the hairs from his nostrils twice every month to make himself pretty—it's true . . ." His voice rose high in indignation at the raised brows and mocking smiles around him. "You may mock, but Amminios has his father's blessing and spends his days drinking wine with the magistrates in Gaul. He already has three horse farms and trading rights in wine and glass and fine tableware and is amassing his own private fortune."

"And slaves." The elder grandmother spat on the fire. "That one makes his fortune trading in slaves. His wealth is in blood, as is his father's."

"Indeed, it may be so." Gunovic nodded, slowly. "Caradoc, however, is of different stock. He is exceptional. If you are in battle, this is the warrior you want at your side. His mother is war leader of the Ordovices and they, as you know, are second only to the Silures in the courage and strength of their warriors."

His eyes were on Eburovic, whose distant ancestors were of the Silures. Eburovic stretched his arms and moved his feet to the fire. "That's a lie," he said pleasantly, "and you know it."

Gunovic grinned. The Eceni smith was his closest friend. What is life if you cannot taunt a friend a little? The others grinned with him, feeling the tension die.

Eburovic moved so the fire lit his face. "You should tell the truth if you would be a singer, smith. The Silures are good warriors, some of us may even be heroes, but the Ordovices are exceptional. It is said that they are born with the battle fever in their eyes and that it never passes from them. Those who fight against them ride out expecting to die. Most of them do so."

Gunovic inclined his head. "It may be so. I bow to your greater experience. Certainly the mother of Caradoc is a warrior of known prowess. Her name is Ellin nic Conia." His voice lapsed again into the cadence saved for the tales of heroes. "She is tall and very beautiful, with hair the colour of corn before harvest and green-grey eyes that take on all the shades of the sea. She wears a tunic the colour of her eyes and is known across the land for her valour in battle. Her horses are the finest of those bred in the west, her sword-cuts the hardest, her spear flies the farthest, or at least"—his voice altered, gathering a sense of portents to come—"they did all of these until last winter when her son Caradoc, at eleven years old, took his warrior tests from her people and won his spear. Now his mother's spear flies second to her son's."

"At eleven? He passed his warrior's tests amongst the Ordovices at eleven?" It was 'Tagos, sister's son to Sinochos, who asked. He was twelve years old, nearly thirteen, and he was due to take his tests at the winter gathering. It was considered a good age with no shame if he failed the first time. To pass, he had to throw a spear and hit the mark nine times out of nine at fifty paces. Less than one in ten who tried it passed first time.

"He did." Gunovic nodded. "It was attested by all their dreamers. None has taken them younger and succeeded. He will take the tests of both the Trinovantes and the Catuvellauni in the next year. His father does not approve and will do nothing to help him, but I have seen the boy, and he will succeed. When he does so, he will be a named warrior of three different peoples. There is no man, including his father, who has ever achieved such a feat."

"And will the son slaughter the dreamers as his father has done, or will he honour them, after the way of his mother's people?"

There was a shocked silence. It was Macha who had spoken. In the same cold voice, she said, "It is ten years since the Sun Hound killed the last of his true dreamers. There were two. He had them skinned alive and their bodies nailed to a hazel tree and took instead Heffydd the False who speaks his master's words as if they came from the gods. Will the firebrand son follow him in his sacrilege, do you think?"

"No." Gunovic shook his head. "The Ordovices hold the lands that lead to the sacred isle of Mona. Of all the tribes, they are bound closest to the dreamers. Caradoc despises his father and follows his mother in everything. He will not drive out the dreamers, wherever he comes to rule."

"Good." That from 'Tagos, who had sat with his fists bunched, ready to fight but with no obvious target. He let them relax and rolled his shoulders as one does cooling down from a fight.

Sinochos said, "So then what of the Sun Hound who has three different sons by three different mothers? Has he finished his sowing of seed or need we warn our daughters to be wary of Trinovantian men with plucked noses and heads thick with wine?"

There was a ripple of laughter, not quite sure of itself. Gunovic stood, stretching his legs. "Oh, he's too old. It's his sons you have to warn them of; they come in threes and are inescapable. And smiths with dry throats and hairy nostrils. Warn them of those as well."

He grinned so his teeth shone in the firelight and the

absurdity of it made them laugh again, which was a good way to finish and wiped away the last memories of the first sun hound and its death at the hands of the Romans. Only Bán did not forget. He slept for the night with his mother as he had not done since he was three years old, and Hail slept in the space between them.

Gunovic left three days later, the richer by three new packhorses, a big bay three-year-old colt that would be trained and ready as a riding horse for him to take when he next passed by, the promise of grain to fill his packs when he came back in the autumn, nine blocks of salt, a tunic in pale undyed wool with a border in Eceni blue, a set of bone needles and a selection of dried herbs that would heal both himself and his mounts if he could remember which were for poultices and which to take with food—and such finished and part-finished weapons as Eburovic felt he could spare in the circumstances.

As befitted his status, he also carried a message directly to the elders of the Coritani through whose lands he was to travel next. It said that the Eceni considered the attack in the autumn to have been the act of rash youth and it should not be allowed to foment ill-feeling between two peoples who should better remain at peace. In evidence of the earnest intent of his words, he showed an armband in gold that was both broader and heavier than the one that had been given Arosted the salt trader when he delivered his message in the other direction. In trading with the warriors of the red kite, he was able to offer a great many brooches of high value but few spear-heads or sword blanks, having already shed most of his stock.

Gunovic passed through the Coritani and on north to the homelands of the Brigantes, fierce-fighting followers of Briga, where he found that he did, in fact, have iron to trade, including several dozen good Eceni spear-heads, together with the rumour, provenance unknown, that the Coritani were massing to attack their northern neighbours. He was well rewarded and enjoyed his stay and turned west towards the mountains a rich and happy man.

CHAPTER 4

Late spring moved into summer and brought an early
drought. The heat was greater than anyone remembered it.
The air sucked moisture from ground and people alike.
Horses stood in pairs in the shade of the hawthorns, flick-
ing their tails in each other's faces. In the roundhouse, the
door-flap was raised to its fullest and the fire damped to a
bare minimum. The elder grandmother slept naked on top
of her furs with her arms stretched out sideways to let off
more heat. In the forge, the fires had been cut to a single
glowing coal. Nobody moved who did not have to.

Breaca found Airmid by the sacred pool beneath the
waterfall. The older girl lay stretched like a lizard on a scoop
of rock. A nine-stemmed hazel grew out of a crack beside
her, its leaves throwing oval shadows equally on the rock, her
body and the water. The patterns shifted with the lift and
stir of the breeze, blurring her outline so that, walking past,
it would have been easy to miss her. Even knowing exactly
where to look, Breaca still had to stand and wait until her
eyes had made the change from sunlight to shadows and

could pick out the dark of sunned skin against the lichen-dappled stone. When she was sure, she climbed up on a different rock and sat for a while studying Airmid, watching the pattern of her breathing and trying to see if her eyes were open. In time, when it seemed clear that the girl was awake and not dreaming, Breaca slid down, laid her gift on the ground between them, returned and settled herself to wait.

And wait. Behind her, a stand of mixed thorns and hornbeams buzzed with life. At the corner of the wood a small, slate-grey bird caught flies and fastened them with careful intelligence to the spikes of a blackthorn bush. Elsewhere, a wagtail moved from stone to stone across the water, filling its beak with insects, carrying them in relays to a waiting nest. On its third trip, it gave way to a kingfisher, a streak of blue light with the sun-bloom on its belly that flashed down over the water and dived for a fish in the centre. Seventeen heartbeats passed before it surfaced, carrying no fish. Frowning, Breaca watched the water close over the place it had been. It did not seem right that a bird should have gone to the realm of the gods and come back empty-handed. She looked over to Airmid, wanting to talk, but the other girl's eyes stared blankly out across the water. It was possible, after all, that she was dreaming. Breaca let out the breath she had been holding and went back to waiting. This time, she did not watch the pool.

Everyone dreams. From before she could walk, from before she could speak more than her own and her mother's name, Breaca had listened to others talk of their dreams and their dreaming. It had come to her early that while her mother had dreams—colourful, vivid, lively dreams with great bearing on her life and her family—Macha and the elder grandmother spent time alone *dreaming* and came back to the roundhouse with their eyes fixed on faraway places and the words of the gods on their lips. At much the same time, it had come to Breaca that she wanted the dreaming far more than the dreams—and that it was granted far less often.

Three times since she had been old enough to understand the nature of what was happening, girls had gone out to spend their three nights alone and come back to tell of it. The sisters Camma and Nemma had gone out in succeeding years and come back with the white goose and the deer respectively as their dreams. Camma, who passed her days keeping Hail from her roasting pans, had been a vague, pale-haired lass who lived with her eyes on another horizon, but motherhood had taught her the truth of her dream and she guarded her two children with a ferocity that proved worthy of it. Nemma, her sister, had returned with the red doe, but it would have been astonishing had it been otherwise. From early childhood she had followed the tracks of the red deer, collecting dropped antlers and moulding deer-shapes out of scraps of hunted skin. Throughout one summer, she had reared an orphaned hind calf, feeding it on mare's milk and teaching it to come to her call, so that now, in hard winters, she fed it as she fed the horses. Sinochos and the other hunters knew its tracks and knew that they touched it at their peril.

Those were the first two Breaca saw. Neither was exceptional; each was happy with her dream and each paid due respects to the goose or the deer at the appointed days and times and hung a token—a feather and a hind foot respectively—on the wall above her sleeping place to act as guardian. It was Airmid, strange, tall, dark-skinned, dark-haired Airmid, who was different. She was the one who, at dusk on the last day of her long-nights, had walked back in through the door to the women's place, stepping across the stones laid in the entrance as if walking on water, with her eyes not in focus and her face wide with wonder and her mouth still not able to make the words for what she had seen. She had not been given a token; she had no need of something external to remind her of what had happened. The gods had spoken. They would continue to do so, and what they had said defined the rest of her life. She was a dreamer.

Breaca had witnessed the full import of it in the spring before her mother died. It was a sharp, clear morning with a good sun and a thick frost. She had risen early, out of habit, and was sitting outside the roundhouse, working on a deerskin. Bán had been with her, plucking a woodcock he had caught in a trap. Everyone else was still asleep when Airmid arrived, running from the women's place, skipping barefoot past the midden without care for the debris, stopping only at the door to the roundhouse because the elder grandmother had spoken to her sharply from inside, saying her name and asking for caution. She had waited then, panting, clenching and unclenching her fingers, with her dark hair, so much like Macha's, still crushed flat from sleeping and her eyes wild and the chaos of the dream hanging about her, making her *other*, in ways she had not seemed before. The grandmother had finished dressing then and come out to listen and, with a visible effort, Airmid had come back from the place her mind had gone. "The rain is coming," she said, and her voice had rasped, like a frog's. "Nine days from now. We need to move everything."

"The rain always comes. Why should we move anything now?" The elder grandmother had been gentle, which was a new experience. In normal circumstances, one roused her early at great peril.

"There's too much. It will flood. The gods' pool beneath the waterfall will not hold all the water and it will spread out across the paddocks like a sea. The river will carry the bodies past the doorway of the roundhouse. The bodies—"

She had stopped then, biting her lips to keep from weeping; Airmid, who wept for nothing and no-one. Breaca had reached for her, but the elder grandmother had risen first and taken the older girl inside to lie down on her own bed and given her a wad of willow to chew until she slept, and Breaca had been set to watch over her while the old woman went off to discuss the news with her peers.

There had followed a scatter of unseasonal activity. Over the next seven days, the people had moved to the higher pastures and carried with them everything that would spoil. On the ninth day, the rains had come as Airmid had said they would. Over the course of the day, the river had swollen and burst its banks and the flood had risen halfway up the wall of the roundhouse and everyone who saw it had given thanks for the timeliness of the warning that had allowed them to move; all except for Airmid herself, who had wept inconsolably through fingers splayed wide with grief because the three frogs that had come to warn her in the dream had floated past, dead, on the water.

Breaca had watched her more closely after that, if from a distance. Airmid had a difficult reputation and it was not entirely undeserved. Four years spent as the eyes and limbs of the elder grandmother had left their mark so that she did not speak much and when she did so, it was with an irony that frequently bordered on rudeness. If pushed, the edge of her tongue was sharper than anyone but the elder grandmother's and that was not something to court without reason.

Other gossip was less accurate. The tale of Dubornos, the redheaded son of Sinochos, and the damage she had done him was plainly untrue although Airmid had made no effort to refute it, which was frustrating. In the early days, when Breaca had realized that it was jealousy that made her peers speak so badly of the older girl, she had tried to defend her. She had fought, twice, and been blooded. Later, after a conversation with her mother, she had stopped fighting another's battles and set herself instead to watch and learn what she could of the secrets of dreaming. If Airmid noticed, she gave no sign.

Everything had changed in the autumn with the death of Breaca's mother. Airmid had been a quiet, solid presence at a time when the world had turned over and she had made the gift of the red-quilled warrior's feather, which no-one else had thought to do. Afterwards, a new respect had grown between them, and then friendship, which went deeper and was worth more.

It was a good day to sit quietly with a friend. Breaca watched the changing flood of light on the surface of the pool. The sun moved and her shadow moved with it, sliding forward by degrees until it stretched to the first reeds that hedged the bank. She considered whether she needed to change her position so that her shadow might not taint the water and decided not. The sun moved further until it shone on her back, warming the place between her shoulder blades that had felt exposed since the morning of her mother's death. She closed her eyes and let the heat move inwards. In her mind, her mother spoke to her, as she had done in her infanthood and, like an infant, she did not understand the words. In the distance, a frog began to speak and the two voices merged. A hand took over from the sun, kneading the muscles that ran up either side of her spine. A voice that was not her mother's said quietly, "Breaca, open your eyes."

She did so. A small frog, less than three fingers wide, sat on a rock in the dark of her shadow. His skin was moss-green with a brown stripe along the side. His eyes were entirely black, and when he blinked the upper and lower lids met in the middle of the brown stripe. He blinked now. Breaca blinked back.

Airmid said, "How did you know that I needed the plantain?"

"I heard you tell Macha."

"Where did you find it?"

"There's a plant in the high paddock, where the yearling colts grazed in spring. I picked the leaves at the old moon and took care to take only one in three. The plant is still living."

"Thank you. That was well done." Next to her frogs, Airmid cared most about the plants. It was one of the things that set her apart from the others. The hands moved from Breaca's spine to her shoulders, working out the knots of a morning's work. "You have been practising with your father's new war spears again?"

"Only for a short while. Macha needed help with the weeding. Afterwards, I took one out to the lower meadow and tried it for balance."

"Was it good?"

"It will be good for Sinochos. He holds them further back. I would need a weight at the butt end to keep the tip up."

"Hmm. Move your arm . . . no, back, like that, to make this muscle bigger . . . does that hurt?"

"A little." Breaca closed her eyes, seeking the spot on the top of her shoulder where the pain began.

"I thought so. Here, do you feel that? You've torn it. You should talk to your father. Ask him to make a spear balanced for you. Is that better?"

"Yes, thank you. He won't make one. I'm too young. If it comes to war, I won't be allowed to fight."

"It won't come to war this summer. The elders will meet at the midsummer gathering to review their decision but it is well known how you feel and if you speak against it nobody will gainsay you. If the Coritani were to attack, they might change their minds, but Gunovic has done his work well; the Brigantes are threatening them from the north and the warriors of the red kite are not so many that they can defend two borders at one time. They will not attack us if we do not attack them, so there will be peace for now. It may be different by next summer, but you will have your own blade by then as well as a spear."

"I might still be a child, and not allowed to fight."

"No. You will be a woman before the winter."

"How do you know?"

"I can read it in the water."

It was a joke. Airmid's voice changed, deepening so that it thrummed through them both. Breaca opened her eyes and looked downwards. In the pool, their merged reflections shimmered. She watched as Airmid's hands moved forward, sliding under her arms to lift the curve of her breasts. She frowned. A cold ache began inside her. "Is it so sure?"

"I think so. You can't stay a child for ever." The fingers worked gently, making her stomach swoon. "Does that hurt?"

"No . . . Yes. A little. Only if you squeeze hard."

"But they feel sore more than they used to?"

"Yes."

"Then it will be two months. Three at the most. You will come to your bleeding by the end of harvest, if not sooner."

They were not joking now, not for this. It was too big to think of. Airmid's hands linked in front of her, squeezing her diaphragm, warming the place where the fear grew. Breaca looked up at the sky. High overhead a kestrel hung on a thermal, a blurred smudge in blue air. Beside her, Airmid said, "Be happy. By this time next year, you will be free of the elder grandmother."

"Did you think that when you went out on your long-nights?"

"No. I was happy with her. I was sad to leave."

"I will be too."

"I know."

The sun moved round and glanced up off the water, achingly bright. They slid off the rock and into the shade of the hazel and lay side by side, their arms stretched out together, dark skin and pale making alternating bands of colour. Breaca turned onto her stomach and drew patterns on Airmid's arm, starting at the wrist and moving up the forearm. At the elbow, she stopped and traced the lines of an old tattoo. The pattern was fading a little with age but it had been carefully done, slightly larger than life, as if the god, in the shape of a frog, had dipped a hind foot in blue-green ink and stepped on the inner fold of Airmid's elbow where the mark of it would be closest to her heart. Breaca drew a loop around it with her finger. With care, because it was not done even for the closest of friends to probe too deeply into another's dreaming, she said: "I have always wondered how the elder grandmother could do this without sight to guide her hand."

"She doesn't need eyes to see the patterns of things. You know that."

"I do. But I thought she might have done it before, when you were a child and she could still see."

"No. I didn't know about the frogs then. They didn't come to me before my long-nights. Nothing came before then. I thought I was barren, that I would be coming back with nothing. I used to lie awake praying to Nemain for a dream, any dream, even if it was one that barely touched me, like Camma's. The elder grandmother told me once that she thought I might dream the earthworm and I believed her I couldn't sleep for nights afterwards, thinking how bad it would be."

"She told me I was a wasp, that I would sleep through the winter and sting people in the summer."

"She has her own reasons. I think the worrying is needed, to leave you open for the gods. But you will dream. You must believe it. It's just hard to wait."

"I know. I have no patience. But it's better when we talk about it."

It had been her utmost fear: that she was so close to becoming a woman and still the gods had sent no sign. It was good to hear that it had been the same for Airmid. The knot in her diaphragm relaxed a little. She sighed and shifted over on the rock, moving her hand on the other girl's hip. A soft kiss brushed her neck. She leaned into it and let her fingers drift down, exploring. It was a day for new patterns, for exploring in the shifting shadows, for merging, sweat-glued, with another. The kisses became longer and more focused and their direction changed. At the pool, the king-fisher dived a second time, unwitnessed, and came up with a fish. High above, the kestrel slipped sideways over the water and began to hunt the rushes on the far bank. Across the river, in the horse paddocks, a boy and a hound whelp played with a leggy dun filly, taking turns to stalk imaginary monsters.

The sun moved on and the shadows made sharper angles. Breaca lay with a palm pressed to Airmid's frog-print and thought of childhood and what it would be to leave it. A new thought came, one that brought back the cold, differently. She rolled over, moving out of the shade. It did not make the thought better. "Airmid. . . ?"

"Yes?"

"What if I don't become a dreamer, and you are called to go to the dreamers' school on Mona? Would you go without me?"

"What?"

The older girl came upright, suddenly, frowning to make sense of the question. Looking her straight in the eye, Breaca said, "The training is twelve years, maybe twenty, if the elders ask it. Would you go without me?"

"No, of course not, how could you say that?" The frown was frozen on Airmid's face. Her fingers, lacing through Breaca's, squeezed until the knuckles were white. "It is not going to happen," she said. "Don't talk of it. You will dream."

"But—"

"But even if I were called to Mona tomorrow, you could still come. Every dreamer must have a warrior as guardian and you are that already. You could come as my warrior and train in the warriors' school."

It was the core of her fear. Since the day of her mother's death, since Airmid's gift of the red-quilled feather, the shadow of it had darkened everything. Breaca closed her eyes. The cold engulfed her. In the darkness of her own grief, she said, "On Mona, the warriors are nothing. They haven't been to war since the time of Caesar. It is the dreamers who sit in the elder council." It was an overstatement, she knew; warriors who trained in the school on Mona were accorded the highest worth, but that was not the point.

Airmid, understanding, did not correct her. Instead, she said, "The dreamers share their council with those born in the royal line of their people. You are the next leader of the Eceni. If I am called, there will be a place for you, too."

It was not what she wanted. Breaca opened her eyes. Airmid sat opposite, her face serious. Sand stuck in a feathered line up the length of her arm, like the rib on a leaf. Her eyes were pools to drown in. Every part of her was beautiful. Breaca reached out and took both her hands. They had shared everything, the deepest part of living. It was right that she give her deepest secret. Here, by the gods' pool with Airmid as witness, Breaca nic Graine, heir to the royal line of the Eceni, gave voice to her secret and made it an oath. "If I go to Mona, it will be because of who I am, not an accident of my birth or a single act with a spear. I will go as a dreamer, or I will not go at all."

It was Airmid's idea that they leave the pool and walk up the river to a place where they could swim. No-one was out in the noon heat to watch as they passed the last of the horse paddocks and walked north up the narrow ribbon of marginal land that joined the forest to the water. Away from the village, the land became rougher; good lush meadow gave way to harsher, coarser grasses and then to sand and scrub with the occasional ankle-sucking marsh. At these places, they skirted into the first ranks of trees, weaving out again as the ground rose and dried back to grassland. Upstream, the river was narrower than the stretch that sang past the roundhouse, but faster flowing so that the tune of it was different and the life it gathered more varied. They watched the reed beds for different kinds of lizards and counted dragonflies in three new colours. The forest became denser away from human settlement and the trees changed. Here, there was more pine and larch and silver birch, less hazel and willow. The hawthorn was ubiquitous, stippling the margins with the wind-tattered remnants of white flowers. Breaca picked some and threw them on the water in memory of her mother.

The sun was lower, casting the shadows over their left shoulders, when Airmid called a halt. The river, caught back by an ancient pinch in the landscape, had broadened out again to form a pool, shallower and wider than the one beneath their own waterfall. The forest grew close to the margin, with a short, steep bank stretching down from the roots of the nearest trees to the water. Airmid put her back to the sun and looked left and then right. Taking a few steps forward, she did it again and was satisfied. Pointing up to where a tall beech stood proud of the first rank, she said, "This is the place. Go on up. Sit between the roots and tell me what you see."

"Are we not going to swim?"

"Later. This is more important."

The tree she had pointed out was older than most of those close to the steading. Breaca dug her fingers into the bank and climbed up to stand beside it. Roots the breadth of her arm arced up out of the loam and made a looping network that reached to her knees. Two of the thicker ones formed a fork facing the river and she squeezed herself between them so that they held her on either side, comfortably, as her father's arms had done when she was younger. She looked down at the river. From this height, she could see through the shining surface and into the lazy, swirling circles of the current as it spread out to form the pool. The beauty of it was perfect, well worth the heat of the journey. She smiled down at Airmid. "Is this right?"

"If you feel it so." The older girl stood at the very edge of the water with her feet braced and her hand shading her eyes from the light. She was serious now, quite different from earlier. "Look across the river to the land beyond," she said. "What do you see?"

Breaca looked. The tree held her facing east, to where the land was flattest. Out on the fen, the sun played tricks. The far horizon was lost in a haze that promised water but did not deliver. Between here and there, the land was flat, stippled intermittently by strips of stunted, wind-angled gorse and swathes of bracken and wild grass. None of it was exceptional. She shook her head. "I don't know. What am I supposed to see?"

"You'll know it when you see it." Airmid grabbed a root and swung herself up. She knelt, putting her eyes level with Breaca's, and gazed out in the same direction. Then she did it again, with her head further down. "You can't see it like that," she said. "Sit lower."

Breaca edged herself downwards. The horizon line rose and the angle of it altered. She peered at the place where land and sky blurred together and, this time, she saw what she was meant to: a long, low mound that sat up just proud of the land around it. "What is it?" she asked.

"It's an ancestor mound. They build them to honour their dead. The important thing is that, if you sit here at the right time, you can see the sun and the moon rise over the top of it. I think that would be good. If it mattered to see them."

Airmid had moved to stand at the side of the tree. Her head was tilted slightly to one side and she was frowning, not at Breaca, but at herself, trying to get the words right. Amongst the laws, some were more clear than others. One of the most clear was that a girl nearing her womanhood should find her own place to sit out her long-nights alone, without help from her peers or her elders. Breaca had spent a good part of the summer, that part not spent with Airmid, looking without success for a place that felt right. Now, cradled by the root-arms of the birch, she knew she had found it, and that she was not the first to sit there.

Airmid had fallen silent. Breaca reached for her hand and held it. The wealth of the gift she had been given sank into her, slowly. "I am thinking," she said carefully, "that this might be a good place to sit for the long-nights of dreaming. That the ancestors might help one who was sitting here."

Airmid nodded, solemnly. One half of her face lit into a smile, having offered her gift and knowing the worth of it. The other half was still serious, bearing the responsibilities of adulthood. "They might," she agreed. "Do you think you could find your way back here on your own?"

"I think so. If I follow the line of the river, it would bring me back here." Breaca wanted badly to reach up and kiss her. Instead, she focused on the serious half of her face and thought it through, trying to see the pitfalls. "I will be walking at dawn, when the light is most difficult. If it has been raining, then the place that was marshy today will be knee-deep in mud. I would have to curve further into the trees and then back out to the river again."

"Good. You should come whenever you can. There is no knowing what weather and light the gods will send, so you must know it so that you can find it in fog and total darkness. For now, you should come down to the river and make your introductions. The water is shallow here, but it's still deep enough to swim in. And very warm."

It was. Their own pool, the one below the waterfall, was unknowably deep. It reached down to the realms of the gods and only the otters and kingfishers swam there. Here, in less sacred water, they could stand up to their necks, squeezing their toes in the eddying sand, and spit fountains at each other or dip beneath the surface and swim in bubbled spirals, sliding skin on skin like fish, or lie on their backs with feet and faces exposed, watching the world as the frogs do, blinking.

Afterwards, they lay folded together beneath the curve of the bank, letting the sun warm their joints, listening to the throbbing boom of the bittern that stood in the reeds further up the river. Breaca played with the loose sand, etching pictures. In the way her father had taught her, she made a wren, a she-bear and a horse. All three were watched by a frog that was of her own design. Airmid reached over her shoulder and added the sweep of a leg and the dot of an eye, to make the frog more real. When it was done, she drew a leaf that might have been a spear-head for it to sit on and a long, low oblong that became, with some added symbols, the ancestors' mound. Without discussion, they drew each other in the space beneath the mound, lying as they were now, with a garland of beech leaves, to keep them together for eternity. Airmid drew a sword and a shield in the doorway, to ward off enemies. She added another Breaca, a smaller one, sitting in the distance with her back to a beech tree, watching the moon rise over the horizon, but that was dangerous and she wiped it out as soon as it was complete.

Because they needed to talk of it, but not directly, Airmid asked, "Have you asked your brother how he came by his dreaming? Bán was not on his long-night when it happened. He could tell you everything."

"I've asked."

"What does he say?"

"He says it wasn't a real dreaming."

They were done with drawing. Breaca lifted a broken reed from the bank and tickled the top of the water. A small fish reached up to kiss the surface where it touched. "His heart is set on passing his warrior's tests and nothing beyond. He doesn't want to be a dreamer." It was inconceivable to Breaca that her brother should not share her heart's need, but she had recognized it to be so. She helped him, when she could, with his warrior training.

Airmid was behind her, resting her chin on her shoulder, watching the reed and the fish. "What does Macha say?"

"To him? Nothing. To me, she says that if the gods want a person to hear them, they will shout louder until he does. Or she does." The fish saw a water beetle just beyond the tip of the reed and snatched for it instead. Beetle and fish vanished together beneath the surface. Breaca laid the reed on the bank where she found it. She reached back and found Airmid's hands and wrapped them around her. The mood of the morning had passed and the fear was returning. She said, "What happens if they only whisper? I might not hear them."

"You'll hear. I promise it."

The kiss on her ear was as light as that of the fish on the reed. The breath was warm on her neck. The sun moved lower on the water and the dazzle of its reflection coloured the world gold, even after she had closed her eyes. The earlier mood was not, after all, irretrievable.

Sometime later, Airmid said, "Everyone fears the same thing. It is only the arrogant who believe the gods will speak to them—and so they hear nothing, because they have not learned to listen. You are not arrogant."

"But I am still afraid."

"Which is how it should be. But still. However quietly the gods speak, you will hear them. Be patient. They will tell you everything you want to know. All you have to do is listen."

CHAPTER 5

Rain shivered on the leaf in front of her. Fine drops gathered together and rolled forward to splash heavily onto her knee. Above her and to the side, other leaves dripped their loads onto her neck, her hair, the bare skin of her arms and legs. It was warm rain, heated by the thunder and lightning, tempered in the forge of the gods, and the feel of it was a relief after the pressing heat of the morning. Now that the first cloudburst was over, Breaca could pick out single drops, pattering briskly through the upper branches, louder than the receding thunder.

Lightning flashed again and lit the group of riders huddled at the edges of the trackway below her. They had run for shelter too late and were drenched, and their horses with them. She counted thirty but there were probably more. They were travelling on the eve of the midsummer solstice, which made it certain that they had not come simply to trade or to visit kin. She eased closer, pushing through the clinging leaves to a place where she could see but not be seen. There were two groups, that much was clear. She had watched them riding in from the southern trackway and there had already been two separate factions before ever they ran for the trees. Those who stood on the near side of the path were led by a big, black-haired man mounted on a solid brown gelding. He was young, less than twenty, but he sat quietly and looked around him with the steadiness of age. If one of them was going to see her, it would be him. She curled herself small and tight and kept her eyes away from his, not to call herself to notice.

The second faction, grouped beneath an oak on the far side, were led by a red-haired youth on a nervous bay colt that started at every shaken leaf and mouthed constantly at its bit. The rider used his hands roughly and there was blood in the frothing spit. She took note of that, and the colour of their cloaks and the style of their torcs and patterns on their armbands and the accents with which the black-haired one swore at the weather and her country and the redhead cursed her people and his own father, and then, as the rain fell harder and the noise of it filled her ears and theirs, she edged back, step by careful step, to the place where the grey filly waited.

The storm was a brief one. It passed before she reached the turf rampart, giving way to rinsed blue skies and a drying sun, so that when she pushed through the gates in the encircling rampart the filly was black with the sweat of the run as much as the steaming after-wash of the rain. Inside, the compound was deserted save for a cluster of hens and a sleeping hound. It was the third day of the midsummer horse fair and every man, woman and child of the Eceni was at the fairground, securing the last of their bargains and renewing old acquaintanceships over jugs of ale, while the elders of each group prepared for the council gathering in the great-house. They were not alone in this; across the country, it was the same. Each of the tribes came together in its own homeland at this time. Even the Coritani must speak with their gods, and daybreak on the summer solstice was well known as a time when they listened most keenly. Very rarely an individual or a group from one tribe might choose to travel to another's great-house for advice from their dreamers or to bring a petition pertaining to war, or its cessation. The truce of the season allowed it and the peace that arose afterwards was understood to be a gift of the gods. Those she had seen on the trackway were not from a people with whom the Eceni were at war but there could be no doubting their intent; they were riding for the sacred land that was the heart of the Eceni nation and their route took them directly past Breaca's roundhouse.

It was not done to run horses at speed within the compound but certain circumstances allowed it. Breaca cantered directly for the roundhouse and the women who remained inside. Airmid had heard her coming. She stood waiting outside the door-flap, with the elder grandmother at her side. Both were dressed for ceremony. Their tunics hung straight and uncreased and smelled of sage. Black crow's wings graced the grandmother's shoulders, their tips falling forward to meet at her breastbone. Airmid wore a necklace of silvered frog bones, a fine, delicate thing that shimmered as she moved. Her black hair, newly combed, was bound at her brow by a thong of palest birch bark, the mark of a dreamer. Gold torcs gleamed at both their necks, giving them added height, making them *other* and sacred.

On any other occasion, the sight of Airmid like this

would have filled Breaca with pride and a desperate longing. Now she was part of the new pattern of the day, a thing to be dealt with quickly. She threw her weight back and the grey stopped neatly as they had practised. Airmid reached up for the reins. Her eyes were crisp and clear, with the added depth that came after dreaming. She said, simply, "Who are they?"

"Trinovantes. Thirty at least, possibly more. They are armed but the leader wears the band of a messenger on his left arm. They are on the trackway and they will pass here on their way to the gathering. They should be met and greeted." She twisted her body to look into the roundhouse. The grey spun and fidgeted under her. She saw nothing and straightened. "Where is Macha?"

"With your father. They rode up to the trading fields to help clear the great-house for the gathering."

Breaca cursed, fluidly. "Sinochos, then?"

The grandmother grinned, showing her lack of teeth. "He is out hunting for the feast tomorrow night. If you were wanting a man and not overfussy about which one, his son is here."

"Dubornos? Why?" Dubornos, when she had seen him last, had been sitting in the trade stands, broaching his second jug of ale and speaking floridly to anyone who would listen of the bargains he had made at the fair.

"He fought with another youth over the trade of a sword belt and they sent him home," said the grandmother. "I daresay they would let him back did he bring big enough news. You'll find him in the men's place, cooling his head. He will be fit to ride as long as he is given a horse with good sense."

"What's wrong with his own horse?"

Airmid said, "They took it from him and made him walk. You would need to give him another." She did not say the grey; she knew better than that. Breaca loathed Dubornos with a fierce passion. In her opinion, he was a bully, a liar and—worst of all insults—an appalling horseman. Her eyes met Airmid's. Breaca's hands tensed on the reins and the filly tossed her head. She said, "I'll bring him to the paddocks. He can take one of the new geldings. They are fast enough and their mouths are better able to take him." It was not true, she knew that, but she would have died before she gave him her own horse to ruin.

She left before the elder grandmother could argue. In the men's place, Dubornos was sulking and refused to believe either that warriors were coming or that he had any need to act as she requested. She let him call her a liar twice and then drew her belt knife and laid the blade across his throat.

"When you have won your spear, you will have the right to argue. Until then, you are a child and do as you are told. Is that clear?"

It was the first time she had used the rank her killing gave her, the first also when she had drawn her knife against another in genuine anger. Dubornos blanched and his eyes widened, showing the whites. He pushed himself back against the doorpost and the movement shaved a sliver of skin from his neck, making it bleed. Holding the blade with excessive care, Breaca said, "Swear to me in the name of your ancestors that you will ride as fast as you can to my father and tell him what I have told you."

"I swear." It came out as a whisper. She did not push for more.

"Get up."

She took him to the paddocks and waited long enough to see him catch and mount a safe, unimaginative gelding before turning back and riding for the gates.

Airmid and the elder grandmother had been busy in her absence. The grandmother held the blue cloak and little-owl brooch that Breaca had laid out to wear at the gathering. Airmid held a comb and a belt with fine tooling that was new and that had clearly been set aside as a gift for later.

"There is no time—" she began.

"There is always time." The elder grandmother spoke patiently, as she did to women nearing childbirth. "The storm has not yet passed over the trees where they shelter. They will not leave until it does so and then they will walk slowly for a while to dry. When they are near we will hear them and, in any case, they will not pass us by. This is the house of the royal line and it is you they have come to see, even if that is not how they tell it. In this, you are your mother's daughter. You will greet them as she would have done, not as a child newly back from rooting out rats' nests in the fields."

That was unfair. She had not been rooting out anything; she had been looking for the green-grey fungus that grew on the elm trees and could, if stewed right, make a lotion to keep off the flies. It was to have been her gift to Airmid before the gathering; they could have stewed it together and had the liquid ready to give to those elders who wished it. She opened her mouth to say so. Behind the grandmother, Airmid smiled and shook her head in a complex gesture that signalled understanding and thanks and the need for haste and acquiescence. Breaca shut her mouth and slid off the horse.

"What do I need to do?"

"Wash, comb your hair, let us dress you."

The grandmother was rarely so patient for so long. It was not something to test by hesitating further. Breaca did as she was bade; washed her face and arms and legs in the jar of water that they brought her and scrubbed them clean and dry with the hank of sheep's wool scented with rosemary. Airmid combed her hair, taking care to tease out the tangles without tearing. The grandmother brought out the stone-grey tunic that had been her mother's and had been cut down to fit. The belt-gift was beautiful. Airmid had tooled it herself, interweaving the shape of the frog with the warrior's spear that was Breaca's sign until she dreamed one more fitting. It had been oiled well and was supple. Breaca pulled it tight and tucked in the ends, cursing her luck and the Trinovantian warriors that she had not had time to find her own gift. She was trying to say it, with her hands and her eyes, when the grandmother emerged from the place beyond the fire where she kept her private possessions. She was holding something out as she might her own gift. "You should wear this. It is what they expect of you." Firelight flickered over the thing in her hands, making it move like a snake.

"What is it?"

"Come outside and see."

She ducked through the door-flap after the grandmother. In the light of the newly washed sun the thing she carried took solid form and shone, brilliantly. It was her mother's torc, the sacred one woven by the ancestors from nine times nine gold wires that was the mark of the leader of the Eceni. Breaca had not seen it since the gathering before her mother's death. The sight of it now made her head feel hollow.

She put a hand to her throat. In the voice of a child, she said, "It is not for me. I am not old enough. Macha should have it. She is leader now."

"Macha is not here. They have come to speak to a woman of the royal line. They will not respect you without it."

"Then let them not. That is their choice."

"No. In some things, the gods have first say. It is yours. You will wear it."

The elder grandmother did not speak now as she would at a birthing, but as she had done in the last council meeting, forbidding war on the Coritani. Elders, dreamers and war leaders from the whole Eceni nation had heard that voice and chosen not to argue. Breaca dropped her hand. Airmid reached from behind to scoop up her hair and hold it high. The elder grandmother spread the end-pieces of the torc and slipped it onto her neck. It settled about her collarbones as if made to fit, and for the first time in her life she understood the change that had happened to her mother when she wore it. Like the sword-blade her father was making, it sang in her soul and lifted her head higher. Wearing it, she knew what it was to walk close to the gods. She turned round. Airmid was biting her lip. There were tears at the corners of her eyes, although the smile that went with them was real and bright. The elder grandmother nodded slowly.

"See; one must trust the gods even when one does not understand them. The torc is yours and clearly so, whatever your age. Go now and prepare your weapons. You must not appear to the southerners unarmed. Airmid will have your horse ready for you at the gates. Don't worry, you will have as much time as you need."

She had more than enough time. She had thought the grandmother had made a mistake and that they were not coming at all when the first noise rolled out of the woodland and the first horses followed. They came at the gallop, leaving the trees and spreading out to ride abreast along the flat race-ground to the south of the rampart. They were dry now and had taken time to dress with the formality required for a meeting. Their shields had been lifted from the saddle bows to hang from their shoulders as befitted warriors riding beyond their own land. Red-quilled crow's feathers fluttered in handfuls from their torcs and their warrior's braids. Their cloaks flew out behind them, yellow as the morning sun. The colour picked the fire from the bronze on their arms and gold at their necks and made it burn more brightly. She would have thought them magnificent had she not remembered the words of Gunovic: *Cassivellaunos's cloak took all the colours of all the tribes, except the gorse-bloom yellow of the traitor Mandubracios.* It was a wonder, knowing that, that they had not chosen to wear a different colour.

Breaca walked the grey filly forward from the gate to meet them. Airmid had braided her hair at the sides in the way of a warrior, weaving the single kill-feather in place. In her right hand, she carried the war spear her father had made for her, ready for battle against the Coritani. On her left shoulder, she bore the shield she had recently finished making. The boss in the centre was of iron, brightly polished to match the spearhead. The surrounding leather was horse-hide, boiled and steeped and painted with egg white to make it waterproof. It had been bare, awaiting her long-nights and the revelation of her dreaming, but today, in order that Breaca not appear a child, the grandmother had dipped a wet finger in woad and drawn on the front face the looping serpent-spear of the ancestors, snake-headed at either end with the spear running across it, joining the gods to the earth. It would come off later if she washed it, but now, newly done, it showed starkly blue against the near-white of the leather and Breaca thought it beautiful. Just before she mounted, the grandmother had painted the same sign on the shoulder of her horse. She felt it pulse like a live thing against her thigh as they walked out onto the plain. The filly felt the same; she moved with her head held high like a colt and her nostrils flaring.

At the centre place, opposite the gates, she halted. The warriors rode fast, at battle pace, and showed no sign of having seen her. She stood the butt of her spear in the thong that hung from the front of her saddle and held the tip straight up to show greeting and no threat. Still they came on. Far back in the paddocks, one of the new-traded colts lifted his head and screamed a challenge, or a greeting. She thought it might be the blue roan with the white hind leg that was going to be her father's next sire horse. The unruly bay in the centre of the Trinovantian line tossed its head and received a jab in the mouth before it could scream back. The filly, better trained, snorted a soft answer.

The warriors pulled to a skidding halt less than a spear's length in front of her. Only the black-headed one on the brown gelding did it well, but she expected that of him. Gunovic's words rang in her ears. *Togodubnos is the first son. He is a giant for his age, with black hair and a hooked nose. He has not yet killed in battle but he earned his warrior's tests in good faith.* He wore a single crow's feather and the quill had not been dyed red. She viewed him with the first measure of respect. His gaze, returning hers, was level.

The rest broke rank, making the line curve around her. Covertly, she searched for the youngest brother, the warrior with the corn-gold hair and the sea-green eyes of his mother. *Caradoc is exceptional. If you are in battle, this is the warrior you want at your side.* Or the one you might have dreamed of facing in challenge-combat, practising in sleep every stroke and thrust until you knew exactly how he could be beaten. Breaca changed her grip on the spear, feeling the thunder of her heartbeat pulse through the shaft. She examined the line of riders twice more and still failed to find the firebrand. The intensity of her disappointment surprised her.

The redhead was on her left-hand side, still fighting with his horse. *Amminios, the second son, is pale, with sallow skin and eyes that water.* His feathers fluttered in the breeze and the many-coloured quills spoke of great deeds in battles. If any of them were true, he was as good a warrior as his brother. Breaca did not believe them. She shifted her shoulder so that her shield faced him and he could see the serpent-spear on its face. He said something in another language and the woman who sat on his right whispered a reply. Breaca did not hear the words but the tone was derisory.

"My brother believes you follow the gods of the most ancient ancestors, that you bear their device on your shield."

It was the black-headed man who spoke. His accent was thick and some of the words were entirely foreign but she made the gist of it. His voice carried more respect than his brother's had done. He crossed his arms and leaned forward on his horse's neck, smiling, with one brow raised, as if it were the redhead who was ignorant and they who shared the joke of it. *He is a good diplomat. He would make a fine leader did his father permit it.* A prince, being groomed for leadership, sent to cut his teeth on the Eceni.

Breaca considered her answer. Macha and the elder grandmother would have responded without thought. She tipped the shield to face forward so he, too, could see it. "Your brother is wise if he knows the gods of the ancestors. I follow the gods and the dreams of my people going back seven generations. To know of the time before that, one must speak to the singers."

"A good answer. Perhaps we will do so." The black-headed man inclined his head. Beside him, his redheaded brother frowned and asked a question. The woman bent and murmured in his ear. The redhead stared at Breaca and sucked his teeth. His hands jabbed the reins and his horse threw its head up so that he had to sit back hurriedly or break his nose on its neck. It took him a moment to settle it.

With her eyes on the elder brother, Breaca said, "Your brother would do better if he used a softer bit and held his hands lower."

The black-haired man closed his eyes, briefly, as if in prayer. Had he been Eburovic, or Sinochos, she would have known he was fighting the impulse to laugh. The woman to the right of the redhead drew a breath and, with some hesitation, translated. The delay gave Breaca fair warning. The grey filly was already dancing back out of reach as the man lunged his colt forward. It was not an honest match. He was armed with a sword and she with a spear three times its length and she had spent her summer practising against just such an attack. He, if Gunovic told the truth about anything, had spent his summer growing soft on Gaulish wine drunk from glass vessels and plucking the hairs from his nostrils. Certainly he did not know the moves by which a sword might hope to defeat a mounted spear, and his colt was not listening to him. For Breaca, the filly moved as if born to battle. The fight was short and brutal and over too fast. They stopped when the tip of her spear rested on the redhead's breastbone and the first thread of blood stained his tunic. His horse might have moved and impaled him but his black-headed brother reached for the reins and kept it steady. He was not smiling now although it was not clear with whom he was most angry.

Breaca said, "Togodubnos, son of Cunobelin, warrior of the Trinovantes, Breaca, warrior of the Eceni, gives you greeting. I was told your brother Amminios had not yet taken his warrior's tests and yet he wears the tokens of one who has killed many times in battle. Perhaps it is this confusion that angers him."

There was absolute silence. The woman leaned forward to translate and was waved back. Breaca had spoken slowly and none of the words was difficult. Moreover, she had used the formal introductions and language of a singer that were universal within the tribes. Amminios flushed darkly, and then paled to less than he had been. Purple shadows stood out under his eyes. The thread of blood at his breastbone spread wider. Breaca clicked her tongue and the filly backed away two paces. Her spear remained level. Somewhere, far behind her, the roan colt screamed another greeting. To Togodubnos, she said, "If you have come to talk in the gods' time, it does not do well to fight. If you have come to fight, Amminios dies first, I promise it."

"And you second? Would you risk that?" Togodubnos

was toying with her. He, too, had heard the colt and knew what it meant.

"Maybe. But this is not a time to find out. I think your brother should put up his weapon. If he is an envoy, he should act like one."

She raised her spear and seated it upright in the holder. Amminios had enough sense to sheathe his sword. High up in the paddocks above the roundhouse, the roan colt called out for a final time and was answered. Eburovic's war-horse had been trained to scream as it rode into battle. It did so now as he crested the hill. One hundred and thirty warriors of the Eceni spread out on either side of him. In line abreast, they hurtled down the slope towards her.

The Trinovantes swung round in a passable line and moved their shields to their backs, showing that they offered no danger. Breaca walked to the front and led them forward at a slow trot to meet her father at the gates.

Bán had enjoyed the fair more than any before it. For the first time in his life, he had been deemed old enough to trade. Macha had given him three of her sapling hounds and he had spent a day securing the best bargains. Two of them had gone in exchange for a proven brood bitch brought down from the north. She had whelped twice already and he had examined her offspring. She threw fast, strong whelps with long necks and good eyes and a vivid, buoyant temperament. Afterwards, Macha had agreed that the bitch would make a good mate for Hail when he was older. The third sapling had been traded for a set of three bronze harness mounts with shining black inlays. He had already tried them on his dun filly with the sickle-shaped blaze and knew they suited her. She was still a foal but she was growing into the early promise. He had brought her to the fair, not to trade—he would not have traded her for the world—but to let people see his father's best brood mare and the wonder of the foal she had thrown. For three days, he had basked in the approval of strangers, as men and women from the far corners of the Eceni lands commended him on the beauty of his foal, on the striking colours of his whelp and on the good training of both. It was the best feeling a young warrior could have, next to being granted his spear for valour in battle.

He had thought that might come, too, when Dubornos first arrived with his news. He badly wanted to ride out with his father and the other warriors but Eburovic had taken him aside and asked him to stay behind and help protect his mother and the other dreamers. Dubornos, too, had been left behind, while 'Tagos, his cousin, had ridden out, but no-one had told the disgraced youth that it was so he could protect the dreamers. He had simply been relieved of the new horse by his father and told not to make trouble. Sinochos himself had stayed; in the frantic moments when warriors abandoned their ale jugs and collected their weapons and horses, he had picked his group to guard the people. Bán was not really part of it, he knew that, but they let him join them as they discussed their defences and then left him with Hail to guard the door to the great-house while Macha and the other dreamers continued their work to make it ready for the gathering.

It was not a hard task. The dreamers came and went without noticing that he was there, and there were so many warriors arming around him that he knew if an attack were to come, he would be lucky to see any of the action. After a while, when no-one spoke to him, he sat on his heels and played a guessing game with Hail, tossing a pebble quickly from one hand to the other and then holding out his clenched fists for the whelp to choose which one held the stone. The pup got it right three times out of four and was getting better but the novelty of it wore off too quickly and neither of them had the stomach to play for long. Bán was thinking of running to check on his filly, or to find Silla, who was under the care of Camma and Nemma and probably much less bored, when Macha walked past with an arm full of newly cut pine boughs and asked him to come inside and help her.

He had never been inside the great-house before. He walked beside Macha, with Hail kept close at heel, on best behaviour in a place of new smells and new people. The great-house was vast, much bigger than the roundhouse he was used to. The making of it was one of the legends told by the fireside on cold evenings. From when he was small, he had heard tales of how the walls and the roof alone had consumed two hundred trees and the preparation before that had lasted for decades; of how the oaks that made the roof beams had been trained by succeeding generations to ensure they grew straight and tall, how the hazel rods woven between them had come from coppices left untouched for ten years at a time to allow them to grow strongly enough to enable a grown man to walk across the roof and not fall through. The thatch that covered the hazel took the straw from every field for a day's ride in any direction. The first time it was laid, the thatchers had worked for three months without break while underneath them teams of carvers cut the images of the people—horse and hare, bear and boar, crow, eagle and wren—onto the great oaks of the door-posts and the arcing beams.

The effect was magical. Walking in behind Macha, with the three fires throwing light out to the farthest edges, Bán felt himself surrounded by the living dreams of his people. Then he saw the wall hangings and passed beyond his wildest dreams. On every surface, wolves ran with hares, hawks flew with swans, deer sprang high over snakes. And there were so many horses; everywhere he looked, Bán saw extraordinary, numinous horses, running past him, running with him, running at him. He stopped, halfway from the door, unable to take it all in. Macha dropped her bundle by the nearest fire and came back to kneel at his side. She put a palm to his forehead and looked into his eyes. "Bán? Are you all right?"

"Yes." He drew a long breath and made himself look at her and not the pictures. "It's the smell, the pine and the rushes and the smoke. It was making me dizzy."

That, too, was true. He walked on a thicker layer of fresh rushes than he had ever known. The feel of them underfoot spoke of luxury and proximity to the sacred. The scent of cut pine was not new to him, but he had never asso-ciated it with the work of the dreamers and had never smelled it so strongly.

"It's the resin for the torches," said Macha. She stood up, taking his hand. "We mix it with tallow and pine needles to make a paste and then we put that on the pine boughs. They burn better and longer like that, and last through to morning. It's one of the secrets of the gathering. Come and see." She led him to the nearest fire. A pot stood on the heat, stirred by a sandy-haired dreamer. The air was thick with the vapour, so that Bán's vision swam.

Macha said, "Bán, this is Efnís, who comes from the northern Eceni, up by the north coast. He is in charge of mixing the resin. Efnís, this is my son, Bán. He has come to help you with the torches."

The dreamer looked up, briefly. He was a young man, not much older than Breaca, with a strained, anxious face and eyes that turned down at the outer edges. "Thank you." He nodded distractedly, his mind elsewhere. To Bán, he said, "Have you a knife?"

"Of course." His belt knife was a small one, shorter than Breaca's but just as sharp.

"Good. The boughs your mother has brought must have their side branches cut off cleanly so we can make them into torches. Can you do that?"

"Yes." He said it quickly, because he wanted to stay. Bán had never been to the north coast but he had heard it was a place of harsh grazing and poor hunting and that the people lived on dried seaweed through the winter. He had spent the three days of the fair trying to find someone he could ask about this without giving offence and had not yet succeeded. The gods had clearly sent him here to find the answers to his questions. He sat down on the far side of the fire, then thought to look up at Macha. She raised a brow and then nodded. He felt the clasp of her hand on his shoulder and the press of her kiss on his head and the warmth of her smile as she walked away, and he forgot, for the moment, about being a warrior and became instead a cutter of pine, assistant to the dreamers, which was almost as good.

It was not hard work but the boughs were newly taken

from the trees and leaked sap on his palms and fingers. The high, resinous scent made his eyes water and his head float. He put a hand to his head to run his fingers through his hair and found that now his hair, too, had sap on it. He cursed, forgetting where he was. Efnís looked up, shocked, and for a moment it was like looking at Macha when she was angry, or the elder grandmother at any time. Then the northerner frowned and became a boy again, or a young man, bearing new responsibilities.

"Oh, the sap. I'm sorry, I should have told you. I did that on my first time as well." He left his pot and came round the fire to look. "Hold still. If you move your hand, you'll spread it further. And don't touch your hound. If he gets it on his pelt, he'll try to lick it off and be sick."

Bán sat like a rock, fixing Hail with a glare that stopped him from trying to sniff out the tallow while there was no-one to guard it. Efnís parted his hair from his fingers. He said, "If we leave it, it'll spread and you'll have hair that sticks up for months. If I cut this bit out now, no-one will notice and the resin will be gone. We can burn the cut piece of hair on the fire as an offering to Briga. Would you mind?"

Bán said he didn't mind. Efnís borrowed his knife, commenting with approval on its sharpness, and deftly cut away the glued lock of hair. They laid it on the fire together and made the invocation to Briga, which always had a wish at the end of it. Bán's was the wish he always made: that he become a warrior quickly. He made it with his eyes shut tight so that he could see better in his mind the image of himself riding into battle with spear and shield held high. He had opened his eyes again when he heard the first horses; three dozen or more coming at a hard canter down the trackway. His heart leaped with hope until, moments after that, he heard his father's bullhorn sound the all-clear. He knew the same twist of disappointment he had in the morning but it was swamped, quickly, by the urgent need to see who was coming. He was on his feet before he remembered his chore. He spun round, breathless. "Efnís? May I. . . ?"

"Go and see? Yes, of course. Just take it slowly. You have been breathing the pine-steam and you'll be dizzy."

He was already running. Carved and painted horses danced about him as he reached the door, gathering other symbols with them. His father's she-bear was there, and Macha's wren, and the bright-painted sun hound that had been the sign of Cassivellaunos when he made his last stand at the river. He was just in time. Ahead of him, the warriors of the Eceni burst from the trees in a scatter of sunlit gold. There were hundreds of them—thousands; every spear the Eceni could muster and others from other tribes. Breaca rode in front, riding tall in spite of her wounds, with her shield on her shoulder and her bloodied spear held aloft and her hair braided for battle and her torc blazing as if the fires of the gods had just given it birth. The blue cloak of the Eceni swirled behind her in the sudden wind, taking up colours from the trees and the moss and the people, gathering patches so that it held all the colours of the tribes except the yellow of the Trinovantes, the colour of the traitor Mandubracios. But that was there too, and the traitor with it. From the moment of Gunovic's story, Bán had known him: a lean man with the nose of an eagle and watery eyes that would not meet his. He wore battle honours he had not earned and braided his red hair deceitfully. He dismounted now, before Breaca, the ultimate discourtesy. He had come, Bán was certain, to betray her.

"Traitor!" He screamed it as his father screamed before battle, as Cassivellaunos had screamed at Caesar's legions when they first fought at the river. Beside him, Hail howled his war howl and the sound of it was taken up, echoing, by the sun hound and the she-bear, the boar and the wren and all the other beasts from the great-house that had followed him out to help. They crowded around him, promising blood. When he moved, they moved with him. Together, they hurled themselves at the enemy.

"Bán, *no!*"

"Get off me!"

"Amminios, don't! It's a child. Leave him."

"*Bán!*"

A horse reared and he was thrown to the ground. Around him, the people went to war. In the confusion and noise of battle, he heard Hail, howling, and the voice of his mother.

"Bán!"

"The hound . . . will somebody get hold of that cursed hound—"

"Amminios, stop!"

The world went black and then red and then all colours. When they settled, he heard Efnís speaking, and then his mother again. Both sounded distant and unhappy.

"I'm sorry. It's my fault. I let him go. I didn't know he was—"

"It doesn't matter. You weren't to know. Get me more water. Bán, can you hear me? Can you open your eyes?"

His head hurt, badly. Cold moss lay on his face, dripping down to his neck. He opened his eyes. The sky was very blue and the sun too bright. His mother made a shadow, leaning over him. Her face was distorted and upside down.

He blinked and tilted his head. She moved round to where he could see her properly.

"Bán? Can you see me?"

He screwed up his eyes. "Yes." His voice was a whisper. He remembered the battle. "Breaca? There was blood on her face. They were going to kill her."

"No. Bán, it was not so." His mother was grieving. He could hear it in the way she spoke and her cheeks were wet. He had never seen her weep for him. She said, "The Trinovantes came as envoys under the gods' peace. You broke the truce and named one of them traitor. It is the deepest insult you could give to them and the gods. You will have to—"

"Stop. That can come later. Let him tell what he saw." The last voice was one he knew but could not place. It washed over him, like the wind through dry grass, surprisingly warm. He rolled his head to the side and tried to see. Dry, bony fingers closed his eyes. The darkness was more comforting than it had been. The voice said, "Tell us what you saw when the warriors came out of the woodland."

The image came to him again: Breaca riding at the van of the Eceni nation, with blood on her face and the snake-spear painted in red on her shield. At her side, the traitor with the yellow cloak raised his sword and swung for her horse's legs. The grey filly screamed and fell. He flinched and his eyes sprang open. The elder grandmother smiled at him and, for the first time in his life, he did not feel afraid of her. "Tell me," she said.

"Mandubracios," he said. "He came to betray Breaca. She won the battle and still he came to betray her."

"If she won, how could he betray her?"

"In the next battle. He would be there, pretending to be on her side, but he would be fighting for the enemy." He pushed himself up. Something else came that he had forgotten. "Her spear. I saw him break her spear."

There was silence. A gust of wind rattled the trees. Tethered horses stamped and jingled their harnesses. A crow flew overhead, calling, and was joined by two others. "Thank you," said the grandmother, distantly. "It is a good answer."

There were more people around him than he knew. Feet scuffed on grass and shadows passed over him as they stood and walked away. He heard the snap of old joints as the grandmother rose. She spoke across his head. "Efnís, let go of the hound before you choke him. He will do no further harm. Macha, you are the lawgiver. You must explain to your son the debt he owes and the manner of repayment. I will speak with Eburovic and prepare him for what is to come."

Efnís let go of Hail and for a moment the grandmother's words were lost in the frenzy of greeting. Bán pushed himself off the ground. His head still spun but with Hail's help and his mother's he was able to sit upright. He looked round and found they were alone, but for Efnís. The young dreamer wound his fingers in the long grass and would not meet his eyes. Beyond him, the fairground, which had been inhabited by every man, woman and child of the Eceni, was deserted. Macha said, "Bán, come inside."

The great-house was busy, but quietly so. The smell of pine was weaker and some of the horse banners had been removed from the walls. They returned to Efnís's fire and Bán found that someone else had finished cutting the pine boughs and the torches had been made. They lay in an ordered pile on a sheepskin to one side. The pot on the fire heated only water. When it boiled, Macha filled a beaker and mixed in some herbs and made him drink it. The taste was of burdock, which he knew, and other, more bitter things that he did not. They made his tongue curl and his eyes sting but his head cleared and he could see better than he had done. Macha sat on the ground in front of him and drank the dregs of his drink. Her eyes were on the fire. He had never seen her so serious. He put a hand to her arm. "Where is Breaca? She had blood on her face. She may need healing."

"No." With an effort, Macha drew her eyes from the fire. "Efnís, will you leave us? I would speak with my son."

The young dreamer did not run, but the flurry he left behind him was the same. When they were alone, Macha said, "Bán, Breaca is unhurt. She exchanged harsh words with the Trinovantes and I believe she crossed blades with one of them, but they did her no harm."

"But—"

Her eyes fixed on his. They were the grey of iron, and firelight danced in the dark of the centres. "Bán, what you saw was a vision, a thing brought on by the pine-steam and your first time in the great-house and . . . other things that we know too little of. But it was not real. Breaca has not yet fought her battle, the first or the second. The man you attacked is not Mandubracios. He cannot be. The traitor lived in the time of your grandfather's grandfather. He is dead long since."

Bán frowned. It made sense but only partially so. He believed in what he saw. "Then who was he?"

"Amminios, second son of the Sun Hound, Cunobelin. He and his brother Togodubnos came as envoys from their father. An envoy is sacred, Bán. Even were it not midsummer, they are not to be attacked."

Her face and her eyes said more than her voice. And she was weeping again. A fist of ice clutched at his chest, making it hard for him to breathe. Her words from before echoed in his head: *You broke the truce and named one of them traitor. It is the deepest insult.* She reached for his hand. "Bán, I know you did not mean to do it but the laws are exact and, for this, we cannot pass them by."

He was going to be a warrior. A small part of his mind told him that this was what it was like to face battle: the terror churning in the pit of his stomach, the dreadful unknowing of what was to come. He tried to ask and found he could no longer speak. He resolved, whatever it was, not to weep.

His mother said, "I have spoken with the elders and they have agreed on a judgement. You owe a debt to Amminios's honour, to his house and to his person. There are two ways it can be paid. The first is for you to serve him for a year, as Breaca serves the elder grandmother."

"But he is not blind, or lame. He does not need someone to be his eyes and limbs."

"No. And so service to him would be different."

"Like a slave?"

"Yes. I believe so." He gaped at her. Neither the gods of the Eceni nor their dreamers permitted slavery. Simply to consider it was to risk the wrath of Nemain. His mother was still talking. "We have considered this and it is not acceptable. For many reasons . . ."

He was a warrior. He could do anything. He squared his shoulders. "I will go if that is what you want of me."

"*No.* No, it is not. Most assuredly it is not. You may owe this man a debt of honour, but he . . ." She was struggling, seeking the words to name a horror, and not finding them. Drawing a breath, she said, "The honour is ours. Amminios does not share it. The elders would not allow you to go to him." He saw the fear in her eyes, more clearly than before, and the effort it took her to face him. She spoke fast, to get it over. "There is another way. You must give him a gift, something that matters to you deeply. A gift from the heart that would be worth as much as a year of your life."

She could not look at him then. Her eyes slid away to the fireside, where Hail chewed on the bare end of a torch. He saw the trail of wet on her cheek again and understanding fell on him, crushing him, choking him, grinding his life to dust.

"Not Hail!" He clutched at her, frantic with terror, grasping the startled whelp with his other hand. "Please, please, not Hail. I would rather serve for the rest of my life."

She caught his wrist. "Don't say that, Bán. Not on a day like this."

"But—"

"Just don't. And no, it is not Hail." He saw the ghost of a smile. "I do not think he would accept Hail. Your battle hound tried to unman him. If Efnís had not caught him, I think he would have succeeded."

At another time, he would have been pleased with that. Now, even as the relief swamped him, he cast around for the real answer. "The new bitch? She is good. A man such as that would not know what to do with her, but I will give her if I must."

"No. Not the bitch. She is a thing you have traded. She is not something you value. There is one other—"

And so he saw it, like a knife-blade too close to be ducked, aiming straight for the heart. "The foal? My dun filly?"

"Yes. I'm sorry, Bán, but it's the only thing that will serve."

"But she can't leave her dam. She's too young. She isn't weaned yet."

"I know. So the mare will have to be given with her. They must go together. Tomorrow morning, after the ceremony of the sunrise, you must give them both to Amminios as your debt-gift, with your apologies."

His day passed in desolation. He sat in the field with the filly, giving her salt and honeyed bran cakes and the other gifts that were brought him. Word travelled fast and people he barely knew—the ones who had come to look at her and admire her during the fair and others he had never seen before—passed by the field and left small gifts: a twist of salt for the filly, a jar of oil to paint her hooves, a sword belt for him to wear in the morning. A day earlier, he would have burst with pride simply knowing that they cared. Now nothing touched him. His father came to be with him for a while. Together, they brushed the mane and tail of dam and foal and polished their hides until they shone. They said nothing. There was no need for discussion. Both knew that she was the best foal Eburovic had ever bred and the dam was his best brood mare. Both knew the years that had gone into making her and that the chances of ever breeding another like her were too small to measure.

In time, his father left and the filly nuzzled Bán's neck and lipped at his hair and did not understand why he did not play as he used to. He twisted her forelock, as he had on the morning she was born, lifting the silk-sand hair away from her face so that the new-moon star showed to the sky. He spoke to her: promising her great things, that she would be honoured above all the other horses in her new owner's herd, that she would be gently ridden and well trained and would see great battles; that when her time came she would be put to the bravest and best of the sires and would breed only the best of foals. He lied and he knew it and the words dried in his throat. She blew in his face and butted his shoulder to cheer him, and he smelled the special young-foal smell of her and knew that he wanted to die.

Breaca came later, nearer to evening. Thunderclouds gathered in the west, blotting out the skyline. The red of the sunset leaked from the edges like blood from a fatal wound. He watched it and tried to remember why he had believed himself to have the courage of a warrior. He did nothing to acknowledge his sister. Of all the people close to him, she was the one he least wanted to see. She stood on the edge of his vision, waiting. Presently, when he did not turn to her, she stooped and laid an armload of twigs and logs at the side of the wall. "I brought wood for your fire," she said. "You should build a fire if you are going to stay out all night."

That was sensible. He had not considered a fire but it was a good idea, for Hail, if not for him. He nodded to show he had heard and waited for her to go away.

"Bán?" She crouched at his side. Shyly, almost tentatively, she laid a hand on his arm. Her voice had a catch, as if she had been weeping, or was going to do so, soon. "Bán, I'm so sorry. I didn't know. . . . They didn't tell me until now. I have tried to make them take other gifts but they say it is in the hands of the gods and they cannot act differently."

He said nothing, not out of rudeness, but because there was nothing to say. Anyone else would have left him to his misery. Breaca was his sister. She sat down on the ground beside him, moving the quiet, disconsolate Hail out of the way. "Bán? Little brother?" She reached for him, wrapping her arms around him. Her fingers linked through his. Without his conscious thought, his thumb sought out the scar on her palm, running down the ridge of it. She laid her cheek on his head as she had always done and pulled him close to her chest. He could hear the beat of her heart through her tunic. In the old days, when he was a child and she had held him thus, he had counted her heartbeats out loud, to show he knew the numbers and could measure the rhythm. Now they rocked through him, echoing in the emptiness.

Her voice moved down through his head. She was speaking, telling him that she had tried to reason with the elders and had failed and that she had come to offer the only recompense she could think of. "I know the grey filly is not as good, but if you want her she is yours. Would you take her as my gift to you? Please?"

He shook his head. He did not want another horse, ever. He had already decided that. He tried to pull free and she held him tighter. "No." Her arms bound him close. "Leave it then. Stay with me. Just stay and be still. We don't have to talk."

He gave up the struggle. She held him tightly, as he had held Hail, pressing her lips to his hair and then everywhere, kissing his forehead, his face, his neck. This, too, was something that would have brightened any other day. Since her mother died, they had not been this close. He was her brother; he had always known that he would have to share her. Then, through the spring, seeing the change in her, he had thought her lost to Airmid and had turned to Hail and the filly in her place. Now he found he had never lost his sister but instead was losing half his heart. He began to sob then, feeling himself a child again in her arms, forgetting that he was a warrior and had vowed not to weep.

She held him for a long time until the crying had stopped. His head hurt again and she brought him clean water and a hank of wool to clean his face. She held him on her knee and ran her fingers across his scalp, untangling his hair. When she found the sheared ends of the newly cut lock and ran over it without comment, he knew that Efnís had told of all that had happened in the great-house. He looked up at her for the first time. She had taken off the torc and the blue cloak, and the warrior's braids had been combed from her hair so that it hung loose in a fine sheen to her shoulders like the vixen's pelt of his horse-dreams. She looked entirely unlike the warrior he had seen wield the red-marked shield and the broken spear in the forest. "I saw you," he whispered. "You were leading the spears. You had a sword-cut on your arm and there was blood on the back of your tunic, all the way down."

"I know. Macha told me." She stood, staring out at the sunset. In the odd, lurid light, her face and her hair were the same shade of red gold. She looked strained, as she had in the winter, and he looked quickly at her hand, to make sure that the wound on the palm had not opened. It did not seem that it had. He looked up again. With her eyes still on the sunset, she said, "I don't want to be a warrior, Bán. That's for you."

She wanted so badly to be a dreamer and go to Mona with Airmid. He knew that. He had always known. He did not think it would happen but today was not the time to say it. "I didn't make up the vision," he said. "It was so."

"I believe you. So does the elder grandmother." She squatted down beside him again, out of the light, wrapping her hands in his. "She told it to the other dreamers so they would know ahead of the gathering. This one will be a bigger council than the one in the winter; the dreamers and singers and war leaders of the entire Eceni nation will all come together with our elders and the grandmothers. Togodubnos has asked leave to put a question: a 'representation' from his father."

"Have they allowed it?"

"Yes. They have to. It is the gods' day and anyone who comes can put a question."

Over by the great-house, a horn brayed, mournfully. Breaca untangled her fingers from his. "I have to go. The council will meet when the horn sounds a second time and I must dress properly."

She kissed him again, on his eyelids, making him squint. He giggled and, just for a moment, forgot the filly. When he looked again, his sister was standing straight and sober. She said, "It is not why I came, but I have a message from the grandmothers."

For a heartbeat, he dared to hope. But if it was a reprieve, she would not have waited so long to tell him. Reading him, she shook her head. "No. Not that. But I am to tell you that, if you want it, they would allow you to sit with the council. You could hear the Trinovantian put his question and there would be time for you to speak afterwards." She smiled, wryly. "It is the greatest honour they can give. You would be the youngest person ever to sit as a member of the elder council. The singers would tell it in your hero-tales after you died." She spread her hands. "They cannot go against the laws, but they are doing what they can to make it better."

It was a great honour but it did not make it better. She knew that as well as he did. He said nothing. After a moment, Breaca nodded. "I told them you would prefer to stay here but I had to offer. Will you light the fire? Please? Tonight is not a night to spend in darkness."

His throat was becoming tight again. He said, "I will light a fire. For you."

"Thank you." She hugged him a final time, as she might were he going to war. Releasing him, she said, "Stay warm, little brother. I will be back before morning." She left before he could weep again.

The night was warm and not dark. The sun sank below the horizon but the light remained, muting the stars. Bats and evening insects flittered in perpetual dusk. Horses grazed as they would of an evening, cropping the grass in circles around where he sat. The greater mass of the people, those not engaged in council in the great-house, cleared away the trade stands and the benches, the ropes and the marker stones, returning the fairground to the flat, open fenland it had been before they came. In due course, they lit fires and sat round them, talking. Only the youngest and oldest slept.

In the field, Bán laid and lit his fire and was surrounded by moths. Hail lay curled tight, dreaming of hares. The dun foal grazed and sucked from her dam and in between came to lie on the other side of him, sharing her warmth with his. He talked to her of the constellations as they passed over-head: the Hunter and the Serpent, the Bear, the Otter and the Spear. She dozed with her muzzle resting on his thigh. A horn sounded faintly in the great-house and raised voices answered in chorus, falling away to a distant murmur, like the sea.

The footsteps came shortly after that, a quiet scuffing on the grass that could have been a horse grazing but was not.

"May I join you?" The accent was rounded, from the far south. A man squatted down at his fire and, without asking further leave, laid a piece of wood on the flames. That was unfortunate; it was not permitted to turn away someone who shares a fire. Bán looked down at the filly's head, resting on his knee, and said nothing. Hail, perversely, raised his head to look but made no attempt to drive the incomer away.

"It is a beautiful night." It was an inconsequential statement, but the tone of it made him look up. The man was young, not much older than 'Tagos, but taller and more loose-limbed, like a colt that will be big but has not yet grown into its body. His hair was black and curled like lamb's wool and his nose, which was too big to go with the rest of him, had been recently broken and reset on the angle. The effect was comical. One could imagine, were he younger and not so big, that he would be taunted for that. Dubornos, for instance, would not let him forget it. As an adult, it marked him out so that his face was one that others would remember. He had discarded his sun-cloak. In its place, he wore a dark, sober tunic and a new cloak of undyed sheep's wool, marking him as neutral, of no tribe. Perhaps, on this night, it was a necessary deceit. Or perhaps the elders had required it.

The man held his palms to the fire, savouring the heat. His presence was an insult and clearly deliberate. If he stayed, it would be necessary to move. Bán looked out across the field, seeking out other places where he could build another fire.

"Who is Mandubracios?"

The words were slipped in between one crackle of the fire and the next so that Bán was not sure he had heard them at all. He looked up. The man's eyes were on his face. They were brown and wide and free of guile. "The traitor Mandubracios," he said again. "I have not heard of him. Can you tell me?"

"I am not a singer."

"I know, but I did not ask for a song, just the bare bones of a story. Was he Eceni?"

"No!" That one could think so was appalling and added to the insult. "He was Trinovantian. He betrayed Cassivellaunos to Caesar's legions. It was because of him they crucified the hound Belin, who was named for the sun."

"Ah." The man reached over and held his hand for Hail to smell. The whelp raised his head, gave the proffered knuckle a perfunctory lick and fell asleep again. The man stroked him as one who cares for his hounds. He said, "I can see that would be a bad thing."

"It was worse than bad. It was against the gods and the people."

It was then that Bán decided not to move. If he was going to be made to talk, he would do so, whether his audience liked the tale or not. He could not make the shadow pictures with his hands in the way that Gunovic had done but he could make the story real, with the colours and the smells and the feelings of the people. He began at the beginning and told it all. When the death of the hound came, he did not weep, because he knew it was coming, but he saw by the sudden stillness in the man's features that he had told it well. "But the gods have exacted their price," he said. "The traitor was cursed by the dreamers. His people are ruled over by the Sun Hound, who is of the line of Cassivellaunos . . ." And, because the stranger raised his brows but did not interrupt, he went on to tell him the tales of the three brothers: of Togodubnos, who was weak and let his father rule in his stead when the leadership should be his of right through his mother; of Amminios, who was without honour and plucked his nostrils to keep in with the Romans; and of the third son, Caradoc, who carried the fighting blood of the Ordovices and was going to be made warrior of three different tribes. He had intended to tell how this last one was a firebrand and despised his father but he remembered Gunovic's warning that the Sun Hound did not deal lightly with treachery and so did not. The enemy of my enemy is my friend. Already, he considered Caradoc a possible ally.

He finished and they lapsed into silence. The fire hissed and spat. The big man stroked his fingers thoughtfully down the length of his nose. "Is it possible, do you think, that Togodubnos is not weak but recognizes that his father and his grandfather and all his ancestors before that worked throughout their lives to bring two tribes together, and that to take his rulership of the Trinovantes now, when the endeavour has just succeeded, might serve only to split them apart again?"

"Then when will he take the oath of his spears? Will he stay for ever in the shadow of his father? Is that the way of a warrior?"

"No. But a man may be a warrior and also a diplomat.

And fathers do not live for ever. Cunobelin is of middling age; he may live for ten or twenty years yet, but when he dies his land will be split between his three sons. If they do not see eye to eye about how to rule it, there will be war and other people will die. You have grown listening to and admiring the great deeds of your warrior ancestors, yet it is not the duty of a warrior to make war for the sake of it but only to protect his people, or to avenge the deaths of others."

"Then why will there be war when the sons take the land?"

"There may not be. But suppose one brother—let us say, Amminios—has spent many years living amongst traders and statesmen in Gaul and believes strongly that his fortunes lie with Rome." Bán looked at him, shocked. Even Gunovic had not stated it so clearly. "And suppose that one of the others—Caradoc, perhaps—hates everything Roman with a passion that boils his blood and will do all he can to remove them and their allies from any place and any people over which he holds sway. Then the third brother—Togodubnos—unless he is a good diplomat may not be able to prevent these two from waging a prolonged and bloody war as each tries to enforce his wishes on the other. At best, there would be unnecessary slaughter. At worst, the legions of Rome might be called upon to intervene as they were by Mandubracios and we would find ourselves facing another invasion such as our ancestors faced. That would be unthinkable."

"And is the third brother a good diplomat?"

"I don't know. I am not the best person to say that. He tries to be. I am not sure that he succeeds."

"Was it diplomacy that brought him here to put his question to the council?" Bán asked it directly, with his eyes on the stranger's face. The man nodded, slowly. He did not look unfriendly.

"Not entirely. In that, he acted as his father wished. His father believes . . ." He trailed off and began again, differently. "Let me tell it as the council heard it. See"—he lifted a stick from the pile by the fire—"here is a stick. We will call it the branch of friendship between two peoples, the Trinovantes and the Eceni."

"It is bare. There are no leaves on it."

"Exactly. The tree from which it came has been allowed to wither, which is not good. The Trinovantes—the Sun Hound—would be as a brother to the Eceni and he is grieving that he has allowed this tree of friendship to go unwatered so that it bears no fruit. He has heard of the loss suffered by the royal house of the Eceni . . ." He looked sideways at Bán, who nodded to show he understood—the man could not name Breaca's mother any more than an Eceni could. The man went on, "Cunobelin grieves most bitterly at this loss but grieving is not enough. A brother who is a true warrior does not simply grieve for the murder of his sister, he rides out and takes vengeance. And so the question put to the council was this: when the Eceni spears ride out to avenge the death of the woman of their royal line, the Sun Hound asks that he be allowed to bring the combined spears of the Trinovantes and the Catuvellauni to aid them in their battle against the warriors of the red kite. Only thus, he believes, may the tree of friendship be brought to bear fruit once more."

Bán had been watching the fire and not the stick. When the man raised his hand again, in place of the bare twig he held a small branch of newly cut hazel, most sacred of trees. Leaves hung about it, and a single crow's feather with the quill painted black, for war. He gave it to Bán, who laid it on the fire. He was not yet ready for gifts from this man.

He said, "Did Togodubnos make a stick turn into living hazel for the council?"

"Yes. They knew it to be a piece of trickery—sleight of hand—but it served to make the point and to ask the question that needed to be asked."

"Togodubnos, speaking for his father, asked the council to make an alliance with the Trinovantes and the Catuvellauni against the Coritani?"

"He did, yes."

"What did they say?"

"Nothing. They asked him to leave that they might discuss it fully amongst themselves. The answer will be given tomorrow after the ceremony of the sunrise. After you have given the light of your heart to my brother."

He understood her worth. That, in itself, was a gift, if not enough to dull the pain. In a while Togodubnos said gently, "Did you know that your sister offered Amminios her grey filly in place of yours?"

Bán had suspected it but had not been sure. He shook his head, dumbly. It did not need to be said that Amminios had refused it.

The man said, "It is a great thing when two who share the same father care so deeply for each other. You should treasure it."

"I do."

There was a long silence. They both looked into the flames.

"The elders will refuse your request," said Bán, eventually. He felt regret, even knowing it was true, and was surprised by it.

"I know. I knew it the moment you attacked Amminios. Until now, I did not know why."

Togodubnos rose. Standing, he seemed bigger than he had when seated by the fire. One or other was a trick of the light. He smiled. "It is almost dawn. I will leave you with your filly. I think I will not tell my brother the council's answer. It will be enough that he hears it in the morning. He will not be pleased."

"He has not been named a warrior. Would he have ridden against the Coritani?"

"He would have led the right wing of the Trinovantian attack. It would have been his best chance to win honours in battle."

The ceremony of the sunrise was brief and very beautiful. It did not involve the relighting of dead fires as at the beginning of summer, nor the opening of the new year as at the start of winter. Now, at the height of the sun, the people lined the river that ran foaming past the great-house and, as the first light struck the water, they gave back to the gods their gifts of grain and gold and asked the questions for which they needed answers. Bán was not at the riverside. His gift was different. Breaca had come as she had promised and helped him to prepare the filly and her dam, but the giving of them was his alone. The elders signalled the time of it. As the sun rose free of the horizon, the elder grandmother lifted a horn and blew it, strongly. The people moved back, making a semicircle round a small knot of grandmothers and elders who gathered in the centre. Togodubnos was called out to join them and, after a moment, Amminios.

Both wore their sun-cloaks and their torcs. Both had been seen to give armbands of solid gold to the water.

Bán came at the second signal. He walked forward, leading the mare on his shield side and the dun filly on his sword side, as he had been taught. Both walked out well, aware of all the eyes turned their way. The people stepped back to make a corridor along which they walked. It was not done to cheer on the day of the gods, but each adult carried a belt knife and most of them, by chance, had picked up a stick or a small log from the fire piles as they left for the river. The noise they made, beating the blades on the wood, was that of returning warriors, beating their sword-blades on their shields to signal victory. It began softly and built in waves to a thunder over which the voice of one boy could not be heard. The elders let it roll until the point was made and then the grandmother raised her horn and blew a third time. The silence that came after hurt the ears more than the noise had done.

Bán felt himself empty, as if his soul still sat by the fire and only his body were moving. He walked the mare and the foal forward the last steps to the elders. The grandmother stood perfectly erect. In the sunlight, her eyes were white, as if poured of mare's milk. The others behind her stood straight and stone-faced. Only Togodubnos smiled—warmly, with some sorrow, as he had by the fire. Amminios's smile was poison, marred only by three scored nail marks down the side of his face. Bán had only Dubornos as his example of what it was to inflict pain and take joy in it. Standing alone before his enemy, he had some understanding of how shallow that experience was. For a frantic, fleeting moment, he wondered if it might not be kinder to take his knife from his belt and kill the filly cleanly, now, before the assembled people.

"Bán, son of Macha, harehunter and horsedreamer." The elder grandmother stepped forward. She had never used his full name before. She had never, as far as he could remember, spoken his name at all and now she was giving him titles he had not earned. "You come before us to make your apologies and to give your gift, the gods' gift, to one who will receive it in the gods' name. You will do so now."

He felt his head grow light, as it had done in the greathouse. Amminios looked discomfited; he had not expected to be standing in the gods' stead.

The exchange was made quickly. Breaca had told him the proper words of apology and the way to make the gift. At a nudge from his brother, Amminios stepped forward to take the lead ropes and give his thanks. His accent was thick and barely comprehensible and the phrases perfunctory. He stepped back, holding the lead ropes as if he were not sure what to do with them. The mare followed with reluctance. The filly twisted her head back and whickered to Bán.

Before he could respond to it, Togodubnos stepped forward. In a voice designed to carry he said, "My brother is not familiar with the language or customs of your people, but I pledge in his name that the gods' gift, made on the gods' day, will be treated with the respect due to Belin, the sun, who is most sacred to us and our father. I swear it on my honour as a warrior." In the crowd, knife-blades beat on wood again, briefly. Amminios frowned.

Togodubnos bowed, with his arm across his chest in the mark of a warrior's respect, and turned to the elder grandmother. More softly, he said, "I came last night before the council with a request from my father, Cunobelin. May I know the council's answer?"

"You may." The elder grandmother's smile held the barest shadow of Amminios's poison. "The council has considered the request and the events that surround it. It is our decision that there will be no war. This you may tell your father—that the tree of friendship does not feed on blood. It requires Briga's earth and Nemain's water to allow it fully to flower. To you, we would say that you are a man of honour who is bound by blood to men who are without honour. There will come a time when you have to choose. If you choose the waters of friendship over the blood of your kin, you will be welcome amongst the Eceni. If you do not, you will be slain, as will all our enemies."

For Bán, the sight of Amminios's face was a flicker of light in darkness.

CHAPTER 6

"He's going to die, isn't he?"

"Everything dies, Bán. Some die sooner than others, that's all."

"But is he going to die *now*—of the sickness?"

"He might do. There's no blood in the scours, which is a good sign, but he's still very cold, which is bad. If we can make the mixture properly, then he might live. If we sit here and talk about it, then, yes, he will die. Keep him close to the fire and watch the water. Tell me when it comes to the boil."

It was midmorning and everyone was awake and busy although not too busy, it seemed, to walk past on their way from here to there to see what was happening, even if "here" was in the far opposite corner of the settlement and "there" only a step or two distant. It had been all right while Bán was out with Airmid gathering the plants, for no-one had known what was happening. Now that they were back and had built a fire outside the harness hut, word had passed faster than he could have imagined until everyone had heard that Hail was sick and Airmid was tending him, and felt the need to visit and see if it was true.

It had started badly, in the time before dawn when all the world was asleep apart from a boy and his sick hound whelp. Bán had been standing in the dark in the river, washing Hail clean of the foul-smelling scour, when the splash of another's wading and an adult shape looming in the darkness had told him he was not alone. He had stood still in the freezing current with pebbles jabbing into his feet and clutched Hail tightly to his chest. A voice floated over the water, dryly amused. "Is he sick, your hound?"

It was a woman, but not Macha. He breathed in relief. All night he had been praying to Nemain who ruled the waters and it seemed she might have answered him. "He's got the scours," he said. "I was waiting for dawn so I could take him to the elder grandmother."

"Were you so?" The woman's voice ran with the roll of the river. He didn't recognize it, except to know that she was laughing at him. She said, "Then you may wait a dawn or two yet. Your sister has come into her bleeding, Bán of the horse-dreams. She's in the women's place with Macha and the grandmothers. They'll be in there for a few days yet, barring warfare, fire or flooding."

Bán stood numbly. The news slammed into him like a fist in the gut. Hail squealed in the sudden tightening of his grip. "When?" he asked, and then, because the timing was less important than the fact that he hadn't known, "Why didn't they tell me?"

"*When* was last night, as the moon rose. As to why they didn't tell you, you would have to ask your mother that. Had you been in the roundhouse, you would have seen them go, but sleeping apart as you are, I expect they did not think it needful to wake you up."

"I was awake," he said miserably. "I was watching over Hail." He thought of his prayers and his promises to the shape of the moon in the water and how they were wasted and he wished that the gods had found some way to tell him before it was too late.

The woman took a step closer. "So. I'm sorry you missed them. They will be sorry, too, if they come out and find your whelp dead. There isn't anyone who doesn't care about him after . . . all that has happened. Perhaps I can help you?"

She was close now, standing at ease beside him in the racing water, as if it were her home, more so than the land. He looked up and saw with despair that it was Airmid and, therefore, he was finished. The cold in his feet had welled up to his heart and frozen it.

"I don't . . . I can't . . ." It was the cold that made him stammer, he would swear it.

"Be still, I won't eat you." Her smile had a knowing slant to it. Her voice was the same as it had been from across the river. He heard it differently now. "You don't have to believe everything you are told about me."

"I don't."

It was true, if only because half of the things he had heard about Airmid contradicted absolutely the other half. The older boys hated her. It was said, when she was out of range and the other girls were not listening, that she had done permanent damage to Dubornos when he had tried too hard to ask for favours. Bán had not been privy to the conversation in which the exact nature of the damage had been explained in detail, but it was widely rumoured that the youth would be lucky if he could sire his own children when he came to full manhood, and certainly there had been a month or so in winter when it was clear to everyone that he was walking lame.

That was one half of it. The other half came from Breaca, which should have made it more reliable but had not. Breaca was the eyes and limbs to the elder grandmother, which was a great honour but also very dangerous. Airmid had been her predecessor and had stayed five years with the old woman before crossing to adulthood and it was this, according to the older boys, that was the source of her madness.

Bán had spent the past two and a half years watching his sister closely for signs of similar insanity and was daily relieved not to see them. Nevertheless, Breaca did not consider Airmid mad and had said so, even after the incident of the spring floods, when the older girl had turned up at the roundhouse with her hair all awry and her tunic not belted and a wild look in her eye as if she had been too close to the gods. It had not been Airmid's fault, clearly; she was a dreamer and they were all known to be different. Bán was lucky, he knew, that his mother was not in any way like the others but then Macha had the wren as her dreaming and the bird of the gods kept her sane. Airmid, by contrast, had missed out on the luck; her dreaming was the frog and proximity to water was known to drive even the strongest of women mad. Dubornos's injury notwithstanding, Bán was not sure that Airmid was one of the strongest women. She was certainly not one to whom he would willingly have entrusted the life of his hound.

He had been considering whom else he could ask for help when Airmid had waded forward out of the river, drawing him with her. She had taken Hail from his arms as he negotiated the bank and walked back to the rampart so fast that he had to run to keep up. At the gates, she had presented him with a choice that was no choice.

"If we go up to the high paddocks to pick some plants that might make him better, will you help me?"

She had Hail. He would have done whatever she wanted.

"I will try."

"Good." Her smile was almost like Breaca's. "That's all the gods ever ask of anyone, that they try."

Bán was trying. It was all he could do. He had picked the plants she had indicated and helped her carry them back to the fire. Dawn had come while they were in the high paddocks, and by the time they returned, word had spread and everyone not intimately involved with Breaca's long-nights had come to see if the rumour were true and to offer help in Hail's nursing. Airmid had thanked them with the same wry courtesy she had shown to Bán all morning and had told them that they would be called upon later if the pup survived the initial dosing. Sinochos, when he came back a second time, had been asked for more firewood and had gone out to gather it. He had sent his son, Dubornos, to bring in the first load, which was an unfortunate choice, if made with the best intentions. The youth had dumped it as far away as he could without dishonouring his father and then he and his friends had stood at a distance taunting Bán, making graphic and insulting gestures when they thought Airmid couldn't see them. Bán kept his attention on the water rising to the boil in the pot on the fire and considered the battles he would have to fight later to prove the madness hadn't tainted him.

"If you don't fight them, it will upset them more."

Airmid was sitting close by, grinding river clay and mallow roots to a paste in a bowl she had dug out from amongst the elder grandmother's private things. Bán studied her, covertly. There was a chance that what she had said did not mean what it seemed. She measured a length of washed root, cut it in pieces and dropped them into her grinding bowl, counting aloud as she did so. When she reached the right number, she began grinding again. Without looking up, she said, "Your friend with the thin hair. It will hurt him more if you don't fight him over this."

He did not risk a glance at Dubornos. It was true that the boy's hair was thin; when it was wet, it straggled down to his neck like rats' tails, just like his father's. It was the rest of what she said that bothered him. "He's not a friend," he said.

"Does he know that?"

He shrugged, as he had seen his father do in the face of danger. "He does now."

"Good. So then you won't have to prove it. There are four of them and they are all twice your age. They'll tear you in pieces and it will serve nothing. Wait until Hail is better and then show them what he is made of. He won't let you down. I was there when he was born; the grandmothers knew before you ever got there that they had seen the birth of the best hound yet born from Macha's line, they just had no idea what to do about it until you walked in with your dreaming. Let your hound get well again, then train him up and show them that he's the best. It will be better than fighting."

She raised her eyes from the bowl, sweeping a fall of dark hair from her brow with the back of her hand. The movement made the sleeve of her tunic fall back to her armpit and the mark of the frog's foot—the one that Dubornos had mocked so savagely—was suddenly visible on the inside of her elbow. Bán had never seen it before. It was not the harsh, acid colour of his imagination, but a deep blue-green, like copper left to weather, picked out in small dots on the place where it would be closest to her heart. He stared at it for too long and, when he looked up, found she was waiting for him, watching, and that she knew what he had been looking at. It seemed likely that she knew also what he had been thinking. He raised his eyes to her face. Her gaze was clear and grey, like the clouds when it rained. Her smile was open, without the earlier twist of irony. Returning it, Bán saw her properly for the first time. He thought again of what it was to be bonded to the water and felt the weight of his opinion swing over, as it had been threatening to do all morning, to the opposite position. Breaca had been right; Airmid was not mad. The wrongness of his earlier thinking stuck in his throat, twisting painfully. Hoarsely he said, "The water is near to boiling."

"Good. You come here and stir this. I'll look after that."

To hoots from the distant Dubornos, he swapped places with her, taking over the bowl and grinding stick while Airmid lifted their carrying sack and tipped the contents onto the grass between them. A scatter of different plants fell out, half of them tall with wide oval leaves and prickled stems and bell-shaped flowers the colour of mare's milk that hung in clusters from the stems. The rest had smaller, greener leaves that shone like a wet river pebble and neat red flowers that flecked the stem like drops of blood. As he watched, she sorted them swiftly into bunches of each kind and began tearing them up to drop in the water. When both bunches had gone, she started stirring. "You can come and look," she said. "Just don't stop grinding the paste or it will stiffen."

He shuffled closer to see what she was doing. The pot on the fire was a wide one with a zigzag band of decoration near the rim and a pinched lip for pouring. As he looked in, she pushed the last of the comfrey under the water and he saw the veined grey-green leaves disintegrate. The rest took longer to succumb. Airmid stirred carefully, watching for the point when the knotgrass leaves lost their sheen and the red from the flowers bled into the white of the comfrey. At the moment the colours merged, she pulled the pot off the heat and scooped in more water until it was cool enough for her to put both hands in and begin shredding the leaves, rubbing them to nothing between thumb and forefinger, squeezing the colour into the water. She was done when the clay paste was just becoming hard to handle and the infusion was a deep, mossy green, flecked here and there with the cream and scarlet of the fragmented flowers.

"There should be an empty flask by the grandmother's bed. Can you get it?" Airmid was frowning, staring at the liquid. Talking was an effort. Searching inside the roundhouse, Bán found a flattened oval flask with a narrow neck stopped with a plug of rolled horse-hide.

"Here." He carried it back to the fire.

"Good." She was biting her lip, still holding the focus. "So now all we need to do is pour the liquid into the clay and mix the two together. When the colour is all the same, we pour it into the flask and it's finished." She looked up, suddenly, her eyes wide and warm. "Do you want to do it?"

"No!" he said, shocked. And then, "Can I?"

"I think so. He's your hound. You want him to live more than anyone. It should be you who does the last thing. Look"—she reached over and took the grinding bowl from him—"I'll pour. You stir. That way we do it both together. Just make sure you imagine Hail well and strong after-wards—it helps the medicine."

She poured, he stirred. The paste flowed in spirals into the green broth of the infusion. The clay slipped off the flowers, leaving them as particles of colour in a steadily greying sludge. The smell was of turned earth and the cud of marsh-fed cattle, high on the vapours of myrtle. When it was ready, they poured it together. Airmid rested her elbow on her thigh, pouring from a height to make a thin stream while Bán held the medicine flask steady below her. When it was full, he pushed the stopper in and she turned it over to check that it didn't spill.

"Right." She grinned like a girl. "That was the easy part. Now we have to dose him. One of us needs to hold him with the head up, while the other tips the mix into his mouth. We give him only enough to make him swallow three times. He needs it nine times in daylight and three times overnight. When the scouring stops, we can go down to three times in the day and once in the night." She eyed him pensively. "Can you do that?"

"I can do anything."

"I believe it." Unexpectedly, she swept her fingers light-ly through his hair. "Let's get started and see if your hound can do the same."

It was long past nightfall and Bán was exhausted but doing his best not to succumb to sleep. Hail lay beside him on a bed of clean grass. The whelp's breathing was slow and level and his eyes were no longer sunk back into his head. The last time they had dosed him, he had sucked the medicine greedily as he had done before weaning when he was still on mare's milk. He had passed no scours since dusk and his urine was normal. Best of all, he no longer smelled rancid. Airmid had said he would live and Bán believed her. She sat beside him now, propped against the wooden wall of his sleeping place, dozing as he did. He felt the weight of her arm round him, pulling him into her side, keeping him safe. The frog's footmark pressed against him and he no longer feared it. It joined the other shapes that came and went from the dreams—of hares and horses and spearmen and Breaca sitting her long-nights alone in the forest. Her hair was a deep red, like oxblood, and it shone in the light of the moon.

Later, he woke without Airmid's arm round him. She was a shadow seen in the poor glow of the fire. He heard the sound of the medicine jar, gurgling. He pushed himself up on one elbow.

"Airmid? Can I help?"

"No. I'm fine. He's taking it on his own. Go back to sleep."

He was awake now, more alert than he had been. Fragments of his dreams disturbed him. "Why are you not with Breaca? She will be going out on her long-nights when the dawn comes. Should you not be with her?"

"She needs to be alone. That's the point of it."

"But don't you need to be there when she goes? To give her your blessing?" He was guessing and she must know it; he had no notion of the rites of the women any more than he had—yet—of the men.

"Maybe later."

Hail finished drinking. With a sigh, he paced a circle on his grass bed and settled back to healthy sleep. Airmid stoppered the medicine jar and put it back on the shelf she had made for it. Now that she was closer, Bán could see that she had changed since the morning. The dark mass of her hair had been carefully combed so that it fell in a flat sheet to her shoulders and she had twisted it back from her brow with the strip of rolled birch bark that marked her as a dreamer. The tunic she wore was a dark one, not the pale wool she had on when she first met him at the river. In the shadows it was difficult to see the colour but he thought it might be dyed green. A pair of bear's teeth on either side of a polished, peat-darkened horse's footbone hung on a thong between her breasts, clacking softly as she moved. Frogs in different poses were carved on the bone. The sight of them brought him back to where he had been.

"Breaca doesn't have a dreaming yet, does she?" he asked. "I mean, there's no one thing that talks to her like the frogs talk to you."

"Not yet. But it doesn't always come before the long-nights. That's why we sit them. And even so she may never have one. Not everyone does." She had lifted a separate flask from the shelf and was mixing things together in a drinking cup, heating it gently. He smelled wormwood and honey, bitter and sweet. The memory of it made him sleepy.

"But she wants one. She's always wanted one. That's

why——" He stopped, biting his tongue. He had been going to say, *That's why she's friends with you, because next to Macha and the elder grandmother, you have the most powerful dreaming.* Yesterday he would have said it. Today, he was not sure it was true. Instead he said, "That's why she has been looking so hard for the right place to sit since last summer."

"Indeed." Her voice carried that edge of irony that had frightened him so much before Hail had been sick. She came to sit beside him, cradling the cup in her hands. "Here. This will get you through until morning." He knew the smell and knew it was true. He did not want to drink it.

"When I am asleep, will you go out to see Breaca?"

"I might do."

"Then wait. I have something for you to take to her."

He had his own special place on the far side beyond the fire. He found it by touch and reached into the most secret corner at the back of it, bringing out the thing that was hidden there. He held it out for Airmid.

"This is for Breaca. Hail found it on the other side of the horse paddocks, beyond where Nemma and Camma planted their barley. I think it will help with her dreaming."

"Do you so?" She was not making fun of him now. The thing slid from his palm to hers and she held it up to see it properly. The firelight touched on it softly, melting the shadows for a little way round. Airmid looked thoughtful. She pursed her lips and nodded slowly. "Do you know what this is?"

"Macha says it's a spear-head, made by the ancestors. They carved stones and used them for hunting before the gods gave them iron. See"——he was kneeling beside her now, so they could look at it together——"if you look at it here, you can see where they would bind it crossways to the shaft. It wouldn't be a big spear, not for boar or bear, but they could take hare with it possibly, or if they were lucky a deer."

"Or a man?"

He hadn't thought of that. "Maybe." He sat back on his heels. Doubt struck him as it had not before, but the first impulse had been so strong, he was not prepared to let it go so easily. He said, "I still think she should have it."

Airmid closed her hand. The spear-head vanished from sight and the quality of the light changed. She slipped the thing inside her tunic and the shape of it made a slender bulge at her belt. "All right. You and I will make a bargain. If you drink all of the cup, down to the grit in the bottom, I will take your gift to Breaca. If it happens that you wake after I am gone, you will not put your head outside the door—saving flood or fire or warfare—before the sun touches the roundhouse. That is my offer. Will you take it?"

It was a long time to stay cloistered, long past his normal waking time, but he reached for the cup. It did not occur to him not to. The taste was more bitter than he remembered from the times his mother made it, as if Airmid was running short of honey. Still, the warmth of it spread outwards from his throat and his stomach, making everything tingle. By the time he reached the dregs at the bottom, the tingling had become a light-headed numbness and he felt the parts of his body lift and spread apart, moving outwards to the far corners and beyond them. He was distantly aware of Airmid supporting his shoulders and laying him down on the bed beside Hail and drawing up the bed-skins to cover him. He did not hear her go out.

CHAPTER 7

Breaca woke to cool fingers laid on her brow and Macha's voice in her ear.

"Breaca? Let go of the dream. It is time to be up."

The dream had been violent, a clashing of swords and a thrusting of spears, and men had died with her waking. She lay in the dark and stared at the roof beams and made the feel of it leave her. In its place came the hollow ache of hunger and the greater twist of anticipation and fear. She breathed deeply and thought of Airmid and then of her father. When the crisis in her diaphragm passed, she opened her eyes. Macha was there, leaning over her, dressed and feathered for ceremony. Her face was lean and solemn, with the laughter confined to the lines about her eyes.

"Here. This is for you." She held out a tunic. It was the grey one that Breaca had worn at the midsummer gathering and not seen since—the one that had once been her mother's. A familiar knife-thrust of grief added to the increasing fear. She reached for the tunic and slipped it on. Macha helped her to tie the belt and ran a comb through her hair, spreading it long and free down her back in the way of a child. "Are you well?" she asked.

It was the traditional question and it required the traditional answer. "Yes, I am well."

Macha smiled and did not believe her. No girl on the brink of womanhood could reasonably be expected to feel well.

"Have you everything you need?"

That was not part of the tradition and was, therefore, more important. "I think so."

Breaca looped her belt tight and slipped her knife in it, tying the hilt-thong to the leather. Her pouch hung on the other side. She opened it and checked the contents: a small, stoppered flask to hold water, a second with a wider neck and a thicker base, to hold the embers from the fire with which she could kindle her own flame, a bundle of dried sage to make the offering to the gods, a smaller bundle containing a wren's wing for Macha and the foot of the small, fierce, yellow-eyed owl that had carried the dream of her mother. In a separate twist of dock leaf was the thighbone of a frog, which had been Airmid's gift to mark the end of summer. She worked the leaf open and ran her finger along the length of the bone, using the memories it brought to banish the last dregs of the dream and the persistent ache of fear. She was Breaca of the Eceni and she was going to become a woman. For close to twelve years her waking dreams had been of this time. Since the day of her mother's death, many of her sleeping ones had been designed to prepare her. She was going to walk out alone and live for three days and three nights with nothing but her own thoughts to guide her, and those thoughts were not going to be mean ones. She took her hand from her pouch and drew the drawstring tight. "Yes," she said, "I have everything."

"Good. Come outside. It is time to be going."

She stepped beyond the door-flap and found she was not, after all, alone with the night. A human snake stretched back from her doorway; the dozen women of childbearing age stood waiting in silence, each carrying a torch to light her darkness, each dressed and feathered, as Macha was, with the precision that spoke of a long night's preparation. Tears pricked at her eyes. She was taking the first of her steps into womanhood, and she should have expected that the women would come to see her leave. That she had not did them no honour.

The elder grandmother stood at the head of the column. A fox skin hung down her back like a cloak, the fall of it weighted with nuggets of raw gold hung about with eagle feathers. The two wings of a crow arced down from her shoulders to meet at the point of her breastbone. This was why she was the elder grandmother and had lived so long; she had the fox and the eagle as well as the crow in her dreaming, for all that she rarely proclaimed it. And yet she had not dressed like that alone, had not woven the small, rounded feathers from the back of the eagle into her hair with such precision, had not washed her own tunic and dried it in sage smoke with her own hands. For three years, Breaca had been the one to dress the old woman. She had known where the fox skin was kept and how to hang the crow's wings, balancing them on the sharp angles of her shoulders, with the weight of the body skin hanging down the back, holding them in place so that the tips met exactly in the middle. In a shock of understanding, she realized that

Airmid must have done it as a gift to them both and that, very soon, the duty would pass to another. The cold stab of dread and loss sought out the place between her shoulders again, twisting inwards, drawing at her warmth. She reached past the elder grandmother's torch and touched the thin stick of the arm that was holding it.

"Why did I not know you would be here?" she asked.

"Because I saw to it that you would not. No woman ever does, nor does any expect it. It is not important. What matters is that this morning you are going out as a child and will come back three days hence as a woman."

The elder grandmother was being kind, which was not her way. Breaca stepped closer, afraid to embrace her; afraid, equally, not to. The torch flared with her movement. Fresh light showed the milk-white eyes as they looked into hers and laid bare her soul. It hurt too much and she moved her gaze away. The banded feathers braided into the hair of the grandmother's temples hung in perfect symmetry on either side of the ancient cheeks. The threads binding them were red, black and gold, tied in bands that matched the rhythms of the eagle. Breaca reached out and touched one, taking liberties. It spun as if she had blown it.

"I should have done this for you."

"No." The beech-bark skin creased tighter in a smile. "You had better things to do. As did Airmid. She has been with your brother."

"What?" She stared, wondering if the grandmother was finally losing her reason. She could think of no reason why Bán would choose to go near Airmid if he didn't have to. The answer came to her suddenly. "Hail?" she asked. "Is he sick?"

"He will live. And, perhaps because of it, you have been sent a gift." She pressed something small into Breaca's hand. "This is from your brother and his hound."

It was a spear-head in stone. She knew as soon as she touched it. The sharp edges of it bit into her palm even as the surface felt smooth and reassuringly cool. It was a pale colour, like the full moon at harvest, and the firelight reflected from it softly. It drew her gaze and all her attention at a time when she needed to be thinking of other things. She closed her fingers, crushing the light away, and looked up at the grandmother. "I thought the laws—"

"—said that you must take nothing of the male with you. I know. We have discussed this." The old woman nodded past her to where Macha stood waiting to escort her to the gate. "In some things, the laws are not immutable. They are there to protect the vulnerable, not bind the strong. We think you may need this and that you will know what to do with it. Take it with you and listen to what it tells you. Learn what it can teach."

The spasm came back to her diaphragm, blocking her breathing. "What if I hear nothing, Grandmother? What if the gods don't speak?"

"Be patient. Listen. They will speak."

She did listen. She had listened. She was listening. The gods had not spoken.

In the first hours, Breaca had been concerned to say her prayers, to gather wood for the fire that she needed to burn the sage and to lay out her dreaming tokens in a circle around it. Later, shrouded in the skin of a she-bear that had been, indirectly, her father's parting gift, she had fidgeted, cursing the late, lazy midges that fed on the exposed parts of her skin. She had built up the fire then, and laid damp beech leaves on it to make yellow smoke that swirled up past her cheeks and kept the biting things at bay. Later still, in the dark part of the night, she had slipped into sleep and let the fire go out and cursed herself for doing so. Her dreams had been as they always were of men with spears and bloodied swords, seeking her mother's life or her own; they were not a real *dreaming*.

The second day dawned slowly, with more rain and a thickening mist. She saw the rising of the sun no more than she had seen the rising of the moon the night before. That which had been black simply became less black and settled finally to a dull, undulating grey. Even the trees on either side became ghosts, vague shapes that loomed in and out of sight with the waxing and waning of the fog. The day grew colder and dead leaves fell with the rain, slithering down the tree trunks to infiltrate her stacked-branch shelter. More rain followed and soaked into the bear-skin until it stank of wet dog and old bear grease and urine. Her mind sang the names that would stick to her when she returned to the women's place without a dream but with, instead, a sheath of bear-stench around her that no amount of washing would clear through the winter. She loathed her father for having made her the gift and herself for having accepted.

Sometime in the third day, time lost its meaning. The quality of the light had not changed since dawn. Without the sun and its shadows she had no way to measure the space between moments. She took to counting the drips that fell from the front of her shelter until the rain fell so fast that they ran together to make a stream and could not be counted. She listened to the forest, to the smothered cries of the jackdaws, the magpies, the crows, the battling jays and the squirrels. As she listened, they left her, one by one, and the woods fell quiet. She turned to the river for solace but it was swollen with autumn rain, thick with mud and dying leaves so that it ran sluggishly and in silence. Its only offering was the mist that hung over it, sickly, like smoke from a poor fire. The ancestor mound sat squat and sullen on the horizon, devoid of the magic that it had held since the day Airmid had first introduced her. Breaca watched it for an age, aching, praying to each of the gods in turn for a sign, and saw nothing.

Day moved to evening and stole the light. Her stomach griped on its emptiness and her spit dried so that she began to pray that the river would flood, simply to allow her to drink. In despair and in memory of something Airmid had told her, she sat still and counted her breaths and her heartbeats, letting her own body set the rhythms of time so that she would know it had not stopped altogether. The world dissolved to a blurring of greys and her life moved with the rush of blood in her ears.

At the end, it was the needs of her body that drove her from the shelter. She had taken neither food nor water since the first hint of her bleeding and had thought herself empty of both. In this, too, she was wrong. She held on until the pressure in her bladder became too much to bear and then shrugged out of the skin and eased herself away from the grasping roots of the tree. When she stood, the urgency was less and she took time to observe the requirements of the ceremony. The dreaming tokens were not to be left unguarded. She walked round the dead ashes of the fire, picking them up.

The west, nearest her shelter, was the place of water and dreaming, Nemain's place, sacred to women and the night; Airmid's frog bone was there. In the north, home of earth and rock and mountains, she had placed the wren's wing from Macha, who had been to Hibernia and Mona and knew the mountains well. South was the fire and the full sun of summer and it held the foot of the yellow-eyed owl that had been the dream of her mother. The east, place of air and wind, home of the eagle and the fleet-running hare, had been empty for most of the first day. In her imaginings through the summer, she had left it free for the symbol of her dreaming, so that she could return from the other world and draw the image first on the empty patch of sandy loam as she had once drawn a frog for Airmid. Now, in the real world, with the earth so sodden and covered in wet leaves that it had taken an age simply to clear a wide enough space to light a fire, drawing on the earth seemed a childish fancy. Sometime in the dark of the first night, it had become clear that she needed to fill the gap and she had placed Bán's stone spear-head there. It had glimmered, gathering firelight and folding it outwards, making the circle whole. Later, after the fire had gone out, the curves on its surface still glistened, catching what light there was and holding it for her. She had been grateful during the day and now, standing, she lifted the stone last and held it in her hand for a moment before slipping it in the pouch with the rest.

Beyond the grasp of the trees, the world was different. The river was running faster than she had imagined it and was less clouded with mud. The mist had thinned and the rain had stopped and the quality of the air was better. The river danced and sang and small fish flashed at the margins.

Out on the eastern horizon, a gap appeared in the clouds showing a night sky. A haze of moonlight brightened the far bank and, in the stars, the shield arm of the Hunter pointed up towards the Hare.

Breaca slid down the bank to the place where she had lain with Airmid and walked forward until the pool lapped at the bare skin of her feet. It was cool but not cold and the feel of it was refreshing after the insidious damp of the rain. She walked slowly downstream, feeling the grate of sand between her toes and the coil of the river around her ankles. At the place where the flow ran fastest she stepped sideways onto a stone, lifted her tunic clear of the surface and squatted to urinate. Small clots of blood slipped out with her water and flowed downstream. She felt better afterwards. The hollowness of hunger had become a part of her and the new emptiness matched it. Standing up on the stone, she turned east to study the stars. The rent in the clouds widened until she could see the spear held aloft by the Hunter. The tip of it pointed east to the far horizon with the crisp imperative of an order. She took a step further out across the river—and stopped.

In all the hours of instruction from the elder grandmother and Macha, in the long talks with Airmid, it had been impressed upon her that she must find a place to sit, to light her fire, to lay out her tokens. At no time that she could remember had she been forbidden to leave that spot; it had been her assumption that she should stay there, but it had not been said. She considered the matter intently. In this, it was as important to abide by the spirit of the law as by the letter. Presently, when she was sure that she was breaking no unspoken rules, she stepped out onto another stone and then another.

On the third, halfway across the river, she turned back to look at the wood. The beech that had held her was shrouded in mist, as forbidding as it had been since she first arrived. The far bank, by contrast, was clear and inviting, the ground was sandy and free of dead leaves, and winter grass rippled under a light breeze. As she watched, a water rat threaded through the reeds and paused to look at her, its eyes bright in the starlight. It was the first living thing she had seen since walking out of the gates, and for one appalling moment it seemed possible that this was it, that she was going to return not only smelling of rancid bear fat but with the water rat as her dreaming. Her mind sang, cluttered suddenly with the grandmother's tales of others whose arrogance had brought them dreams they did not want. Even the least of them had not dreamed a rat. She swayed on the stone, light-headed with fear, paralysed in ways she had not been by the Coritani spearman or Amminios and his sword.

Then a white owl screeched close by in the woods, a dog fox barked and a vixen answered, a stag grunted in the far distance and suddenly the night was alive with all the things that had been missing. The rat stayed a moment longer and vanished. It gave no message and was, therefore, neither her dream nor her dreaming. The shock of relief crushed the air from her chest, leaving her dizzy. In a burst of unstable energy, she ran the last half-dozen strides to the far side of the river, skidding on the crossing stones, throwing herself with outstretched arms onto the crumbling sand of the bank. She collapsed onto the turf, breathing in ragged bursts, laughing and crying together, weeping her thanks to the gods and the rat and the river. Only later, as she calmed, did she remember something Airmid had said, long ago, in the summer. *Be careful of the river. It is not for nothing that men say it has the power to drive women mad. Don't cross when the moon is on it if you don't have to.*

Wiping her face, she made herself sit upright and look at the water. White foam curled innocently around the margins of the stones. The truncated circle of the moon lipped at the one on which she had been standing. She could return. If pressed, she would do so, but it would be better to do it in daylight, or later at night when the moon had passed on. In the meantime, she was free to follow the call of the Hunter. Standing, she put her back to the river and set off east, towards the dawn.

Without the rain, the night was surprisingly warm. She crossed scrubland too poor for horses but with signs that deer had grazed on it recently. Stunted hawthorn and rowan, growing singly or in small stands, dropped leaves in the breeze as she passed. Islands of gorse and broom grew more strongly; the late flowers of the gorse glowed faintly yellow in the starlight. Everywhere, the land was completely flat, without even the gentle undulations of the paddocks beyond the roundhouse. The mound was the only feature: a dark, brooding bulk that became darker and more brooding as she approached. She did not make for it directly, but it was in her path and she made no effort to avoid it. Even so, she might have passed it by without a second glance had not the clouds split apart as she came near and the full moon burst through, flooding the mound and the land around it with light.

It was not a beautiful sight, but it was arresting. She stopped and drew breath once at the spectacle of it and then again, more sharply, at the sight of the great stone that stood at the mound's end. It was granite, which was not common: a single slab of it taller than she was by a spear's length and half a spear wide, tapering to a rounded point. From a distance, it had the same proportions as the spear-head in her pouch, but it was not the size that caught her eye, that brought her up close to run exploring fingers across the surface, but the markings on it. There, at a height level with her eyes, was boldly carved the sign of the serpent-spear, the one the grandmother had painted on Breaca's shield and the shoulder of her horse as she rode out to greet the Trinovantes on the gods' day in the summer. She ran a finger along the lines, cleaning the edges. It was not newly cut, nor was it, on close inspection, as deep as it had first looked. The whole thing, from the end of the serpent's head to its tail, was the length of her hand, and the lines had been softened by generations of sun and wind and rain and the furred coverings of lichen. Had it not been for the high angle of the moon, she would have missed it altogether.

"Is it a good likeness?"

Breaca spun round, her knife coming clean of the sheath even as her ears made sense of the words. The elder grandmother stood behind her, grinning as she did whenever she had caused the greatest discomfort in those around her. She was not dressed as she had been in the women's place. She was, in fact, not dressed at all but for an elaborate necklace of eagle skulls and fox teeth that clattered on her breastbone. Her thighs were slickly wet almost to the hip, as if she had crossed the river elsewhere than the stepping stones and had misjudged the depth of it. Her eyes, caught in shadow, were black.

"It has taken you long enough to find the place. I was beginning to think I would have to seek you out." The grandmother cocked her head. "Did you bring my spear-head with you?"

"Is it yours? I thought . . . yes, I have it here."

She was too shocked to answer more fully. Nothing, none of the lessons, none of the elliptic conversations with Airmid, had prepared her for this. She reached in her pouch and brought out the gift Bán had given her. She had taken it lightly but now did not want to part with it. The grand-mother took it and turned it over in her hand.

"Good."

She handed it back. Breaca received it with relief. The grandmother smiled again, brightly. Her step was light, as if, by shedding her clothes, she had shed many of her years. "Come. You are late and there is a great deal to see."

Reality moved back another pace. The old woman stepped round behind the standing stone and vanished, much as the water rat had done. When Breaca did not fol-low she called, sharply, in a voice of fast-waning patience, "Come. Quickly. You're wasting time."

It was not good to try the grandmother's temper. Breaca stepped round the standing stone, sucking in a breath to squeeze into the narrow space between the rock and the grass of the mound. On the far side, she let the breath out again, sharply, and grabbed for the support of the standing stone. Her stomach lurched as she stared down at where the ground should be and saw only space. Here, hidden from prying eyes, was the entrance to the mound: a shelving pit that slanted down and into the earth, its walls bounded by more slabs of granite. The grandmother waited inside it, glaring.

It had taken more courage than Breaca knew she pos-sessed to face the water rat. Entering the mound was easy by comparison. It was not, as she might have expected, a cave of earth, but rather a wide, open-ended tunnel lined with cut and dressed stone. Standing at the entrance, she could see through the length of it to the shadowed scrub at the far side. Moonlight leaked in from both sides so that the interior was no darker than the roundhouse in an evening. She stepped slowly in. Three steps led down the entrance slope, all of stone and all worn by many generations of passing feet. It felt good to be walking in the tracks of the ancestors. She caught up with the grandmother, who turned and led the way inside.

The interior of the mound was surprisingly dry. Outside, the world was saturated after two nights of steady rain. Here, on the inside, the great slabs of the walls and ceiling fitted so closely together that neither earth nor water could seep between them and the packed earth beneath her feet was parched as in the height of summer, crumbling to dust between her toes. Here, too, were worn the grooves of many generations' passing, although in the tunnel they ran parallel, as if those walking here had done so in pairs, shoulder to shoulder, or else had kept to one side going in and the other coming out. Breaca kept to the left, the shield side, out of instinct, her hand on the hilt of her knife. The grandmother walked ahead of her in the centre, ignoring the long-trodden paths.

The exit came soon and without any sign of the honoured dead of which Airmid had spoken. Breaca followed the grandmother up three steps into full moonlight. The land beyond was unremarkable. Scrub stretched away to the horizon. The river foamed and sang to their left. To the right grew a thick hedge of gorse. Breaca was looking for a way to get past it when the grandmother tapped her on the arm and, crouching, motioned her forward to a fox run that was wide enough to crawl through. The grandmother was small and naked and came through unscathed. Breaca had her tunic for protection but still emerged with long scores on either arm and a triangular tear on her shin.

She drew breath to speak, to advise that they walk round the hedge when they left, or at the very least to ask that she be allowed to go first with a knife on the return journey. The words were not formed when the grandmother clamped the claw of her hand across her mouth and forced her to silence. She pressed her lips to Breaca's ear. Her voice was a breath of wind. "Say nothing. There are men in the hollow. If they know you are here, they will kill you." She unclamped her hand. In the moonlight, her eyes shone yellow, like a hawk's.

Breaca had not noticed a hollow. She looked for it now, lying flat on her stomach in the shadow of the gorse. Creeping forward, she saw a wide, round-ended valley sunk into the earth like a bowl to feed the gods, the slopes of it lush with grass and berried rowan. A small stream threaded down one side and spilled into a pool on the valley's floor. Near the centre, a fire burned with high, leaping flames. Two men stood on either side of it, each with a stock of dried boughs.

More men walked in from the east down a path that coursed alongside the stream. They were small men, the tallest no bigger than the elder grandmother and some not even that. Had they been clothed Breaca might have believed them children but, like the grandmother, they were naked, brown-skinned and dark-haired, and all were assuredly adult. She saw no women. From a place behind the rowans, a dozen of them dragged a vast cooking bowl, of a size to feed an entire roundhouse, and set it to heat on the fire. Presently, rising smoke carried to Breaca the mellow, meaty smell of bear fat, boiling.

The taller of the two fire-keepers gave his place to another and went to draw water from the pool, carrying it up in an oversized ale jug. When added to the larger bowl, the water hissed and made steam. On the ninth such journey, the taller man stood over the bowl and began to speak. Breaca could hear the tone of his voice, faintly mournful, like birdsong at dusk, but not the words. As he stopped speaking, the water hissed violently and fell silent.

A third man, one with a sun symbol drawn in yellow on his chest, was called forward to tip the contents of a belt pouch into the mix. He stirred it using the butt end of a spear and the smell ripened, gathering the tannin of hawthorn berries and the sweet-sour of spoiled hay until it settled to something Breaca recognized; they were mixing woad, the most sacred of plants, guardian of warriors and women in childbirth. Her mind was drifting, bringing images of the serpent-spear on her shield and the preparations for her mother's childbirth, when it came to her, suddenly, that she was watching one of the men's rites and that it was forbidden, absolutely, by all the laws of gods and dreamers, for any woman even to think of it, still less to lie on the damp turf and watch while it happened. In panic, she thrust an arm across her eyes and began to squirm backwards. The grandmother's claw clamped her wrist, holding her still. The whispered voice was acidly painful, for all that she could barely hear it. "Would I bring you here did the gods not permit it? You will stay. There are things you must see."

She stayed. She had no choice. Beneath her, the last of the men had entered the hollow. Their exact numbers were hard to count but thirty or more gathered close to the fire and a handful of others squatted by the stream. At a signal from the fire-tenders, spear-hafts were brought from the shade of the rowan and distributed, one to each. Spear-heads of stone were collected from a central pile, chosen with care so that, even when each warrior had taken the best he could find, there were as many left behind that were not quite perfect.

The leading fire-tender turned to the group and clapped his hands. As one, each man knelt with his right knee to the earth, settled the spear-haft across his left thigh and bound spear-head to haft with a leather thong taken from his hair. They worked quickly and in silence. At the end of it, the leader clapped again. The warriors stood and made a ring round the fire. Names were called in the same fluting birdsong. At the sound of each one, a man stepped forward, presenting himself and his weapon to the cauldron and the keepers who stood beside it. What came next stopped Breaca's breath in her throat. The vat had not seemed big enough to take a whole man, but she saw each of the warriors step in and duck down until only the top of his hair was visible, and when they stepped out they were no longer men but glistening half-ghosts, silvered grey to match the coming dawn, sliding as wraiths through the mist rising up from the stream. They gathered at the shores of the pool, taking care not to enter the water, standing in silent ranks with their spears held away from their bodies. There were seven yet to enter the vat when the first bloodred edge of the sun lifted over the eastern horizon. Seeing it, one of the men set up a song in a minor key with many repetitions. Before the second phrase, the others had joined in.

Breaca felt the grandmother stir. Her voice was less harsh than it had been, and more easily heard. In all the noise down below, they could speak aloud without risk of detection. "Look at the patterns," said the grandmother. "It is the pattern that matters."

She looked. The woad gave the grey, Airmid had taught her that; when mixed with melted bear grease or horse fat, it turned a warrior's skin to the silvered, trout-belly grey that offered perfect camouflage at dawn or dusk. The heroes of the past had used it often; the singers' tales told of them rising like ghosts from the mists of a river to confront their enemies. In the dark of the night, Breaca had not seen beyond the transformation it wrought on the men. Now, looking with care and with the added light of the dawn, she saw that the fire-leaders had used also the blue woad, mixed perhaps with spit or egg white, to draw signs on chest or back, or, in a few cases, the forearms of the warriors. It took a long time before the patterns became anything more than random lines. It was only when the men lined up again by the fire, closer and all together, that she saw what they were.

"They are wearing the serpent-spear. The sign you put on my shield." Breaca felt stupid for not having seen it sooner. She said, "It is different. Not as you drew it."

"No. In this, the serpent head is on both ends, facing both left and right, looking back and looking forward. For these men, that which has happened is as important as that which is to come. The past carries the seeds of the future and both must be honoured. For you, it will be the same.

When you return, you will repaint the sign on your shield to match this one."

"Is it my sign?" She felt a spasm of the old fear. The spear was not a living thing. It could not talk to her in the dream the way the frogs spoke to Airmid or the wren to Macha.

The grandmother was ruthless. "It is yours until you earn another. Now look at the leader."

The fire-leader entered the cauldron last. He drew his own sign, working on his forearms. Breaca saw the outline as he began and her heart leaped, knowing it. "Is it a hare? The leader has the sign of the hare?" The hare was Nemain's beast, as sacred as the wren. It could cross between the worlds at will, carrying word from the gods to the people and back. Only in her moments of greatest hope had Breaca imagined the hare might be her dreaming.

The elder grandmother said, "Yes, it is a hare. He has earned it. It may save him yet. Watch, now. They are nearly ready."

The old woman sat upright, peering into the hollow. The warriors were grouped at the fire again. The song had died away and the leaders had set up a new, harder chant, tossing phrase and counterphrase back and forth between themselves and the warriors, beating their spear-hafts on the empty cauldron to keep the rhythm. The tone of it was quite different from the birdsong of their earlier music. This was a promise of war and death, not a welcome to the sun. The power of many voices poured into it, raising strength and hope. Breaca felt it rock through her, calling an answer from her heart. Without thinking, her fingers matched the rhythm, tapping it out on her thigh. "When are they going to fight?" she asked. "And whom?"

"They will fight as soon as the sun is fully up. It will not be long now. When it happens, you will watch and learn. You will not go down." The grandmother reached back into the fox run in the gorse and drew out a spear-haft, such as the men had used below. "Did you see how the binding was done to fix stone to haft?" she asked.

"Yes."

"Do it now."

Breaca's belt pouch was tied with a leather thong of the right length and weight. She unthreaded it and used it to bind back her hair, tying it loosely at the nape as the men had done. It was not perhaps necessary, but she wanted to follow the ritual exactly. The grandmother clapped as the leader of the warriors had done and Breaca knelt with her right knee touching the earth, balancing the spear-haft on her thigh. The position was awkward, but became easier with time. As the men had done, she swept the thong from her hair with one hand and held the stone spear-head next to the haft with the other. The winding of the thong, too, was harder than it had looked. Twice she dropped the stone to the earth. Twice the grandmother picked it up and handed it back without comment. In the hollow, the chanting reached a climax with a wild pounding of feet and stopped, cleanly, on a beat. Breaca finished the final turns of the thong in silence. It was not perfect; she could see how it could be done better, but it was tight and she knew in her heart that the spear would kill for her if she asked it. The haft felt light and vibrant in her hand. In first greeting was the promise of things to come. The sun blazed fully over the eastern rim of the bowl and caught the milk-blue of the stone, turning it gold. A breeze ran over the top of the valley, bringing the smells of smoke and blackthorn and rowan and the wild-bitter war scent of woad. Breaca smiled at the grandmother. The life of the sun and the spear sparked through her. The old scar on her palm, relic of her first kill, began lightly to throb. "Where is the battle?" she asked.

The grandmother nodded, with the patience she granted importunate youth. She lifted her hand and gestured east to the sun. In the last moment of silence, softly, she said, "It is here."

The screaming was almost human, a long, piercing ululation that could have been a war cry from the throats of a hundred warriors. Breaca stared down the valley, out onto the path at the eastern edge, seeking its source. Only when the first bird stooped from the sky did she realize that she was not to witness a battle of equals; not man against man, warrior to warrior, a battle of heroes; but men—small men—against eagles, the greatest of birds.

The numbers were not even. From the beginning, the sky was dark with the flooding barrage of wings. She saw the first of the warriors die in the hollow below her, his eyes pierced through to the brain, his head crushed in talons that could break the neck of a deer. His cries, choked on blood and pain, were the signal for the greater mass of the birds to strike. They did not stoop from a height, wings folded, as falcons do, but flew in at a shallower angle, powering on wings that spanned far more than the spear-lengths of the men who opposed them. They struck out in passing, raking eyes and arms and shoulders, and flew on, wheeling at the valley's walls to come in again. They did not mark flesh on every pass, nor did they escape each time unscathed. The warriors fought in pairs and for every man wounded or killed, one was left to stab upwards with his stone spear. Birds fell, screaming harshly, to have their skulls beaten by the spear-hafts or their bodies impaled. Even so, they did not give their lives cheaply and more than one man was injured beyond hope of rescue by the strike of a dying eagle from the ground. The warriors fought bravely and with a sense of long practise. Each time one of their number died, his surviving partner sought out another, similarly bereft, to make a new pair. Still, the numbers dwindled and the spaces between them became larger. The eagles were uncountable and they knew no fear. It was never going to be an even battle.

Breaca watched in horror. Had the grandmother not kept a hand clamped to her arm, she would have run down to help, whatever her orders. Instead, she put her fist to her mouth to keep from crying out, biting on her knuckle as, one by one, the men of the serpent-spear fell to the eagles. "The woad grease is not helping," she said. "Why did they use it?"

"Because it is what their fathers used and their fathers before that and still they have not learned to do otherwise." The grandmother was scathing. It was not clear if the scorn was aimed at Breaca for her ignorance or at the warriors for their blind faith. "The woad is not useless. If you watch, the talons slide on skin where otherwise they might strike, and even those that strike leave wounds that would heal faster with less chance of infection were the men to live. But they will not live. It takes more than good camouflage and sliding skin to defeat the eagles. Watch the warriors. Learn from them. They work in pairs when they should work in larger groups; they use spears alone when swords would give them a wider strike and shields offer safety. They are learning, but not fast enough. These are the last. After them, there will be no more."

"*What?*" That caught Breaca's full attention, as the rest had not. "How can they be the last? This is Eceni country. We are everywhere, like the stalks of corn in a field."

The grandmother smiled, thinly, like a snake. "Breaca, these are not Eceni. They are the ancestors, do you not see? The Eceni are tall and fair-headed and they use weapons of iron and bronze. These are small and dark and their weapons are stone. Their blood runs in your line, else you would not dream as you do, but there is not enough of it to bring them back. If they lose here now, there are none to follow them. And they are losing."

That was clear. And, although the grandmother's hand had fallen from her arm, it was also clear that to run down now with only a spear would be suicide, and achieve nothing. Breaca said, "These are only the men. There must be women and children. If they live, then the people live with them."

"Perhaps, but the eagles will kill them. The women are already preparing to fight but they will not win. After them, the children will die."

"Then we should go to them, talk to them, help them to escape."

"Maybe." The grandmother tipped her head sideways, considering. "It would be a good thing to save the children. They would carry the blood at least."

"That is not enough. There must be those old enough to carry their ways, their dreams and their tales. How else does a people know itself?"

"How indeed?" The grandmother smiled happily, as if a point had been well made. She looked down into the valley. Three warriors were left, standing back to back in a triangle, their spears held aloft, facing the death that was coming. One of them was the fire-leader with the symbol of the hare on his forearms. He set up the war chant and the others followed. The first of the circling eagles tipped its wings and began the powered descent.

"We should leave now," said the grandmother. "It will not serve them to have another witness their deaths. The gods know this has happened. They will deal with it as they can."

"And the women and children? The bearers of dreams?"

"Are beyond us. I am sorry. Truly. If it were possible, I would take you—"

"Get *down!*"

Breaca screamed it, throwing herself forward, thrusting the grandmother back. The eagle was above them, the great wings curving round, thrashing the air, as the talons swept forward to strike. In that moment, all Breaca could think of was the size of it; that the valley had distorted her sense of scale and she had not been prepared for the crushing, overwhelming immensity. There was no time to plan. The spear leaped like a live thing in her hand. It was piercing upwards as the first of the talons struck. She did not aim for the chest, as the warriors had done, but for the head, for the sungold eyes and the shrieking maw and the shining red road of its throat. The flint sang as it flew, mournfully, as the warriors had done. She saw the glance of the sun on the stone and the fountain of blood and smashed bone as it bit into living flesh. The climactic, bittersweet joy of the kill washed through her as it had never done before. The throb in her palm waxed and waned and was still.

The eagle died at her feet. The weight of it dragged the spear down, smashing the haft against her arm. She was already on the ground, kneeling at the grandmother's side.

The old woman lay on the turf, her eyes wide and white. Dark blood flowed freely from a puncture wound on her shoulder. It pumped, faster and more brightly, from a gash on her neck.

"Don't move . . . don't. I'll bind it." Breaca's belt knife hung from its thong. She wrenched it loose and cut along the hem of her tunic, making a ribbon of wool. Fear made her careless and she cut the heel of her hand. The grandmother turned her head. Breaca put a hand to her forehead, holding her still, fighting for words and reason and a way, any way, to stop the bleeding. "Don't. You mustn't move. You'll make it worse . . . hold still. Let me bind it. When it's stopped, we can leave. I'll carry you—"

"Breaca."

It was the voice she knew, the one that brooked no argument. She let fall the strip of wool. "Yes?"

"Give me the spear-haft. It is my staff. I would hold it."

She had not thought where it came from. The staff was to a dreamer what the blade was to a warrior. She wrenched it from the throat of the eagle, cutting the bindings of the stone free with a flick of her knife. The end was stained with blood and spattered with flesh and bone. She rubbed it clean on the grass.

"Now help me to stand."

"No, you mustn't, really, you mustn't. We have to get you to Airmid. She'll know what to do. Please let me bind it . . ." Breaca was weeping hot tears of panic. Her hands were shaking. She lifted the strip of tunic and pressed it tight to the wound. "Please, you can't heal it alone. You must believe me."

The old woman was a pale grey, the colour of wet chalk.

Her breathing came in short and ragged gasps. Every bit of her energy went into her voice and the effort of it was heart-breaking to watch. Struggling to sit, she said, "I am not going to heal it alone. Nor is Airmid within reach. You must get me to the mound, the one we came through. In there I can dream."

"But dreaming won't—"

"Breaca . . ."

"Yes, Grandmother. I'll take you. It's not far."

It was not far and they did not have to crawl through the gorse hedge. In the hollow, the last of the warriors died, their deaths solitary and private. The eagles were feeding or soaring in lazy circles. They showed no interest in the old woman and the girl making slow steps to safety. The elder grandmother walked as far as she could, bearing her weight on her staff. When she stumbled for the second time, she consented to be lifted and carried, as she said, like a wailing babe.

"Into the mound. It is not far." The grandmother's voice was the rustling of mouse grass; a shape in the air with no heart behind it. "In the centre is the dreaming place . . ."

"There was nowhere, Grandmother. It's a tunnel. We walked through it. The walls were smooth. Please let me bind the wounds and carry you home. I can do it. You weigh nothing. I mean . . ."

"You mean you are a strong young woman and you can run for half a morning carrying my weight for all you have neither eaten nor drunk for three days. I believe you. But I must dream. Here now . . . no, to the left, through the grasses. We need only go a little way in."

The mound sat, brooding. There was no stone at this entrance, only a rounded opening half hidden behind the spreading foliage of the mound. Breaca would have missed it had not the grandmother directed her to it. She ducked down and eased in sideways, protecting her charge from the dew-damp grass. Inside, it was darker than it had seemed in moonlight, or perhaps the contrast was greater under the sun. It smelled of earth and ancient dust. She felt the floor crumble under her feet. When she leaned on a wall to steady herself, it, too, fell to dust. She jerked upright. "Grandmother. . . ?"

"Trust me. We are nearly there. I will not lead you into danger." She sounded faintly amused. "Last night, you were still in your dreaming. Today, you are a woman. It is time for you to see the world as it truly is. Go forward nine paces and stop. . . .Good. Now turn left, to the heart side. There should be a space."

She was right. There was a space where before, under the moon, there had been unbroken stone. Low down, cut into the earth of the wall was a chamber. If Breaca crouched, almost to sitting, she could ease inside it. The grandmother tapped her arm. "Thank you. Let me down now; this is far enough I would lie on my left, with my head to the west . . . Have you my staff?"

"Yes, it's here. Grandmother, *please*, let me—"

"No. Thank you. I have enjoyed your company, but we must part. I must stay here and you must return to Macha and Airmid and those waiting. It is well past dawn. If you don't run now, they will set out with the hounds to find you."

"Then I'll bring them here. Swear to me you will still be here."

"I will swear if you will swear not to turn back until you have seen Macha."

Breaca sat back on her heels. It was completely dark. She

touched the old woman's face. It was smooth now, the oak-bark skin bound tight to her skull. Breaca had seen enough of death to know when it was close. Tears flowed unchecked down her cheeks. She scrubbed them away with the back of her wrist. "I swear I will not return until I have seen Macha. Please live till I get back. Please? I don't want to lose you."

"You won't lose me. I swear that, too." Her smile was a bright thing in the black space around them. "You must remember to redraw the serpent-spear on your shield. If you forget, ask Bán how it was in his vision. Hang the shield where you can see it and remember what it tells you."

"To look to the past as well as the future?"

"Yes. Both. The dreams of a people carry its heart. Without the dreams, you are nothing but the walking dead. But if you have only the dreams and no children to carry them, then you are nothing but dust. Remember that. Go now. It is time for me to dream and for you to run."

She sounded, at the last, composed and reasonable; the elder grandmother one most loved and most feared. Breaca eased back out of the chamber. Standing, she hit her head on the roof. It had not seemed so low when they walked through it before.

"Grandmother. . . ?"

"Run. Go all the way through to the entrance stone. Don't turn back. Be strong. I will not leave you."

She ran. The darkness closed in around her. The faint and laboured breathing passed to nothing before she reached the light.

The sky changed as she ran. Bruised clouds rolled in from the east, full of rain. The sun leached out through the cracks between, making shadows where before there had been none. She crossed the river at the stepping stones and did not pause to give thanks to Nemain or the water or to the stones for keeping her dry. The path down the side of the trees was cluttered with knotted roots and rocks and pitfalls that she had not seen walking up. She ran over them, bounding, as a deer runs when hunted, and only remembered them later. The blood pulsed in her chest and her head and clouded her eyes until all she could see was the serpent-spear and the hare; the one undulating in the air before her, the other running along at her side. She ran half the morning, without stopping for water or to sense the way. It was a path she knew well by now and only at the very last did she remember that the eastern gate was closed to her and she must go in at the west, through the women's gate that was only used in this and one other ceremony. She veered sharply upwards and ran along the sides of the paddocks. The grey filly saw her and came forward at a run, only to prop and wheel and snort and race away again as she passed.

The gates were closed before her, but then it was always so for a girl-woman returning from her long-nights. One of the others waited inside, ready to put the traditional questions. They had told her many times that the returning woman was like a child newly born and that her first entry back into the world of her people must be handled with care, that the traditions must be followed else she would risk losing all she had found. She had believed them and had practised until she could speak the phrases in her sleep. But she was not sleeping now and she could not think of the words, could think of nothing but how to run and how to breathe and the need to fulfil her vow to find Macha before she could return to the grandmother. The gates were planed elm, carved with the symbols of Nemain. She fell against them, hammering with the heel of her hand. Wood built to withstand fire and the attack of massed spears rattled faintly at her touch.

"Who comes from the realms of night?" It was a voice she knew, distantly, but could not give a name.

"It's Breaca. I must find Macha. Bring her, quickly—"

The gate opened, suddenly, so that she fell inside. Airmid caught her before she hit the ground. "Breaca! What's the matter?"

She could barely breathe. Her lungs were on fire. Her spit tasted of blood. Speaking took more effort than she had ever imagined. She folded into the arms that held her. "The elder grandmother...You must come quickly. She's bleeding. And Macha. I swore to find Macha—"

"I am here."

Macha had never seemed so forbidding. She stood in the door to the women's place, a tall shape framed against the fire beyond. Her eyes pierced, like an eagle's. Her eyebrows arched. "To whom did you swear, and what did you promise?"

"The grandmother...the elder grandmother. The eagle killed her... tried to. I can take you to her..."

Macha stood back, sweeping the door-skin aside. "Breaca, come in. We must talk."

"But—"

"Inside. Now. Quickly." It was not a voice with which she could argue.

She could walk, with help. They sat her by the fireside. Airmid held her from behind, her hands linked at her diaphragm, easing the pain of breathing, her legs stretching forward so Breaca was contained on all sides, like a child. Macha brought water and made her drink. Someone else brought malted barley, roasted and drizzled with honey; it was the greatest of all foods and it tasted of sawdust and sand. She ate it because they would not leave her until she had done so. When she tried to speak, she was stopped and made to eat more. They would not listen until she had finished it. She thought she would die, or break apart with the pressure inside, until Macha said, "It is enough. Let her see now." Then the women left to sit in their circle round the fire and Airmid helped her to stand and took her to the place at the back, furthest from the fire, where a curtain of black-tanned horse-hide kept a sleeping place apart. The women sat in silence. Macha and Airmid alone moved forward to the curtain.

She was shaking now, all over; her hands and feet were quite numb. She spoke in a whisper, denying the truth before it was shown her. "It can't be," she said. "I *saw* her. I talked to her. She gave me her staff to make the spear . . ."

"It was the third night of your dreaming. She had been waiting a long time for this."

Airmid was weeping, silently. Macha, it seemed, had been and would be again but needed, now, to be able to speak clearly. "In a moment you will tell us what she said to you and how you left her. But before that you must see her and know the truth."

They lifted the curtain aside. The elder grandmother lay on her left side, with her head to the west. Her hair was thin, almost gone, but her skin was tight and smooth as a young girl's and the smile on her lips promised the advent of all things one least expected. She held her staff in both hands, as a warrior might hold a spear in the final moments of battle. Bending, Breaca touched the end of it and found it dry, with no debris of blood and shattered bone. It was her fault; she had not followed the ceremony for returning and all that had been predicted was happening. She was going mad and the only one who could help her lay beyond reach on the floor. Reason slipped away from her, flapping wildly, leaving her empty and sick and unable to think. When she spoke, her voice came from other parts of the room and bounced back at her. "I left her in the mound," she said. "She promised she wouldn't leave me, she *promised*—"

"She won't leave you. She came to you at your dreaming. She will be with you in that, always."

Airmid had changed, as if something inside her had broken and she needed comfort, more than she had done in the past. They sat together, joined, and wept for what they had lost that none who had not served the elder grandmother could understand. Presently, Macha bade them move and take their places by the fire and pick up the lost threads of the ceremony of one returning. Had Breaca followed the tradition, she would have met with the elder grandmother and the other dreamers and told them her story so that they might understand it and bring out the truth it held. But there was no elder grandmother and it was not right to keep the old woman's last words from the others who had loved her, so Breaca sat at the head of the fire and told them all the tale of her long-nights, from the empty desolation of the cold and the mist to the journey across the river and the meeting with the water rat and all that had happened on the other side of the mound.

She ended in silence. One of the older women spoke—
Eburovic's mother's sister, who was the oldest amongst them,
next to the elder grandmother, which made her, when one
thought about it, the new elder grandmother. She was a
maker, not a dreamer; she wrought her magic with leather
and wood, and took things that Eburovic made and gave
them a meaning and presence that silver and gold alone did
not. In the last year, arthritis had set into her hips and she
was losing the power in her legs. Breaca listened to the
rhythms of her voice, not the words she was saying, and
wondered if it was a requirement of the elder grandmother
that she need the eyes and limbs of another to help her and,
if so, who it would be. For the first time, she was glad that
she had crossed out of childhood and become a woman so
it could not be asked of her.

"Breaca?" Macha had said her name twice and she had
not heard. She lifted her head. The world swam, slowly, and
her thoughts took too long to catch up. She made herself
watch the shape of Macha's mouth and, that way, made out
the words. "Breaca, you must paint your shield now, before
you sleep. We will find the dye and help you, but you must
draw the serpent-spear as you saw it. Can you do that?"

Breaca closed her eyes and saw the warriors of the
ancestors with the serpent-spear painted on their bodies. In
her mind, they stepped closer so she could see all the detail.
She opened her eyes again. "I think so, yes."

"What colour do you need?" That was what the elder
grandmother—the new elder grandmother—had been asking. She knew the dyes better than anyone; she would have
whatever colour was required, did Breaca only know the
answer. But she did not. "The men drew it on themselves

with woad—the blue woad mixed with egg white, not the silver mixed with bear grease."

"So then did the— Were you told that you should draw it in blue?" Airmid was at her side again, no longer weeping but speaking slowly, with care, because she had been this way most recently and knew what it was like and also, perhaps, because she cared most that it be done right.

Breaca shook her head. "She didn't say. Only that I should ask Bán how he saw it in his vision. But we can't do that now. He's a boy and we can't bring him in to ask him . . ."

Her words fell in silence. All eyes turned to Macha, who moved her shoulders, flexing them as if testing a new weight. She was the oldest of the dreamers now, and the position carried responsibilities all its own. She stared into the dark at the back of the room, frowning. In time, she said, "He was born at the autumn equinox. That has not passed and so he is still only eight years old and is permitted to enter the women's place. It will not be the first time this year. Airmid, would you find him and say I asked him to come? He will be helping Eburovic and Sinochos to make the death platform for the elder grandmother. They are in the barn just outside the gate."

Bán might still be only eight years old but it was half a year since he had last been in the women's place and his life had changed immeasurably since then. Last time, he had been a frightened, disoriented child, with the dream still heavy about him, seeking comfort from his mother and the new life on the floor. Now he followed Airmid with dignity and respect, keeping his eyes level and his back straight. Breaca watched him walk in through the flap and take his place by the fire as if born to it. His eyes swept the circle, resting on his mother, on the new elder grandmother and finally, in a sudden blaze of recognition, on Breaca. Airmid had not told him, then, that Breaca was home. She made herself smile for him, watching as he took in the full measure of her: the tangled hair and the recent weeping, the cuts on her legs and bruises on her arms, the tears on her tunic. Whatever else of her long-nights had been a vision, the crawl through the gorse had been real, and something, at some point, had hammered into her arm to leave a mark such as might be made by a spear-haft, falling. His smile folded as he saw it so that he frowned, like his mother, with a creased line over each eye. She leaned across the circle and touched his arm. "I am well. I will come and talk to you later. Now, the elder grandmother would ask you some questions."

His eyes flared wide in alarm. He knew, as well as anyone, the taboo that forbade one to mention the name of the dead. Breaca nodded sideways and he settled. Word had passed already: *She who was the elder grandmother is with us no longer. There is a new one in her place.* It would take a while, though, for everyone to adjust. Even amongst those who knew and had had longest to come to terms, it took a moment for all eyes to turn the right way. When she was sure of their attention, the new elder grandmother nodded, slowly.

"Bán harehunter." Her voice was quite unlike her predecessor's. She still spoke as Macha did, or Nemma or any of the other women—with the song and lilt and laughter and sorrow of everyday living. She had not yet learned the lift to the tone, the weight to the words that meant everyone stopped their own talk to listen. Still, they could hear the beginnings of it as she spoke, and it came through more at the end. "This will be hard for you and we do not ask you lightly, but it is necessary for your sister, for the completion of her dreaming. I have some questions to ask you. For her sake, will you answer them?"

Bán grew very still. Breaca saw his fingers flicker in the sign that gave thanks to Nemain and, at the same time, asked her help. "Yes," he said, "I will answer."

"Thank you. This summer, at the midsummer gathering, you had a vision in which the war host of the Eceni returned from battle. You saw your sister in the van, dressed for war, is this correct?"

He nodded. When it was clear he was required to speak, he said, "Yes."

"Good. Thank you. How well do you remember the vision?"

He closed his eyes. His head moved, as if someone beside him had spoken, or waved to catch his attention. When he faced front again, he opened his eyes and said, "I remember it well."

"Good." The new elder grandmother gestured to Airmid. The shield which had hung over Breaca's bed was brought forward, still in its covering. They passed it round the fire to its rightful owner. Bán watched his sister take it and saw on her face the same relief he felt whenever he came again to Hail after a time apart. She slid off the calf's-hide cover with its painted symbols of she-bear and wren, and underneath, painted brightly in blue, he saw the serpent-spear as the elder grandmother had drawn it back in the summer, for Breaca to meet Togodubnos.

"That's not right!" He had spoken without thinking and knew himself out of turn. He sat back, apologizing

before the words were truly out. "I'm sorry. I didn't mean
. . . it didn't look like that in the vision. This is not the one
I saw."

"That's good. Can you draw for us the one you did see?"

The new elder grandmother was less abrupt than the
old one had been. When Bán looked puzzled, she smiled
and gestured to the ashes at the side of the hearth. He
picked a small stick from the pile and broke it, to make a
clean end. Closing his eyes to check the vision, he bent forward and drew in the ash. His new drawing was not so different from the old one, but there was more of a curve on
the tail of the serpent and both ends had a head. He sat up
and looked at them both, shield and sketch, comparing one
to the other and then both to the picture in his head. His
likeness was better. He nodded to let them know; no need
to make too much of it. "And it was red," he said, "dark red,
like Breaca's hair when it's in shade. As if it had been drawn
in horse blood that never dried."

The new elder grandmother smiled for him, warmly.
"Thank you. You have done well. You may go now. Tell
Eburovic that his daughter the warrior has become a woman."

II

WINTER–SPRING A.D. 37

CHAPTER 8

Luain mac Calma, known to the world as the Hibernian merchant, dropped to his knees on the heaving deck of the *Greylag* and felt his stomach invert. His guts looped and twisted and wrung themselves dry as they had been doing for as long as he could remember. The boat wallowed drunkenly on the swell and the vomiting started again. He put his head down and retched until his chest ached and his head burned and the sweat ran from his body and all he brought up was a spit's worth of green froth that barely touched the sides of his throat on the way. It had been the same the last time and the time before that; his stomach had long since emptied and all that came back now was the brine he had swallowed the last time. Bile dribbled between his fingers and he watched it puddle on the deck before another wave smashed over the bulwark, slamming him into solid oak, drenching him, pouring cold into his throat and eyes and nose and down into the marrow. A second wave followed the first, lifting his body and swirling him back towards the stern. He nearly let go of the guard rope then and let the ocean take him over the side.

It was fear that kept him holding on. Luain the Hibernian was not afraid of death, even death by drowning, but he was very afraid indeed of not keeping the oaths he had made to the gods he believed in, and the thought of facing them prematurely with his life's work unfinished made him grab at the twist of hemp and hold on.

The boat rose higher, fighting the wave. The deck tilted further, rearing like a colt in a temper until it seemed likely that the whole ship would go over backwards. In the hold, the horses screamed and no-one was there to tend them. He took a step towards the forward hatch and stopped. The thought of losing the red Thessalian mare hurt more than the pounding of the sea but going down to her would not save either of them. He was forming the prayer for lost souls, his and the mare's, when the sea subsided and the *Greylag* slapped back on the water and rolled in a backwash of swell. He lay still where he had fallen and let his guts do their worst. Somewhere down in the darkness, a mare with a foal in her belly made all the noises he wanted to make.

Mac Calma had believed himself a good seaman. For two years he had sailed the trading route between the south coast of Britannia and the markets of Gaul, taking great brindled war dogs, ripe corn and raw, uncured hides south to the continent where the prices were best. On the return journey, he brought back all that newly Romanized Gaul had to offer: fine wheel-turned tableware, green glass, tanned leather and—better than all these—good vintage wine from the warm vineyards of Rome. He sailed his goods into the ports on the banks of the great river and carted them inland to sell in the courts of Cunobelin, the Sun

Hound, half a day's ride to the north, and Berikos of the Atrebates, three days south. These two wanted the luxuries of Rome if the rest of their world did not and Luain the merchant had a reputation as the man who could get hold of anything—almost anything—if you asked him right and he liked the colour of your money. It was, perhaps, surprising that he had been asked to transport horses only once before and that had been in high summer, sailing them across the short half-day stretch from the river mouth to the port of Gesoriacum in Gaul. Even so, one of the mares had panicked and kicked a hole in the planking not far above the waterline and the entire crew, mac Calma included, had been called to put their backs into baling to keep the merchantman afloat for the last leagues of the journey. It occurred to him now that a kick below the waterline might be the fastest and cleanest way to end the current voyage, but he had bound the horses' feet at the start of the journey to keep them from harming themselves or the *Greylag*. Even had he not, there was not one of them left with the strength to kick a hole in an eggshell, still less a foundering ship.

The retching stopped. Luain rose, sweeping the water from his face, and fought for a foothold on the swilling deck. To his right, Segoventos, ship's master, grinned a rueful greeting. The Hibernian waved back, yelling, "Will we make it to the shore?"

The master stared at him, uncomprehending. Luain cupped his hand to his mouth and shouted again. The gale took the sound of his voice and ripped it to shreds, hurling it back in his face with a fresh thrashing of brine. Segoventos of the Osismi, free man and ship's master of Gaul, shrugged and ran his thumb in an eloquent, slicing line across his throat before turning his attention back to the rigging, which had already snapped in two places, to the mast, which had not, and to the seas ahead, that he might keep his ship—his heart's joy—from breaking her back on the next running wave. It was not an even match. Even as he turned, a wave crashed over the prow, swamping the decks. The ship bucked and kicked. Segoventos fought with the steering oar. Down in the hold, a yearling colt squealed in terror and was cut off, sickeningly fast. Luain cursed and let go of his guard rope. He took a single sliding step towards the helm and cupped a hand round the ear of the master.

"I'll see to the horses . . ." Even this close he had to scream it against the wind.

Segoventos shook his head. "Forget it. They're sea mad. You'll not get near them. . . . Hold *on,* for the gods' sake, man . . ."

The master flung him a fresh rope and he caught it by instinct. Another wave bore in from a different angle and caught them broadside. The ship screamed this time, louder than the horses. The timbers gave out noises Luain had not known they could make and three ropes snapped together in the rigging. High overhead, the sail cracked free in the wind. Even in the heart of the storm, with the wind and the sea doing their best to deafen them, every man on the ship heard the crack and looked up, knowing what it meant. All of them, to a man, looked back to Segoventos to save them. The big man stood stunned for a moment longer than he should have done and then braced his feet on the side board and bent his full weight on the steering oar, striving to bring the ship round out of the wind.

The *Greylag* was his wife, his mistress and his daughter.

He loved her as Luain loved his red Thessalian mare and he had lived with her, slept with her, trained her for lifetimes longer than the merchant had his horse. Now he brought the whole of his considerable strength to bear on the helm, forcing her by will and weight to turn. For a single, shuddering moment, there was a chance he might do it. Luain prayed as he had never prayed before and knew he was joined by the rest of the ship. The horses fell silent. Even the rain held off for a moment as the tiny, brave peapod of wood fought to give her master what he wanted—and failed. The gods of the sea are not so readily diverted. With a snap like a breaking armbone, they reached up from the depths and broke the steering oar in mid-shaft. Freed of the sea, the end of it swung wildly and the master cracked back on the foot boards, striking his head as the *Greylag*, honouring the voice of her new masters, turned broadside on to the sea and ploughed into the murdering waves.

"Segoventos!"

The call came from near the bow but Luain was already there, kneeling at the master's side, lifting his head away from the oak, running his fingers through the salt-matted hair, feeling for breaks and finding none. The big man shook him off and hauled himself upright.

"We're dead." The words came through the dark on gusts of wind. The broad, bearded face of the master was turned to him. In two dozen hard crossings and ten times that many nights spent mired in drink on shore, Luain had never seen the man weep. He was weeping now, so that the tears washed the sea from his face. "She'll go now till she breaks and that will be long before we see land. I've lost you your horses. I'm sorry."

There was nothing to say. It was always the risk and drowning was not the worst of deaths. Luain the Hibernian, who was not exclusively a merchant, felt the proximity of his life's end and changed the manner of his prayer. In the maw of the storm, with the salt-laden rain whipping the skin from his face and the vaulting deck doing its best to break his legbones, he did what he could to make peace with himself and his gods. Because he was going to die and it didn't matter, because it was dark and the noise of the storm was overwhelming and somewhere up beyond the clouds there was a moon he would have liked to have seen, he spoke out loud and weathered the level stare of the master.

Pulling on an arm rope, he found that he could stand. The square rig of the sail flapped in the storm above his head. Once, it had shone white, with its black goose gliding out from the masthead so that they would be known long before they reached port. Now the rain had turned all of it black and the outline of the goose had blurred and merged with the rest. Still, it was something he could pray to and he let the full range of his voice out into the weight of the storm. He had a good voice, better when he let the tones loose and began to sing. Around the ship, men stopped their own praying to listen. Somewhere, a higher, lighter voice joined his. In the back of his mind, he tried to work out whose and was only partially surprised at the answer.

He was singing still when the lad at the bow cried out. At first, thinking the other had been washed overboard, Luain enlarged his prayer to include the newly dead. Then another voice joined the boy's, louder and saying the same things. To his right, the singer saw the master drag his gaze away from the thundering seas and crimp his eyes free of water and then do it again as if what he saw was not possible.

"*Yes!*"

The word hit Luain broadside as the wave had done. He faltered and his voice stopped. Segoventos spun round, jabbing his finger like a spear in the dark. "Keep singing, man, it's working." Then, "Math! Get up that mast, if you want to live. Brennos! Curo! Bind the rigging. The rest of you, get the sail into the wind. Whoever said we needed an oar to sail a ship when we have a good wind and a sail we can turn with?" He swung back to Luain, grinning. "Hold tight. It'll be a bumpy ride and you may have to swim a few strokes at the end but we'll see your horses safely landed yet."

The ship was a new place. Men moved who had been beaten into the timbers. The lad at the bow, a willowy fifteen-year-old with corn-gold hair and skin like a girl's, scaled half the mast and brought down a snapped end of rigging. Others lashed broken timbers in place and made new fixing points. Luain mac Calma, singing, kept hold of his rope and what solid wood he could find and stared off the side into the dark, trying to see what the master and his men had seen. The ship came under control slowly, fighting them as a bull fights a halter, but she was outnumbered and outmastered and the wind had changed allegiance, veering round to buffet his right shoulder, not his left, driving them through the waves, not across them. In a moment of relative calm, the master turned and smiled, brilliantly. "You haven't seen it, have you?"

"What?"

"There." The man pointed left, swinging his arm with the swing of the ship so that his finger marked a fixed point in the dark. "Land."

Luain stared where he was shown. The world was black. He kept his eyes where he thought the horizon might be, looking for the white mark of breakers on a shore to show him what the others had seen. He saw nothing.

"Not there. *There.*" The arm swung backwards, heading towards the stern. "Your friends are waiting. We're half a moon early and still they're waiting. They've lit us a fire."

"A fire? In this weather?" Hope died in his heart. They would not be the first to drown happy, believing they were sailing to paradise. "Who could keep a fire alight in this weather?"

"I don't know. But I can see what I can see and if it's Eburovic of the Eceni come to buy your Thessalian mare, you'll tell him a fair price or I'll have you tied to the mast-head and give her away as a guest-gift."

The master was laughing breathlessly, shouting orders and waving his arms and still holding on to the steering oar as if there were something useful to be gained by it. The boat shuddered and fought but she was moving west, the way he wanted. "If you would make yourself useful, go to the bow and be ready to cast a rope out to whoever it is that is waiting. It might be better if they see a known face early on and hail us as friends, not as slavers."

CHAPTER 9

The first of the men came ashore dead. Breaca was at the headland when the surf piled him in. The flaccid body surged higher with each wash of the waves until he came to rest at her feet. He was young, close to her own age, with sweeping gold hair that glimmered like cut corn in the fire-light and his face was at peace, as if the ocean had sung him to sleep as it stole his air. She hooked her fingers under his armpits and began to drag him clear of the broken timbers and storm-frayed ropes that gathered at the waterline. His head lolled against her hand, his skin colder than the water he had come from. She looked around for help. Eburovic was waist deep in the sea, pulling in someone else. Bán was with Hail and they, too, were dragging a body up the shore be-tween them. She looked around for longer, darker hair, bound back by the dreamer's thong, and saw it, a spear's throw down the headland. She waved both arms above her head. "Airmid! Over here! This one needs help."

"Here, I'll get him." 'Tagos was at her side. He was always at her side, or just behind her whenever she turned; it had been so since the day in late autumn when she and Airmid had said in public the things that before had been said only in private. Or rather, Breaca had screamed them at the packed mass of grandmothers, warriors, elders and dreamers in the great-house, and Airmid, white and tight-lipped, had listened, pleading for calm with her eyes until she, too, had reached the point of no return and had replied with the single statement that had broken everything between them. "You're not a dreamer. I can't make it so. The serpent-spear was a warrior's dream and one to be proud of, but if you will not come to Mona as my warrior then I will go alone."

They had both left then, Breaca to ride the grey battle mare harder than she had ever ridden her before or since, Airmid to the deep woodland to the place where they had scattered the ashes of the elder grandmother. They had come together later and apologized stiffly, and they still shared a bed, but nothing since then had been the same.

In honesty, Airmid had not been at fault; every dreamer of the Eceni nation had gathered for the council that autumn and they were of one voice in their opinion that Breaca nic Graine, heir to the royal line of her people, was a warrior of exceptional skill but that the dream of the ancestors and the war eagles and the mark of the serpent-spear did not constitute a true dreaming and she had shown none of the other signs of a born dreamer. There were four hundred and sixty-three dreamers at the gathering; even had Airmid ignored the words of the gods and her own dreams to speak against the overwhelming tide, her voice would have counted for nothing. But Airmid was the one who knew of a vow, spoken aloud by the gods' pool on a summer's morning, and she should have known better than to name Breaca as the warrior she wished to have at her side when the call finally came to journey to Mona. The call had not come yet—they were still waiting for that—but the question had been asked and the answer given and all had been said that should not have been said in the wake of it and 'Tagos padded at Breaca's heels like a hound whelp, trying to fill a void that was not his to fill.

He ran to her now, skidding down the shingled slope, his face fresh in the wind, his voice eager. Grasping the lad's ankles, he hauled him up the slope, saying, "Come on, he might not be dead. Let's get him up where it's dry."

"No. He's drowned. He needs a healer, or someone to say the prayers for the dead. Get the next one, down there, can you see?" The gale howled around them. Driving sleet made Breaca temporarily blind. She shoved the hair from her eyes with the back of her hand and pointed to where she had last seen movement. A lean figure with long dark hair like seaweed was struggling to find his feet in the racing surf. "There's one out there who can stand. Go and help him. If he falls in the waves, he'll be lost."

'Tagos ran where she pointed. Airmid joined Breaca, taking hold of the drowned youth's ankles, and together they dragged him, buttocks scoring the shingle, up onto the headland. The turf made a harsh, cold bed, but there was no snow as there was further inland and he was out of reach of the sea. They laid him flat and Breaca knelt at his side with her head to his chest, cupping her free hand over her upper ear to keep it from filling with rain. The rub of her hair on his skin rustled like mice in wet leaves but the gallop of his heart was not there.

"He's not been gone long. We need to clear him of

water." Airmid was kneeling at his other side. She brushed his eyelashes and felt for the pulse at his throat. Something in his response gave her cause for hope. "If we can pour the water out of him, there may be time yet."

They lifted the body between them and turned him over and a life's worth of sea drained out of his throat and his nose. Airmid said, "We need to breathe for him, like you did for Hail when he was first born. Do you remember?"

Breaca nodded. "Of course." It was not something one would readily forget.

They laid him back on the grass with his face to the sky. Airmid lifted his chin and stretched out his neck. "Tip his head back to make a straight path for the air. Lift the weight of his chest with your breath. Like this . . ."

It looked easy when Airmid did it, but that was ever so. In the three years since the elder grandmother's death, she had taken on the full mantle of the old woman's healing. It came to her now, as the dreams did, with an easy familiarity. Breaca, for whom neither dreams nor healing were easy, knelt and placed her mouth as she had been shown over the blue and salted lips. He tasted of seaweed and fish skin and faintly, on the surface, of Airmid. Grains of sand pushed themselves between her teeth, grating along her gums. When she breathed for him, the air wheezed wetly from his nose and the sides of his mouth. His chest made no movement. She sat back, frustrated.

Airmid said, "Try again, harder. Pinch off his nose. You're driving fire into wet boughs, not nursing a new flame on dry tinder."

"You do it."

"No. This one is for you."

"Why?"

Sometimes, Airmid could look exactly like the elder grandmother. She said, "Because he will not return for me. Nor for anyone if you leave it much longer. Just do it."

Breaca bent lower and blew harder and the lad's chest began to rise.

Airmid watched and then bent to other tasks. They worked well together, with the ease and comfort of practise and only a dull residue of pain. Breaca did what she could to light the fire in the youth's chest while Airmid did what else was necessary to draw his soul back to his body. When his bones had been checked and his internal organs felt through his skin and none of them seemed out of place or broken, she sat at his head and began the prayer for healing in the wake of battle, which was the closest thing she knew to a drowning. Macha heard and came to sit at his feet, adding her voice so that the sound of the two together lifted over the wind and the driving lash of the storm.

Down on the beach the sea gave up the rest of its bounty. Pale echoes of men found land beneath their feet and dropped to their knees, weeping their thanks to Eburovic for the size and strength of his fire and to the gods for the size and strength of Eburovic. Soon after that, half a herd of horses churned up and out of the surf. Breaca heard Bán cry out the way he did at the beginning of a hunt and then again, shortly afterwards, in wonder and joy. This once, she ignored him. The fire she nursed was gaining heat. Under her fingers, grey skin became less grey. The mouth clamped under hers moved convulsively and the dead youth bit his own tongue. His eyes sparked open. In the flaring light of the fire, they showed a thin rim of silvered grey round a central dot as round and wide as the moon. Breaca looked into them and saw only the limitless void.

"It's no good. He has left us." She rocked back on her heels. Macha let go of her prayer and sat still near his feet.

"I don't think so," she said. "Airmid, ask him the question."

Airmid reached out and took hold of one sea-cold wrist. Moving her head so he could see into her eyes, she said, "Welcome, seaman. Would you stay here on land with the living, or shall we give you back to the sea?"

It was not a trivial question. Anyone, adult or child, who has journeyed to the gods may not be made to live against his will. Not all of them, given the choice, will choose to return to the life they have left. The youth, it seemed, might do so. Breaca felt him stir under her touch as he fought to take breath for his answer. The words rattled in his throat and were lost in a paroxysm of coughing. With Airmid's help, she rolled him onto his chest and levered him up to his knees and waited while he retched himself clear of another life's worth of water.

They were not alone now. Shadows gathered, hunched against the sleet, and on the far side of the headland men fresh from the sea gathered more wood to feed her father's fire. Further back, on the edge of her vision, horses huddled in a corral bounded by a low hedge of gathered gorse, shaking water from their hides and reacquainting themselves with each other and the sense of land beneath their feet. Hail paced the perimeter of the gorse ring, giving them a reason to stay in safety. On the near side of the headland, Eburovic was coming to see her, bringing a tall, lean-faced stranger with long, dark hair, the one 'Tagos had helped from the sea.

They stopped just behind her and a careful, resonant voice, only slightly hoarse from the swimming, said, "We're all alive, even the horses. The *Greylag* is breaking apart on a sandbar and Segoventos will be lucky if there's enough of her left to build a rowboat, but if you are back with us and planning to stay, we can say that the sea claimed no lives tonight."

At the sound of his voice, Macha looked up, like a hound at the right note of the whistle. Slowly, she rose to her feet. "Luain," she said, softly. "Luain mac Calma. Welcome."

It was the voice Macha used when she was with Eburovic and then only when she believed they were alone. Breaca watched her take the stranger in an embrace as close as any she had ever bestowed on Eburovic. With her father standing by, smiling his quiet smile, the tall man buried his face in Macha's neck. His hands clasped and unclasped in the well behind her shoulder blades as if they could talk in ways his voice could not. His hair mingled with hers, black in black, both drenched by the night, and for a while it was impossible to tell which strands came from whom.

At length, they let go of each other and stood a little apart with their fingers interlinked as lovers do on first knowing their love. The man lifted Macha's hand and kissed her fingers and let it drop away. "How did you know to build the fire?" he asked.

"Breaca had a dream."

"Did she so?" He turned to look, appraising. He had the stance of a singer and the eyes of a dreamer and he knew more of Breaca than she did of him. She weathered his stare, seeing him match her against those on either side. She was Macha's height now and they looked alike. It was her hair that set her apart from the others; even a night such as this could not soak all the red from it, and since the row with Airmid she had given up hope of earning the dreamer's thong and begun to braid it at the sides so that she was marked beyond doubt as a warrior, not a dreamer; one upon whom dreams are thrown, not by whom they are called. His eyes bored into her and he raised his brows but he did not ask, as she had, why the gods had chosen to throw her this dream when there were others who could have understood it sooner and better so that they would not have had to risk their horses riding hard through the night to light a fire with wet wood in the teeth of a storm. Instead, he nodded, as Macha had done when she first heard of it, and said merely, "Thank you. We owe you our lives," which was not what she expected at all.

The youth was coughing again. Breaca bent to help him and so caught the moment when he turned fully to life. He smiled at her, a flash that came and went like a leaping fish and made them conspirators together against the dark, then his gaze slid past her to Luain mac Calma, the merchant who was far more than a merchant, and suddenly he was not a youth part-drowned on a headland, but a warrior and perhaps an enemy. He took no trouble to hide what he felt and she was battle-trained. In the troubled, angry eyes she read recognition and the memory of betrayal and a sudden decision, so that when he bunched himself tight and rolled to his feet and would have grabbed for the blade at her back, she was already up on her feet and back and out of reach.

"There now." Her blood raced as it had not done since the Trinovantes had galloped on the roundhouse. "Is that any way to thank those who have saved you?"

The lad shook his head, not trusting himself to speak. The others made a ring round them, loosely and perhaps not by design. He stood on the balls of his feet, streaming water from tunic and hair and shivering like a child under the lash of the rain, and yet, without doubt, he was a warrior of a calibre to match her father, who was the best Breaca had ever known; family pride would not allow that he might be better. Each weighed the space between them and the chances of success and neither chose to test the other. His eyes granted a half-apology and swung sideways, raking the length of Luain mac Calma. "You sang the song of soul-parting," he said. "You are not a merchant."

"And you joined me." Mac Calma nodded, carefully. "So we are neither of us exactly what we seem—Math of the Ordovices." He spoke it in a different tone, weighting the name with a singer's emphasis, and it gave Breaca the piece she needed to make the whole. If he was not Math of the Ordovices, then she knew who he was and with the knowledge, god-given, came the certainty of what she must do.

Drawing her blade from her back, she held it across her hands in a gesture recognized from one coast to the other as the pledge of honour between warriors. Remembering the teachings of the elder grandmother on the ways by which a member of one royal line should address another, she said, "Caradoc, son of Ellin of the royal line of the Ordovices, son of Cunobelin, Sun Hound of the Trinovantes, spear-bearer of three tribes, you are welcome in the lands of the Eceni."

She had expected a nod, a smile of recognition, a warrior's weighing of herself and her honour, and in all of these she was confounded. She had offered her blade as a gift and she could as well have plunged the length of it into his chest. Caradoc turned perfectly white. To the merchant who must now, at the very least, be a singer, he said, "You told her."

Luain said mildly, "I didn't. There has not been time."

"But you knew."

"Of course."

"When?"

"A long time ago." The singer smiled, crookedly. "I was present at your birth."

"So Cunobelin set you on to me." Loathing scalded them all. "Nursemaid and spy rolled into one."

The singer's smile remained unchanged. "Hardly. Your father and I have a degree of respect for each other but not so much trust that we would enter into something like this. To the best of my knowledge, Cunobelin still believes you to be in the far west with your mother's people. If he hears otherwise, it will not come from me."

"Mother, then?" That was less acid; more surprise tinged with unwilling hurt. "How did she know of it? Conn swore to me he would say nothing."

"Conn has said nothing."

Relief swept the angry, fair-skinned face. Whoever Conn was, his betrayal would have hurt. "Maroc, then? The dreamer who is also a singer. Of course. I should have known when I heard you sing the song of soul-parting on the boat." He smiled tightly, mocking himself. "You hid that well these past few months."

"Only from those who choose not to see what is before them." Mac Calma began to twist the sea from his tunic. The wool was wrecked; pulled out of shape by the sea. Nothing he could do would repair it. "Segoventos knows who I am," he said. "And Brennos, the mate."

"Do they?" Caradoc was scathing. "That was brave. With all of Gaul under the heel of an emperor who has outlawed 'barbarian soothsayers, seers and bards' and the ports full of men desperate to prove their patriotic ardour? Or perhaps you haven't seen a man crucified yet and think it no risk?"

He was pushing deliberately beyond the boundaries of acceptable behaviour. Three Gaulish dreamers had been crucified at the behest of Rome in the past year. All three had trained on Mona and, given his age, it was likely that Luain would have known them. Even had he not, the shadow of their dying still hung over the land. As a sacrilege, it defied description, but more than that, it confirmed the uncomprehending brutality of the enemy.

Luain mac Calma abandoned his tunic and stared out to sea. "I have seen it," he said. "It is not something I would court unnecessarily. In this, I believed I was taking no more risk than was wise. Some men I would trust with my life. Segoventos is one of them." He looked up. "I had considered that you might be another."

Caradoc of the Ordovices, acknowledged warrior of three tribes, tilted his head, as if testing the thought. He was calmer than he had been, enough to smile with due irony as he said, "That would presuppose that I knew who you were."

It was not the proper way to ask for an introduction but nor was it overly rude. The singer looked across at Macha, who nodded; a man should not have to make his own introductions in the presence of another who can make them. She, too, could raise the singer's lilt when she chose.

"Caradoc of the Three Tribes, warriors and dreamers of the Eceni, let me introduce to you Luain mac Calma, once of Hibernia, now merchant, singer, healer and dreamer of the elder council on Mona."

So they shared them both, Mona and Hibernia, the two

islands blessed by the gods. You could hear it in their voices, a blending of lilt and intonation, as if they had learned
at the same knee—or over many years sharing the same bed.
It should not have been surprising. The training of Mona
was twelve years from beginning to end, and there was no
reason to suppose that Macha had spent all of it chaste, any
more than one could suppose that Airmid would do so. All
summer, Breaca had feared the arrival of a dreamer from
Mona and the summons he must bring. Now, with Luain
mac Calma standing on the shingle and arm's length from
Macha, Breaca looked, not to Airmid but to her father. He
felt her eyes on him and smiled his brief, flashing smile. It
warmed her, as it had always done.

Caradoc was watching her. The anger had drained from
him, leaving him thoughtful. She felt him weigh the fact of
what he saw against the fictions he must have heard of the
child-warrior of the Eceni. He, of all people, should know
the difference between the truth and the myth that grew
around a single act. Her blade still lay across her hands, an
offered pledge, untaken. The laws of the warrior's oath were
clear; in accepting, he would bind them both to mutual protection on the field of battle and off it, to be broken only
in case of death, dishonour or blood-debt. It was neither
offered, nor taken, lightly. Caradoc stepped forward and laid
his right hand on the hilt. With no formality at all, he said,
"Thank you. I accept the oath." His smile leaped between
them, privately.

The night was ending. On the far horizon, dawn slipped like
a silvered knife between the storm and the sea and the textures
of the light began to change. Things the night had hidden

came shadily into view: the rope burns and bruises of the shipwreck and the white scar of an old burn on Luain mac Calma's forearm. Further back on the headland, the fire had grown and the snap of burning driftwood brought sparks and drifting smoke. The men of the *Greylag* had stopped work on it and were sitting in a circle, putting effort into drying their clothes and their hair and making it clear they had no interest in the small group gathered closer to the shore.

Eburovic said, "We should join your shipmates at the fire before the idiots kill the flame with wet driftwood and we find ourselves sitting out the rest of the night by a heap of cold—"

"No. Wait." Breaca stood very still, so that her eyes did not lose the thing they had just found. "There is another ship, a bigger one." The light changed, making the shape more solid. Her eyes widened. She pointed out to sea. "A much bigger one."

They gathered round her, following the line of her sight to where, far out on the horizon, the ghostly outline of a ship big enough to hold ten herds of horses sat low in the waves. Luain mac Calma was first to see it with her. "It seems we are to be honoured with more company." His voice was run through with other tones than a singer's. He turned to her father. "May I take it you are not trading directly with Rome?"

There was a moment's silence. Eburovic did not move his gaze from the ship. "We are the Eceni," he said shortly. "We do not trade with Rome."

"Of course not. I apologize. And in any case, that's not a merchant vessel. It's a legionary troop ship, and the last time one of those came on our shores it was an accident—

one of Germanicus's ships blown off course and foundering. Caradoc's father rescued the survivors and returned them to the grateful arms of their emperor."

"And the time before that?" asked Caradoc, softly. He must have known the answer.

Mac Calma turned and spat against the wind. "The time before that it was Caesar and the first wave of a Roman invasion. Let us pray to all the gods that it is not so again."

If it was an invasion, it was destined for early failure. The ship wallowing offshore was three times the size of the *Greylag* and her crew five times as numerous. In familiar water and with a favourable wind she was one of the fastest ships in the known world. In foreign water, in catastrophic weather and with a master who knew nothing of the coastline, she was doomed. With the growing light of the dawn making the unfolding disaster plainer, Breaca joined the others by the fire and listened as a frantic, grieving Segoventos bellowed orders in the teeth of the wind to a man who was never going to hear them, about the sandbar and the tidal race and the need to steer between these two to bring the ship aground within reach of the land. The moment of impact was inevitable and painful and many of those who had lived through something like it turned away. Those who did not saw the ship foundering far out beyond the *Greylag*, and knew the distance to shore was too great for any to survive. By common consent, they waited, to see what could be done for the dead.

The first bodies washed up with the turning tide. There were not many; the ocean, having lost one crop, was not ready to give up the fresh one. A woman and a child came in together, clad only in underclothes as if woken in haste.

Macha reached them first. She carried the child as she might a newborn infant, laying him at a safe place above the tide line. Breaca and Airmid together carried the mother. Luain and Eburovic made a stretcher of paired beams and laid planks across it and waited down at the shoreline for the rest. A mariner came presently, lashed by a single turn of rope to a fractured beam. It, or one like it, had crushed his skull before he was washed ashore. Others followed: a handful of Roman legionaries who, extraordinarily, had thought to keep their weapons with them as they swam and, more extraordinary still, had not simply sunk to the bottom but had fought clear of the ship and kept themselves afloat long enough to be caught and carried by the tide. The swords had slipped from their sheaths and gone to feed the ocean but the rest of their armour was sound. Breaca, 'Tagos and Caradoc stripped them in silence, working their knives into water-swollen buckles and knots, freeing them up slowly so that none had to be cut. Four scale-on-hide jerkins and as many good leather belts were removed whole and set to dry by the fire with Hail guarding them, while the bodies were freed of seaweed and laid out with the rest.

A long time after that, two boys came in, no more than Bán's age. Each was naked and bore on his shoulders and back the scars of slaves. The men of the *Greylag* gathered them up and carried them to join the others; all were accorded the same respect regardless of rank, as strangers would be who were not enemies in battle.

Breaca was by the fire turning the rescued armour when Curaunios, the *Greylag*'s second mate, called out from the shore.

"Here! Help me here. There's one alive. Where's the healer?"

It was an odd thing to call, but she learned later that Curaunios was from Gaul, of those families amongst the Aedui for whom Rome was not always the enemy. Breaca ran with Macha and found the two men kneeling in the sand, the one spewing water as Caradoc had done, the other supporting him gently. It was the first time she had seen either a living Roman or one of the warriors of southern Gaul. The Gaul was vast, a great blond bear of a man, with skin that had reddened under the lash of the sea and hair that was already streaked with grey.

The Roman was younger, not much older than Caradoc. He was naked, his skin summer dark to match the oak brown of his hair. Even from a distance, Breaca could see the marks of rope burns on his palms and strips of waterlogged skin that hung free from his shoulders. More spectacularly, a network of battle scars laced back and forth across his upper body. Unlike the slaves and more like the legionaries, he carried the bulk of these not on his back but on his chest and right forearm where enemy blades had passed his guard, and all of them were old. On his left side, below the ribs, a puckered cavity big enough to take a balled fist showed angry purple lines around the edges. Better than words, it said that he had spent his summer fighting and may have learned how to block the sword-cuts coming for his throat but was less adept at avoiding the spear aimed through his ribs for his heart.

Caradoc, who had direct experience of Rome, said "Equestrian," as if that explained it, and spat. The others gathered with him, watching with curiosity, uncertain of what to do. Segoventos pushed past them to stand before the man, explaining in heart-rent detail all the ways the ship could have been steered to safety. More than any of the others, he carried the guilt of watching a ship die and not having died himself to save it. He spoke to the Roman as a way to cleanse his soul, not because he expected to be heard.

The Roman had not been the ship's master and he had no feel for the sea. He knew only that he was alone and surrounded by strangers in a land he had never intended to visit. When he could take a full breath without choking, he shook off the helping hands, bunched his fists on the shingle and pushed himself to his feet.

And stopped. The tip of Breaca's blade drew blood from the water-softened skin at the tuck of his chin. Caradoc, warrior of three tribes who had killed at least once in battle, held the hilt and kept the blade level. Breaca stood ten paces away with the empty sheath strapped to her back and her hands by her sides; she had pledged him the blade, and she would not stop him taking it unless his enemy was of the Eceni. Her scarred hand throbbed.

"You are Roman?" Caradoc spoke in Latin, levelly and without emotion. Even for Breaca, with no knowledge of the tongue, the meaning was clear.

The foreigner stared at him and said nothing. Caradoc nodded. The lethargy of the sea was completely gone, replaced by a balanced keenness. His gaze floated easily round the gathered group. His eyes, seen in the odd, snow-dense light, were of the same metallic grey as the blade beneath them. His hair was drier than it had been, and paler. "This man is the enemy of our people," he said. "Does anyone wish to dispute that?"

No-one did. Seamen and Eceni alike shook their heads. Without thinking, Breaca reached for her belt knife and drew it clear. Caradoc saw it and nodded his thanks, lightly, to her and then to the group.

"In that case, I claim blood-right; for the death of my mother's grandfather, for the men who fought beside him against Caesar, for the dreamers of Mona who died last year in Lugdunum, capital of the three Gauls, for all those unnamed of our people who have died in slavery under the yoke of Rome since they first brought their warships to this land, for all these and more, his life is mine."

He raised the blade with both hands. The man on his knees before him, who was both Roman and a soldier and had just survived certain death in the sea, thrust himself to his feet in the space before the killing stroke and made a grab for the hilt.

Caradoc smiled and stepped wide and took his left hand from the sword, changing grip from that of an executioner to that of a man entering battle. He nodded with a detached respect. "Good. Thank you. I would not have liked it like that."

The blade swung in a long, singing arc with a man's neck at the apex—and passed on and through without drawing blood. The Roman lay on the shore, spitting sand from bloodied teeth. A red mark showed on his shoulder where he had been thrust to the ground. Caradoc frowned and changed his grip for the back swing. Segoventos, ship's master, who was bigger than both of them put together, reached a hand to the younger man's arm so that the blade stopped still as if grounded in oak. "No," he said. "He is not yours. You have not the right."

Caradoc freed his hand. He took a step back and kept the blade, but the tip was lower than the hilt and he was not within reach of his victim. He shook his head, like a dog out of water, gaping.

"Segoventos? He's a *Roman*. He needs to die."

"He is a shipwrecked man, as you are. If the gods wanted him dead, they would have taken him. You have not the right to say otherwise."

"I have more right than you. This is not your land, Gaul."

"Nor yours—son of the Sun Hound." It was said quietly; Segoventos only bellowed for the important things, like the life of a ship. For the rest of the time, his size spoke for him.

Caradoc let his breath out in a rush. He spun to face the others. The men of the *Greylag*, who had known him for six months as Math, boy of the Ordovices, were eyeing him with undisguised curiosity, waiting for him to deny the parentage that had been named and then, when he did not, making all the assumptions that went with it. Caradoc looked past them to Eburovic and Luain mac Calma. His nostrils flared tightly. "This is your land. Will you do as my father did and let him go with guest-gifts and the promise of trade?"

"No." Macha stepped forward to stand in front of the Roman. She did not point, or gesture or raise her voice, but Breaca had never seen so clearly the authority of the dreamer used at will. "You know that is not the way of the gods. Your father acted against the will of the elders in what he did and I have no doubt he will be called to account for it, in this world or the next. But what you are doing is no better. You are not facing this man in fair combat. He is not even armed. He is not responsible for the acts of his fathers, any more than you are for yours, and even less so for men whose blood he may not share at all. If he is an enemy, it is in his own right and it is not for us to say so here. We will not compound your father's error. Instead, we will take this man back and call a meeting of the elder council and let the gods and the grandmothers decide his fate."

"You will call a council in this weather?" Caradoc spread his arms wide, taking in the snow and the ice and the aftermath of the storm. "Can your dreamers fly through the air like the deer-men of the northlands and join their councils in the deepest drifts of snow?"

"Hardly." Macha smiled, thinly, and he was reminded yet again that he faced a dreamer. His eyes dropped before hers did. "We can do nothing while the snow holds us bound. It was enough to come here and we are not yet back safely. If we return without loss, there will be eighteen new mouths to feed and sleeping places to find and that will keep us occupied until the snow lifts. When it does, the council will meet. In the meantime, the man is a guest, as you are. He will not leave us; he is a lone man in a strange land and if we can find little food in it, he will find none."

"You think so?" Caradoc chewed on the flesh of his cheek. Slowly, he reversed the blade and returned it to Breaca. "And if he does not understand this and still tries to run?" he asked quietly. "The Romans believe themselves masters of everything. Would you let him roam free in the Eceni heartlands?"

"No." Macha paused and turned round. Luain mac Calma had moved down the shore to stand beside the Roman and was translating her words into Latin as they spoke. She spoke slowly, so her meaning was not lost.

"I believe this man to be intelligent. On that basis, he will be allowed to live. If he is stupid and tries to run, then you may hunt him down as you would hunt a wolf who has broken into the foaling pens. The elders will not prevent you."

The Roman stood upright on the shingle, ignoring the cold. He was a head shorter than Luain mac Calma and the contrast made him seem smaller still, but he stood like a warrior and did not show the anger Breaca might have expected. He thought for a moment after Macha finished, then answered briefly in Latin.

Unexpectedly, mac Calma grinned. Inclining his head with elaborate courtesy, he said, "Our new guest thanks you for your offer of hospitality and is honoured to accept. He assures you he will not break into the foaling pens."

"Good."

Macha turned away from the sea. Those who had been watching turned with her and began the long walk back up the shore towards the horses. Bán and Hail went ahead, driving the new animals, keeping them well away from the home herd in case of fighting or disease. Eburovic brought up his spare riding horse and offered it to Segoventos, ship's master, who accepted. Others were mounted, some two to a horse, until none were left walking. The foreigner rode double with Luain mac Calma, with 'Tagos riding alongside.

Macha held back until Caradoc and Breaca, coming last, caught up with her. The warrior rode as if born on horseback, his hands guiding the beast along a path barely seen in the opening dawn, his mind clearly elsewhere. He made space for Macha beside him, granting the deference due to a dreamer. When there was no-one but Breaca to hear them, she said, "You will not fight the Roman, I will not permit it. But you may like to give thought, before we return to the roundhouse, as to how you will respond when our young bloods find it necessary to challenge you."

"You think they will do so?"

"How could they not? It's winter and the nights are long. If they were bored before, their condition will not be improved by the addition of eighteen men, one of them a warrior whose deeds have been sung in the roundhouse since they were children." Macha was not angry. If anything, she seemed mildly amused. "What do the Ordovices do when the tedium of winter becomes unsurpassable and someone throws a firebrand into the kindling?"

Caradoc took it in good humour. "We throw spears at the mark," he said. "If that fails, we run races and try not to kill anyone." He turned to Breaca, who rode on his other side. "Amongst my mother's people, if a warrior's pledge is made on a blade as we have made it, those between whom it is shared may not fight each other, even in play; they are bound as brother to sister, to defend and protect unless one acts in such a way that the other is bound to break the pledge."

Breaca said, "It is the same among the Eceni. We can neither fight nor race unless one dishonours the life or family of the other." She had known it when she offered him the blade, and had seen before Macha had that it would be necessary and why. For the first time in her life, she had met someone with whom she was evenly matched; they could spend their lives splitting hairs over the results of each race or risking their lives in endless winter challenges—or they could avoid races and challenges from the start.

Caradoc nodded, thoughtfully. "We could still race on horseback," he offered. "That would not offend the gods."

His glance held buried laughter and the certainty that she would lose, which was ridiculous.

"We can't race in winter," said Breaca. "The ground is too hard. And . . ." She smoothed a hand down the grey mare's neck. In three years, the beast had grown into all her hidden promise. Even thick-coated for winter, her breeding showed clearly in her lines and paces. "There would be no point until you have your own horses. There are no others amongst the Eceni that would match against this."

Caradoc grinned back, pushing his borrowed horse to a trot. "Maybe not. In that case perhaps we should all pray to the gods for a quick and easy end to the winter and a peaceful start to the spring."

CHAPTER 10

The end to winter that year was neither quick nor easy. Too many bodies sleeping in too little space made the days long and the nights uncomfortable. As Macha had foreseen, the arrival of the Roman caused less of a stir than the firebrand son of the Sun Hound. The foreigner may have been a warrior and an enemy, but his lineage was unknown and his name had not been three years a watchword for skill and fighting ability as Caradoc's had been. The young warrior was challenged within days of arrival, with the sea still in him and the skin still peeling in strips from his arms. Predictably, it was Dubornos who made the challenge and, predictably, he lost. 'Tagos was next, because he had to be, and he lost too, if not so badly. The seamen began to take sides, swelling the factions that grew at the end of every winter as those newly made warriors sought to prove themselves against their peers. Fights broke out more often than was acceptable and the dreamers were called in more than once to break them up and heal the injured.

Caradoc, to his credit, did not take sides. Instead, he

gathered the ringleaders and talked them into a series of crazy, impossible competitions, telling them that this was how his mother's people, the Ordovices, spent the months between solstice and spring. In this, clearly, he was stretching the facts; if the warriors of the war hammer competed thus throughout the frozen winters of the west, there would not have been enough of them left alive and uninjured come the summer to make war in the way that legend had it. Still, the half-truth served well. On a freezing afternoon with the sun bright and the snow caked to ice, he showed them how to build sledges and had them race, six at a time, down the long, curving track between the paddock rails, throwing spears at straw targets as they went.

He won, but then he had raced a sledge before, on mountains far steeper than the paddock slope. Spirits ran high and 'Tagos, who had come closest to him, gained in stature. When the charge of that wore off, those who had lost the snow race most dismally borrowed axes and cut down a pair of pine trees, cutting the side branches to make poles of them so that they could race in knock-out heats across the river. There was less snow now, the wind had backed round to the south, warming the air. In places, the ice on the river was leaf-thin so that one could look through it and see the fast water beneath. For the final heats, the poles were greased with tallow, to make it more of a challenge. Two of the sea-men fell in. One of them hit a boulder on landing and broke his shoulder. The result was a tie; 'Tagos matched pace throughout with Caradoc. Dubornos came close behind them. No-one else cared enough to finish.

Spring came with a rush after that and suddenly they were too busy to race. The warm wind continued, soothing the last of the snow and ice into water. The river ran in spate, flooding the low ground on either side, carrying away the debris of the winter and leaving churned mud in its wake. Higher up, on the southern edge of the forest, the meltwater washed over the sandy loam, dragging long streaks of sand down through the pastures and into the settlement, where it found its way into the cooking pots and the sleeping hides and was, everyone agreed, worse than the mud.

The trade routes opened as soon as the snow allowed it. Runners were sent out to summon the council, and Eburovic harnessed his cobs and forced his wagons through the mud to bring back grain from those who could spare it and ale and—joy—a deer's bladder full of salt. In the paddocks surrounding the village, the home herd grazed on the green shoots that pushed up as soon as the pressure of snow lifted. At the top of the hill, separated by two clear fields in case they brought disease, the new horses were fed the last of the winter fodder to supplement the poor grass. Under the warming sun, they lost the hollows behind their ribs and above their eyes and began to shed the harsh coats of the sea crossing. Each day, as the moon grew smaller, they rubbed out more, itching it away in handfuls on the ageing thorns that bounded their paddock to reveal moth-eaten patches of rich, shining hide. Then one day the last of the old hair was gone and the last of winter with it so that the air lost the damp smell of rotting rushes and wet wood and was filled instead with the lift of new leaves and the sound of the cock redbreasts fighting.

The council was set for the full moon. For five days before, elders, grandmothers and dreamers began to gather. In the high land above the steading, the great-house was cleaned and cleared; the old rushes, laden with rodent droppings and white with fungus, were dug out and burned in noisome heaps at the far edge of the trees. Those at the river had not yet grown to replace them, but grandmothers with fore-thought had brought dry barley straw from those communities that could spare it and the smell of it filled the vaulted space beneath the roof.

Efnís arrived on the day before the council. The young man from the harsh lands of the north had grown in three years to be the foremost dreamer of his people. Bán found him in the evening, sitting alone on a horse-hide in the great-house surrounded by half-made torches. Bán offered to help and they sat together in the half-light, sharing news as they worked; or rather, Bán shared the news and Efnís listened, since all that was worth hearing had happened south of the lands he had left.

Bán was the acknowledged expert on the Roman. It had happened by accident; the foreigner was clearly very taken with the red Thessalian mare and Bán had been in love with her from the moment she emerged from the sea, so it was natural that they should talk once they found a common language. The man had tried to learn Eceni but had found it difficult. Bán, out of courtesy, had tried Latin but the feel of it twisted his tongue and made the muscles of his jaw ache and he had stopped as soon as he had found that they both spoke Gaulish. Bán had been learning it from Gunovic in order that he might do business with the horse traders on the far side of the ocean and not be cheated, and the Roman had learned it from his unit's posting there. Neither was fluent but time and the help of the sailors had improved them.

Bán's other area of expertise was Caradoc, although for different reasons. The boy had discovered early that he did not like the young warrior. The memory of Amminios's visit and the loss of the dun filly came between them, so that their eyes never met and any conversation was so formal as to be worthless. With time, they had stopped trying to speak and Bán had watched from the outside as the factions brooded and changed in the overcrowded men's house. In the beginning, not knowing of the sword-pledge made on the seashore, he had pleaded with Breaca to challenge the newcomer and cut his legs from under him. Later, he had come to realize that, even without the warrior's oath, each would have found a reason not to test the other, that neither she nor Caradoc was certain of winning and the fight, if it came, could only be in private and would not be in play. After that, he drew back, and was careful when talking with Efnís to complain chiefly of Caradoc's reaction to the Roman.

"Caradoc hates him." Bán took a torch from Efnís's hand and dipped it into the vat of bear grease, twisting it to work the fat into the straw. The earthen smell enveloped them both, richly. "It's because of his father. The Sun Hound favours Rome and Caradoc hates his father so he hates the Romans, too."

"He has good reason. Were it not for the influence of Rome, the Sun Hound would not have driven the dreamers from his land." These days, Efnís was inclined to see everything through the mask of the dreamers.

"But that wasn't this man's fault. All he's done is get shipwrecked and run races and everyone hates him for that, too, because he holds back and lets Dubornos and 'Tagos beat him when he could run them into the ground. Dubornos would see him gutted and be happy about it. It's the only thing he and Caradoc agree on."

"I heard your young men hate Caradoc as much as he hates the Roman."

"Not all of them. Only those who think they should be able to beat him, which is Dubornos and his friends. The rest love him. It's disgusting; like watching a bitch in season walk through a pack of dogs. If he walked through fire into the depths of the ocean, they would follow him just for his smile."

Efnís grinned. "Men are like that. They see something good and they either want to be part of it or to be better themselves. Sometimes the only way to be better is to destroy what is good——" He looked up, sharply. "Who's that?"

It was Breaca. She stood in the doorway with her hair wild around her head and she was panting, as if she had been running hard, or riding. "Bán? Have you seen Airmid? Or Macha? They're not in the roundhouse."

"No. Macha was outside a while ago. I haven't seen Airmid since this morning."

Airmid had dreamed badly. It had shown in her smile and the dark hollows under her eyes. Bán had not asked her about it, nor had he spoken of it to Breaca. One did not, these days, speak of one to the other, except now, when something had happened to change things. He stood, the torches forgotten. "Why? What's the matter?"

"They're racing again. Dubornos and his friends have set it up. The fools have made a route along the river track—up one side, across at the fallen oak and down again to cross on the greased logs at the bottom."

Efnís said, "But it's nearly dark. They can't race now, surely."

Bán shrugged. It was insanity. The greased poles were a nightmare and had been proved so. No-one with a head on their shoulders would choose to walk across them in broad daylight, still less run them at night. The river flowing beneath them was once more within its banks but it still ran white and wild and angry; anyone falling in would be lucky to come out alive. "So let them race. If they drown, we can ask Airmid to sing the water from them afterwards. If she fails, it will be no great loss."

"No, you don't understand." He had rarely seen Breaca so upset. Her fingers were white where she gripped the doorpost. "They're going to cross at the oak log above the sacred pool. If one of them falls in or tries to swim the river, he will be swept down to the pool. Airmid dreamed it. It must not happen."

"*What?*"

The blood drained from Bán's head, leaving him giddy. What she said was unthinkable; everyone knew that the pool was Nemain's, that to enter it was utterly forbidden, that a life was forfeit and the death appalling for anyone who broke the taboo. Worse than that was the devastation that would be visited by the gods upon the people. The last time a man fell in was in the grandmothers' time and the war with the Coritani had started soon afterwards. Even the far southern Gauls, who had not understood the ways of the midden and had left piles of human ordure and the stench of male urine around the roundhouse, would have known not to enter the pool. "But, Breaca, they won't go in the river. They wouldn't dare—"

"The Roman would. They're making him race. Dubornos held a knife at his throat and told him to race properly or he'd carve out his guts before the council had a chance to vote on it."

"But someone will have told him about the pool."

"Did you? You have talked to him more than anyone."

He had not. The pool was a part of his life; it had not occurred to him that anyone might not know about it. Even had he thought of it, his few words of Gaulish were for trading horses, not for explaining the complex balance of honour and obligation that maintained the relationship between the gods and their people. Aghast, he said, "Dubornos is mad. He is doing this to kill the Roman and he hopes it will bring war so he can prove himself a warrior in battle. We have to stop them. Where are the horses?"

"The grey is outside." He had heard it arrive earlier in a hammer of hoofbeats and a wrenching stop, but had taken no notice. "Yours is in the paddock. It's too far to go and get it. You can ride behind me."

They were already running. Hail bounded ahead of them at the door. Bán called over his shoulder to Efnís, "Find Macha or Airmid. Tell them what's happening. Get them to the pool."

"What if I can't find them?"

"Then blow the horn that calls the council. That will bring them."

"That's sacrilege!"

"Only if done without good cause. This is the best cause. Do it." The mare wheeled, standing straight on her hocks. Bán whistled Hail and they were gone.

The race had begun. The route followed a track up the side of the river, then turned inland and wove through the woods. To run it was difficult, but possible. To ride it, flat out, was insanity. Bán kept his head low and his arms locked around his sister's waist as Breaca pushed the grey battle mare to her limits. Branches whipped at them raising welts and the path twisted viciously, but they did not die.

The path broke out of the trees close to the river. The smell of mud and surging water flooded Bán's senses. The perfect disc of the moon lit up the water so that he could see twice over the shape of the hare that lived on the surface; Nemain's beast. Usually, it was her signal to him of good hunting. Tonight, it felt as if she held her breath, waiting to see who profaned her pool.

"There, at the crossing. Caradoc is ahead."

The river ran wild and white. Bán made himself look up to the narrows, where the oak trunk spanned it. The figures of running men were small in the distance and their bodies merged with the land. Caradoc was most easily seen; even had he not been at the front, his hair marked him out from any distance. On the headland, soaked from the sea, it had been the colour of old straw. Now, dry, cut and combed, it caught the light of the moon and shone like burnished metal. 'Tagos was a pace behind, then Dubornos. The Roman was harder to see. His hair and his body were so dark that, had he stood still, he would have been all but invisible. As the pack spread out, it could be seen that he ran an arm's length behind the other three.

"The Roman's still holding back." It was clear from the way he ran. Bán shouted it out loud, not sure if Breaca could hear him.

"He was. Not now."

She was right. The man had taken Dubornos's threat to

heart, or perhaps, with his death less than a day away, he had chosen to show who he really was. Either way, having paced himself up the side of the river, he let loose with perfect timing and put in a startling sprint as Caradoc slowed to approach the log. 'Tagos was taken by surprise; he neither saw nor heard the shadow closing in on him until it was past. Dubornos had been running closer and had, perhaps, been expecting the move. He lengthened his stride to match the foreigner and passed 'Tagos on the other side.

The fault for what happened next was Dubornos's, everyone agreed on that later. He had walked across the oak log uncounted times in the summers since it first fell and he knew that it was rotten and unstable and could not take more than one man at a time. The Roman could not have been expected to know that and so, when they reached the trunk together, it should have been Dubornos who held back.

He did not. Caradoc was midway across, running neatly and with an economy of effort that could be seen from the riverbank. The trunk shuddered beneath him but did not tip until the Roman and Dubornos—in that order—leaped onto it, running. Then it rolled.

Eight men, and a boy and a woman on horseback, shouted a warning. The runners had already acted. Caradoc flung himself bodily at the far bank. The Roman dropped to one knee and took hold of the rotting wood, digging his fingers deep for a handhold. No-one saw clearly why Dubornos fell. Some said later he had already lost his footing on the rolling timber, others that he simply ran headlong into the Roman and that was enough to trip anyone. Whatever the truth, there was a moment of silence as his body arced over the river and then a scream that ended as he hit the water. His red hair flashed once above the surface and was gone.

The race dissolved into chaos. Men flung themselves belly down on the bank, reaching out across the water. Dubornos's friends shouted his name, achieving nothing. In the jumble of moving bodies, Bán saw a gilded head on the far bank rise and fall out of sight. Caradoc, true to his reputation, had chosen action instead of words. He was naked already and greased against the cold. Sleek as an otter, he dived. Breaca was a heartbeat behind him. Bán was pushed backwards as she dismounted. Her belt and tunic were thrust up into his hands. She said, "Don't let the mare follow me," and then she, too, dived in.

"Breaca, no!" Bán grabbed for the reins. The grey fought him, plunging for the bank. She had been trained to follow her rider and did not understand, or did not care, that to do so would kill her. The boy pulled her head round to her flank, sawing viciously on the bit, cursing. Blood flecked the spit that foamed from a mouth that had never known pain. He kept his grip and forced her head away from the river. Men jostled around him, still shouting. A dark head forged through them and stopped at his knee.

"Does it narrow anywhere else?"

It was said in Gaulish, too fast. The language swept past him. He gaped.

"The river's too strong." The Roman spoke again. "They're under. We're going to lose them. Does it narrow anywhere else?"

"Just above the sacred pool. They must not go in. It is death." He could have wished his language better.

"Then we ride." The man was a horseman before anything

else. He could mount at the run, without help. Bán was pushed forward on the withers, as a child would be. Stronger hands than his took up the reins. The grey fought and met a grip that brooked no argument. She struck out once and settled. A foreign voice, full of humour, said, "Show me the way."

The ride came from Bán's worst nightmares; his ears were filled with the noise of the river, his mind with the echo of Breaca's voice screaming his name, he saw her hair in every moon-cursed glint of the river. In his ear, the Roman said, "Is she doing this because her warrior's oath would not let her race against Caradoc and she must find another way to test herself?"

It was what Bán had feared most since she plunged into the water. He said, "No. She would do it anyway. They think the same, those two," and realized that it was true.

"Still, it may let them decide who is best without having to die for it."

"We can pray so." And he did, because that, too, was true.

They came to the bend in the track, where it entered the woods. The Roman pulled the horse to a halt. "Must we go through the trees? It will be slow."

"No. There is another way. Very difficult."

And very dangerous. He did not say that. They turned hard left and pushed the mare down a muddy slope and into the marsh on the far side. She slid and staggered and plunged through, hock deep, fighting the sucking bog as gamely as she had earlier fought the bit. They urged her on with voice and heels and, once, the flat of an open palm. On the far side, they pushed her harder. She had a great heart but she had run doubly laden for a long time now and she was tiring. Bán felt her falter and spoke to her in the voice

Breaca had used, asking for more. At the back of his mind he remembered that she was pregnant and that the foal was promised to Airmid—if it lived, if it were not dropped early, if Airmid were still here to see it and had not already left for Mona by the time it was born.

It did not seem to him likely that all those things would happen. With increasing despair, he offered a prayer to Nemain for the life of an unborn foal because it seemed more likely to be answered than any prayer for his sister who was in the water that would soon fill the god's pool. The mare heard his voice and found a way to run harder. The man at his back leaned forward to slacken the reins. Bán pressed his face to the streaming mane and prayed for speed. Beside him, the river roared.

"Give me your belt. And the reins."

They pulled to a halt on the flat ground at the head of the waterfall. The mare stopped, spent. The Roman dismounted at the run and ran onto the rocks that overlooked it, assessing the flow of the water and the cleft that funnelled the power of it over the drop and into the pool. Bán slid to the ground and felt his legs crumple. The foreigner caught him. "I need your belt," he said again.

Bán stripped off his belt. It was a good one, made for a warrior. The Roman bound it round his own waist; his own was mere string. Holding the mare, they unfastened the reins and made of them a rope, two spear lengths long.

"We can stop them here, do you see?" The man pointed. Below them, the rock of the riverbank pinched together to narrow the flow. Water poured through the cleft, creaming white. Bán said, "You mustn't go into the pool."

"I know. Caradoc told me before we raced." The man

knotted the free end of the reins through the belt and tied the other end firmly in the girth of the mare. "Keep the horse there. If she does not come forward and the reins do not break, we are safe." He smiled, brilliantly. His teeth flashed as white as the water. "Can you do that?"

Bán's heart lurched. He felt sick. He looked up into steady brown eyes. They did not seem to him reckless, as Breaca's could be, or bitter, as Dubornos's certainly were. He said again, because he had clearly not been understood the first time, "The dreamers will kill you if you enter the pool."

"I know."

"They may kill you anyway."

"I know. And I may drown. The gods will see to it, mine as well as yours. If the reins hold and you keep the mare still, it may be that we will all live. Think of your sister and pray to whoever you think will listen."

The man did not dive. He eased himself into the river, feeling his way with his feet. The weight of the water pressed him flat to the rock, foaming as it coursed around his chest and arms. He found a ledge he could stand on and edged sideways until he reached the gap. The leather rope stretched taut between man and horse. Bán ground his heels into the earth and put his back against the mare's chest. He spoke to her, explaining what they were doing, buoying her spirits at the expense of his own. The man looked up. His breathing was short, crushed by the weight of water. "Tell me if you see them."

"I will." He peered into the darkness. A cloud slid over the moon, so that her light spread only from the edges, as sharp silver streaks. He thought it an omen and prayed for the cloud to move.

"*Bán!*"

He thought it was Breaca and turned too fast. The mare took a step forward to ease the pressure on her girth and the Roman swore, viciously. The boy pushed her back and looked round. Airmid stood at his side.

"Where is she?" Her eyes were terrible. He had never seen her truly angry. She was beyond that now, in the place where the gods spoke and she answered. He found it a wonder that Breaca could ever have argued against her.

"In the water. Dubornos fell in. Caradoc went in to rescue him and Breaca after. They were swept away."

"What are you doing?" His mother was there behind Airmid, and Luain mac Calma. Curved knives gleamed dully at their belts. He did not want to think about the implications of that. Efnís hung back, an unwilling accomplice.

"The Roman is there." He showed her the man in the water. "He is going to——" He broke off. A gilded head showed above the water, soaked to darkness as it had been on the headland but still lighter than any others. "*Now!*" He yelled it over the noise of the water. "Now! They're here! A spear's cast. Less——"

He threw his weight back against the mare's chest and promised her death if she failed him. In truth he had seen only Caradoc. The warrior was battling the current, trying for the bank and failing. He swam with only one arm; the other was broken, or weighed under. Beyond him, towards the centre, a figure rose up. Bán saw fox-red hair, streaming water and an arm thrown high, as one drowning and calling for help.

"*Breaca!*"

His voice was lost in the surge of the river. Airmid's, higher and more piercing, rose above it.

Both were too late. The arm disappeared. For a moment, the red hair spread wide on the flowing current, then it dipped beneath the surface and was gone.

The water was cold, like liquid ice, and the power of it shocking. The first dive took her under, pressing her down until the breath burned in her lungs and bright lights flashed before her eyes. The gods did not come to her as they had in the dream of the shipwreck, but her father spoke in the voice of her childhood, teaching her to swim, reminding her not to fight against a current this fast, to let Nemain of the water lift her. She kicked, pushing up for the moon.

She broke the surface a long way downstream. The riverbank was deserted. Men called her name, distantly. It was impossible to see anything but water. She kicked up again, rising higher, and looked around. A flash of pale flesh spun past. She grabbed for it and hauled in. It twitched, pulling against her. A shock of gold-straw hair surfaced beside her, and the smooth skin of a youth, streaming wet. Grey eyes opened wide and recognized her. Caradoc spat water and fought for breath. "Not me. We can't . . . rescue each other. Not . . . the point." Absurdly, he grinned.

The current dragged them round a bend. Letting him go, she struck out sideways. The bank was within reach. Caradoc swam with her, strongly. His face emerged again, close to hers.

"Where is he? Where's Dubornos?" She had to shout it, over the noise of the water.

". . . don't know. Can he swim?"

"I think so. Look out!" A branch swept past, striking them both. A numbing pain shot up her arm. She flailed, fighting to keep her head free. The current pulled her back into midstream. The bank was lost. "Caradoc!"

"Here . . ."

A hand flashed closer to the bank. Beyond it, a paler face broke the surface.

"Dubornos!"

She threw herself back against the flow. The limp body smashed into her, driving the breath from her lungs. She grabbed for it without thought, dragging at hair and flesh alike. Her fingers scored his skin. His head came free of the surface. She shook him by his hair. "Wake up, fool. Swim!" He made a choking noise and swore, pulling away from her. She released his head and kept hold of his arm. The water spun them together, like lovers.

"He's alive." She called it out, in case Caradoc was near.

"Good . . ." His voice came from behind her. His arm swept past hers and grabbed Dubornos and for a moment they both held the drowning youth, a trophy, evenly caught. Their eyes met and she felt a bubble of laughter that was swept away by the water before the current snatched at them afresh and Dubornos was torn from her grip.

Caradoc caught him as he spun away. They were dragged under and emerged further away, still together. His voice carried back to her. ". . . get him out . . . mustn't go into the pool."

She had forgotten the pool. Terror impaled her soul. Not for herself, but for the deaths piled upon deaths that Airmid had dreamed would happen should a body enter the god's domain. It had been her dream of last night and they had argued in the wake of it, because it was unthinkable that anyone should fall into the pool and it was easier to argue over that than the other things that came between them. She would have wept now, had she the breath for it. She tried to see where she was but the crushing water held her down. Cold and the constant battering drained her strength. Her mind demanded action and her body replied late and poorly. Her limbs were of lead, worked too often; they folded and would not unfold. She kicked herself upwards to look ahead and found she was no longer alone. People gathered on the bank. She saw the grey battle mare and was grateful; Bán had ridden her well. She saw Airmid in silhouette against the moon and her heart bled. She saw the white creaming foam of the waterfall's head, closer than she had thought possible. In the dream a man's body had been swept into the pool and Nemain's wrath fell on them for generations. It must not happen. Rising high above the surface, Breaca took a breath, doubled over and dived for the second time.

The water was her friend. It understood the meaning of sacrifice. For all time, her people had known that. Her lungs did not hurt. The current was warm now, as if in summer; the threads and strands of it wove around her, cushioning her from hurt. The power of it filled her, narrowing into a spearhead as it drove towards the cleft in the rocks. She felt no fear now, at the end. The water drummed an echo of her heart. She heard her mother's voice, singing. She spread her arms wide, to catch the edges of the rock and not be swept through. Her body slammed, crushingly, into a wall where the cleft should have been, driving the last breath from her lungs. The world, already black, shattered into crimson, emblazoned with a thousand stars. Spinning, she fought for the rock, to hold it. Her knuckles smashed on stone. She wedged her arm against it and spread her feet, bracing, to make of herself a barrier. It was all she could do. It was up to Caradoc to get himself and

Dubornos to the bank. A body crashed onto her back. She screamed and the river filled her. Her mother sang in the tongue of the ancestors. She let herself go.

"Breaca? Breaca, please, please, will you *breathe* . . ."

"She's gone. I am sorry. I was too slow to lift her."

"No. She *can't* go now. I won't let her. Her heart is still beating. She must be made to breathe."

"Let me . . ."

There was a great deal of pain, but she had expected that. Periodically, it burst into her lungs, like raw fire poured into her throat. Other fires, slower and longer burning, ate at her feet and fingers. She ignored them and looked about. The gods, in their mercy, had taken on the faces of those she loved. Airmid leaned over her, weeping, and Macha. Bán held the grey battle mare, his face a study in grief; Hail could not comfort him. Caradoc knelt, streaming water, as he had when she first saw him, and the Roman stood close by. Luain mac Calma, whom she did not love but might have come to respect, gazed into her heart and rammed his fist for the second time into the soft space below her diaphragm. White pain exploded within her. She coughed and it became a paroxysm of choking. In agony, she swore, cursing them all. Many hands helped her rise, pulling her up to her knees. She retched and tasted the spent mud of the river. A solid palm clapped on her back and more water spilled out of her, and more; she retched for ever. At the end of it, breathing was easier, if no less painful. A hand gripped her jaw, holding her head still. Black hair, bound back with a dreamer's thong, came into view. The face so framed was one she knew, but not Airmid's. She frowned, trying to focus. A heron feather spun on the breeze, holding her attention. Luain mac Calma said, "Welcome back to the land, warrior. Will you stay amongst us now, or would you continue your journey?"

It was more than a question. Worlds hung in balance, awaiting her choice. Far away, the elder grandmother—*her* elder grandmother—laughed, pointedly. Closer, Airmid squeezed her hand. Bán released the grey mare; a soft muzzle lipped at her hair and a wash of warm breath enveloped her. She thought of a foal that was due and how much it had meant. The eyes in front of her cleared and were brown. They saw into her soul and through to the gods beyond. They did not allow for self-pity, or delusion. She pulled on the hands that held hers and sat up, properly. "Is the pool safe?" she asked. "Did anyone enter?"

Airmid said, "The pool is safe. The Roman had already put himself in the cleft. He caught you. Caradoc held Dubornos and brought him to the side. He will live, though his pride is dented. If you come back to us, no-one has died." Her voice was steady, the voice of a dreamer who has dreamed the worst and whose vision has been averted. Her eyes said other things entirely. Breaca looked into the depths of them and smiled.

"I am already back," she said. "I couldn't leave now. If nothing else, I am needed to vote at the council tomorrow."

She looked around for the Roman and saw him kneeling in the mud beyond mac Calma, watching her evenly. Caradoc was with him, one hand on his arm; there, too, a boundary had been crossed. She let her brows rise up in a question that was meant for him as much as for Macha. "If it is still necessary to hold the council after this?"

CHAPTER 11

They still held the council. The elders had made the journey and it was not seemly to send them away without a gathering. Then again, there were those, particularly amongst Dubornos's faction, who said that the Roman had engineered everything that had happened expressly with the council's decision in mind. They were balanced by others, less fool-hardy, who said that he had taken a good chance when he saw it and that the question was not whether he was a fine warrior with a sharp mind but a man who, if left alive, would return to the ranks of the enemy with his head full of detail and his heart full of the need for revenge. The memory of an invasion three generations old ran fresh in their minds and the Roman's actions had done nothing to dispel the dread of it.

The day dawned bright and free of mist. Spring was fully upon them. Because it was a full council, people dressed for the gods. Breaca wore a new tunic that had been a gift from Airmid; a deep russet, one shade darker than her hair, with an edging of mossed green. Her hair had been rinsed clean of river mud and combed out and she wove into the braiding the single crow's feather with the band of red on the haft for the man's life she had taken. It was too early in the year to find a new hide for her shield, but the elder grandmother—the new elder grandmother—had given her the pigments to repaint the serpent-spear on the old one and it glistened now with the rich red of newly spilled oxblood that would not turn brown as it dried.

Not long after dawn, she sat on a bench outside the doorway to her father's forge and worked a hank of sheep's wool dipped in river sand up the length of her sword. Her whole body ached. Black, red-edged bruises flared across her shoulders and back, and her hand had stiffened and was causing cramp. Airmid had given her a drink before they slept that had served to ease the worst of the aches, but it had made her drowsy and unaccountably weepy and she did not want to risk it again on the day of a council. Accordingly, she sat in the sunlight and burnished her sword and did her best to ignore the pain.

"Are you well?"

Her head jerked up. The Roman leaned comfortably against the corner of the forge. She had not spoken to him after the river. Caradoc had taken him away while she was still trying to stand without coughing. The other runners had begun to reach them and it had been thought best for the man's safety if he did not meet with Dubornos's supporters in advance of the council. Even without that, she would not have sought him out. Since the shipwreck, she had avoided him when possible and held to the necessary courtesies when not. She had no doubt that the council would condemn him and had not wished to come to like him before the vote. Still, she could not refuse to answer a direct question.

"I am well, thank you, yes. And you?" Her Gaulish was not good. It added to the awkwardness of their exchanges.

"Bruised, but not broken." He rolled his shoulders reflexively and fingered the old spear wound at his side and she was reminded, as clearly as if he had spoken, that he had not always been an unarmed man, staring his own death in the face. It was not an accidental act.

She pulled a hank of fresh wool from the bag at her side and rubbed it absently up the length of her blade until the woven patterns of her father's forging rippled blue-grey, like a fish under water. The Roman felt around on the dew-wet grass for a place where the sun had dried it and, finding one, sat down. It put him lower than Breaca. He tilted back against the wall so he could see her more easily. He was not here simply to pass time. She worked the wool over the bronze serpent-spear that formed the pommel of her sword and let him choose his moment to speak. He was, after all, the one who could count his remaining time in days, or less. She remembered the river, and what it had felt like knowing that she was about to die. It had not been unpleasant. It would be good as a warrior to hold to that feeling in battle. If Bán was correct, this man had fought in more battles than he could count and it was possible that he felt like that all the time, which would explain his lack of fear. She looked up to see him better and found his eyes already waiting.

"Your blade is very beautiful," he said.

"Thank you. I believe so." She balanced it on her knees. It looked as good as it had ever done. The blade was straight and true, the perfect curves of the pommel gleamed as only good bronze can, and the ancestors' spear-head embedded at the heart of it shone milk-white. Only the calf's-hide binding on the hilt showed patches where the lanolin had leached from her fingers. She wrapped the wool round it and rubbed to make them disappear.

The Roman said, "I am told that a blade holds the soul of the warrior for whom it was made. Is that true?"

She frowned, working through the unfamiliar Gaulish. "Not soul." She shook her head. "It holds our dream. Or the dream of the ancestors, passed down the line, and the deeds of those who have used it." She used the Eceni word for dream, knowing no other.

"So it is impossible for another to use it?"

"Not impossible, but it must be done correctly—with honour." She remembered her pledge to Caradoc on the headland and all it had meant and tried to think how to explain the bedrock of a lifetime and the wisdom of the ancestors to one who knew nothing of either. Slowly, testing the words, she said, "If one offers another a blade, in the oath of the warrior, it is in recognition that they are of the same blood, although different; of the same gods, although the names may sound strange; of the same honour, although their paths may never cross."

"It binds them like brothers—or sisters?"

"Something like." She thought of Amminios and his reputed hatred of Caradoc. From what she had come to know of the latter, the depth and passion of loathing was mutual. She said, "Closer than that, I think. Sometimes brother will fight against brother."

"But you would never fight against a man who had lent you his blade, nor he against you?"

"Of course not."

"I see. That is . . . a pity." He was silent and very

thoughtful. She finished her work and let the weapon rest between her palms. It was the best sword her father had ever made. Glancing sunlight sparked along the metal, piercing the air between them.

"Caradoc has explained the points to be put before the council," he said. "There is a balance, for and against. Because of that, if they vote my death, it is possible I may be allowed to fight a chosen warrior."

She had not considered that. It had merits, not least of which was that the dreamers would not be called upon to kill a man they had come to respect. Airmid, she knew, would be relieved beyond words if it were so. The Roman was still watching her. She said, "Caradoc would be that warrior?"

"He believes so. I suspect he may have to fight Dubornos first for the privilege." His tone was still tinged with irony but he was not smiling now. This close, she could see that the skin was tense around his eyes, making crow's feet where before there had been none. Under the sunned brown of his skin, he was pale. A pulse beat at the angle of his throat, faster and harder than her own. She regretted, suddenly, not having spoken with him sooner.

"You would defeat Dubornos," she said.

"I know."

"But maybe not Caradoc."

"He believes not." One corner of his mouth twitched upward. "I, of course, believe otherwise."

"Really? Even fighting in a strange land, without your gods and with a weapon you have never held before . . . Ah—" She stopped. Sudden understanding made her cough. When she could breathe again, she said, "My father's blade would be too big for you. Even Sinochos's would be—"

"Far too big. Even two-handed, I could not wield it fast enough. And Dubornos would die before I used a blade of his line." He pushed himself upright, taking care not to snag Macha's good tunic on the stone wall of the forge. His lips made a tight, straight line. "I am learning some of what binds a blade to a lineage. They told me yours was newly made. I thought that because of this, and my friendship with your brother, it might be easier for me to borrow it. Forgive me, I had not fully understood."

He turned away. Breaca put a hand out to stop him. All of her most important decisions were made on the turn of a moment; this one was no different. The rightness of it filled her.

"Why not?" she said. "My father has other blades that he can lend to Caradoc. He has no need of mine, and it will not dishonour our pledge for you to use it against him. Here. Take it; test it. It is a good size for you. See if your blood sings for it as mine does." She passed the hilt towards him. "Take it," she said again. "With this blade you could at least meet Caradoc on even terms, and he would not want it otherwise. You should try it now, before the council starts. Wait . . ." She pressed it into his hands. He was no taller than she was; the blade fitted him well. "I will get another and we can practise."

"I can't." His hand closed once on the hilt and she saw that he did, with certainty, hear the song as she did. The light of it showed in his eyes, in the sudden catch of his breath, in the spark of danger and easy death that passed between them. She could have stepped back and did not.

"No." He forced his palm open. The blade spun from his hand. She caught it before it hit the ground, her eyes on the man. His breathing was not controlled now, nor his face. He gave a small bow. "Thank you. It is truly magnificent, as you say, but I cannot try it yet. If your council votes for a fight, then I will accept and be grateful. But not before."

"Why?"

"Because I have hopes that they might still let me go. My gods may be weaker here, but I have put my life in their hands more times than I can number and they have never let me down. I don't believe they saved me from shipwreck so that I could die now. If I am right, then I may yet return to my unit a free man."

"Then you will return having known a blade of the Eceni. Is that such a bad thing?"

"It would be a bad thing if Tiberius orders another British campaign. What would we do, you and I, if we found ourselves on opposite sides in battle, and you wielding your blade?" His eyes were steady; the panic she had seen was gone, or better controlled. His smile held genuine regret. "I may not follow your gods, but I have no wish to offend them when I rest on their mercy. If I took your blade in good faith now, knowing that this may happen, I would do so."

It was not at all what she had expected. In shock, she said, "You would go from here, having known us, and yet if your people asked it you would fight against us in another invasion?"

"Yes. Would you do different?"

"Of course. I am Eceni. We do not invade the lands of others."

She would have left him then but a horn sounded at the great-house, calling the start of council. The guest-laws forbade her to abandon him to walk alone. She offered him a horse and he accepted and they rode in silence up the track between the paddocks to join the gathering council.

The elder grandmother stood in the doorway. A badger-skin robe fell from her shoulders in a wave of black on white, making her seem broader and stronger than she was. The hawk-skin clasping her head was feather-perfect and hid the thinness of her hair. The beaked skull that she held to use as a pointer was chalk-white and drew all eyes. Bán, who had dressed her with especial care, burned with pride. The old woman had grown into her role in the years since her predecessor died and she made a good leader. She turned now to face the quiet mass of elders, speaking the words of invocation to the gods that made the great-house a place of sacred meeting and bound everyone who entered to accept what took place within.

Others stood around, more or less striking according to taste. Dubornos was conspicuous in a tunic of fine Eceni blue and an excess of gold. He had been one of the first to trade for Gunovic's blue enamelled armbands and he had added a new one each year since. He wore them all now and the metal clashed on his arms. His torc, too, was the product of a southern smith; he did not trust Eburovic to make one of sufficient ostentation. In this, he was probably right. Bán had watched as his father spun out the last of his gold, mixing it with judicious quantities of silver to make a torc for Caradoc that he might come before the elders with the decoration he was due. The result was a thing of breathtaking beauty and strikingly simple. Even without it, Caradoc would have stood out from the crowd. With it, he was regal, and Dubornos was a blue jay, cackling in the branches. Someone should have told him before he shamed his people.

Luain mac Calma stood further back, picked out by his height. His dreaming was the heron; one could see the easy interchange between the tall, long-legged spear-bird and the man. A blue-grey feather the length of his thumb dangled down from his temples, fitted neatly so that the curved tip lay exactly level with the line of his chin. It spun gently in the morning air.

Breaca was near him, blazing in the sheen of the sun. Her hair could have been cast in bronze, her eyes were copper-green and alive with the morning, the white of her shield was snow against the rust of her tunic and hair. Bán smiled at her and she smiled back but her mind was elsewhere. The Roman stood at her side and one could see they had been talking. The tension strummed between them, taut as a drumhead. The foreigner was paler than he had been and he stood too still. He looked grateful as Luain mac Calma pushed his way forward and translated the elder grandmother's words into Latin. The discordant jumble of vowels and consonants clashed with the soft flow of Eceni around them. Everyone else stopped speaking. In the silence that followed, the Roman bowed. "It is clear," he said in Gaulish so they could all hear. "I will abide by the rule of the council."

It was never going to be a quiet meeting, nor a brief one. Had it been called quickly, in the first days after the shipwreck, there might have been fewer with strong opinions to voice. As it was, everyone who was eligible to speak wished to do so. Bán, who was not eligible, found suddenly that he had no stomach to follow the crowd inside. The day was bright and fresh, while the great-house was airless and the smoke from the torches already stung his eyes. It would be more full of people than he had ever seen it. His harness hut had been taken over by Segoventos and the second mate and Bán had been forced to move back into the roundhouse to sleep; he found that he missed the solitude and the company of his hounds. He needed the peace of the forest more than he needed to listen to the old anger of adults, bound up in the language of singers and given credence by the elders. He knew what the arguments were; he had heard them rehearsed too long and too often in the past month.

He looked round, searching for a known face. The crowd flowed and changed around him. Caradoc had taken the Roman into the dark. Airmid was quite close, standing alone. The dreamer had a haggard look as if she had either dreamed badly again or not slept at all. Reaching forward, Bán tapped her on the arm. When she looked round, he signalled himself, then Hail, who lay in the sun at the side of the great-house, and finally the forest. She raised her brows and then nodded. He edged sideways to the rim of the crowd and broke away, running. Several people saw him go but none made any move to stop him. Had he looked, he would have seen that more than one envied him his freedom.

Bán was far into the trees by the time the last of the elders filed in through the doorway and sat in the appointed place. Luain mac Calma, being of Mona, held rank above all of those present and could have led the council had he chosen. He had not. He sat by the door-flap, in a position from which he could be seen and heard and could readily translate if required. He hitched his borrowed cloak to a bracket on the wall and settled back to listen with his ears to the voices of men, with his soul to the voice of the gods and with his mind to the memories of his past, seeking their parallels in the present. It was this last, more than anything, that occupied him.

Luain mac Calma was in his thirteenth year when the last Roman warship ran aground on the eastern coast. There had been no gathering of the elders then. The ship had foundered in Trinovantian waters and Cunobelin, war leader of the Catuvellauni and recently made leader of the Trinovantes, had ignored all requests to place the matter before the elders, choosing instead to put himself in good odour with Rome by returning both men and boats to the Emperor Tiberius intact. More than anything else in his reign to date, that one act had marked the Sun Hound as a friend of the enemy. Word had swarmed across the country like fire through dry grass, spreading west from the dun at which he held court, through the Catuvellauni as far as the Dumnonii in the western toe of the land, before turning right and running up the coast, through the Silures to the Ordovices and across the short, choppy straits to the sacred groves of Mona itself. Luain had been in attendance on the elders when the messenger arrived. He had seen the man given an oak leaf in gold for his services and seen his splay-hoofed gelding exchanged for a mare of far higher quality, in foal by a good horse. Beyond that, he had seen nothing. The elders had called the council with a speed that astonished him and when they emerged two days later, hot and grubby and short on sleep, not one of them felt it necessary to answer questions from a curious youth.

It was the first time mac Calma felt the timing of the

gods pull against him. If the general Germanicus had waited one year more to lose his troops to the ocean, the young dreamer would have been a full member of the council and would have heard the laws teased out and examined, heard the balancing arguments made on both sides and understood the final judgement with its train of penalties and actions. As it was, he sat now on the edge of another council led by other people, and found that his heart sent him one way and his head the other, while the laws of the gods twisted both ways, or neither. Which was unfortunate, because they were asking him questions.

". . . if we may hear the thoughts of Luain mac Calma, Hibernian, more lately of Mona?"

It was the second time the elder grandmother had spoken his name, and the sound of it brought him back to himself. She made a good leader of the council. For all the shrivelled skin and the lame leg and thinned-out hair, she had a voice that could reach the far edges of the circle and she carried the undoubted authority of age. In the hours since the horn had signalled the opening, she had ridden with great skill the delicate balance between the factions. She sat in the west, in the place of deepest dreaming. The badger-skin robe flickered patchily white in the darkness and the hawk-skin on her head took on its own life. Even from this far back, one could see the strength of the god in every gesture and if it cost her life-days to do it, there were few present who would notice and still fewer who would say anything afterwards.

"Well?" She was not a dreamer, but she had seen more years than any present and the effect was much the same. Her voice caught a place in his chest and made it vibrate.

"You have heard the arguments on both sides. We are evenly matched. You are not of the Eceni, so cannot pass a final judgement, but you come to us from the great council of Mona; you know the laws of gods and men as well as anyone here and you have your own dreaming, which is not inconsiderable. It is known that you have dreamed on this. We can hope that you have an answer. Is it so?"

The tall dreamer rose to his feet. It was late afternoon. He had lifted the door-flap a long time ago to let in the light. The torches guttered, sending threads of black smoke up into the roof space. The scent of it filtered down, mingling with wool and leather and sweating humanity to create the familiar smell of winter and warmth and comfort. He breathed it in and looked round. They were tired now and wanted an answer. The young men wanted blood, even 'Tagos. Surprisingly, he had sided with Dubornos on this. Caradoc had been evenly balanced and had argued better than the others; he had the makings of a good leader if he could be taught to curb his pride. Breaca had surprised him, and the Roman too. The Roman was long gone. He had asked to be excused not long after Breaca's speech, and his request had been granted. None wished to force him to listen to the words spoken against him. In the time since then, none had offered any new arguments although many had chewed over the ones already made.

Luain mac Calma stepped forward into the space reserved for the speakers. From here, he could see and be seen, hear and be heard. He nodded towards the elder grandmother. "I have dreamed," he said. "What I have seen will not be welcome and it has bearing far beyond the question before us now. Nevertheless, I believe there may be an answer within it." He touched a finger to the heron's feather hanging at his temple and led them into the world of his dream.

The hind fed on a young larch, reaching up to tug on the new foliage with her tongue. Her breath warmed Bán, carried on an eddying breeze. A woodpecker drummed on the bark above his head. A magpie screamed obscenities from an upper branch. Hail shifted at his side, his tail thumping twice on the ground. The deer flicked ears as big as a boy's hand. She stopped feeding. A spray of larch flicked upwards. The magpie screamed again.

A voice behind him said, "Do you not need a spear to make the kill, Bán harehunter?"

He had no need to turn. The voice was as familiar as the light, careful tread had been. "I have Hail," he said. "And this." He tapped the handle of his belt knife. It had long been a source of pride that he did not need a spear, that he could stalk closer to the quarry than any other and kill before it began its flight. He pushed himself clear of the holly bush under which he had been lying. The deer watched him with limited interest. Turning, he said, "I don't hunt with three dogs to every spear as others do."

The Roman sat with his back to a small ash. He looked tired. The crow's feet at his eyes had deepened with the strain of the day. He nodded, as if a boy's hunting were an important consideration in his life. "You mean as Dubornos does. I would not think that of you. But this deer lives." He said it as a question, with a brief upturning of his brows.

"It's Nemma's friend. She raised it from a calf. To kill it would be like killing one of the horses." Bán grabbed a branch and hauled himself to his feet. The deer flicked her ears, snuffing the breeze for a scent of barley meal, or salt. "See, she is not afraid of us. Not even of Hail."

"I see." The man made no move to stand. "So have you caught something else?"

"No. I followed another deer, a young buck, but it didn't seem a good day to kill."

Bán sat down with his back to the same tree as the Roman. The man did not question why it might not be a good day to shed blood without reason and Bán did not feel the need to explain. Today, such things were obvious. Hail lay between them. Remarkably, the man pulled a twist of smoked hide from his tunic and gave it to the hound. The cracking of dried skin filled the clearing. Bán watched, chewing on a nail until his impatience overcame him. "Why are you here?" he asked. "Is it over already? Have they decided?"

"Hardly." The man smiled, crookedly. "They will be in there until night falls. It would not surprise me if they were still arguing at dawn tomorrow. I came away when I had spoken. It is better for Luain if he does not have to translate for me. I asked if I could come out for some fresh air. They trust me enough not to run now so they let me go."

"But you could run. The horses are there. Today of all days you would be long gone before the hunt began. They would not know you were gone before they came out." Bán did not have to say "I would not tell them"; that was understood between them.

"I could." The Roman had thought about it; that much was clear. He stared at the hind, who stared back. As if to her, he said, "Where would I go?"

"South, to the Trinovantes. They are friends to Rome. The Sun Hound has returned lost seamen to Gaul before."

"Perhaps. But it would not help the enmity that exists between the Sun Hound and his son and, in any case, I have given my word to abide by the ruling of the council. I would not go to the gods an oath-breaker."

There was nothing to say to that. Bán sat awkwardly and dug his toe into Hail's flank. The silence lengthened. In the clearing, the hind stripped off the last of the new larch and wandered, soft-footed, into the deeper wood.

The man stood. He peered south through the trees, angling his hand against the sun. "Why don't we go and see the horses that came off the ship? The red mare is gentling now. She might let you mount her."

It was something to do. They followed the deer track until it met the wide swath of the trackway leading south towards the horse fields. Hail led, searching out rats' nests and deer tracks with unfocused abandon. The breeze was warm, lifting their hair and blowing away the clinging scent of smoke from the great-house. For Bán, it could have been an ordinary day, but for the knot in his stomach and the difficulty he had with swallowing. He asked, "What else did Caradoc say?"

"What he was always going to say: that it is not myself who is the danger but what I represent. He was very generous in his estimation of me. I was to understand that if I would agree to remain with the Eceni, or to travel west with him to the Ordovices, then he would vote for my life and the granting of land and horses."

"Would you not agree to it?"

"To avoid the death they have planned for me, I would agree to anything asked of me by a man, but I would not swear it on oath before the gods and he knows it. He would not swear to stay in Rome if our positions were reversed."

"Why not stay? You could be happy here."

"Perhaps. But I would no longer be me. Who we are depends on where we are. Some people are not so readily transplanted."

"So Caradoc will vote against you?"

"Of course. He was always going to do that. He was more pleasant about it than Dubornos."

"Dubornos? Ha!" Bán grimaced. "You saved his life. He should be grateful."

"I saved his life, therefore he hates me more than he has words to express. He was purple with anger. I thought he might fall into fits from the passion of it."

"That would have been good." In spite of himself, Bán grinned. "They might let you go if you managed that."

"Maybe I should have smiled at him harder."

They reached the paddocks. An old yew trunk as wide as Bán was high blocked the entrance to the first field. Great plates of orange fungus grew from the bed of furred moss and lichens that patched its surface. They clambered over and walked up the hill to the last and largest of the paddocks. A beech tree, generations old, stood in the centre amidst the scattered leavings of such mast as had not been stolen by squirrels or collected by the children in the autumn. The herd grazed nearby, or stood in its shade. Bán and the Roman strolled up to sit beneath it. The red Thessalian mare saw them coming and raised her head. She had rolled recently and was coated in mud. At Bán's whistle, she left the safety of the herd and trotted over to meet them. As always when he saw her move, the boy was speechless. Even on that first night as she came out of the sea, her stride had been longer than any he had seen and she had floated across the shingle on cushioned air. Now, with the winter behind her, she matched his dream so closely that it raised the hairs on his arm.

The Roman sat on the turf, watching. "She's learning to trust you," he said.

"I think so." Bán nodded. In the beginning, newly off the boat, she had rolled her eyes and kicked at the sight of him. For half a moon, Luain mac Calma and—oddly—Airmid were the only ones she would have near her. All through the early part of spring, Bán had sat still in the slush and the mud with barley meal scattered around him, waiting for her to take the first steps in his direction. Recently, she had begun to come to his whistle. He carried a twist of salt and a comb inside his tunic. Sitting beneath the beech, he emptied the salt onto his palm and held it tight in a fist so she had to tease his fingers open to reach it. When she was done, he brought out the comb and began work on her mane; it was not as tangled as her tail so he was less likely to scare her. Hail quartered the empty field behind them, searching for mice. The Roman lay back on the grass, cushioning his head on his hands and closing his eyes to the sun.

Bán asked, "What did Breaca say?"

He did not necessarily expect an answer. For a while, it seemed he would not get one. He worked on with his grooming. The mare grazed peaceably and did not kick as he moved to her hindquarters and drew the comb down her tail. Each day, he passed small boundaries such as this. Beside him, the Roman stirred.

"Your sister said that if they condemn me for what I am, not who I am, then your people will have sunk to the level of Rome and the taint will never clear." The man opened his eyes and stared at the open sky. "She insults me and still votes for my life. I think she hates me as much as Dubornos does, but what she does with it is different."

"She doesn't hate you. She is not Dubornos. You saved her life, too."

"True. But she has a particular sense of honour and I have offended it."

Bán did not ask how. He would get it later from Breaca if it mattered. He pulled a handful of grass, twisting it into a wisp, and began to work the mud from the mare's hide. Since the winter, she had not been fully clean. It seemed a good day to change that.

"Did you know she was pregnant?"

"What?" Bán looked down, surprised.

The Roman was lying with his head beside the mare's hind leg, staring up at her udder. "The mare," he said. "She's pregnant."

"Oh. Yes. To a black Pannonian horse with a white star. Luain mac Calma told me. She was in season when he bought her and he took her to be covered straightaway. The foal will be born in the month after midsummer. Airmid says it will be black with white on its face and I will ride it in battle." He did not mention his dream.

"Then she must be right." The man grinned, suddenly. "You might do better to ride the mare. She has seen enough battles."

"How do you know?"

"She has the brand of a legion, see?" He reached back to point out a mark on her neck; a jumble of angular lines and cross bars showed sketchily through the mud. "*LVIIIA*—the Eighth Augustan. If you clean all the mud off her sides, I'll bet the white flecks on her flank there will turn out to be the spur marks. She has been ridden hard. Either her rider hated her, or he had trouble on the field and needed to leave it quickly."

Bán ran his fingers across the flank that was closest. There, behind her ribs, he felt a ridge of tissue. The mare flicked her tail and stamped and he took his hand away. He worked his grooming wad down, freeing the clotted mud. The scars, thus revealed, stood out like chalk marks against the rich red of her hide. It was a wonder he had ever seen beyond them. He passed his hand down again, feeling the extent of the damage. "Did you know her?" he asked.

"No. I've never been with the Eighth. But I have known many like her. They live short lives and brutal ones. She is better off where she is. You could . . ." He trailed off. In a quite different voice he said, "A crow. How very tactless."

He named the bird in Eceni although they had been speaking Gaulish. Bán had been working under the mare's stomach. He straightened. The Roman had moved. He was lying with his back against a small knoll, his fingers laced loosely behind his head and his eyes open, staring in grim fascination at a crow that hopped across the turf a spear's throw from his feet. As Bán watched, the bird jabbed its beak into a pile of decaying horse dung and dragged out a worm.

"Shoo it off." Bán lifted his arm, to throw the grooming wad.

"No. Leave it." The Roman lay very still. Small pearls of sweat stood up on his temples. Tracks of it threaded down to the rim of his tunic. His jawline was tight, cording the muscles on his neck. For the first time, Bán saw fear in a way he understood. The implications of it sent a slick of cold down his back. Abandoning the mare, he walked carefully to the man's side and sat down. He put a hand on the shoulder beside him and felt the muscles flinch.

"How did you know the name of the bird in Eceni?" he asked, gently.

"Your sister told me." The man made no move to throw off his hand. "We saw one this morning, riding up to the great-house, and I asked her. It's my name, or something like it. In Latin: *Corvus*, the raven. It's the name of my house."

"So we could have called you Corvus instead of 'the Roman' or 'the foreigner' all this time. Why did you not tell us?"

The man smiled. His lips stretched tight over white teeth. There was no humour in his face. His eyes stayed on the bird. "With what is coming? With your dreamers seeing messages in the flights of birds and the patterns of leaves on the grass? Do I look insane?"

Numbly, Bán said, "They don't see messages like that." He was beginning to feel sick and had no knowledge of what to do about it.

"I know that now. I didn't know it when I first came. Caesar wrote it and I believed him. I'm sorry . . ." The man rolled his shoulders. It did nothing to ease the stiffness of his muscles. The crow speared another worm and tore it in two. The Roman shuddered, like a horse shaking off flies.

Bán said, "Who told you what is coming? Not Breaca?"

"No. She is more generous than that."

"Dubornos, then?"

"Of course. He said the last man condemned by the elder council lived for a day and a half before the birds finally killed him." His voice was oddly hollow.

Bán wrenched himself upright. "He said *what?*"

The crow fled into the upper reaches of the beech, croaking displeasure. The Roman craned his neck to watch it.

Furiously, Bán said, "Don't listen to him. He doesn't know. He couldn't. It happened in his grandfather's time. He wasn't born then. His *father* wasn't born then. It's not true. And it won't happen now. They will let you fight Caradoc, they must do."

"Must they? I don't see why. I wouldn't." The man's eyes, unseeing, rested on the crow. As one emerging from a dream, he said, "The dreamers broke his limbs and bound him to the platform and opened his abdomen with a knife, crossing the cut so the crows and ravens could feed without hindrance. They said he lived a day and a night and on until dusk of the next day, that he died only when one of the birds tore at his liver and made it bleed. Even then—"

"Stop it!" The gorge rose in Bán's throat. Swallowing hard, he said, "Dubornos may be mad but you don't have to join him. It doesn't matter what happened then. It was different. Verotagos had betrayed us to the Coritani. Six warriors died because of what he did, his father and his sister amongst them. We were in a war and losing badly. There were others who might have followed his lead. The dreamers were making a *point.*"

"And what are they doing now, if not making a point?"

Bán was weeping. Hot tears of anger and frustration streaked his cheeks, pooling at his collarbone. "It's not like that. You have done nothing to offend the gods. You even stopped Dubornos from falling into the pool. They would have skinned him first, before they broke his limbs for the platform, if he had gone into the water. He was trying to upset you. Don't let him do it." He made himself think, seeking a source of reassurance. Only one came to mind. "Have you spoken to Airmid?"

"No. It hurts her to look at me. She does it, but the effort is painful to watch. I don't think it would help either of us to start threshing through the details."

Bán knelt. He took the man's hands in his own. He made himself look through the eyes to the soul that rested inside. The will that it took made him calmer. "Corvus, listen to me. They will not do that. If you have to die, it will be fast. There are ways to angle the knife so that it pierces the heart before anything." He had never been told it, but in the deepest part of his soul he knew it to be true. He made a cutting motion upwards to the base of the breastbone and felt the short shock of the other man's breathing. His hand moved on down to where he knew the old wound to be, at the side. Touching the pit of it, he said, "I promise you, it will be faster than a spear in the side could ever have been. Was that so bad?"

The man twitched a small smile. "No. I didn't feel it until later. But then I was busy and I didn't expect an attack from that side. My Vexillarius was supposed to stop it coming but he was already down."

"What happened to him?"

"He raised his arm too high. A spear took him in the space beneath it, where he had no armour."

"Did he die?"

"Eventually. The field medics had him for a day or two first."

"A day or two?"

"Four."

"And this would be worse?"

"Maybe not." The man laughed, short and hard and bitten off before the end. "Thank you for that." He freed his hands from between Bán's palms and lay back on the turf where he had been before.

Looking up, Bán saw that the crow had gone. He closed his eyes and felt the warmth of the sun and tried to be calm.

"At least you don't have prisons here," the Roman said, dreamily. "I couldn't bear that, not being able to see the sky, or hear the birds. They say Julius Caesar kept Vercingetorix in an underground dungeon for years before he had him killed. The man was broken long before they brought him up into daylight."

Bán shuddered. The red mare moved around, grazing near his feet. He reached out and touched her, for the feel of something real beneath his fingers. "Why would he do a thing like that?"

"Because he could. Because he wanted to make a point. I suppose because he was a general and he had seen enough men die in the field to know that there are few things you can do to a man that war cannot do worse. It's true. I had forgotten . . ." The man sat up, slowly, and looked round. "Do you hear a horse?"

Bán did. They turned together, sitting on the knoll. The figure that emerged from the forest was too distant to see clearly but a banner of red hair and the reckless speed marked Breaca as clearly as if they had recognized her face. The Roman pulled himself to his feet and watched her go. "It's your sister," he said. "She's borrowed your dun colt again." He spoke lightly, as if her choice of horse was the most interesting point of it. Breaca reached the corner of the wall and gave the colt his head. He was half-brother to the filly that had been taken by Amminios. He wasn't as good, but he was close. He ran almost as fast as the grey mare.

"She's very angry," said the Roman. He stood very still.

"She's unhappy. It is not necessarily because of you."

"And that is why Airmid and your father have followed her?"

Bán looked back to the trees. Airmid stood with Luain mac Calma on the trackway. His father was not there. It was a mistake that had been made often in the last month by those unfamiliar with his family. Today, it was not important. He let it go. "That's Luain, the dreamer. He brought news from Mona that Breaca did not want to hear. He will have spoken it formally at the council, to seek the approval of the elders."

The Roman nodded, absently. "Would she leave before the vote?"

"No. They would only discuss it after." Bán felt sick again. Down at the trees, a flash of gold caught the late afternoon sun and Airmid turned as if someone had hailed her. "Caradoc is there," he said.

"Then he will have news." The Roman sat down, suddenly. Bán stood and raised his arm. Luain mac Calma saw it and waved, pointing. Caradoc emerged from the trees and began to walk up the slope towards the yew log that blocked the gateway to the lower field. He walked fast, not quite running; it would not take him long to reach them. The red mare nudged Bán and he did not reach for her as he would have done.

Caradoc vaulted the log, easily. Hail saw him and trotted down the slope to greet him; the young warrior, too, had found ways to get on the right side of the hounds.

"I think——" Bán stopped. What he thought did not matter. The Roman's attention was focused entirely on the man walking up the hill towards them. The Roman's skin was grey where before it had been brown and sweat ran freely from his temples. His hands were clasped at his knees, tightly. Bán tried to swallow and found his mouth too dry. His senses expanded overpoweringly. The rush of his heart pulsed in his ears, deafeningly loud. The mare straddled to urinate and the spiked, earthen smell of it, normally so familiar, made him heave. His skin tingled; every place where his tunic touched him became a deep-rubbed sore. The flashing gold of a man's hair became the source of the sun in a world gone suddenly mad. He rubbed the palms of his hands on his tunic and regretted it. "Is this how it feels before battle?" he asked.

"Yes, but in battle one has a weapon, and at least the illusion of choice."

"Of course." And there was no choice. By now it would have been decided whether they would let him go to his death as a warrior bearing a borrowed sword, or if Dubornos held enough sway to see him die broken on the platform. They should have discussed the ways to escape such a fate and had not. Caradoc passed behind a whitethorn hedge and was out of sight for the space of two strides. Without moving his eyes, Bán drew the knife from his belt and held it out on the flat of his hand. "Take it," he said, shortly. "It gives you choice." The hilt made a brief pressure on his palm and was gone.

The warrior was close. Hail trotted at his side, grinning. The man reached down as he would with his own hound, fondling the great ears absently. A spear's length from the

Roman, he stopped. The world stopped with him. Bán felt his throat clench and the tears burn in his eyes. He tried to speak and nothing came. The Roman was still, like a statue. His face was quite white.

For one moment longer, they held like that, then Caradoc threw his arm out in the salute of one warrior to another and inclined his head and it was enough.

It was more than enough; words would not have been better. Bán looked away, his eyes still burning. Beside him, he felt the man draw in a breath so deep it might have been his first in the world. In the space after, he swore, softly—a long stream of foreign words in the middle of which Nemain was invoked as a saviour and then Briga, whose bird was the crow. When he ran out of words he looked up at the warrior.

"Thank you," he said. "Can you tell me why?" He spoke Gaulish, out of respect.

"Mac Calma spoke of his dreaming." Caradoc crouched neatly on the turf. "And then Airmid told of hers. They are our two most powerful dreamers and what they saw was the same. It is not you that we have to fear and your death will do nothing to stop an invasion, if one is coming. Knowing that, it was only damaged pride and the memory of your ancestors' actions that called for your death. Neither of these was enough. The dreamers would not do it."

"You mean Airmid would not do it?"

"No. None of them would. They said so and it swung the vote. Some still voted against, but the majority was with you."

"And you? May I know which way you voted?"

It mattered to him, one could see it. Caradoc nodded. His eyes were alive with a striking humour, brighter than they had been since the day of the shipwreck. "You may," he said. "It has changed since the day of our first meeting. When the sea threw you up at our feet, I would have killed you, you know that. Even after your actions in the river, I would have voted for your death because I believed it necessary to preserve our people. But the dreamers spoke against it and I trust them. If they say there is no reason for your death and that it would offend the gods to kill you, then I believe them. I voted to let you go and I am glad there were more of us than the others."

"What about Dubornos? He will not be glad."

"No. Not in the least, but you are still a guest. If he kills you, it is murder, which also draws the dreamer's death, and he will not take that risk. You have the right now to wear a sword but I suggest you don't do so unless you want him to challenge you. That would be . . . complicated."

"Indeed. Thank you."

In the lengthening silence, the Roman brought his hand to his face and pinched the bridge of his nose. He had done that in his first conversations with Bán, when he was lost for words and they had run out of useful hand signals. He said, "And now? Do you give me a horse and tell me where to ride?"

"If you wish." Caradoc pushed himself to his feet. "On the other hand, if you want to get home before your daughters bear granddaughters, then you will allow us to escort you south to the port beyond my father's dun and take a merchant ship from there."

The Roman laughed, loosely and not very controlled, so that one could read in him the first waves of relief, barely held. "Could you say that again in Latin?" he asked. "I think my Gaulish is failing me. If nothing else, I have no daughters, no children of any kind—but are you telling me that *you* will ride into the city of your father and your brothers? I thought you were at war with him?"

"Not yet. I don't fight unless there's a good chance of winning."

Caradoc said it again in Latin, taking longer, elaborating as the other asked questions. Bán watched his friend's face change as the world opened out before him. When the questions ran out the Roman stood and, turning, bowed to Bán. In Gaulish, he said, "Forgive me. It is not every day a man is given back his life. If it is not a discourtesy, I think I would spend some time alone with the gods. I thank you for your company."

Bán found himself grinning widely, like a fool. Tears streamed down his face and he didn't care. "You don't need to thank me."

"No. But I am not certain I have any other way to repay you."

It was said hesitantly, with wrong words, and in any case repayment of a debt to a friend was too complex a thing in any language. Bán stood and offered his hand to be grasped, in the Roman way. He put his arm on the man's shoulder. "Go," he said, smiling. "Hail and I will hunt now. There will be meat to eat this evening. Make sure you are back in time or Camma will be mortally offended. She is far worse than the dreamers when she's angry."

"You would have liked him to stay?"

Bán sat on the knoll under the beech tree. The Roman was a small figure in the distance, walking along the horizon. Caradoc lay back on the grass and peered up through the branches as the Roman had done before him. He thought carefully before he answered.

"I think it would have been better to fight at his side than to fight against him."

Bán rolled over, resting his chin on his fists. More things had passed, it seemed, than a Roman's dance with death. He found a withered beechnut left behind after winter and prised it open with his fingers. The mast within was small and shrivelled. He held it up for the red mare and she lipped it delicately from his palm. "Is that what they dreamed?" he asked. "That you were fighting against him?"

"Maybe. It's hard to tell. You have known a true dreaming; I have only known dreams and all of those confused, but it seems either way nothing is precise. Everything is shapes and shadows and there are a hundred different interpretations, all of which may be true, or none."

"But there will be war?"

"Yes. There will be war on a scale such as we have never known it. A brother will be the spark that lights the flame and a brother will be the one to fan it."

A name hung in the air between them. Bán was the first one to speak it.

"Amminios." He spat it out. The taste of it soured his mouth and the sound took the shine from the day.

"They think so. I am certain of it. As soon as my father is dead, he will act."

Caradoc rolled over onto his side. A faint scar on one jaw reminded Bán that he was a warrior with a dozen kills to his credit. His grey eyes searched deeply as Luain's had done once, on a headland. There was an offer of friendship there if one chose to look for it. He said, "My brother will be at the dun. If you want to come with us, you must be prepared for that."

Bán stared at him. He had not thought past the day and the death he had believed must follow it. "Will I be allowed to go?"

"If you wish to. Your father will go, and Macha. Airmid has been given leave to travel that far. Mac Calma named her Airmid of Nemain, which I think she was not expecting. It sets her higher than any dreamer of the Eceni for the last three generations."

"But she still has to go to Mona?"

"Yes, of course. She will ride with the Eceni as far as the boundaries of your land and then turn west."

"Alone?"

"Hardly. Breaca refused to take the oath of the sworn warrior. The offer was passed to 'Tagos, who also refused. That left—"

"Dubornos." Bán let the full horror of it roll over him. "Dubornos will be sworn warrior to Airmid in her years in Mona? Did she accept it?"

"Do you think she cares? Breaca had already gone out by then. She would have accepted Amminios if it would have ended the council and let her follow."

"Maybe." Bán was only half listening. He remembered his sister and the speed she had called from the dun colt. From that he remembered other things. He chewed on his lip, building courage to speak. The grey eyes were patient, waiting. "Will she be there at your father's court?" he asked. "The dun filly?"

"No." It was a short word. The eyes said more. Bán read anger and a deeper rage beneath it.

"Is she——"

"She's dead. I was not there. Togodubnos did what he could but he was unable to stop it. It was fast; 'an act of sacrifice to the gods of Rome.' I am sorry."

"Don't be. You are not to blame."

Bán lay back and looked up at the sky. The sun hovered on the brink of the horizon. Opposite it, the first edge of the moon showed in the east. He offered a prayer and the promise of vengeance. Presently he sat up and held out his arm. The other clasped it, as a friend would, gripping at the elbow.

"Will you kill him?" Bán asked.

"Amminios? Oh, yes." Caradoc of the Trinovantes smiled tightly. "Without question, I will kill him. But not until after my father dies. Nothing can happen until then. In the meantime, we will travel to my father's dun and see what it has to offer."

CHAPTER 12

It will be bigger than anything you have ever imagined.

Caradoc had warned her, and then Macha, in the days of preparation before they left the roundhouse. Gunovic had laid the groundwork over the years with his winter songs and Arosted had fleshed it out in laconic monosyllables, sprinkled like his salt. It was her own poverty of imagination, therefore, that had left Breaca so utterly unprepared for the reality that was Cunobelin's dun.

"It is meant to do this to you. Don't let it."

Caradoc rode at her side as she led her delegation out of the ranks of coppiced hazel onto the long, shallow slope that led down towards his father's land. He was used to it, had grown up with it, watching the improvements and extensions as his father had sought to make his land secure. Coming on it for the first time, Breaca was rendered speechless before the endless acres of grazing land, the richness and order of the planted fields, the height and the span and the haze of smoke and heat hanging in the air that told of more fires—of more dwellings—than she had ever seen in one place.

She was a warrior and it was the dike that struck her hardest, as it was supposed to do: the long, straight, ditch-fronted rampart that marked the first defence of the Sun Hound's land. It was vast, impossibly so, and stretched further than she could ever have envisaged. Seeing it, she could understand, finally, why the dun was said to be impregnable.

Caradoc, who was also a warrior, sat still at her side, seeing it afresh through her eyes. "It is a long time since these defences to the north were manned; my father does not believe there is any risk of attack from the Eceni. The greater threat now is from the south, from Berikos and his Atrebates who wait on the far side of the sea-river and would plunder my father's ports if they were given the chance. What you see here is old and not well maintained."

Breaca said, "But effective none the less. The banks would be hard for attacking warriors to cross in any numbers."

Caradoc raised a brow, smiling. "If you came with a war band, would you continue?"

A shiver of goose-flight brushed across her spine. She let it pass before she answered. "Yes. But I would do it with care and I would make sure I knew the weak points before I started."

"Good. If it were me, I would consider bribing the guards at the gates. A wall is only a barrier if it has no gaps." Caradoc pushed his mount forward. "Today, that should not be necessary. The spies have been following us since we left Eceni lands. My father should know everything down to and including what we eat and drink while travelling." He was already ahead of her. He turned back, one brow raised. "Shall we go down and see if he will let us in?"

They rode down the long slope together. Caradoc was mounted on the dun colt and looked good on him. The horse had been Bán's last gift before the party left the round-house and if it was offered as much in provocation to Amminios as in honour of his brother, none had chosen to remark on it. It was widely known by then that Amminios had sacrificed the filly to the Roman gods and that her spirit was therefore lost, unable to find its way to the lands of the dead. Even those who had not known her were appalled by that.

Bán himself rode the red Thessalian mare, a mount that surpassed any the Eceni had ever seen. Because of her value to the breeding herd, the elders had been required to give permission before Bán took her south but the vote had been unanimous in his favour. On the journey, the mare had proved skittish and prone to bouts of unnecessary nerves, but Bán had sworn he could bring her safely through a thunderstorm if he had to and they had let him alone with her.

A cattle market occupied the flat plain before the dike. Beyond it the warriors of the Trinovantes waited in a row, all alike in the gorse-yellow cloaks, with burnished helms dull in the early light. Their shields were bronze with circular decorations and their harness mounts matched them. None bore spears but even at this distance Breaca could see the hilt of a sword projecting above the shoulder of each one. She scanned the line, seeking those she knew. Togodubnos was near the centre, recognizable by his tumble of black hair and the breadth of his shoulders. Amminios, red-haired and flashily mounted, was beside him. After that, they were all the same.

Caradoc pointed out his father. "The golden shield is his. To the left of Amminios." She had passed over the shield, thinking it bronze; in full sunlight, it would have been more impressive. She marked it in her mind so she would not forget.

Others were named whom she knew by reputation. Heffydd son of Eynd was the only one who mattered; the false dreamer who got his dreams from the Sun Hound and not from the gods. Airmid had watched him all the way down the slope, but distantly, in the way that said she had been dreaming and had not yet come back to the present. She was already dressed for the longer journey beyond this one; the shield hanging from her saddle was the plain hide of the dreamer and her cloak the hearth-smoke grey of Mona. The brooch at her shoulder was cast in the shape of the serpent-spear, and Breaca wore its partner. That much remained between them.

They rode through the market, doing their best to maintain order. Breaca, as bearer of the royal line, took the lead as she had done since they entered Trinovantian territory. Caradoc, as the returning son, rode beside her. After them, a long column of warriors, dreamers and seamen snaked behind, the order defined by complex rules of rank and status. It had taken a long time to assemble a company that was both safe and balanced. Warriors from all over Eceni lands had put their names forward for the journey— some to honour Breaca as she led her first formal delegation, some for the sake of the Roman, most because they wished to see Cunobelin's dun and this was their best opportunity. The elders had made the decisions in the end, picking those who would acquit themselves well in case of danger and yet be a credit to their people if there were peace.

It was not a peacetime delegation. Macha, Airmid and Luain were the only dreamers, Bán the only child. The rest were adult warriors and most had seen battle. Cunobelin's men waited ahead of them. In any confrontation it is easier to let the enemy come to you; better still if you are organized and they are not. Breaca looked down at the calf pens and wicker hurdles hemming her in on either side and swore, with feeling.

"We can form the line when we're clear of here. He has left you room." Caradoc rode easily with one hand resting on his thigh. He was facing away from her, nodding acknowledgement to muted cries of recognition from the crowd, and he spoke without turning his head. From a distance, were it seen at all, it could be taken that he spoke to the small group of sheep traders that crowded his horse's flanks.

She followed his lead, glancing outwards to left and right, nodding at those who hailed her. "I'll call the others up as soon as we're all through. If any of us gets through. Gods curse these people. Why do they all have to get in the way?"

Caradoc grinned at a man selling ale and signalled that he had nothing to trade. "It may be they have orders to do so. This is the first time I have known a cattle fair to be called before the first day of summer." A he-goat ran at the walls of his pen, splitting the wood, and the dun colt shied at the noise of it. He fought to bring it under control.

Breaca said, "If the horses bolt, it will not look good."

"If the horses bolt, it will be taken as an excuse to attack." Caradoc laughed, breathlessly. He did not seem unhappy with the thought of battle. Seeing her, he sobered, biting his lip. "We must hope that your brother is handling his mare well."

"I am praying for it." Breaca turned back from a minor altercation with a potter and saw why her own horse had faltered. "We'll know soon if he isn't. That bull doesn't like horses."

Two men straddled the track in front of her, arguing over the price of a tall, blue roan bull. The animal had not wintered well; ribs and hipbones showed sharp-edged with no padding of fat or muscle to cushion them and the white tracks of scars showed where it had fought and, perhaps, not won. Its horns were the length of her forearm and gracefully curved. The tips tapered to fine points and had been capped in silver. It was not a decoration she knew but she had heard that the Romans marked their beasts thus for feast days.

"Does your father worship the bull?"

"My father worships power. If he believed a bull would lend it to him, he would take it, but that is not one of his. Say something pleasant. They think you're angry."

"They're right. But not with them." She smiled a false greeting to the handlers and edged the mare to the left, away from the loop of the horns. The bull eyed her malevolently. The mare jigged forward, snoring. A bawling calf, left alone in a pen built for many, lifted its tail and gave vent to a liquid jet of hot, sour faeces. In the pen beside it, a sow rooted at the wicker walls, endeavouring, with apparent success, to dig her way out. The smell was overpowering and the noise worse but the horses passed it and suddenly they were clear of the pens and had been neither gored nor goaded into unseemly action.

With her eyes on Cunobelin and her face set, Breaca lengthened the mare's stride, counting the paces as she walked across the plain; three forward: Macha and Eburovic were past the bull and safe; six: Luain mac Calma and Segoventos the Gaul came within reach. The latter was not a good horseman; she heard his curse and the chink of his harness mounts but nothing more. Nine: Airmid and— Nemain help them all—Dubornos with his excess of arm- bands and gaudy dress came within reach of the bull. Since leaving Eceni heartlands, he had placed himself on Airmid's left as if by right. If Breaca thought about that for too long, she would be too angry to think of anything else.

She smoothed the front of her tunic for something to do. She had not known, until that moment, how much of her rode three rows behind. Her mind counted the twelfth pace and Airmid was safely past the calf and the penned pig and riding in open land. Relief plumbed the depths of her, clouding her vision. She lost count of the strides and had to measure the gaps between tufts of grass or the fat, spread- ing cattle turds. The remaining seamen and warriors were all of a stature to handle their mounts. It was Bán, riding at the end, for whom she held her breath now.

Caradoc sensed it. Without turning, he said, "The mare is behaving better than she was in the forest. He has a spear's throw to go, maybe two. I'll tell you when he's through. Look to your right; someone brings you a gift."

Breaca looked down. A woman walked by her knee. A dark woollen cloak covered her hair and most of her face. Underneath it, she was young and had recently given birth. Milk stains darkened her tunic at both breasts although there was no sign of a child. The gift she offered was a slate- grey whelp of less than weaning age. It squirmed blindly in her upturned palms. Breaca glanced behind her; to refuse it would be an insult but she had no intention at all of riding forward to meet her country's most powerful war leader cradling a puking, whining whelp on her lap. Airmid could have been trusted to take it but she was too far away, pushing her horse past a man herding a brace of ewes and lambs. No-one else was within reach.

Breaca leaned down. "Thank you. I am honoured, but I have nowhere to carry such a gift. If you could perhaps give it to—"

"I'll take it."

Surprisingly, Caradoc reined back the dun to ride behind her. Smiling shyly, the woman dropped back to greet him, or, perhaps, to engage him in proper talk. She spoke rapidly and her words were too fast to follow, exhorting, possibly, and admonishing. Her accent was highborn and did not accord with the quality of her dress. Breaca heard Caradoc's amused reply and the heavy sound of bronze tapping iron. Three strides on, the warrior was back at her side, bearing his gift and lacking his armband.

"Did you know her?" Breaca asked. The armband had been a gift from her father. It was worth more than any whelp.

"A little." His grin glittered more brightly than it had done, over a bedrock of sudden, unexplained anger. She had expected there to be undercurrents here—enmities, old feuds and loyalties of which she knew nothing—but the sight of them so readily exposed left her uneasy. She would have asked for an explanation but the sharp edge to his smile did not allow it. He was closed to her, as he had been on the headland, still wet from the sea.

Caradoc tucked the whelp into the crook of his elbow, wrapping it in a fold of his cloak. Warm and dark after the chill of the morning, it fell silent. "It's a good whelp," he said. "Odras is the last of the old royal line of the Trinovantes. She is niece to Togodubnos's mother through whom my father rules. She is known throughout the land for the quality of her hounds. Your brother will like this one when it grows. Just don't expect me to care for it if there's fighting."

"There will be no fighting. I will not allow it."

An oath sounded in Latin and she turned in time to see Bán's mare face the bull. The men had changed sides and the beast stood four square on the track, its head lowered so that the silver points were horizontal. The Roman, blessedly, had got past. He waited on the far side, giving advice in low Gaulish that was ignored by both men and boy. The bull-men had given up all pretence of trading; the coming sport was too good. At a prod from the larger of the two, the bull took a step forward and scored the ground with its horns. The silver bent at the ends, twisting inwards.

"Bán—" Breaca reached for her sword. She had never yet drawn it in anger. Her palm itched at the thought.

"No. Watch. He can do it."

Her brother laughed brightly and called something that she didn't hear to the Roman. The red mare spun on her hocks and sprang like a deer, passing over the scouring calf and into the pig pen. They paused for less than a heartbeat, only enough to raise a flurry of outraged squealing that drew eyes from the four corners of the market, and then the mare was out again onto clear land, and Bán was riding her neatly at a hand canter to join his sister. There were cheers from the less constrained, or less tactful, amongst the traders.

"Isn't she good?" He rode up to Breaca's right, the side of the dreamer. Airmid held back to let him through. "Do

you think they set it up for us to show what she can do?"
His eyes were alive, his smile brilliant. In many ways, he was
a mirror to Caradoc, lacking only the simmering anger.

"Assuredly." She tried to be sober, as befitted the
greater occasion, and failed. "Caradoc has been honoured
with a gift from his people. If you are good and do not
offend any more of the Sun Hound's prize swine, he may let
you have it."

They had left Hail behind for an assortment of good
reasons, not least of which was the fear that Amminios
would harm him, but the parting had not been easy. Bán saw
the whelp and his eyes grew round.

"It's a bitch," said Caradoc, lifting the edge of his cloak.
"You have a new mate for your foundation sire."

Bán's eyes grew wide. "Can I have her? Really?" He was
a child still. She forgot that sometimes.

"Later. If we survive the meeting. Just now, we have
something more important to do." Breaca looked left to
Caradoc. "Are you ready?"

"Of course. We are all ready."

"Good." She raised her arm above her head. Forty-two
riders spread out in a line on either side: seamen to the left,
dreamers to the right, warriors on either end. They moved in
something close to silence. She felt the hiss of their breathing
and the pressure of concentration. New bridles creaked and
harness mounts clashed mutely, but the curses and oaths of
practise were absent. For days they had worked through
this—on the meadow at the roundhouse, on the flat plains of
the horse lands and, later, on the open stretches before and
after the tracts of woodland that marked Trinovantian territory. She had planned it, remembering Togodubnos's arrival at

the roundhouse. Caradoc and the Roman had helped make it happen. Between them they had achieved something remarkable: A group of seamen who were not riders had learned to mesh with men and women who had ridden alone or in competition with others for all of their lives. Each of them had learned something, if only how to work as part of a team with those they despised. Even Dubornos had accepted his part in it. They lined up now with a precision and pride that made Breaca's heart ache and her hand clench on the reins.

"Go." The Roman spoke softly from further down the line. She dropped her arm to the horizontal, pointing forward, and sent the grey from a standing start to a full gallop. The entire line matched her pace. She felt the Roman pushing his gelding at the same time as Bán held back on the red mare and Caradoc tempered the dun. All three kept their noses level with the grey. As Togodubnos had once attempted to do with a smaller band in front of a deserted steading, she swept her people forward in a level line towards the warriors of the Trinovantes. At the last possible moment, she threw up her arm and called the halt.

It was good, possibly perfect. She reined in the grey opposite Togodubnos and not his father. The Sun Hound, lover of all things imperial, faced the Roman. Caradoc, smiling warmly, looked down from the height of the dun colt on Amminios. To his right, Bán sat taller than any of them and the red mare shone like the setting sun with the blue of his Eceni cloak making the sky about her. In the beginning, it was impossible to look elsewhere.

"Brother." Breaca addressed the man opposite as he had addressed her when he came to offer armed aid in their war against the Coritani.

Togodubnos acknowledged it, nodding. "Sister. What brings you here?"

He would know that; he would have known for days if not months. Trinovantian spies were everywhere. Nevertheless, he required a reply, given and heard in public.

Formally, she said, "The gods have seen fit to honour us with a number of shipwrecked seamen. It is the wish of our elders that they be delivered to a suitable trading ship bound for Gaul. We have pledged their safety until such time as they board ship. As you have spoken at our council on behalf of your father, we would ask your leave to pass beyond your gates and south to the sea river."

"And you return to us our brother, Caratacos." It was the first time she had heard the Gaulish rendering of the name. Togodubnos made it a statement, not a question, and a means not to answer her request.

Caradoc himself answered. "I was on the *Greylag*," he said, and they had known that, too. "I am alive only with the aid of Breaca and her family. They are, as you have long said, our close kin in all but name."

"Indeed."

"And I hear I have other kin—that you have sired a son. My congratulations."

He spoke lightly, with only the barest edge of the earlier glitter, but she was not alone in hearing the sting in the words. She held the grey still. It was the steady brown mare opposite her that flinched, and Amminios's bay. Togodubnos himself was good. Had she not known him before, she would not have seen the sudden brush of colour high on his cheeks, nor recognized the warning in his eyes.

Evenly he said, "Odras sends you her highest regards and

her apologies that she could not be present to greet you in person."

"I should think so, when she can ride better than the rest of you put together." His smile was tight and the mockery was directed inwards as much as out. "Nevertheless, I am honoured. And I trust your son is in better health than his late sister?"

It might have been a genuine question. Togodubnos took time to gather an answer. Another, harsher voice filled the void he had left. "He is very well. The succession is secured. You are free, therefore, to continue your career as a merchant seaman."

The words fell into the still air like a thunderclap, rocking through Breaca's chest, pushing the beat of her heart from its rhythm. Because she was of the royal line and the pride of her people rested more heavily on her than on the others, she made herself look left to their source, to the man whose name had been both a threat and a promise since her childhood: to Cunobelin, Hound of the Sun, guardian of his people, pitiless destroyer of his enemies, hawk of diplomacy and wolf of the trade routes.

"Greetings, princess." He had grey eyes, exactly like his youngest son, and they were laughing at her.

He was not a broad man—both Togodubnos and Heffydd, his dreamer, were broader—nor was he especially tall. His hair was a nondescript, late-harvest straw, streaked with the white badger stripes of age. His torc and his shield were of gold, intricately worked, and the bands arrayed up both arms were studded with pink coral and enamels in colours she had never seen. Beyond that he had not chosen to turn himself out with particular ostentation; Dubornos had outdressed him without effort and Bán was by far the better mounted. What he had was a presence that allowed no room for manoeuvre, that inspired not so much fear as a certainty that his will was law and could not be gainsaid; that she was nothing and he was the world. Like his stronghold, he was everything she had been told and more. *It will be bigger than anything you have ever imagined.* How could the man who had taken it by force of character and held it for thirty years without recourse to war have been anything else? And he had called her princess.

She gave the salute of one royal line to another. "Cunobelin. Sire of the Catuvellauni and caregiver to the Trinovantes. Your presence honours us." It was the most formal greeting she knew. She spoke in the neutral dialect with which Togodubnos had opened, forsaking the broader vowels and softer consonants of her homelands.

"No more than yours honours us." He smiled now with more than his eyes. Like Caradoc, it changed his being and the air around him so that the sun grazing her skin seemed warmer. "We have a ship in dock at the southern harbour. She has neither the speed nor the oarage of the *Greylag* but she is believed to be a good vessel none the less. We would be honoured if your mariners would accept her as our gift."

He means to give them a ship? As a gift? A whole ship?

She was speechless and doubtless meant to be so. Segoventos was well within earshot; half the meadow was within earshot. She heard the rattle of harness mounts and the jig of a hard-held horse towards the far right-hand end of her line where the Gaul sat his pied cob. Opposite her, and out of his father's eye, Togodubnos inclined his head and raised it again in an unmistakable nod. She could have loved him for that.

Raising her voice, she said, "I am sure the *Greylag*'s master would be overwhelmed with gratitude at such a gift."

It was the right answer. The glitter of excess fell from the morning. At her side, she heard Caradoc's soft snort of amusement. His father simply nodded.

"Good." Still smiling, if more thoughtfully, the Sun Hound swung his horse. "The ship has not yet been named. She is in dock at the deep river berth. We will visit her later to ensure that she is acceptable to those who will sail her. Perhaps then they would like to name her. Before that, my people have prepared a meal. You will accept our hospitality and join us?"

That, too, was not a question. Breaca bowed her head. With consummate dignity, she said, "We would be honoured."

She had expected Rome, or Gaul, in counterfeit. She had prepared to be offered wine and to refuse it, to be faced with fish and waterfowl and other of Nemain's beasts and to refuse those, too; to be served by slaves and to refuse their service. She had done what she could, with the help of Caradoc, Luain mac Calma and, latterly, the Roman, to understand what it was to eat from a single platter, leaning sideways on a bench raised from the floor, and had readied herself to eat with apparent enjoyment the fruits and vegetables, sauces and spices of another continent. She had seen the vulgarity of southern jewellery and was braced to see it reproduced in the hangings and carvings, the pottery and the dress of those who greeted her.

What she was given was home—a magnificent, understated, perfectly replicated version of home.

The great-house of the Sun Hound could have been

that of the Eceni, had they chosen to build it with the door facing south and yellow hangings on the walls, and to have only the sign of one dreamer carved on the doorposts. Because she needed to find fault, she decided that the carvings of bears were oppressive and oddly inept, as if drawn from the outside by one who feared what he saw, rather than from the inside with the understanding and soul-mingling of the dream. She watched Airmid and saw her note it, and saw her, too, pick through the meal with care, testing and tasting for other evidence of failure. There was none to be found. Everything else was in order, and more than that. The Sun Hound displayed his wealth with restrained good taste, letting the quality and quantity of the fare speak for him. At the end of a good harvest, the Eceni could have prepared a meal of this size for numbers such as this but not in early spring, at the end of the hardest winter in the grandmothers' memory. They were given oatcakes and honey— *honey*, in spring—and malted barley and good, fresh ale that had not soured with storage and a whole roasted boar with a bull calf for those who preferred it and salted hams that had not yet dried. There was more meat than she would have liked but it was served as a courtesy and they would have done the same, if they could, had the Sun Hound paid visit to the roundhouse. The only clear difference was the absence of women. Togodubnos's mother was there, a quiet, watchful woman with the height and dark colouring of her son, and a younger woman who fawned on Amminios, but no others.

They finished on more ale and a story from Heffydd, the dreamer, involving a young hero shipwrecked on a foreign shore, who returned home with new companions. The mariners liked it, particularly the vivid, overblown description of the new ship granted by the overjoyed father. Caradoc sat it out impassively. At the end, he stood up and left the room while the others were still complimenting the singer. Presently, the seamen were invited to leave the circle and join in small clusters to discuss trading with certain of the merchants. Segoventos bloomed visibly and his voice swelled to fill the roof space. Dice and a handful of gaming boards were brought out for those not immediately involved in the negotiations. Breaca turned to find Cunobelin at her elbow.

"They will be well here for a while. We will visit the ship later when the torpor of the meal has passed. Meanwhile, the gods have held the good weather for us. There is wind, but no rain as yet. Perhaps you would care to visit our trading stalls and workshops? Our people would be grateful to meet you in person."

"We would be honoured. Thank you." She said it automatically; the formalities of conversation had come more easily as the meal progressed. Glancing round, she counted off those who could be relied upon to accompany her. Macha and Eburovic were nearby, enmeshed in an animated, if vacuous, conversation that allowed them to listen to others. Luain mac Calma was arguing with Heffydd; from the far side of the circle she could see the tension in him. The Trinovantian dreamer was subdued but not overtly angry. Airmid sat with Bán playing knucklebones, neither of them paying attention to the game. Further away, 'Tagos and Dubornos had been seduced by the gaming boards. Already, 'Tagos had laid his dagger on the ground at his side as a wager. She considered them, thinking. The Sun Hound grinned. "Let them stay. They will lose nothing of worth but their pride. In any case, you are safe here, or if not, two untried warriors will make no difference."

It was what she had thought, repeated exactly as if she had spoken it aloud. The skin prickled down her spine and the mellow aftertaste of the meal soured in her mouth. She wished she had drunk less ale. The Sun Hound raised a brow. "The young people are busy. I think we need make no special exit. Caradoc is outside and the grooms hold your horses, waiting. Unless you would prefer to walk?"

"The Eceni very rarely prefer to walk," she said, tightly. Airmid would have recognized the edge to her smile. "If they are ready, we should not keep them waiting."

They made a small party: her family, including Airmid and Luain, accompanied by Cunobelin and his youngest son. Caradoc had relaxed since the end of the dreamer's tale. His voice had mellowed and the savage glitter was gone from his smile. Sometime in the space between the meeting at the gate and the start of the meal, he had passed the hound whelp into someone's care and regained his armband. She took care to comment on neither. He rode easily along the path, pointing out the things that were new or different: the layer of ashes strewn across the path to soak up the mud and make it easier underfoot; the line of ancient oaks left behind from the days when the dreamers held sway; the river in the far distance and the flat-bottomed barges that ferried merchants and their wares down to the trading ships moored in the deeper docks to the south. She studied him as they rode, seeking the small signs of danger she had come to know. He had seemed relaxed like this before the river race, and on the morning of the elder council, and neither time had it reflected the reality underneath. He glanced sideways at her, amused, and broke off from his description of barges. "Have you ever played the Warrior's Dance?"

He asked it in Gaulish, for no obvious reason; everyone around them spoke it well and if they were overheard it would not give them privacy. Still, she answered as best she could in the same language. "The board game your brothers were playing when we left the great-house? No. Gunovic plays it but I have never tried. I am told it takes great subtlety."

"It can, although not everyone plays it that way. Togodubnos, for instance, wields his pieces as weapons, marching them down the board like horses running down defeated warriors. Amminios can spend all day playing as if he is moving the pieces for the feel of them in his hand or the beauty of the patterns they make on the squares. One could almost forget he was playing to win."

"But he does win?"

"Of course. Every time. He is unstoppable—like a butcher wreaking slaughter in the killing pens. It is painful to watch. If he loses, it is only to lull his opponent into a greater gamble."

"Does he win even against you?"

They rounded a corner and met the wind face on. Caradoc narrowed his eyes against the sting of it, looking out past the workshops to the ruffled ribbon of the northern river. "The Ordovices have a saying: 'A man gains no honour who plays at killing.'" He said it without rancour. "I have not played with my brother since I won my first spear. Before that, yes, he won against me from the day I was old enough to play until the day I was old enough to put an end to the games." He smiled at her, brightly. "Competition is heavily encouraged in the court of the Sun Hound," he said. "Losing is not. My brother does not take well to it." He had changed his language, sliding easily into her own tongue and carrying it north to the broadest vowels and most lyrical form—the one least likely to be understood by his father. "The one to observe is my sire. He is the master but he does not play with a board. Watch him. It is an instruction in the dance of life."

"I will."

They rode on in silence. The wind blustered in from the side, clearing the thick dregs of ale from her head. The path to the trading stands was straight and lined on both sides by workshops and trading stores. Breaca counted four separate forges, marked by the heat of their fires and the paler colour of their smoke. In between them stood leatherworkers, potters, weavers and brewers, traders of salt and, yes, merchants offering the spices and sauces and olives and wine of which she had been warned. None of them was pressed on her and she was spared the discourtesy of refusing.

They stopped at the forges as they passed. At the first, the smith offered her a dagger with a stone in Eceni blue inlaid on the cross-piece and a dolphin leaping on the pommel, and she accepted. The second remarked on the serpent-spear brooch at her shoulder, which she had made. She would not give it away, but offered to come back and cast one similar in his workshop. The third made much of her torc and, on finding that Eburovic had fashioned it, insisted her father remain at his forge to discuss methods for drawing gold and perhaps to engage in some practical experiment. Cunobelin, who was required to approve the visit, gave his consent without demur. Shortly afterwards, Macha was similarly seduced by a weaver who remarked on the fine stuff of her tunic and then Airmid by a woman bearing a small child whose urgent need for vervain was all too apparent. Luain mac Calma went with her, to help in the healing.

Soon they were four: Breaca and Caradoc, Bán and Cunobelin. None or all of it could have been orchestrated, and there was nothing to do but nod and smile and listen as the Sun Hound demonstrated the overwhelming wealth of his kingdom.

The fourth forge was set back from the path on the other side from the rest. A slight, blond boy with astonishing blue eyes stood ready to take the reins of their horses. Cunobelin dismounted and threw him the reins as if he were no more than a hitching-post. To Breaca, he said, "This is the mint. We strike our coins here. If you would care to join me inside? I believe you would find it interesting."

The one to observe is my sire. He is the master but he does not play with a board.

"Thank you. I would be honoured." She slid down from the grey and passed the reins with a nod of thanks to the horse-boy. The mare balked at the strange hand on her bridle and had to be calmed. Cunobelin waited beside her, his hand on her arm. His features were clear and free of guile and she could see how he had won an entire kingdom by charm alone. They were at the door when he turned back to his son.

"Caratacos? You, too, would find it of interest."

Caradoc shook his head, smiling. With perfect courtesy, he said, "I doubt that, Father. I have never been one for the use of coins. They lose their value too easily."

"Nevertheless, Heffydd assures me these are different."

"Heffydd? A man who knows me well." His brows arched to his hairline. "Nevertheless, in this he is wrong."

"I think not. And it would upset him to hear that you think so."

"Indeed?"

Breaca had the sense of watching hounds fight for pack precedence, or deer clash horns in the rut, except that, here, the circling and snarling and gouging of turf was done with minor inflections in tone and the dip or rise of a brow. The Sun Hound, it seemed, had won this particular round although she could not have said why. After the briefest of pauses, Caradoc swung his leg forward over the dun colt's neck and dropped lightly to the ground. Bán moved in to take the colt before the horse-boy could grab the reins.

The Sun Hound ducked under the lintel and led the way into the forge. The interior was dark after the afternoon sun. Breaca let her eyes rest on the warm edges of the fire until she could see and then squinted past it to the corners. A smith stood near the back wall, a featureless shape in the gloom, invisible but for the scorched, fire-puckered frame of his apron. The fire itself was white-hot in the centre; the man had been working his bellows and had only recently stopped. A mould stood ready but she could see no crucible of molten metal. The smith stepped forward.

"Now, my lord?"

"If you please."

Grains of gold, ready weighed, were already seated in the mould. She had never seen the process of casting coins, nor believed it useful to learn; true traders knew the value of their goods without the need for gold as intermediary. For the sake of form, and because it was the reason she had been invited, she made a show of studying the tongs and the way the smith angled the bellows to draw the heat of the fire across the tip of the mould. In doing so, she used the time to watch Caradoc and his father and to feel the pressures growing between them. She had not been disarmed and the smith did not have the look of a fighting man. If it came to it, they were two against one, three if she counted Bán, and their horses would fight with them. The smith drew his mould from the fire. She eased a step backwards, closer to the door.

"It is done. Now we must stamp the two faces of each."

The mould was cooling fast. At a tap, nine discs of shining metal fell out to scorch the workbench. The smith lined them up on his block and moved across swiftly, placing a stamp on each and tamping down with his hammer. He changed stamps for each side, creating different faces. The metal glowed, hotly. Wood smoke added to the drifting threads of burned metal so that she felt more at home than she had in days. It was not a safe sensation. Breaca focused on the fire and was glad of the hiss and fizzle of steam as the smith doused his work.

"They are complete, my lord." The smith stood back, moulding to the shadows. Nine parts of the sun flared on his workbench.

They were coins, nothing more. Breaca had seen a few; Dubornos had an armband with one set in the face of it. The horse worked on its surface was childlike and she had not paid it great attention. These, however, were more weapons than coins. Cunobelin and his son leaned over to look, each affecting more interest in the gold than in the other.

The smith had expected more than silence. "It may be difficult to see them clearly," he said. "Here, let me set the torches." Light flared in the darkness. The smith was a thinner man than she had realized and more nervous. The acid bite of his sweat sharpened the air.

"Am I right in thinking they are not all the same?" Caradoc made it such a question as a man might ask his friends on seeing a strange flower bloom at dusk—pointless, but polite.

The question was not for the smith but the man was too nervous to notice. "If my lord please, there are three different designs, as commanded by my lord your father."

Caradoc said "*Three?*" rather sharply, and the smith knew he had overstepped the mark. Cunobelin sighed.

"Thank you, craftsman. You may go."

The smith left, hurriedly. He did not look like a man whose worst hurdle was behind him. He was not, however, Breaca's greatest concern. Caradoc was leaning back on the forging block by the workbench, his legs crossed at the ankles and his thumbs hooked in his belt. "Why three?" he asked. "I thought all lands were one land and all coins one coin."

Cunobelin arranged himself on the far side of the fire. He was more visible than the smith had been but only barely so. His voice rolled out of the darkness. "I am not as young as I was and I have three sons. It is time for them to begin to administer their own lands. For this they will need their own coins."

"Really? And how long have your sons had lands of their own?" He was discussing his birthright and he made it sound like a bull, or a dray horse of limited value.

Cunobelin said, "They have none as yet, but on my death each of my sons will require a territory that befits him. I have acquired some lands south of the great river amongst our cousins the Atrebates. Amminios will have those. The trading rights on the southern ports are his, plus the farms he has already inherited from his mother's Gaulish kin. He has always had more interest in trading than either of his brothers and he will do well by this. To mark it, Heffydd has placed a boat on one side of the coin and Amminios's name on the other, with my barley sheaf above it."

He turned the coin over. The torchlight flickered on the crude image of a boat, with many oars and two masts. Had Silla drawn the *Greylag*, it might have looked like this.

Cunobelin moved to the next coin. Tapping the ear of barley on the upper surface, he said, "As the eldest of my sons, Togodubnos is heir to the lands of the Catuvellauni." He turned the coin over. "From his mother, he inherits also the leadership of the Trinovantes. It is my wish that these two peoples remain together, and I believe he is the one to sustain this. His sons will have it after him, through Odras. Her symbol is the moon. I have put it near his name, so that there is no confusion."

Breaca knew Caradoc better than she had before; the complex layers of his character were more visible to her than they had been on the headland after the shipwreck, or even in the elder council. Nothing changed outwardly, there was no defining frown or catch to his breath that she could have pointed to and said, "This is what betrays you," but it was clear that his father had landed a telling blow and that it was not the dividing of land that had done it.

On the surface, the grey eyes washed across hers, warmly. Caradoc smiled and nodded genially to his father and said, "I trust you sought Odras's permission before you used her mark?"

"Of course. Heffydd dreamed it and we took her the outlines before the stamp was cut. She had just given birth to her son, and was glad of this acknowledgement."

"She would have been." Caradoc picked one of the coins from the workbench and flipped it high in the air. It tumbled, spinning, onto his palm. He held it faceup and both Breaca and Cunobelin could see the ship that was Amminios's sign. "I hear the child is to be named Cunomar, Hound of the Sea. He, too, will need a boat one day."

It was the only weapon he had and it drew no blood. Unimpressed, the Sun Hound said, "You gave your armband for his name? You should have asked me and I would have told you it for nothing. I had thought you were paying for the whelp. It will be a good one, worth the price. Odras still has the best eye for hounds."

It did not seem likely that the armband had been given as the price of anything, but rather as the gift of one long absent to the woman whom he most values. And then it had been returned. Breaca remembered the warmth in Caradoc's voice as he had addressed the young woman in the marketplace and the clash with his brother afterwards and suddenly it was hard not to walk out to fresh air and freedom, away from the complications of others' lives. She held her place at the doorpost, waiting. They had seen only two of the three coins and the last was the one that mattered most.

Caradoc reached towards the remaining coins. The fire had died down and the metal shone less brightly. He lifted one and held it in his clenched fist, not yet looking at the surface. Softly, he said, "You have no need to make a coin for me, Father. You know they have no value in the lands of the Ordovices."

"Nevertheless, a son of mine has value wherever he goes. And his mother's memory must be honoured. These have your name on one side and the symbol of the war hammer on the other. I am told that Ellin of the Ordovices had no daughters and that you are her heir in the west until such time as another woman is chosen to replace you."

His mother's memory . . .

The one to observe is my sire. Watch him. It is an instruction in the dance of life.

The fire had sucked in all the air and burned it. Breaca's fingers gouged into the wood of the doorpost. She bit her lip to keep from crying out.

Caradoc stood quite still, staring at the coin lying flat on his palm as if by doing so he held on to his place in the world. "There is news I should know of my mother?" he asked. His voice was deeper and softer and shorn of all humour.

"I'm sorry, but it is better that you learn it here than outside in front of others. Word came to us from the west only recently. Your mother is dead. She was taken by a spear in battle against the Silures and died with the end of winter. It was a warrior's death."

The silence held them tight. A log shifted slightly on the fire. Outside, the rain, which had been falling for some time, began to beat more heavily on the roof tiles. Inside, they stood in a place of utter quiet, broken only by the soft sounds of breathing. The Sun Hound leaned forward a little, moving into the light, the better to see and be seen. His features displayed just the right proportions of sorrow and dignified regret—the mix of a man who has lost a woman he loved, of a war leader who must maintain the dignity of his station and of a father who cares for his son's welfare.

Only knowing the nature of the game was it possible to see deeper, and Breaca was not certain she knew enough to see it all. Cunobelin had not done this on the spur of the moment; coin moulds are not drawn and cut in a morning. He must have known of the death since the end of winter and he could readily have sent someone north to the Eceni lands with news. He had not kept it a secret until now without a reason. In this dance, the final winner was the one who found that reason first.

"Who else knows this?" asked Caradoc, quietly. His thinking was faster than hers and there were other things at stake. Odras had told him the name of her son and the identity of its father but not the news of his mother; he would need to know why she had not spoken.

"Heffydd knows. No-one else. The messenger who brought the news is dead."

Gods. The thought rocked Breaca as nothing else had done. *He has killed to keep this silent.*

"Who?" They were not playing games now. The layers of pretence had curled back like bark from a birch log, laid wet on a fire. Cunobelin was frowning and watchful. Caradoc stood upright, his fingers splayed on the forging block. Strands of hair, dark with sweat, clung to his brow. He asked his question again, spacing the words, giving each one due weight. "What was the name of the rider who brought the message?"

His father said, swiftly, "It was a woman. One of your mother's sister's kin. She died in a fall from her horse as she was returning with my death-gifts and news of your safety. The warriors of my honour guard who had accompanied her rode on to complete her journey."

Breaca thought, *I have seen Caradoc ride. The Ordovices fall from their horses no more than do the Eceni.* And then, *His father has oath-sworn men in the land of the Ordovices. Why?*

Caradoc said merely, "Her name?"

"Cygfa. Her mark was the swan."

The swan was a powerful dreaming; the bird carried word from the gods of light and sun to Nemain of the waters, and those who dreamed it were favoured by both. By itself, the name meant nothing to Breaca and she regretted that she had not listened harder to the kin-deeds of the Ordovices when they were told by the fire. Caradoc closed his eyes and she believed that he prayed. The firelight played on his cheeks, cutting deeper shadows in the hollows beneath the bones. The spark of danger was gone from him and it seemed certain that his father had just made the killing move. Time, then, for the Eceni to enter the game.

Letting go of the doorpost, Breaca stepped forward into the circle of torchlight. She played the game openly, after the manner of Togodubnos. In this place, it was not safe to do otherwise.

"Why did you tell him now?" she asked. "It would surely have been possible sooner."

She was a guest. She could appear naïve and could display, even, a little righteous anger. The guest-laws limited how he could answer.

The Sun Hound turned, frowning. He had counted her an observer, not a player. "My lady," he said, "to receive news like this, I felt it best that my son be amongst his own people."

Caradoc laughed, harshly. The smith had left the bellows beside the fire. The young warrior pumped the handles, raising the heat in the core. With his face turned away from her, he said, "He had to tell me himself to make the right impact. He needed me malleable and open to direction. My father has dreams that one day the house of the Sun Hound will extend from the eastern shore to the west and that his grandsons will rule it together. He wishes me now to ride west and take leadership of my people."

My people, not *my mother's people*. It was not said by accident. The fire lit him harshly from below. His face became a skull, flaring with the gods' light. His hair, this once, was not the brightest part of him. He looked up at his father. "Is that not so?"

"Close enough. Will you do it?"

"No, and if I did, they would not accept me. You forget that the people of the war hammer pass the line of their rule through the women, as do the Eceni. It is not a question of a man stepping in to take over before they choose another woman; it will be done already. Cygfa has younger sisters who will have succeeded her, and even if she had none, I am your son and I carry the blood-guilt for her death. From the moment I cross the border, I am dead."

"That is not so. The woman died in an accident. My men will attest to it."

"Your men, I am sure, will say what they have been ordered to say, but faced with the dreamer's death even they may find it in them to tell the truth. If you are guilty, I am guilty. It is the law."

Breaca said, "Caradoc, you were with us through the winter. You had no idea what was happening and no means to stop it. Luain carries the authority of Mona. He will absolve you of the blood-guilt."

It might not have been the right thing to say but she had witnessed Caradoc's sense of honour, and it was too easy to imagine him riding west to pay the price in his father's stead for an act he could not have prevented.

"Thank you. We may have need of that." Speaking to her, Cunobelin said, "Caradoc misreads my dream. I am not so enamoured of Roman ways that I think only of grandsons ruling. If the Ordovices pass their line through the women, that is their choice. But they will still need a man to sire their daughters. I may have only sons, but there is no reason why I should not have granddaughters."

Caradoc laughed, openly. "So I am to be a studhorse for hire to the highest bidder? I don't think so. Togodubnos may accept that and Odras may have allowed it, but the women of the war hammer choose their own men and I doubt they would choose me even were I there to make the offer."

Three of the nine coins were his. He scooped them up now and dropped them, one at a time, like falling sunlight, into the white-hot core of the fire. They held their shape for a moment and she saw the war hammer, rendered better than the ship or the horse had been, and the outline of a head drawn from the side in the Roman fashion. It lengthened as the coin melted and then, with one last pump of the bellows, burst into flames. The air was filled once more with the bite of burning metal. Breaca sneezed.

Caradoc pushed himself away from the fire. His composure had returned, however thinly. He addressed his father with the formality of a singer in the place of the elders. "Thank you for your news. I will leave it to you to pass it on to my brothers and . . . those others who might wish to know. I will discuss my position with the dreamer from

Mona. If Breaca is correct, I will accept his absolution. I have no wish to die early, nor by that manner. But I will not return to the Ordovices. Cygfa's sisters will make their own choice when the time comes to bear children. I will have no part in it."

"You would become landless, without kin?" It was said baldly, the ultimate threat.

"Yes, if the gods will it." In a gesture as clear as any in the convoluted figure they had danced, Caradoc stepped past Breaca towards the door. To his father, he bowed. "With your leave, and that of Segoventos, I will pursue my career as a merchant seaman, as you advised me." His smile mocked. "You have, after all, just given us a boat."

In the stunned silence that followed, he looked out of the doorway and turned back frowning. "Bán's gone," he said to Breaca. "And the horses."

CHAPTER 13

The weather was not good. A light rain began to fall shortly after Breaca and the others ducked under the low lintel of the coin forge. The door-skin fell into place behind them and blocked the warmth of the fire. Bán reined the red mare back under the shelter of an aging, fire-struck oak tree, tugging the dun colt after him. The horse-boy joined them soon after, squatting down on the edge of the track where the mud was least and his tunic would not stain. They sat for a while, not speaking. Bán thought of his new hound whelp and what he might do with her. She was special, a prize worth five days' uncomfortable riding, more tangible and therefore more valuable than the look in Amminios's eyes when he had seen the red mare.

Bán had seen the bitch who was the dam, and that was very good because it let him see how well she would turn out. It had happened in the morning, shortly after they had arrived. They had been walking towards the dining hall when Caradoc had taken him aside and given him the whelp, pointing out a wicker-walled hut in which the dam was likely kept. He had been right; the hound bitch lay inside on a bed of fine straw and her pups stumbled and play-fought around her. She was an elderly bitch but not too old and her milk ran well. The whelp, when returned to the bed, had found its feet and pushed its way through her litter-mates to the teats. It took after its dam; both the colour of aged slate with a scattering of white hairs along the flanks and a white flash at the chest. The head was good and broad and the ears well set on top of it. The dam had a rough, thorn-defeating coat and the whelp showed the first signs of it in the bristle around her muzzle. She was not Hail, but she would be an excellent brood bitch for later; better than the young brindle he had traded at the horse fair who had proved good on the hunt but barren to the dog. He had been about to pick up the whelp to look in her mouth and check that she was whole when the door had opened suddenly. The hound bitch had raised her head and thumped her tail on the ground in greeting.

Bán drew his hand back from the straw and turned to see his visitor. The woman on the threshold had recently given birth but she was slim again and she held herself well. She had black hair that hung past her shoulders and wide, oak-brown eyes. Her hair was braided in a way he did not recognize, she wore rings on three fingers and the cut of her tunic showed white skin at her shoulders. She was the first woman he had seen, barring Arosted's daughter, who was not of the Eceni and he made an effort not to stare. She came in and crouched at the head of the hound bitch and spoke to her, warmly, as he might with Hail.

"I brought back the whelp," said Bán. His presence needed some explanation.

"I know." Her voice was smooth and flowed over him the way Airmid's did. The whelp had sucked itself to sleep and lay mouthing at the nipple with white milk dribbling from the corner of its mouth. The woman reached in and picked it up. The pup squirmed lazily at her touch but did not wake—a sign of good handling.

"You are of the Eceni?" she asked. "The boy with the red mare?"

"Yes." If it was a label, it was a good one. With luck Amminios would have heard it.

"Togodubnos told me of you. He said you had a good hound already."

"Thank you. I have. But we have need of a good brood bitch to go with him."

"Of course. One always needs a good brood bitch for the hound. She doesn't always have to be good at the hunt." Her smile was tight and showed fine, white teeth. Had she been Eceni, Bán would have thought he heard irony in her answer and strands of other, more bitter things beneath it, but she was Trinovantian and he was not certain. He said nothing and the moment passed.

The whelp was persuaded to wake. She stood at the edge of the straw, blinking. One of her siblings took it as provocation and fell on her, growling ferociously. She threw off the torpor and fought back with commendable courage. They fell apart presently and both wandered off to find others to spar with.

"She is a good whelp," said Bán. "Stronger than the others."

"She is the best I have ever bred. Tell Caradoc that. And return this to him." The woman straightened her arm and drew a band from above her elbow. Holding it out, she said, "Give him my thanks. Tell him I mean no disrespect, but too many will notice if he is seen without it and as many will know where it came from if they see it on my arm."

The band was twin to the one Bán wore above his own elbow. His father had melted down three of his own and others collected from the Eceni warriors to garner enough bronze to cast a simple band for his family and each of their guests. It was something to unite them, more tangible than the quality of the horses, and the mariners had taken them up as a badge to be worn with pride. Bán had not considered that they might be used for barter, or that one might become a message in its own right. He took the thing and fitted it on his right arm, which had no decoration.

"Caradoc shall have it," he said. He had not needed to add that he would make the transfer covertly. That much was obvious, together with the fact that he had been trusted to do it well. The weight of it pressed on him, pleasantly.

The return of the band had been achieved as the warriors and the mariners milled around the midden before the start of the meal. Bán had joined them, slipping between Curaunios, the ship's mate, and Caradoc, and it had been easy in all the swirl of cloaks and tunics to return the band. The grin and the clap on the shoulder and the warmth of shared secrecy sustained him through the meal. It was coming to Bán, slowly, that he liked Caradoc a lot and that his approval was worth more than that of most men. He had begun to dream of travelling west, to the land of the Ordovices, of taking and passing their warrior tests—after those of the Eceni—and being pledged to Caradoc in the way Breaca was. The sharing of the whelp between them had been a step along the way and it had left him buzzing with an excitement that the rain did not dampen.

Sitting in the rain with the horses, he had been considering the journey west when the smith emerged from the forge. The man was ill, clearly; his skin was the colour of old tallow and his eyes had the fixed, unseeing quality of a cornered deer. But he was not open to the offer of help, nor did he seem prepared to stay and talk of what was happening inside. When the horse-boy hailed him by name, he flinched as if struck and sprinted away from them to vanish amongst the huddle of smaller, less tidy workshops that flanked the track. Watching his departing back, Bán considered the possibilities and decided on action.

"Here." He slid down from the mare and passed the reins to the horse-boy. "I'm going inside. Breaca and Caradoc might need help."

The child stared at him blankly. Bán said it again, pointing, and took a step towards the door of the forge. The boy fell on him, grabbing at his tunic with both hands, gabbling in a frantic, incomprehensible patois. His gestures made more sense than his words. One of them, or both, would die if the door-flap were lifted.

"That's not true." Bán prised the clutching fingers from his forearms. Some of the words sounded Gaulish. In that language, speaking slowly, he said, "I am a guest. I can go where I wish."

"No." The possibility of common understanding calmed the lad. A measure of terror left his eyes. In stilted Gaulish, he said, "The Sun Hound will not permit it. You may not go inside."

"My sister is in there, and my friend. They may be in trouble. I have a duty to help them."

"No." The boy could not have been more than eight but he was fierce for his age. His fingers gripped with the strength of one much older and his mouth was set firm. "The smith was the only one in the forge when we came. If he has been dismissed it is because they wish to be alone."

"You mean Cunobelin wishes to be alone."

"It is the same thing." The boy was very blond, paler than Caradoc or any of the southern Gaulish mariners, and his eyes were an intense, vibrant blue. He smiled, tentatively, offering consolation. "Your sister is armed, your friend also. If there is trouble, you will hear it. Besides, the young lord is a warrior like no other. Even his father would not attack him without other warriors at his back."

It was true. Bán had forgotten that Caradoc's reputation would have preceded him, particularly here. He relaxed and, after a moment, the lad calmed and withdrew his hand. "We will wait here," he said. He sat down on the grass by the feet of Cunobelin's horse and, reaching up, pulled Bán with him. "My name is Iccius. My people are the Belgae. You are Eceni?"

"Yes." Bán edged in under the shelter of the red mare's belly. "I am Bán mac Eburovic, also known as harehunter." His belt buckle was cast in the image of a running hare. The elder grandmother had made it for him. He loosened it to show it off.

The boy admired it, shyly. "And this mare, she is yours?" The question was tentative, as if the mere suggestion was ridiculous.

"Yes. She was Luain's guest-gift to my father after the shipwreck of the *Greylag*. Eburovic passed her on to me."

It was a long story and it had to be told from the begin-ning, with interruptions for Iccius's wide-eyed questions. The rain fell more heavily as it progressed and they both moved further under the shelter of the horses. Even so, by the end of it, they were drenched, the horses with them. Rain ran in a continuous stream from the mare's hocks. It dripped under her belly and spilled in sheets onto Bán's hair and shoulders. Wiping the water from his eyes, he consid-ered the welfare of his mare, his harness and his new friend, in that order. He leaned over and tapped the Belgic boy on the shoulder.

"How far to the stables?" he asked. "We should get the horses in before the saddles are ruined."

The lad gasped. "No! We—I—cannot leave . . ." He gestured towards the forge.

"Not even if I asked you to take me? I am a guest. I might get lost. Is it not your duty to direct me?" It would have been so in Eceni lands, but then, in Eceni lands, no child would have been left out in the rain holding another man's horses.

"No." Iccius was emphatic. "But you can go. I can tell you the way."

Bán knew the way; that had not been the point. He chewed his lip, considering the options. Thunder rang over-head and the mare sighed, shifting her weight onto her other hip. The gods spoke, occasionally, in ways even he could hear. Grinning, he lifted his shoulder in an exaggerated shrug. "If you have to stay here, then I should stay, too," he said. "We should keep each other company. And the rain might pass soon."

"It might."

Neither of them believed it.

Bán reached into his tunic and pulled out the small calf's-hide bag that Airmid had given him after the meal. "We could play knucklebones," he offered, "if you know how to play?"

"Of course. Everyone knows that."

The lad was nimble-fingered and had a quick mind. Bán was losing the second game when he heard footsteps on the path. The tread was less measured than the Sun Hound's but had a similar cadence. He looked up, blinking the wet from his eyes. His gaze passed over a tunic dyed a deep purple that appeared to be running slightly in the rain and a cloak of brilliant Trinovantian yellow. The armbands were gold, inlaid with coral but not overly gaudy. The hair hanging in sodden ropes at the shoulders was red, darkened to the colour of dead oak by the rain. With a tightening foreboding, Bán craned his neck beyond the belly of his horse. The man crouched down, bringing his head level so that Bán looked into eyes the colour of snakeskin and a smile that haunted his dreams. It was Amminios and he was laughing.

"I thought I might find you here." He jerked his head back in the direction of the forge. "They'll be in there arguing for ever. It's my father's way of ensuring they're not overheard. You don't have to stay out in the rain and wait for them." He was wetter than they were and he had walked from the great-house to find them. His tone was conciliatory, almost conspiratorial, as if they were old friends, and Cunobelin the only enemy. Bán hooked his elbows round his knees and edged back towards the mare's head, where he could make a quick grab for the reins.

"I have to stay here," he said.

"Then you should let the slave take your mare into the horse barn. She is too good a horse to let her go stiff standing out in the rain, and my brother's colt, also."

Bán stared. He hoped, sincerely, that his ears had deceived him. He was not certain it was so.

Amminios grinned, his eyes wide with a deliberate, mocking frankness. "Iccius is a slave. Of course he is. Did you think we sold them all before you came? Or that we have them hidden in huts awaiting your departure? Grow up, child. This is not the horse lands. My father will only go so far to avoid offending Eceni sensibilities, and freeing the slaves is a step beyond his limits. The child is Belgic. His father sold him when he was six years old. I brought him from Gaul to decorate my hearth and table and I would say he fulfils his purpose amply. Today, however, he is a horse-boy and he is going to take my father's horse to the barns."

The man had spoken in fluent, flowing Gaulish. Beside him, Bán felt Iccius flinch. The knucklebones had dropped from his hand. His skin turned the colour the smith's had been: a pale grey, tinged with an unhealthy yellow. In a voice quite different from that with which he had been speaking earlier, he said, "My lord, I have to await the great lord—"

"No, you don't," said Amminios pleasantly. "You're mine. If I order you to take my father's horse to the barns and rub it down before it stiffens and tears a muscle, then you will do so. If our guest has any sense, he will let you take his horses with you."

The boy was caught, miserably, between two conflicting orders. The difference was that Amminios was present and could enforce his. The battle lasted only a moment. Iccius ducked his head and took the reins of his charges.

Amminios rose, extending his hand. Rainwater coursed unheeded over his bare head, blotching the fine wool of his cloak. "Bán? We are older than we once were. We are both younger brothers who will have to make our own way in the world while our elders lead the warriors of our people to battle. We should be allies, not enemies. This is not an attempt to wrest your mare from you. The guest-laws forbid it and I would be a fool even to try. I am concerned for your horses and for you. At the very least, you should stand out from under the oak tree. The fact that it has seen lightning strike before does not necessarily mean that it will not do so again."

It was a day in which the gods spoke often. The thunder sounded again, closer, and a flash lit the sky. Bán might have stayed for himself but he was not going to risk the life of his mare and Caradoc's colt. He ducked out from under their feet and reached for the reins.

"I'll bring them," he said. "Iccius has enough to contend with leading my sister's battle mare and your father's horse."

"As you wish. In that case, perhaps we should run? The weather will not improve with our standing here and we are all of us wet enough already."

They ran back along the path to the horse barns. Iccius ducked into a neighbouring house and brought out warmed mash and good hay. He fetched wads of rolled straw and pads of sheepskin and together they swabbed the rain from the horses' hides. Amminios worked on the dun colt and it took to his handling as well as it had to Caradoc's. Breaca's grey mare would not have him near her but there were many, even amongst the Eceni, whom she treated the same; it was not necessarily a reflection of integrity or worth. Iccius was better. The mare snuffed him suspiciously but allowed him to dry her down. The saddles were stacked on harness stands at the end of the barn and another boy—another slave—of Iccius's age was called out to dry and grease them. The air filled with the warm smells of boiled oats and neat's-foot oil and steaming horses. But for the presence of slaves, it could have been any Eceni horse barn in the aftermath of a storm.

Amminios stood to the side, his hands on his hips and his sodden cloak thrown back over his shoulders. He turned to Bán.

"Happy now?"

"The horses are better, yes. Thank you."

Iccius seemed better, too. His colour had improved and the shy smile was back, although there had been a warning in his eyes, and a plea, and Bán had not yet made sense of either. Until he had, it was best not to talk of it. He took a comb and began to tease out the mare's tail, stripping out the mud and grit of the journey. Amminios laid a restraining hand on his arm.

"Leave that. It will wait. You are as wet as the horses. We should find you dry clothes and something warm to drink and a place to sit out of the rain until the others come back."

"Where are they?"

"Your family, I believe, are being entertained by our craftsmen. The mariners have gone to see the new ship. Segoventos would have ruptured a blood vessel if he was made to wait any longer so Togodubnos took them all down to the anchorage on barges. They will have met the rain so their return may be delayed until the worst of it has passed. We will gather again in the great-house when they are back. In the meantime, would you like to see the whelp again? I understand she is to be a brood bitch to your war hound. Is that not so?"

"If she grows into her promise, yes."

"Then you should spend time with her. Come, it's not far."

It was the stuff of fevered dreams and nightmares. Bán found himself drawn steadily away from the horse barns to the small harness hut near the great-house where the bitch lay with her whelps. The dark-haired woman had gone, for which he was grateful, but otherwise the place was as he had left it.

Amminios, the man who bought and ordered slaves, lit the torches himself and kindled a small fire in the corner, well away from the pups and the straw. He took Bán's cloak and hung it up on a wall hook and put his own beside it. He left for a moment and returned with two dry tunics and a jar of hot honeyed ale flavoured with wormwood and stinging nettle, and some oatcakes. None of these was pressed on his guest. Of his own accord, Bán stripped off his sodden tunic and slipped on the dry one. The food was left at the side where it could be reached by either party. Amminios sat in the straw by the bitch, who knew him as well as she knew the dark-haired woman, and lifted one of the dog whelps to eye height. "Odras has said I can have the pick of the dog pups from the litter. I had rather thought this one would make a good war hound. What do you think?"

It was the biggest of the dog whelps and a good iron grey. Bán lifted up one of its smaller, paler litter mates and passed it over. "This one will be better. That one picks fights with anything that crosses him but he gives up too easily. This one only fights when the others push him but he doesn't stop until he has won."

"Let me see."

They placed the two whelps in the straw. As Bán had said, the larger picked the fight with the smaller and lost. In the short time of watching, the pattern was repeated twice over.

"You're right," said Amminios, thoughtfully. "I had only seen that he fought well with the others. I had not noticed that the other waits and then wins. Was your war hound like that?"

"He was born alone," said Bán. "He grew up with me as his brother. We don't fight."

"Of course not. Brother should not fight against brother. The gods speak against it." Amminios smiled as he had done all along, warmly and with an unnerving intelligence. He clasped his hands and tapped the extended forefinger to his lips, thoughtfully. "You are not a warrior yet. It is right that you do not fight, but do you play?"

"With Hail?"

"No, with other men." A square board stood in the shadows beyond the fire. Leaning over, Amminios lifted it and the leather bag beside it. He laid both in the flat earth by the straw. The board was finely made, with a chequered pattern of pale and dark wood and bronze bindings at the corners. The playing pieces were red and yellow tablets, like small, flattened pebbles, smooth to the touch and uniformly made. Amminios tipped the bag and they spilled out, mutely clashing, onto the board. "The Gauls and the Romans call the game Merchants and Bandits," he said. "My father's people call it the Warrior's Dance. I prefer to think of it that way. Have you ever played?"

"A little. Gunovic the iron trader brought a set with him

these last two years. He taught me the essence of it—enough to see that it takes greater skill than I have got."

"A pity." Amminios scooped the counters into his palm and slipped them back into the bag. The board folded in half to protect the smooth inner surface. He laid them both against the wall. "In that case, we will have to content ourselves with watching the whelps test each other's weak points until the seamen return."

He reached for the ale jug and drank. It was a breathtaking breach of protocol, not to offer it first to the guest. Bán watched, speechless, as the man finished and wiped his mouth with the back of his hand.

"You don't trust me," said Amminios. "You would have thought it poisoned and turned me down, which would have been difficult for us both. I drink, therefore it is safe, I swear it. Will you share it with me?"

He held the jug out, one-handed. The smell of it was dizzyingly good, the rich, fiery, bittersweet memory of winters at home and kin-deeds told by the fire. Bán took it and drank; it would have been a gross discourtesy not to. It was stronger than the ale given out at the meal and more recently heated. The wormwood sang through his head and lit the fires in his guts. It was a pleasant feeling, but not a safe one. The elder grandmother—the old one—had used wormwood when she needed urgently to speak with the gods. It was not advisable to drink to excess when one needed to settle the affairs of men. Bán closed his eyes and let the heat spin out to the ends of his fingers and toes. He remembered Iccius and the second game of knucklebones. The lad was good and would have won had Amminios not interrupted them. He remembered the way the boy's voice had changed when confronted.

Opening his eyes, he reached for the gaming board and bag of counters. "I would like to play with you," he said. "It does not take so much effort that we cannot watch the whelps at the same time."

It was a simple game on the surface; a child could have learned it. Twelve counters of each colour were placed in a row along either edge of the board. The thirteenth was smaller and more densely coloured and Bán was not familiar with its use. Amminios, who played yellow, held his up between finger and thumb. "This is the dreamer piece. It can move three squares at a time, jumping sideways at will, but if it is taken, the game is forfeit. Have you played with this?"

"No. Gunovic played only with the twelve. They can move one square or jump over another to move into a space. A piece is lost if the enemy warrior jumps over it. The winner is the one who clears the board of his enemy's pieces."

"Then we will play that way. If you win a few, we may bring in the dreamers. As in life, they make the dance more interesting."

The dreamer pieces were removed and placed carefully at the side. The remaining counters were lined up along the edges of the board. Bán, playing red, took first move. It was nearly a year since he had last seen a board and he moved slowly, as one waking after a long sleep, feeling his way into the strike and clash of the dance. He played the first game unimaginatively and lost. His first six counters were swept from play in a single, skipping race. The remainder were cornered and taken in pairs or singles. It was a swift, neat execution, achieved with no sense of hostility. At the end of it, Amminios scooped his own counters into his palm. He had lost three. "Again?" he asked.

"If you don't mind playing against a novice."

"Not at all. You played well. You were learning to look ahead by the end. You will improve quickly with practise."

The second game passed less swiftly but the result was the same, and the third. The fourth took longer. Towards the end of it, both were reduced to three pieces. The space on the board made it more difficult to trap an opponent into making a mistake. The brood bitch stood and stretched, yawning, and squeezed out through the door-flap to relieve herself. The players abandoned the game to deal with the sudden flurry of squalling whelps. On her return, soaked to the skin, they agreed on a draw.

That was the turning point. Bán won the fifth game. The joy of it surged through him, fiercely, like throwing a spear and hitting the sweet spot of the mark at its centre. Amminios, smiling, left him and returned with a fresh jug of ale. "This is not as strong as the other," he said, "but it is hot." He placed it on the ground between them. "Shall we play again?"

Bán won the next two games in a haze of elation and ale. They introduced the dreamers in the game after that and he lost. The new pieces had greater flexibility than the warriors and, as Amminios had said, they made the dance more exciting. It took Bán three games and another draw to become easy with their use. Soon, Amminios offered a second variation where a warrior reaching an opponent's corner could, for one move, become a dreamer. The games moved faster and the play became more subtle.

On the twelfth game, with the fire built up and a whelp lying asleep on his lap, Amminios said, "Winning is good, but we should play for something more than this. I will lay my armband on the next game. Will you wager against it?"

They played Bán's bronze armband against Amminios's gold and Bán lost. He lost his dagger and his belt in quick succession and then won them back; his sword changed hands three times in as many games; Amminios placed his horse—a sharp, fine-blooded bay—and lost it. The game in which he won it back was played faster than any before it and left them both sweat-soaked and shaking.

They played on. Time stretched and lost its meaning. The world shrank to the swooning firelight and the shadows of the pieces on the board, to the rush of blood in the ears and the trickle of sweat down the back of one's neck. Bán heard his name called, distantly, and changed his mind on the piece he had been going to move. The game had hinged on that move and he won it, thanking the gods for their timely warning. Beside him lay everything that had been bet; each game had been cumulative and all was placed on each win. In his tally, he owned the bay horse and its saddle, Amminios's sword and its belt, a dagger, two armbands and a torc. Amminios stretched his arms, hooking his fingers back and cracking the knuckles. "One more," he said. "You were lucky on the last one. I want my horse back."

Bán grinned. Runnels of sweat streaked his forehead and soaked the neck of his borrowed tunic. His legs were cramped and his bladder strained. His fingers reached for the counters even when they were not in play. He had rarely been so happy. "You lost your horse because you wanted your sword back, and lost your sword for your dagger. You should give up while you can. You have nothing else to lose."

"Oh, but I do. I have Iccius. I will lay him against my horse and the rest of my war gear." Amminios spoke easily, with disarming frankness. His grey-green eyes rested on the board, avoiding confrontation. A log cracked in the fire. Rain ran heavily from the roof. The hound bitch rolled over, sighing, and the whelps mewled in frustration at the temporary loss of the teats. Bán felt the sweat grow cold on his neck. The remains of the oatcakes churned in his guts.

"You cannot rest another man's life on a board game," he said.

Amminios arched a brow. "He's not a man. He's an eight-year-old Belgic boy who was sold by his father to a Roman in Gaul and I can do with him as I wish. I won him in a game; there is no reason I should not lose him the same way." He arranged the pieces on the board, smiling. "Except that I don't plan to lose."

It was the smile that made the difference, and the memory of the terror in a boy's voice, and the backwash of the ale and wormwood, cold now, but no less potent. Bán lifted the two dreamer pieces from the board. Spinning them in his cupped hands, he held them out, one in each closed fist. "Your turn to pick for start."

"You accept, then?"

"I do."

"What will you place against him?"

"All of this." Bán swept his arm along the collection of worked gold, enamelled bronze, studded iron and leather at his side. "Mine as well as yours."

"And the horses?"

It was a careful trap, as well set as any he had sprung on the board. The jolt of it made Bán shudder, as if more than his mind had to swerve to avoid it. "I will place your horse," he said. "Not mine."

Amminios grinned, sharply. "That's not enough, warrior. If you have nothing to lose, you have no reason to play well. I have seen that. You take the most risks when you have the edge of fear behind you. It is no contest otherwise."

It was true; they both played better when there was the greater loss on losing. It was not, at this time, the point. Bán said, "We are gambling with a boy's life. That is fear enough."

The man laughed. "With his life? You think that I will kill him if I win? Or you think that freedom with you would be better than slavery with me? Do not overrate yourself, Bán of the Eceni. Life in your roundhouse is not so good that those brought up in a civilized court would rush to join it. Iccius is happy with me. He would not thank you for suggesting otherwise."

He was backing away from the board. Bán dropped the dreamer pieces onto the wood. They rolled together into the central hinge, red and yellow, the colours of blood and treachery. He felt the pulse throb at his temple. "You will not play?"

"No. Not if you will not wager something you value. As it stands, if I win, I am no better off than I was when we started."

"If we do not play at all, you have lost your horse."

Amminios shrugged. "I can buy other horses. In fact, I can gamble for other horses. There are those who are not afraid to wager that which they value." He stood, taking a step towards the door, then turned, shaking his head, as one shakes off bad feeling. His eyes were warm and bright; those of a friend. "Forget it. I take that back. You played well and it was a pleasure to match against you. My horse is yours and you may take him when you ride out. I will give Iccius your greetings and your best wishes for his future. He is a beautiful child. He will live better here where he is appreciated."

Amminios lifted the door-flap. The rain had stopped. The afternoon had darkened into evening. Bán heard Airmid's voice calling his name. It was not the voice of the gods, but of the one person he knew who could reach them most closely. The sound brought back the dream of the red mare and her white-headed colt. He imagined riding either of them with the memory of intense blue eyes and a shy smile and the fear on a boy's face as he tried to hold his ground against Amminios. He remembered the dun filly and the details of her death that Caradoc had chosen not to tell him.

Amminios said, "Your friends are looking for you. You should go out now. They will be worried."

Bán stretched forward. His mouth was dry. His pulse raced as if he had run since morning. The dreamer pieces, blood and treachery, came into his hand. "Sit," he said. "We have one more game to play."

The man turned in the doorway. The flap fell behind him, cutting out the cool of the evening. "You accept the wager? The red mare for Iccius?"

"For your horse and Iccius. He will need something to ride when we leave." Bán pushed the pile of armbands and weapons to the side. "You can have these back. They would not fit me and I have no need of them. We will play only for the horses and the boy. Do you agree?"

"I do." Amminios leaned forward and tapped Bán's left hand. Opening it, Bán saw the yellow of treachery wink back at him. The Trinovantian smiled, sharply. "The first move is mine," he said.

It was a game like none that had gone before it. From the first move, Amminios attacked, wielding his dreamer with a savagery and precision that was new to them both. Bán lost three of his warriors in as many moves and came breathtakingly close to losing his own dreamer and the game. The power of it hit him with a force that was physical, dashing the blood from his head and leaving him breathless. He gathered himself and fought back, setting a trap and springing it while Amminios's attention was on his own assault. It gained him two pieces and forced the yellow dreamer to flee for cover. Amminios countered with one of his skipping runs that took a piece from one far corner of the board to within a square of the other and spun left at the end. Bán had seen it coming and gave away another three of his red warriors. A moment later, in a move as sweet as any he had made, his dreamer took five of the opposition.

They became more circumspect, circling each other, moving pieces in feints and counterfeints, pushing the dreamers around the board in defensive moves that drew no blood. The warrior pieces became more valuable. Each lost another one and became more wary still. Neither of them wanted a draw; to take the dreamer, each needed at least three counters on the board. Amminios began to move his pieces as if at random. The board became an ice-covered pond and his pieces children playing. The patterns of it carried a lethal, fluid grace. It was hard not to be sucked in, to dance for the beauty of the dance. Bán dug his nails into his palms and bit the inner edge of his tongue. He pushed his warriors into an ugly, condensed block and made them move in a massed charge, sweeping the ice dancers to the far side of the board, breaking the patterns. It took time, and Amminios wove circles about him, taunting.

Neither spoke. In other games, there had been a quiet background conversation. They had talked of the horses, of Breaca's battle grey and the races she had won, of the red mare and the foal she carried, of the Sun Hound's breeding projects and why Amminios believed his father's blood lines to be tainted with faulty stock and what he planned to do on his three farms in Gaul. Bán had told of Hail and their hunting. Amminios had relayed a story of Odras's hound bitch and her lone run against a full-pointed deer.

This time, there was silence. On the outer edge of his mind, Bán was aware of other voices besides Airmid's calling his name but he was beyond the point where they dictated his moves. Partway through the ice dance, he felt a draught as the door-flap lifted and he knew he had been found. Shapes gathered in the doorway. Someone brought another torch and the shadows of the counters changed direction. Voices murmured like the morning babble of wood pigeons and made as much sense.

Someone asked, "What have they wagered?" and someone else—Caradoc, or the Roman; their voices were uncannily similar under strain—said, "The horses. It will be for their horses," and a third voice, which must have been Amminios's, said, "Brother, you demean me. We play for our honour. And for the boy." Not long after that the door-flap shifted again and he knew that Iccius was there.

None of it touched Bán. He was in a place beyond reach. His soul belonged to the board and he would have played on if they had told him that Iccius had escaped and was riding the red mare over the ocean to Gaul, or that he was dead.

They were both dancing now. He had broken his warriors' march and sent them outwards, probing for weak spots. He found one and took a piece and then found himself cornered and lost his own warrior in turn. His dreamer sheltered behind the remaining three pieces. Amminios had four. It was not impossible—each had won from this position before—but it was dangerous and neither could afford mistakes. Patterns grew before Bán's eyes: replays of the afternoon's games and of others, earlier, played with Gunovic. The ghost of an idea tugged at his imagination and caught hold. A path formed in his mind similar to one he had seen before and failed to take. He believed it worth trying now.

In a new break from the dance, he moved his dreamer into the open and began a curving slide across the board. Amminios's pieces moved like wolves on a trail. They split into two groups and came after him. They were well disciplined, keeping close together, never allowing the single space between that would enable Bán's dreamer to turn and skip across them, wielding death. The yellow dreamer sat alone towards the left-hand side of the board and did not move. The red hit a corner and the wolves began to close. Bán brought his three remaining warriors forward defensively, to cover the gap. If one looked ahead, one could see that there was enough time, just, for him to bring them into square formation around the smaller piece. He could protect it from attack but he would lose the flexibility of the dreamer's sideways movements.

He sighed and shifted in his seat. The crowd had grown quiet. Caradoc, or perhaps the Roman, swore quietly in the name of Briga. Bán did not look up. The pieces moved swiftly. Neither player took the time to stop and consider all other openings. Both were intent on the wolf pack and its kill. Bán hopped his warriors forward as fast as the play allowed. On one move, he risked a gap. To have taken advantage of it would have slowed the yellow advance and he knew Amminios better than that; the wolf does not stop to snap at dayflies when the deer is running on the trail. At his next turn, Bán was able to bring one piece four squares forward, gaining ground. Another moved sideways to fill the void. Amminios smiled thinly and arched his brow. He had done it once or twice before as a way of offering a clean end to a game already forfeit. In this game, he would not do it so soon. It became instead a quiet signal between them; he was winning and they both knew it.

The wolves were three squares away when the red dreamer made a break for cover. It was the highest risk Bán had taken throughout the entirety of their play and he heard a hiss of indrawn breath from the doorway. He struck sideways and down, bypassing his leading warrior and slipping sideways behind it, out of reach of the yellow counters. Amminios frowned and stared at the board. It was not a move he had considered. The rhythm of play faltered briefly as he studied his options, then he lifted one of his warriors and moved it, skipping, back and forth across its fellows in the zigzagging strike that marked his most elegant play. It came to rest within two squares of the red dreamer and the new position changed the tenor of the game. Even the least experienced of players could have plotted out the ending. Hesitantly, Bán brought his warriors in a ring round his key piece. He moved his pieces more slowly now and it made no difference. Soon, the yellow counters surrounded the red, one move away from the kill. The red dreamer had two moves left and either one placed it in mortal danger. To move either warrior would bring it within reach of the yellow and Amminios would clear the board. In each case, the dreamer was forfeit and the game with it.

Amminios rested the tip of his finger on the tiny red counter. Quietly, just between them both, he said, "Must we go through with it? You played well. I would not inflict the final indignity of the kill for no reason."

"What will happen to Iccius?"

"He will continue to serve as horse-boy. Your red mare will improve my father's blood lines, and the colt that she carries will be mine when we ride to war against the Ordovices."

"It might be a filly."

"Maybe. Then I will have a battle mare to match your sister's."

Bán laid his hands flat on his knees. The pressure of the play had left him more drained than he had ever been. Looking up, he met a forest of eyes: Breaca was there with Airmid, Macha with Luain; Eburovic stood to one side near the Roman. Odras, the woman who owned the hound bitch, leaned against the wall, nursing a silent infant. Searching further, he found the face that he wanted. Caradoc stood in the shadows behind Amminios. His father stood on his left. In this light, one could see the likeness of the eyes, and the difference. The Sun Hound's gaze was reflective, a bottomless pool to be explored only by the gods. Caradoc's was more open; laughter simmered in the iron-grey depths, to be seen only if one chose to look for it, and approval.

Bán wiped his hands on his tunic. His head felt hollow

and his ears rang. It was possible that a boy might feel like this at the end of his long-nights, having passed the warrior's tests and won his spear, although he thought not; none of those he had seen welcomed back to the men's place had looked as if the gods had blessed them, and he felt that way now.

He became aware that Amminios was looking at him, that he had asked him to yield and was awaiting his answer.

He frowned and checked the pattern of the dance; exultation was unhealthy in a warrior and led, always, to defeat and humiliation. His father had taught him that long ago and Caradoc had demonstrated it endlessly in the races. Only by fitness and skill, careful planning and with the aid of the gods did one succeed. He had planned and prayed and the gods had heard him. It was Amminios's last move that had made his pattern possible. He placed his elbows on his knees and leaned forward to touch his rearmost warrior, tucked beyond useful play in the corner. He had placed it there some time ago, one move among many in the frantic flight to support his dreamer. Amminios, if he had seen it at all, had dismissed the threat.

"The way you have taught me," he said, "when a warrior reaches the corner furthest from whence it came, it grows in stature. For one move, it can act as a dreamer. Is this not so?"

It was not necessary to lift the piece. As soon as the words were spoken, the dance was clear. For a piece with the power and scope of a dreamer, a path lay clear across the board, skipping all three of the remaining red pieces, taking out two of the yellow warriors and making a final double jump to the yellow dreamer sitting alone and forgotten at the back of the board. It was a clean and beautiful kill and he had learned the basis of it from Amminios.

"So it would seem." The Trinovantian placed the flat of his two palms together and touched his fingertips to his lips. When he looked up from the board, his eyes were as blank as his father's, his features set in bland irrelevancy. "Congratulations," he said. "The gods have spoken on your behalf. My horse is yours."

"And Iccius."

"Of course. With the horse goes its boy."

Bán looked up. Breaca was angry with him, and proud at the same time. Beside her, Macha was having some trouble not laughing. Between them stood Iccius, a thin-faced child with a shock of white-blond hair and vast blue eyes, turned the colour of jewels in the lamplight. He was weeping.

Bán stood, feeling the urgent need to drain his bladder. He pushed through the crowd and clapped Iccius on the shoulder in passing. The moment was pure in itself and he had no wish to milk it.

"Segoventos will leave soon," he said, quietly. "If you wish it, you can return to Gaul and thence to your people. If not, you will be welcome amongst the Eceni."

The feast held in the great-house surpassed that which had preceded it in the quality and quantity of food and ale, wine and entertainment. The atmosphere was less restrained than it had been. Slaves served, but discreetly. Wine was passed to the mariners and those of Roman mind who wished it. It was not pressed on the Eceni. Two men and a boy excused themselves early, stepping outside for fresh air and solitude. As if by chance, they found each other and walked awhile, coming to rest on the slope beyond the northern gates that marked the entrance to the dun. The night was cool and newly washed with rain. The storm clouds of the afternoon had thinned to stranded gossamer, looping weblike between the stars. The Hunter rose from the east with the Hare over his shoulder. The Ram's Horn lay low in the west. The moon hung between them, a coin cast poorly in silver with one side lost to the heat of the forge.

The turf had been cropped close by uncountable numbers of sheep. It smelled of sage and silverweed. Hedgehogs, rats and foxes rooted amongst the debris of the cattle market. Caradoc lay back with his hands cushioning his head. "You'll sail soon?"

The Roman, too, lay back against the rising turf of the bank. A small white flower grew at his head, reflecting the moon. "Segoventos says we must be on the evening tide in two days' time when the moon is full. It is too soon for propriety, but if we leave it longer we'll lose the tides."

"He is anxious to see how she handles."

"Of course. And as anxious to be safe in Gaul before Cunobelin changes his mind and takes her back. Segoventos will not admit it, but she is a better ship than the one he lost."

Caradoc said, "I had heard they were going to name her the *Raven*. Why did they not?"

"It was an idea of Curaunios's, not any of the others. Briga's birds are unlucky at sea."

"So they named her instead for my father?"

"He may think so, but no. They named her for a horse that nearly changed hands in a board game this afternoon. And for her rider."

•

Bán sat up slowly. Earlier, he had drunk too much ale and felt ill. The spinning of his head had cleared with the fresh air but not the heaving spasms that tied in his guts. "What have they called her?" he asked.

"The *Sun Horse*."

"Why?"

"Because they didn't know you were going to try to give away your best mare to a man who is known to kill horses," said Caradoc, dryly.

"Would you have walked away if he had offered to play you for the boy?"

"My father has a lot of slaves, Bán. You can't fight my brother for each of them."

"Leave him. He won when he needed to. It is enough." The Roman came to sit between them. He was growing fitter, visibly, as he came closer to Gaul. The band on his arm, which had fitted perfectly when they left Eceni lands, was tight and dug into the flesh. To Bán he said, "They named the ship for your red mare. She came with us through the storm and she is staying here with you. It seemed right that she be remembered. You must send word when her foal is born. I would like to know if it is as you dreamed."

Bán thanked his gods that he had found true friendship twice over in men for whom he had total respect. "How will we find you?" he asked, sleepily.

"Segoventos will return to Eceni lands before the summer is out. He wants to try for the north river again some time when there is no storm. He feels it owes him a good landing. I think you will see him often when the weather is right. He should be able to leave a message at a place where I will find it."

"Will you not come back with him?"

If Corvus heard yearning in the question, he had the decency not to show it. He said, "I would come back if I could, really, but I think it will not be possible. When I return to Gaul I will return also to the legions; where I go and what I do then is up to those who command me. It may be that I come back, but I think we should hope that Tiberius does not decide to send the legions into Britain. I would not like to fight against you."

That was impossible. They were friends and would never fight. Bán said, "You could come on your own."

"Maybe. If I am not reposted immediately, there may be time."

Caradoc said, "Bán sits his warrior tests in the autumn, six months from now. He requires two men, neither of them his father, to speak for him before the gods."

It was an offer, and a promise, and a gift of greater worth than he could ever have dreamed. Bán saw the moon blur and slide sideways, becoming two. At his side, Corvus pursed his lips and whistled, thoughtfully. At length, he nodded. "If the gods will it, I will be there," he said.

CHAPTER 14

The Eceni departed before the mariners. They gathered at daybreak, two days after the Warrior's Dance and half a day before the newly named *Sun Horse* set sail with the evening tide. The morning dawned bright to welcome their leaving. A cold mist lay on the ground, pushed back by the fires of the great-house and surrounding dwellings. The horses stamped and snorted and the fog of their breath added to the white in the air.

Breaca sat the grey mare at the gateway while the others in her party spoke their last farewells. Cunobelin waited with her. She had expected him to turn out in full ceremonial dress, clashing gold on bronze and iron with enamelling and jewel-work between. As was his way, he had confounded her. He stood bare-headed, his hair straw-soft in the sun, his cloak the simple gorse-flower yellow of the Trinovantes, stripped free of other adornment. His sword hung from his right shoulder in the way of a warrior and his shield was bull's-hide on wood with no mark of tribe or rank so that he could have been one of the wandering heroes from a singer's tale, brought back to mortal lands for the length of a dawn. He stood at her horse's bridle and offered short, acerbic comments on those who gathered to leave.

The partings were not all easy. Macha had spent three nights alone with Luain and looked strained as she mounted her mare. Mac Calma had business in Gaul and had accepted Segoventos's offer of a berth on the ship's maiden voyage. He had promised to return to the roundhouse on his way back to Mona but no time had been set for his arrival. It was a pattern that had been played out before and the pain of it was old and plain to see. Habit had not made it smoother.

Bán was happier. He stood tall by the Roman, his face aglow with pride, joy and the grief of parting. Since the day of the dance they had been together, riding or training with swords and spears. Breaca had noted the care with which the Roman had taught her brother the ways of the legions, that he might be able to defend himself should they ever come face-to-face. He was saying something now in his accented Gaulish and Bán, laughing, replied. His voice cracked mid-sentence and jumped down the scales, finishing in a register that matched Luain's. It was not deep, but it was resonant and one could hear where it might go.

Without thinking, Breaca said, "He is no longer a child."

"So it would seem." She had forgotten Cunobelin was there and might hear. The familiar acid humour laced his voice, overlying other more serious things. "We go to all lengths to set tests of manhood that will stretch those newly grown so that they will feel as if they have truly achieved against great odds. Then sometimes the fates—you would say the gods—intervene and the workings of man are left redundant."

"He will still have to sit his long-nights in the autumn. The elders will not grant him his spear without it."

"Of course. His manhood must be seen before the people; he would want that. But in his heart he knows the truth and knows that others have seen it."

He was right. It was there in the way that Bán held himself, in the ease with which he shrugged off the sudden slide in his voice and accepted the gift of a knife from the Roman, giving a spear-blade in return. A small sliver of pride burned in Breaca's heart, a lost thing in all the cold parting. "He won well," she said.

"He did, but it was his care for the boy Iccius that made him a man."

That, too, was true. Iccius waited behind Bán, a fair-haired child, overhorsed on Amminios's highbred bay. The touch of freedom had already changed the way he looked.

Others were gathering. With a jolt, Breaca saw Airmid waiting far back near the great-house, dishevelled and distracted and not yet mounted. She had spent the final night collecting plants in the woods and meadows beyond the walls of the dun and returned in the fading light of predawn carrying a wrap laden with fescue and sage and the first pale yellow flowers of agrimony. A woman—Lanis—who was sister to the one with the sick child, had gone out with her and had returned with her hair bound back by a thong of birch bark at the brow and the wistful, far-distant look of a dreamer—or newly made lover. They walked together towards the horse barns. Dubornos scowled viciously as they passed, which might, in other circumstances, have been amusing. Breaca busied herself with the fit of her girth strap and said nothing.

"She is not riding with you."

She looked down in surprise. The Sun Hound jutted his chin towards the women. "Lanis," he said. "She is not riding with you. Her sister's child is still close to death and she is the only one with any chance to keep it alive."

Danger pricked down Breaca's back. Healing was the work of the dreamers and Cunobelin had skinned his dreamers alive, leaving them nailed to their sacred trees. Only Heffydd had lived, and that because he had forsaken his dreaming. She looked at the Sun Hound, considering. In all of their dealings, he had never failed to answer a straight question. "Is she safe to stay here?" she asked.

"Yes. I have spoken with Luain mac Calma. He has accepted my word, sworn on the eagle of Rome and the badge of the Sun Hound, that I will not harm her. She will travel to Mona in the autumn. Mac Calma will have warriors sent to guard and guide her."

It was not said with ill intent. The facts signalled a change in the way of things as the first foal signals spring, and none of it had any bearing on Breaca or her life. Her choices were her own and their consequences hers to bear. Still, she was glad to see Caradoc ride over to take his leave of his father. If nothing else, it gave her reason to look elsewhere.

She drew back, not wanting to witness the final parting between father and son. She had not forgotten, nor would she readily forget, the skill with which the Sun Hound had manipulated the news of a death and the lengths he had gone to keep it secret. Word of it had travelled after Caradoc's meeting with his father and seemed spread throughout the dun by nightfall. Certainly it had moved fast enough for Odras, when asked to name the hound whelp on the night before their leaving, to choose to call her Cygfa in honour of a dead warrior of the Ordovices, and no-one had thought to question it.

The parting between Caradoc and Odras had been private and no-one had questioned that, either. Caradoc had not returned to her his armband but they had exchanged other less tangible gifts and it had not made the last day easier. There had been a while when Breaca had been afraid Caradoc might stay and that there might be difficulty between the young warrior and his older brother but it had not happened. As she had predicted, Luain had absolved Caradoc of the blood-guilt, after which the youth had been equally free to take ship with Segoventos, to remain in his father's dun or to ride west to his mother's people. His request to ride north with the Eceni had been unexpected, but not unwelcome. In the strange anticlimax that marked the end of the visit, she had been grateful for the offer of companionship.

Caradoc was the last to bring his horse up from the barn. With his arrival, the group was complete. Eburovic rode up behind Breaca, with Macha and Airmid following. Dubornos, silent this once, rode at his dreamer's side. For two days all of their paths lay together. Then, at the border with the Eceni lands, Airmid would turn west and ride for Mona. None knew, nor had any way of knowing, when she would return. It was easiest not to think of it. The last riders joined the line. 'Tagos and Sinochos brought up the rear, leading a string of riderless horses, each laden with gifts from the Sun Hound, and it was time to go.

Cunobelin returned to her side, his hand once again on the grey mare's bridle. He had spent the night in feasting and talk with Eburovic and looked none the worse for it. His breath smelled faintly of wine overlaid with horsemint but neither to excess. His eyes were as Breaca had first seen them: full of dry humour and a depth of understanding that was both alarming and perversely comforting. It occurred to her, too late, that if she could have learned to trust this man, he would have been a peerless ally. She tried to imagine it and failed; after the forge, it was impossible to view him as anything other than dangerous.

Nodding as if she had spoken, he raised his arm and gripped hers at the elbow in the simple parting of warriors. "Are you ready?" he asked.

"No. But we are unlikely to be more so. I think we should leave."

"Good. Then I will clear your path." He signalled behind him and eight men pushed on the beams that held the gates. With a groan like falling timbers, the two halves swung outwards. The meadow below was silent and empty. It had not been thought necessary to order a cattle market for their leaving.

He walked with her as she pushed the mare forward through the gap. "You will be back?" he asked. As with everything he said, it was both a question and a statement.

"If the gods will it."

His eyes mocked. "I will pray for their intercession."

They passed through the gate. The others threaded behind, saying final goodbyes. The Sun Hound reached up once more and clasped her hand. She felt the ridged calluses of sword and spear and then, surprisingly, the swift press of a ring. Looking down, she saw a flash of gold with the emblem of the sun and its following hound raised on the surface. He had worn its twin on the small finger of his left hand throughout the visit. She twisted his hand round, trying to see if he wore it still, and for the first time his face creased in an open, honest smile.

"It's mine," he said. "I would not permit it to be copied. Take it. The gods have not seen fit to grant me a daughter. Now, perhaps, I have the beginnings of one. If you need help in the name of the Sun Hound, it will be given, even to the ends of the earth and the four winds." It was an old oath, and it fell oddly from the mouth of a man who had made clear his disdain for the gods.

She might have answered directly but Caradoc reached her, drawing up on her other side. His presence touched her, warning.

"Thank you." She tried the ring on her fingers. It stayed well on the fourth of her right hand. "I will take care of it. If the Eceni have need of your aid, I will remember."

"Not just the Eceni," Cunobelin said. "You. There is a difference."

They rode in subdued silence, following tracks that ran along the edge of the Sun Hound's coppiced woodlands, with patchwork fields of newly planted corn and beans to one side. It was late spring, the time of hardest weeding, and the fields were full. Workers paused to hail them as they went past. Caradoc was recognized by his hair and the colour of his cloak and he paused often to wave and call a greeting. Late in the morning, a man recognized him from a distance and sent his son, a boy of less than Iccius's age, to beg a ride with him for a few hundred paces so that he could say later in life that he had ridden with the greatest warrior ever to come out of the dun. The lad was unwashed and had hair lice and Caradoc lifted him up and set him down again like a cherished son.

Further out, on the higher, less fertile ground, they passed fields of livestock, bounded by ditches. Long-horned roan cattle fed straggling calves. Nursing ewes, taking umbrage at the unseasonal heat of the day, rubbed themselves clear of wool on the hawthorns. Here, too, there were shepherds and cowhands and always someone to hail them, to talk and exchange news of the dun and its occupants. It slowed their passing, but not badly.

At noon, they forded a stream between two stands of willow and stopped in their shade for a meal. Sinochos organized it; he had saddled the packhorses and knew where the most perishable supplies had been placed. Breaca hobbled the grey with the other horses and walked alone along the riverbank until she was clear of the trees and could sit freely on the sandy bank with her feet trailing in the water. The river ran fast for its depth and the touch of her heels made sinuous wavelets on the surface. Small fish crowded at her toes, thinking them insects. A heron passed overhead and came to rest on long-stilted legs upstream of where she sat. She looked for frogs, or signs of their young, and found none.

She lay back on the bank and closed her eyes. A clatter of ducks took off downstream, roused by the horses, or one of the men splashing in the water. 'Tagos shouted and Dubornos replied, then Sinochos joined in and one of the women from the northern coast, and it seemed suddenly that all of them were bathing, hurling water and oaths and washing away the smoke and smear of three days under a foreign roof.

Breaca stripped and slid into the spring water alone. The cold made her gasp. She plunged her head under and stood with her feet on the bottom and her arms spread wide, letting the current strip her clean of the dun, of Cunobelin and his machinations, of Amminios and his sneering evil. She opened her eyes and saw the light from the surface made green. Her arms were ghost limbs stripped down to nothing, flesh pared from bone until all that was left was the core of her, and the grinding pain of Airmid's leaving. She let her breath out in a stream of uneven bubbles and kicked for the surface. The world came back, light and loud and full of others' laughter. She kicked for the bank and pulled herself out onto the warm sands to dry in the sun and then to dress in a tunic that had been clean and no longer felt so.

Lying on the bank afterwards, she listened to the familiar rise and fall of Iccius's questions and Bán's succinct and careful answers. Underneath them, at the edge of her hearing, someone walked softly over sand. She thought of frogs and kept her eyes closed.

"You did not wish to eat?"

It was Caradoc. It could have been worse. She opened her eyes and rolled her head sideways. "No. Thank you. I have had meat enough for a lifetime. I can live without more."

"It's not only meat. There is cheese, and malted barley, and oats ground with hazelnuts wrapped around with dock leaves." This last was a Trinovantian delicacy and he knew that she liked it. She might have eaten it for his sake but the thought of food made her stomach clench.

"Thank you, but no. I would rather not eat for now."

"As you wish. It may all be gone now in any case. Dubornos is eating like a bear in case food is scarce on the journey west to Mona."

He said it plainly, with the familiar bite of humour, and she was grateful. The others had stepped round the topic of Mona for days, as if it could not be mentioned in her presence. Not even Eburovic had dared speak of it openly in her hearing. She said, "Food won't be scarce. They will be travelling under the protection of the grey cloak of Mona. Wherever they stop, they will be fed as if they came from the gods."

"Dubornos thinks Airmid should avoid contact with the Catuvellauni or the Coritani. She might be wise to listen."

"I don't think so. Only your father dares ignore the sanctity of Mona and he has promised them safety. They will not be harmed by warriors of any tribe and even Dubornos can see to the wolves."

"Possibly." He sat at her side. He had changed his tunic for one in darker wool of coarser weave and his neck was bare of the torc. Seeing it gave her a warning of what was to come.

"You are leaving us?" She felt a twist of disappointment. She could laugh with Caradoc as she could with no-one else; his presence would have brightened the spring.

"Yes. I'm sorry. Segoventos will hold the ship for me at a port halfway down the river, but only as far as tomorrow morning's tide. If I don't reach him then, he'll sail without me."

"So you are going to Gaul with Luain?"

"Only briefly. Whatever I said to my father, I must go west and speak with my mother's people, if only to let them know the facts of Cygfa's death. There are ships that sail from Gaul up the west coast. At this time of year, two or three leave the ports every month. I will find passage on one of those."

"You could ride with Airmid. The route to Mona passes through the lands of the Ordovices."

"I could, but I am too easily recognized to pass for long unnoticed. My father would hear of it and send men on my trail. This way, I can be at the dun of the war hammer before he has word that I am not still with the Eceni."

"Lest he try to make you a studhorse." She smiled faintly. "I remember." She remembered other things of the conversation in the forge. "Your father has men already with the Ordovices," she said. "They will return with word of your arrival."

"No. He may have other spies, but he will not hear anything further from those who killed Cygfa."

There were many ways in which he mirrored his father. The ability to speak of death without emotion was not yet one of them. He tried, but the edge of it hardened his voice. She studied the set planes of his face and the grey expanse of his eyes. "Dead men bear no witness?" she asked.

He shrugged. His gaze did not flinch from hers. "The elders will meet in council as they did for the Roman. The decision will not be in my hands."

"I think your voice will count for something. It did so with the Eceni and you were not one of us."

"Then I will think carefully before I speak."

He would vote for their death. It did not need to be said. She would have done the same.

She picked another stalk of grass and chewed on it idly. With her forefinger, she drew a war hammer in the sand, followed by the symbol of the sun hound. "Did you know them?" she asked. "Your father's men?"

"I believe so. Three men of his honour guard were

missing for the duration of our visit. They would have been present had it been possible." He leaned over her drawing and smoothed out the sun hound, replacing it with a serpent-spear, well drawn. "They are of an age between Togodubnos and my father. They taught me my weapons as a child. One of them gave me my first battle mount. I would have trusted all and each of them at my side in war before any other man alive."

"But they killed Cygfa and so they must die." She drew a frog, because she was not thinking, and rubbed it away with the heel of her hand. "She was your cousin, is that not so?"

"She was to me what Bán is to you."

"Ah." That made it different. "Did Odras know that?" she asked.

"Of course."

"And your father?"

"It is wise to assume that my father knows everything. It almost always proves to be true."

"Then he will know that you are taking ship tonight."

"No. In some things we are careful. Of those left behind, only Luain and Segoventos know I am coming. No-one else."

"And of those here?"

"Bán knows. And now you. When I am gone, you can tell the others. Dubornos might wish to betray me out of spite, but I do not believe he will ride back alone into the dun, not with the journey to Mona so close."

He stood, smiling in a way quite unlike his father's. His cloak was lined with raw, undyed wool on the inside. As she watched, he took it off and turned it, so that the plain side faced outwards. The brooch with which he pinned the shoulder had no real shape to it and would not arouse attention. He took a leather cap from his belt and set it on his head, hiding the sunlit gold of his hair. His blade was the one Eburovic had made for him. It hung across his shoulder and the hilt was covered with calf's hide, concealing the war hammer that stood proud on the hilt. She looked for his horse and saw the pied cob that Segoventos had been riding on the journey down. It was a good mount, but it was not the colt. They walked together to where it stood by the edge of the birch stand and she made a cradle of her hands for him to mount with.

"You should have taken the dun colt," she said. "At least then we could have raced one day."

It was something to say and not important. Still, he grinned. "Bán and I have agreed a temporary exchange," he said. "I will return, in due course, for the colt. In the meantime, the beast is safer with the Eceni than on a ship bound for Gaul. I will take the cob and sell him. Segoventos will return the proceeds to Bán in kind. He will buy a mare for Iccius so the lad can set up his own herd. Bán will give him use of the dun colt as a sire."

He settled his cloak behind the saddle. She patted the cob on the rump. Caradoc reached down and offered his hand and she took it. "You have it all worked out," she said.

"Of course. I am the son of my father." His smile was light. His grip was cool and firm and touched the depths where she felt most empty. His eyes were the colour of clouds and their patterns as complex. He withdrew his hand and made the salute of the warrior. "You could still ride for Mona," he said quietly. "The elders did not confirm

Dubornos as Airmid's warrior and she will hardly be unhappy if he is supplanted. You should speak to her. She fears tomorrow's parting as much as you do."

"We have said all we can ever say. There is nothing that words can change."

"Maybe." He kicked the cob on. Breaca walked at its shoulder, pushing the trailing birch out of the way. He looked out over the top of her head, his eyes narrowed, searching the distance. As if to the horse, he said, "Lanis was the daughter of the last true dreamer of the Trinovantes, one of those my father had flayed and hung on an oak. She has reached her womanhood with no-one to guide or teach her. To have three dreamers present at once was a gift greater than any she could ever have prayed for. You can't blame her for taking all they can give."

The spit dried in her mouth. Had it been anyone else, she would have walked away. Because it was Caradoc, with whom she was oath-sworn, and she trusted his integrity, she said, "There is no blame. Airmid chooses where she will. We all do."

"Indeed."

They reached open ground. She stood in the shade of the trees. A deer track passed east towards the sea. She could see no roundhouses, or herders' huts, at least as far as the next rise in the land. Beyond it, the air held the bright, reflective quality of sky over water. The smell of the sea mingled faintly with crushed turf and horse-sweat. She thought of his last meeting with the gods of the ocean and the courage it would take for him to board ship once again. On impulse, she unpinned the serpent-spear brooch from her tunic. "Here." She held it up. "For protection."

"Against shipwreck?" He read her too easily. "Do you think I'll need it?"

"No. Segoventos will do nothing that might risk his new boat, but it doesn't hurt to be sure."

"No, it never hurts." His smile was crooked, as it had been in the forge. He pinned the brooch high on the left shoulder where, until these last days, Airmid had worn its partner. Luain would know what it signified, and possibly Segoventos.

The horse stamped under him, needing to be gone. Caradoc reached down one more time and laid his hand on her arm. His touch was warmer than it had been and his palm damp.

"We will meet again in the autumn," he said. "I have promised Bán I will speak for him when he sits his long-nights."

"Thank you. It matters to him."

"And to me." He swung the horse away. His voice came back over his shoulder. "Briga keep you safe."

She watched the path for a long time after he was gone.

CHAPTER 15

The Eceni travelled faster once Caradoc had left them. The track was broad and the horses were more closely matched than they had been. From the first, Breaca pushed the grey mare forward into a canter, seeking freedom in the rhythms of movement that stilled the need to think. The others followed at their own pace, always keeping her in sight.

Caradoc had chosen his place of leaving well. For the rest of the day and on into the one that followed, they met no-one. The track passed through great swathes of managed woodland, dotted here and there with the huts of charcoal burners and signs of recent felling, but no men hailed them for news of the dun, or sent their children to beg rides. If word were to travel to Cunobelin that his son no longer rode with the Eceni, it would not do so by chance.

Late in the second day, they reached the Place of the Heron's Foot, named by the ancestors for the pattern of three rivers running into one that made the land look as if the great stilted bird had walked across it, leaving a single footprint deep in the plain that stretched on either side. The rivers themselves ran through wide, wooded valleys, making singular contrast with the surrounding land and marking convenient boundaries. Here, the boundaries of three tribes came together. To the north and east were the lands of the Eceni, stretching as far as the north coast. The Trinovantes, on whose land they had travelled, held everything to the south. Westward were the Catuvellauni. The valley of the heron's print itself was owned by no-one, being the preserve of the gods and granted freely to all who passed, that they might rest for a time without fear of attack.

They crossed the river late, swimming naked through the cold, fast-flowing water, and made camp in a clearing on the far side.

Breaca made her bed in the shelter of a briar some distance from the main clearing. Night mist gathered at the base of the trees. The air hung heavy with the scent of cow parsley sharpened by thyme and the beginnings of bloom on the thorns. She sat for a while, wrapped in her cloak, and watched the moon rise towards the top of the thicket. The hare who lived on the moon's surface showed her face so that the ears and the one eye looked down to the earth, watching the watcher. Breaca's shield hung on the stub of a cut branch close at hand, the round whiteness of it mirroring Nemain's light. The old scar on her palm ached and had done so since morning.

"May I join you?" It was Airmid. She could always walk more quietly than the others when she chose.

"If you wish."

She had not placed her back to a tree, believing there to be no threat. Airmid came to sit behind her and wrapped her arms loosely round her waist. Her chin rested close to Breaca's shoulder in the way it had done in the beginning when they had wanted to speak together and not be heard.

One could wonder, now, why it might be necessary. One could remember a woman emerging unclothed from a cold, fast-flowing river, and the earthen smoothness of her skin, like sand newly washed by the sea. In doing so, one could note, in retrospect, that there were none of the marks that such a woman might carry had she taken a new lover and wonder if it was tact that made it so, or the absence of cause.

"She is a dreamer. She is also pregnant. We dreamed the birth of her child and how it should be named. It was her first dreaming. She could not do it alone."

The words throbbed through Breaca, carrying the air from her chest. "You are talking about Lanis?" she asked.

"Yes."

"She didn't walk with the joy of a woman who has seen her child grow in the dream."

Airmid said, "She saw his death. It was not good."

"On the orders of the Sun Hound?"

"No. He died at the hand of a Roman and a warrior of the tribes and those who could have stopped it stood by and did nothing."

Amminios, then. Neither Caradoc nor Togodubnos would do such a thing, whatever the circumstances.

Breaca leaned back into an embrace that carried no guilt. The hands that circled her waist knew her better than any, and the voice in her ear asked presently, "You gave Caradoc your brooch?"

She nodded. It was not a time for speech.

"Did he give anything in return?"

He had given his armband to Odras and she had given it back. He had nothing of like worth that he could have given Breaca, except his word, which was worth a great deal. "He said he would come back in the autumn, to speak for Bán at his long-nights."

"Good. I'm glad." The hands moved from where they had been. "Do you want me to leave you?"

"Do you want to go?"

"No."

"Then, stay. Please."

She had sworn to herself a long time ago that she would spend the last night alone. She was older now, and understood more of the world and her place in it, and an oath made privately, in anger, carried no weight. The night was cool but not cold and the wind softened as it coursed through the briar to brush feather-light across her skin. An otter took a fish from the river and carried it past them, still wet and garlanded with weed. Somewhere in the forest an owl hunted and a dog fox made a kill. Rain fell, but softly so that it did not penetrate the briar. These things came distantly, as facts in a dream while her mind and her soul were elsewhere. She remembered at the end not to weep.

Breaca dreamed of war. It was not surprising, but it meant that when she woke to shouts of alarm she did not respond as quickly as she might have done, believing herself still sleeping. She rolled over lazily, reaching for Airmid and not finding her. The memory of the coming day closed on her, bleakly. Without opening her eyes, she said, "What is it?"

"Eburovic." Airmid stood at the edge of the briar, look-ing out towards the clearing where the remains of the night fire burned. "Get up. Quickly. We're under attack."

"Did you dream it?"

"No." There were shouts again from the riverbank and a horse screamed in anger. Airmid spun back. "Where's your blade?"

"Here." She would not sleep without it, as her father lived always with his. She had never used it in anger, had never unsheathed it save for burnishing or, once, to offer it to Caradoc. Drawing it now, Breaca felt the difference as a song in her blood. The throb in her palm screamed as she reached for the hilt. It hurt less when she held it. Her shield hung by its shoulder strap from a stubbed branch of a beech nearby. The lower edge had touched the water as they swam the river and the red dye had run then dried overnight, fix-ing it so that the serpent bled across the haft of the spear. She settled her hand in the grip behind the boss and this, too, felt different.

Men shouted one to another at the riverbank. She heard Bàn's voice shifting register again, starting high and finishing deep, and then Iccius's shrill scream, cut off prematurely. Airmid was beside her. They ran through the hazels towards the noise. Breaca asked, "Who is it?"

"Coritani. Who else?"

"But this is the gods' place."

"And your mother was giving birth, which is sacred. It didn't stop them then, either."

Airmid spat. She had forsaken the grey cloak of Mona and armed herself with blade and helmet. Of itself, it said she would not be taken alive as a slave. If they died, it would be together: a dreamer and her warrior. In adversity, there was some good.

They broke from cover into chaos. The enemy far outnumbered the Eceni. Their green and black striped cloaks blurred their outlines in the poor light of dawn. The mark of the red kite stood proud on their forearms, new, as if freshly done in the night. They made a half-circle, blocking the way to the river. The Eceni warriors stood in a knot before them, half naked and poorly armed. Eburovic was at the fore, shieldless, wielding the great she-bear blade of the ancestors with both hands, cutting arcs in the air that kept the enemy back but would not do so if they built the courage to come at him together. 'Tagos stood to his left, guarding his side in place of the shield. Sinochos stood before Macha and Dubornos kept fast to his flank. All bore blades and nothing else; their shields had been set by the fire to dry overnight and were out of reach.

Airmid spun on her heel. "They need their shields. I will get them."

"No! It's too far. You'll die before you're halfway there. Stay with me. We need to get the horses."

Their mounts milled on the riverbank downstream of the ford, herded by one of the Coritani. Breaca whistled and the grey battle mare screamed an answer. She struck out at the man beside her. He fell and water ran red on the shingle. Another warrior grabbed for the mare's halter and was knocked from his feet by her shoulder. He died underfoot. Warrior and battle mount met at the foot of a willow and the crash of blood, more powerful than the horse-sweat, stung them both. Breaca whistled again and two other horses pushed through the trees. The herders stood back in fear and let them go.

"Airmid, get the colt. And Bán's red mare. They know how to fight."

Breaca mounted and the height gave her a better view. Bán stood to the left of the others between an oak and a cluster of brambles. Iccius knelt at his feet, clutching a blade wound on one thigh. Three warriors closed on them, grinning. She kicked the mare forward. Two of the enemy died without honour, caught from behind by a blade that sang as it killed. The third looked to his left where a horse struck at his shoulder and did not see Bán's blade as it swept through his throat. Blood sprayed in a fountain where he fell. Breaca shouted, "You have killed. I saw it. If we live, you've earned your spear."

Bán grinned wildly and made the warrior's salute. There was no time for more. Airmid was there with the red mare and the colt. Breaca shouted at whoever would hear. "Get Iccius mounted. He'll die if he's left on foot." They put him on the colt and he clung to the mane, weeping. Bán was up on his Thessalian cavalry mount. Breaca reached down and pulled Airmid up behind her on the grey. A shadow moved at her left. She thrust out with her shield and drew back her blade for the swing. The red mare moved ahead of her and the enemy warrior died in a plash of blood and splintered bone. Bán shouted, exultant, and punched the air. His mare's feet streamed blood. Breaca screamed at him, "Get the other horses. Bring them to the fire."

"What are you going to do?"

"Fight!"

They wheeled and separated. Iccius followed her brother. As they parted, her last thought was that the Belgic boy was unarmed and would die.

•

Bán rode with fire in his heart, circling the encircling enemy. The red mare killed for him. In every way, she was the mount from his dreams, faster and more savage than he had dared hope. Lifeblood stained her teeth, and crushed fragments of men clogged her hooves so that when she turned fast to catch a warrior who came at her shoulder she slipped and fell into him, and Bán, for once, had the chance to use his blade in defence of them both. The man swung at him, backhanded, and Bán had to duck. His mind held the impression of a wide grin and a single crooked eyetooth. The image jarred, prodding at his memory as he grappled to hold his balance on the spinning mare. He put it aside and gave thought to fighting.

The enemy warrior was still off balance. His cloak fell away from his shoulder, exposing the blue edge of a mark drawn at the nape of his neck at the point where the collarbone met the great vein. Bán swung his blade backhanded, aiming for the blue line, but the grip slipped in his hand and he struck low on the shoulder and drew no blood. The man sneered as he might at a child and drew his own blade back for the killing blow. His attention was all on the strike; he never saw the snaking teeth that came forward and smashed the angled bones of his face so that the laughing grey eye split open like an egg and the roots of his teeth showed clean through the rent in his cheek. He fell backwards, bellowing, and the mare screamed with him, throwing herself forward. The crack of his ribs breaking underfoot was the sound of an axe splitting wet wood in winter.

Bán hauled the mare to a halt and hurled himself at the ground. The man lay flat on his back, clutching at his face. Blood pumped crazily from the wound on his chest and air bubbled through it, foaming. The mare came in to finish what she had started but Bán shouted her back. The enemy warrior lifted his head and gargled on blood. The noise was an animal one, of pain and death and inchoate terror. His guts had been caught by one of the murderous hooves and the smell of split lights was appalling. Bán ripped the brooch and the cloak from the warrior's shoulders. There at the neck was the mark for which he had aimed; not the red kite of the Coritani, but the war eagle, wings flung high in the stoop and feet braced for the kill. It was an old sign, recently resurrected, with the oaths of the ancestors renewed and respoken, reworded for a man who favoured Rome. Bán had seen the sign often in the past days, had taken meals with men—only men; their leader did not take the oath from women—who bore it with pride, had played the Warrior's Dance with their leader and won. These were Amminios's men, he was sure of it. Memories of a broad smile and a single crooked tooth gave him a name that might go with one that lay at his feet.

"Decanos?"

He was not sure. He could not be sure. A man's face changes so much when he is dying. Bán laid a palm on a death-cold forehead and avoided the one good eye that searched for his. He had not seen death in battle before, had imagined more glory and less time taken dying. The reality curdled his guts, but he had no time to consider it. Already the black birds of Briga circled in the dream to carry the man's soul to the river. Bán could feel the beat of their wings, hear the carrion call tear into his own soul with a promise for later. He shook the stiffening shoulder. "Decanos," he said, more urgently, "is it you?"

It was too late for speech but the amber eye held his and blinked twice before the white rolled up and was gone for ever. He felt the truth as a punch in the stomach and the duplicity of it swamped his reason. Standing, he slashed his blade across the lifeless throat.

"Bán!"

Iccius called him, frantically. Men were running at him, all in the green and black striped cloaks of the Coritani. Bán hauled his blade clear and threw himself at the red mare, running with her for three strides before mounting. A hand caught at his tunic. He hacked down twice and severed two fingers before it let go. Free, he wheeled the mare in towards the centre of the clearing, calling Iccius to follow him. On the other side of the fire, Macha was down. Bán could see her black hair fanning the turf and the white of her face below it. A bubble of pain rose through him and was washed away, to be brought back later, when the gods gave more time. Further over, beside the smouldering remains of the fire, Breaca was fighting on foot, with Eburovic on one side and Airmid on the other. It was impossible not to feel awe at the sight of her. She blazed as a single point of fire amidst the carnage. Her hair burned like molten bronze. Her eyes gathered the rising sun and made it brighter. She killed with a wild precision and the ravens of death danced over her, singing.

Bán came to himself. "Breaca!" He pitched his voice high and saw her glance in his direction. "They are the men of the war eagle—Amminios's men. Trinovantes, not Coritani."

His sister grimaced and raised an acknowledging arm, then gestured again towards the horses. The entire Eceni herd had been gathered together on the margins of the river. Three Trinovantian warriors were walking in on them, whip-handed, trying to drive them across to the Sun Hound's territory. Not while he lived. He was Bán hare-hunter, warrior of the Eceni, brother to the serpent-spear, and he would die before they took his horses. Yelling his sister's name as a battle cry, he spun the mare and kicked her on and they broke through the circle of enemy warriors as a spear through a straw target. At his side, Iccius clung to the dun colt as it fought its way through beside him. Ten strides and he was there.

"*Bán!*"

The scream came from his left, where Iccius had been. He could not turn; an ageing warrior with white-streaked hair and the stealth of long practise had come at him from the right. The mare, unaccountably, had missed her killing stroke and it was left to Bán to save them both. It was the stuff of his daydreams: true combat, fought between heroes. He felt an absence at his side, like a gap in a wall that lets in the wind, and knew that Hail should have been there to make things perfect. Still, it was close enough. He raised a wordless yell of hope and fury and swung on the forehand at the white skin of the warrior's throat.

"Bán! Behind you. It's a trap!"

The words reached him but made no sense. His blade bit clean air, pulling him off balance. The grizzled warrior grinned. Bán twisted his arm for the backswing. A shadow fell beyond his shoulder. Too late to turn, he saw it and delayed his swing. The blow to his head struck like lightning. The sun exploded and ushered in night, catching the pain and folding it in before he could cry out. The mare screamed for him, or maybe it was Iccius, and he felt himself fall. Somewhere, in another world, Amminios stood over him, laughing.

"Breaca!"

She heard the shout distantly, filtering through the clash and chaos of battle. She was going to die; she was certain of that. It was the dream of her long-nights all over again and she stood in the place of the ancestors, preparing to die with dignity and honour against insuperable odds. The war eagles were too many, too well armed, too well prepared, and the Eceni were none of those things.

Earlier, seeing the parallels, she had prayed to the elder grandmother, asking if there was anything she could do, any change she could effect that would make the sides more even. The only answer had been silence, and that was enough to let her know that she neared the end and the best she could do was to die well when the time came. The knowledge of it brought a peace that swooped through her in the still moments between the fighting, when one man died and another had yet to take his place, or in the long spaces between heartbeats when the singing blade gave some respite and she and the enemy breathed.

At those times, she stepped beyond herself and saw the carnage as Briga did, from outside and above and with a sharpness of interest that did not allow feeling. It was not as the singers made it; no-one had sung of void bowels, torn intestines, blood and splintered bone and the agony of time taken dying if the blow is not a clean one—but nor had they captured, however hard they might have striven for it, the absolute, immaculate, crystalline ecstasy that filled her, the certainty that it was for this she had been born.

Briga, mother of death, rode the small space of the clearing, casting her ravens at those fated to die, and Breaca, warrior of the Eceni, did the god's bidding with a joy that threatened to rend her heart.

"Breaca! Bán is down. Amminios has him—"

Bán. He mattered. And it was Airmid who spoke, so she was still alive. Breaca smashed the boss of her shield into the face of the man who threatened her father's sword arm and took a step back.

"Where?"

"On the far side of the river, beyond the ford. Amminios has his body. He'll desecrate him as he did the dun filly."

She had heard of that; Caradoc had told her. It defied all the gods and left the spirit wandering without a home. For a horse, it was obscene. For her brother, it was appalling; unthinkable. She turned. A flap of yellow, bright as a hawk's eye, showed amongst the dusky greens of the riverbank. Above it, limp red hair flowed out from beneath an iron helmet. An unstained, unused shield showed the mark of the war eagle, so like the legionary eagle of Rome, as did the shields of the three men with him. Alone amongst the attackers, Amminios and his closest honour guard had not taken the guise of the Coritani. It was an unnecessary conceit. She would have known him anywhere.

"*Amminios!*"

The man wheeled his horse. Her brother lay across his thighs. Blood splashed, life-bright, from the dark mess of his head. Behind, a grizzled warrior on a bay gelding held Iccius by the hair, one arm blocking his mouth to stem the screaming. On the far side, a youth with a bronze helmet led the red Thessalian mare and the dun colt, keeping a safe distance from both.

The grizzled warrior spoke and Amminios laughed. He raised his arm in mocking salute. His voice carried over the water in tones that aped his father. "He is dead. I will honour his body. My men will do the same for yours." He wheeled his horse and pointed ahead. As one, the four men spurred their mounts forward.

"No!"

She would have tried to follow then, but Amminios had planned well; his parting salute had been for his warriors, not for Breaca. The cold wind of the god warned her so that she dodged the blade that sought her life and spun left into screaming, lethal mayhem. Grimacing, Airmid struck past her shoulder and a man with grey hair lost his right eye, and then, howling, his soul. Breaca crushed her shield against the dead man's chest, using the weight of her shoulder to throw him down. She trod on his face as she moved forward and felt his cheek break. In that moment, Bán was forgotten; every part of her strove to kill and not to die. Eburovic, the solid core of her life, came to her right side and she offered herself once more as his shield, freeing his sword arm to strike.

So long ago, Airmid had offered to go for the shields. She should have let her; she might have lived to bring them back and the odds would have been much better. Too late now. To her left, a bull of a man with the eagle large on both upper arms rushed Sinochos and his nephew. Iron smashed through flesh to bone and 'Tagos went down, squealing. Sinochos danced to the right, stooped to grab the boy's fallen sword and straightened, swinging both blades like threshing scythes. His battle cry cracked with the edge of madness.

The bull-man lost his vitals and half his face. He crashed to the earth on the body of a young Eceni who had lain there so long he was slick with the gore of others. They embraced in death.

"Together. We must stand together." Eburovic bellowed it in Breaca's ear. He shoved her towards Sinochos and pulled Airmid along behind. He was tiring; she could feel it in him, a dragging of the reflexes that said the song of his blade ran weaker. Briga hovered by his shoulder, a raven on each wrist. A small part of Breaca denied it and was crushed to silence.

"Where's Macha?"

Macha was down, he must know that. Breaca pointed with her blade's tip. "There. By Dubornos."

Dubornos had been amongst the first to fall. Macha had gone to tend him and had been caught by a thrown spear. There had been few of those; the Eceni had wrenched them from the turf and thrown them back and they had stopped coming. Only the foolish make a gift of weapons to the enemy and the men of the war eagle were far from that. They stood now in the same half-circle that had begun it—fewer of them, but harder to kill. These were the survivors, warriors who had lost count of the battles fought and won and had long ago lost their fear of the dark. The first rush had not succeeded and now they held back, shedding the green-striped cloaks of the Coritani and wiping themselves clean of the false marks on their forearms. There was no honour in pretence and these were men for whom such things mattered.

Breaca counted the odds. Seven still stood of the Eceni, counting herself; two were wounded and would fall at the next clash, which left five. Amminios's eagles were eleven, who had once been too many to count. Pride buoyed her heart; her people had fought fiercely and when the bodies were found the tale would speak well of them. Her father felt it, too. She sensed a tightening in him, a promise sworn to the dead and the living in the presence of the god. He clasped her shoulder briefly and slid his hand down her arm.

"Give me your shield."

He was her father; it was his right to die shielded. She shrugged off the shoulder strap and felt the sudden floating lightness of her arm, and the cold. Without thinking, she cast about, searching for a spare blade to bear in her left hand.

"Here." Airmid nudged her elbow. The blade she offered was an enemy one, longer than the serpent-blade and wider. A bronze fox ran on the pommel, its brush curved over the line of its back. Blood made the hilt slick. Breaca took a chance and knelt to wipe it clean on her tunic. The eagles were not yet ready. When they came together, it would be in the old way, fighting in pairs until the last ones left standing held the field. She believed, because it mattered to do so, that the enemy would kill the wounded cleanly, as Briga and the old laws dictated, and would not take slaves. It occurred to her that Airmid should know it, too, and her father. She pushed herself to her feet, the better half of her attention still on the fox-hilted sword in her left hand. "Eburovic, they . . ."

He was gone. Her eye caught the blur of white that was her shield and the fine, high keening that was the sound of the she-bear blade sweeping down for the kill. Her mind fed her the action piecemeal; the war eagles had been as inattentive as she, and her father had chosen, this once, not to shout. Still, the noise of his feet on the turf had given some warning and the leading man had time to raise his sword.

That one died. The one beside him was caught by the edge of his shield and spun round into the full edge of Eburovic's blade. It sheared the cap of his head like the broken top of an egg and, alone amongst the dead that day, he died without a sound.

Her father spun on his left foot. The shield—her shield—smashed outwards with his fist behind it and the face of a blond-haired warrior was dashed to fragments on the boss. The serpent-spear became invisible, one more smear in a crazy wash of red.

These three her father killed before the enemy came to themselves and closed on him and the first of their blades caught him above the belt in a sweeping cut that gutted him, cleanly, like a deer. They had not expected to catch him so easily and the shock of it brought them up short. In the sudden rush of silence, the quiet sloop of his body, spilling, was the sound of the world as it ended.

"Eburovic, no!"

Breaca passed beyond honour, or even sanity. Scything twin blades as Sinochos had done, she hurled herself forward, killing without care.

The men of the war eagle died in pairs around her and she chose not to count. Airmid and Sinochos stood together, guarding her back. Others came in from the edges, stabbing. It lasted moments, or lifetimes, and the last of the enemy died as the ravens took her father's soul.

She would not believe he was gone. Kneeling, she held his hand between her palms and pleaded with him to talk to her. His eyes were open, his face folding in on itself, exchanging pain for peace. A man so at ease with himself could not really be dead. She kissed him and tasted the salt of her own tears mixed with blood that was not all his.

"Breaca, let him go." Airmid came to kneel at her side and pressed a finger to the wide-open eye. The surface was clear but the lids did not close at the touch. A cool hand closed over both of hers and drew them away. The one voice she could hear said, "He is gone. You must leave him for Briga. We have the living to care for, else he died for nothing."

The words reached her slowly and made little sense. She was in a different place, walking with her father to the river. His shade walked with the resilience of youth and there was a joy about him she had not seen since the death of her mother. She watched him with awe and wonder and felt herself smile.

Airmid said, "Breaca, listen to me. Macha is still alive. If we can get her home, she may remain so. He would want her made safe."

She frowned. She cared for Macha. Her father had cared for Macha. "How badly is she hurt?"

"A spear took her in the chest. She can breathe but only with great pain and she can neither walk nor ride."

"We will make a litter and drag her."

"Sinochos has made it. You have to come. We can't leave you."

So she had been with Eburovic longer than it seemed. She tried to think. Airmid was there to help. Brown eyes searched hers. Cool hands gripped her wrists. She looked up from her father and met a strength that shamed her. Making an effort, she said, "How many others wounded?"

"Eight who will live. 'Tagos is the worst. He will lose his sword arm, but he will live if we can stop the bleeding and the stump does not rot. The others' wounds are deep but not fatal. I can begin work on them here, but we should take them to the roundhouse immediately. Forgive me, but there is no time to build platforms for the bodies. We will take their shields and honour them as battle-dead. Eburovic would have understood."

Eburovic. The voice swam and faded. Her father stood on the bank of a river. Water the colour of moonlight hushed past his feet. Hazels, nine-stemmed for Nemain, dipped their leaves to brush the surface. An otter swam midstream. A salmon rose, bearing an acorn in its mouth. The far bank was hidden in mist although Eburovic stepped out as if it were only a stride away. He turned and waved to her, his face alight with memory and the promise of home. Weeping, she lost her sight and when she found it again he was gone.

She blinked and looked around. Airmid was at her side again, although in a different place. It was later than it had been; the sun stood higher over the trees and the mist had burned long ago from the water. Someone had caught the horses, killed those too badly injured to move and saddled the rest. The grey battle mare waited for her, still wet about the forelegs and muzzle where she had been washed clean of blood. A flap of skin hung loose above one eye where a sword-tip had caught it and the long, scored mark of a spear-thrust showed along her ribs, but she could stand and walk and could be ridden. Breaca raised her eyes. Airmid's met them, waiting. The dreamer was deathly tired; it dragged at her, turned her skin grey.

Breaca became aware that others were ready to go, waiting only for her. She pushed herself upright. "You have done all the work. I'm sorry."

"Don't be. You were with the gods. It takes time to come back."

"Maybe." She looked around. The clearing was quiet. There were more dead than before; their shades filed past in twos and threes, slowly.

"Who killed the wounded?"

"I did. Sinochos helped. We made the invocations to Briga."

They were at peace; it could be seen so. The living bore the pain of it, the hard decisions of who amongst friends might be saved and who not. Airmid's exhaustion became clear, and the greatness of heart that had taken on the task without hesitation. Old pain twisted in familiar places, a thing to be dealt with later, when there was time.

Breaca gripped an offered arm and was helped to rise. Her blade lay sheathed and silent on the bank. Her shield had been cleaned. Her spear had broken early on; the two pieces had been found and brought together. A memory pushed at her, of a boy's voice predicting a broken spear and a betrayal by one who wore the yellow cloak of the Trinovantes. She caught sight of Macha lying nearby on the litter, eyes closed tight to hold in the pain. The hound whelp, Cygfa, burrowed amongst the bandages at her chest, a minor consolation for a son lost in battle. Bán's death and the theft of his body sawed suddenly at Breaca's heart, demanding vengeance. She began to think more clearly.

"How many of our people are still alive?"

"All of those who fought at the end. Of the wounded who may live are Macha, 'Tagos, Dubornos——"

"Dubornos? But he's dead. He fell first. I saw him go down before the first wave of spears was over."

Airmid said, sourly, "He fell. He was not badly wound-ed. He could have fought on but he chose to feign death. It is a good way to stay alive for one who would not die a warrior."

Their eyes met. Something that had been settled was settled no longer. Breaca said, "You still have to go to Mona. You should have left with the dawn." A day ago, it had been all that mattered, the only source of pain.

"I can't go now. The elders will understand. With Bán gone, I am the only healer. I will return home with the wounded. When everyone is mending, then I will leave."

"Alone?"

"I don't know. Maybe." Airmid turned away and then spun back, wearily, as Breaca caught at her shoulder. "Leave it. It's not your business. You can't come. You won't come. You made an oath and that's an end to it. The elders will decide who—"

Breaca said, "It was a mistake. I renounce it."

The moment hung around them, carelessly. Airmid blinked. "What?"

"It was a mistake, a child's dream made in ignorance and preserved in pride. You knew that, everybody knew it. It has taken me too long to learn it."

"But—"

"I renounce it. Here, before the gods, I renounce the false oath of my childhood and pledge instead that I will travel to Mona as warrior, protector and friend to Airmid, dreamer of Nemain." It made a change in the day to see Airmid smile.

The grey mare had come close without being called. Breaca mounted and helped Airmid up behind. The others began to ride north, moving slowly for the comfort of those on the litters. She said, "It will take me all summer to persuade Hail that Bán has gone and he must follow me instead. Do you think the wounded will be well enough for you to leave them by the autumn?"

"Probably. Those that live."

"Good. We will go then, you, me and the hound. We'll be in Mona before the first snows of winter."

III

SPRING A.D. 39–SPRING A.D. 40

CHAPTER 16

The night was too warm and the room lacked air. The darkness groaned to the unsettled sleep of a dozen men. A pot of stale urine sat in the corner, the smell of it overlaid by the thin, sour stench of vomit. Bán lay naked on a pallet, sweating greasily. He ached for the chance to bathe, for the lash of river water on his skin, for the piercing cold and the scouring cleanliness that it brought. On other nights he would have escaped into sleep, or made the attempt. This night, he lay awake watching the walls and the visions came at him as they had done in the fevers. A smiling Iccius was crushed under a rock fall; Breaca died on Amminios's spear. Both rose and came towards him, pleading with him to cross the river in their company and join his people in the realms of the dead.

He resisted; Iccius was not dead and Breaca had died on the blades of the war eagles, not a spear. Amminios had said so when Bán first woke on the ship to Gaul and Iccius had confirmed the tale in private later, telling of that moment when the war eagles had fallen on the Eceni in overwhelming numbers so that there was no doubt that all the defenders had been slain. Bán would dearly have liked to have joined them. In the first months in Gaul he had thought of little else, planning the many different ways in which he could induce Amminios to kill him and so travel that last step into the arms of his family. It was Iccius who had stopped him; the child was Bán's responsibility and he could not have left him to suffer alone as Amminios's plaything. Once, when things were worst, he had considered killing them both, but the gods did not look kindly on a warrior who took his own life to no purpose and Bán's own heart would not allow him to kill Iccius, even to keep him from harm.

Bán explained all of this to the phantoms as he had done many times before, promising that he would die as soon as the opportunity presented itself, but only when it could be done with honour. They backed away, shaking their heads in sorrow. He stared hard at the plastered wall until he could see it through their bodies. It was a long time since the ghosts had held the power to frighten him. Even his mother could come and go now and he felt her presence as a gift. It had not been so in the beginning; they had come to him first in full daylight in the hold of Amminios's ship and the terror they wrought had been worse than the pain from the wound in his head. Bán had spent days cowering in the bilges, pleading with them to leave, and so had failed to kill Amminios when there might still have been the chance. Other visions, more vividly painful, had followed the early floggings of slavery and the brand they had burned onto his upper arm after the first time he had tried to escape. The wound had become infected in the days after the event and the flesh around it had melted to leave a putrid, stinking ulcer, and Bán believed his wish to die might have been granted had Iccius not sold himself to one of the grooms for the price of a salve and herbs for a poultice and had risked further beatings to nurse his friend through to sanity and health.

That had been a mistake. Amminios might have known the depth of care that bound Bán to Iccius but until that moment Braxus, the Thracian overseer, had not. Amminios owned them in law, kept them as toys for his amusement, his daily proof that in the greater game of Warrior's Dance he had not lost, but Braxus was the one who truly owned the measure of their days. The overseer was a hard man who measured pain as he measured the barley gruel he fed to his charges, carefully and with forethought. He had measured Bán well in the time after the brand-wound had healed. When the young warrior had escaped a second time, it was Iccius who had suffered the branding, although he had been with one of the men and could not possibly have taken part in the flight. They had taken more care with the iron so that the letter stood out, the A of Amminios permanently imprinted on the thin flesh of the boy's upper arm.

After the third escape, Iccius had been mutilated beyond repair, with Bán forced to watch. Two men skilled in the gelding of bulls and horses had brought sharpened knives and heated plates and three other slaves, similarly cut, to hold the boy still. Braxus himself had held Bán, speaking in his ear the things they would do next if Bán only gave him the opportunity and the excuse.

There had been no escapes since then. For nearly two years Bán had passed his days taking orders from men he despised and his nights lying alone, nursing a need for vengeance that kept at bay the need to die.

The visions came and went and he watched them with little interest, fighting off the pull of sleep. There was no sleep this night. Iccius had been summoned to Braxus's presence and had not yet returned. The child had never asked for anything, but Bán had set it on himself as a sworn duty since the first time he had understood what was happening; whenever the summons came, he would keep himself awake through the night, until dawn if necessary, so that there was a shared bed to come back to and safety and an embrace that offered no pain.

A horn sounded far in the distance: the night watch of the legions, marking time outside the walls. Durocortorum was not a legionary town, but it served as a billet for passing detachments. In the summer, the officers and men crowded through in their thousands—for trade, for exercise, in transit along the broad roads east to the German border or north to the coast. Now, with autumn looming, the units were fewer; a single detachment consisting of an officer and a few dozen cavalry had arrived two days ago and chosen to pitch its tents outside the walls rather than take beds in town. Word said they had come for the horse fair and had gold to spend in profusion. Other better regulated rumour said that the new emperor, Gaius Julius Caesar Germanicus, known to his men as Caligula, was due to visit in the spring and that the troops were organizing the advance preparations.

Iccius had heard the truth from Braxus: that Gaius was intent on subduing the free tribes who held the east bank of the Rhine and was recruiting local Gaulish tribesmen to act as scouts and screening forces. That was more believable. It was well known that the mighty Caesar would rather throw away every able-bodied man in Gaul than lose one more

Roman life to the tribes who had already wiped out the three legions sent by Tiberius's esteemed predecessor Augustus.

Bán smiled in the dark. He had heard a great deal about the tribes of the eastern Rhine and their ferocity in battle. He turned back towards the plaster wall where the visions clamoured for his attention. When he gave it, they rode the wave of his thoughts. The shapes that assailed him became vast, blond-maned warriors wielding swords that could cleave a horse in two and still cut on through the rider. In his mind, a dozen of them set on a single man, slicing his guts from his corpse, leaving him to die the dreamer's death with the crows taking his eyes first and his heart last. The face of the victim changed as he died: lean, lupine features broadened in the cheekbones and the chin grew stronger; a hooked nose became broken and bent to one side; red hair became mud-brown and curled back on itself. In the last breath of his life, pale yellow eyes darkened to oak and Amminios, son of the Sun Hound, became fully Braxus of Thrace, overseer and slave.

The horn sounded again; another watch closer to morning. Soon after, the cockerels crowed. Bán rolled over to face the dawn. A line of faint light beneath the door grew slowly brighter. A greying of one corner of the ceiling showed where a handful of roof tiles had been dislodged and not yet replaced. A blackbird woke, scolding in the same tone as its cousins had done in the woods of the Eceni. Somewhere beyond the walls of the villa, a foal called a greeting to its dam in the universal tongue of all young everywhere and suddenly the morning was alive with breathtaking, crippling memories of home. It happened most days; if Bán were going to weep, it would be now. He stared, wide-eyed, at the gap in the ceiling and made himself listen, and not feel.

Without warning, the door swung open. Iccius stood on the threshold, a small figure in a linen shift not yet out-grown. He had been growing fast when they gelded him but had barely made a hand's breadth since.

"Iccius." Bán whispered the name, not wanting to wake the others. He sat up and held out his arms. The child walked to him as if he were dreaming, eyes level and unsee-ing, arms straight at his sides. In the beginning, he had been like that every time. Later, there had been occasions when he had come back able to speak and share memories. The regression did not bode well for the rest of the day.

"Come and lie down. Let's get rid of the tunic. Shall we do that?"

At times like this, it was best to treat him as someone very young. Bán slid the tunic over the tousled blond hair and folded it at the end of the bed. The linen smelled of rosewater and cedar smoke. Underneath, the boy stank of sweat that was not his own and another man's semen. His skin was alabaster white with a greyish tinge and that, too, spoke badly for the day ahead. Sometimes he had good colour and could smile a little. This morning, the only colour was in the blue hollows beneath his eyes and the handprints that showed on his ribs where he had been held overtightly by a man who did not care what damage he did. The worst bruising was internal and invisible, and Bán would not be able to judge the severity of it until they walked together to the stables. In the beginning, it had been crippling, rendering the child useless to anyone but the cooks. They had set him to cleaning pots at the cistern where he could kneel close to the water and not have to move. More recently, if they talked about it, he had said he felt nothing.

"Would you like a drink? Here . . ." The beaker that stood by the pallet had been poorly thrown by an apprentice, leaving it ill-shapen with a crack down one side. Holding it carefully, Bán poured water between slack lips and watched for the swallow. In the first days, that, too, had been impossible.

"Good. Now these. I saved them for you." They were grapes and he had stolen them from the kitchen—a flogging offence. Fear shone in Iccius's eyes, then a memory of a smile. He ate them one at a time, savouring the sweetness. A wash of colour returned to his cheeks. His eyes warmed and brightened, not to what they had been before the gelding— that was never to be expected—but to something better than when he had walked through the door. Bán hugged him gently, holding him close until he could feel the beat of another heart overlaying his own. Small, strong hands closed over his shoulders and Iccius laid his cheek on Bán's shoulder. It was a signal between them that it was all right to talk.

"Was it just Braxus?" Bán whispered still. He thought that at least one of the others in the room was awake, but they could share the pretense of privacy.

He felt Iccius nod on his shoulder. "Yes."

That was something. "Did he give you any news?"

"Some. You know Braxus—no-one comes or goes from Durocortorum but he knows about it."

"What of the Romans camped outside the gates?"

"What he said before was right: They're recruiting for a new wing of auxiliary cavalry." Iccius repeated it exactly, having learned the words, and followed with the flicker of a smile, knowing he had momentous news. "They have come with an order to buy two hundred and fifty horses. Amminios wants all of them to be from his farms. He has given his word to the magistrates that he will provide them."

"Two hundred and fifty?" Bán forgot to whisper. Men woke, belching and demanding quiet. He lowered his voice. "What will they do with so many?"

"Ride them, what else? There are five hundred mounted warriors to each wing. They will get all of the men and half the horses here. The rest of the horses have been sent up already from Spain. They are in Germany now, being trained by the horsemen who ride already with the legions."

It was good news and better with retelling, but Bán's mind was already elsewhere, scouring the paddocks that surrounded the villa. "We don't have more than eighty ready for sale." The horses were not his but he felt them to be so. He counted on his hands in bunches of ten. "We could do eighty-five if we were really pushed but the last half-dozen would be two-year-olds, not fully broken. They would not be safe for cavalry."

"Amminios has ordered all the three- and four-year-olds sent down from the farm at Noviodunum and others brought up from Augustobona. With them, we will have the full number."

"Then the Fox will be here. That's good." He gripped Iccius by the shoulder, feeling more cheered than he had done. "Are you to go to the horse fair? Can we go together?"

"No. I can't go." It was said tightly, with a slight clenching of the hands. Everything Iccius did was controlled now, as if he was afraid that real movement might betray him.

"What? Is it Braxus? Did you not please him?"

There was no answer, which was answer enough. Then a small fist clenched at his shoulder, suggesting more. "It's not only that. I have to help in the kitchens this afternoon."

Bán felt his stomach tighten. He said, "That's all right. You like the kitchens. And you can help me with the yearlings this morning. That will be good, too."

"Maybe."

"Who is coming that you are needed in the kitchens?"

He knew the answer. Iccius's reticence had told him. By asking, he held it at bay that moment longer. Then Iccius said, "Amminios is on his way down from Noviodunum with the horses. The visiting prefect—the Roman officer who is buying them—is invited to dinner. He has ordered that we both be in the serving party."

"Gods, no." It was Amminios's favourite game, to show off his "barbarian savages, tamed to domestic service." Bán's head swam and the visions came back, stronger. Dead Iccius stood in front of him, more vividly than the Iccius he held alive in his arms. In Eceni, so the others could not understand, he said, "I *will* kill him."

He had said it before, and had meant it then, too. Just as last time, Iccius's vast blue eyes looked up into his. Tears floated on the rims. "Then you must swear to kill me first. Bán, please, swear it."

The child was close to panic. His fingers gripped with the desperation of one dangling over an abyss. Bán held him tightly until he felt a small grunt of pain. When he let go, Iccius said again, "Do you swear it? Swear you will kill me. You *must!*"

"No." He pressed gently over the bruised ribs, trying to ease away the hurt. "I could never kill you, you know that."

He bit his lip. The visions pressed closer, asking for blood. They would not leave unless he gave them something. He said, "I swear not to kill Amminios while you live. Will that do?"

There were no words, but it seemed that it would. The hands relaxed their grip on his shoulder and the moment passed. They had walked this circle so often before. If Amminios were to die and there was the slightest shadow of suspicion that his death was not a natural one, every slave in the house would be tortured for information and then crucified, up to and including Braxus. It was the law. In the days after Iccius's gelding, when it had seemed he might not survive, Bán had stood beneath a full moon and sworn to his ghosts and to Nemain that he would kill Amminios and live long enough afterwards to see the Thracian nailed to the wood. Braxus, somehow, had known it and had ridden the three miles to town himself to bring back the healer to see that the boy lived. She had worked well and the wounds had healed cleanly, but Iccius's soul had fled and only half of it had come back to live amongst them after.

Bán hugged him again, more peacefully. "It is better for you when Amminios is here," he said. "Braxus will leave you alone and there will be more horses to care for. We can spend the days in the stables and forget about everyone else. Come on. If we are up first, we can let the horses out into the paddocks. It's always good to watch."

The morning foreshadowed the rest of the day. The clear skies of dawn clouded over early and the fresh breeze brought a light drizzle that strengthened later to stinging rain. Even so, the horses were at their best. It was a year after his capture before Bán realized that Amminios had taken every word of their conversation on horse breeding and was making it happen. The red Thessalian mare and the dun colt, now grown to adulthood, had formed the foundation of the new stud. The mare had thrown three foals since the landing. The first—the one she had been carrying when they were captured—had not been the white-headed colt of Bán's dream but it was breathtakingly beautiful none the less. Its hide was perfectly black, streaked at irregular intervals with long, lean patches of white, like liquid moonlight poured on polished jet. Its conformation was close to perfect; the chest was wide between the forelegs to give good space for the heart and lungs, and when it stood its legs were clean-boned and straight with a perfect angle at hock and stifle. It was born in a thunderstorm on the night of the full moon, and Bán had felt the gods gather to watch as he had sat in the pouring rain and given the colt its first lick of salt from his hand.

Milo, the stud manager, had not found the new colt beautiful. Milo was Italian, from one of the northern provinces far from Rome, and in his world piebald horses were a bane, a sign of the gods' impending wrath. He had brought the killing hammer with him on his second round of the morning and it was only the unexpected arrival of Amminios—who had liked the colt's colouring and seen the promise in its lines—that had stopped him from crushing the newborn skull to pulp.

Milo had nursed his resentment and, when the time came for weaning, had ordered the colt north to Amminios's second farm at Noviodunum. Bán, bereft, had begged to go with him. Amminios's refusal had prompted the third and final attempt to escape. News had come afterwards that Milo had recalled the foal, intending to have him slain, but Amminios had forbidden the waste of his future racehorse. The weanling had continued its journey north and there had been no news of it since.

The stud had grown steadily since then. Now in its third year, it boasted two hundred breeding mares with eight studhorses, all in use. The young stock from the last season's breeding was close to weaning, and Bán watched them as a falcon watches her chicks as they balance on the nest's edge. The red mare's most recent colt was his most difficult charge. It was a dark, solid chestnut with a white flash between its eyes, too heavy in the bone to be perfect but with the prospect of carrying more weight than its dam when it was older. The problem was one of temperament. The mare's first two foals had been sharp, as their mother was, but not mean. This one was savage and fought for the sake of it. In the paddocks, it bullied the other foals. In the barns, it struck without warning at those set to handle it. The sire had been Amminios's choice—he had taken to the good bone and had ignored the wall eye and the vicious temper. Bán had spoken once against it and not wasted his breath after that. He spoke as little as he could to Amminios and only on the topic of horses. They made his life bearable. Were it not for the stud, he would have been harvesting corn or driving bullocks behind a plough. In the worst event, he would have been digging rock for the widening of the road that stretched south from the town towards Lugdunum. The slaves who worked on the chain gangs lived in hell, taking comfort only in the knowledge that they would die before the season's end. In his bleakest moments, when death seemed a welcome release, the ghost that came most often to Bán was the old elder grandmother, the one he had feared most, cackling a reminder that life could always be worse.

He was carrying water to the troughs in the weanling paddock when he heard Iccius's cry. The boy was at the barn grooming three-year-olds for sale. At first Bán thought that the impossible had happened and Iccius had been kicked. That would have turned a bad day into a disaster—even the chestnut with the evil temper had not yet tried to kick Iccius. The second cry was shorter and more despairing and he heard his name couched within it, in Eceni. He threw the water into the trough, dropped the buckets and ran.

It was warm and dry in the barn. The rain had damped the dust and the horses were eating new season's hay. The air smelled of their breath, sharpened by the wet of their coats. The nearest was a black colt. His hide had been polished until it reflected points of light from the harness mounts hung on the wall.

Iccius stood in a corner, holding a grooming brush, his face awash with terror. Over him stood Godomo, the southern Gaulish freedman who acted as secretary for Amminios and had charge of the farm in his absence. He was a long, servile lizard of a man with one leg shorter than the other and a testicle missing so that he bore a grudge against every whole man who crossed his path. Iccius, who was no longer whole, was his favourite plaything.

"You will go," he said. "Braxus commands it." His voice had the high pitch and taunt of a starling.

Iccius pressed himself into the brick of the wall. "I can't! I won't do it. You can't make me."

Only one thing aroused in him this level of terror, made

him lose his mind to the extent that he would say something so stupid.

Bán stepped in front of him before he could repeat the calumny. To Godomo, he said, "It's the hypocaust, isn't it? You can't make him go in there again. It's not safe."

"Ah, the shadow's shadow." The lizard smile stretched far under his cheekbones. Loose strings of saliva threaded the corners. He stepped sideways, back into the line of Iccius's frozen stare. "It's as safe as it needs to be. The master requires that the baths be working by this evening. It is up to us to make it so. The flue is not drawing air and the fires will not take. There may be an obstruction in the hypocaust."

"Then send someone in who knows what they're doing. Iccius hasn't the first idea."

"Did I just hear you offer to take his place?"

Bán would have done it. The thought of crawling into the blackness with no air and old insects biting at his hands filled him with terror as great as the boy's, but for Iccius's sake he would have tried his best. "I tried before, in the spring," he said. "I am too big."

"Shame." Godomo had known that. He had been there to watch. "Then it will have to be the little catamite, who fits. I will count to three. If he is not on his way to the hypocaust by the third count, I will call Braxus." He leered. Braxus was his best and only weapon. "One . . ."

They ran together. Braxus was waiting for them at the side of the baths. The entrance to the hypocaust was a small gap an arm's length across and half as much high, blackened with soot and grime. The walls above it were of thin marble, poorly cut and badly fixed to the stone behind. Up above, weak roof tiles clattered under the rain. Already, they showed cracks at their fixings. In the first frosts of winter, they would shatter.

The whole structure of the baths was a disaster and had clearly been going to be so from the start. The problem was that Amminios trusted Godomo. The lizard-man stood straighter in his master's presence and his voice was firmer. Moreover, once in a while, at clear cost to himself, he told the truth. Thus, in Amminios's absence he had been entrusted with the supervision of the project; he had been left to handle the budget, which was barely adequate, and had failed signally to restrain himself from creaming off the better portion. The surveyor had followed his lead, and the architect who claimed to be from Rome itself but was not, and the engineers he brought in from the town to ensure the building was up to the highest standard. Every one of them had taken his cut and what was left had not been enough to pay for the materials, never mind the men to build it. Bán himself had been drafted in to help construct the tiled pillars of the hypocaust and lay the floor across them, and the fact that it was the first building work he had ever done, and the first under-floor heating system he had ever seen in his life, had not been considered a handicap.

It should have been. Bán's part of the floor remained solid; he had the wit to understand what was required of him and a pride that would not let him finish a job badly. Others were less scrupulous, or less competent, and the place had been barely six months from opening when a series of pillars beneath the caldarium had fractured and the floor had subsided. That was when Bán had tried to crawl in to the hypocaust to see the extent of the damage and had failed to worm his way through the gaps between the remaining pillars. Iccius, being smaller, had succeeded.

He was still small enough and there was no question but that he would be sent again; Braxus would do it for spite, whether it was needed or not. The doubt lay in the danger, in how much of the floor had fallen and how much was left to go. Bán ran round to the front door and let himself in.

Inside, every surface shouted colour. There had never been a question of affording mosaic, but the one place Godomo had spent his full allocation was on the glazes for the floor tiles and the artist who had painted the ceilings and walls. The man had worked without pause through the whole of May and the result was considered tasteful to Roman eyes. In the hallway, dolphins in shining turquoise sported with blonde, fair-skinned nymphs with rose-red nipples and gold leaf on their fingertips. Elsewhere, the gods became men, or vice versa. Jupiter became a red-haired Trinovantian, reclining on a couch. Dark-haired, pale-skinned Minerva waited on his bidding. On another wall, a hook-nosed Pan played pipes before a gaggle of blue-eyed virgins. The god's eyes were pale yellow, like a hawk's.

Bán pushed through a curtain to the steam room. Here, heroes rode in painted chariots under a citron sun. On the longest wall, Alexander of Macedon grew from his shining, golden childhood to become the armed god-man who tamed the world. In this, the artist had taken other liberties with history: the golden boy-child dancing in the Dionysian groves of his mother was classically Greek, but as he grew older his hair darkened and his features changed until the adult, the world's greatest general and builder of empires, bore the straggling straw-coloured hair, bulging eyes and weak chin of Gaius, son of Germanicus, for the past three years emperor of Rome.

The caldarium was musty and damp and a film of early mould spattered the lower walls, staining the yellow of Alexander's desert sand. Warped benches in white beech lined the walls. Bán followed the line of them to the southwestern corner. The last time the floor had collapsed, the first warning sign had been cracks in the plaster between the tiles there. The builder called in to do the repairs had done a good job but he had said more than once that it would have been necessary to demolish the lot and start again to do it properly. He had pointed out the paucity of the foundations and the impossibility of making the pillars of the hypocaust stand firm on weak earth. His prediction, made in Godomo's hearing, was that the repairs would break down before winter.

He had been right. A single crack, half a finger's width across, ran in a jagged line from one wall across the corner to the other. Bán traced it with his finger, then prised loose a chunk of plaster at the angle of the floor and the wall to reveal the greater crack beneath it. The floor curtain whispered and booted feet trod heavily on the tiling behind him. He turned to see Braxus standing on the threshold, watching. If the overseer had not already noticed the crack, he could not avoid it now. Bán pointed. The Thracian nodded, turned on his heel and strode back out into the rain.

Bán caught up with him round the side at the entrance to the hypocaust where Iccius was kneeling at the opening. Bán put himself in the way.

"You can't send him under the floor. It's not safe."

"It's safe enough."

"At least let him go in with a rope round his waist so he can follow it out if he gets lost."

That had been the source of the worst of Iccius's nightmares: the time spent worming his way round in absolute darkness, unable to find the way out. Later, they learned that Braxus had closed the opening for a while and the boy had almost certainly passed it in his frantic search for air.

"And let him wind the rope round the columns and bring the whole floor down on his head? I don't think so. Amminios would be sorry to lose so willing a slave." His words were acid, designed to wound. Whatever Iccius had done, or not done, for Braxus, it still festered between them. The man was the soul of malice and the boy's shell of obstinacy perilously thin. Bán opened his mouth to offer another alternative—any other alternative—and shut it again when Iccius reached up to touch his arm.

"Don't. It's not worth it. I'll go in." He spoke in Gaulish, because Braxus was there and it was forbidden to do otherwise. Still, as he bent down and squirmed in through the gap, he said, "Pray for me," and that was in Eceni. Bán did so, in Eceni, silently. Braxus sneered and ordered him back to the horses.

The morning passed slowly. The rain eased and stopped and was replaced by a southeasterly wind. In the barn, the horses were fed and groomed. The first batch of two-year-olds arrived from the north in the charge of the small, wiry Dacian slave with the unpronounceable name who was in charge of the horses on Amminios's third and biggest farm, based in the south, near Augustobona, the heart of his mother's lands. Early on, Bán had named the man Fox, for the colour of his hair. Not long after that, Fox, in his broken Gaulish, had begun to refer to Bán as his son.

They greeted each other warmly and shared news of the stud. The new horses were inspected for soundness, wind-tested and sent on their way to the temporary corrals that had been set up around the auction ring on the outskirts of the town. The eighty horses Bán had selected as fit for sale were similarly inspected, haltered and sent on.

The mares with foals were in the lower paddocks. Fox leaned on a fence and watched them graze. "Yon chestnut colt will be a bastard." He said it with relish, as if he were looking forward to the fight.

"He already kicks at Milo when he's leading them in."

"Good. Intelligent as well." Fox hated Milo with a passion and made no effort to hide it.

They watched the colt a moment longer and then Fox pushed away from the fence. "Where's the grey studhorse? The new one from Parthia that we bought last— What was that?"

It was the sound Bán had been waiting for all morning—the crack of falling masonry and the cry of a boy in terror and pain.

"The baths." He was already running. "It's Iccius at the baths."

It was worse than last time. No-one was waiting at the entrance to the hypocaust. He shoved his head and shoulders into the gap and shouted into the stinking, fire-baked darkness. He smelled brick dust over the soot and ash and knew the worst. "Iccius! Iccius, it's me! Are you all right?" His voice echoed over his head and back but there was no answer. Fox tapped his shoulder.

"They're inside. The floor's gone in the steam room."

He ran for the entrance and through to the caldarium. A knot of men had gathered in the southwestern corner. Godomo stood, white-faced, on the margins. In all ways, the baths were his responsibility. Freedman or not, if Amminios came home to a broken building and no hot water, there would be hell to pay and Godomo the debtor. When Braxus waved at him, shouting, "Get the builder, you fool. Now!" the lizard-man thrust past Bán and out into the courtyard, shouting orders to the others to make themselves useful. The cluster of onlookers wavered and dispersed until only Braxus was left.

The builder was a good man, but he would have to be a god to mend this in the time allowed. The hole in the floor was bigger than it had been in the summer and that had taken half a month to mend. A crack ran up one wall and a slab of marble had fallen from it, shattering the floor tiles and itself on impact. Braxus stood at the edge of the void, peering in. Bán crashed down on his knees at his side.

"Where is Iccius? Is he all right?"

The Thracian sucked on a back tooth. His face was oddly still. He nodded downwards. "There."

Iccius lay on one side, his head cradled in a nest of broken tiles, one arm bent out at his side like a peeled and folded stick. The greater bulk of his body, such as it was, lay under one half of another marble slab that had plunged through the cavity and smashed onto the floor of the hypocaust below. It was not as thick as it should have been to face the wall, but it was enough to crush the bones and flesh of a slight, unmuscled boy.

"Iccius!"

"Don't waste your breath. He's dead."

"No!"

"*No.*" The word rose up on a fine column of dust. Iccius opened an eye. In the dusted gloom of the hypocaust, the blue flashed dimly, like unwashed glass. He had been weeping before; clean tracks scored down the grime of his face, but he was not weeping now. Seeing Bán, he smiled, crookedly, with the half of his face that was uppermost. In Eceni, he whispered, "Now you can kill Amminios."

"No." Bán clutched at the edge of the gap. "Iccius, don't say that. You're not going to die."

"Yes, I am. You can't . . . No, Bán, don't . . ."

The floor was not safe. He brought more of it down as he swung over the edge. Above, Braxus cursed him for a fool and promised a flogging, but did nothing to haul him out. Bán crouched in the rubble. Fractured slivers of tiling sliced into the bare soles of his feet. The columns on either side leaned in at dangerous angles. He knelt, ignoring the cuts to his knees. Iccius rolled his head towards him. His face was alabaster white as it had been in the morning. Even the hollows beneath his eyes had lost their colour.

Bán kissed a cheek and then the cold, bruised lips. He was weeping. His tears scalded them both. "Don't move. I'll get you out. Iccius, listen to me. You are *not* going to die."

"I am . . . just waited for you . . ." It was less than a whisper—a barely heard breath. The great blue eyes lost their focus, swimmingly. When the boy smiled again, it was at shadows seen in the dank dark of the hypocaust and Bán had no share in what he saw there. Pain racked his heart. He lifted the broken head and cradled it to his chest and felt the shuddering of a soul holding on to life. He kissed him as he had never done, a lover's kiss, passionate with desperation.

"Iccius, don't. I love you. You can't die. You mustn't."

The boy smiled. His breathing rasped. Fresh blood and a clear, straw-coloured fluid leaked from one ear. He frowned, struggling to speak again.

"Iccius, don't. It takes too much from you."

"No. Listen . . ." Bán bent low to hear and felt the spider's touch of a kiss on his ear, then a single phrase stored and given up with all the breath that was left. "Promise me you won't die for nothing."

He sighed once, softly, and was gone.

It was harder to climb out than it had been to jump in. Braxus stood watching and did not offer help. Bán emerged, scraped and grazed, and felt none of it. Black rage ate at his heart. He stood before the overseer on legs that shook.

"You saw the crack in the floor. You knew it wasn't safe. You killed him."

The Thracian smiled, colourlessly. "He was a slave. It was a quick death. You could pray for the same." He could have been discussing a deer caught hunting, or a sow freshly slaughtered. "His blood will seal the floor. Perhaps next time it will hold the columns." He turned away, chewing on his lip, and began to pick his way over the debris. "It is fortunate that Amminios has been called back to his father's court. The child was to have been offered to the visiting prefect at dinner after the sales. It would have been difficult to find another so well trained at such short notice—"

Bán aimed the blow from behind—a coward's strike that gave no chance for defence. His father would have disapproved of it. Iccius, who had never been a warrior, would not. He used a fragment of marble as big as both his fists and sharp at one end and he drove it with a strength that surprised him. The spike broke through the Thracian's skull as through an eggshell and buried itself deep in the soft matter within. Braxus dropped without a sound. The slap of his body echoed off the walls and raised more dust from the cavity in the floor. His head dangled over the edge of the broken tiles, dripping gobbets of blood and brain onto the marble below. He twitched once. There was no chance that he was alive but none the less Bán knelt and jerked the man's knife free from his belt and grabbed his hair, pulling his head back to bare his throat for the cut.

"Don't." The voice came like a snapping branch. Bán rose to a warrior's crouch, the knife weaving in front of him ready to kill. Iccius's words wove round his heart. Braxus was nothing. Amminios was not here and not coming. If he was going to die now, he would have to take Godomo with him at least to make it count and it was not Godomo who had spoken.

"Stop. It is me. Father to the son." Fox stood in the doorway, part hidden beneath the fall of the curtain. It was possible he had been there all along. "The boy, your brother, is dead?" he asked. His Gaulish had never been fluent. His accent was more pronounced now than ever.

"Yes."

"Then leave this one. He is dead also. You should not have his blood on you when you run."

Bán stared at him. Thinking was impossible. He wanted to kill and go on killing and then to die.

The Fox took a step forward, his hands loose at his sides, his eyes steady. "Go out to the yard. The four-year-olds are being saddled up ready to leave for the sale. Take Sentios's horse, the big bay. Tell him I said so. Ride for town with the others and leave them when you reach the market. By the time this one is found, you will be gone."

"What about you? They will know you were here."

"No. I am with the horses. Everyone knows that. Of you, they will believe only that you were with the boy. Run now. It is your only chance."

In two years of friendship and teaching, it was the best advice the Fox had ever offered. Bán hurled the block of marble through the hole in the floor and ran.

CHAPTER 17

The livestock marketplace was a solid but temporary structure, erected at the beginning of summer and taken down again at the end of autumn. The horse sale was the last event and the one with highest prestige. Breeders, farmers, gamblers and racing men came from the three parts of Gaul, Belgica and the two German provinces to trade horses at the Durocortorum autumn sale. Rumour said that some of those trading each year came from the free Germanic tribes from the eastern side of the Rhine, but it was impossible to know the truth of that.

Bán hid beneath the stands. They were of oak and ash, cut by carpenters of the Parisi who knew each tree and spoke its language. Every spring, they built an arena and five tiers of seating that would have lasted decades and every autumn they pulled it down and distributed the weathered planks as firewood. The space beneath was used to store fodder and grain for the horses, stacked back as far as the third tier. Behind that, the space was too low for ease and a gap was left, narrowing down so that the space beneath the lowest tier was less than the height of a man's forearm. There was less fodder now, at the end of the season, than there had been in spring. Bán forced his way past old hay and sacks of barley and crawled forward into the dark, oak-scented cavity beneath the lowest seats.

It was dark and airless and the noise made him ill with terror. The boards above his head made a sounding-box so that the skittering cries of the rats were as loud as the booted feet running on the stairs between the rows of seating, and the voices of the crowd came up at him from the beaten earth even as the infinitesimal creaks of his moving cracked like thunder so that he must be heard.

He edged forward, a hand's breadth at a time. Every scrape of his tunic against the unplaned wood above him rasped like a saw on oak knots and he stopped, trembling, his palms drenched, his mind trapped in a white cataract of fear, waiting for the legionaries, or the town magistrate, or—worst—Godomo, to find him.

It was impossible to think or to plan. A part of him needed to kill again, many times—to hear the crack of broken bone and see blood running free as men died to avenge Iccius and Eburovic and all the others of his dead. The remaining part, nearer the surface, wanted very badly to die. Death was a place of no pain and many friends and in this place, in the humid, rat-ridden bowels of the stands, his friends had abandoned him. He was as close to fever as he had been since the branding and the visions did not come, even when he pleaded with them to show their faces. All he could see was Iccius, white with pain and lost blood, and all he could hear was the whisper *Promise me you won't die for nothing.*

The crowd was reaching capacity. The front rank of seats had been filled not long after dawn. By now, those at the back were filling with those who paid for the cheapest seats and drank the cheapest wine and so felt entitled to make most noise. At the entrance to the arena, a drum padded out a two-time rhythm. In moments, the sound of it was drowned out by the beat of trotting horses. Even those in the rearmost seats hushed and sat at quiet attention.

Bán pressed himself to the boards at the front of the stands. Shrinkage and knot gaps let in cracks of light and some of them were wide enough to make good viewing ports. He pressed his eye to one and then drew back a little, fearful that the shine of it would be seen and give him away.

The four-year-olds were first—those fully trained for war and transport. They came in squadrons of twenty, crossing the arena forward and back, with mounted grooms dressed as auxiliary cavalry, showing off their weapons training and steadiness under attack. They ran sorties, one group on another, throwing blunt-pointed wooden spears and catching them on padded shields. The men were performing as much as the horses; a good many of them were freemen hired for the season, and if the visiting prefect really was recruiting local tribesmen for a new cohort of auxiliaries they would do well to catch his eye. Knowing this, Bán looked for the area of the stands before which the best performances took place and so found where the Roman officer sat in the second row of the crowd with half a dozen of his guard around him. He wore minimal armour and no toga and avoided the private seats of the magistrate. Braxus would have known the politics of that, or would have made it his business to find out. But Braxus was dead, and when they found him his murderer would die as slowly as they knew how to make it happen. Amminios would see to it, or Godomo in his absence.

Bán's bowels cramped in terror. In the first months of his slavery he had been forced to watch a crucifixion and the memory of it had woken him for nights afterwards, dry-mouthed and retching. With the passing months, his mind had healed over the horror, in the way the body scabs over a wound, giving him false courage. Now the absolute reality swamped his mind and paralysed his limbs. With no effort at all, he could feel the nails scrape between the bones of his arms and the days and nights of screaming agony that followed as his body succumbed to the drag of its own weight. Pressing his brow against the boards in front of him, he breathed, whistling, through a windpipe tight as a straw. The world flashed scarlet and black behind the seal of his eyes.

The four-year-olds were leaving the arena by the time he could breathe freely again. The drumroll sounded for the three-year-olds. In another time and a different world, he would have been riding the good solid bay with four white socks that was the best horse from his own group. He made himself peer again through the crack; it was better to make the world normal, to think about the mounts and how they were turned out, than to let his mind run free.

He heard the horses before he saw them and knew from the jagged rhythm that something was wrong. The first rank was perfect: four greys turned out in black leather harness with riders in black and polished bronze. The crowd gasped its appreciation. The second rank were chestnut and the third bay, and every one of them was perfect. The problem lay in the fourth rank, the second from last. The colours were mixed—a patchwork of piebalds and skewbalds, none of them from his farm. The black and white horse at the far end of the line was fighting its rider, had been doing so since before they ever entered the arena and continued as the squadron wheeled to the right, to face Bán and the magistrate, and halted. The rider of the pied horse was not one that Bán knew. From a distance, he looked Batavian, one of the hired mercenaries from the tribes on the western, imperial side of the Rhine. He should have been a good horseman—Batavians were amongst the best—but this mount had the better of him and anyone watching could see it.

Bán knew the opening drill well enough that he could do it—had once done it—blindfolded. In theory, the riders saluted and moved immediately into a canter, riding straight for the wall beneath the magistrate's box. Less than a horse's length from the boards, they split down the centre and wheeled hard, half left and half right, making two long columns that raced the length of the arena parallel to the stands. Four phalanxes of four-year-olds—eighty horses in all—had done it perfectly. The lead group of three-year-olds managed for four strides before the fractious piebald colt exploded beyond all control.

The result was chaos. Horses from the front two ranks crashed into the boarding that protected the side of the arena. Others shied, bucked or wheeled to be clear of the danger. Bigger horses barged into smaller ones and knocked them from their feet. A young chestnut filly with thin legs fell to the ground, screaming. Bán saw her rider struggle to throw himself clear of the saddle horns before his leg was crushed beneath her. A short while later they both rose, unharmed, but no-one was watching them by then. The crowd's attention—and Bán's—was focused on the centre of the arena where a pied colt with a hide like milk-streaked jet fought a blond giant with hard hands, a harder bit and a cutting whip, and it was clear to anyone who knew anything that the horse would die fighting before it gave in.

The crowd loved the scent of blood. The magistrate, who had been to Rome and seen the games, felt the mood change and sent swift orders. Slaves and freedmen ran from the box and messages were shouted ahead to the other riders. Some of them, those who had fought in battle and could think, had already ridden close with ropes to restrain the colt and were waved back. The remaining three-year-olds were cleared from the arena, leaving the colt and the man alone on the sands. Above him in the tiers of seating, Bán heard men and women begin to wager on the winner and how long it would take and whether it would be allowed to go all the way until the horse killed the man or if the magistrate would stop them first and have the beast slaughtered.

Bán heard only snatches of the betting. He squirmed his way back under the tiers of seats and out through the grain store far more fluidly than he had entered. The fear of earlier vanished like dew under a hot sun. He knew how Iccius had felt each time he walked back into the dormitory after a night with Braxus; the worst had happened and nothing else could touch him. Better than that, he was free to die, if it could be done with honour, and he thought now that it could. He crawled out into daylight, crouched for a moment to let his eyes adjust to the flood of light and colour and ran for the arena.

Nobody stopped him. The noise of the stands receded, as if his ears had been plugged with loose wool. The world stood on the other side of a gauze curtain through which air and light filtered slowly, deadening sight and sound, except in that one place, in the centre of the sands, where a colt he had known was fighting to the death, and would take him with it. A dun filly cantered on the edge of his vision, dead a long time since and newly present amongst the ghosts as a promise of what was to come.

He reached the front of the stands. Still nobody saw him or tried to hold him back. He was invisible, wrapped in the care of the gods. He remembered a conversation on a hillside in another life. *Is this how it feels before battle? Yes, but in battle one has choice.* He had not known, then, what it was to choose death over life, or how it freed one from care. He vaulted over the oak palisade and landed lightly on the sand.

He was three strides out into the arena when the first of the magistrate's servants saw him. The man carried a horn-handled knife at his belt—and then didn't. Bán crouched, carving the air in front of him, as he had done in the bath-house. The blade was sharp on both edges and honed to a fine point.

"You can die if you want. It makes no difference to me."

It was the truth, spoken without bravado and recognizable as such. The man weighed the cost of a possible flogging against the certainty of a knife in his chest and made the wise choice. Bán grinned at him. "In war you can choose." He said it aloud in Eceni, because that, too, was possible now. The man backed away, holding his hands before him, his eyes showing white at the rims. No-one else took his place.

In the centre of the arena, the Batavian was in trouble.

He was trapped in a saddle designed for cavalry riders in war. Every part of it had been adapted over the years to hold a rider in place without need for hands in the face of an enemy whose main task was to unseat his opponent. Padded horns at front and back bent inwards and pressed down on his thighs, holding him in place as the colt threw itself into a series of spine-jarring bucks. To dismount with any grace at all, he would need the beast to stop and it was not going to stop.

Faced with death or dishonour, the man chose to fight and, because he had no other weapons, he was using the bit and the whip without recourse to reason. The bit must have been Milo's doing. It was a harder one than Fox would ever have countenanced, with a high port that could pierce the hard palate and sharp edges that had already lacerated gums and lips so that red foam splattered back over the shining white-on-black hide. The whip was thin and left long, lacerated cuts and the horse took as much notice of them as he would of a mosquito. There is a staging post in rage which no amount of pain will extinguish. Bán had experienced it once, flogged by Braxus, and had never forgotten. The colt had been angry before it entered the arena; with calm handling it might have been settled but the Batavian had thrown calm handling to the gods; he was as angry as the colt and every cut and jab and backbreaking buck spun them both deeper into a mindless, lethal frenzy.

Blood spattered freely on the sand. The smell of it, briefly, was the smell of the hypocaust, until a wall of horse- and man-sweat flooded everything else. Bán stood very still. His heart swelled. The overwhelming power of the colt filled him with pride and awe. He remembered an old tale of the ancestors who had sacrificed horses to the gods before they had come to know that horses *were* the gods walking on earth and that to kill them was sacrilege. He could believe of this horse that it was a god, or a gift of the gods. The Batavian on top was a mortal man who could see his own death approaching.

Bán raised his arm. In the neutral Gaulish of the region he called out, "Do you know the cavalry dismount?"

The colt reared from the sound of the new voice. The man threw himself forward, hugging the neck. Every rider's fear is the horse that throws itself backwards. Without a chance to dismount, the rider dies, crushed beneath a writhing mass of horseflesh. For a heartbeat, the pair hung high in the air, the horse and his clinging parasite, and death hung with them.

The crowd cheered, distantly. The spectacle was perfect. The man had been picked for his colouring as much as his skill as a rider; his hair was white blond, paler even than Iccius's, and it flowed like a flag over his black leather corselet. The horse was bridled in black with a halter beneath of bleached white rope. Its hide was night black with streaks of poured milk. From a distance, the sweat gave a polished shine to them both and the freckles of blood were not visible.

The colt teetered on the brink and came down again, forefeet smashing the sand into dust. Bán skidded sideways to avoid a striking hoof. Over the bruising hammer of a standing buck, he shouted, "They will not stop this. The magistrate himself has bet two thousand denarii on your death. Can you do the dismount?"

"Yes." The word was thrown over his shoulder, lost in the churning spray of a turn.

"Good. I will throw sand in his face. He will stop when it hits him, then flinch, as if from the wind. Do it then."

It was a trick Fox had taught him to get the better of the big chestnut studhorse with the foul temper. Then Bán had not had to mount after, only catch a halter rope. He prayed and felt the gods at his side and knew that he could not fail. At worst, the colt would kill him; at best, he would kill himself. He had yet to decide whether to kill the colt. It, too, deserved release from slavery.

He stooped and caught a fistful of sand. The colt reared again, screaming. Heartbeats passed with it high in the air. As it came down, Bán moved round to one shoulder and, as the forefeet hammered into sand, he threw.

All things happened at once. The crowd rose to its feet, sensing a climax. The colt, following the instinct of a thousand generations, propped and spun away from a desert wind that did not exist. The Batavian, to his credit, executed a perfect cavalry dismount. All he needed was a horse that stayed level for more than one stride and he was up and off, tucking his shoulder in and rolling on the sand to come up on his feet. That half of the crowd that had bet on his survival cheered. The rest booed. The magistrate signalled his servants, who began to run onto the sand. The colt, freed of its burden, looked around for an exit and saw it, an open gap in the distance with none but a skinny boy in the space between. Scenting freedom, it sprang from a standing start to a full gallop. At the second stride, its shoulder brushed the boy. Bán gripped his stolen knife in his teeth, reached up with both hands for the curved horns of the saddle, kicked up, once, twice, and was on.

The mount at full gallop is the most difficult manoeuvre

a cavalryman can be asked to make. To be successful, he must land in the saddle exactly between the horns and slip his legs into place beneath them. In full armour, it is almost impossible. For a lean, lithe boy who had practised half his childhood, albeit with a less difficult saddle, it was an act aided by the gods. Even with a shield, he could have done it.

The colt did not stop. The boy was lighter than the man had been and he did not grab at the reins or attempt to stop the onward rush to freedom. On the contrary, Bán leaned forward with the knife in his hand and cut the bridle at the poll, sweeping the ear loops free. The horse spat the bit to the arena floor. The halter had a single rope, coiled up and knotted under the chin. It gave a handhold, nothing more. Bán left it in place and held on to the mane, leaning forward and shouting encouragement. They reached the gates and they were flying.

Men of the three- and four-year-old phalanxes were waiting for them. Milo, of all men, had known both colt and boy and had seen what might happen. Eighty mounted men stood strung out in an arc on the rain-damp turf of the collecting area. The horse saw only gaps between others of its kind. Bán saw the trap—a rope held taut at neck height, too high to jump and too low to duck under. He had no reins and no way to pull the horse round. With perfect pre- science, he saw the colt's death of a broken neck and his own, infinitely slower, nailed to wood. He looked to both sides. There was a gap of sorts on the right between the end- most rider and the arena wall. He reached forward along the colt's neck.

"*Hai!*"

He slapped a cupped palm on the colt's left eye. The

horse jerked violently to the right, saw the gap and forced it open. They broke free. Open grassland stretched out before them. The legionary camp lay ahead and to the right. A fringe of oak darkened the northern half of the horizon. Beyond that, there was nothing but space. The colt lengthened his stride.

"Stop them!" Milo whipped his own horse into a gallop. It was slow and kind and stood no chance. He wheeled round and raised his whip hand, pointing. "Freedom or his worth in gold to the man who takes them alive!"

He could have made no better offer. One hundred and nineteen mounted men, over half of them already free, kicked their horses forward. One hundred and nineteen war-trained horses threw their hearts into running. The spectators fighting to reach the gates of the arena felt the reverberating thunder as the race began. The betting began afresh, on the pied colt or the hunters.

Bán knew himself blessed. He hung in that gap between life and death, awaiting the call to cross the river. He regretted his failure to kill Amminios, or even Milo, but nothing else. In his fist, he gripped the stolen blade, the point turned in to his heart, and he knew without question that he could use it when the time came. Given time, if the gods so willed, he would kill the god-horse first, slicing open the great veins in the neck as the ancestors had done in their sacrifice, and they would ride together across the river to the world of the dead. He did not feel it to be sacrilege.

The colt ran with a long, fluid stride. Iron clouds hung low in the sky, except in the south where a blade of sunlight lit them yellow, showing the path to the gods. Bán pushed with his legs and the colt answered, swerving slightly right to follow the line of the light. Their speed was more than Bán had known, except in dreams. Small bushes and single trees whipped past in the wind. Behind them, a horn blared a legionary command. Six different notes split the air in the language Bán did not know. It was repeated again and answered, harshly, from the camp to his right. He pushed the colt left, away from the noise.

A small wall with a ditch beyond it reared up in front of them. They jumped it and landed neatly and found that the flat land seen from the arena had been an illusion. Ahead, the ground sloped gently down to a thin, trickling stream shrouded on both sides by a wispy, green-grey woodland. They dipped down, running on turf that smelled of sage and wild mint. Bán heard the sharper shouts and another horn and knew he had dropped from their view. He grimaced and yelled to the colt, cheering it on. Two ears flicked back, one black, one streaked with white, and he told himself the beast knew his voice.

They jumped the stream. Bán prayed aloud to Nemain of the waters and to Airmid, who had been named for her and was dead. The land beyond was flat and sandy and the colt kicked up dust. To their right, willow and hazel trailed leaves in the water. Both were trees of the gods. The colt slowed, unsure of its direction. Bán leaned forward and tugged on the halter rope. He clucked his tongue the way he had always done when leading foals in from the paddocks. The colt dipped its head and turned to the pull of the rope. On the slope, the first of the following hunt crested the rise and saw them. Bán freed his thighs from the grip of the saddle and slid to the ground, pulling the lead rope until he and his mount stood with their backs to a stand of hazel. The colt shoved against the boy's shoulder, using him as a scratching post to clear the itch of the bridle, then dropped its head to graze. Bán looped an arm across its neck. His free hand held the stolen blade, sharp as a skinning knife, against the patterned black and white of its hide. He pressed his palm into the neck groove until he felt the bounding rhythm of a pulse and knew where to start his cut. In the willows by the stream, a blackbird chucked a warning as it would have done at home. He heard it and his heart filled and he did not weep.

The hunt was close. Their thunder swamped all other noise. The blackbird fled, soundless in the chaos. The first of the riders was the Roman cavalry officer from the arena. He had ridden well to get ahead of the hunt. His mount was built for speed in battle. He shouted as it jumped the stream. The colt raised its head and called. Bán reached under the great arced neck and changed his grip on the knife. He held his breath, awaiting the word of the god. The Roman pushed himself high in the saddle and raised his arm and shouted in Latin, *"Now!"*

Bán was stronger than he had been when Amminios took him. The men who stepped out of the woods at his back had to hit him twice before he fell.

He woke to the sound of a legionary trumpet, calling the watch. The pain in his head consumed him. He opened his eyes and found dim shapes in dusky light and even that was too much. He pressed his palms to his face and sought oblivion. Iccius came to him in the blackness, and then Macha. Neither of them spoke. Memories crowded in: of Iccius and Braxus, of the sounding-box beneath the stands, of the colt and their flight to freedom, of his capture and what must come after, which was worse than any headache. He would die, now, without honour. He took his hands from his eyes and made himself look around. They had neither bound nor stripped him. He was not incapable; if there were the means to bring an early death, he would find it. What the gods thought, he would find out after.

He had looped his belt around his neck and was standing on a box, reaching for the ridgepole of the tent, when they found him. There were three of them against his one—two Gauls and a Batavian. He threw himself at them, gouging at the pale eyes, biting whatever flesh passed his face, kicking for an exposed groin. The first grunts of pain brought the prefect running. He stood beyond the door-flap. His shadow spread before him, wavering in the light of a fire. His voice was dry and cutting.

"Civilis, he's a boy, not an armed man. Hold him steady. If you kill him, I'll have your hide for a tent-covering. Rufus, stop playing the fool and make him safe."

Their pride would not allow them to keep fighting after that. Civilis—the Batavian—trapped Bán's wrists and held them behind his back. The other two wrapped him over and over like a chrysalis in the cloak on which he had woken. One of them whipped off his belt and buckled it round, holding the wrapping fast. Another swept his legs from under him and laid him flat on his back on the floor.

"Gods, must you— Never mind." The tribune snapped his fingers. "Rufus, get me a lamp."

The lamp came quickly—a steady oil-lit flame that burned cleanly, with little smoke. The taller of the two Gauls swept back the door-flap and held the lamp aloft, shedding light all around. Bán screwed his eyes shut. The brightness of it seared through to the soft parts of his brain. He ground his teeth at the pain but made no sound. The officer stepped in between them, shielding the flame with his body, and set the lamp on a bedding box at the end of the tent. In Latin he said, "Leave us. Don't go far. Civilis, find out what happened to the guards. I gave orders he was to be watched. Find who was on duty and deal with it."

Bán lay on his side, trussed like a hunted boar. The pain in his head defied comprehension. Despair settled in his chest like a dead weight, crushing his heart and his breathing, draining the will to fight. He heard the prefect lift the lamp and set it again on the turf. Warm light flickered against his closed eyelids. A cool hand touched his brow and swept back through his hair. A dry, firm voice said, "Bán mac Eburovic, will you open your eyes for me?" In Eceni.

Visions slammed into his mind: a deer grazing in the forest near the great-house; Eburovic standing on a headland beside a fire that was in itself a miracle; a naked man kneeling on sand with Breaca's serpent-blade at his throat; that same man, waving from the stern of a ship that bore a flaming sun horse on the sail.

"Corvus?" He tried to raise his head and failed. He said it in Gaulish and then in Latin. "Corvus? Is it you?"

"It is. Quintus Valerius Corvus, prefect of the Ala Quinta Gallorum—or I will be when it is fully formed."

Bán would have known the voice before if the humour had not been absent. No-one else spoke Gaulish with that lift to the final vowels. In a confusing cascade of long-forgotten feelings, he remembered a promise, made under moonlight.

"Did you go back for my long-nights?"

"No. I'm sorry." The voice softened and lost the humour. "There was no chance. I was posted south as soon as I reported back. If I'd been able to, I'd have found out sooner what had happened and come to find you and maybe Iccius would still be . . . Shh, now. I'm sorry. I'm so sorry. Let's get you out of this nonsense and see what's to be done."

Bán was not weeping—he would not weep—but he could not speak, either. Strong hands loosened the belt that bound him, unwound the cloak and raised him to sitting. A beaker of well-watered wine was pressed into his palms and he was held until he could swallow without choking, then simply held, his cheek pressed close to leather worn smooth with years of exposure to weather, his hair stroked down and down as he had stroked Iccius's, soothing, in a morning that seemed a lifetime away and was not. He smelled leather and lamp oil, sheep's wool and horse-sweat and the warm breath of a man, sweetened a little with wine. He felt safe as he had not done since he was a child in his father's arms. The arid ache inside him swelled with grief and compounded loss. He looked up and found brown eyes, made amber in the lamplight.

"Why are you here?" he asked.

"Fulfilling the will of the gods?" Corvus smiled as he had done a hundred times in the roundhouse. "According to my orders, I am here to buy horses and to recruit men. The emperor is building a fresh army and he needs both. I have been forgiven the dishonour of losing a ship and they have given me charge of a wing of Gaulish cavalry, for which I am very grateful. You only have to march once with the infantry to realize why every other civilized nation makes war on horseback." He smiled inwardly at a joke Bán did not under-stand and shook his head.

"Never mind that. Just believe me when I say that I have the necessary authority and it matters to me that I use it wisely. I have concluded an agreement of sale with a partic-ularly unpleasant Gaul named Godomo; I will buy from him two hundred and fifty horses of mixed age, both colts and fillies, at the full asking price—that number to include an irregularly marked black and white three-year-old colt and the youth who so effectively demonstrated the cavalry mount in the arena."

Bán felt his heart stop. He remembered Braxus and all that went with him. "He can't sell me. He really can't. Even if Amminios would let him, he can't. I killed—"

"No." The hands soothing his head fell still, grasping his temples. "Don't say it. Even in private, say nothing."

"But—"

"Bán, listen to me." He was pushed upright and made to look into eyes that were nothing at all like his father's. "At the villa of Amminios, a Belgic boy-slave named Iccius was sent into the hypocaust to find why the fires would not draw. In the process of looking, he dislodged a badly made pillar and caused a floor to collapse. He was fatally injured by falling masonry. A Thracian overseer named Braxus, who had a carnal fondness for the boy—"

"Corvus, you *knew* Iccius. How can you say that?"

"Because he's dead and you're not and whereas I can do nothing to bring him back, I can stop you from following. Hear me out. I am telling you what has been recorded. The Thracian slave jumped into the cavity and tried to save his catamite. He was struck on the head by a block of marble in a secondary fall and he, too, died of his injuries. That's how it was. Godomo has sworn it in front of the magistrate. He has agreed to undertake the repair of the baths at his own expense."

"But—"

"Bán, will you listen? A slave cannot give evidence against his master except under torture. Do you really want to suggest that Godomo has perjured himself?"

"How can he testify to anything? He wasn't there."

"He may not have been, but in the absence of his master he has ultimate responsibility and, according to all the witnesses, the only two people who were present are dead. It is understood that the Thracian had sent all others from the building on a pretext before he tried to save the boy, so the truth will never be exactly known. In the meantime, if Godomo wishes to conclude the sale of Amminios's horses—and I understand that he wishes very badly to do so—then he must agree to sell me the pied colt and give me the papers concerning his rider. I have made it very clear to him that this deal is all or nothing. I get you, or he makes no sale to me or any other Roman officer. He has no choice. Therefore, it must be that no-one else was involved in the deaths or his sale will founder."

"He can't sell me. I'm not his to sell. Amminios will hang him if he comes back and finds me gone."

"He may do, although I doubt it. Amminios is interested primarily in money and power and I am his route to both. I think it is a risk Godomo is prepared to take. In any case, he hasn't sold you. He has passed your papers to me, which is different."

The Roman rose and crossed back to the blanket box.

He drew another beaker and a flask of wine from inside and dragged the box across to act as a seat. A rolled scroll lay on his knee, ignored by them both. "Did you know Amminios was going to host a dinner in my honour tonight?"

"Yes, Braxus told me. They were going to offer you Iccius after it."

"Gods. Were they?" A muscle jumped in Corvus's cheek. "I would not say I am glad the lad is dead, but I am glad I avoided that." He poured for them both and Bán drank unaided. Wine was a habit he had come to late and only in small quantities, but it warmed him now and he would not have done Corvus the dishonour of turning him down.

The Roman said gently, "Godomo told me that Amminios's war eagles slaughtered your family. Is it true?"

"Yes."

"I'm sorry." He sat down on the blanket box, keeping the wine at his side. "And Caradoc, is he dead also?"

"No." The spit grew sour in Bán's mouth. "He left us a day before the attack. He helped Amminios plan it."

"What?" The Roman stared at him. "Are you sure?"

"Yes. Amminios told me on the boat when they first brought me over. I didn't believe him then but I heard him talking about it later in the bathhouse with Braxus; they forgot I was outside stoking the fire and could hear it all. He was laughing at the old-fashioned superstitions of the Eceni, about how Breaca had been taken in by something as meaningless as an oath made on a blade and the rest of us had followed her blindly, like children. He said—" He choked and had to gather himself. "He said it was what made us so easy to kill."

The memory burned at the scar on his arm. It was what

had sparked the very earliest attempt to escape and had earned him the brand. In the white-hot fury of the moment, he had dropped his wood and run for the stables to steal a horse, with no better idea in his mind than to get back to the land of the Ordovices and kill Caradoc or die trying. His choice of horse, made in haste, had been poor and Braxus's men had run him down before he reached the gates but, for the brief span of his freedom, it had mattered more to Bán that Caradoc die than Amminios. Searching inside now for that same flame of anger, he failed to find it; Iccius's death had extinguished everything.

Still, he wept—for the memory of Iccius and his family more than for himself. Corvus came to sit beside him, sharing the dignity of silence. In time, when the worst of it had passed, he said, "I am truly sorry. I had thought better of Caradoc. But whatever might have been between him and his brother, it will be different now. Cunobelin is dead and Amminios has sailed home to attend his father's funeral. If you are right and he has made a pact with Caradoc, then the two of them will kill Togodubnos. If they survive, I would bet everything I own that Caradoc will go on to kill Amminios. He may have made a passing alliance, but he has nursed a hatred since his childhood and I can't see him letting go of it easily. I would say that if your former master makes his way home alive he will be concerned about greater things than a freed Eceni hostage."

Corvus refilled the beakers and laid them on the blanket box within easy reach. Bán stared at him.

"Hostage?"

"Indeed." The Roman was trying not to smile and failing. "I have the papers here. They, too, have been attested in my presence by the magistrate. You are a prince of the royal line of the Eceni. It is not uncommon for a younger son to be sent in good faith to be reared in the homes of men who oppose his people. It is a means to ensure that treaties, once signed, will be adhered to. Half of Gaul sent younger sons as hostages to Caesar. They fought at his side and made a good part of his cavalry in later wars."

"I wouldn't fight for Amminios if he tore my teeth from my head to make me do it."

"No-one is asking you to. I am simply saying that by the laws of Rome you are not a slave, and you are free to go home whenever you want to. I don't want you as a hostage, and neither does the emperor; he's not at war with your people. It's late in the year for ships to be crossing the ocean but there's one leaving Gesoriacum in ten days. I can get you onto it and I'll pay for your passage. If the ship's master can be persuaded, I'll see if they'll sail all the way up to the lands of the Eceni so you won't have to travel through enemy territory." Corvus grinned in a way that Bán had forgotten. "My only stipulation is that you take your mad killer colt with you before it does someone an injury. Civilis nearly lost an arm to its teeth when he tried to take its saddle off. The halter is waiting until you feel well enough to try, or it can rot off where it stands. No-one else will go near it."

It was a dream, obviously. Bán stared at the lamp. A winged horse flew round the base of it, given life by the undulating flame. It was a long time since he had dreamed with such precision. Iccius was present, as he had been throughout the day, but none of the other phantoms. Bán called a vision of home, of the roundhouse and the paddocks and his father's forge, and found it came only dimly and was empty of people—a ghost place, lacking even the ghosts.

He called to the river and the sacred pool and the memory of the waterfall in summer, thinking that here, at least, he could expect to find Breaca, or Airmid. The dust in his mind told him that the lands of his past were dead to him, closed off for all time. He thought he should weep for that, but the ache inside did not allow for further weeping. He looked to Iccius for advice and saw him, indistinctly. The blue eyes were the same as they had last been in life, and the message that went with them: *Don't die for nothing.*

He brought his dry gaze back to Corvus's face, seeing afresh the contrast between the vital, vibrant intelligence of the man and the dry husk that was himself. The prefect smiled at him and crooked his brow. "What are you thinking?"

With all that had been done for him, he could not tell the truth. Instead, he said, "That I have no home. That home was given meaning by the people who lived there and all of them are gone. That there is nothing for me to go back to."

"That's not true." Corvus turned to see him better. He stretched out and took Bán's hand in his own. There was not so great a difference in their size now, nor the colour. Three summers in Gaul had baked Bán brown and he had grown in height to match any Roman.

Corvus said, "You're upset because of Iccius, I understand that, but you'll feel differently with time. You must believe it. Do you still miss Eburovic as you did? Or Macha?"

Bán said nothing. With more time to think, he might have found the words to explain that Eburovic was a warrior and had died with a blade in his hand and Macha was a dreamer who could call on the gods to sell her life dearly, but that, like the dun filly, Iccius had been Bán's to look after and he had failed.

In the space of his silence, Corvus said, "What about Efnís? He was your friend; his people would take you in if you don't want to live amongst your own. You have so much to do—you could sit your long-nights and take your spear-tests and become a warrior and then, if the elders agree it, you could pursue Caradoc for his blood-guilt." He used the Eceni words and they came stiffly to his tongue, rusted from lack of use. Still, he cared enough to try.

Bán said, "I am too old to sit my long-nights. It must be done at the right time or the gods will not send the dream."

"Sit your spear-tests, then. You could still become a warrior."

"A warrior is nothing without a dream. Could you imagine Eburovic without the she-bear? Or Breaca without the serpent-spear? I could be a hunter, perhaps, or a smith like my father but it wouldn't be the same."

Corvus frowned. His hands were steady, feeling a truth that ran beneath the words. Quietly, so that it was just between them, he said, "I won't let you die, Bán. You're worth too much for that."

There was nothing to be said. The gods, too, were not ready for Bán to die. He had seen the chance twice in less than a day and twice it had been taken from him. He thought of life without Iccius and did not see how it could be borne.

Corvus held his hands in stubborn silence. The man was a friend, perhaps the only one. The ache inside parted to give Bán an answer. He said, "Make me a warrior of Rome."

"*What?*"

"You are recruiting men for your cavalry wing. I may never be a warrior of the Eceni, but I passed my fifteenth birthday at the full moon before the autumn equinox and in the eyes of the Gauls that is all it takes to be a man. You are recruiting men. Take me. If it is to be said that I was a hostage, then let me follow in the footsteps of my predecessors, the Gaulish hostages to Caesar, and enlist in the emperor's army." He did not say, *And go to war, and fight, and die as did my father and sister, with a blade in my hand.*

The silence counted his heartbeats. Outside, an owl cried, the carrier of dreams, and a horse screamed in anger. Even after so little time together, he recognized the voice of the pied colt. A name came to him, as it had done with Hail. "He is the Crow," he said. "The pied colt is called Crow." He said it in Eceni, when all the rest had been in Gaulish. It made more sense that way.

A hand fell on his shoulder. Corvus stood over him, shaking his head. "Go to sleep. You're overtired. We'll talk of it more in the morning."

"You'll not let me enlist?"

"I won't stop you from doing anything your dreams tell you to do, but you're not a citizen, you can't enlist in a legion and I can't appoint you directly to the cavalry; that's not in my power. To do as you say, you'd have to go through four months on probation, which is not something to be taken lightly. If you grew tall enough over the winter, and if the assessors thought you good enough, you might get a cavalry posting, but if not, you'd be in the infantry cohorts or discharged and left with nothing."

"But you must need men to serve in other ways. I can

build. I can cut corn. I can run a stables and a stud farm. It would still be home."

"Bán, that's not necessary. We do have need of servants and many of them are freemen, but even so, the best I could offer is to take you as my groom, or teach you to write and make you my scribe, and neither of those is a fit life for a warrior of the Eceni."

"I can write already. Amminios had me taught. It made me more Roman."

"Even so."

The box was pushed back to the wall. The lamplight wavered with the movement and was snuffed out. Outside, firelight cast smudged shadows. Bán found himself lying down with a folded tunic as a pillow and a cloak laid across him for warmth. The beaker of watered wine was left by his head.

"Sleep now, and see what the dreams bring you. You can make your choices in the morning."

Bán slept and dreamed of nothing. The morning brought him a pied colt called Crow who had stood through the night in a halter because nobody else had dared take it off. By noon, bitten once and kicked, Bán had changed the halter and the colt had eaten in his presence. In the evening, he met with Corvus, and told him his decision.

CHAPTER 18

"The Sun Hound is dead."

Word spread from the dun with the last days of autumn. "Cunobelin is dead. Amminios is returning from exile in Gaul. He has sworn alliance to Berikos of the Atrebates, enemy of his father. Togodubnos will oppose them both. There will be war." Everywhere, dreamers and elders who had waited all summer for the news gathered their warriors and prepared them for battle. The wisest among them were less urgent. "Be patient. Hone your blades but do not expect to use them yet. The Sun Hound held on to his life long enough. It is too close to winter to fight now; there will be no war before spring."

On Mona, in the warriors' school and the council of dreamers, they heard the news sooner than most. Since early spring, Luain mac Calma had sent reports of the wasting disease that was slowly draining the Sun Hound's life, couched in language that the bearers thought to be trivial but was not. The fact itself was brought to the council directly by Lanis, sole dreamer of the Trinovantes, who rode without rest from the east coast to the west, changing horses every half day to keep the speed. She arrived at the straits in the early evening of the third day after the death and lit a signal fire to summon a ferry from the island. Two men waited with her on the foreshore: Gunovic, the travelling smith, whom she knew of old, and a stocky, straw-haired youth of the northern Brigantes who spoke in an accent so thick that it defied comprehension but who carried as evidence of his good faith a blue stone carved in the shape of the leaping salmon, the mark of Venutios, who was Warrior of Mona, second only in rank to Talla, Elder of elders. When the ferry came, those who handled it had orders to take all three across.

The evening was cool and still. Midges danced in clouds above the jetty, dark patches reflected in darker water against the greyed background of the sky. Breaca stared through them to the cloaked shapes on the ferry. She was one of a dozen, handpicked by Venutios to act as welcome party to Lanis and the two unnamed men who travelled with her. The Warrior himself stood to one side, the strong planes of his face showing in profile against the water. He was not a tall man by Eceni standards, but he had a solid strength that made him seem so. He radiated a calm that on most days would have spread to them all but today did not. The scar on Breaca's palm itched as it had done all day so that she felt high-strung, like the grey mare before a race, and had no idea why. Those on either side of her stood at ease, expecting no trouble, nor did they have cause to do otherwise; whatever the events in the east attendant on Cunobelin's death, they posed no immediate danger to Mona or to those who lived and studied there.

The ferry swirled in the grip of a current. It was well

known that the gods protected their own and Mona was nothing if not the gods' isle. If those on the ferry had offered danger, Breaca did not believe they would be allowed to cross the straits in safety. Still, she could not settle. She had stepped forward to speak of it to Venutios when the larger of the two unnamed travellers stood up at the bow of the ferry and a flicker of late light on the water showed his face.

"Gunovic!"

The craft was less than a spear's throw away, swinging against the current. Breaca ran forward to the end of the jetty, the shock of welcome swamped by a wave of unreasoning panic that came close to unravelling two years of Mona's training. She stretched to catch the ferry rope and turned it round an oak post and hauled it in, calling to him, "Gunovic, are you well? And Macha? Is there ill news of the Eceni?" and he was with her, leaping up onto the jetty with the agility of youth and holding her in his great bear's embrace and for a moment she was a girl again, greeting her father after a year's absence and the world was as good as it could ever be. Gunovic was not her father, but he had cared for Macha through a summer's long illness and had lost his trade because of it and stayed the winter and the spring after that and he was the smith of the Eceni now in Eburovic's place. She could imagine no-one better. He grinned and the panic ebbed, leaving only the joy and the needling itch in her palm.

"Gently now, there's no bad news from us." He ran his fingers through her hair in the way he had done when she was young. "In fact, I think there might be good news if the elders confirm it."

"Really?" She stood back, holding him at arm's length

to see him better. The late sun lit his armbands and the gift-brooches on his cloak. Nothing had changed of the man but the peace in his face, which was new. Hope made her rash. "Gunovic—is Macha pregnant?"

"No. Not that I know of. And perhaps not ever. I think she would be by now if it could happen." An old pain cramped round his eyes; he had lost one family to slavers in his youth and had sworn never to love again. To find himself loving and loved and yet be denied children would be the hardest irony. She squeezed his arm and would have apologized for asking but he shook his head and gave a half-smile that took the loss and made it bearable. "With news that good, you would have heard me shouting it from the other side of the straits," he said. "But it is good all the same. Macha has asked me to be singer of the Eceni in your mother's place. I have come to ask permission of Talla."

He was grinning like a boy with his first hunted hare. Breaca hugged him fiercely. It was not news; she had heard it already in the summer, one of the half-rumours that blew to Mona on the backs of the gulls, but there was no reason for him to know that, and to hear it confirmed made her day perfect. There was no-one else, ever, who could have taken her mother's place. She pulled him close, pressing her face to his shoulder. "Talla will give permission," she said. "It is long past time we had a new singer."

"And a new sire for the horse herds. See, I have brought him all this way for your approval."

Gunovic clapped her on the shoulders and turned her round to show off the big bay horse that stood on the jetty. A straw-haired youth in the black cloak of the Brigantes passed behind her back, leading his own horse. The hand-itch died away as he passed, leaving only the fluttering anticipation that had been with her all day. The stranger spoke with Venutios, who knew him and greeted him gladly. When they stood close, a degree of kinship was clear between them in the wide, blunt faces and the grey eyes. Only the hair was different: Venutios's was dark, streaked with grey at the temples, while the other was fair. Breaca watched as the Warrior smiled and put a hand on the messenger's arm. She had never yet known Venutios to make a mistake in his friendships.

"Who is he?" she asked.

"His dam won a race against Sinochos's white-socked chestnut and his sire has bred at least a dozen good—"

"Not the horse, the youth. The one talking to Venutios. Who is he?"

"The lad? His name's Vellocatus. He's from Venutios's people, sent with a private message."

It may have been private, but it was not welcome. She saw the warmth pass from the Warrior, leaving him still and unnaturally stiff for one who lived his life in the fluid forms of battle. The straw-headed messenger pressed his point, cutting the air with the edge of his hand for emphasis, and then stopped, leaving a silence that spoke as strongly. The warriors of the welcome party stood away and turned their backs, giving the pair privacy. The gesture passed unnoticed. Venutios gazed past them all, staring vacantly at the sun-stained horizon as if he stood on the jetty alone. He looked older than he had done, more burdened, like a man who has been given a shield heavier than is sensible and must carry it in a fight not of his choosing. Seeing him, Breaca made sense, suddenly, of a recent dream of Airmid's in which a salmon had swum upriver to the spawning grounds, bearing a crow's feather in its mouth. Her heart jolted within her. Horrified, she spoke aloud, forgetting Gunovic was not of Mona and might not be privy to its secrets. "Gods. They're calling him home. What time is this for Mona to be choosing a new Warrior?"

It was the time set by the gods and could not be changed. On Mona, more than anywhere else, the gods walked the land and life moved to their rhythms. Every part of the island was sacred. Breaca had felt it when she first stepped off the ferry with Airmid and it struck her afresh each time someone she knew came to visit: a quickening of the pulse and a strengthening of the blood that lifted her higher and sharpened her vision so that she saw more clearly the threads that bound each of them to the land and to each other and understood once again the small place of her own cares in the greater pattern of the world.

In the normal course of things, the renewed clarity would have passed by nightfall on the day of Gunovic's visit, lost in a flurry of greetings and gifts and gossip. Breaca had news of those things that mattered in her tight-woven world: of her progress in the warriors' school; of the grey mare's latest filly foal, which was not turning out as well as it might have done; of Airmid's new lover, who was the greatest of the school's warriors, and what Lanis had said of her in open hearing.

Gunovic, for his part, had news of the tribes beyond: of Macha and the progress of her healing, which was as complete as it might ever be; of 'Tagos, who had found that he could wield a sword left-handed, but not a spear; of the Coritani, who had declared a truce and sworn oaths at the autumn council not only of neutrality but of friendship and alliance in the face of possible war in the south. All of this would have taken the best part of the night and the sharpness of vision that was Mona's would have blurred again by morning, but for two messages, brought together, which changed the face of the world for ever.

Breaca had felt the change before Venutios raised his hand to gather his group at the jetty. In the moments of meeting, she had exchanged with Gunovic the news of a year, condensed into half-sentences and shorn of all drama. There had been no time to reflect on it after. The horns had sounded as the travellers reached the settlement, summoning the warriors, dreamers and singers of Mona to council, and there had been barely time to gather up a cloak and brooch before she was queuing to enter the largest of the greathouses and then standing in rank order with the other warriors behind a fire pit that spanned half the width of the hall, beneath torches that filled the air with pine smoke and burnt tallow, watching, with startling clarity, the play of flame and shadow on the gathered faces.

She heard a murmur pass through the ranks of dreamers gathered on the far side of the fire and looked up. The front line parted and when it came together Talla stood in the space before the fire pit. The Elder could barely walk without aid and yet she was there now, standing erect as the youngest of dreamers, her hair moon-white in the torchlight and her eyes warm with the glow of the fire. Maroc stood at her side, the dreamer who all believed would be her successor. He was a slight, wiry man with thinning wheaten hair and pale eyes. At first glance, he had the look of one who should be casting pots or stitching harness and he had passed as such more than once out of necessity in the lands of Gaul and amongst the tribes south of the sea-river who had turned their backs on the dreamers and the gods. On Mona he made no effort to hide who he was, so that, waiting under the arc of his gaze, Breaca knew the same sense of awe as she did in the presence of the standing stones of the ancestors. A shiver passed down her spine and a high whine, like the hum of summer bees, began to play in her ears. She looked for Gunovic and found him, far out on the side amongst the singers. He was staring straight at her. She smiled but saw no response.

Maroc signalled behind him. Two of the apprentice singers dragged forward a hide-covered vessel and set it on a slate on the dreamers' side of the fire pit. In its presence, the quality of the silence changed. Breaca felt the tension around her rise to battle pitch. None of the others had hand-scars that warned of battle, but each of them had been proved best in the testing grounds of the tribes and none had come to Mona without sufficient experience of war to sense the changes in the air. They held themselves ready, like dogs straining against a leash, and each felt it as the last moments of battle before the spears are thrown, when life is sweetest and Briga fills the air with death. Breaca swallowed on nothing and reached for Hail, who was not there.

"Warriors of Mona." Talla's voice was thin as a hollow reed. In the air above the warriors, it gathered strength, and echoed from the back walls. "Warriors of Mona, you know by now that Venutios, who has been your Warrior, the greatest of his generation, has been recalled by his people. He goes in honour and with the blessing of the elders. He has served for twelve years beyond the ten of his training and his honour guard served with him. All are free now to return to their tribes, but we would ask one last service of them."

Talla gestured to her right. Venutios stood in the shadows and none of them had seen him. He had changed from the formal dress of the welcome party, replacing it with a short hunting tunic the colour of dried bracken. Newly hung round his neck, was a leaping salmon carved in blue stone, and a bull's horn hung from a thong at his side. This last, above all else, was the symbol of the Warrior, the badge that set one above the rest. It was hard to imagine it borne by anyone else.

Talla acknowledged him with a nod and went on. "As with the Elder, Mona can never be without her Warrior. Before Venutios leaves, one must be chosen from amongst the two thousand of the school to take his place. The laws of the choosing come from the ancestors; they are clear and precise. You need not know them, save as they affect you directly. Maroc will guide you through the first steps."

The Elder stood less straight than she had done. Maroc took her place at the edge of the fire pit. The logs burned red at his feet and cast his shadow upwards, giving him height. His voice was deeply resonant and reached them all without effort.

"Warriors of Mona. Of the two thousand, thirty will be chosen to take the tests. Of those thirty, one will be Warrior. The first part is in the hands of the gods alone. The tests that come after are yours for you to prove yourselves before the gods. They last a night and a day and will be harder than any you have encountered. There is danger. At each time of the Warrior choosing, some have died. You are not bound to take part in the first selection, but if, having taken part, you are among the thirty, you are bound to continue. Those who wish to leave may do so now."

He looked out into silence. Two thousand warriors looked back. Nobody moved.

"Good." He reached down and stripped the hide from the vessel at his feet. The skull of a bull shone white in the firelight. Between its horns sat a wide copper vessel the mouth of which was sealed with a black horse-skin, bound drum-tight across the top. At Maroc's signal, Venutios stepped forward and stabbed his knife in the centre to make a single incision, five fingers wide. The blade flashed once as he lifted it clear. Breaca flinched and felt the ripple of it pass on and multiply, two thousand times.

Maroc said, "The cauldron holds a pebble for every member of the warriors' school. All are white but thirty, which are black. Venutios will call the names in rank order. When you hear your own, you will step up to the mark, reach across the fire pit and take a stone from the vessel. If your stone is black, you are one of the thirty and must remain here. If it is white, you are free to go."

The preparations took moments. The bull's skull was moved to the very edge of the fire pit. A long, narrow slate already gave a mark on the warriors' side of the fire. On the dreamers' side, Maroc stood to one side of the vessel, Venutios to the other. The Warrior spoke the first name gently, as if they two were alone, sharing news across a campfire.

"Ardacos of the Caledonii."

A small, wiry man with the dark colouring and high cheekbones of the ancestors stepped up to the fire. Ardacos had been on Mona a decade, longest of all those

in the school. He would return to his people at the spring
equinox unless he had reason to stay. Without question, he
was unmatched by his peers for skill with the spear in battle or in the hunt. In the moments before the gathering,
when rumours had flown fast as larks and the betting
faster, over half of those present had bet that he would
take Venutios's place as Warrior. Breaca had not been one
of them but Ardacos would have been her second choice.
She had no doubt that the gods would want him to take
part in their tests.

Ardacos stood at the slate and leaned over the fire. The
flames washed red along his arm. He touched one finger to
his forehead in homage to Briga and slid his other hand
through the slit in the hide. When he opened his palm the
pebble that lay on it was black. Two thousand sighed, less one.

Maroc's voice echoed over their heads. "Ardacos of the
Caledonii is first of the thirty."

Venutios was already speaking the second name.

They passed through forty stones, the remainder of
those warriors who had entered the school in the same year
as Ardacos. Two of his comrades joined him, a man and a
woman, both of northern tribes, although none as far north
as the Caledonii. Breaca, watching with the clarity of Mona,
saw in those who drew white a diffidence, or an absence of
confidence, that betrayed each in the moment of reaching
across the fire. By the time Venutios called the next name,
she could tell before a hand was opened what colour stone
would lie on the palm.

"Gwyddhien of the Silures."

Black. It would be black. Breaca would have known it this
time simply from the name. There were only two amongst the

school who were in genuine contention to be Warrior and Gwyddhien was, in Breaca's opinion, the better of the two. She had bet as much with Airmid, staking a silver brooch with coral inlay on the outcome. The only surprise was that Airmid had accepted.

A tall woman with blue-black hair and eyes that spoke to the soul stepped back from the fire pit and opened her hand. The stone on her palm was black.

"Gwyddhien of the Silures is fourth of the thirty."

That half of the warriors who had not bet on Ardacos let out a collective breath. Across the fire, in the front rank of dreamers, Breaca saw Airmid's sudden smile and returned it. Airmid may not have bet on Gwyddhien to win the tests, but she had badly wanted her to be part of the thirty.

The night took on its own rhythm. Venutios spoke through the nine-year warriors to the eight to the seven and on. The names ran through hundreds to thousands. On Mona, where the dreamers learned songs and laws that could take days in the telling, two thousand names remembered in order was no great feat, but the man was neither a dreamer nor a singer and if he had put effort into learning the names of each year's new intake as they arrived at the school, Breaca had seen no sign of it. The list came now from a knowing that went beyond rote learning and was part of what made him Warrior: the care for those whose lives he might one day hold in his hand. It was what set him apart from the others, what, for Breaca, set Gwyddhien apart from Ardacos. The latter excelled as a lone hunter or single warrior—if one had need of a man to set an ambush, or to steal from the enemy, Ardacos was that man—but it was Gwyddhien who could lead two thousand into war and wield them as a single force. It was not hard to imagine her, ten years from now, speaking two thousand names as if each were a valued friend, and meaning it.

"Cumal of the Cornovii is twenty-second of the thirty."

Cumal was of the fourth year, the only one of his intake to have drawn a black pebble and deservedly so; he had a fine eye for a spear throw and was best of all the island with a slingshot. Breaca had fought at his side in practise battles and had found him sharp-witted and dependable; a good choice for the thirty.

The next name was an uninspiring warrior of the Dumnonii, the first of those who had been on Mona three years. Surprisingly, he picked a black pebble as did the woman who came after him, so that in the space of a dozen breaths, there were six left black in a vessel of nearly six hundred white where before there had been nine.

A soundless sigh passed through the thinning ranks of those remaining. Somewhere, a voice calculated the new odds out loud. Breaca had no need to listen. She could feel the shape and size of the black stones in her core, as if each one nested in a long bone, cushioned on marrow and laced through with her blood. They sang to her in high voices, like curlews, and she had no way to answer in kind. She prayed to Briga and watched the changing textures in the air above the fire until her mind ached.

Venutios named the warriors of the third year and the pebbles came out in their dozens, each one white as an eye. The first of the second year's intake reached through the horse-skin and when he, too, brought his hand out with white on the palm, six black pebbles remained amongst three hundred and eighty-seven white. Breaca was last of the second year. The summer of Amminios's attack had been long and full of caring for the wounded and she and Airmid had set out late in the autumn, reaching Mona long after the equinox on a ferry that had been launched from its winter dock to carry them across. One month longer and Breaca would have been considered the first of the next year's intake.

Another new hand reached into the horse-skin and her mind said to her, "Black."

"Cerin of the Votadini is twenty-fifth of the thirty."

Five black pebbles lay among two hundred and fifty-four white. Three warriors of the second year remained to take the call.

Two.

The whine in her ears grew louder and reached a higher pitch. The pulse rushed in her head, lifting her clear of the ground. The tension could be tasted, metallic on the tongue. Her heart slowed, and each beat crashed against the cage of her ribs. Venutios's mouth made a shape and the name floated towards her, slow as a leaf on a pond. She stepped forward to meet it.

"Breaca of the Eceni."

There was warmth in his voice and a recognition of the battles she had fought, the one against Amminios that had changed her life and those others, smaller, staged as tests in the school. In the silence after was a smile and a reminder of a sword fight, one on one, when she had broken Venutios's blade on her own.

Three steps to the fireside and three more to the slate. The elder grandmother waited on one side, as real as the heat. Eburovic was less real, less solid, but she remembered the smell of him, fresh from the forge. Both of these were a part of her; on Mona, she could find them with ease. She set both feet on the slate and gazed across the fire pit and her heart cried out for the one she had never seen, for the one she sought in the quiet of every night and had not yet found. In the last moments before stretching across the fire, she could have prayed to Briga to give her a black stone and did not; she prayed for Bán.

Who was not there.

Airmid was there, surprisingly close, and one other, not clearly seen, and then her arm was bathed in melting heat and her hand was slipping through a drum-tight hide and if the vessel held dozens on dozens of stones she did not feel them, just the one that came to her hand as if made for it. She closed her fingers and drew out her arm and her mind said to her, "Black."

"Breaca of the Eceni is twenty-sixth of the thirty."

She turned left and walked to the waiting group. Twenty-five pairs of eyes watched her, weighing her worth and her chances of success. The stone burned like red iron in her hand. Her soul wept.

A warrior of the Cornovii joined her shortly afterwards and there were three stones left. Those still to choose had been on Mona a year or less. In a while, all that remained were the dozen who had come across in a single group at the equinox. They clustered together like sheep, raw from the crossing and the change in life that was Mona. In their own tribes, they had been the best of their age, possibly the best in living memory. Now each was simply one amongst many, all equally good, all still unproven.

"Braint of the Brigantes is twenty-eighth of the thirty."

A lean, black-haired girl took her place on Breaca's left, her face stiffly white. She was one of the northern Brigantes, distant kin to Venutios, and her name was that of the goddess in the far northern tongue of her people. Breaca knew nothing else of her history or skills. In a moment, the girl's cousin joined her, a broad-shouldered boy with red hair and fair skin: twenty-ninth.

Those left dispersed, one by one, white after white until only one warrior remained. He was the youngest and the newest to Mona and he approached the fire with the smile of one who sees his destiny clear before him. Breaca watched him stretch across the fire and knew herself split. The part of her that reasoned said that if there had been two thousand pebbles and only one was left, then that one must be black. The other part, which saw the greater pattern of things, said, quite clearly, "White"—and was correct.

The boy stared at his palm in horror. There was no doubting the colour. He had drawn white and must leave. Close to weeping, he stepped back from the fire and began the long walk round to the dreamers' side and the way out.

Numbly, Breaca watched him go. She had no foreknowledge of the testing but her life's experience had taught her that if the gods required thirty warriors to set out together, they should be given exactly that. She saw Maroc share a look with Talla, who nodded. A pile of white pebbles lay at Maroc's feet where the departing warriors had placed them. Bending, he scooped them up and counted them in handfuls through the cut in the hide so they landed, ringing, against the copper floor of the vessel. As the last few fell to silence, Venutios raised his head and said, "Caradoc of the Ordovices."

He was not there. He could not be there. Breaca had seen his face and felt his presence when she had picked her own stone and had known him a ghost of her past, not her present. When the movement began far back in the still ranks of the dreamers, she was certain it was someone else coming forward to explain to Venutios his mistake. It was well known that Caradoc had spent the autumn in the land of the Ordovices; he could not be in the great-house.

She had forgotten that Venutios was Warrior, and did not make mistakes. The front row of dreamers split and swayed and when it came together Caradoc stood on the dreamers' side of the fire pit, his face calm, his hair dulled to straw by the torchlight and his eyes bright as ice. She felt his presence as a mule kick to the chest.

She was not alone. Surprise hissed through the ranks of dreamers. Far back, a woman said, "He is not of the warriors' school. He cannot take part in the choosing."

"That is not so." Talla's voice cut through the rest. "The laws are clear on this. Those who train with the Warrior are of the school for that day if for no other. Venutios." She turned, raising an arm. "Have you trained today with Caradoc of the Ordovices?"

"I have. He came to me this morning and we practised with sword and spear before the work of the school began." Venutios was Warrior. None doubted his word.

"Then it is so." Talla turned back. "Caradoc of the Ordovices—had all thirty been chosen, your name would not have been called. As it is, there remains one black pebble between the bull's horns. Sufficient white have been added to make one hundred in all. Your test will be no less great than the others'. You may approach the slate."

He had a long way to walk round the edge of the fire pit. Breaca watched him, feeling sick with a dread that had nothing to do with the choosing of pebbles. She did not doubt that he would pick the black stone; the gods had spoken merely by his presence and they would want him of all people among the thirty taking the tests. The sickness came rather from his presence as it had done each of the few times they had met since the death of her father and the theft of Bán's body.

Caradoc had not come to see her in the long summer months immediately after Amminios's attack as Breaca had thought he might. She had spent the time helping Airmid with the wounded or working out in the fields, trying to plant and weed and gather the same harvest as they might have done before losing so many people in the battle. The work left her exhausted and irritable and she would have made poor company, but the thought of him gave colour to days that might otherwise have passed in shades of grey and she was grateful for it.

In the space of his absence, the elder council of the Eceni had met, absolving him of blood-guilt, together with his father and Togodubnos. Maroc had crossed the country from Mona to attend, to ensure that this was so. The dreamer's word had not swung the council—no-one with sense wished to declare war on the Trinovantes—but his presence had spoken strongly for the need to maintain an amicable peace. Cunobelin had sent blood-gifts of untold worth and had declared in public, before a gathering of elders, that his middle son was no longer welcome in his presence and that the lands and ports south of the sea-river which had formerly been granted to Amminios were to be given instead to

Cunomar, son of Togodubnos, to be held by the latter until the child came of age. Togodubnos himself had ridden up alone to offer his own heartfelt regrets and to restate his wish for continued friendship with the Eceni. Caradoc alone had neither visited nor sent word.

When he came, finally, it was with a shipload of yearlings on the back of a summer's trading in Hibernia and the west coast of Gaul. He rode in through the gates with the dawn on the day of the equinox with Segoventos for company. Breaca had been awake through the night, sitting watch over Airmid, who had been seeking Bán's soul in the grey lands of the unsettled dead. The attempt had failed, as it had done nightly since the attack, and Airmid had fallen into an exhausted sleep from which it was not safe to wake her. Breaca had called Hail to heel and, without waiting for the hound to join her, had walked down to the river to wash away the dust and disappointment of another night. She met Caradoc outside the men's house. He was wearing her brooch with red horsehair dangling from the loops and grinning like a child and playing with Hail and looking around for Bán, or for signs of his long-nights. His first words, thrown out in play, were "I thought the Eceni honoured the men returning from their long-nights with greater ceremony than this?"

He had been trading with strangers for three months and had travelled without pause from the coast; it was not reasonable to expect that he would have heard the news. She knew that, even as she drew her blade and laid the edge of it against his neck, pressing into the skin so that the great vein beneath stood out blue. He stopped smiling before the iron touched him, but did not move. He had sailed for days without break and ridden through the night and was pushed to the edge of exhaustion and he still thought faster than any man she knew. While Segoventos blustered, he raised a hand, his eyes wide and fixed, his mouth set, saying only, "Bán is dead?" And then, when she nodded, not trusting herself to speak, he said, "Amminios. I'm so sorry. I should have known. Tell me what happened."

The tale of the battle took far less time to tell than it had to fight. At the end of it, he had borrowed a fresh horse and ridden south, giving no reason but promising to return before the moon was out. He did so, within a time that meant he had ridden without rest. The horse was ruined, but he brought back others and, more important, details of the ceremony Amminios had used when he had sacrificed the dun filly to the Roman gods.

Of all the blood-gifts from his family, it was the only one of worth. Luain came shortly after to join Airmid and the recovering Macha in the search for Bán's soul. When it was clear they could do nothing alone, they called in all the dreamers of the Eceni, from the northern coast to the far southern border, and together they spent three nights without break hunting between the worlds to find a boy and his horse. They succeeded in the smaller part; the dun filly was found and guided to rest in Briga's care, but Bán was beyond them and they stopped their search in the end, fearing to lose dreamers in a place whence they might not return.

The warriors sat vigil throughout and Caradoc with them, eating nothing and drinking only water for three nights and three days while the dreamers worked. When news came of their failure, Caradoc wept as if Bán had been his own brother, or son. Breaca was beyond weeping. The loss was too great; it burned a wasteland in her soul that no amount of tears would heal. She left the vigil grounds and went hunting with Hail and when she came back she spoke to no-one.

Airmid took nine days to recover from the search. At the end of that time, Breaca gathered the horses and Hail, ready for the journey to Mona. Caradoc stayed to see them go. On the morning of their leaving, he sought her out alone near the paddocks. It was the first time she felt the aching dread at his presence although she was not clear, then, why it should be so. She would have walked past him if she could, but he stood in the gateway and reached to take the bridle of Airmid's colt so she had to stop. His eyes were too bright for the morning and his colour high. His hair, bleached to white gold by a summer's sailing, was darkly damp from the stream and recently cut. The wind twisted it across his face, sticking it to his cheek. He held out a small offering wrapped in deer-skin and said, "This is yours."

She met his gaze evenly. It was the most she could do. "There is no need. You brought the only gift you could. What happened was not your fault."

"I know. This is not a gift." He offered it again. "Take it. See what it is."

She did as he asked. Courtesy and the guest-laws required it. Inside the wrap lay the serpent-spear brooch with the tokens of red horsehair still hanging free from the lower loops. He had polished it and replaced the pin but it was the same otherwise as when she had given it—an impulse born of a moment that had come to have meaning only afterwards, and had held it, until now.

He was waiting for her to speak. Baldly, she said, "Don't you want it?"

"Of course. What I want is not at issue . . ." He stopped and began again on a new breath. "If I kept it, would it have meaning, as it once did?"

Comprehension came on her slowly, with visceral force. Since the battle, she had not known the loss of him, only the pain of Eburovic's absence and the crippling desolation that came from the theft of Bán. Throughout the long summer, his promise, and her certainty that, whatever had happened, he would keep it, had nurtured a spark of life in her soul when everything else was dead. Now, in his presence, standing close enough to touch, a physical sickness gripped her. It was impossible to be with him alone without the intervention of the dead; he smiled and she saw Bán smile; he tilted his head to the side with his hair stuck to his cheek and it was black hair, not gold, and she wanted to stretch forward and smooth it away as she would have done for Bán; he wept and she saw Bán, grieving for the dun filly; and because she saw Bán in him, she saw also Amminios commit the ultimate act of desecration and take from the battlefield a body not offered to Briga. Even here, with Caradoc so close that she could feel the warmth from his skin, could smell the sheep's oil on his tunic and the smoke from last night's fires, he bore a shadow that was not his own.

The morning grew cold around her, pinching the flesh of her face. When she needed it most, her voice failed.

"Thank you." Caradoc nodded as if she had spoken. His brief smile was polite, the product of years at his father's court. "It is best to be clear." He let go of the colt and reached instead to touch the hilt of her blade as he had done once before when life was quite different. "The blade-oath—"

"Is void." She recoiled from his touch. Her voice, renewed, came too fast and harshly. "The blood-debt makes it so. Even did it not, I would absolve you of it."

"Then I would renew it." One finger remained on her blade and would not let go. His voice matched hers, but was slower.

"Why?"

"Because the world contains more people than just us two and someday it may matter that the Eceni are bound to the Ordovices. We do Bán's memory no honour if we forgo those things that bind us before the gods." His eyes were level with hers. His face was raw, stripped of the irony and the striking intelligence that were his defences, leaving him open to see and be seen for what he was: a warrior on the cusp of adulthood, struggling to make himself understood in a field that was new to them both. Only once before, fresh from the sea, had she seen him so unguarded, and that had not been within his control as this was now. The exposure unnerved her, and the strength of purpose that drove it. She had experienced his courage in the river-rescue of Dubornos and again facing his father in the forge; she had never thought to face it from the other side. Stricken, she said, "I would never dishonour Bán's memory."

"I know." His eyes were the colour of stone and as unyielding. "Then will you let the oath be renewed?"

"Yes." At the end of a long, stifled impulse to touch him, she folded the deer-skin back over the brooch and pressed it into his palm. "And keep this also. If it comes to mean what it did, I will tell you."

"Thank you." Surprise and pleasure lit his smile. "If the time ever comes, you will know where to find me."

She had always known where to find him, or had thought so. He came and went from Mona as the dreamers did, as if the greater part of him resided there. In the spaces between, he was in the land of the Ordovices, or sailing with Segoventos, visiting tribes from the Brigantes and Caledonii in the north to the Dumnonii in the far southwest, trading and gathering information and finding who favoured Rome and who did not. Always, the ultimate enemy was Rome; his hatred had never waned.

On Mona, he had taken a regular place at the warriors' school and whereas it had been impossible to avoid him completely, she had always been given warning of his coming. They had met sparingly and always with cause and the pattern had been the same each time: a brief exchange of courtesies and small fragments of news but nothing more. The ghosts of their past stood between them and nothing could be as it had been.

Until now, when he was about to become one of a handful sent on the greatest of warrior's tests: Caradoc, son of Cunobelin, who had won his spear with three different tribes by the age of twelve; who had never yet failed any test of man or gods; who was bound to Breaca of the Eceni by an oath that prevented each from competing directly against the other.

Venutios's voice came distantly and with a different tone from all the names he had called before.

"Caradoc of the Ordovices is thirtieth of the thirty."

"We will hold a feast in honour of Venutios. You will hunt for the table. A boar would be good, or a deer."

"Is that all?"

"It is enough. Venutios will guide you. He remains Warrior until a successor is chosen."

Talla had said it, speaking to the thirty in the grey light before dawn. It was the boy-cousin of the Brigantes who had asked the question—a forward youth, unused to Mona's ways. No-one else had spoken. To hunt was enough, and whatever came after. At Talla's command, they had run to collect their hunting spears and knives and whatever dream-tokens would bring them closer to the gods. They were forbidden kill-feathers or any other tokens of war. Breaca, with two others, had been permitted to bring a hound.

Maroc had spoken to them as they gathered again at the gates but he had been no more explicit than the Elder. "You can hunt alone or together; the choice lies with each of you. Only know that you must stay together. Venutios will ensure that you do."

They had filed out through the gates in the order in which they had been named. Maroc had made a mark on each as they passed—a thumb-sweep along the brow of woad thinned with water and egg white, naming them for the older gods of the ancestors. The mark was too pale to be seen but Breaca had felt it dry as she ran, tightening so that the pressure was a constant reminder of his words.

You can hunt alone or together; the choice lies with each of you.

It paid to listen to Maroc. In two years, she had never known him to speak without reason and his words rarely had only one meaning. There were no boar near the settlement, that was well known. It gave them time to make decisions. Venutios had led them westwards, setting a fast pace, and the others had settled behind, moving into the wide crescent favoured of harehunters, close enough for each to see and be seen, but not so close that they had any cause to speak.

Breaca was grateful for the chance to run and not to talk. In normal circumstances, she would have hunted alone. She had Hail, who had been taught from the first to hunt in a team of two; the hound was her last living remnant of Bán, and his joy in the hunt made it hard to share him. And yet she was one of thirty and even as they gathered before the gates she had felt the threads of them weaving together: the dark, silent knot that was Ardacos with his soul rooted in the ways of the ancestors; the focused vitality of Gwyddhien, shining like polished jet amongst river pebbles; the sharpness of Braint, the black-haired girl-cousin of the Brigantes, and the obduracy of her redheaded kinsman. Strung out in a line in the heather, they made jewels on a thread, each of them a different colour, each necessary to the whole. Even the dullard of the Dumnonii, who was named in his own tongue for the badger, was revealed, running out in the open, as solidly dependable. Only Caradoc was different, the one not truly of Mona, who, without asking, had put himself on the far left, the place of the shield, the most vulnerable to any attack. He was not part of the weaving, any more than the ghosts who ran in his shadow. She thought that Caradoc, of them all, might choose to hunt alone and waited to see if he did so.

By any standards, it was not a successful hunt. The thirty quartered the island together through the morning and into the late afternoon and found nothing. None of them, in ten years' experience, had ever known the land so barren but the very fact of frustration knitted them closer, so that, when the cry finally did go up for quarry, they responded as one.

They were near an outcrop within sight of the sea, on the westerly tip of the island, when it happened. The curve of the rocks faced east and was backed by a small hill, from the top of which Gwyddhien called down to say she could see Hibernia, that island on the far western edge of the world that was made visible only on days blessed by the gods. Venutios took it as a sign from the gods and called to Breaca and the others to loose the hounds. They were good hounds, all keen and well tested in the hunt, and in defiance of the empty morning each found a different trail, running forward with a single-minded determination that spoke of deer at least, if not boar. Venutios whooped, or possibly Gwyddhien, and the hunt began in earnest.

The thirty were spread wide and Breaca sprinted down through scrub in Hail's wake with few others for company. Caradoc ran with her, keeping level with her left shoulder as he had done since morning. His presence marred the sudden exhilaration of the chase, but not so greatly that she could not ignore it; too much was at stake.

"To the south! Down there in the thorns!"

Gwyddhien called from the top of the outcrop, pointing down into the trees. It was late in the afternoon and the low sun cast her in silhouette, sharply. Her hair had come free of its bindings and flew wild in the wind, black as a crow, the bird of Briga. In this hunt more than any other, the marks of the gods were omens. Calling Hail, Breaca altered the line of her run and plunged into the broad straggle of wildwood that spread out round the base of the crag. Brambles snagged her skin and beech-brush whipped at her eyes. Caradoc left her. She felt a nakedness at her side where he had been. His loss, her gain, if she made the kill without him. Still running, she ducked under the low branches of an ash and saw Hail ahead of her, stock-still and snarling. Slowing, she crept to him, her spear tight to her shoulder, and looked where he looked, into the depths of the blackthorn.

Tiny, flesh-folded eyes glared red with loathing. Heat and boar-stench filled the space. A tusk glanced white. A grunt gave warning of certain death.

Danger consumed her, perfectly. A full-grown boar could kill a bear, ripping it open from gullet to guts. Songs were sung of lone hunters who had faced one with a spear and made the kill unaided, becoming heroes as they did so, but none knew of it happening in truth. Breaca had heard more honestly, from a singer she trusted, of two hunters who had taken one between them, killing it cleanly with the first cast of each spear. She looked about for Gwyddhien and found instead Ardacos, crouched to her right, still as a stone. His spear was clasped straight at his shoulder and the hunting knife in his left hand was smeared with mud, not to shine in the sun. He was naked but for a loin-kilt of fox pelts and his skin was so brown, he could have been part of the shadow. This was how the ancestors hunted, she could feel it.

She had no idea how long he had been there but it was long enough, and he was the second-best choice for Warrior. She opened a palm, asking direction. He put his finger to his lips for silence and made a curve of his arm, showing where she and Hail should go. She nodded and was gone, Hail at her heel.

The sounds of others hunting crashed through the woods. The boar grunted a second warning. A stoat chittered—the sign of Ardacos. She loosed Hail at the thicket and stepped in with her spear—and stepped back, shouting, "No! It's a sow with young. Leave it!" and was in time to stop Hail but not Ardacos, who was fast as his dream and had already made his cast.

The gods smiled on them. The dark man's spear struck but did not kill. The sow, enraged, charged in defence of her young. Breaca found she could perform miracles and climbed the blank face of the outcrop, spear in hand, pulling Hail up behind her. She heard Ardacos's grunt of pain.

They were hunting in the gods' wood on the gods' isle and the gods exacted their penance for a mothering beast injured in defiance of their laws. Breaca's spear had made no wound and so she was not wounded. Ardacos's had scored along the sow's shoulder and he was scored as deeply and in the same place, but he had not killed and so he did not die. He rolled away from the strike as a hedgehog rolls and leaped up to catch the lower limbs of an oak before the beast could turn. An adult male would have circled the tree, waiting three moons if necessary for its quarry to come down, but the sow had young to feed and the scent of hounds fresh in her nostrils and she left him, grumbling, to return to the thorns.

In time, when the beast showed no sign of returning, Breaca climbed down and found a different path out of the wood, skirting wide of the sow's den. The after-thrill of danger pulsed through her, powerful as winter ale. Hail ran at her side, desperate to hunt again. Ardacos had found a different path, quicker. She met him at the place where the woods stopped and the outcrop began. He was crouched on the heather peeling moss from a rock to seal over his wound. She held the moss for him and cut a strip from the hem of her tunic to bind it on. He took his time, as if the day were young and the outcome still uncertain.

"You have lost your spear," she said. "I could go back and get it."

"No. It's not safe to go back. I can make another."

It was the most she had ever heard him speak. He was ten years her senior and as distant as the most taciturn of elders. She had been on Mona twelve months before he had acknowledged her existence and then it was only to push his blade past a weakness in her guard and land a strike on her wrist that would have severed her hand had it been meant. His face was leathered and closed, like a bat's. She had never seen him smile. He did so now, disarmingly, pointing back towards the southern end of the outcrop.

"We lost," he said. "They've taken a different beast."

"I know." She had heard the death-squeal as the sow attacked. Now she heard Venutios sound the Warrior's horn in the signal for the rest to gather. "Caradoc and Gwyddhien have made the kill." She felt it as a change in colour of the weave, a brightening of two threads and a dulling of the rest. She tied off the frayed end of her tunic and picked up her spear. Ardacos was slower, taking time to stretch his shoulder and test the feel of the wound. He caught her arm as she passed.

"No hurry. They'll gut the boar and clean it before we move on. It'll take no more than three of them to manage the beast and the same again to cut a tree to carry it. The rest of us will only sit and watch. We may as well take it easy."

He was right. The beast was a young male of last season's brood. They were known sometimes to return to their birth-den for wintering and if the sow was farrowing she did not always take the time to drive them away. It was a good size, big enough to justify two for the kill, not so big as to need three; more than enough to grace the leaving feast of Venutios. The Warrior, who was soon to be merely a warrior, stood back and let Gwyddhien organize the gutting and preparation of the kill while Caradoc led a party to select a tree for the carrying pole.

In the distribution of work, Breaca saw the beginnings of the new Warrior's retinue. Always there was an inner core of those to whom the most needful tasks were entrusted. With no reason to join them, she sat on the margins and watched others take on new roles. Ardacos, unconcerned, went about his own business. He roamed the outcrop seeking a stave to make a spear-haft and, having found one, lit a tiny stick-and-heather fire to harden the point. By the time the two cousins of the Brigantes had lashed the boar to the carrying pole and hefted it onto their shoulders, he was armed again. He smiled again at Breaca as they set out, and said, "Don't let your guard down now, lass. This is more than a boar hunt. It's not over yet."

CHAPTER 19

They were too far from the great-house to return before nightfall. The option remained to walk through the night or to find an encampment and wait until dawn. Venutios, who had led them this far, gave over command to Gwyddhien who, in turn, consulted with Caradoc. At his suggestion, they chose to walk until dusk and then stop for the night at a place they both knew.

The light faded winter-fast, leaching the colour from the day. Clouds of midges rose from the scrub to feast. The hunters ran in a column, as fast as the boar-carriers could go, taking turns with the pole to keep up the pace. Breaca ran near the end, twenty-fifth in line, and took her turn to carry the pole. Hail dallied at her heels, licking the fallen blood.

Gwyddhien led them round a bog and through another tract of woodland, up a gentle slope and over more outcrops to halt on the summit of a low, crater-topped hill in the centre of which a small lochan lay still and clear. Under her direction, they split into groups to gather wood for fires and bracken to lie on. Ardacos waded waist-deep into the loch and speared fish. Others gathered roots. Venutios sliced the liver of the boar, which would not keep well in the warmth of the night, and shared it equally amongst them so that it became like a true victory feast. Later, they swam in the loch by firelight, cleaning off the blood of the hunt and confounding the last of the insects. The boar, still on the carry-pole, was hung high between two rocks, out of reach of the hounds.

It was not a night for sleeping. They lay in small groups, talking by firelight. Those with hounds shared them for warmth. Venutios lit his own fire high up on the crag top. His peace spread over them, but thinly, as if the mantle of it were already passing to another. At the lochside, Gwyddhien moved from group to group, praising each for its actions in the day, taking the threads of the thirty and weaving them tighter. Ardacos walked alone round the water's edge, his spear on his shoulder, constantly vigilant.

Breaca lay alone with Hail at her side and stared up at the black night. The moon had not risen and the stars were brighter for it. She found the dreamer's star sitting low on the southern horizon and thought of Macha and then of Airmid, who was lover to Gwyddhien and yet had still bet against her becoming Warrior. In doing so, she had refused to state her alternative choice, except to say that it was not Ardacos. What had seemed surprising seemed less so now. The bet had been made in the evening, just before the choosing of the thirty; Airmid would have known all day that one extra had trained at the warriors' school in the morning. By evening, she would have had time to discuss its implications with Maroc.

Nudging Hail to follow, Breaca rose from her fire. The

thirty were spread in a half-moon around the shores of the loch. She had not taken note of where each had chosen to spend the night, but she could find the important ones, by instinct, or a half-heard word, or the shape of an outline against the embers' glow: Cumal and Ardacos, Venutios and Gwyddhien—and Caradoc, who was far out on the western side, alone. She picked her way carefully round the rocks at the water's edge. Hail recognized their destination from a distance and bounded forward joyfully, spoiling any chance of surprise. She could have called him back but not without drawing attention from the wider group, which she preferred not to do. In any case, she had no wish to lay constraints on Hail that would dampen his spirits. It had taken a long time for the great hound to acknowledge Bán's loss. Even now, he cleaved to certain boys at the time when their voices were breaking. For the rest, he was selective in his affections—generous to those whom she liked and aloof with the rest. Only with Caradoc did he find friendship where she did not.

She stopped just beyond the circle of light. Caradoc sat on the far side of the fire, jumbling Hail's ears with careless affection. The poor light darkened his hair to black and changed the shape of his face. He looked up and his eyes were the ones she had known since childhood, full of care and Bán's unconscious grace. The nausea rose in her throat, predictably. She sat on a rock, quickly, before her nerve failed her. Caradoc shifted his head in the firelight and his eyes became grey again, searching hers, seeking a reason for her presence and failing to find it. Presently, he said, "I'm sorry you were not with us at the kill."

"So am I." She pulled her knees in to her chest and

hugged them tightly. "How did you know Ardacos and I were going for the wrong beast?"

"I didn't. I saw Gwyddhien jump down from the crag and she was not near Hail. I had the choice to go with the hound's nose or the hunter's eyes. Nine times out of ten, I would go with Hail. But this was Gwyddhien." The hound heard the sound of his name in the words and leaned into his hand, crooning pleasure.

"You think she should be Warrior?"

"With what is to come? Yes." He picked a stalk of old grass and chewed the end of it. "If we were at peace, Ardacos would be unbeatable. He carries the lore of the ancestors and we can never learn too much of that. But he is too silent, and takes too long to trust those around him. If there is to be war, we will need a Warrior who can gain trust and give it on first meeting, or know that it will never be given. Gwyddhien will do that."

Breaca looked across the loch to the last murmuring group with Gwyddhien at its heart. She said, "She is doing it already."

"I know."

He had laid a pile of dry bracken and heather roots neatly to one side. Breaca leaned forward and set a handful of each in the fire's heart. Flame washed her face and his, as it had done once in a forge. They sat in silence, testing the edges of tension between them. There was a third option and neither had said it: Caradoc had been one of two who killed the boar, and he could mould two thousand warriors to his will as readily as Gwyddhien ever could. Airmid had known that when she laid her bet. On the far horizon, the dreamer's star flared, holding its secrets.

"Why are you here?" His voice came out of the dark.

"To ask a question. Or, perhaps, to test a theory." She looked at him across the fire. He sat calmly, but with an edge of caution, as if she were part of the Warrior's tests. She said, "It seems to me that the hunt is not the choosing, that the choice has been made long since by Talla and the elder council and the hunt is to bring the thirty together, to begin the weaving of the new Warrior's honour guard. If that were so, and if you were asked, would you pledge your life for Gwyddhien's?"

She had thought it might be a question he had asked himself. Looking at him, she knew she had been right but that, having asked, he had not found the answer; the conflict was clear on his face. With honesty, he said, "I don't know."

"You have too many responsibilities amongst your mother's people?" She knew nothing of his life among the Ordovices, save that he had not been held responsible for the death of the messenger slain by his father.

"Yes, but it's more than that. If there is war, I would wish to be part of it, and Mona has only once in recent history sent the Warrior and all two thousand into battle."

"Against Caesar and the legions."

"Yes. They rode in support of Cassivellaunos at a time when the sanctity of the land itself was threatened. The songs of Mona say that, of them all, only three came back alive. They were the greatest warriors our land has ever seen and they were the ones who held the banks of the sea-river against the onslaught of the legions, whatever the singers of other tribes—my people and yours—may say. If it comes to war with Rome and if Mona sends her warriors into the field, then it may be that I would join the honour guard if I were asked—but if not, I would wish to be free to fight alongside whoever will join me."

In the still night, a cold wind stroked across Breaca's back. Maroc had spoken of this, but not so directly, nor with such a sense of urgency. "Will it come to that—to war with Rome?"

He shrugged. "It could do. Amminios has all the ambition of my father and none of his diplomacy. Cunobelin trod a fine line; his wealth was based on trade with Rome and her subject peoples but he did not take on everything Roman. In these last two years, he returned to the dreamers and the ways of the gods. Amminios will never do that. He wants control of the trading ports on both sides of the sea-river and will stop at nothing to get it. In this, he has the support of Berikos of the Atrebates. That man has waited thirty years to get the better of my father. If Amminios gives him a reason, he will take it."

"And Amminios has reason in the ports south of the sea-river that your father gave to Togodubnos's son as blood-guilt for my family." Memories of battle crowded the night. Amminios laughed from horseback and the roll of hooves rocked her head. She stared into the fire and made herself hear only the wind ruffling the loch and the murmur of other voices at other fires, none of them enemies. When she could think clearly, she said, "The loss of the southern ports would give neither Amminios nor Berikos due cause to call on Rome for aid."

"Not unless they fight for them and lose. Amminios, as you have found, does not like to be seen to lose."

She raised her head, sharply. He met the heat of her gaze without comment. He could have been taunting her, but was not. Both knew it to be true. She said, "He may not like to lose, but if he wins, then the whole of the southeast is in danger. He will not stop at the river, and if he takes the dun, he will move next on the Eceni. We have wealth greater than he has ever seen, in land and corn and horses. Just because we choose not to trade it with Rome does not make it worth less."

"So he must not be allowed to win, or to escape to Rome. The only chance is for Togodubnos to reach the southlands before Amminios. The spears there are sworn to my father. While his body lies whole and for three days after they burn him, they cannot forswear, it is the law. After that . . ." He spread his hands.

"Would they swear faith to Amminios?"

"The Atrebates are nothing if not a practical people. They changed allegiance from Berikos to my father because a debt was owed. They will change back again as easily. I think they will swear to whoever gets to them first with enough spears to make a convincing argument."

"Does Togodubnos know that?"

"We have to hope so. If he fails, then the southeast will take fire like pine boughs dried over summer."

He sat up and moved his hands above the fire, making shadows as the singers did. Bold shapes stalked others across the blur of his face. Like this, because she had to fight to see the face behind the shadows, she saw only him. He smiled and it was not Bán's smile. His hands made a blade and shield, moving round in thrust and parry. Softly, he said, "The elders of the Ordovices met in full council at the equinox. I brought a petition before them and it was accepted. If war starts in the east, I have permission to lead the warriors of the war hammer in defence of my brother's lands."

It was what his father had wanted. She refrained from saying so. Instead, "And so we come full circle to my first question and you have given its answer. You could not lead the Ordovices if you were sworn to protect the Warrior."

"No."

"Nor if you were the Warrior."

"Not unless Mona and the Ordovices were one, which is unlikely."

"So then why are you here?"

"I don't know. You would have to ask Maroc."

"Maroc would answer as he always does: to learn the will of the gods, which may not be the will of man."

"Nor even the will of Maroc, whatever that may be."

Behind the shadowplay, she could see the dry smile, so like Airmid's. Maroc's plans were known only to a few, though any could discern them by looking and as many could appreciate the breadth of vision that sought to bring the warriors of west and east together in defence of the land. Breaca had heard it in outline from Macha before she left the Eceni homelands. Since coming to Mona, she had begun to understand the detail and the extent to which the dreamer had found in Caradoc a willing vessel, the one man who might achieve his dream; who might, if the gods were good, one day go beyond it. Caradoc would not unite the tribes to bring power to his father, but he would strive to the last breath in his body to do so if it would keep back Rome and its supporters.

There was only one flaw Breaca could see. Standing to leave, with Hail at her side, she said, "You are Ordovician only on your mother's side. Will the sworn spears of the war hammer follow you in a battle that is not of their choosing?"

He was lying back, with his hands laced behind his head. She heard his voice in the darkness, dryly amused. "I would stake my life on it," and then, more reflectively, "If they don't, it is not only the east that will fall."

Breaca was in the Eceni great-house, petitioning aid in war from the elders, when Ardacos's fingers gripped her ankle. By her own fire, she woke to blackness, and a canopy of stars. The creased bat-face blocked them out. Fingers danced in front of her eyes, making the sign for danger and then good luck. She rose silently and was handed her spear. Hail stretched and followed.

They ran along the edge of the loch. The smell of still water mingled with sphagnum moss. Her bare feet splashed in shallow water where she missed the rocks. At the northern edge, they turned uphill and ran to the lip of the crater where they lay flat behind the rocks. He pointed over the rim and she saw what he had seen: a shape that was not a rock, moving amongst the crags below.

"A bear?" Her heart flipped over in her chest. "I thought there were no bears on Mona."

"We were told not. In eight years, I have seen none." He glanced at her sideways. The edge of his eye showed white in the starlight. "Maroc's dream is the bear."

"And my father's." She laid her spear on the rocks. "We must not kill it."

"I would not suggest it. But the beast has smelled the boar and will take it if it can." He sat back on his heels and flashed her a smile. His face was more animated than she had ever seen it. He said, "This is the choosing, not the other. The danger is great. At every Warrior's choosing there have been deaths, and they do not come from hunting boar. We may not kill it, but we must still drive it away. And it may kill us."

He did not look like a man preparing to die. The whine of bees began again in her ears, the gods' warning, and Maroc's voice faintly, *Only know that you must stay together.* Warily, she said, "You were not thinking that it was sent for us alone—giving no chance to the others?"

The bear was the colour of the night. Even with the clear sight of Mona, it was hard to hold it in focus. In the time she waited for Ardacos to speak, it stood up and made of itself a silhouette against the stars. She heard the man sigh beside her, a nasal whistling of breath. "No," he said, "I do not think it is just for us. Where would be the honour in that? To become Warrior because none else had the chance." He squirmed back from the edge and tapped her wrist. "Go, then; we must act quickly. I will fetch Gwyddhien. You rouse the others."

He regretted the decision. Even as he ran ahead along the edge of the water, she saw it in him. She sent Hail ahead for Caradoc and worked along the edge of the water, waking each group as she came to it. The hounds were full of boar offal and somnolent and unwilling to stir themselves. Their warriors were little better. One in every four she left to feed the fires and wrap dried bracken onto sticks to make fire-clubs. The rest she told to leave their spears and arm with rocks of a good size to throw, impressing on them the need not to kill; they knew the laws, but only she and Ardacos had been given a living reminder of the penalties. Midway through, Caradoc joined her and they divided the rest between them, meeting back at the place where the boar was kept. Gwyddhien was there already, standing on the crag above the carcass. Ardacos was nowhere to be seen.

Breaca climbed onto the rock and looked about. The bear was downwind and had caught their scent. It rose on its hind legs, the blunt snout raised to the sky. Breaca said, "Where's Ardacos?" and the words were barely out before she saw him and realized that the bear did not stand as she did just for the scent of a handful of warriors hidden among the crags, but for a small, wiry man, naked now and weaponless, who stood before it, swaying.

"Gods, what is he doing?"

Gwyddhien grimaced. "Bear-dancing. It is a tradition among the Caledonii, apparently, handed down from the ancestors; they dance with the bear and ask it to leave them in peace and it does so." She spoke softly, with the singing lilt of the west. Even shouting above the noise of battle practise it was the same. It was this that had first drawn Airmid to her, that and her outstanding skill.

They watched the dancing warrior together. Breaca said, "He's mad."

"Or supremely courageous. If he dies, they will say it is the former. If he lives . . ." The tall warrior grinned and spread her hands, as a garner might at a lost bet when the contest has been hard and fast. "We dare not interfere. If we go down, we will break the bond between them and he will die. All we can do is stand and watch."

Venutios jumped the height of the rock and stood beside her. He alone gripped his spear. Whatever he might become, he was still the Warrior and no-one had the power to tell him to abandon his weapons. He leaned on the haft and watched the dance as bear and man edged sideways, away from the crag.

Breaca watched Venutios rather than the bear. She had reached him last in the round of waking and had found him sitting by his fire, honing the blade of his hunting knife. He had not asked why she came.

"Were you expecting this?" she asked.

"Something like it."

"Is it always a bear?"

He ran his tongue round his teeth, considering the limits of what he could reveal. "No," he said, eventually. "Not always."

She wanted to ask what else they could expect but he would not have been permitted to answer and to ask did him no honour. She stared out into the night. The more Ardacos danced, the harder he was to see. Starlight made him grey, the colour of rocks, and the bear the same. She felt the others gather behind her, scaling the crag slowly. Not all of them saw Ardacos. Twice, Breaca had to hold back a warrior who thought to take on the bear alone.

She was holding the arm of Braint, the girl-cousin of the Brigantes, when she saw the other shapes, smaller and more ghostly, that followed the larger.

"Cubs!" She let go of the girl. "Gwyddhien, Ardacos must be warned. He can't take his eyes from the she-bear but either of the cubs is big enough to kill him."

She spoke too late. The boy-cousin of the Brigantes had acted even as she let go of his cousin's arm. He sprinted down from the crag, yelling his war shout and hurling the stones he had carried. Seeing him, the smaller cub turned. The bigger reared up like its dam and advanced on Ardacos. He may have seen it, but a man can only dance with one bear at a time. He made no move to turn, to engage it or to defend himself.

"No!" Breaca was already running. She held the two rocks she had collected and she had Hail. It was not enough. She felt Caradoc at her left side, the place of the oath-bound, and was glad of him. Gwyddhien joined on the right. Others ran, strung out behind. Venutios stayed on the rocks, observing.

"Go!" With a prayer for his life, she sent Hail to harry the she-bear. From a distance beyond spear-throw, she cast the first of the two stones. With the gods' aid, it bounced on a rock by the bigger cub and shattered, spitting debris. The cub yelped and fell to all fours. Ardacos turned, letting go of the dance. The she-bear reared higher and slashed the air. Hail launched at her from behind, ripping a mouthful of pelt and turning away before the claws could smash him to rags. The bear yarled, a small noise for one so vast, and spun to face the new threat.

Breaca shouted, "Ardacos! To your right. There's another cub!" and knew she was too late.

There were six of them within striking distance and all had hurled their stones. One of the younger warriors had a fire-club and threw that, too, but all of them had aimed for the adult or the bigger cub; none had taken heed of the smaller as it threw down the youth of the Brigantes and came to the aid of its dam. It was not large for a bear, but Ardacos was not large for a man and he had no defence but his guile. He rolled away from the strike as he had rolled from the boar and so was not disembowelled. The claws caught him on the shoulder where the boar-tusk had already struck. With a crack like breaking greenwood, they broke his arm and ripped the flesh beneath. He fell without a sound.

"Ardacos?"

He lay belly down on a bed of moss and green bracken with his head to the west in case he should die. The boy-cousin of the Brigantes was already dead. Venutios had spoken the invocation to Briga to accept the soul of one lost in the hunt, although it was his own fault and the god would know it as well as they. His cousin mourned him alone and silently. Of the rest, three had been wounded such that they could not walk unaided. The remains of the thirty had made a crescent about the fallen bodies and driven the bears off with the noise of stones clashed on rocks and the fire-clubs spun in the air to make rings of flame. Hail had harried the beasts into the distance and had not been injured. For that Breaca gave thanks, privately, even as she was sending others to search for the plants she needed to begin the treatment of the wounded. In the time it had taken to make a drag-litter to carry Ardacos safely to camp, she had found she was the one with the most knowledge of healing. Three years with the elder grandmother was worth a lifetime of others' teaching. She had described what she needed and where it might be found, and half of the thirty had run at her bidding.

By the time she had made him comfortable, she found that three years of anyone's teaching made no difference when those looking searched in the dark at the start of winter on the far western edge of the world. None of the plants she wanted had been found and she had to make do with green moss, lifted whole from the rocks and laid in the wound as Ardacos had done in the morning. She was binding it in place on the warrior's back when she felt him move.

"Ardacos?" His head was turned away from her. She moved round and bent to look. His eye was open and held a question. "You succeeded," she said. "The bears have gone. The boy of the Brigantes died, out of recklessness. All the rest are alive. You were wounded and have bled greatly but you will—" The eye closed. She was saved from speaking platitudes that might yet prove untrue.

She looked up. To Gwyddhien, sitting on the rock above, she said, "I have done what I can. His arm is set and bound. The wound is closed but still bleeding. He needs Airmid or Talla if he is to live. We should leave now."

"Do you think so?" The tall warrior was silent a moment, then shook her head. "We can't move out yet. It's already too dark and clouds are moving in from the east. We will have rain soon, or mist. The route back to the great-house is not without its own dangers, and none of us knows the way well enough to find it at night. We had better wait until daylight."

"We can't. It's too long." Urgency gave a bite to her tone.

Gwyddhien smiled, halfway to the peace of the Warrior. "I think not. It's past midnight. Morning is not far."

"But still too far. If we leave now, we will reach the great-house at dawn. If we wait until dawn before we move, we won't get there before mid-morning and he will be dead by then."

"Better one dies than many. We have three who are weak and will need to be carried, and there is a body that cannot be left—"

"We can leave it. If we bury him with rocks, the bears will not take him. I will come back with others tomorrow—"

"*No.*"

They faced each other across the injured man. Breaca found she was shaking. The blood coursed hot in her veins and her palm-scar ached again. She drew a breath and hissed it back through closed teeth. With careful clarity she said, "Then I will run alone to the great-house and bring a healer back with horses and a litter. We will be here before dawn. He *cannot* be left longer."

"No." Venutios shook his head. "You can't go alone. The thirty must not be separated. It is the law of the choosing."

He was still Warrior. She would have trusted him with her life. But Ardacos had been a friend and had woken Breaca when he could have danced with the bear alone and perhaps succeeded.

"Who will stop me?" she asked.

"I will." Venutios sat on a rock with his spear held loosely across his knees. His quiet eyes promised death if she defied him. He shrugged an apology. "I'm sorry. I would let you go if I could but the law on this is certain and not open to discussion. Either all of you go or none."

Breaca was breathing too fast to think clearly. She slowed and thought of Eburovic, who had always counselled calm and the need to find the reasons behind the words in any conflict. To Gwyddhien, she said, "This is not about finding or losing a path. We have all hunted here at night many times, you more than any. We could find our way blindfolded if we had to. Why do you not want us to go?"

The warrior nodded, the heat going out of her. "I have lived here ten years," she said. "There are no bears on Mona."

Breaca said, "There were bears tonight. We saw them."

"This is the night of the Warrior's choosing. What we see may not be there. Only with daylight will we see the truth. We have lost only one of our group, maybe two if Ardacos dies. The elders predicted three or four times that number. If we walk through the night, we risk more than him alone. Dreams come in other shapes than bears."

"Ardacos was not wounded by a dream-shape."

"Are you sure?"

"Yes. Hail does not see dreams. There may have been no bears on Mona before, but there are three now. We will deal with them later, or leave them to live in peace."

As she spoke, she vaulted up onto the crag beside Gwyddhien. Her knife was in her belt, a better weapon than none. Hail would follow her, if no-one else. She stepped round to the side, putting Gwyddhien between herself and Venutios. Clearly, so it could be heard by the full group, she said, "If the dreamers are sending dream-shapes, they will send them to us here as much as on the walk back. Ardacos needs help and the laws are not fit if they condemn a man to death for no reason. Those who agree with me may follow. I am leaving, *now*."

She jumped. She ran. Hail bounded beside her, so close she could smell the heat of his breath and the bear-stench on it. In three strides, Caradoc was shielding her left. By ten, Braint, the girl-cousin of the Brigantes, was on her right with Cumal of the Cornovii just beyond. By the foot of the hill, there were more running behind her than she could readily count, certainly more than were left up above. She paused and looked back. On the crag top, Venutios raised the Warrior's horn and blew the recall. Breaca knew a moment's exultation, as she had done on the day when she broke his blade. Taking only Caradoc and Braint, she ran back up the hill. Venutios met her, his face still as an elder's pronouncing law.

"You may not go alone but the greater number have chosen to leave. It is Gwyddhien, then, who must follow."

The tall warrior stood behind him. In her hand she carried her own spear and Breaca's. She passed the latter over, butt first, in the sign of good faith. "I am ready." The lilt to her voice made it a prayer.

Breaca offered her hand in the warrior's greeting. She said, "If we are to carry the wounded, we will need more wood for stretchers. Give me half of the thirty and I will get it."

"You have them." The clasp was accepted and returned. Gwyddhien grinned. "Get a new pole for the boar also," she said. "We will halve the carcass and it will be less weight to carry. We can go faster like that."

They ran through the night; not fast, but fast enough. No dream-shapes threatened and they made good time. Clouds covered the sky but did not shed rain. Without stars to guide them, they sought for and found a hunter's path marked with cleft sticks and followed it. Gwyddhien ran at the head of the column, checking the route. Venutios ran at the back, keeping pace with the stragglers to ensure the group was not split. Breaca and Caradoc made a team with Braint, who needed work to keep her from grieving the loss of her cousin. Between the three of them they carried Ardacos, rotating so that two carried and one ran, and they swapped places often to keep fresh. The injured man passed in and out of consciousness as they ran but even when awake he lay silently and did not cry out when they stumbled or had to pass him hand over hand across a stream.

They were on a downhill slope, taking care to keep Ardacos level, when Breaca realized she could see the outline of her hand and her foot beneath it and that dawn must be coming. She looked for Caradoc and saw his hair, pale as waving corn. He smiled and his teeth showed white. Black-haired Braint, at the far end of the stretcher, was still too dark to be seen.

At the foot of the slope, Gwyddhien gathered them. "We will be at the gates by full light. Even with wounded, we must make a good entrance."

They were tired and untidy, a ragged cluster of half-seen shapes. She sharpened them into three rows, ranked by age and experience, with spears slung behind in the sign of peace. Of Ardacos, she said, "We will stop at the oak before the gateway. Bring him forward then. He is still the greatest of us. He should enter first."

It was an act of honour worthy of them both. In the eyes of some, he may have been greatest when they left, but Gwyddhien was returning as the Warrior, none of them doubted it. Breaca bent down to the stretcher and found the wounded man awake. He winked as he had once before. She kept her hand on her spear and did not let down her guard.

The remaining ground was known to them all: a brief run of rolling gorse-covered hills and minor valleys filled with willow and hazel. Of the two streams, the nearer was crossed with stepping-stones and the farther by a bridge.

The first of the spears fell as they passed Ardacos across the stones. Breaca heard the grunt and wheeze of a hit and jumped the last two steps to the far bank without thinking. Caradoc, who held the back end of the stretcher, jumped with her and ran as she did. They sprinted untidily for the shelter of a hawthorn. Braint dashed to join them, hurling herself facedown in the turf.

"Venutios is hit," she said.

"What?"

Caradoc said, "I saw him go down. The spears were aimed at him."

"Gods. Why?" Breaca stretched out from the hiding place and tried to count heads. On the open ground, she might have seen them. Here, in the shelter of the valley with the trees still in autumn leaf and the remains of night still upon them, it was impossible. Only Gwyddhien was visible, lying flat in the poor shelter of a rock. Breaca put her cupped hands to her mouth and blew the cry of the night owl, the call of the warriors of Mona. Gwyddhien returned it and ran to join them.

Breaca said, "Venutios is down."

"I know. I saw. You were last to cross apart from him?"

"Yes."

"Then at least we are all on the right side of the river."

Gwyddhien made the owl's cry, louder. Others answered in twos and threes and gathered, slowly.

Cumal of the Cornovii arrived first behind the rock. "Ordovices!" He spat on the ground at Caradoc's feet. Their peoples were ancient enemies. "I would know their spears anywhere. Did you know of this?"

Caradoc stared at the other man. With quiet deliberation, he turned to look across the river at the fallen shape of Venutios. The Warrior lay sprawled on his back, his limbs at unhinged angles. The shaft of a single spear rose above him. Turning back, Caradoc was stiffly formal. "Forgive me. The light is too poor to see from here but I was close when the spears fell and I believe they bore the mark of the horned god on the haft."

"No, they were Coritani," said Breaca. "Unless the Cornovii have taken the mark of the red hawk for their own?"

Braint said, "Votadini. They mark them black and use poison stewed from mushrooms on the points. I have known them since childhood. They killed my mother's uncle."

There was silence. A jackdaw flew down to Venutios and was scared away by a flung branch.

Stone-white, Gwyddhien said, "Then the spears are sent by the dreamers, as were the bears. Why would the dreamers kill their own?" Unspoken, but more clearly, was, *Why would Airmid?*

Breaca said, harshly, "Ask Venutios if you should happen to meet him in the lands of the dead. He must have known of the risk and we should have thought of it. Many more died in other years than would have been killed by a bear." She blamed herself, because it was safer than blaming anyone else, even a dreamer who had taken a bet when she might instead have given a warning. A bitter anguish curdled her guts, but dully, as if, once faced, it might prove overwhelming.

"Then what now?" asked Gwyddhien. "We can't kill the dreamers."

"Can we not if they can kill us?" Breaca rounded on the group. Two dozen faces doubted her. In the grey light, even Caradoc looked uncertain. She had thought him immune to fear and was shocked to find it not so. The dreamers of Mona were sacred, bound in a web of peace; they could walk through war from one side to the other and no warrior would lift a blade against them. She felt the unravelling of the weave that had made the thirty whole and prayed to Briga, and to

Nemain, who cared most closely for Airmid. In answer, she saw only Ardacos, dying, and the Warrior already dead, and the wrongness of it chilled her to the core. She called for Eburovic and the elder grandmother and neither came. Despairing, she called for Airmid, not for the living dreamer, but for the sense of her that enfolded like a second skin and gave support when it most was needed. The night gave nothing back, and less than nothing; in the dark was an echoing silence that leached at her will. Here on the gods' isle, on a night warped by the gods' touch, she was alone, abandoned by those she trusted most, who wielded instead the gods' power against her.

The knowledge of betrayal was crippling. She stared out beyond the stretch of hawthorn to the willows that flanked the second stream. A fine mist drifted forward at knee height, coldly insidious. She had never craved death, as 'Tagos had done in the first months after he lost his arm, but she saw it approach and did not have the will to resist.

Hail nudged at her hand, shoving his head against her palm. Alone of all of them, he did not harbour doubt or fear the dreamers, did not distinguish between the good and bad of a battle. He lived only to hunt and kill, to fight and win. Crouching, she dug her fingers in the harsh hair of his neck. Eburovic might be denied her but none could rob her of the memory of the hound's birth, of the sight of Bán in the doorway of the women's place, fresh from the dream, wild-eyed and lost, aching for a soul he barely knew, but already loved; her little brother who had yearned to be a warrior when everyone else had clearly seen that he was destined to be the greatest dreamer the tribes had ever known, until a single act of treachery cut him short. From Bán, it was a short step to anger, to fury, to a consuming rage. Two years of Mona's teaching had schooled her to prevent passion from overriding reason, but Mona had brought her to this and her teachers had known of it and said nothing. In defiance, she nurtured the spark that burned in her core and could be fed so very easily: by her loathing of Amminios, by the memory of their first meeting, of his sacrifice of the dun filly, of his final act of desecration, by the sound of his laughter ringing in her ears, until there blazed within a fire that could destroy anything that stood in her way.

Shaking, she stood and looked round with a clarity that made nonsense of the indecision just past. The mist burned away, a phantom of her fear. The remains of the thirty watched her, warily, as if she, too, might be unreal. She smiled and saw those closest flinch. Choosing her words with care, she said, "If this is the dreamers' work, then it is part of the test. We are the warriors of Mona. They have spent years training us for battle. If we are to die, then it should be with honour and in action, not standing like bulls in a pen awaiting slaughter." She lifted her spear with the point upright, for battle. "I will fight the dream-spears alone if necessary, but it would go better in company. Who will fight them with me?"

The pause could be counted by the hammer of her heart and might have been eternity. At the end of it, a voice behind her said, "I will," and Caradoc stepped forward to her side, closing a door too long left open. She smiled at him, light-headed, and he returned it, and she was reminded of a moment in a river when death had held them and had chosen to let them go. With commendable practicality, he said, "We'll need other weapons. Spear against spear is no way to win a fight. We need blades and shields to do it properly."

"The armoury is on this side of the compound. We are twenty-nine, less the wounded. Ten will be enough to carry what we need." Braint stood not far away. Breaca put a hand on her shoulder. "Will you risk your life to retrieve your blade?"

The girl was vividly alert. Her grief at her cousin's death had turned readily to anger and the need for action. She grinned, savagely. "Anything."

"Good. That's three. We need seven more. Not the wounded."

Braint was youngest of them. The others would not allow her courage to be greater than theirs. None refused to join her.

Gwyddhien recovered her composure and her ability to plan ahead. She said, "The armoury is too exposed. If they are waiting, you will need a diversion to keep their attention elsewhere." She pointed through the gloom. "There's a stand of willow that leads to the edge of the second stream. You take your ten to the armoury. I'll take the rest and we'll make as if to cross there. You can break in while we do it."

Breaca felt herself balanced, as if on a high wall, with a clear view of those gathered below. Without conscious effort, she could place each of the twenty-five warriors that remained uninjured of the chosen, and sense the quality of their courage. Ardacos lay in the lee of the hawthorns. His dark eyes met hers with no hint of fear. She said, "Someone must stay with Ardacos. We have not brought him so far to lose him."

"I'll stay. If you help me move him behind the rocks and

give me six others, we can keep him safe for as long as you will need." It was Caradoc. Even as she regretted the loss of him, she knew he was the only one she could rely on to protect the wounded man. She nodded. "We'll leave our spears with you. We'll have enough to carry coming back and you'll use them better here."

They moved Ardacos without difficulty. As the groups began to part, Gwyddhien raised her hand to hold her group. "We need a signal to time the diversion right."

"Wait here."

Nine spears fell as Breaca sprinted the breadth of the river stones and another dozen as she returned. Each, to her, had the stench and style of the Coritani, remembered from her youth. She flung herself into the lee of the rock and held her prize aloft for all to see.

"The Warrior's horn." It was the length of her arm and gently curved. The two ends were bound with plain, unadorned silver and the horn itself had been polished over the generations to a warm translucency that caught the first cold glimmer of dawn and made of it a fire that joined her own. Looping the thong about her neck, she said, "I'll blow the call to war when we have the blades. Meet us back here to collect them. Then we will see who throws spears that change in the dark."

"And before that?" asked Gwyddhien. "You can't blow the horn when you reach the armoury. You'll call trouble on yourselves too early."

Breaca grinned. The promise of battle coursed through her, burning clear the threat of betrayal. "Has Airmid taught you the call of the croaking frog?" she asked.

"Yes."

"Then use it. Three times and three again. When the last one calls, we'll break in. Pray for us and we'll bring you weapons."

A brown-skinned frog croaked in an eastern marsh and was answered by its mate. In the colourless predawn light, a hand was raised in long grass and swung forward. Ten warriors and a hound slid, belly-down, like lizards, across dew-sodden turf.

The compound was quiet. Smoke rose thinly from night fires. Hounds and cockerels slept. A small, stone-built hut, slate-roofed for protection from fire, stood midway between one great-house and the next. The door was wooden and hinged and prone to squeal whenever it moved—except this time, when a young, black-haired warrior of the Brigantes clamped fat from a hunted boar to the openings and silenced them. Three warriors entered, one wiping boar-fat from her hands. The interior was blacker than the night had been but they had practised many times finding their weapons blindfolded for an occasion not unlike this. They sought out blades and passed them, hilt first, to those waiting outside, knowing each by the shape of the pommel. Shields were harder to name. Each bore the Warrior's mark of the leaping salmon on the face, blue against grey, with personal marks etched only lightly on boss or handle, too faintly to be seen. In the absence of better direction, twenty-nine shields were picked at random and handed out, and the one found that was different and special. Bearing three blades and three shields each and with the hound leaping ahead to warn of danger, they ran back to the rock whence they had come. Those protecting Ardacos had been attacked. Two of the defenders lay wounded but not dead and were left on guard with those three already injured. With the blades and shields passed to those who could use them, Breaca raised the Warrior's horn to her lips, filled her lungs and blew the call to battle.

Breaca ordered her half of the line. They walked forward, shields overlapping, blades raised and ready. For the last time, they bore the leaping salmon in blue that was the mark of Venutios, who had been Warrior and was dead. His shield alone had been different from theirs: The salmon was etched deeply on the boss and inlaid with blue stones. Breaca had wanted to take it to him but had been overruled by Gwyddhien and Caradoc together; it was too close to dawn for her to do it unseen and the horn had been blown with a force that could be heard across the island; they were at war and the time for the dead was later, if there were any left alive to tend them. The shield had been left instead with Ardacos, who had been given his own blade and helped to sit. At his own request, they had strapped the shield to his side so that his wounded arm would not be the death of him. He had grinned as they left and pledged his life to theirs, as a warrior should.

The remains of the thirty made a steep-sided crescent, like the hunting but steeper, a formation that gave each protection by a neighbour but offered the chance to win honour alone with a single charge. Gwyddhien took the centre as was her right. Breaca, by virtue of her actions, had won the right flank, the place of next greatest honour. Caradoc had been given the left and had tried to take Braint as his shield-mate but had resigned her to Breaca and taken instead Cumal, the Cornovian who had spat at his feet.

He and Breaca had parted at the edge of the trees, just before the first steps out into open ground. Caradoc had stood with his back to the dawn. The remains of the mist had scattered a fine spray on his hair and across his shoulders and the cold morning light made of each drop molten metal, to match his eyes. He was troubled. Breaca could see it in him, but not the cause. For the first time in two years, she found she welcomed his presence. Reaching forward, she had touched a fingertip to the hilt of his blade, returning the warrior's oath as she had never done before. She had not spoken. She was not sure if, in that moment, she could have spoken, but they were interrupted in any case by Brock of the Dumnonii who was unsure of his place in the line and when he had been reassured and was settled, the moment, and the queer trick of light that had cast Caradoc in silver, had passed.

They parted, each to take either end of the line. In the last instant, he had stopped her, saying, "Don't think about who is in front of you. If we are truly facing the dreamers, what you see may not be real."

She had said, "I will know Airmid."

"Be sure that you do."

The group walked uphill out of the valley, moving slowly not to break the line. All around them, night was giving way to morning, greys and blacks to the pastel colours of the dawn. A blackbird followed them beyond the last hazel, chucking a warning. In the paddocks beyond the great-houses, grunting sows roused themselves and ewes called to their lambs. High in the upper fields, a colt squealed in irritation and raced the length of a wall. The hammer of his feet rolled from the hills.

Braint said, "We should have got the horses. I would have rather died on horseback."

"It was too far and dawn too close. We would have been seen before we got there." Breaca looked east. A gap in the clouds showed a lining of molten gold, awaiting the first real rays of the sun. She thought of Venutios, dead, and the peace he had brought and was glad that it was gone and not dampening the wild, clear fire that burned in her, quite different from the battle fever that had gripped them all in the great-house when the choosing of the thirty had begun. The field was sharp in her mind and the ordering of the warriors. The weave that bound them was sound, and each shone with a defiance and certainty that made the whole stronger than if each were fighting alone. Braint was her only worry; the girl blazed with enthusiasm, but lacked the training of Mona.

Breaca said, "Be careful when the sun rises. If they are good, they may use it to blind you. Don't look to your left without raising your shield hand for shade."

"I won't."

They skirted a patch of gorse, shield locked to shield. The land lay open to the first ditch and wall of the dreamers' compound. The warriors' school had practised here often. Breaca had once held off an attacking party of ten with only Cumal for company. To Braint, she said, "If we are split from the rest and there are more than four against us, turn your back to mine and— What is it?"

"Warriors! Look! A whole line of them!"

They rose from the ditch, fully armed and decorated for war. Kill-feathers hung from the ends of their torcs in the manner of the ancestors. They wore the tokens of their dreams about their necks and in their hair. Their shields were solidly grey, denying allegiance to the Warrior. Their blades were steady.

Breaca swallowed the bile that scalded her throat. "It's the honour guard. They have sent against us those who survived the last choosing. They are too many. We can't meet them in a line like this."

It was the worst she could have imagined. Caradoc was far to her left, Gwyddhien ten paces back, deep in the arc of the crescent. Breaca could see him but not her. They should have planned for this and had not. It was too late to make a new signal that the honour guard would not know. Cursing, she raised the Warrior's horn to her lips and blew the call for a spear-head. Pausing to make sure Braint had understood, she began to run.

They were twenty-three, one untrained. They made the transition from the crescent to the spear-head as fast as any might have done it, coming together in a wedge focused on the horn-bearer. Breaca would die now, that was certain; none lived from the first rows of a spear. She felt sorry for Braint, who was behind her right shoulder in the second rank. Caradoc had stepped into the shield space on her left and once again the door closed that had been open. She had no need for the Warrior's horn now, except to show defiance, which was reason enough. Raising the serpent-blade that had been the gift of her father, she put the horn to her lips and blew so that the sound gathered them and hurled them forward, like a pack of hounds loosed for the hunt or horses given free rein to race. Her only regret, as the mass of the wedge built speed behind her, was that she had not had time to engrave her own mark on the boss of the borrowed shield.

A contrasting horn sounded in the dreamers' compound, with higher notes and more delicate than the one just blown. The sun broke through the gap in the clouds, streaming light onto the field of battle. The morning came alive with colour and sound. The warriors of the honour guard threw down their shields and sheathed their blades. Those at the edges dropped to one knee. Those in the centre moved aside smoothly as a well-greased gate and they, too, knelt. Behind them, the gates to the compound stood open and the ranks of dreamers waited, dressed for ceremony. At the front, alive and whole, stood Venutios. His shield was iron grey marked with red, the colour of freshly spilled blood. The symbol painted on it, still wet so that the edges blurred, was the serpent-spear.

Talla stepped forward to meet the charge of the warrior's wedge—which halted, quivering, as a spear might when thrown into oak.

"Welcome, Warrior of Mona."

The Elder's voice was thin and dry as an autumn leaf. Her eyes and smile were those of the elder grandmother so that one might weep, unguarded, on the field of battle, which would be unforgivable but might be unavoidable if the driving fire inside could not be quenched, or stilled, at least.

Shaking, Breaca sheathed the serpent-blade and noticed, late, that her hand had not throbbed with the promise of combat. The warriors of the wedge crowded round her, swearing their lives for hers. Caradoc was there, who was already oath-sworn. Braint and Cumal joined him. Gwyddhien stepped out from the third rank of the spear. She spread her palms wide, as a gambler might on losing a close-fought game. Her smile showed no resentment. "You took the horn and blew it when no-one else did," she said. "I would have died for you then, willingly."

Talla nodded. Breaca looked past her. Airmid stood just behind with Venutios and there was no question of betrayal, of anything but care and an overwhelming love. She wore the silver brooch with the coral inlay she had just won in a bet and she wept, which was heartbreaking, but not badly so; a dreamer could be forgiven tears on the battlefield where a warrior could not. Because speech was unsafe and the questions too difficult, Breaca asked only, "Ardacos?"

Airmid said, "He lives. He is being tended, as are the others. He says to tell you that it is only now beginning. He will join your honour guard when he is fit, if you have need of him."

"I will always have need of him. He carries the soul of the ancestors." A flash of yellow caught her eye as a cloak lifted in the breeze. Among all the clamour and the movement, Gunovic stood waiting with Lanis, whose very presence was a reminder of the Sun Hound's death.

Without turning, Breaca knew that Caradoc had seen it and made his decision. She felt the rightness of it settle on them both. To him and to Airmid, to Braint and to Gwyddhien, to any who listened, she said, "With what is to come, we will have need of you all, however you choose to serve."

The ferry bumped against the oak pilings of the jetty, pulling against its tether with a gentle insistency. Two horses stood ready, held by the white-cloaked warrior of the Ordovices who had taken the last ferry of the evening to bring a private, urgent message. Breaca sat on a rock a spear's throw away, not quite out of sight. In all the havoc of the Warrior's naming and the swearing-in of the honour guard and the preparations for the delegation to the Sun Hound's funeral, it was good to take Hail away and spend some time alone. The late sun warmed her back and the berries hung ripe from the rowan. The water of the strait furled against the rock at her feet. Straggling willowherb dusted seeds on the surface. If she narrowed her eyes and glanced at the water— just so—the flow of the current against the rock and the scatter of seeds and the reflection of the berries made the shape of a spear, thrown against—

"Am I interrupting?"

"No. I was waiting for you." She opened her eyes. Caradoc stood a short distance away, dressed for travel. His cloak was the white of the Ordovices, like that of the messenger waiting on the jetty. He was strained, as Venutios had been, a man carrying a new weight. No word had spread of the nature of the message that called him away, but she could guess.

"You are setting out for your father's funeral?" she asked. "Do the Ordovices want you to lead their delegation?"

He nodded. "They do, but not immediately. There is something else I must attend to first." On the jetty, the messenger turned his back to them, giving privacy. The urgency still showed in the way he stood. The horses moved, restlessly, flashing their harness in the sun. Caradoc squinted against the sudden brightness. "Breaca, I—"

"You have to go. I know. We seem always to be parting on riverbanks." She smiled. In the chaos, some things were simple, and very wonderful. "Sometime, perhaps, we might correct that."

It was the pain in his eyes that warned her. He was more than strained; almost, he looked as he had done at the paddock gates back in the Eceni lands, when she had refused to take from him her brooch. She searched his face for a reason and failed to find it. Confused, she said, "Have I changed so much? I am Warrior, but it was luck made me so. You could have gone for the horn, or Gwyddhien—even Braint had it in her to think and run—and I would be in the honour guard now, swearing my life for theirs. Or yours, if you had been prepared to give up the Ordovices for Mona."

He had not been; of all those who had picked a black pebble and survived the tests, he was the only one not to have joined her guard. She had not been sorry; she could see the shape of a battlefield in her mind's eye, with Mona on the right flank and the spears of the Ordovices making a solid wall on the left. The only questions were the names and numbers of the enemy and the timing of the battle but that was the future and the present was Caradoc, who was unsettled and unhappy and was staring at her now in a way that mixed disbelief with a dangerous, unguarded hilarity, as if he might begin to laugh and never stop.

"What is it?" she asked.

The clear, grey gaze raked her full length. "Do you really not know what you did?"

"I cast aside two years of Mona's training and allowed myself to get so angry that it overwhelmed my reason. If Maroc knew how shallow grew the roots of his teaching, he would be horrified. It was nothing special. If Gunovic tells me one more time how proud my father would be, I will throw him into the straits."

Caradoc raised a brow. His self-control was returning. Both were glad of it. "Would he not be proud?" he asked.

She grimaced. "The dead have the advantage of the living; they can see the truth of things. Eburovic would be more concerned, I think, that I did not give way to arrogance."

"Which, being aware of it, you won't." He lifted one foot up on the rock and rested an elbow on his knee, thinking. Looking up, he said, "When you argued with Gwyddhien after Ardacos was wounded and ran down from the hill, why do you think I followed you?"

"You were oath-sworn. You had no choice."

"No. I did it because it was so very clearly the right thing to do. I would not have gone against Gwyddhien and Venutios but when you did, the least I could do was follow. The same when you faced the dreamers' fog and made the decision to fight; it may have been nothing special to you but none of the rest of us could do it. I have never in my life felt as helpless as I did then. Even on the deck of the *Greylag* as she broke apart and sank, I knew that if I could jump clear and swim, I had a chance. The power of the gods was everywhere and I did not believe I would die. Last night, the gods were nowhere and I was paralysed. I could hold the stand around Ardacos, I could lead the left flank of the advance, but I could not have faced the fog and made the decision to fight, and I did not run back for the horn."

"But I am nothing like Venutios. I don't carry the peace of the Warrior as he did." The fear of it had gnawed at her soul since the morning. She had hidden it from Gunovic's teary joy, from Maroc's knowing smile, even from Airmid.

She could not hide it now, before one who had been there, who must be made to understand.

He was gentle with her, as a man with a child on its first horse. "Breaca, you don't have to carry the peace. What you carry is quite different. If you listen to the singers with the right ear, you'll find that each of those chosen has brought a different quality to their time as Warrior. Venutios *was* the peace. It was a part of him; he spread it without effort, simply by being. You couldn't do that even if you tried."

"But then what will I carry with me? Anger? Is that what Mona wants? What she needs? Do you really think so? It's what I felt when the dreamers' fog was closing on us."

"Was it? I don't think so. It may have been at the start but it is not what we saw. What did you feel when you blew the horn to call the wedge? Don't tell me anger. I won't believe it."

She might have done; it was easy, if untrue. She thought for a while, letting the notes of the horn blast afresh through her mind, and the pure, sweet moment after. In time, she said, "I felt as I did just before I broke Venutios's blade—as any of us does when we cast a spear and it flies true and there's that moment just before it hits the target when we know, with absolute certainty, that it will pierce the centre. It's the battle joy that comes before the killing starts and the screams of the wounded. It burns through, like wildfire, and nothing can stop it."

"That's it." He was intent, in a way she had seen him only rarely before. "You carry the wildfire, the battle joy; you blaze with it. When you stood up in the dreamers' fog, it was as if someone had lit a pitch-torch and thrust it in our eyes. When you led the wedge, you could have been poured from the forge of the sun, you burned so brightly. Gwyddhien was not the only one who would have died for you then, but we didn't follow you believing we were going to die—we shared the battle joy, the moment of certainty. Ask anyone in the wedge—we knew, with absolute conviction, that we could hit the old honour guard and live."

"Nobody lives in the front rows of a wedge."

"But we believed we could, and that was enough to make us try." He was not saying it out of pity, or the need to curry favour. There was no irony in his voice, taking away from the meaning. He offered his honesty as a gift and his eyes, holding hers, held an integrity that told her he believed it, if nothing else. He was leaning forward, close enough to touch. The wind and the evening sun were both at her back. Her hair blew across his, copper thread laid across corn, and the sun welded them together. The decision, then, was simple. She reached up and took his hand. "You have a brooch that was given once as a gift," she said. "Perhaps it is time—"

She stopped. The fire had died in his eyes. The strain she had seen before returned, magnified. Fortuitously, or perhaps not, the man on the jetty made the horses move so that the harness jangled in deliberate and unsubtle reminder of the need for haste.

Caradoc was not one to take the easy path, even when offered. Ignoring the interruption, he said, "I can't, not now. I'm sorry, truly. If I had known there was a chance you would . . ."

Each time she thought she knew him, there was more. This she should have expected. She said, "You have someone else? Someone amongst the Ordovices?"

"Yes."

His hand was still in hers, cold suddenly and too white. She squeezed it, kindly, and made herself smile. "She is fortunate. I wish you well of her, and she of you. You and I are still oath-sworn, are we not?"

"Yes."

"Then that will be enough. I have learned as much from Airmid; lovers may come and go but the oath that binds a warrior to her dreamer—or to another warrior—lasts beyond all of these. Come on." Standing, she freed her hand from his and turned him by the shoulder. "The ferrymen are waiting and it doesn't do to keep them long. Go now. We will meet at your father's funeral and see what can be done to cull the poison that is Amminios. That is the thing that matters most."

Saying it, she could believe it was true.

CHAPTER 20

The death platform stood at the top of a small rise to the north of the dun. A pack of red brindle hunting hounds with harsh coats and wary eyes lay guard about the base. Three men with the mark of the Sun Hound painted on their forearms and the black spear of mourning on their brows laid green boughs and grass over a fire pit the length of a man's body. Dense, fragrant smoke rose and billowed beneath the platform, seeping through to the linen-wrapped body above so that, even downwind, it was hard to detect the taint of decay.

Breaca pushed her mare close to the nearest upright. A blanket of pre-dawn mist hovered at knee height, hiding the ground. Smoke obscured the sky. Between them, they trapped her in an otherworld of whiteness and death. Echoes of the dreamers' fog sent cold fingers down her spine that took time to shake off.

She was not the first to visit the dead. Others had been before her, bearing gifts for the journey: a shield in leaf-thin bronze with flying herons on the boss swung against one of the pillars; a rope of red coral hung in loops from the woven hazel of the platform; a silver horn clashed against it, the sound muffled by the mist. Everywhere there was gold: rings and coins and armbands hung suspended in the smoke. The wind and the rising heat of the fire played games, spinning them slowly. The smoke dulled them all to baser metal.

Her own gift was a torc of woven gold bought from Gunovic for just this occasion. The metal was not worked with the skill of her father, but it was as close as any living smith might achieve: intricate without being fussy and well worth the price. She reached up from the saddle and tied it under one corner of the platform where the smoke would not blacken it too soon. The oldest of the fire-tenders nodded approval.

A rider emerged from the mist behind her. She backed the mare away from the platform and waited. Even had she not been expecting him, his size would have given him away. He was broader in the shoulder than she remembered and his hair was streaked with grey but otherwise he had not changed.

"Togodubnos, greetings. Your father is well honoured in death."

"So far." He smiled a brief greeting. The ritual welcome of the delegation had been performed in full when they arrived at dusk the night before. There was no need of formality between them; as Warrior she was his equal and even without that their past bound them close enough to speak openly in private. He said, "We will take him to the grave mound tomorrow. Luain mac Calma designed the place where he will lie. If the sun shines, Cunobelin will go to his resting place encased in living gold."

"And even if it does not, the majesty of his wake-march will still be greater than anything the world has known." She had seen the preparations; there had never in all the histories of all the tribes been a funeral on the scale of this one. If nothing else, the number of mourners and the variety of tribes from which they came made it unique.

He said, "I hope so. That is the intention. Whatever mistakes he made in life, my father brought security and unimagined wealth to more people than any one man has done before. We owe him a last remembrance even if we cannot keep his peace."

Hail ran to her, breasting the sea of mist. He had killed and eaten; the marks of it showed stickily dark at his throat. He carried the back quarters of a hare, sacred to Nemain, and delivered it into her hand. If it was an omen, it was a good one. Togodubnos watched as she slid the bloody meat into the pouch on her saddle.

"Togodubnos, I am unarmed." She spread her arms, lifting the edges of her cloak to show the unadorned belt underneath. "I left my weapons with the gate guards when we arrived last night. Even had I not, this is your father's time. While his body lies aboveground and for the three days of his funeral, I will honour his peace."

He nodded. "Of course. I expected no less."

"Then what is it that disturbs you?"

He eyed her, carefully. "I have heard," he said, "that you made a vow before the standing stones of Mona that you would challenge Amminios and kill him or die in the attempt. Is it true?"

"It is. And I have heard that Caradoc has sworn the same. If you listen in the dun, you will hear warriors of a dozen tribes taking odds as to which of us will kill the other for the privilege of fighting Amminios alone."

He smiled, faintly. "That would be a challenge worth watching."

"But it will not happen. Caradoc and I are oath-sworn and cannot fight. Even if that were not the case, the pledge to kill Amminios was taken in youth and in anger when I first arrived on Mona. I have grown since, and in any case I am no longer Breaca of the Eceni, free to act as I alone see fit. I am the Warrior and Mona is my first regard. If the opportunity presents itself, I will kill Amminios, but I will not seek him out. Nor, I think, will Caradoc; he, too, sees the bigger picture."

"That would be good." Togodubnos walked his horse away from the platform. Breaca pushed the grey mare to follow. At a safe distance from the listening ears, he said, "Amminios is here. He, too, has given up his weapons, although he uses gold to speak where a blade may not. Without question, he will ride south as soon as he may. If that were to happen and we were to pursue him, there is a risk that he might flee to Berikos of the Atrebates or to Rome."

It was old news; only the immediacy of the threat was new. She said, "Can you stop him?"

"I don't know. When the risk is all or nothing, then, no, I don't think so, but I believe that if he is offered something he may take it, rather than lose the whole. I propose to offer him stewardship of the largest of the ports on the south bank of the sea-river; it is not the only prize, but it is the greatest of those he seeks and it would be better than nothing. If he takes it, we may avoid war."

The plan had the feel of his father about it, but that did

not make it bad, or unacceptable. She said, "How will you ensure that he takes only what he is given?"

"I will ride south with him. I will take a small force; my honour guard and perhaps two hundred others, enough to match those spears he may muster directly, but not to outface him, or provoke the Atrebates to battle before we are ready."

"What will you do if he turns you down and runs to claim the oaths of the spears in the southlands?"

"Follow him and try to reach the spears before he does."

"And if he arrives first?"

"Then we have lost. At best, we will spend the winter preparing for war against the Atrebates; at worst, we will face Rome."

He rested his palms on his saddle and looked out over the land that was now his sole responsibility. He was not a slow thinker and he did not lack education or the means to interpret what he knew. Above all, he had been instructed daily in the game of Warrior's Dance by the man who had made it his life's skill. He was not a natural player, but he had learned more than most men. He looked at her and made his offer.

"It is in my mind that if the Warrior of Mona and her honour guard were to be part of the force that rides south with Amminios, those whose minds were inclined to war might be moved to reconsider. It could tip the balance in our favour." His gaze was honest and open, lacking both Caradoc's irony and Amminios's malice. With a small shrug, he said, "I am aware what this would cost you personally. If you would prefer not to spend time in my brother's company, I will not think less of you for it."

"No, but I will." The sky overhead began to brighten. The great plates of mist sank and thinned as the air warmed. Down in the dun, men and women of two dozen tribes woke, rose and, each in their own way, greeted the dawn. Breaca of the Eceni, Warrior of Mona, felt the fire of the morning sun rekindle the fires of her soul. She reached out and gripped the arm of her friend and ally.

"Give me warning when you're preparing to ride. We will be with you."

The funeral spanned three days. Just before dawn on the first day, Cunobelin, Hound of the Sun, friend to Rome and protector of his people, was carried from the platform to the grave mound in a chariot driven by his eldest son. Red horses drew it and the red hounds ran at the sides. The harness mounts were of bronze, mirror-bright and inlaid with amber and coral, the body was bound in cloth of gold, and the great yellow cloak was laid on top.

Togodubnos drove the chariot at walking pace, following the traditional route taken by the rulers of the Trinovantes for uncounted generations. Small changes had been made to the landscape in the spring before the Sun Hound's death. Gorse had been planted along the route and it flowered now, so that the chariot and its tail of mourners passed along an avenue of yellow; dandelions made an acid carpet through the grass.

The procession that followed was longer and more dignified than any that had gone before it. The royal lines of every tribe attended, each bringing the foremost dreamers and singers of their people. Mona alone had sent a delegation of two hundred in addition to the Warrior and her honour guard, half of them dreamers. Behind them rode the people of the Trinovantes and the Catuvellauni, and behind them the merchants from Gaul, Iberia, Greece and the three Germanies who had made their fortunes trading at Cunobelin's ports.

At the grave mound, the deceased was laid to rest on a bier of oak, surrounded by more wealth than had ever been seen in the realm of the dead. Luain mac Calma, who had responsibility for what was to follow, was visibly uneasy. For the best part of three months he had been directing the engineers and carpenters of the Trinovantes in their construction of the wooden chamber that would house the departed body and then of the grave mound that would sit over it. For the three days before the funeral, he had overseen those bringing into the chamber the shields, weapons, food and gold with which the departed soul was honoured, ensuring that each piece was placed at the right angle to achieve his ends. On the first day of the funeral, in the dim light before dawn, he ordered the pallbearers who carried the body from Togodubnos's chariot to take their lord into the chamber and then he closed the entrance behind them with a vast flap of stitched hides, sealing the interior from view.

The moments of waiting were long and tense. Three nuggets of raw gold had been embedded in the turf above the entrance of the chamber, one beside the other, a hand's breadth apart. The rising sun caught the edge of the first, palely uncertain. With time, and the absence of cloud, the glow steadied to a focused point of fire. The second joined it and the third. When all three glittered like glowflies, Luain ordered the hide to be stripped aside, exposing the heart of the mound and the body lying in state within it to the dawn.

The result was blinding. As the cover fell away, the full face of the risen sun blazed through the entrance, glancing off each piece of polished gold, reflected and multiplied until the man, the cloak and the bier on which he lay were encased within a sheath of living light so radiant that it made mere gold look coarse. Pure sunlight washed out of the darkened mound and drenched those who stood watching, raising a single unconscious gasp of wonder. It was a testament as much to Luain mac Calma's skills as a diplomat and counsellor to the dying man as to his achievements as an engineer. If the Sun Hound had need of an accolade, or a single symbol to show his reconciliation with the dreamers—if those dreamers had need of a sign to show that they walked with the gods and the rulers of the people—then both needs had been satisfied. It was as perfect a passing as any could ask for and not one of those present would forget it, or tire of retelling the moment to those whom the gods had not called to be there. They stood in respectful silence until mac Calma signalled the horns to blow and they filed back whence they came.

On the second day of the funeral, the dead man was lifted from his bier, carried outside and laid on a pyre of dried oak and ash. Cunomar, the three-year-old son of Togodubnos, lit it with the studied solemnity of the very young. The spaces between the logs had been packed with straw and tinder and small nuggets of minerals sent by Maroc from Mona so that the flames leaped up in scarlet and gold and bright green, and those few amongst the crowd who might have forgotten they stood in the presence of majesty were reminded once again that they had never seen his like.

On the third day, the ashes from the fire were lifted from the pit beneath the burned-out pyre, placed in a jar of baked, unfinished clay and returned to the heart of the mound. Everything inside the chamber—the shields, the blades, the spears, the food, the wine, the caskets of clothing—was broken, torn or ground underfoot. Their spirit forms had been carried across the river by the departing soul, and there was no need now for them to remain whole in the land of the living, as temptation for any who might desecrate the grave. The tomb was left open for the day, to be closed at the rising of the moon, under Luain's command. Those who wished to do so were encouraged to spend time in the presence of the dead. The walls between the worlds were thinned here and now, the words of the gods more easily heard.

Through it all, one name ranked alongside that of the dead man. Caradoc, warrior of three tribes, had not chosen to honour his father's passing, and his absence left a bigger gap than his presence might have filled. In a gathering of this size, rumours buzzed and spread like flies on a carcass: he was said to be in Gaul, assaulting Amminios's holdings there while his brother paid homage to their sire; he was in the far western toe of the land, forging alliance with the Dumnonii who controlled the tin mines, persuading them to cut back on their trade with Rome; he was in Hibernia, the vast island beyond the mists at the western edge of the world, raising warriors to sail east and challenge both of his brothers; he was in the wild lands of the north, paying court again to Cartimandua of the Brigantes, who held the spear-oaths of more warriors than any man, including the one recently departed.

This last was both true and demonstrably false: Cartimandua did hold more warriors than Cunobelin had done but Caradoc was not in her company. The leader of the Brigantes had led her own delegation south and had been conspicuous both by the size of the offerings left at the grave—she had given a chariot bound in gold and a shield of the same metal—and by her conduct. She was not a subtle woman and, whereas Caradoc was manifestly not in her retinue, she let it widely be known that he had spent a recent winter in her great-house, "paying court" as assiduously as his father had ever done to any woman.

Breaca, who had more reason than most to know which of the stories were false, watched from a distance. She had known little of Cartimandua until the day of her choosing, when it had become clear that the Brigantian woman was, indirectly, the reason for Venutios's recall.

It had been an odd time, that hazy period when the mantle of Warrior had not fully left one or passed to the other and neither the past incumbent nor the present had grown used to the change. In the days immediately afterwards, Venutios had taken Breaca into Talla's great-house and given all he knew of the Warrior's teaching, passed down in an unbroken line since the days of the oldest ancestors. He had, without difficulty, named two hundred of his predecessors, each of whom had held the title for a decade or more, and under his tutelage Breaca had learned not only the names, but also the dreams and the power each had held and the stories of their choosing-nights, going back through uncounted generations. The sense of age and veneration and the responsibility it embodied had left her silent with awe. There were things she knew now that even Talla had never heard, nor would she ever do so.

On the first day, the day of the choosing, it had been different and less easy. Breaca had come across Venutios in mid-afternoon, sitting in the shade of the hazel trees by the stream eating an apple. From a distance, he had looked content enough; closer, the grief and dragging resignation had been clear and Breaca would have walked away had he not hailed her and invited her to join him. They had sat quietly and she had tried to gauge the limitations of his peace and had found it whole, but thinly so. She had not known, then, that she would not be required to carry it as he had.

Presently, he had split another apple and given her half and, as if to the water, had said, "My people are the northern Brigantes, the smaller part of that nation. It is the wish of my elders that, together with Cartimandua, who rules the larger, southern part, we make a whole which is greater than either alone. This is why I have been called home." He had thrown the apple core into the stream. His blunt, open face had been closed. "Cartimandua has never set foot on Mona, nor will she ever do so. She believes that her will and Briga's are one and that she needs no dreamers to interpret or to intervene. She teaches this to her people and has them treat her as a god."

Breaca had said quietly, "No-one rules for ever."

"No. And it is the wish of our elders that her child, if she has one, be brought up with an understanding of the difference between the gods' will and the urgings of the human heart. This I will do with all my strength while there is still breath in my body." And so she had seen the full extent of the task he had accepted on the jetty, had felt the weight of it dragging him down. It had seemed then, and did so still, unbelievable that the one who had been Warrior could be shackled so easily.

"If there is war," she had asked, "will you lead your people south against Amminios and his allies?"

"I believe the people of the north—my people—will listen to me, and, yes, if it is necessary, I will lead them in support of the Trinovantes. As to Cartimandua's people—" He had stopped. Soft feet had brushed the grass behind her. Venutios had pitched his voice beyond Breaca's shoulder. "Caradoc has seen her more recently than I. Caradoc, in the event of war between your brothers, will Cartimandua of the Brigantes lead her warriors south, do you think?"

There had been quiet. That Caradoc had spent a winter with the Brigantes was well known. No word had spread to Mona of his activities there. Breaca had turned and found him lying back on the grass at her side with his head cushioned on his hands. His eyes, empty of feeling, had reflected the sky. With uncharacteristic venom, he had said, "That one will do whatever suits her and that is not something any of us can predict." Sitting up, he had softened his voice, but not his eyes. "Cartimandua is one who believes respect is earned by an accident of birth. In consequence, she demands it unearned and does not give it, even to those of her people who act with greatest honour and courage on her behalf. She will act as impulse drives her and there is none can say how that will be, not even herself." His gaze had met Venutios's and what passed between them had been private. "I don't envy you your place."

The man who had been Warrior had smiled, thinly.

"No. Neither you, nor any man. I wouldn't wish it on another, but I will make of it what I can."

Venutios had not been part of the Brigantian delegation to the Sun Hound's funeral and what he made of Cartimandua remained open to conjecture. Breaca found very quickly that she shared Caradoc's opinion, and her pity for the one who had been her predecessor deepened over the days. Irritatingly, she had found herself more than once caught at table listening to descriptions of Caradoc's physical attainments. On the most recent occasion, she had been with Odras, who had waited quietly for a gap in the talk before asking, in a clear, carrying voice, how, after an entire winter spent in rampant coitus, the Brigantian ruler had managed to avoid conceiving a child. The laughter was loud and had lasted longer than perhaps it should have done and the topic of conversation had been abandoned, never to return in Odras's or Breaca's hearing.

It was in the lull after that, privately, that Odras told Breaca the last of the rumours, the one that had gained least circulation and that seemed, on the face of it, most likely to be true. Breaca left and sought out Airmid, who should have been able to tell her the truth of it but had not. In the absence of answers from the living, Breaca walked up to the grave mound to consult with the dead.

The burial chamber faced east, but Luain had constructed a second opening tunnelled out to the west, by which the mellow light of the setting sun might enter and warm the remains. Breaca arrived near dusk and found the place empty of the living, filled only with still air and the single square-edged beam of light that fell onto the funerary urn and the torn yellow cloak below it. The chamber within the grave mound was larger than she had imagined, and smelled of timber, not earth and stone. Newly planed oak lined the walls and ceiling, carved on all surfaces by the whorls and lines and strange dancing beasts of the ancestors. She rested her back against the mark of a running deer and untied her belt pouch, tipping the contents onto her palm.

The keepsakes of her life were here, such as could be carried: a ring in gold, a piece of carved amber that had been a gift from Airmid when they first crossed the straits to Mona, a fragment of leather cut in haste from the end of her father's belt before they had left him by the river, the dried foot from the first hare that Hail had killed for her after Bán had gone. She tipped them all back again, keeping only the ring. It lay cool on her palm. She stood for a while, feeling the imprint of it, then leaned forward and laid it on the centre of the yellow cloak in the last of the slanting evening light. The small, engraved image of the sun hound showed black in a sea of gold.

Footsteps whispered on the grass outside. A shadow fell in from the entrance. A voice she would have recognized in the midst of battle, or in the blindness of a closed grave, said, "Of all the gifts he ever gave, he would not have wished that one to be returned."

She lifted her head. The chamber became colder. The skin on her face stretched tighter across the bones. "Caradoc." She made herself turn to face him. "I hear you are sire to a child by Cwmfen, who leads the Ordovices. I had thought you followed only Maroc's urgings but it seems not. Your father will go happy into the lands of the dead with his dearest wish fulfilled."

"Not by me." He stepped further into the room. His voice was stilted and oddly formal. "Yes, I have a daughter, newly born. I stayed to see her first breath before I rode east; it is why I am late. We have named her Cygfa. Bán had a hound whelp of the same name and for the same reason. She will grow knowing why her mother and not her aunt leads the people of the war hammer. It will not make of her a vassal of the Trinovantes."

"And what will she know of her father?"

"As much as you knew of yours. More, I hope, than I knew of mine. Or, at least, what she knows will be different."

He moved to the far side of the bier to face her. In the resinous air of the chamber, he smelled of travel, of horse and harness and mud and clothes worn too long. He had taken the time to wash the dirt from his hands and face and to throw on a fresh cloak, creased from the saddlebag but clean and crisply unweathered. It was white, the colour of the Ordovices, and brooched with a war hammer in silver. His face was worn and lined from lack of sleep. It was a man's face, not a boy's dragged wet from the sea, but then that had long been the case. Still, she could not imagine him a father.

I have a daughter. Pain twisted inside her as it had not done at their parting on Mona's jetty when she had taken it as a passing fancy, and had said so, and, in pity, he had not told her differently. Lovers may come and go, but fatherhood does not. Caradoc was not one to sire a child by accident; to have done so spoke of a bond as great as any warrior's oath. She knew him well enough to know that, if nothing else.

We have named her Cygfa.

We.

Cartimandua, at least, would be silenced by that.

It was best that she leave. Nodding down at the bier, she said, "I will leave you alone with him."

"No." His hand stopped her. "Don't go. It was you I came to see. My father and I have said everything we were ever going to say."

He lifted the ring from the dead man's cloak. It lay on his palm, warm in the sunlight. The gold became something for them both to watch. "He would not want you to renounce him now," he said.

"I didn't intend to. He valued his alliances more highly than that. I would not stoop to do less." She spoke of the dead in words for the living and the living understood.

The grey eyes were wide, holding hers. "We are still oath-sworn."

"I know. Did you wish to renounce that?"

"Never. Did you?"

"No." She took the ring and slid it onto her finger, studying the carved image on its surface. She was the Warrior, a pupil of Mona. She did not believe he could know how she felt.

"How did you know I was here?" she asked.

"Airmid told me. I would not have disturbed you but Amminios has gathered those loyal to him and left the dun."

"What?" She raised her head, sharply. For a moment, she was only the Warrior. "He has rejected Togodubnos's offer?"

"It would seem so."

"Then he must be stopped. If he reaches the south-lands and takes the oaths of the warriors, there will be war. Unless . . ." Even given the day's news, she still believed she knew Caradoc better than most. By consent of the elders, he had command of five thousand spears of the Ordovices; he would have brought at least some of those and yet she had not heard the horns sounding greeting nor the chaos that the arrival of many horses would have caused. An appalling certainty beat into her mind. "Where are your warriors?" she asked.

He paused a moment, looking at his father's urn. The sun shining through the western port bisected his face, making it difficult to read. With a studied neutrality, he said, "They are already in the southlands. Those warriors who were previously sworn to my father have transferred their spear-oaths to me. It is the other reason I was late."

"Gods—" She gaped at him. "And Amminios? What do you think he will do now?"

"He will ride into the southlands believing them to be a safe haven and he will find it is not so. My warriors will take him and hold him alive until we reach them. If we ride now, we will not be far behind."

We. The casual assumption that Mona was at his disposal. Anger was too easy, too near the surface; it became important to leave. Caradoc stood in the way and caught her arm as she passed.

"Breaca, don't. It was necessary. The warriors of the southlands are Berikos's Atrebates, only lately sworn to my father. Their loyalty is anything but certain. You know this, you said it yourself. If Amminios had reached them ahead of us, we would have ridden into a battlefield with the ground not of our choosing."

"And instead, if you are wrong, we may ride into a war. Did Togodubnos know you were going to do this?"

"No."

"So he, too, does not play the Dance as well as the masters?" The control of Mona was gone. Anger scorched the air between them—a just and righteous fury, given cause by his actions in war, not in love. She said, "What if Amminios plays the game better than you? What if he does not ride into the waiting arms of your Ordovices? What if he sees them, or is warned and takes fright and seeks refuge with Berikos behind the borders of the Atrebates, or sails for Gaul and his Roman friends, what will you do then?"

He had ridden too far, too hard and was too tired to match her. Wearily he said, "It's nearly winter, the seas are too uncertain for him to sail for Gaul now. As to Berikos, I think my brother's pride will not let him seek help so early. He still believes he can win on his own."

"Does he? Do you believe that? Or will your pride not let you consider defeat?"

It was not a question that allowed an answer. He let go of her wrist, suddenly, and stood in silence as she walked past him into the clamour of the evening.

Airmid, who knew her best and held strong opinions on the matter of Caradoc, had saddled the grey battle mare and slung the serpent-spear shield from the cantle. The honour guard were already mounted awaiting word to leave, all except Ardacos, who rested on Mona, nursing a broken arm. She would have liked him here now, for the strength of his silence. The rest felt the heat of her anger and thought it was for Amminios. In good heart, they mounted and followed her towards the gate to join the queue of those waiting to retrieve their weapons. Hail ran at her side, eager to hunt. Of them all, he was the only one to look back at the grave mound.

———

Rain fell at a slanting angle, driven by the wind. The grey mare stood with her tail to the worst of the weather. Breaca sat tall in the saddle, held erect by anger. Without turning her head, she said, "So much for Amminios's pride. It does not outweigh the sight of five hundred spears and the white cloaks that wield them."

Caradoc was at her left. He too kept his eyes on the enemy. "It was a gamble. We lost. I still say it was a necessary risk."

"And is it part of that necessary risk that we now face the combined warriors of the Atrebates and their allies, the Dobunni, and that we are outnumbered eight or nine to one? You can fight them. I would not ask the spears of Mona to die for the sake of another man's pride. We are going home. Send word if you win. I am sure I will hear if you die."

Rage had sustained her for the two days' hard ride and the crossing of the sea-river at the end; it did so still. She sat the grey mare on a long, low slope looking down into an empty valley. Behind her waited the honour guard of Mona and seventy additional warriors plus the two hundred of the Trinovantes, supported by Caradoc's Ordovices. They were nearly a thousand in all, not an inconsiderable force, but they were as cockles in a cornfield compared to the thousands upon thousands who filled the slope opposite. Even those spears who had sworn to Caradoc were ranged against them; it had taken less than half a day for them to forswear and change sides. The Atrebates wore pale brown cloaks, the colour of sand; the Dobunni, on the left flank, wore green checked with grey, like lichen on rocks. At their heart, between the two, Breaca could see a single splash of gorse-flower yellow. Across the gulf that divided them, she could hear Amminios laugh.

The other two sons of the Sun Hound flanked her, one on either side. To her left she said, "You wanted a war. Are you glad now you have it?"

"We won't fight them now, it's too close to winter. This is for show. They know we can do nothing before spring." Caradoc rode a dun horse like the one Bán had given him. The white cloak spread across its haunches, sodden with the mud and sweat of the ride as much as the rain. He was as angry as she was and making no effort to hide it. Tight-lipped, he said, "I apologize. The fault was mine. Does that make you happy?"

From her right, Togodubnos, who had lost most and handled it best, said, "Stop. There is no fault. We tried and we lost. From the moment Amminios refused my offer of the single port and rode south, the rest was inevitable. He lost some men in taking back the southlands from Caradoc's Ordovices and now we have fewer to fight in spring. That is as good as it could be." Staring out at the spears ranged against them, he said, "Think; it could be worse. He could have journeyed straight to Rome and asked the new Caesar to give him the legions to take his land back."

"What makes you think he won't?" Breaca cleared her throat and spat. In the rain and the wind, facing an uncertain future, her rage began to wither. Without it, she was empty, hungry and cold, and none of these things mattered as much as the need to weave a solid alliance that would grow into a force that could fight and win. She sighed and, for the first time since the desperate race from the dun, the

Warrior balanced the woman. To whichever of her companions chose to listen, she said, "It's nearly winter. Not even Caligula is mad enough to send troops across the ocean now. We have a full winter to prepare. Our smiths can beat weapons and our warriors can train to use them as they have not done since the time of Caesar. Between us, we can raise an army that will cut down the Atrebates as a blade cuts corn. If the gods are with us, it will be enough to hold the weight of Rome."

CHAPTER 21

In Germany, on the banks of the Rhine, under the gaze of the Emperor Gaius Julius Caesar Germanicus, also known—although never in his hearing—as Caligula, the probationaries from Gaul put on their best display.

March. Watch the dress of the weapons. The spear's slipping. Keep your grip and don't let the tip waver. March.

A circular horn wailed at the rear of the ranks. The cohort paused for a heartbeat and then, to a man, wheeled left. Relief rippled down the lines. Only since midwinter had the probationaries begun to learn the horn notes along with the spoken commands, and only since the first day of February had they worked with the horn alone; to do it now, and perfectly, was little short of a miracle. Bán noted the relief as he noted everything else, dispassionately. A small part of him marched mechanically in time with the rest. The greater part, his soul, watched and judged and felt nothing.

It had taken some time in the early days after Iccius's death for Bán to understand the change that had taken place within him. In the beginning, he had thought the void in his soul was a body's natural response to shock and would pass with time. Slowly, on the journey east through Gaul, he had come to realize that he had lost also the foundations of his life that had held him together in the two years of slavery to Amminios—that Breaca no longer came to him, nor Macha, and that he missed them both. In their place, he grew accustomed to the sense of Iccius walking at his side, or rather, of himself walking with Iccius in the lands of the dead, both of them shades in a land of shadows, saying nothing, but sharing a quiet companionship.

It was not an unpleasant sensation and, having no fear of death, he had found himself insulated from the many fears that beset the Gauls who had joined up with him. He had acquitted himself well so far in the infantry training— he had, in fact, found parts of it challenging, even exhilarating, and had some hopes that he might attain the cavalry, although that was as much for Corvus's honour as his own. The prefect had almost completed the recruitment for his newly formed cavalry wing, the Ala V Gallorum, and had made it clear that he expected Bán to join his unit as soon as the probationary period was over. It was a hurdle to aim for and no harm in it and it did nothing to hinder Bán's resolve to find, in time, a means by which he could join his family and Iccius in the lands of the dead; his only constraint was that it must be done with honour.

The Crow was his greatest hope in this regard. The colt had not mellowed on the journey east towards the Rhine. Indeed, it still fought to kill anyone who tried to mount it and Bán spent every moment of his spare time in its company, playing out a complex dance where he provoked danger but must do his best to overcome it. So far he had succeeded and could now mount without fear of serious injury, but nothing was certain.

Keep pace. Maroboduus is stepping short on his left foot. Don't let him put you off your stride.

The horn brayed again. The mass of men paused briefly and Bán with them. They were nowhere close to the polish of the battle-hardened legions who moved reflexively at the first flutter of notes. Perulla, their centurion, raised a threatening arm and movement returned to the ranks of trainees. Bán wheeled right and found he had to skip a step to bring his rhythm in line with the rest.

Hell and damnation, he will have noticed that.

Don't look back.

He had looked back once during practise and found himself running the first five miles of the training route in full kit for days on the strength of it. Reparation for a missed step in the emperor's parade would be worse than that, without doubt. He marched on, his eyes fixed on the bobbing helmet of the man ahead and his attention on the silver and scarlet knot of Praetorian Guard standing to attention in the stands, and the man who sat in state amongst them.

He's asleep. Or he's dictating to the scribe. Why are we doing this if he's not paying attention? Look at us, damn you. Or don't. We don't need to be noticed. Just let us march and get it over and go back to where you came from. Tell them the Rhine armies are invincible, it is what they want to hear. Better than the truth, that the forest will never yield to Rome, nor should it. What would your Senate say if you told them that, Gaius Germanicus?

Gaius Julius Caesar Germanicus. Caligula. Two names for one man. Before Corvus's men had ever set foot in Upper

Germany, his actions had touched them. They had been travelling through Belgian Gaul when news had reached them that the emperor had ordered the execution of Germany's governor and that his replacement, Lucius Sulpicius Galba, was in place. Until then, Corvus had kept his men travelling slowly. Bán had found later that the prefect had known what was coming, that he had served under Galba in Aquitania and it was on the incoming governor's orders that he had begun raising the new cavalry wing. Corvus had been sent west to keep him clear of the trouble and had been ordered to keep his recruits out of the way until the carnage had ended.

Corvus had quickened the pace with the news that the new governor was in place, but still the group did not travel overfast. In the half-month it took for the new recruits to reach him, Galba had swept like grassfire through the legions of the Rhine, discharging the lame, the indolent and the old with a ferocity that had left the remainder bruised and cowed. Having broken them, the governor set to building them up again. Men who had thought service under the eagle a pleasant way to pass the time had learned their mistake. By the last days of autumn, when Corvus led his men and their long strings of new mounts into the cavalry stockade at Moguntiacum, the legions were buzzing. By late winter, they had built two new legionary forts and the ranks had been able to execute their manoeuvres with a precision not seen since the days of the republic.

In the first days of spring, a new legion had marched in and taken up residence in one half of the newly built quarters. The men of the Legio XXII Primigenia were Roman citizens and they believed themselves as far superior to the Gauls and Germans with whom they exercised as their emperor was to ordinary men. Within five days, they had revised that notion. Within ten, the evil of the river had touched them and the desertions had begun.

Every one of the incomers feared the river. It swept hissing past the camps, a sucker of souls, bearer of bloated carcasses and home to biting insects, and each dawn it spewed a clinging mist that spread out in flat planes that hid the defects in the ground so that the cavalry rode out daily in fear for their horses' legs. Only those born and raised on the banks of the Rhine found it tolerable. The Batavian auxiliaries could swim it in full armour with their horses beside them and not break ranks. They did it for bets, for training and displays for the senior officers, or simply for the thrill of immersing themselves in its embrace. They loved it for itself and for the one name that was woven inextricably in its history: Arminius, son of Sigimur, destroyer of the legions, the man whose soul, it was said, had taken strength from the river and returned it a hundredfold.

Here, too, the men were divided. The Romans and Gauls would make the sign to avert evil at the sound of Arminius's name and spit against the wind. The Germans were more discreet and saved their opinions for those whom they trusted most. Bán heard the details from Civilis, the big, broad Batavian with the freckled skin and the washed-gold hair who had clubbed him to unconsciousness at Corvus's command and been apologizing for it ever since. The Batavians were an emotional people and Civilis, like all his kin, was prone to expansive friendships. Since Durocortorum, he had taken to Bán as a son, or a younger brother lately come to manhood, and the tale of Arminius was one more piece of his heritage that must be learned. He told it sitting on one of the three bridges over the river, dangling his feet over the edge and tossing in pebbles for luck, one for each of the three legions destroyed. "The Seventeenth, Eighteenth and Nineteenth are gone with their cohorts and auxiliaries and all their camp followers. They will not be heard of again."

Bán had spent two months with the legions by then. They believed themselves invulnerable and he had seen no reason to suppose they lied. Politeness constrained him from saying so. "How were they defeated?" he had asked.

"It was Augustus's fault. He put Quinctilius Varus in charge of them and the man was a lawmaker, never a warrior. But they would have died anyway; Arminius had fought with them and seen their weakness. They had not learned that to march in lines with armour polished to dazzle the sun is not a good way to fight in a forest. And then, too, they trusted Arminius because he had once been an officer. It was impossible for them to imagine that any man could forsake Rome and return to the tribes."

Civilis grinned his contempt, showing white teeth in the moonlight. His own sword belt was polished to outshine the stars and he, too, was an officer in the legions, if only a decurion of an auxiliary cohort.

Bán said mildly, "We still fight in lines."

"Of course. The legions will never learn from that mistake. To do so would be to admit their weakness, and Rome can never be weak. But she will also never again seek to bring Greater Germany, that part east of the river, into her empire. Because of Arminius, the tribes of the forest live free of the yoke of Rome."

"The same Rome that you fight for."

Civilis shrugged. "The pay is good." He had leaned forward. "And I believe in the river. It is said amongst our people that it holds the spirit of Arminius. While the river flows, Rome and her allies may not pass."

In that, Bán believed him. He had watched as the evil sucked at the hearts of the Gauls who had accompanied him from Durocortorum. Men who thought themselves warriors or hoped to become so turned to whimpering children when made to stand watch in pairs overnight. Forage parties sent across the bridge to cut timber for the new camps came back silent and white-eyed, shying like horses at any sudden noise. An army camp is full of sudden noises. Those sharing their tents, and later, once built, their wooden huts, passed unpeaceful nights. Bán alone had been untouched, his soul safe with Iccius in the lands of the dead.

Then the Roman legionaries arrived and, by the end of the month, Bán had witnessed the first execution of a deserter caught and returned three times to his unit. His headless body had been cast into the river and the remainder of his cohort were made to stand watch as it floated downstream on the grey, malice-ridden water. The losses had slowed after that, but never fully stopped.

With spring the snows had cleared and it had become possible to travel, and the river had become a minor irritant, a thing to be scratched off along with the mosquitoes and head lice in the face of the greater, more tangible threat of the emperor. The news had come with the first day of February. *He is coming. He will be here in ten days' time to inspect the legions. He has banished his own two sisters and executed Marcus Aemilius Lepidus, who was his lover. He will kill any man who catches his eye. Death from Gaius comes slowly.*

The Romans of the new legion had known Gaius first-hand and were the most afraid. Their training had fallen apart as men panicked, and had come together again as the centurions flogged the sense back into them, or greater fear.

They had reached a peak of polish at the time it was required. Gaius had arrived in the early morning on a day of no cloud and the two legions of Moguntiacum had waited in perfect ranks with the winter sun sparking a million pin-prick fires from their armour. For the honour of their emperor they had spent a day in manoeuvres and Galba, the governor, had marched amongst them, taking personal charge. They had marched for twenty miles up the banks of the river and back again, dug a ditch, built a rampart, attacked and defended it, and not a single man had faltered in a display that lasted all the hours of daylight. The emperor had let it be known that he was impressed.

That had been the first day. The second was given over to the cavalry. It was not a day in which Rome could excel, save by proxy. Romans did not make good cavalrymen but they had the gold to buy the loyalty of those who did, and so squadrons of Gauls vied with Germans for superiority in the speed, precision and daring of their displays. The day rocked to the thunder of mounts pushed to the limit, and the cries of men in triumph.

Later, close to evening, the legions gathered to watch a parade of a different kind. The emperor had need of new warriors for his German horse guard and Moguntiacum had the honour to provide them. From amongst three thousand volunteers of the Ubii and the Batavi, five hundred had been handpicked by Galba. They were big men like Civilis, with the same sun-flushed skin. Mounted on matching chestnut horses, they had ridden out in their war dress, their red-gold hair knotted above the right ear, faces streaked with white clay and tunics hung with horse tails and the dried scalps of their dead.

Their display had been breath-stopping. In every respect, it had surpassed all that had gone before and, this once, Gaius had shown his approval in a way that could be seen by anyone who watched. He had ridden down the ranks congratulating the riders personally, adding, every now and then, an additional instruction so that, when the five hundred left the field, half of their number did so knowing that they would henceforth spend their lives bound to their emperor, closer than the Praetorian Guard. The legionaries and probationaries had watched and approved. Gaius might have a limited understanding of warfare, but he had a sharp sense of what it took to protect his own hide. It would be a brave man who took on the horse guard, and even so he would not reach the emperor alive.

Nearly finished. Don't look up. Corvus said not to attract his attention. "What he likes he wants and what he wants he takes. You are different. You stand out the way your killer colt stands out in a field of brown mares. If he sees you, he will want you and the colt both. Don't give him cause to look."

He hasn't looked yet.

The morning of the third day had been devoted entirely to the probationaries and they were nearly halfway through. Two horns sounded together, a semitone apart, calling the halt.

That's it. We're done.

They were not the horse guard. It was not given them to see their emperor face-to-face. An order was given through the tribune of the Praetorian Guard and Perulla, centurion to the probationaries, stepped forward to an unknown fate. The emperor had not yet ordered the execution of a centurion for the failings of his century but it was not unknown. The recruits waited in utter silence. They had a respect for their centurion, if not a great love. For four months he had bullied, cajoled and flogged them into order. None had liked him but they recognized an evenhandedness in the way he had behaved. He had not chosen favourites, or bullied the weak more than their comrades, and all had grown into a measure of respect. More than one realized now that it would have hurt to see him die.

The Praetorian tribune stepped down from the stands. Bán held his breath and, behind him, heard a god named in Gaulish. An order was given in Latin, too far away to hear, and it seemed that Perulla was not to die, or even to be dismissed, but that those of the recruits who hoped to win a place amongst the cavalry were required to fetch their mounts and conduct their display. Bán risked a downward glance. Greying river-mist sculled at his ankles, the river's bane come out in force. With a brief prayer to Iccius, he turned and ran to fetch the brown mare whose colour and bearing would attract no attention.

"How did it go?"
"Badly."

The mist had cleared. The parade ground had been so smooth a man might have pressed it with a flat iron, but neither of these facts made any difference to the quality of the display. Bán reached in under the brown mare's belly and brushed dried sweat from her girth. It was not her fault that she was mediocre, or that he had spent all of his spare time with the Crow, making the infinitesimal progression towards mounting and riding, when he could have been practising with her. The mare was safe and had nothing to recommend her beyond her colour, which had matched the others of the troupe and had lent them a temporary uniformity, at least until the cantered circles had started.

"Did Galba say anything?"

Rufus leaned against the post that marked the stall's edge. The Gaul had been made a decurion in Corvus's new cavalry wing, and one would have thought he had better things to do than lean against a lump of oak talking to a probationary who had yet to be placed in a unit. Corvus had charged him to keep an eye on his protégé, that was well known. It was not always appreciated.

"Galba said nothing." Bán stooped under the belly of the mare and began to work under her mane where the lathered sweat had dried in creamy waves. "The emperor called for his meal before he had a chance to step down from the stands."

"He'll do it later. You'll get your place in the cavalry yet. He's seen you in practise, and he knows who you are."

"He hasn't the slightest idea who I am. He never comes down here. Perulla will make the decisions, and whatever he might have thought before he's just seen enough to change his mind for ever."

The mare had changed legs unexpectedly just before the end of the charge and come raggedly to the halt half a pace ahead of the line. It was not the only mistake, but it was the most obvious and had made of Bán a spectacle that he never wished to repeat. Bán said, "If I spend the next twenty-five years marching in line with a hundred stinking Gauls, it will be my own fault. If you see Corvus, tell him that from me. And he can have the Crow. I wouldn't wish on him the life of an infantry packhorse."

"Corvus wouldn't take that mad bastard beast as a gift if you died and left him in your will. In any case, it's not over yet. Don't give up hope." Rufus patted the mare on the rump, raising dust. "Don't stay too long here. Get yourself to the parade ground and find something useful to do. Unless Civilis is lying through his ugly German teeth, there'll be something worth watching before the emperor finishes his lunch."

If Civilis had lied, more men than Rufus had heard him. Bán took a shovel and basket to gather horse dung from the parade ground and found three ahead of him doing the same, with more brushing the turf free of straw and others repairing a board in the stands where a nail may, or may not, have been loose. Gaius had retired to Galba's headquarters within the legionary camp of the XIVth half a mile upriver. If anything did happen, there was little chance of their seeing it, but still they worked on the parade ground and Perulla did not stop them.

The sun rose above the top edge of the forest as they worked. It was the best time of day; for a while, the river livened, became a rippling of molten silver that lit the trees along its banks so that what had been black became green and one could imagine the forest, if not a friend, then not so implacable an enemy.

The alarm was raised first by the Praetorian guards stationed outside the door to the governor's lodgings half a mile upstream. The German horse guard had been dismissed, which had offended many of those so recently instated, but they had retired to their quarters and stabled their horses to await a further command. The source of the commotion was not immediately apparent. Galba's residence was the best guarded in the whole of Upper Germany, and only one truly desperate to die would risk attacking it. Still, it seemed that someone had, and that men on horseback were riding out in defence of their emperor. It was a while before the probationaries, leaning on their shovels and brushes, saw anything but a knot of hard-ridden horses, with cloaks flying behind. Some thought that the horse guard were back but there was too much armour and it flashed too brightly and, as the group came closer, it could be seen that there was gold at the head of it—that the emperor led himself, on his flashy white war-horse, with every piece of harness metal bar the mouth-bit in gold and his cuirass embossed with images of Alexander. The man was no rider; he kept his balance by his hold on the horse's mouth and the bit was savage. Blood ran freely in the foaming saliva. Bán turned away and so was first to see the attackers.

"*Chatti!*"

He thought he screamed it but his voice had lost its power. In his place, the pied colt screamed for him—a shattering challenge that took all the fury the beast harboured and gave it voice. The horse was far back in the lines, but the sound of it reached them as if he were close and the noise alone made the rest of the probationaries turn towards the river. To a man, they paled. Everybody knew the Chatti—the tribe of men bred for war, descendants by reputation if not by blood of the renegade Arminius, who emerged from deep in the forest to harry the villages and settlements on the Roman side of the river. They knotted their hair as the horse guard did, but wore the scalps of their vanquished dead in knitted capes about their shoulders and hung rotting skulls from their belts. Bán saw thirty or more of them surge up out of the water with their horses, shake themselves like dogs and mount, swinging rust-dulled greatswords of a size that could part a man's skull as a hand knife parts an apple. He had opened his mouth again to shout the unnecessary, reflexive warning when they thrashed their horses to a gallop and the war howl began.

It had been different when the horse guard had raised the cry on parade—more ordered, less terrifying. Hearing it now, one could begin to understand why the Gauls said that their champion Vercingetorix had been defeated, not by the Roman legions, but by four hundred Germanic horsemen riding for Caesar. It was said they had hacked limbs from men for the joy of it, leaving them to die slowly on the field, and now, hearing their cry, Bán could believe it. The sound carried death in the heart of it, more certainly than the river. A man would have to be tired of life, or supremely self-confident, to ride against the Chatti.

The Emperor Gaius Germanicus, it seemed, was such a man. Riding hard at the head of his Praetorian Guard, he raised his voice in the cavalry paean, realized he could not be heard above the clamour, and wheeled his sword above his head instead. Light flared on iron polished to silver and an edge as fine as a man could make it. It was not a weapon that would last against the killing blades of the Chatti, but none could tell him that.

The men of the legions had seen the danger. The XIVth were fastest to respond but even the probationaries were dashing for their weapons. Bán hesitated, wanting to go to the Crow, but there were tales of what happened to men who deserted in the face of the enemy and he would not have it said he showed fear in the first attack. In any case, the Crow, of all horses, could look after itself.

He was halfway across the parade ground when the horn sounded from the riverside, a long, sighing note with another just after. He sprinted on, trying to remember whether the command to charge had that second shorter note beyond it or if what he had heard was, instead, the order to regroup on the standard. He was at the gates when it sounded again, louder, and the actions of the men around him told him all he needed to know. He clung to the gatepost, doubled up and panting and struggling for breath to speak.

"He's stopping us? We're not to go out to help?"

He asked it of the air and the gods because he had thought Galba neither a coward nor a traitor, but the command did not make sense. Perulla the centurion answered.

"That's the 'hold firm' they're sounding. If you want to hear it as the charge, you're welcome. Myself, I think we should hold firm exactly where we are."

The centurion was not a tall man—the Romans never were—but he was broad and he wore his parade ground armour as if born to it, the mail shirt long ago moulded to his shoulders and back, wearing thin beneath the arms and in the folds above the belt. He stood upright between the gateposts with his left hand on Bán's shoulder and his right arm thrust across the opening so that none of his charges, turned dull-witted by the war howl or the promise of action, might throw themselves out.

None of them did. They gathered in a ball behind him instead, crunched together, swaying. Bán was at the head, the unvoted spokesman. "What do we do?" he asked.

Perulla smiled, dryly. It was the first time Bán had seen him do so.

"You should go to that bloody horse of yours and see if you can shut it up before Gaius orders its throat cut. After that, I think perhaps we might get ourselves in a line and march over to hold firm by the governor's residence. If we get a move on, we'll be in place in time to hail our emperor's courageous victory when he returns from his battle."

It was Civilis.

Word spread quietly and with care amongst those who had stood along the length of the via principalis and burst their lungs shouting "Gaius *Germanicus!* Gaius *Germanicus!*" as their emperor rode past. It filtered down as a disbelieving snigger from the stone-built dormitories of the XIVth to the half-finished wooden huts of the probationaries, gathering credence as it went. Bán was in the remount lines, making the most of the quiet time to settle the Crow. He heard the whisper and chose not to believe it. Rufus arrived to lean on the stone manger at the head of the stall and put him right.

"Of course it was Civilis. Who else would it be? Not even the Chatti are howling mad enough to cross the river in broad daylight when every sentry's on knife-edge in case Gaius walks past and finds him asleep on the job. It's why they stood down the horse guard—half of them are Batavians. They'd have recognized their own kin and pulled away. The Praetorians have had their brains addled by the river; they'd fight their own sisters if the lasses turned up with red hair and swords in their hands. All they needed was the boy at the head cursing them for cowards and they waded in as if their lives depended on it."

"Did they kill him?"

"Civilis? Don't be daft. He led them a dance up the river, tripped a couple of their horses and dived back into the water with his men. Praetorians don't swim and the emperor wouldn't let them try. He had them decorate a few trees to mark the location of his victory the way Caesar did in the old days and rode back in triumph. You know the rest."

He did. Bán had been one of the many strung along the length of the main street bursting his lungs as the emperor rode past. The euphoria of it had caught him in spite of himself and he had found he wanted to believe that some kind of battle had happened and the enemy had been routed. The reality left him with a sour taste in his mouth.

He turned his attention back to the Crow. There was no knowing why the colt had become so angry but, with time and quiet and no people to harass it, the beast had calmed. Bán took a chance and lifted one hind foot that had seemed hot in the morning. A bruise showed on the sole near the point of the frog. He reached in his belt for a hoof knife and pared away a sliver of horn. Rufus chattered on, talking nonsense about the Chatti and the horse guard and Civilis, who was now, apparently, going to be made prefect of his own Batavian cohort on the strength of his "services to the emperor."

Bán spat onto the sole and rubbed the horn clean with his thumb. The bruise was an old one, nearly grown out, and the heat he had felt, if it had ever been real, had gone. He dropped the foot and eased himself upright, stretching the knots from his spine. The Crow fly-kicked and he dodged without thinking. It was part of the way they were together. He gathered the hoof knives and grooming brushes and, with Rufus, began to walk back up the horse lines towards the camp. He had grown over the winter, and was almost as tall as the Gaul. Walking beside him, he was pleased with the difference. If Rufus noticed, he said nothing and they crossed the empty parade ground in silence.

It was not yet evening. The sun slanted from the west, casting long shadows across the packed earth. Bán pushed open the gates to the compound and stood back to let the Gaul go in ahead of him, asking, as he did so, the question that had been burning in his mind since the imperial visit began. "Do you think we'll go to war? Perulla was saying he thought it would happen this summer; that if Galba could promise to secure the frontier against the Chatti, Gaius would build a fleet and sail for Brit—"

He stopped because Rufus had stopped, and Rufus had stopped because Perulla was waiting on the other side of the gate, with Civilis and a trio of the emperor's horse guard behind him. Bán tasted bile in the back of his throat.

Perulla stepped forward. He raised his right hand in a salute that made no sense.

"Bán son of Eburovic? Hostage of the Eceni?"

Bán felt the air leave him. Not since Cunobelin's dun had he been so addressed, and never in Latin. Rufus jabbed an elbow at his arm. He nodded. His voice was lost.

"Your presence is required by the emperor."

"Now?"

"Immediately."

The horse guard flanked him. He no longer felt himself tall.

Until that moment, he had believed Amminios's new bathhouse to be the epitome of Roman ostentation. Then he stepped through the doors of the governor's residence at Moguntiacum and his memories fell to dust. He walked too fast down wide, airy corridors, past unblemished marble and skin-smooth plaster, treading on sweeping, lyrical mosaics. Amminios had done his best to ape his adopted culture and fallen so very short. He had aspired to display his wealth and had, instead, displayed its absence. Here, in Galba's mansion, restraint was everything, fuelled by wealth beyond measure. It showed in every perfect line and arch, in the marble busts of the ancestors settled in their alcoves and the single springing athlete in bronze. Colour was used with subtle elegance; the floor mosaics mingled fluid blues and greys and aquamarines so that Bán walked on running water with Neptune at its heart. On the walls above, a single narrow-banded frieze ran at head height along the length of the corridor. Achilles slew Hector, Scipio vanquished Hannibal, Octavian destroyed Antonius. They passed one after the other in flashes, separated by the heads of the guards.

They came to a double door of yew, carved with the pegasus and boar locked together, symbols of the XIVth and XXth legions. The guards halted, not quite in step. The tribune of the Praetorian Guard saluted. Nobody spoke. Bán might have thought himself suddenly deaf but for the trickle of water from a fountain somewhere close by and the cackle of two cockerels fighting in the world beyond the walls.

The tribune knocked once. The door swung open. The room beyond was quite different from those through which they had passed. Restraint had been abandoned in favour of an opulence Amminios would have recognized. Silks in scarlet and gold adorned the walls. The fountain Bán had heard from outside sang in the far corner, playing water onto golden dolphins. A dais had been raised on the northern wall and the chair standing on it had lions carved into the armrests and an eagle above the back.

The emperor wore purple and the cuirass of gold with scenes of Alexander's victories in relief across it. Eight men of the Praetorian Guard, in scarlet and polished armour, stood in pairs on either side. Other men, not in armour, stood ready to take notes. One, with the look of a Greek, was permitted to sit. Behind them, Galba stood below the emperor's right hand and to his left, still and tense, stood Corvus.

They brought Bán to the foot of the dais, so that he would have to crane his neck upwards if he wished to see Gaius properly. No-one had ever schooled him in the manners of address to an emperor, or even whether it was permitted to look him in the eye. Bán gazed at the legs of the chair. They ended in carved leopard's feet, with the claws extended. He did not look up.

"This is the Briton? The hostage who would fight for Caesar, as the Gauls did for our honoured ancestor of that name?" The voice was deeper and less brittle than his reputation suggested, more the adult than the spoiled child.

Corvus answered him. "My lord, yes. He is of the Eceni, who hold land to the north of that held by the late Cunobelinos."

The emperor was familiar, it seemed, with the politics of Britannia. He raised a brow and nodded. "His name?"

"My lord, he has no Roman name as yet; it will be given only when he receives his posting. In his own land, he is called Bán, which means 'white' in the tongue of Hibernian, the island where he was conceived. His mother had a dream of a white-headed horse on the night of his birth and he was named for it."

Bán stared at the leopard's feet. In his head, he counted the toes over and again. In all of his life, he had heard his mother's birth-dream related only twice: once to himself in the summer after Hail was born and he had his own horse-dream, and then again by the first elder grandmother, shortly before she died. Only Macha could have told Corvus. Or perhaps Luain mac Calma, who knew too much and spoke too freely . . . *Hibernia, where he was conceived* . . . His mother had not told him that. He searched for Iccius to ask if it was true and failed to find him. A stranger's voice washed over him.

". . . Does he not hear? Or perhaps he does not understand? Tell me he speaks Latin. It is enough that we recruit barbarians into our forces. I will not have it if they do not speak a civilized language."

"My lord, he understands—"

"I speak Latin." Bán raised his head and looked into the stone-still face of Galba, governor of Upper Germany, whose eyes, famously, were of a blue to match the mosaic of his floors. Beside the governor, Gaius Julius Caesar Germanicus, Emperor of Rome and all its provinces, sighed through pinched nostrils and snapped his fingers, and Bán felt his head turn to the sound as a hound to its master's whistle so that, whether it was permitted or not, he stared up into the dense, clouded gaze of the emperor.

"White. Very good, for one so black." There was amusement there, and so much more. The eyes and the voice and the light, curving smile all spoke differently. Bán watched the eyes with their promise of death and let the voice sweep past. "They tell me you are a prince among your people. Is that true?"

He felt the fraction of Corvus's nod and said, "My lord, it is almost true. My sister was firstborn of the royal line." He could have said, *I once thought I would be warrior to her dreamer,* but it would have made no sense here. "We do not accord ourselves princes as Rome does. I would have been a warrior in my sister's war host, and perhaps if I had daughters and the other branches of the royal line were to wither, one of them would take her place."

"A warrior. Indeed." The eyes flayed his mind. Pain sat at the seat of them, as well as murder. Bán could feel the colours of it, and the pressure behind his own eyes. It was said this man had been a hero, much beloved of his people until an illness struck him down and he became a tyrant. One could imagine what such pain as this, if it were constant, might do to one already drunk on too much power.

His brows were gold, paler than his hair. They arched with practised precision, fair warning of a change in temper. He licked his lips, leaving them too red. With shock, Bán realized they were painted. The emperor asked, "Have you won honours in battle?"

"My lord, I have fought only one battle and I was taken . . . hostage at the height of it. Before that, I killed two men in fair combat and it was witnessed by my sister. Were she not dead, she would attest to it."

"And you would become a warrior for Rome?"

"My lord, yes. It is an honourable choice."

The emperor laughed. Half a heartbeat behind, Galba, Corvus and the attending clerks laughed with him. The Greek—if rumour was correct, he was a freedman of Tiberius's, passed on to his successor—leaned forward and whispered in the ear of his liege. The emperor nodded and flicked his hand. Whatever had been said was already decided, but the man was a favourite to be indulged in public, not dismissed. The cavernous eyes narrowed. They drew the life from those they touched, leechlike. Bán, who had thought himself already a husk, felt himself become feather-light under their gaze. The painted lips smiled, thinly.

"We, too, were held hostage, in this very country, by men of the First and Twentieth. In time, they will pay for their temerity, but it made of us a warrior. Thus we look favourably on your path of honour, for we know, as you do not, that service in the armies of Rome is the greatest honour available to any man, and that soon the opportunities to win praise in battle will be manifold. Already those who fight to preserve us have been rewarded. You may have heard of our skirmish yesterday . . ." He paused, giving Bán time to nod and those others around him to make gestures of awe and mild reproof at a famous victory reduced to a skirmish. Throughout the room, men who had risked their lives in real battles murmured their approval.

The emperor raised his hand for silence. "The men of our guard who travelled with us from Rome have thus shown their metal. Our horse guards, however, have not yet had the opportunity to do the same and their loss weighs heavily on us. We have decided to rectify that, and to give you that same chance."

He crooked a finger. The larger of the two horse guards stepped forward. He was a head taller than Bán, with upper arms that matched the width of the boy's thighs. His sword was twice the length of Bán's torso, the blade wider than any he had ever seen. The man himself stank of horse and sweat and hair-grease and when he grinned, as now, he showed the canines and one molar missing from the right.

The emperor nodded benignly. His gaze pierced, like a snake's. "We are already called Germanicus, after our honoured father. It would please us to add Britannicus to our name, and that province to the empire, thus completing the vision of the deified Julius, our most honoured ancestor. Our commander, Galba, believes that we must not remove our war-hardened legions from the Rhine until the hostile tribes of Greater Germany have been subdued, and this grieves us greatly, for without them we cannot hope to defeat the fiercer tribes across the ocean. Your presence, however, is fortune's gift, for now we can match those two countries and see which is the winner. Thus will we let the gods and your valour guide our action. If our horse guard wins, we will know that Galba has gauged the metal of the Germanic tribes correctly and we will accept his decision. If you win, we will consider that fortune has smiled on our endeavour in showing us that Britannia is the stronger. In that case, we will take our armies north to march against the ocean and the barbarian tribes beyond it."

It was spoken for the scribes, to be taken down for posterity and talked over in Rome. Bán fought to find the meaning beneath the words, then saw Galba and felt the waves of rolling anger that spilled from the man and realized there was no meaning beneath them; what he had heard was everything.

Galba said, "My lord would match a boy against a man? A probationary against an officer of the horse guard?"

He was a brave man. Others had died for questioning lesser decisions than this. Bán saw the possibility of it grow and recede. The clouded eyes closed a fraction, hiding the dragging lust. The emperor said only, "He has killed men in battle and that some years ago. He is old enough to kill again. Or to die with full battle honours at the hand of another. What better way is there to live but on the edge of victory? We envy them both. If our health and life were not pledged to the people of Rome, we would wish to take the field ourselves. It will be decided then—tomorrow, before noon."

Gaius glanced sideways and down at Corvus, who had not moved; who, perhaps, could not move. "You signed his recommendation, I believe?"

"I did, my lord."

"Then you will see to it that he is appropriately armed. We would not have it said that he was unable to do himself justice."

They were dismissed. Corvus walked ahead of Bán to the door. Galba spoke as it opened. "And you will find him a mount better than that cow-hocked brown mare if you wish him to live."

CHAPTER 22

"You can't do it. It's madness. He'll kill you."

"I don't think so. The Ubian will do that. But it will be done with honour."

Bán walked in a shell of euphoric detachment. The part of him that breathed, that had picked over the quail's eggs in saffron and the delicate, grilled river fish he had been served in Corvus's quarters, that had listened to the advice from Civilis, that had ignored, time and again, the offer of good and better horses from Rufus—that part had become a wraith, so loosely tied to the earth as to be invisible. It had occurred to him in the night, as he lay in Corvus's guest room, that perhaps Gaius, of all men, had known what it was to live without a soul and was doing him a favour. Or perhaps the emperor had sucked the last vestiges of life from him and was casting the husk to the Ubian wolf as his gift to a man upon whose valour his life depended. Either way, the result was the same. When he rose in the morning, with Iccius clear at his side, he felt himself floating on a flood-tide of battle fever, light-headed and superbly sensitive, so that his fingers tingled and his skin felt the press of his tunic as if he had gone his whole life naked and today was his first time in clothes. Around him the camp was already drifting away, bleached of colour and with sound that echoed from a world not his own.

Only Corvus had colour—in his eyes and the flush on his cheeks and the scarlet plumes on his parade helmet. He stood in the horse lines with his helmet under his arm, doing his best not to upset the colt, while still speaking against him. His brow creased with the effort of making himself clear without causing offence. "I know he's your horse and you care for him but he's not safe. You can barely saddle him without risking your neck. Four times out of five he throws you when you try to mount and the fifth time it is only because he is waiting until you ask him to walk. You can't do it. He'll kill you before you ever get to the Ubian."

Bán grinned. "And then what will the emperor do? A victory to the Gaulish horse? He'll have to return to the Senate and tell them that Caesar was wrong and all of Gaul is not subservient to Rome."

"Bán—"

"I know, I'm sorry. Spies are everywhere and the water butts have ears. But what else can he do that he has not done already? I am going to die, that is not in doubt. I would rather die in the company of the Crow than anyone else, that's all. Your bay mare is wonderful and I am grateful to you for the offer. I have no doubt she could outrun anything the Ubian may have in his stable but this is not a time to run, or to rely on fancy footwork. All I ask is that you kill the colt cleanly afterwards and don't let Gaius haul him back to Rome to grace his stables. He's damaged enough. He doesn't need that to make it worse."

"Then at least take the sword. Please."

The sword had been Corvus's first offer, before the bay mare, and it had tempted Bán more. It was the last blade Eburovic had ever made, given to Curaunios and passed to the Roman as they boarded the *Sun Horse* all that time ago. Corvus held it out now, balanced across his palms. The bull's-hide sheath held all the strength of the Eceni nation. The bronze she-bear on the pommel carried the core of his father's soul. Bán touched the hilt with genuine regret.

"I can't. I'm sorry. It was made for Curaunios; it's too big for me. I would not go out there looking like a child and disgrace good Eceni handiwork. Civilis has found me weapons and a shield made for a Batavian youth. They're my size and they look right for those who know no better."

Civilis had given him more than that. The leather corselet he wore, and the shirt of chain mail that settled over it, were both gifts from the Batavian. He stepped forward now, a big, shambling bear of a man, rendered suddenly uncoordinated by the weight of what was happening. His eyes were bloodshot from too much drink and the smell of it soured his breath but his voice was steady, as much as a Batavian's could be when immersed in grief.

"Bán, little brother, you must not go out believing you will die. The Ubian has weaknesses. He raises his arm too high in the backstroke and leaves the space beneath it exposed. If you use the spear first and hard, you can strike him as he lifts his arm and he will be dead before he can complete the blow."

Bán laid an arm on the man's shoulder. "Civilis, my friend, if I were fresh from the Eceni heartlands, maybe I could do that. But I have spent four months learning to be one shield in a cohort of hundreds, one gladius in a line of thousands. I could no more fight single combat after that than you could fight as part of an infantry cohort. It will be slaughter, and Gaius knows it. He is looking for a reason to give way to Galba with good grace and we will give it to him."

"Then why are you so bloody happy about it?"

"Because by noon today I will have joined Iccius and my family. Why should I not be happy?"

The pied colt threw him the first time he tried to mount. It was because Corvus was still there. When the prefect left, despairing, the colt steadied and let Bán lead it back to the mounting block without resistance. At the second attempt, it danced sideways, tossing its head, hating the chiming iron of Civilis's chain mail. Its eyes showed white at the rims. The red fire in their centres raged as brightly as it had ever done. Bán spoke in Eceni, which calmed him if not the colt. At the third attempt, he was allowed to ease himself into the saddle.

So little of him was present in the lands of the living. Iccius rode with him, mounted on the dun filly, which was good. They rode side by side, each as substantial as the other. The promise of death held them together.

Corvus waited for him with Rufus and Civilis and, surprisingly, Perulla, the centurion. Bán rode towards them, holding the Crow lightly. He was focused entirely on the horse, on the set of its ears, the rhythm of its walk, the tension in its shoulder that would give him due warning before the buck.

"Bán . . ." Corvus's eyes held more pain than Bán could

remember in any man. The prefect stroked his palm down the colt's neck. "You look good," he said. "Both of you."

"Thank you." It may have been true. The colt, at least outwardly, was perfect; its hide gleamed like oil-smoothed jet with lightning streaks across it and the white half of its face blazed like frost under moonlight. Inwardly, the beast burned, as it had done from the moment Bán had met it in the arena at Durocortorum.

He pushed the colt forward, already walking the road to oblivion. Perulla stopped him.

"Here." The centurion offered up a wafer of lead, rolled thin and folded to a square. "It's a curse," he said. "I have written his name on it three times. If you drop it, he will fall."

Perulla had always been the first to denigrate superstition amongst his Gaulish probationaries. He had the grace to look discomfited. Bán took the wafer and pressed it into his shield hand. It moulded itself to his palm and warmed there. He lodged the spear at his knee and saluted as he had been taught when taking leave of a senior officer. "Thank you," he said. "I will use it well."

They stood back after that and let him pass.

Drumbeats resonated from the far side of the river. Gaius had decreed that the combat be fought on that side—a Roman games on Germanic ground, proof that the Chatti had been defeated. A cohort of Batavians were in place, lining the marked arena.

Three bridges spanned the water and each was manned by legionaries. Downstream, the Ubian had already crossed the lowest of the three, passing through an honour guard of his brethren to reach it. At the upper bridge, a detachment of

Corvus's cavalry wing, the Ala V Gallorum, joined with Civilis's Batavian cohort to make a corridor of silent men for Bán. There was respect in the way they stood and he had not expected that. He set the pied colt to walk between the twin hedges of human flesh. The men were quiet for him, knowing his mount's reputation. They need not have been so. The Crow had changed as they rode towards the river, becoming more fluid, lengthening and softening his gait. For this he had been born, and to ride him was to ride a wolf, or a wildcat, stalking. Bán looked forward between the up-pricked ears, at the right one, which was all black, and the left, which was bisected with white. A breeze lifted the fine hairs at the crest of the mane. The clouds released the first drops of rain.

The Ubian waited at the end of the lower bridge and they rode together towards the battleground. The part-finished shell of a fort provided a backdrop to the arena, making it seem more truly Roman. A stage had been raised at the western side of the space and decked in imperial purple. The officers of the legions had been permitted to join the royal party. The men stayed behind on the Roman side of the river to watch.

The arena was marked with sawdust at its perimeter. Bán and the Ubian stood side by side, awaiting their emperor's arrival. The tribesman hummed his war-song, ignoring the boy. His shield was of bull's hide and he wore it slung from his shoulder. The great killing blade hung naked from his hand and his chain mail shivered in the faltering sun. His head was bare after the manner of his people and would be a good target if one could get close enough to make a strike.

Bán shifted the spear in his hand; he had no reason to believe he could win, but he did not intend to have it said that the Eceni did not know how to fight. Peripherally, he became aware of movement at the bridges, of Corvus crossing the upper bridge behind Galba, riding in a knot of prefects and tribunes, of the Praetorian Guard preparing to cross the central bridge on foot surrounding the mounted dazzle of gold and white that was the emperor. A horn sounded and the stamp of marching men rolled across the water.

The Romans were closer to the forest than they had ever been. Ranks of winter-bare larch rasped bark against bark in the growing wind—but there was no wind. Instead, the air carried the stench of ancient flesh, as of skulls worn for decoration. In the dense dark of the woodland, a single spear flashed. The hairs sprang erect on the back of Bán's neck. On a reflex, he spun the Crow, screaming, "*Chatti!*"

Hell ran at him from the forest. Warriors flowed from the trees as rats from burning stubble, tumbling, screaming, urging each other forward in a frenzy of bloodlust. This was the brutal reality on which Civilis had based his jest; their capes of tanned skins were not scalps, but whole parts of a human, stitched together; the heads hanging from their belts, bouncing from their thighs, were not the dry skulls of the ancestors, but freshly dead with the pulped and swollen flesh still hanging from them in strips; their war howl was like nothing Bán had ever heard from the throats of men and it was matched, with a desperate, primal joy, by the Crow. This much Civilis had achieved; the colt knew the enemy, and it wanted to kill.

Still screaming, Bán swung the colt and forced it back towards the emperor. Chaos ruled the river as five thousand men of the XIVth, all in parade dress, jostled into battle formation and pushed their way onto the bridge. It took five men abreast. A legion of five thousand would take half a morning to cross it. The XXIInd were already mustering at the lower bridge, but slowly and without the benefit of battle experience. In the centre, the officers and Praetorian Guard formed into battle formation before the emperor. They were pitifully few. If the Chatti had sent a battle plan, asking Rome to divide her forces, it could not have been done better.

Already the killing had started. Bán saw two Praetorians die, their heads split from crown to jawbone and the grey matter of their minds spilling out. A blade scythed the air by his head. He ducked, stabbing out with his spear, the craving for death overwhelmed by a battle instinct that came from the core of his being. The weapon scored and was tugged from his hand by the falling body. He drew his borrowed sword. Screaming, the colt rose up and killed without effort as one born to it. Bán slashed out with his blade and felt it bite and had already turned away before the man went down. He sought Corvus amongst the crowd and found him, easily. A miracle happened and the Crow went where it was told to go, coming alongside the bay mare.

Spears flew like arrows, darkening the sky. The emperor's horse went down, threshing. Corvus threw himself from the bay mare and offered it. Gaius mounted. The bay mare, too, went down, the emperor wailing like a child as one of the Praetorian guards pulled him clear of the heaving carcass.

Bán spun the Crow, letting him strike with his hind feet. Corvus held his shield high, sheltering his emperor from the rain of spears. Galba fought to reach them, cleaving skulls with his sword as if it were a hammer, his mouth opening and closing like a fish until he was close enough for the words to be made out, and the governor was saying what everyone had thought but had not dared voice. "Send him back. Send the emperor back. They will kill every horse from under him."

Corvus was bleeding from a spear-wound on the arm. He sheltered Gaius as if he were a lover. A Praetorian shouted above the tumult, "The bridge is blocked. He cannot pass."

"Then lift him up. Pass him over the top. Does he matter or not?" Bán found he was shouting in Eceni, the language of war. Men around him took no notice. He screamed it again, in Latin. "Send him back, across the top of the men, or he is lost." The colt killed, and Galba. A Chatti blade sang as it cut for the emperor's head. Bán took the blow on his own shield and felt the bones give in his hand. A Praetorian took the Chatti head. Others had heard the cry and acted on it. The emperor was a glitter of gold, passing over the heads of men who raised their shields to shelter him and died as they did so. Corvus had still not remounted. The bay mare was gone. Bán reached down and grabbed his arm.

"Get up."

He could think only in Eceni. Corvus shook him free. In the same tongue he said, "Your horse won't take it."

"You're dead if you stay on foot." He spun the colt. The horse guard were over the river and it was hard to tell them from the Chatti. He nearly killed one and stopped in time and saw the same man run through by an enemy spear with a violence that ripped him from the saddle. Bán stabbed and hacked and grabbed at the reins of the newly riderless horse. "Get up, man." In Gaulish this time. The colt paced sideways to give Corvus space. Bán saw the run and the warrior's mount, neatly done, and heard a bellow that was his name and turned into the raised blade of a tribesman who was not a horse guard and the world became black.

He woke to pain, and the scents of sandalwood, citrus and cedar, with an undertow of festering flesh. In time, lying with his eyes shut, he came to realize that the putrid flesh was his own, and the pain in his left shoulder and hand. With more time and some searching, it was clear that he was not a ghost and Iccius had left him. He opened his eyes.

The world was white, with sunlight in one corner. A frieze of Roman gods, of women with hair piled in high cones and clean-limbed youths, defined the junctions between walls and ceiling. A brazier burned in a corner, wisping smoke. The heat wrapped him like a blanket but did not make him hot, which was a relief. He had been, if he thought about it, very hot.

He lay on a low bed under a white linen sheet. A wide-rimmed pitcher stood to the side, half full of water. Experimentally, he rolled over and reached for it with his good arm.

"I don't think so. That might be a little optimistic yet." A man spoke accented Latin to a mind clouded with Eceni. Feet scuffed the floor and a lean, bearded face gazed down from a great height. A charm in the shape of a staff bound with snakes swung before Bán's eyes.

"Theophilus of Athens. Doctor to Gaius Germanicus. At your service." The man's phrases were neatly clipped, like his beard. His voice was throaty, as if recently cured of a cough. He smiled, showing eyeteeth crooked inward. Bán stared at him, unable to speak.

"You took a sword-cut to the shoulder. The bone is broken and the wound is not good. These men"—he grimaced—"they do not keep their weapons clean." Bán remembered the giant who had tried to kill him—the knotted hair, the shoulder-cloak of human skin with hair woven across it, the trophy head with its foetid flesh. He imagined such a man taking time before battle to rub sand along the length of his weapon. He grinned, and stopped because it hurt him to do so.

"Yes. Also a crack to the jaw. I would recommend silence for the immediate future. And the left hand—no, don't move it—the left hand would be pulp had you not held within it a lead tablet which— Be calm, will you?" The eyes held a humour that undermined the sharpness of the command. The strange, hoarse voice said, "The man to whom it applied died in the first moments of the battle and you had not dropped the tablet, therefore the blame for his death does not rest with you. Nevertheless, I believe it would be better if our emperor were not to find out that you rode onto the battlefield armed with a curse and therefore I have thrown the thing into the river. The gods of the Ubian may do with it what they will. You, in the meantime, will lie still when you are told to and you will stop trying to move that hand if you want to retain its use in later life. You have a crack along the small bones, which will heal if you give it time. There are many of your comrades who would wish to be as lucky." Long fingers closed on Bán's wrist and forced him back onto the bed. The dry voice continued above him, numbering the wounded and the dead. "One hundred and fifteen of the Chatti dead for the loss of eighty-seven men of the Fourteenth and Twenty-second, forty of the Praetorian Guard and thirty-three of the emperor's new horse guard. Not a single horse guard wounded. These men fight to the death or not at all. Of the wounded, twenty Praetorians, fifteen boys of the Twenty-second, barely out of swaddling . . ."

Bán's mind came back to him in pieces, throwing disconnected images of battle, of Corvus, of Galba, of Gaius Germanicus whimpering as horse after horse died beneath him. He had not offered the Crow, would not have done so if asked; that fact would have been noted. He wanted to ask if he had a future and did not know how. Better, in any case, to ask if death came swiftly in that future, or with pain spread out before it. The legionaries from Rome had been all too ready to detail the deaths visited upon those who incurred the displeasure of their emperor. They did not say what happened to an Eceni ex-slave who denied the emperor a horse. As the doctor examined the wound and re-dressed it, inflicting a thousand small, bearable pains, Bán's imagination filled the gap and made clear the greater one that was the loss of Iccius. The euphoria of the morning had gone and left only emptiness in its place. He should have died; he had crossed the bridge expecting to die and when the Chatti had come he had thrown the chance away, responding instead to the imperatives of battle. The doctor moved from his shoulder to work on his hand and pain enfolded him, pressing down. Bán sank into it, praying to Iccius to take him.

Darkness came and went. Light became purple with yellow swirled through it. He saw horses with wings and others with human torsos. Voices passed him, shunting words along like cattle in a market. He watched them go and made sense of it after.

"He has a fever from the flesh wound. Beneath it, the collarbone is broken in two places and if the centre part between the breaks festers it will never heal. I have given him poppy to hold him still while I treat the infection. The emperor may wish him dead, but not of his wounds."

"Does the emperor wish him dead?"

"The day I know what the emperor desires before he tells me is the day I will have joined the gods."

He did not know whose the second voice was. He thought maybe Corvus, but his ears had slurred the language until all Romans sounded the same.

Later, he dreamed of the Crow. Of men catching the colt, and herding it into a corral, of others trying to remove a gore-splattered harness and saddle. He felt a presence near him that smelled of blood and horse-sweat and tried to reach out, to say that young Sigimur, one of the Batavian lads, too young to sign up but ready to help, was the only one who could get near the beast without dying. He opened his mouth and moths flew out with wings of brown silk and bodies as broad as his thumb. He watched them circle. On the wings of one was written Sigimur's name. It surprised him, because he could not read Batavian.

"Wake up. Will you wake up, lad?"

A cool hand lay on his good shoulder. He tried to open his eyes. A godly hand pressed down on them, sealing them shut. He tried to summon the moths again, because they had helped him, but they would not come.

"My lord, I'm sorry. I don't think—"

"Let me see him. He will know the presence of his emperor."

He knew the voice, if nothing else. Miraculously, the god released his eyes. Those gazing down on him sucked at his soul. Fear prevented him from retreating back to the dark. He felt his bowels loosen and saw the nose above him wrinkle in distaste.

"My lord, he is not yet fully recovered—"

"Clearly, Theophilus. You may leave us."

The emperor was attended by his horse guard. The stench of them had been muted by frequent use of the baths but there remained a taint of lanolin and poorly tanned leather. Gaius gestured and two stepped forward with the carved, eagle-backed chair. The emperor sat at the bedside, angled so that his head was in sunlight. Bán tried to push himself up in the bed and was forestalled.

"No. Don't rise. We are aware of your afflictions." The grey eyes drank deep. "You are afraid. That is good, but not necessary. I have not come to inflict more pain."

Had he been born among the Eceni, Gaius might have been a dreamer, such was his prescience. The man was smiling at him, which was worse than the stare. A clammy hand touched his forehead. He held himself rigid and did not flinch.

The strange, arid voice said, "The physician is competent else I would have disposed of him years ago. He nursed us through our illness but he believes he alone is capable of healing. We know that Alexander, our ancestor-in-spirit, spent as many hours in the hospital tent as he did on the field and his men recovered the better for it. It is for this reason they followed him to the ends of the earth and won him an empire. You will recover better for our presence." The hand withdrew. It did not seem likely that healing would result.

The grey eyes were eating his mind again. Gaius said, "Would you follow us to the ends of the earth, act as our interpreter in the lands of the barbarians and serve as a shining example to all that the barbarians can be civilized?"

Bán wanted to say, "Only under compulsion," but his voice betrayed him. He opened his mouth but could make no sound. He shut it again, feeling foolish. The emperor nodded as if a thought had been confirmed.

"No. Not yet, we can see that. Be still. We do not punish men for honesty, only for lying to save their skins. A craven life is not worth living, but you have shown yourself far from craven. In our defence, you were prepared to sacrifice everything—your honour, your life, your horse—"

The Crow? The image smashed his mind. Without the Crow, he would truly be dead.

The hand descended on his shoulder, pushing him back. He was not aware that he had risen.

"Be still when you are told to. You were prepared to sacrifice your horse. You did not succeed. He is alive and is being tended by the boy who knows him. You spoke the child's name in your delirium. . . . Good, you can smile. We did not think it impossible."

His vision blurred at the edges. Fog invaded his mind. The gods sealed his eyes.

The voice said, "It was on my orders that the physician did not give you the news of your horse. I wished to bring word myself. With your aid the Chatti were defeated and you will find us munificent in our thanks. We have had medallions struck for those who fought in our defence. Yours will be presented when you can stand to receive it—at which time you will also be confirmed in your posting as an auxiliary in the Ala Quinta Gallorum, a position which— Lie still. We understand your gratitude and will ensure that you have the opportunity to repay us fully when you are fit to do so. There is one more gift, greater than any posting." The acid voice sharpened. It may have been that the emperor smiled. "We believe that your people can be brought within the boundaries of civilization and that you are the first of many. To mark this, we would make of you a Roman citizen. You will leave behind you the name which means 'white' and all that it represents and you will be known henceforth as Julius Valerius, the first name for your emperor, the second for your sponsor. It is an honourable name and you will bear it with pride."

The chair on which the emperor had been seated was pushed back, the leopard feet scraping the floor. A cloak in purple fanned the air above his head. From an impossible distance, Gaius said, "Galba was wrong. The lands of the barbarians will fall to him who has the courage to take them. We are that man. We would have your assistance as interpreter and guide in the lands of Britannia. We would have you come willingly, however, not under compulsion.

"We have a duty to inspect the other garrisons along the Rhine. It will take ten days. At the end of that time, you will be fit to travel. You will come with us to the far northern coast of Gaul. There you will see that which may encourage you to join in our venture."

CHAPTER 23

The sea wind lifted Bán's hair, spreading it behind him. The salt spray soaked it. The trireme bucked beneath his feet, breaking the spines of the oncoming waves. Behind him, three banks of oarsmen sang as they rowed with a high pipe wailing above. The sail, which would have powered them more smoothly than the oars, if more slowly, remained furled. A loose corner snapped in the wind.

Bán clung to the forward rail and watched the tilting line of the horizon and the seagulls drifting sideways over the bow-foam. The whipcrack of canvas tugged at his mind, rekindling memories that were best forgotten. He was alone, at least. That much was good. They had wanted him to stay belowdecks with the emperor and his guard, but the rolling motion had caught at his gut as soon as they left the shelter of the port and he had been excused to take the air on deck.

The ship made good headway. Gesoriacum faded back into the fog that had shrouded it since they arrived. Gesoriacum: refuge for fishermen and traders who braved the encircling Ocean to reach the barbarian lands beyond, or were about to do so; resting place for merchants with cavalcades of mules and armed guards and amphorae of wine and olives and fish sauce and pottery packed in straw, for traders of men or horses and those who would buy from them; and now, with all the pomp and terror and lip-wetting avarice it brought, site of the emperor's northernmost visitation.

News of Gaius's imminent arrival, accompanied by the XIVth and IInd legions, with attendant cavalry and auxiliary cohorts, had wrought its customary panic. Given little warning, the citizens of Gesoriacum had not had time to build a palace, or even a new bath. The artisans and architects had devoted their limited time and boundless energies to creating living quarters fit for a god on earth, and then, more problematically, to the new quay and the lighthouse that the god required to be built, the one for his trireme, the other to light the ship back to harbour should the inevitable coastal fog hamper her safe return. They had achieved the quay but the lighthouse was still under construction when Gaius arrived. Two men took ship and fled across the Ocean to the barbarian lands beyond rather than be held accountable for this failure.

A prefect of the navy was summoned immediately and his sailors completed the construction. Under their ministrations, the tower gave light on the second evening after Gaius's arrival. The emperor's ship *Euridyke*, one of the fastest in the Roman navy, sailed out of port two days later. The emperor, one understood, had business that could not be kept waiting.

Bán held on to the bow rail and did not think about the emperor's business. It was enough simply to ride the ship and not fall. He had fallen more than once on the journey westward from the Rhine until, in the end, Theophilus had ordered him down from the brown mare and into a litter. For five days he had been fed peas and dried figs and made to drink infusions of centaury until he had tipped the last beaker of it away and said that henbane would be better for the fever and he could find it himself—and had gone out at dawn in strange country, found it and been proved right. Theophilus had regarded him differently after that. He began to ask questions that were not exclusively clinical and to provide answers that went deeper than "your wound is healing too slowly."

In honesty, his wound was not healing at all. They changed the dressings twice a day and each time the old ones came away soaked in a stinking yellow-green matter that sputtered on the fire and turned the air bad. The pain ground at him, wearing him down. It is one thing not to care for life but another to be held within it, unable to think clearly past a nagging, knifing ache. They were two days short of Gesoriacum, with the inland gulls already following their wagon train and the salt-sweet scent of seaweed and beached shellfish tainting the air, when Bán took the doctor's three-legged stool and the iron probe and set both by Theophilus's fire and said, "The bone fragment between the two breaks is going bad. You'll have to take it out or I'll be taking space in your sickbed for ever."

The physician had peered at him through the lingering smoke of his evening meal. "So you have decided that you are not the walking dead after all? You have come to claim life?"

"No. I have simply come to claim freedom from your infirmary."

"So?" Theophilus's eyes were grey, red-rimmed with smoke. "It's a start, at least. When you wish fully to claim life, you must let me know; it's something I would not wish to miss." He stood, stiffly, favouring his left knee. "Get me some water and a boiling pan. And call your friends. This will take more than the two of us."

The pain of the surgery was greater than anything he had ever known, including Braxus's brand. Civilis had been there to help hold him, and Rufus; one on either arm. Corvus had come at the end and held his head so he didn't knock Theophilus's arm while he was trying to remove the piece of bone. In the beginning, they gave him wood to bite on but he broke it and so they put a wad of leather between his teeth instead and showed him the marks on it afterwards. Theophilus had stitched the wound with linen thread, leaving a wad of boiled cotton inside. When he took that out, on the first day in the new quarters, it was blood that soaked it, not infection.

He had healed more quickly after that, although his legs were still weak. On the day before the ocean voyage, they had let him visit the Crow and the colt had not kicked him. He had inspected the sword-cuts on its shoulder and washed them with rosemary water and the beast had done little more than lay back its ears.

Later that evening he had been summoned before the emperor, who had bestowed the medallion and the citizenship and the place in Corvus's cavalry wing as he had promised and had explained what was required in return, the last element of which was entirely unexpected but should probably not have been so. Fever and fear of the coming day had kept Bán from sleep all that night. In the morning, he had prayed to Iccius and then his mother for a means to escape what was asked of him but neither had come. Standing now under the lash of the sea and the wind, exhaustion dragged at him more than the pain or the nausea. He ached for a return to the river. He had been immune to fear then, or had believed himself so.

"You don't have to do this."

Corvus had come up behind him, the sound of his footsteps lost in the oarsmen's chant. The prefect braced his arms on the bow rail and narrowed his eyes against the wind. A greening bruise discoloured his jaw where a Chatti blade had struck his helmet flaps; his left arm bore another where the shield had been smashed back by the force of a blow. To balance them, his hair was newly trimmed and he wore the medallion of valour that had been the personal gift of the emperor following his actions in the attack. Bán wore its twin, hung on a thong from his neck and hidden, temporarily, beneath his tunic.

Corvus turned sideways to the rail, appraising. Since the battle, he had never been far away, nor left it long between visits. More than Theophilus, he knew the black pit into which Bán had fallen. Unlike the doctor, he chose to ignore it and deal instead with the necessities of life and the small hooks of challenge and friendship that would lead Bán back into living. Bán had not engaged with any enthusiasm but it had been impossible fully to resist. Then he had been given new orders by the emperor and the upsurge of fear had destroyed in moments the patient work of half a month. He could hide it from Theophilus, but not from Corvus. Nor, particularly, did he want to.

The grey eyes narrowed. "Look at you. You have a fever,

anyone can see it. You should have stayed ashore, and failing that you should be belowdecks in the care of the physician."

"You think so?" Bán wisped a grin. "I had peas and lentils for dinner last night—Theophilus's remedy for the convalescent. It would be colourful were I to spew it on the walls, but I'm not certain it would make me more popular. Anyway, can you imagine what it would do to the crew? You know what it's like when you're living on a diet of fish and one man chucks it back—all the rest catch the smell and their stomachs rebel in sympathy. The emperor would have me flayed alive for turning his prize battleship into a two-man rowing boat with its own vomitorium."

"You know what I mean." Corvus was not in the mood to be diverted. He frowned into the horizon. "You could have told him you weren't fit. You still could."

"You tell him for me. I'll come and weep at your crucifixion." Bán spat. The wind caught it and smeared his face. He wiped himself dry with his sleeve. "Forget it. It's not as bad as you think. The Bán who was enslaved is not the Bán who woke in your tent in Durocortorum, and that one is different again from the one who has been dragged back to life by Theophilus. Besides, you forget. I am not Bán. From last night, I am Julius Valerius." He tried to smile, but the wind had numbed his cheeks and it was enough to move his lips to speak. He shook his head and turned back to the rail. "Go back down below. You have a speech to make. You should be practising it."

Corvus said nothing. His eyes roamed empty space beyond the bow where grey sea and grey sky merged on the grey horizon. The gulls were a sound without shape. Bán tapped the Roman's shoulder and pointed over the shield-side rail. "You're looking the wrong way. It's over there. We are making our own wind. The other ship is under sail and must travel at the behest of the gods."

The merchantman they sought was close enough to show her markings. She tacked sharply and wallowed in the apex of the turn. Her single square sail flapped and bellied in the wind, filling to show the image of the war eagle freshly painted across it. As she came about, the yellow eye and the painted beak showed on her prow.

Three more turns brought her within hailing distance of the trireme. The prefect who had completed the lighthouse had the *Euridyke*'s command. His grandfather had been a Phoenician slave in Augustus's navy at Actium. His father had been granted Roman citizenship on completion of his service to the navy of Tiberius. It was the grandson's intention that he live long enough in the favour of the newest emperor to sire the sons who might follow in the family fortunes. He stood amidships, watching the approaching sail, and issued orders with a calm that quelled the fomenting panic on his ship.

Commands were shouted between one ship and the next and the merchantman changed her angle to the wind and slowed. Men moved on her deck, hauling in the sail. A single man stood at the bow, where he had been all along. His shield boss caught the flat light from the sea and made it gold. His yellow cloak buffeted the changing wind. Straw-red hair, one shade darker than the Batavians', flagged out above it. Behind Bán, on the *Euridyke*'s upper deck, the tone of the oarsmen's pipe changed and was echoed on the decks below. At a single high blast, the shield-side rowers lifted their sweeps from the water. Eighty-five oars rode high, dripping foam onto the sea, then plunged in again at a harder angle. On the sword side, the great beams swept wide. At the stern, the steersman threw his full weight on the oar. Bán felt the deck swoop beneath his feet as the ship leaned into the turn. His stomach followed. He reached out and gripped Corvus's arm.

"Go down and put on your good cloak. Tell His Excellency that the Chieftain of all Britannia awaits his pleasure."

"Are you coming?"

"I'll be in the right place when he wants me."

The Chieftain of all Britannia. Amminios, son of Cunobelin, brother to Togodubnos and Caradoc, recent owner of two slaves and a pied colt, stood in the prow of his merchantman, watching as the *Euridyke* came alongside. Under the Phoenician's direction, the oarsmen shipped their oars on the shield side and the two ships came together, gunwales kissing as lightly as men could make them.

The captain of the merchantman stood by with a rope. One of the *Euridyke*'s men, a Hibernian who spoke Gaulish with a flat, southern dialect, shouted at him to stand clear but either the man's accent was too thick or the master was too overwhelmed by his first sight of the emperor to take notice. He stood in the same spot, gaping, and only a lifetime of rapid reflexes caused him to step smartly sideways as the plank dropped from the trireme fell forward onto his ship. Even so, the edge of it caught him on the shoulder and the bronze spike on the end that smashed into his deck nearly cost him a foot.

He was a big man, as were all ship's masters, and there was no doubt that he had a comprehensive command of seafaring vernacular. He had taken breath to air it when he remembered in whose company he stood. He stopped, suddenly, his mouth flapping. His gaze skipped from the wreck of his deck to the person of His Imperial Majesty, cloaked in scarlet and wearing, ludicrously, a cuirass of solid gold.

The emperor smiled. He glanced sideways at his escort. "The captain takes issue with our first corvus. We believe his sponsor will take more issue with the next."

The men of the escort laughed, as men will laugh who have been ordered to wear full armour aboard ship in mid-ocean and who have heard the man who gave that command make a jest. Corvus, who was wearing his own newly silvered cuirass beneath his cloak, smiled tightly. Bán had decided long ago that he was not going to laugh at jokes he did not understand. He kept his eyes on the master of the merchant ship and said nothing.

The emperor had a way of reading men. He gestured expansively to Corvus. "Our new citizen does not understand the source of our levity. You should explain to him."

"My lord, of course. Forgive me." The prefect turned with a care he never showed on land. In formal Gaulish, he said, "The boarding plank is known as a corvus for the spike at the end, which impales enemy ships as a raven's beak impales carrion flesh. It was used as far back as the first Punic Wars and recently to great effect by the deified Augustus as a means by which legionaries from one ship could march across and give battle on another."

Bán nodded, to show he had listened and understood. He said nothing. His whole attention was fixed on the bow of the other ship.

The emperor was in a buoyant mood. "It is an outmoded

means of naval warfare, as our naval prefect will inform you if you give him time. Still, we believe that in this instance it serves to anchor our ship securely to the enemy's, and it will embolden those who feel themselves at risk on the high seas, allowing them to cross from one ship to the other in safety."

Gaius looked around him. His escort stared fixedly ahead. No order had been given to cross to the other ship and they would not march a step without one. It was Amminios who made the move. One could imagine that he had always been good at sea; from early childhood he must have made the crossing regularly between his father's court and his mother's holdings in Gaul. He sprang down from the foredeck of his ship and leaped lightly onto the bridging plank. By accident or design, a space had grown between the ships before the corvus fixed them, leaving a spear's length of dead water that sucked and gurgled beneath. Amminios wore no armour, but his sword alone would have dragged him under were he to fall.

"Your Excellency . . ." On a swaying plank above the Ocean, he made the obeisance. "My messengers will have brought word of my coming. I would have come to you sooner but the shipping lanes have been closed for winter and this is the earliest I could find a man prepared to travel. I have paid twice the worth of this boat to persuade him to leave the safety of the white cliffs, and even so he complains it is too dangerous. Seeing the ease with which you have travelled out to meet us, and"—his eyes comprehensively surveyed the gilded armour and the polish of the escort behind—"observing Your Excellency's supreme command of the Ocean has shamed him into behaviour that is not becoming a ship's master. Allow me to apologize on his behalf.

I would not have something so trivial spoil the joining of our endeavours."

His Latin was excellent. Bán could have told them that had he been asked, but Gaius had not been interested in Amminios's linguistic skills. His only question, in an evening of orders, had been to ask if the Chief of the Britons could swim. Bán's reply that it was possible, but not certain, was the sole reason the *Euridyke* had not made use of her bronze prow-ram to sink the merchantman on first meeting.

. . . joining of our endeavours . . . Gaius stared in thoughtful silence. He was a man brought up in the world of flattery and deceit, where every sentence held layers of meaning. Had he not been able to see to the heart of things, he would have died in childhood with his brothers. He raised a brow and nodded to Corvus, who raised his arm in command. The escort party stepped forward to the edge of the deck, marching as if on dry land. On the side decks, a party of eight Scythian archers nocked their arrows, raised their bows and waited for the order to draw.

Corvus took the final step up onto the planking and saluted as one Roman officer to another. In perfect Trinovantian, he said, "Amminios, son of Cunobelin, leader of the war eagles and Chieftain of all Britannia, in the name of Gaius Julius Caesar Germanicus, Emperor of Rome and all her provinces, I accept the unconditional surrender of your lands, your ship, your warriors and your person. You will lay down your sword and deliver yourself to the authority of Rome." He repeated it, redundantly, in Latin.

The sea sucked and hissed between the boats. A single gull mewed, higher and more plaintive than the oarsmen's pipe. Amminios said nothing. His eyes held those of the emperor for longer than any man still living and when they drifted sideways, as if by chance, it was to fix on the newly made auxiliary behind him, a man not in armour but bearing a medallion of valour in gold on his chest.

"*Bán?*" The silence lasted a heartbeat longer. Then the Chieftain of all Britannia, to the surprise of those who did not know him, threw back his head and laughed. The echo of it warned off the gulls and made the archers tense at their bowstrings. The escort, their commander and the emperor waited him out. At the end, sobering, he made the warrior's salute. In perfect, unaccented Latin, he said, "Bán of the Eceni. How the dead get around."

Bán was kneeling at the edge of the latrines, vomiting, when Theophilus found him. He had long passed the point where his stomach had anything to give, but the retching continued and he was too far gone to notice who came to help him, or to care. Long fingers wrapped his shoulders and sat him upright, wiping the bile from his nose and chin. A goblet was pressed into his hands and retrieved and refilled when he dropped it.

"Here, I'll hold it for you. Now drink . . . good. Yes, take it. Drink as much as you can. You have a fever. I said it yesterday. You should not have gone on the ship. Come inside now—"

"No, not inside. I need fresh air."

It was already dark. The spring equinox had not yet passed and night drew in more quickly here in the north than it had done at the river. The coastal mist rose to make low cloud, so that the sunsets were short and startlingly vivid but the moon and the stars were invisible. In the legionary camps on the outskirts of the town, the lighthouse made a mockery of the dark. A fire roared furnace-hot at the top of it, showering sparks at the night, casting an unwavering light across the town and the emperor's residence. Out in the camps the light was softer, and kinder to the elderly. Theophilus lost ten years in its glow; one could see that he had been striking in his youth. His eyes searched Bán's.

"You were part of the procession," he said. "I was busy with some men of the Second who had food poisoning so I did not watch. Did it go well?"

"It went well for Gaius. The town magistrates were not about to be caught sleeping a second time. And Amminios still hopes for his support later. He played his part well."

In truth, Gesoriacum, given an extra day's warning, had shown that she knew exactly how to welcome a glorious general home from his victory over the Ocean and the barbarian hordes. Had the deified Julius himself ridden into town with Vercingetorix bound in chains in his chariot, they could not have made a better spectacle. It was not an official victory parade—that was Rome's prerogative—but the citizens who lined the street leading up from the quay waved boughs of laurel, or such alternatives as could be found in the second week of March, and a chariot had been unearthed and gilded and white horses found who could lead it without jibbing at the noise so that the god on earth might ride ahead of his army with his captive, bare-headed and stripped of his weapons, walking behind.

Bán had not expected Amminios to carry it off with such dignity. He himself had marched in his place in the escort and had received the accolade of the crowd and had hated himself for it afterwards. His sickness came in part from that. He had been on his way to find a blanket in his tent when the urgent need to empty his stomach had overwhelmed him. He crouched now, shivering, and remembered.

"Theophilus, this is not a fever. There is not an infusion or a salve that will heal it. When I am gone from here, or he is, I will be as I was before. In the meantime, I will keep out of his way."

"Out of Gaius's way, or Amminios's?"

"Both. They are men of a kind. They recognized that when they met on the ship. Neither of them is safe to the rest of us."

"Did he know you?"

"Amminios? Of course."

"But he did not betray you?"

"What is there to betray? Gaius knows all there is to know about me. I am his living proof that the barbarians can be civilized; that what is needed by the lands beyond the Ocean is the civilizing hand of Rome and, in time, her people will become model Roman citizens. Had he known how Roman Amminios was, he would not have needed me as proof. It was there already."

The beaker he held contained only water. Steadying one hand with the other, he swilled his mouth and spat. The taste of bile lingered behind his teeth. He stood and did not sway. "I am going to bed. I'll see you in the morning."

"You could sleep indoors. I have an empty bed in the infirmary and a brazier lit."

"I don't think so. You forget, I'm in the cavalry now. I share a tent with seven Gauls. So far, I am their mascot, their good-luck charm who will bring them the emperor's favour. It will not take too many unearned privileges for that to change. Besides"—Bán smiled and was surprised to find it real—"I am still a barbarian at heart. I prefer a night spent out of doors, sleeping in the company of others, to one in a room on my own. The day that changes, you can account me fully Roman. Or Greek."

"Never that." The old man stood. The caduceus hanging at his chest took life from the glow of the lighthouse. The snakes writhed up the staff, sleek as eels. "Take care. You are right in your assessment. Each of these men is dangerous, but only Amminios is abroad tonight."

"*What?*" Bán's chest closed, denying him air. "He's not in the magistrate's mansion? Where is he, then?"

"I don't know, except that he is not inside. They had him eat as a guest at the banquet—Alexander feasted those of his foes who surrendered voluntarily, and so Gaius must do the same—but he was given leave to go out afterwards."

"Where, Theophilus? Where has he gone?"

"I don't know. He has given his word to remain within the boundaries of the two camps and I believe he will keep it. As you said, if he wants Gaius's help next summer when the Rhine has been tamed, he won't run for cover now. But equally, he won't harm you, not when you are so clearly in the emperor's favour."

"No. He won't have to. It's not how he works."

"The colt?" Theophilus was always quick to understand; it was what made him pleasant company. "Corvus is inside. He cannot be reached but Civilis and Rufus will be close by. Should I find them?"

"No. This is for me alone."

The shaking had stopped, and the nausea—both luxuries too far. Bán smiled, differently, with the warmth of the lighthouse full on his face, and saw the change reflected in the physician's eyes. He had forgotten what it was truly to hate, and to have the freedom to act on it. He took care to put warmth into his voice for Theophilus's sake. "Thank you, but this is not their business, nor yours. Go back to the infirmary now and be seen by those whose word will count if they are required to testify. Whatever happens tonight, you are not a part of it. You have been good to me. I am grateful."

"Are you?" The man turned and the shadow gave back his years. Only his eyes were the same, a lifetime's wisdom tempered by sorrow. "Then take care of yourself. I would not lose a patient to the flaying knives just because he took a wrong turning. Remember, whatever else he may be, Gaius is a good judge of men. He tests those around him, seeking their weak points. Don't show him yours."

"He knows them already: Amminios and the colt."

"Then do not act as he would expect you to. Be sure he will have planned for it."

Iccius returned to Bán as he passed the last of the tents. The child ran ahead to the bridge, skipping and turning cartwheels and laughing freely as he had begun to do in the few days between leaving Amminios and being taken captive again. The river that bordered the camp was substantial but it was not the Rhine; it did not suck souls, nor make a barrier between civilization and barbarity. This river, in as much as it made a boundary, divided the tents from the horse lines. By an accident of the gods, the glow of the lighthouse reached to its edge and no further. Bán crossed the bridge into darkness. The river flowed beneath him, dreamily, its noise just enough to cover the sound of his feet. He felt light as thistledown, and hollow. He had to pinch the back of his hand to make sure he had not already passed into the world of the spirit. Then he looked up and any certainty left him. Eburovic was waiting at the bridge end, the first time he had appeared to Bán since the battle in which he had died. He carried his war spear and the she-bear shield and his smile was enough to stop the world. He took his place at Bán's spear side, the place of the elder warrior. Iccius stepped up at his left. A new shield hung from the child's shoulder, bearing the shape of the colt etched out in black on a white bull's-hide covering. Bán felt his breath hiss between his teeth and by that alone knew he was still alive. It was clear to him now why he had lived this long, and he was grateful beyond expression that the gods had granted so much. Stooping, he picked a stone from a pile by the bridgehead. It was not a warrior's weapon, but it was enough. He stepped forward and felt the shades of his kin step with him. "Let's go," he said.

The horses stood in rows in wicker-backed stalls with half-roofs covering their heads and good hay in squared wooden troughs to pick at through the night. As in the legionary camp the men were divided, so the cavalry horses were kept apart from those of the cohorts and these were separate again from the baggage train. Two legions had come together outside Gesoriacum: the XIVth, which had marched with Gaius, and the IInd, which had joined them from Argentorate. The two had held competing manoeuvres along the coast in the days before their arrival at the port, demonstrating their readiness for battle. To these were added four cavalry wings, eight cohorts of mixed infantry and cavalry, the emperor's horse guard, two cohorts of the

Praetorian Guard, the entire vast array of the emperor's travelling household and a delegation from Judaea, which had caught up with the emperor at Nemetacum and had, perforce, joined the train. In excess of thirteen thousand men had travelled from the Rhine to the coast and each night the order of encampment had been the same. By force of habit if nothing else, Bán could find the colt in any weather or at any time of night.

He felt his way forward, breathing in the warm, bakery smells of bran mash and barley, hay and horse dung, that hung over every camp. He reached his own row and stood at the end furthest away from the colt, listening. The horses fed, or dozed in peace, hips tilted and hind feet resting. He did not believe there was a stranger amongst them.

The colt was picketed, always, in the endmost stall. They had found early on the ride east from Durocortorum that he kicked the men tending horses on either side and was safest when placed against the wicker end wall. Since leaving the Rhine, Bán's brown mare had been tethered each night at his right, with a space between for safety

Bán was within sight of the mare when the Crow began to move. The white on its face showed in the almost-light of distant campfires as it tossed its head and took a half-step backwards. At the second step, it tugged at the halter rope and snored, a deep, guttural sound that inevitably presaged violence. A man swore softly in Trinovantian. Bán spoke in the same tongue. "Theft of a cavalry horse is a capital offence. Have they not told you that?"

The colt jerked its head as if the halter had been pulled. Amminios said, "It is no offence for a man to claim his own property. The colt is mine, a gift from the emperor."

"You lie. If the emperor believed any other man could mount that horse and live, it would be in his stable. He has seen it fight. He will not give it away."

"Not even for the promise of a kingdom? You do him greater justice than he deserves." The colt struck at the voice. A half-white forefoot flashed in the dark. Amminios sidestepped with the ease of long practise.

"You haven't mellowed him, I see. The question we always asked was whether he was born like this, or made like it during the trip to Noviodunum. Only foals sired by him would have given the answer. We had plans to put him to twenty different mares in his first season. If the first crop had turned bad, we would have poleaxed him before the second."

He had let go of the halter. His voice was moving. The colt knew where. Bán followed the lie of the part-white ear. "He was kind as a foal," he said.

"They say Gaius Germanicus was quiet as a child. Look at him now. Men of Corvus's calibre quake at his glance."

"Corvus doesn't—"

"No, of course not. A man who has lived through one shipwreck will always choose to wear full body armour aboard ship. Don't be ridiculous; Gaius is a monster and everyone knows it."

"You're still alive." He sounded like a child, pleading. He stopped.

"I am useful. He will parade me through Rome and the Senate will vote him a games in honour of his victory and set his statue in the temple of Mars Ultor. Next year, if Galba believes he can spare him the legions, I will be his excuse to invade Britannia, and when the legions have won I will be his client king in the lands of the Trinovantes and the Catuvellauni. I can wait."

"I saw you in a vision once as Mandubracios, the traitor. If I had known how true it was, I would have killed you."

"And brought on yourself the dreamer's death? No, you wouldn't." The voice flowed from beyond the brown mare. Bán edged away from it, towards the colt. The scents of the baths drifted past him: of rosemary oil and lavender, of steam and smoke and Iccius's death. But Iccius was beside him, vividly. His father balanced his spear in his hand, his dead gaze fixed on one place. Amminios said, "Did you know that in Trinovantian legend, Mandubracios was a hero who fought to the death with his comrades? It was Andurovic of the Eceni who betrayed the tribes to Caesar. It is why we never trusted you."

He was close, perhaps in the stall beyond the mare. Bán moved past the colt. He spoke towards the wall, making his voice echo. "You're lying. The Eceni have always hated Rome. All of the tribes know it."

"Of course. Which is why Bán of the Eceni has accepted a place in Caesar's cavalry. I hear you are newly posted to the Ala Quinta Gallorum. Favourite of the prefect and his emperor, granted full citizenship by the god on earth in person." They had been speaking the tongue of the tribes. He changed to Latin, mocking. "Julius Valerius. Does Gaius know you hate Rome and everything it stands for?"

"He'll find out."

"Only if you live long enough. I am tempted to leave you alive. Gaius will take far longer killing you than I have time to do."

"But when it's over I will be free. You will be hunted through the lands of the dead by those you killed by treachery."

"If I believed that, my poor barbarian savage, do you suppose I would have— Oh, no, not yet, my beauty . . ." He had circled back, behind. The colt had kicked out, at the shape as much as the sound of the voice. Amminios slipped past him. His voice spun on, softly malevolent. "Ah, he's a fighter. It will be good to have him back."

"You couldn't take him. He would never work for you."

"Of course he will. Who do you think broke him to ride in the first place? It wasn't your Dacian friend. He could never get near him."

"Liar. Fox was ten times the horseman you are."

"Maybe, but I broke the colt. See, he knows me . . ."

Amminios was at the head, fingers tugging at the halter rope. Hemp whispered past the tie post. The Crow stood rigid, with his feet braced wide, snoring a warning. Bán counted a handful of heartbeats, his eyes wide in the dark for movement he could feel but not see. As the rope came loose, he snapped forward, slapping his hand against the dark hide. The colt jerked back, found his halter rope loose and spun sideways, snaking his head. Bared, murderous teeth showed dimly white. Amminios ducked, laughing. "Bán, Bán—you are so very predictable. But then, so am I."

Bán rolled sideways, into the space between the horses. Iron hissed in leather. A knife called light from the dark. Iccius shouted a warning that had no sound and swung his shield, wielding the edge like a club. Eburovic stabbed with his spear, blocking the escape. The Crow, freed of all restraint, struck with its forefeet as it had done against the

Chatti, striving to kill with a raw, unhampered passion. It screamed its rage, covering the truncated noise of human death. The smell of blood rose and fled down the line, stirring the other horses and, soon, the watch. Voices and running torches gathered on the far side of the bridge. A single shadowed figure squeezed out between the horses at the far end of the line and ran for cover amongst the thousands of other mounts wakened by the sudden presence of death amongst them.

CHAPTER 24

He was lying awake in the tent when they came for him:
eight men and a centurion of the IInd Augusta, all of them
strangers. The men of his tent would have fought for him
until they heard the charge; then they stood back, pale in the
morning, and let the others take him. Bán walked in the centre of the eight, matching pace effortlessly with the men on
either side. He was awake. More than that, he was fully alive.
A fierce joy flared in his chest. Beneath the mist and the blis-
tering flare of the lighthouse, the morning was sublime. The
camp woke around him, busily organized. Bán smelled the
smoke of a thousand campfires and baking bread and the
latrines and thought them equally perfect. He imagined his
death and the pain that would come before it and did not
care. Iccius and his father had departed from him, but he
lived with the certainty that he would join them by nightfall
or perhaps the next dawn. Nothing else mattered.

The emperor was not prepared to deal with judicial
matters at daybreak. The guards beat their prisoner carefully,
leaving no bruises on his face or hands, and locked him in a

storeroom in the magistrate's residence until the summons came. Bán lay back with his head on a bale of undyed linen and his feet cushioned on cards of raw wool and watched a pregnant female rat make a nest in the centre of a neighbouring bale and did not disturb her. He remembered the gods of his childhood and gave thanks to Nemain of the waters and to Briga, goddess of death. He did not ask their favour. In granting Amminios's death and the manner of it, they had given more than he could ever request; his world was perfect, and nothing could diminish it. When they came for him again, he was singing the death-song of his people.

He was by now used to the realities of an imperial audience room: the fresh limewash on the walls, the excess of gold, the ravishing silks that could be packed and unpacked at need. Only the people standing to attention near the dais had the capacity to surprise him. He had not expected Theophilus to be at the hearing, or Corvus. Temporarily, their presence took the shine from the morning; it was no part of his plan that others should suffer because he must. The physician frowned as the prisoner entered; already he regretted the loss of a promising pupil who lacked the sense to heed good advice. Corvus was standing rigidly to attention, his eyes locked on nowhere, with dark rings in the olive skin beneath. Bán knew himself to be radiant and felt a moment's guilt; then the emperor entered and it was impossible to look elsewhere.

Gaius walked at ease, making the Praetorians ahead and behind slow their pace. He wore the toga, the first time Bán had seen him do so, and carried a scroll. The great, carved eagle chair awaited his presence. He passed it and stood in front of the prisoner. He was always taller than one remembered him; not the height of the Batavians, but taller than most Romans. As once before, Bán saw the extraordinary pain locked in his eyes. They fixed on him now, drawing the joy from the morning.

"A good night?" asked the emperor, softly.

"My lord, yes." He did not intend to lie.

"Good. Hold to it. The memory will sustain you through the rest of your life." Ever the master of ambiguity. Smiling, Gaius ascended the throne.

Men of the IInd Augusta had found the body and one of their junior tribunes read the charge: that during the first watch of the night, the accused, Julius Valerius Corvus, did loose his horse, a pied colt known for its unstable temperament, and did set it to kill one Amminios, son of Cunobelinos, against whom he was known to hold a grudge, this man being under the protection and care of his most noble majesty the Emperor Gaius Julius Caesar Germanicus.

The charge was known to those present. Theophilus closed his eyes. The caduceus rose and fell on his chest, raggedly. The rest stared straight ahead and offered no views. The emperor leaned forward, his elbow on his knee, his hand balancing his chin. His smile carried a hunger that Bán had not seen before. For the first time he understood the full magnitude of the promised pain. Terror thrilled through him, jangling his nerves. He felt the life drain from his heart.

The emperor sat back, slowly. He made a tent of his fingers and tapped them to his lips. Time became a space between them. At the end of it, he said, "Did you loose the colt?"

"My lord, I did not."

"Will you swear in the name of Jupiter, best and greatest, and on the genius of your emperor, as the most sacred of all things you hold dear, that you did not loose the colt?"

"I will." He did so. It would make no difference later. The emperor glanced sideways at Corvus. The prefect could have been cast in marble, so little had he moved. The emperor's index finger tapped at his thin, unpainted lips. Around him, men awaited the relevant questions and the inevitable verdict. Only the sentence remained in doubt.

Gaius kept them waiting. His smile was indulgent. He nodded more clearly at Corvus.

"The prefect tells me that love between men is a disgrace amongst your people. Is that so?"

"My lord?" Bán could feel himself frown. It was not a proper expression to bring before one's emperor. He fought for the earlier calm. Gaius gave him no time to find it.

"I have seen you together. At the river fighting the Chatti, on board the *Euridyke,* here and there about the camp. Seeing how you fought for his life, I had thought it had happened long since, but I am told last night was the first time. I am also told that you would die before you admitted to it, which would be unfortunate, and a denial of that which is beautiful."

"*My lord?*" Bán felt the world tilt beneath his feet. For a moment he stood on the edge of a precipice, denying the evidence of his ears. Then understanding flooded him, bringing its own destruction. A door crashed shut that had been open and in its place he felt the weight of a new obligation, a life held in balance by his own. He could deny what they palpably believed to be true and they would not believe him, simply label him a child; or he could provide them with evidence of the truth—that he had killed Amminios—and Corvus's life would be forfeit with his own. On the periphery of his vision, Iccius shrugged and departed.

"Corvus—" He rounded on the prefect. A single muscle jumped in the man's cheek. Grey eyes fixed their space on the wall and would not leave it. Of all men, the prefect understood the depth of his betrayal.

Bán forced his gaze back to the gilded chair. The emperor was smiling as Amminios had smiled on winning the first hard-fought game of Warrior's Dance. He said, "We have men skilled in the asking of questions. I do not believe you would die before admitting it, but you would not be fit to repeat your experience, or to fight for your emperor afterwards, and we still have need of you. And"—the cavernous gaze circled the room; none escaped it—"there are other ways to arrive at the truth than pain. His words might deny the reality, but his body cannot."

The emperor's eyes fixed, at last, on the tribune of the IInd. "Titus Pompeius, we commend your prompt action, but we do not believe the charge as brought bears up to scrutiny. There are factors of which you are not aware, not least of which is that the dead man had requested the pied colt as a gift and had been denied it. It is clear to us that he attempted to take what he desired and that the horse, knowing its duty to its emperor, would not be taken. It is a lesson to us all, that we should trust the integrity of the beast, which knows only its true master. Is that not so?"

It may have been a rhetorical question but it was not safe to assume so. The tribune nodded. "My lord, it is."

"Good. The guilt lies with the dead man and he has paid his price. Your legionaries, however, allowed a thief to enter the horse lines and lay hands upon our property and therefore stand guilty of dereliction of duty. The punishment should be exemplary and swift and should encompass the full chain of command up to and including the centurion. Do I make myself clear?"

"My lord, you do." The tribune had been expecting other things. Ashen, he saluted and was dismissed.

Bán had not moved. He opened his mouth. The emperor smiled and he shut it. Fear churned in him, threatening the hold of his bowels. The emperor glanced down at the scroll in his hand.

"One year from now, our commander on the Rhine believes he will be able to spare us the legions we require to complete the business begun by our honoured predecessor, Gaius Julius Caesar. We will have need of you then, for you are our most reliable guide amongst your people. Today, however, is yours and you should celebrate. I envy you. Love such as this—the truest love that neither betrays nor is betrayed—comes only once in a lifetime. There is no shame in it. Do not feel it base. Equally, do not feel it to excess, for we would not lose you to sleepless nights, either." He grinned, lewdly. From behind the throne, the Greek freedman laughed.

Bán nodded. He was beyond speech. The laughter crawled across his skin. Looking round, he saw it echoed in the eyes of those less favoured, who must, perforce, remain silent in the presence of their emperor. He had heard the same, in the same tone, of the women and boys who sold themselves to the legions and heard in it now the ruin of his pride. If he could have died simply by wishing it, he would have done so.

Gaius's eyes flayed the raw pulp of his soul. His emperor, who owned his life, said acidly, "Julius Valerius, you have not been betrayed."

"No, my lord."

"You may go. Prefect"—he turned to Corvus—"take him home and take care of him. He has been misused by the guards. If you have need of my physician, call him. That is an order. You are dismissed."

"Corvus—"

"Don't say it."

"But—"

"Don't." Dry lips pressed on his head. A warm voice, full of love and longing, said, "My dear, I'm sorry. We agreed not to speak of it but what else could I do?" They stood in Corvus's lodgings, in a room that had once aped the opulence of the emperor's audience room, but from which the glitter had been summarily removed. It was clean and spare and smelled of harness leather and lamp oil and polishing sand. The servant hovering in the doorway had been airily dismissed, leaving them alone.

Bán stood rigidly where he had been led. Warm arms embraced him. A hand caressed his hair. His flesh crept from the touch. The man he would have trusted with his life—and the certainty of his death—laughed warmly and said, "Julius Valerius, I would not lose you to the flaying knives for the sake of barbarian proprieties. As you heard from the emperor's own lips, this is no cause for shame in Rome."

Corvus ruffled his hair once more. The teasing smile lingered on his lips. Above it, lit by the morning sun, his eyes snarled. In the hidden space between them his free hand sketched the Eceni sign to ward against evil, or the telling of lies. Bán felt the floor sink away from him a second time. He swayed and was caught and held. With genial clarity, in a voice that could pitch across a battlefield, or keep close between the two of them, but was set to carry to the walls, Corvus said, "My dear, my dear, we are private here, as we were last night. We don't have to keep our distance."

"No. I'm sorry." It was the best he could do. His world was fading at the edges, as if the sunlight bled the colour from it. He swayed again and was helped to sit. He looked afresh round the room. Two arches were screened with hangings. Either one could have led to another room, or an alcove; there was space behind each for a scribe and his parchment. He brought his gaze back to Corvus and made himself smile. "Thank you," he said. "I would not have asked it of you. But I am truly grateful."

"Good." The relief he saw was real. "Did the guards do you much damage?"

"I don't know." He had not given it thought; it had been nothing compared to what lay ahead, to what may still lie ahead for both of them if he could not learn to act his part in time.

He had never been required to lie before. With a grimace any watcher could have read, he flexed his arms experimentally and said, "I think they may have opened up the wound on my shoulder."

"Have they? Bastards. After all the care we took not to damage it. In that case we will go and see Theophilus before we go to the baths. Everyone knows now. There is no need to hide away and you will feel better after a soaking and the ministrations of a masseur. After that, I think we had best go and see to that mad bastard horse of yours. They have him corralled but he's wilder than ever. I'm told even Sigimur can't get near him." A hand took his good arm at the elbow and raised him into another careful embrace. The lips that brushed his hair chattered nonsense in Latin, and in amongst it, more dryly in Eceni, "And you will need to act better than this, my friend, or we will both hang."

A three-flamed lamp flickered from the small alcove above the bed. Beside it, a gilded statue of Horus, a palm's length high, stared at the night with ebony eyes. A copper horse, smaller and with the green patina of age, reared and pawed the night. Bán had not been in Corvus's sleeping quarters often, but enough to know that these three things, the lamp, the falcon-god and the fighting horse, travelled with him everywhere, as constant as his armour; he had never expected to wake beside them. He lay still, feeling the spring of the bed and the unaccustomed luxury of linen. His shoulder burned, but only if he gave it thought. A tight-lipped Theophilus had dressed it for him. Bán had tried to speak and had had his mouth shut for him by a forefinger levered beneath his chin. The physician had smiled at the muffled indignation that had followed. "Call it raw, unbridled jealousy," he had said, "but I don't want to know the details. You can tell me all about it when we are both free of the army—if we are alive to talk of such things." He had stopped at the sight of Bán's face, and then, with a soft, surprising anger, had said, "What is it upsets you most? The laughter of Greeks or the fact that you are still in possession of your skin?"

It had been both, and he would admit to neither.

Theophilus had glared at him. "If you live in the army, you will have to get used to being the subject of gossip and laughter. Your pride will suffer daily else. And as to the other— you should not crave a death such as Gaius offers until you have seen it happen. If you want it so badly, I will give you an infusion that will take three days to kill you and you may relish every moment of your dance with pain; but not in public, in front of those who care for you."

Bán had said, bitterly, "And would the emperor let you live after that, do you think? Or Corvus?"

"Do you care?"

It had not been a question he could answer, nor was it yet. A draught from the doorway caught the lamp, sending tripartite shadows scurrying across the ceiling. He looked up. Corvus stood by the bed. His shape had changed, and the way he stood. The masks of the day had slid from him, leaving only the strain of their weight. He drew a long breath through tight lips. "You can relax," he said. "It's over."

"What is?"

"The charade. That was Civilis. He had urgent news that couldn't wait until morning. He brought his trail-hound with him. It's not of Hail's quality, but it is good enough to tell us if the listeners had been replaced."

"Was there more than one?"

"Yes. That was the news, or part of it. One of the emperor's freedmen left the house next door at the change of watch. Rufus has checked outside. There was one by the window but he left at the same time. The roof is flat and has no room for a man to hide, and there is nowhere else. We are alone now, genuinely so." Corvus stood awkwardly by the bed. Three flames flickered in each of his eyes, making them impossible to read. "I don't think you should leave yet, but you can go at dawn and you need not come back. Gaius departs for Rome at noon tomorrow. I doubt he has spies set to report to him on something so trivial as the relationship between the prefect of a cavalry wing and his master of horse."

"His what?"

"Master of horse. That was the other thing Civilis came to report. Gaius decreed it last night. You have been promoted. You are not ranked as high as decurion but you will no longer be required to take guard duty or dig the latrines. More important, it means you will no longer have to share a tent with seven Gauls." A half-smile flickered across his face, and something that might have been an apology. "After this, that may be wise."

Bán sat up. The bed linen wreathed at his waist. His heart ached. "Gaius will read the spies' reports come dawn. He may decree something quite different if he thinks he has been deceived. Have you a blade if they come for us?"

"Yes." It was a dress dagger, the blade a foot long and sharp on both edges. It had lain on the tiled floor beneath the bed all along. Corvus slid it into view and held it across both palms. "You are free to use it. That has always been so, but we will not need it on Gaius's account. He waited up for the reports. If he were going to act, he would have done so by now. He is leaving in the morning and he would want to stay to watch; he has never been a man to rush his executions. Civilis would not have come with his hound were he not certain it was safe."

Corvus crossed to the window and pushed open the shutters, letting in the cold, misted air of the night. The lamp spread soft light across his back, showing the sunburst scar beneath his ribs where the Pannonian spear had nearly taken his life in the summer before the shipwreck. Other scars laced across it, none of them as deep. When he spoke, it was without turning round.

"Bán, you—"

"Not Julius Valerius?"

"Hardly. He's a creation of Gaius. He is not the Eceni horseman who rides a horse whose name means 'Death.'" They were talking Gaulish. They had slipped into it from the Latin as Corvus opened the shutters and Bán had not noticed.

"How did you know that 'crow' means 'death'?"

"Your sister told me."

"Ah." He had not thought of Breaca since before they left the Rhine. It took time to build the image of her face in his mind. The colour of her eyes eluded him.

Corvus abandoned the window. When he sat on the edge of the bed, the lamp no longer masked him.

Bán pulled the covers tighter around his shoulders. His nerves were frayed beyond anything Amminios had achieved and he was long past making sense of what he thought or felt. He was offered friendship and he was not certain, any longer, that it was enough. Nor did he know what he wanted instead.

Because it was simplest, he said, "You were going to ask me something?"

The prefect laid the knife on the sheet. The lamplight warmed it. "I was going to say that you gave me a blade once, an escape from the dreamer's death. I had thought to avoid that for you, but it is here if you feel the need of it."

It was an apology, masked in details of the past and still not enough. "There are things worse than death, however it comes. Ask Iccius."

"Bán?" Corvus stood, abruptly. The Horus rocked in its alcove. "Have I offended you? Dishonoured you in any way?"

"You told Gaius—"

"I told Gaius what he and every other man in the legions believed already to be true. And is it so bad that you would rather die over two days than have your name attached to it? Really?" Corvus spun on one heel and took himself back to the window. Anger made him animated where fear and relief had not. "When I told the emperor it was a cause for shame amongst your people I believed that I lied. I spent a winter in the men's house and it did not seem a great cause for shame amongst those I shared with. And here—" He gestured out into the mist. "If you read the scholars, they will tell you that in the Germanic tribes it is a capital offence, that they press such men facedown into marshes under wicker hurdles and tread on them until they are dead. Does it seem like that to you? Does it?"

Unwillingly, Bán smiled. "If it is, someone should warn Civilis."

"Exactly. Thank you. So then why—why—" He was by the bed again. The shutter banged behind him. The knife lay flat on his palm. "Why is this better?"

"I'm not afraid to die."

"No, I should say not. You're obsessed with it. You have been so since Iccius was killed. I had hoped we might give you reason to live."

"By lying?"

"Dear God, what did you want me to do? Tell him you brained Amminios with a rock and he should crucify you for it?" Corvus stopped, breathing hard. "Bán, listen to me. Titus Pompeius has never been on a battlefield and the Second has a cohort of new recruits who haven't worked out how to bribe their way out of sentry duty yet. Were it not for that, you would have got your slow death and there would have been nothing we could do about it. The colt had his blood-frenzy, but he was smashing a body already dead. The killing blow to the head was not made by a horse. No man who has fought against cavalry—no man who lived through the Chatti attack last month and saw the bodies after—would make the mistake they made. The watchmen of the Second saw what they wanted to see and Gaius was not in a hurry to have it checked. He had no need of Amminios and he has you in his debt. All he needed was a reason to let you go. I gave it to him."

"And so I am in your debt, as well as his."

It was this that hurt, more than anything. He did not care about Gaius, but he very badly did not want to be in debt to the man who sat now on the edge of the bed, who stretched out two hands and stopped just short of touching and withdrew them again, clenching and unclenching the fingers; the man who said, "Oh, gods, Bán, do you have to be so very stubborn? You owe me nothing. You never have, you never will. Even had you not given me the knife when we thought Caradoc brought news of the dreamer's death, you would still owe me nothing. This is not about debt and the tally of favours, this is about caring. I love you. Do you not know that?"

Bán sat still, not daring to move. Like mist rising with

the dawn, the fog in his mind lifted to reveal only the thing he had felt, but not seen, when Theophilus first asked his question.

Do you care?

Yes, very much. But I don't know if that care is returned.

And so he had covered it with injured pride and old anger and the last dregs of a need to die, fearing that to abandon this last would be the ultimate betrayal of the dead. He felt for Iccius now and could not find him, but felt no rejection in his place.

The quiet stretched on. Bán felt a touch on his good shoulder and did not flinch away from it. Presently, he stretched out his own hand and met another, surprisingly cool where his own was slick with sweat. They held together for a moment, then he was squeezed and quietly left, and when he was joined again the hand held a wineglass and he found he could sit up and take it and drink without spilling. The wine was the best, the emperor's own. The glass was green with a long stem and his fingers left prints on it. The drink rushed to his head, making his ears sing. Through the noise, he heard Corvus, speaking carefully in the measured, thoughtful tones he used before manoeuvres.

". . . don't have to stay. I won't push for what you can't give. I know what it is to be loved and not to love in return. You may stay in the legion and we will be as we were before. Or, if, knowing this, you can't bear to be even that close, I can get you a boat to take you home. It will be hard and we will have to invent a reason, but it's not impossible . . ."

He wasn't listening. He didn't want to listen. He shook his head. His heart battered against the cage of his breast and the pain was unbearable.

Corvus said, "Bán, look at me."

He was looking. His eyes were wide open. He could see nothing through a blur of tears. He dashed them away with the back of his hand.

"Bán, what is it? Have I—"

"Don't, just . . . will you stop being the prefect for a moment and hold me? Please?"

He woke again in daylight with fingers of sun parting the mist. Corvus lay beside him, already awake. The Horus gazed over them, wide-eyed in the sun. Bán reached up and stroked the dome of its head.

"He watches over you," he said.

"Over us. Yes."

"He was a gift? And the horse. Horus to protect and the horse to fight." An image formed in his mind, of a fair head lying in the place of his own, of a leaner, older face. "What was his name, the one who gave them?"

"Marcus. Marcus Aemilius. He died in Pannonia."

"When you got this." He touched the sunburst scar. The skin around it was more sensitive than that elsewhere. In the night he had run his lips across it, exploring the knots and purpled pits, tracing the outline from ribs to spine and back again. He brushed his finger across it now and watched what it did. The name did not matter, nor what he had been. The past was what built them and brought them to this. He smoothed his palm out and down and heard a breath caught and held.

"Should I stop?"

"Not for me. Do you want to?"

"No. Never." He smiled, remembering things of the

night. "Perhaps now it's light we could manage not to spill the wine?"

The morning moved on. Outside, men's voices roamed back and forth, preparing for the emperor's departure. In the fastness of the bed, Bán leaned into the arms that held him. "If we can hear them," he said, "they can hear us."

"Do you mind?"

"No. Not unless they think we're still acting."

"Hardly that." A kiss stole the laughter from them. "Don't ever volunteer to act. You'd be the death of us both."

"I know. You carried the weight alone and I knew it and let you. I'm so sorry."

"Don't be. You did what you could. It was enough."

"Were you afraid?"

"Terrified. Could you not tell? I'd rather have fought the Chatti single-handed. It is one thing to die in battle but quite another to live for a day and a night for Gaius's entertainment." Fingers lifted strands of his hair and spread them out above his head. "And I thought I'd lost you, what little I had. You should have seen your face in the audience room. I thought you hated me for it."

"I didn't hate you. I hated Gaius for the way he smiled, and his freedman for how he laughed, but not you. It was a shock. I wasn't expecting it."

"You should have been. Everyone else was."

"Maybe, but the dead love only each other; they have no room for the living. I wanted so much to be with Iccius, I didn't notice anything else."

"Bán, you're not dead."

"I know." He lifted a palm and kissed it, tipping it towards the light. There were women among the Parisi who were said to see a man's life in his hand. He rubbed the ball of his thumb across the lacework of calluses and scars and followed them through to their conclusions. "When Gaius is gone, what will we do?"

"This. And march back to the Rhine. And train. And see if we can take that mad killer colt of yours and turn him into a cavalry horse. And wait until Galba says he can spare the legions, and sail back across the Ocean to fulfil Gaius's promise to Amminios."

"Will he still do it, with Amminios dead?"

"He has to. It is what will save him. The Senate may loathe him, but if he can bring them Britannia, the people will let him keep his head." Corvus rose on one elbow. "I was serious last night. You don't have to take part in the invasion against your people. This notwithstanding, you can leave if you want to. I will find you a ship that will take you home."

"Corvus?"

"Yes?"

"My people are dead. Iccius was the last and my soul died when he did. I was born anew yesterday, in this place, with people who are my own. I was Bán of the Eceni. Now I am simply Bán, who rides a horse named Death. Wherever that takes me is home."

IV

LATE SUMMER–AUTUMN A.D. 43

CHAPTER 25

The salt marsh lay on the far eastern coast, south of the sea-river at the place where a single ship—or an invasion fleet—sailing from Gesoriacum or the mouth of the Rhine, and seeking the shortest crossing with the best tides, might make landfall.

On the day of the last new moon before the autumn equinox, there were no ships in sight. The sea rocked with unhurried rhythms and the occasional whitecap flashed on the waves. Such wind as there was blew from the shore out to sea. The land was as quiet. The salt flats simmered under the mid-morning, late-summer sun. Wading birds stilted over tidal mud. A raft of reed-billed oystercatchers, called sea-pies by the local Cantiaci, stirred and settled, piping in high fluting notes. Breaca, seated on a rock, turned to see what had disturbed them. The horizon remained free of ships but, after a while, she felt through the soles of her feet the throb of approaching hoofbeats. The birds made good guardians, if not as good as they had been in the late spring when the tribes had first gathered. In the beginning, they had billowed up in great pied blankets, shrieking at every cough and call. Four months on, they dipped and piped among the pools even through sword practise and were roused to flight only by the hounds.

The incoming warrior dismounted at the canter. He landed heavily and did not have his hands free to balance himself. Breaca listened to his few steps of unsteadiness but did not look round. Those who mattered had gathered at daybreak and stood strung along the shoreline, staring out to sea. Caradoc was there with fifty of his Ordovices as honour guard, his hair a spark of gold amidst the white cloaks. It was eighteen months since he had led the warriors of the war hammer in the left wing of the battle against Berikos of the Atrebates and the patina of victory still sheathed him.

Togodubnos and his cluster of yellow-cloaked spear-leaders stood not far away—a grizzled badger, showing his age and the strains of leadership. For the two days of that same battle, the massed spears of the Trinovantes had held the centre ground solidly against the enemy when the wings had been forced, temporarily, to retreat. They, too, radiated a palpable pride.

To their left, Gunovic and 'Tagos shared the blue of their people but little else. The Eceni, led by Gunovic, had merged with the spears of Mona and had won honour for both on the right flank, particularly on the second day. 'Tagos had not fought then.

Further back, Ardacos and Gwyddhien, Cumal and Braint, Maroc and Airmid made a solid block of grey as they had done on the battlefield—the first time since Caesar that the Warrior had led the spears of Mona in conflict. Breaca, at their head, had felt an echo of the certainty she had known on the night of the choosing and had seen it touch those who followed her. It had not swept them to immediate victory, but it had woven them together into one tight unit and fewer had died than she had expected. Now, a year and a half later, the serpent-spear showed fresh again on their shields, in preparation for a greater war.

The incomer was not any of these, but still acted as if he were owed a place at their council. He strode past Breaca, shedding straw like a poorly finished thatch. At the meeting stone, where the speaker should have stood, he hurled his burden to the ground. The sheaf-ties broke, scattering late-cut wheat, white from too much sun and blued at the edges with mildew. The threshing had been done badly, if at all. A full ear fell against Breaca's leg and dropped a patter of corn round her feet. As if the quality of the harvest was her only concern, she picked a kernel and bit into it. The outer layer was slimed with mould and slipped unpleasantly between her teeth but the inner core was dry and hard; if the good weather lasted, it would not be impossible to salvage the crop. Tilting her palm, she dropped the kernel back to the grass.

"What does it tell you, Warrior of Mona?"

The man's shadow cut across her legs. His voice made of her title an insult. She looked up, shading her eyes from the sun. Beduoc of the Dobunni, oath-breaker and untrusted ally, had been handsome in his soft, southern way until the weight of his treachery had marred him. The lines of his bones still stood well under the drink-slackened skin and the twisting mouth. His eyes were red from the dust and heat of the ride. Sweat greased him. Stubbornly, he threw his question again. "The corn, Eceni. What does it tell you?"

That, too, was an insult did she choose to take it so; she was of Mona first and of the Eceni second for as long as she was Warrior. To say otherwise was to deny her station. She met his gaze and he broke away first. "That the Dobunni gather their harvest late?" she offered.

"Late?" He spat onto the stone at her side. "It is not late. It is not in at all. I cut this with my skinning knife as I rode away from the homelands. The rest stands in the fields, feeding the rats and the starlings."

He stepped away and ran his gaze across the stubble behind them. "You see nothing here." He spread his arm, casting guilt on them all. "You have cut every standing ear along the shore and for two days' ride inland so that you may eat and the Romans, when they land, may not; but everywhere else, from here to the far western shore, uncut corn stands in the fields feeding the birds. In the lands of the Dobunni, the pigeons gorge from daybreak to dusk. By noon they are filled beyond flying so that toddling children can lift them off the ground and carry them home to have their necks wrung. Our grandmothers cut them open and take the corn from their gullets so that we may have bread to eat in winter, knowing that they will have none from the harvest. Our land is empty, tended by infants and cripples, while every able-bodied warrior waits here, watching the empty sea for an enemy that will not come. Our children know hunger and the first frosts are a month away. It is time to act while we can still salvage something for the winter."

That part of Breaca that was dedicated to Mona listened with an ear that said if his life had been different Beduoc of the Dobunni could have been a singer; the tones were there in his voice, patterning the anger. In a corner of her heart, she mourned the loss of a talent. The rest of her watched the beginnings of agreement build in the main body of warriors, if not the leaders and dreamers. Beduoc was neither liked nor trusted but they listened to his word. His people, the Dobunni, were only lately allies and even then only his half: the portion whose land bordered that of the Catuvellauni and who could most easily forge new bonds. On the first day of the battle, they had fought with Berikos and his Atrebates. Their warriors had swung their blades with a single-minded savagery and the bloodshed on the left flank, where they held their ground, had been terrible. Caradoc had led the Ordovices in charge after charge against them and neither side had given quarter, so that the bodies had piled high on the death pyres that night.

The cost had been repaid. On the morning of the second day, Beduoc himself had come into the camp to swear allegiance to Togodubnos and his allies. No-one trusts a man who will break his blood-oath, but of necessity they had accepted his offer and all had agreed that it had been good not to face the war spears of his people through the second day of battle. In likelihood, it was this that had swung the day in their favour and it was not Beduoc's fault that Berikos had escaped and made his way to Rome.

A ripple passed through the gathering. 'Tagos, who had gained a place on the council of the Eceni, stepped forward. He stooped under the pressure of perpetual pain and his right sleeve hung empty below the elbow. His voice was clear and carried to the far reaches of the gathering.

"There is another matter. The Cantiaci have been our hosts throughout the summer but we cannot presume too far on their goodwill. We eat their corn and drink their water, we hunt their game and burn their wood on our fires. And for what? A year and a half have passed since we reclaimed the land south of the river for Togodubnos's son. It has taken that long for the new emperor to raise his legions and now he holds them at the brink of the Ocean and still they do not come. Claudius is no different from his predecessor. Caligula, too, was a showman without the stomach for a battle. I say it is time to go home. In the lands of the Eceni, also, the corn stands uncut in the field and our people fear the white bear of winter."

'Tagos was not the man he had been before the battle. His gaze rode the circle, daring them to call him a coward. None did so. He was no longer a warrior, but in letting go of the name he had earned their respect. It had not been so on the first morning of battle when he had ridden out at the head of fifty Eceni spears. His loss of an arm to Amminios's war eagles had made him a hero of sorts amongst those who had previously honoured Caradoc and he had worked doggedly afterwards, teaching himself to wield a sword left-handed. Gunovic had made him a shield that could be strapped to the stump of his right arm and he had fought well with it in the challenge fights against the young bloods of the Eceni, who stood in awe of his warrior's braids and his kill-feathers and the clear evidence of his part in the greatest massacre of their age.

It had been different in battle against the Atrebates. The warriors of the southlands knew nothing of his past nor cared for the red-quilled feathers in his hair. They saw only that he was a one-armed swordsman and that a spear thrust from the right stood a better chance than most of biting flesh. He had lived through the first day because his friends had linked shields and made a wall around him. Two had died that he might live. It was the loss of Verulos that had changed him—the halting lad with the lame foot, father to Nemma's child, who should have been fighting from horseback but had chosen to stand and defend his friend instead. That night, 'Tagos had lit the fire in honour of the dead. By its light, in front of everyone, he had uncombed the warrior's braids from his hair and laid his feathers in the heart of the blaze. His battle friends had sat with him in silence until the fire died down and then had left to make their own peace with the gods. It had been a good deed and the right one, but it had clearly marked the end of his warrior's road. It took more courage than most, then, for him to put his voice to going home and, because of it, his words carried weight with those ranged round him on the salt marshes.

Gunovic stepped up to join him. He had fought like a bear; no-one could impugn his courage. His eyes slid past Breaca's and came back, pained with the need to straddle both sides of a line.

" 'Tagos is right. If Claudius's troops take ship now, they risk being caught by the autumn storms on their return as Caesar's did. They know this better than we and it affects their actions. I have word this morning from Luain mac Calma to say that the two German legions have set down roots in Gesoriacum and are refusing to take ship. Further east, the Spanish legion waits at Juliobona and it, too, has not yet embarked. There is not one legionary willing to put to sea. If the new emperor wishes to buy credibility from the Senate to shore up his claim to rule, he will have to find other coin than the lives of his men or the conquest of Britannia."

If it had been anyone but Gunovic, Breaca would have rejected his reading of the situation outright. Because she could not, she said, "Claudius has spent all summer gathering his army. He has twenty thousand legionaries and as many cavalry and auxiliaries standing idle at his ports. He has commandeered a navy greater than Rome has ever seen. Are you seriously telling me he does not intend to use it?"

"Not this year."

The gathering cracked apart. It seemed that even the youngest warriors—particularly the youngest—had known of it, or had dreamed it, or had seen it in the movements of merchants along the coast.

"He'll come in the spring—if he ever comes at all—"

"Caligula did not have the courage to attack and Claudius is the lesser man. He has no stomach for a fight he knows he will lose. Caligula at least had accompanied his father to the army; this one knows nothing—"

"It's all for show. Rome does not care what lies beyond the encircling Ocean; they need only feed the imaginations of their people—"

Only the dreamers sat silent, and the two sons of Cunobelin. The rest clamoured like gulls fighting over the midden scraps. Behind them, real gulls in their thousands rode the turbulent winds beyond the salt marsh, whitening the sky. The sea rolled beneath them, too gently for the time of year. The sun fell on the polished waves and shattered, blinding bright. A horn sounded distantly and the gulls moved at its command, flashing like shoaling fish as they wheeled and dropped to settle on the water. In an ordered fleet, each one raised a wing to catch the wind. Invisible currents sailed them in to beach on the marshes. Their eyes were red, bleeding, and when they shook their heads the spatter of it stained the sand. Above them, a war eagle soared on a thermal.

"Breaca?"

She had slipped from the rock. Airmid knelt in front of her. Maroc was at her shoulder. He was the Elder now—had been so since midwinter when Talla died—and it changed the feel of him. His eyes carved hollows in her skull and let light into her soul. Calmly, as if it was part of an interrupted conversation, he said, "Breaca, the gulls have not yet come."

She could see that. Exhaustion drained her. She nodded, lacking the will to speak.

Caradoc was closer than he had seemed. The summer had tempered him, bleaching his hair paler than the straw and making smooth leather of his skin. The complex grey gaze studied her with a warrior's judgement. She expected no less. In the four years since she had sat the grey mare on a hilltop and put aside anger and hurt in the face of a greater threat, she had reached a pragmatic accommodation with Caradoc that worked for both in their service of the land and its people. He treated her as a distant half-sister with whom there had been an unhealed family rift, no longer spoken of. She treated him as she might have done Amminios if, after losing the Warrior's Dance to Bán, the middle brother had joined his siblings in the war against Rome and proved himself a competent leader of men— with respect and a necessary distance. Now he crouched on his heels with his palms on his knees and she felt the pressure of his scrutiny.

From her left, Maroc asked the single necessary question. "When do the white sails make landfall?"

She stared up, lacking an answer. Airmid came to kneel at her side. Airmid's dream in the night had been of herons by the thousand, killing all the frogs, and she had been gathering the courage to tell it. The gulls were worse, but not for her. "Look at the sun," she said. "It will tell you."

Breaca closed her eyes to think. The day had been too bright and the sea too smooth—god-smooth, not the real thing. She had not seen the sun. She shook her head.

"The shadows, then."

She looked down. The answer lay at her feet in slanting shade. "Afternoon, midway between noon and dusk."

It was not what they wanted. Maroc sucked on a tooth and Breaca was a novice again, learning to read Latin and doing it poorly. Shame flushed from her neck to her hairline. Patiently, Airmid said, "Not that. Look at the sun's angle. What is the time of year?"

The sun gave no answers. In her mind, Breaca looked at the turf and at the leaves on the small, wind-weathered birch that grew alone on the rise behind. The grass was harsh and brown and crusted with sea salt. The birch was near naked, a thing of straggled silver bark and sparse, sun-green leaves.

She opened her eyes. The real grass was less brown, the birch had more leaves, but their colour was the same. A strong wind would strip them and make the tree of her dream. "Not long from now. A month. Maybe less. After the first storms of autumn."

The warriors had fallen silent. Those of the Dobunni whose grandparents had rejected the gods made the sign to ward against evil. Others raised a palm for Briga, or Nemain. Gunovic watched her like a hound guarding its whelp. With clear regret he said, "Breaca, are you sure it was this year? Could it not be next?" He was a man of integrity; he could do no less than ask the questions that seemed obvious to him.

She glared, unreasonably angry. "Would the gods send warning now of danger a year away?"

He shrugged, unconvinced. Maroc, who should have known the answer, said nothing.

Beduoc said, "We should still bring in the harvest. The gods do not give luck to warriors who ride to the battle-ground starving, on unfed horses with hounds whose hearts are set on hunting rather than the battle ahead."

Around him, others nodded—men and women who had more to lose than a single life and less than a nation. Not one of them led less than a hundred spears. They were weary of waiting. They turned as one on those clustered round the speaker's stone and their message was clear.

"Go." Togodubnos spoke for the others. He turned his shield to face them so that the mark of the Sun Hound, gold on white, gave weight to his words. "Take your warriors. All those who have corn still standing should ride home now and bring it in. I will return to the dun. If the moon turns and you have not enough for winter, send word to me there. The granaries of the Trinovantes are far from empty I will ensure that stores are sent to those who need it."

Airmid asked, "If you are north of the sea-river, who will keep watch here for Rome?"

Caradoc did not rise. Quietly, from his place crouched by the rock, he said, "I will stay, and the oath-spears of the Catuvellauni; they are not needed at home."

He led that people now, having been granted the blood-oath by his brother after the battle against Berikos. He had spent his last two summers amongst them and his daughter saw him only in winter. If her mother wished otherwise, none knew of it. Once, in a moment of careless inattention, Breaca had reminded him of a pledge that his child would grow knowing more of her father than Caradoc had known of Cunobelin. The strength of his anger had surprised her, and her response to it. In nearly four years, it was the only time they had argued. She had never mentioned the matter since.

Caradoc was looking at her, pensively, as if he read the stream of her thoughts. He said, "Those of the Atrebates who owe me allegiance will join us. They have few warriors and a great many who tend the fields. As, I think, does Mona?"

"Of course." She nodded. He knew it, as did Togodubnos, but it needed to be said again, as often as was necessary, in front of those who might harbour doubt. "The elder council has given its word; the warriors of Mona will remain in the east until the war begins or winter closes the Ocean. We will return in the spring and each year until the threat has passed."

"Thank you." Caradoc smiled a little. To the wider gathering, he said, "Any others who choose to join us will be welcome. When the legions come, we will send runners. Then will be the time to arm yourselves and ride."

Gunovic asked, "You still believe they are going to come?"

"Oh, yes." His gaze was bleak. "They, too, are waiting for the harvest. When the corn is in and they can feed the legions on the profit of our labours, they will come."

CHAPTER 26

The rain fell lightly, fine as mist. The dandelion seed-head trembled. A single wisp shook free and launched upwards, catching the breeze. Others jigged looser in their moorings. Breaca lay on her belly and watched them. The judder took on a rhythm, like ripples on still water. In the trees, a magpie shrieked alarm. Behind her, an owl called in daylight. At the sound of it, Hail flagged his tail from side to side and turned an ear backwards. Breaca wiped her palm clean on the grass and signalled the beech wood at her quarter. A shadow-mass of grass-stained lamb's wool and muddied skin sprinted forward to lie panting at her other side: Braint.

"They're coming." The girl's voice was hoarse with excitement and haste and the need for concealment.

"I know. I can hear them. How many?"

"Twenty riders with spears and swords and big shields. They guard as many others on foot armed with spears."

"A hunting party?"

"It must be. You have left them nothing else to eat."

"They can eat fish."

"Exactly." The girl grinned, teeth flashing white in the mud of her face. She was of the Brigantes, who ate only meat and corn, and she loathed the taste of fish. She squirmed back down below the brow of the slope and knelt up. "There were no hounds and no slingers," she said. "Can I go?"

"Yes. Take Ardacos. He's expecting you."

The girl merged with the scrub. Presently, the dandelion puffball shuddered to a new rhythm. Breaca tapped Hail on the shoulder and they moved sideways and down to where the grey mare was tethered with the other horses, feet bound with sheepskin, harness and muzzle muffled with rags. She stripped the rags away and mounted. Hail ran on one side; Gwyddhien, quietly undemonstrative, took the other. The honour guard of Mona followed. They were thirty, twenty-two of whom had shared the choosing on Mona. The remainder came from the warriors' school, picked to broaden and strengthen the skills of their peers.

They strung out in a line—grey-cloaked ghosts riding padded horses uphill through a quiet wood. In the month since the meeting on the salt flats, they had lived exclusively off the land, lifting the weight of their presence from their hosts, the Cantiaci. In that time, even more than the summer that had gone before, the sun and the wind had annealed them, forging a leathern uniformity that made each alike, but for height and the colour of their hair. They were well armed with fresh-bladed spears and good swords and shields of bull's hide marked with the serpent-spear. Most wore iron helmets, save Breaca. From the beginning of the battle against Berikos, she had known that her hair was her best standard and that her warriors would fight strongest who could see her most clearly in the field. It was more striking now than then; the summer sun had burnished it to a fiery gold-threaded copper that flared even under cloud. In the brief time since their landing, the Romans had come to know and fear it.

The warriors reached the edge of the beech wood and fanned sideways to make a single line abreast. Dismounting, they stripped the sheepskin padding from their mounts' feet, discarding secrecy in favour of sure footing and speed. Breaca signalled and five of their number slung their spears behind, shook loose their slings and opened the pouches of river stones at their belts. They were her secret weapon, trained and led by Cumal, who was master of the sling. On a good day, they could fell a man and his mount in the space of two heartbeats. Leaning down, Breaca placed her palm flat on the serpent-spear painted in red on the grey mare's shoulder and prayed to the elder grandmother for a perfect day.

The riders were Gauls; that much could be seen from their size and the sallow gold hair falling in long braids beneath their helmets. In all other respects, they were armed and armoured as Roman cavalry, with spears and long swords and curving oval shields painted black with thunderbolts and the mark of the eagle in gold. They saw Braint gathering wood in the open and thought themselves blessed by the gods. She had cleaned the mud from her face and unbound her hair and her tunic flapped in the wind above her belt, showing one brown-nippled breast as she bent for another branch. The Gauls yelled from a distance. The girl screamed and dropped her wood and sprinted for the beech wood, gathering her hair behind her as she ran. She was the best runner of her age group on Mona but the Gauls were mounted and she was not. Breaca, watching from her high vantage in the beech wood, clenched and unclenched her right hand, swearing a slow death to any one of them who touched her.

The girl scurried amongst the trees, and when the Gauls next saw her she was in the company of a man, her father perhaps or her brother; he was neither big nor obviously armed. They were both mounted and fled up a clear-felled valley with woods on either side and a steep rise at the far end from which there was no escape. The Gauls howled thanks to their gods. In the woods above, a grey mare stamped and was silenced. A white-flecked hound crooned a war threat, too low for hearing, and the hair rose on his neck like a mane.

The girl and her father reached the end of the valley and turned at bay. This late, it could be seen they were, in fact, both armed but that only added to the sport. The Gauls slowed and called to their comrades, the hunters, whistling them back from the trail of a deer. These were smaller, swarthier men and they swore viciously in Latin until they saw the girl. Then one of them made a jest in Gaulish about feasting on human flesh. On the slope above, a wheaten-haired youth of the Coritani bared his teeth and said, "That one is mine."

The first of the Gauls was within a spear's throw of Ardacos when the sling-stone spun down from the heights and dashed his brains. His companion took his eyes off Braint's sword arm and died with his throat cut, whistling air. The would-be cannibal choked soon after on the end of a thrown spear from the neck of which hung the feathers of a red hawk.

The Gaul who led the group was not a stupid man; his was not the first patrol attacked and he had read the reports of those of his predecessors who had escaped with their lives. Shouting orders, he spun his horse to face the wave of grey-cloaked warriors, looking urgently about for the flame-hair who led them—and found it, too close. He raised his blade high to fend off a killing stroke to his head and saw it turn at the last moment to strike, impossibly fast, for his neck. In a final act of stubborn courage, he looked beyond the blade to see whose hand killed him, and, wide-eyed, saw what none of those who had survived had been close enough to report. His last sight in this world was the face of the goddess, fiercely radiant, framed in wildfire, and the white-speckled hound who fought at her side.

The leader's horse was a bay of strong Gaulish blood, well trained to steadiness in battle. Breaca marked it in her mind as she dragged her blade from the neck of its rider and turned to confront the remaining enemy. Their numbers were thinning fast. Hail and the grey mare killed one of the Roman hunters between them and Breaca took his Gaulish shield-mate with her blade. Her palm thrilled to the action, but only mildly. It was the second ambush of the day, the sixth since the legions had first landed; killing came easily. The air hung thick with the moans of the dying and the stench of lifeblood and void faeces and she barely noticed. Two of the hunters closest to the edge tried to escape up the slope into the wood and found themselves facing Braint, who had abandoned her horse in the valley and run through the trees to outflank them. Shock slowed their reflexes—they had never faced a woman in battle—and they died before they had time to think past the impossibility of it. The wheaten-haired warrior of the Coritani hailed the girl for her first taste of true Roman blood. She saluted, grinning, and bent to cut a lock of hair from each of the dead men, adding them to her bulging belt pouch before running down the slope to help with the rounding up of the enemy's horses.

When all was clear, the enemy dead were dragged to the wood's edge and skewered to the tree trunks with their own spears, their throats cut and their manhood severed in warning. The Coritani youth stripped the shirt from the leader and carved the sign of the serpent-spear on his chest. Breaca saw it and did nothing to stop him. It had been done five times before.

The remaining Roman weapons were divided amongst the warriors. The grey cloaks of Mona left as they had come, silently, on padded feet. Behind them, carrion birds were already gathering. Far back towards the coast, the smoke of a thousand campfires stained the sky.

A small stream ran on the far side of the beech wood. They dismounted beside it and washed themselves, and ate goat's cheese wrapped in nettle leaves and cold meat that had been a gift from a family of northern Atrebates. Breaca sat with Hail at her feet and bathed a graze on his foreleg. He pressed his head on her arm with the teeth tight against her skin and crooned as he did when they were playing. She found it hard to remember a time before she had loved him and he her. She closed the wound with spiders' webs and fed him meat from her saddlebag. Downstream, Ardacos tended to one of the honour guard who bled from a spear-wound above the knee. Others bathed their own wounds or stood in the stream with their sword hands immersed in the water to take down the heat and swelling of the battle. Dubornos, once of the Eceni and now of Mona, brought a flask of water and came to sit at her side.

"There were more this time," he said, "and they were better armed than the last. The next group will be greater still."

It was not an accusation; that was no longer his way. Dubornos was one of those she had chosen to make up the honour guard's strength, recognizing the change in him. It had begun immediately after the battle with Amminios, in which Dubornos had brought disgrace on himself and his family by feigning death in the face of the enemy. Because of it, he had been the first of those to change and the one in whom the difference was most marked. In shame, he had renounced his warrior's spear on the first night of their return and had pledged himself to hunting and the provision of food for the people. Later, when eyes were elsewhere, he had given away his gold ornaments and his styled cloaks to the families of the dead and had taken to wearing coarse-woven wool and a single armband made from the pelt of the red fox, which was his dream, although he had paid it no heed before. He had become a good hunter, but no-one remarked upon it. Then, in the spring before Breaca had been chosen Warrior, he had gone to Macha with a dream and she had named him a singer and sent him west to Mona for training.

He had been there nearly a year before Breaca had noticed him. In the autumn after her choosing, on her return from the Sun Hound's funeral, Maroc had asked her to school the singers in use of weapons and she had found that the singer of the Eceni was also a fighter of quietly consummate skill. He fought without arrogance with no wish to win, and so won against all but the few whom the gods had set apart as true warriors. In the wake of the victory over Berikos, she had chosen him as one of eight to make up the numbers of the honour guard. She had never regretted it. On the battlefield, he fought with a controlled passion, self-lessly. Off it, he sang as well as Gunovic, and possibly—although Breaca was not the best to judge—as well as Graine. In council, Breaca trusted his judgement.

She accepted the water he offered and let it wash the taint of blood from her throat.

"You think we should not be doing this?" she asked.

"No. It is necessary. It pricks their morale and makes them realize they are in enemy territory; it deprives them of food so they must live off the sea, and each one dead is one less to fight when the army moves against us."

"But?"

"But we are thirty and most carry wounds. We should know in advance the numbers against which an ambush will not succeed and be prepared for it. There are some amongst us who would die for the chance to kill another Roman."

"Braint?" It was obvious. Breaca had seen it before, and again in the flanking move on the two Roman hunters.

He nodded. "And, I think, Ardacos. He has taken the invasion as a personal affront."

"He understands what they will do if they gain a foothold. He will not be alone in that."

"No. But that is the reason we cannot afford to lose him."

They looked along the stream. Ardacos finished his bandaging and rose smoothly to his feet. More than ever, the last few days had made clear how strongly ran the blood of the ancestors in him, in the lithe movements and the fierce, unyielding battle anger. Watching him, Breaca felt her heart lift. For nearly a year after Berikos's defeat they had been lovers and she still felt the world brighter in his presence.

He caught her eye now and, smiling, she raised a hand to beckon him over—and stopped because his gaze had moved beyond hers and his face grown still. She turned. Braint was running at her without caution or quiet, waving her arms to show danger. When they were close enough to hear her over the song of the stream, she straggled to a halt, saying, "They're coming. I saw their standards from the top of the rise."

"Who are coming?"

"The legions, the cavalry, the Gauls, the Germans . . . all of them. They've struck camp and they're moving west." She looked up. Her eyes were wild with hate and impotent anger. "They are thousands. Tens of thousands. The line goes back all the way to the sea. We can't stand against them."

A shadow passed over the group. Dubornos made the sign against evil. The girl paled and put her hand to her mouth. "I meant, we who are here cannot—"

Breaca put a hand on her arm. "I know what you meant. We can stand against them only if we stand together. We have always known this. Call the others to mount. We will go back and join Caradoc and his warriors at the eel-spate."

The eel-spate was the largest river the Romans had to cross as they moved in from their landing on the far eastern coast. Tides moved at its mouth, making the land treacherous on either side, but it narrowed quickly so that, by half a morning's ride inland, there was a place where a horse could ford it easily and a warrior standing on one side could cast a spear to the other and expect to make a kill. It was the obvious place for the legions to cross, and Caradoc and his mixed troop of Catuvellauni and Ordovices had been preparing there since news of the first Roman landings. He had not brought them all, by any means; if the warriors of both tribes were counted together they came to over five thousand and he had brought less than a thousand, enough to guard a river crossing but not so many that if they were overwhelmed they would weaken the main force. To these was added the bulk of the warriors of Mona, acting under his orders; they would not be separated from their Warrior, except for minor skirmishes.

In all, the defenders made nearly three thousand and they had been working for three days without break. The result was as good as it could be, better than Breaca had expected. Riding down from the hills behind, she could see the rows of fire-hardened stakes that reared out of the water to point at the enemy. Boulders as big as swine littered both banks, making a cavalry nightmare of the terrain so that no horseman could readily approach the water for a spear's throw on either side of the ford. Mats of woven branches covered narrow trenches that would delay both infantry and horse. Behind the defenders, a long wooded hill stretched to the south and west, making a wall at their backs and hiding their full strength, or lack of it.

Breaca had led her thirty across the river far upstream and looped back to come down through the trees. Emerging now, she saw below her mounted warriors racing their horses along the western bank, hurling shouts and taunts at the enemy. She barely looked at them. On the far side, the army of Rome was gathering. So many men, so well armed, so rigidly disciplined; it was easy to see why Braint had lost her courage on seeing them for the first time. Rank upon rank, line upon line, six deep in their centuries, the first two cohorts of the XIVth and XXth legions waited, resting on their javelins, easing their swords in their sheaths. Rain pearled on shoulder and helm, making jewels of dulled metal, creating uniformity where it might otherwise have been lacking. They were inhuman—or Breaca would have thought so, had she not slain a score of their brethren in the morning.

The legions saw her as she rode out of the trees, halfway down the hill. A murmur rippled down the line, growing to a growl. Not inhuman then, but prone to fear and anger. She grinned, savagely, and hoped they saw it. They would have found the ruined carcasses of their dead on their way here. There had been no survivors to tell of the tall, copper-haired warrior and her grey-cloaked killers, but she was known from the earlier attacks and the mark cut on the chests of the dead had been the same, like the message it left. *You will die here and go to your gods unwhole. Leave us.*

In case they should doubt it, she moved her shield to her right arm so that, coming down the hill with the trees to her left, the sign of the serpent-spear would be plainly seen. Behind her, the thirty of her honour guard did the same. She raised her spear above her head and saw the flicker of iron as the gesture was repeated along the line. Hail ran ahead of her, head and tail high, a war hound greater than anything Rome could offer. He was her living memory of Bán and she used him, as she had done on Mona, to strike the spark of loathing and anger that could be directed at Rome as easily as at Amminios and that became, as it grew within her, the certainty of victory. She felt the mantle of it settle on the honour guard and spread to the warriors beneath her so that the swarms of activity paused and became instead a carpet of upturned faces, and raised spears and blades that flashed in the light and promised death to the enemy.

On the opposite bank, the growl grew. Men began to hammer their blade-hilts on their shields. A pattering noise rose over the music of the stream, like hail on sheet iron, gathering strength. At the far left of the Roman cavalry, a black-haired man in the chequered cloak of the Atrebates tugged at the sleeve of a mounted commander and pointed. Breaca threw up her arm and made a sign in the air as she had seen Maroc do, naming the Atrebatan a traitor and marking him for Briga. The man flinched and fell back, shielding his face as if she had flung stones across the water. The rattle of sword-hilts became a wall of sound, like the roar of a battlefield. Breaca set her teeth and grinned and felt her spear leap in her hand like a live thing. The grey mare raised her head and screamed, as a colt might, giving battle.

Caradoc met her at the foot of the slope. He, too, was leaner and browner than he had been at the meeting on the salt marshes, and even in the rain his hair shone star-gold as if lit from within. He still bore the colours of the Ordovices; the white cloak fell from his shoulders, part covering the stolen mail shirt she had sent him after the first skirmish, and swept back across the haunches of the bay cavalry horse that had been the mount of the Gaulish leader killed earlier in the day. She had sent this later on with the scouts who had ridden to him directly after; a gift because his own dun colt had been killed beneath him, but also a further warning to the enemy: *We have fought against you and won. We are ahead of you, at your sides and behind. Nowhere are you safe. Go home.*

He had understood, as she had known he would. Even before she reached him, she heard the familiar voice, dryly amused, with the edge of danger to it that she had known in battle against Berikos and earlier, in a river, swimming against the current. "Breaca, welcome. The horse is perfection itself, thank you. Rome knows what it has lost."

The knot of his honour guard parted to let her through. The drizzle plastered the gold threads of his hair to his forehead. His eyes sparked, like fire struck from flint. He, too, had waited four years for this. He offered her the hand-clasp of a brother for his sister and she returned it, gladly. In this, they were as kin, fighting a common evil. Parting, he studied her without rancour. "You look as you did on Mona, on the night of the choosing. Do you feel it?"

She grinned. "A little. Enough for today, and whatever comes after it." She did not burn as she had on Mona—the rain, or the presence of the legions, or the will of the gods damped the edges of it—but it was enough; she felt that in her marrow. Those who had known the real thing would feel that—Caradoc and Ardacos and Gwyddhien and the others of the first thirty who followed her. For the rest, word had already passed that the Warrior of Mona had come, bringing the wildfire, and that Rome could not prevail. Above all else, she wanted the enemy to know that, and to feel fear from the start. Glancing down at the stolen cavalry mount, she said, "I'm glad they recognize their horse. Does he ride as well as he looks?"

"Better. Airmid says the hurt of his loss and his presence with us will change the course of a battle. Was his rider of high rank?"

Airmid had stayed with Caradoc; not safe, but safer

than riding with the skirmish party. If she knew of the horse, then it mattered. Breaca cast her mind back to the morning and saw nothing momentous. "I don't know," she said. "He might have been. He led a forage party of forty. His armour was good. Cumal is wearing his mail shirt."

"Then he was big, if nothing else. Cumal is the only one I know as big as Gunovic and your father."

"But he lives and the Gaul died," said Breaca. "As they all will."

Caradoc grinned and she swung the grey mare in beside him. Side by side, they rode to the safe mark scored on the riverbank that kept them out of range of the javelins and faced together the army of Rome, so long awaited. On the opposite bank, the ranks of the legions rippled and steadied as bundles of javelins were handed down the ranks and distributed amongst the first three rows. Each man took four, adding to the two he had carried on the march. The front rows drove theirs into the ground to stand upright at their feet for easy reach but showed no signs of immediate action. The ranks at the rear made bundles, threw them down, and then sat. Some began playing dice, others ate from their packs. On the high ground beyond, yet others were raising tents and lighting fires. The breeze carried the smell of roasting horsemeat and thousands upon thousands of sweating men, waiting.

They were quiet now, but for the mutterings of orders and the necessary clash of movement and the occasional hurled oath. On the defending side, also, the warriors had settled. Had they been fighting their own, the individual spear-leaders would have called challenges across for single combat. If the cause for war were weak, it might have been decided by that alone. Against Rome, where the cause was strongest, there would be no single combat; Rome did not allow it, and even if it did, the outcome would make no difference to the battle or greater war. And so the massed ranks waited and neither side chose to make the first move.

Breaca screwed her eyes against the wet. "If I read the standards right, there are only two legions and those who travel with them."

Caradoc nodded. "Two legions, six wings of cavalry and eight auxiliary cohorts, most of them Batavian horsemen. They are twenty thousand and we are less than three. I could wish for better odds."

"Always. But as long as they stay on the other side of the river their numbers make no difference, and you have laid your boulders well. They can't come at the ford more than a century at a time. There isn't room."

She saw a movement on the edge of her vision; a warrior had stepped up to the boulders strewn along the defending side of the ford. His cloak was green plaid on brown, the colour of the Catuvellauni, his hair hung in war plaits in a pattern she did not know, laden with kill-feathers that spoke of a lifetime of battle. Caradoc, watching him, narrowed his eyes. "He's offering single combat," he said. "And it has been accepted."

It had. A man was riding forward to the boulders on the Roman side. At their margin, he dismounted and began to thread his way through to the riverbank. The warrior did the same. They stood a spear's throw apart, with the water a bright, foaming ribbon between them, swirling round the stakes that made it safe. As they matched up, a collective gasp ran through the ranks of both sides as each saw the impossible: the men facing each other were a pair. Breaca looked at Caradoc, the question implicit.

"Chanos's line is of the Belgae. He has traded for years with Gaul. The other may be a cousin."

"Or a son?" The one on the Roman side was younger. Beneath his helmet, his fair hair flowed longer and brighter.

"Maybe."

Whatever the relationship, the insults had been made and returned, the threats and the promises, all in Gaulish. The Romans could have called their man back, but not Caradoc or Breaca. Theirs was not an army amongst which orders could be given but a gathering of warriors, men and women fighting for their own honour, their lives in the hands of the gods.

The hurling of insults continued, as it had to do. Looking past them, thinking beyond their single, small challenge, Breaca said, "Can we hold them, the twenty thousand?"

Caradoc shrugged. "I don't know. We have to try. Togodubnos needs time to gather the tribes at the sea-river. We can defeat them there, if anywhere, but not before the tribes are ready."

She said softly, "And the rest, the other two legions? Will we have to hold them, too?" That was the question that had nagged at her since the landings. All summer, the spies had sent word that Claudius held four legions waiting to cross the ocean; so far, she had seen only two.

Caradoc said, "These are the Fourteenth and the Twentieth, come from the Rhine. The Second and Ninth were due to sail from Gesoriacum but if they have landed no-one can tell me where. Runners have been sent for three days' ride down the coast and they report no other landings. The cohorts would have to fly on the wings of the gods to out-flank us here and I don't think they have that power."

"Good," said Breaca. "Then we may still win. If Chanos can kill his kin, then we have a good start." By the river, the hurling of insults had stopped. Both men had discarded their shields and shed their mail shirts. Both raised their spears. By tradition, they would cast together. It was possible both would die. Breaca said, "Is he good with a spear?"

"The best."

He was not only good, he knew the other's ways. Both men threw, then dodged as the spears were airborne. The Gaulish mercenary had cast straight, not expecting a dodge. Chanos had cast to the left, knowing it would happen and guessing the side. The Roman spear bounced harmlessly on a boulder, cracking the haft. The Catuvellauni buried itself an arm's length up the haft in the unarmoured chest of its target. The enemy fell, choking on blood. Around Breaca, the defending warriors erupted in cheers. Chanos raised an arm in triumph and hurled a final insult—and fell under a triad of legionary javelins thrown by three men who had run forward to the boulder line—an act of unthinkable dishonour.

For a heartbeat, Breaca felt the warriors around her freeze. Nothing had prepared them for such an abnegation of the codes of war. In silence they stared, denying the evidence of their eyes. Then those closest to Chanos reacted, surging forward, shields held aloft, to drag him to safety beyond range of the raining death. Confusion ran along the lines on both sides. Warriors and legionaries howled encouragement and anger. Caradoc pushed his mount forward, his shield raised, shouting over his shoulder to Breaca, "Gather the spears of Mona. Don't let them——"

"Get back!"

The grey mare sprang forward with her thought, slewing sideways, using the weight of a shoulder on the big bay horse. The cavalry mount crashed back, sliding on wet turf. The sky whickered and darkened. A thousand javelins fell as lethal rain, thrown by legionaries who had been waiting just for this. The riverbank sprouted staves like the spines on a hedgehog. Warriors and horses screamed—and one hound who had run forward to attack an enemy he could not possibly reach—

"Breaca, no! Leave him——"

—and a youth of the Coritani who had slain a Roman in the morning—

"Braint! No! Come back! Breaca . . . Gods, are you both insane? Gwyddhien, hold Braint. Don't let her go. Breaca, come back where it's safe. What were you thinking of?"

Breaca looked up. Caradoc was off his horse, as she was, kneeling at her side with his shield over both their heads. Javelins at the furthest reach of their arc skidded on the grass at either side. The hot, grey gaze scalded her with pain and hurt and impotent fury and the excoriating self-reproach of a leader who lets warriors die without reason. She answered in kind. "It's Hail. What would you have had me do?"

"Leave him where he lies, as we must leave them all. It was a trap. We didn't see it. Would you die here for no better reason than a hound?"

It was Hail, who was Bán; she would die for him and Caradoc knew it. She had opened her mouth to say so but Ardacos was there suddenly, a steady presence in the boiling hell. Kneeling at the beast's other side he stretched to feel for a heartbeat and said, "He's alive anyway," which is what she needed to know. With the skill of the ancestors, for which she loved him, the small man ran a practised hand over the white and crimson pulp of the wound and found what Breaca had seen as she ran out to pull the hound to cover. "His left foreleg's broken. He'll not walk again without help." He looked round. "Where's Airmid?"

Breaca said, "Behind the lines, in safety," because that was where she should have been, and heard the quality of Ardacos's silence and looked up.

"No, I'm here." Nemain, walking on earth. She, too, knelt and her fingers on the smashed and broken leg were already seeking out the detail that could lead to healing.

They were in battle; they could not give time to the wounded. Standing, Breaca said, "Keep him safe. You, too. I'll find you later." To Gwyddhien, she said, "What's happened to Braint?"

"Her man is hit."

On the riverbank, the screaming of the wounded drowned the noise of falling iron. Around the boulders, an arc of warriors and horses lay dying or dead—those who had been caught too near the river when the volleys began. The margin was so small between the ground that was safe and that which was not. Halfway from Breaca to the boulders, a wheaten-haired warrior of the Coritani lay on his belly, clawing the turf. Braint twisted and fought in Gwyddhien's grip. "Let me go to him!"

"No. One of you dead is enough. He'll die at the next volley. Nothing lives out there."

The girl was weeping, in fury as much as pain. "He will live. They have seen that we know him. They're aiming away from him. Can you not see?"

Ardacos said, "They're running out of javelins."

The air grew clear.

Caradoc said softly, "He's still alive."

A horn brayed and the death-rain ceased. The Romans rested on their shields, grinning. Along the western bank, the moans of the wounded rose in the sudden silence. A hundred Catuvellauni warriors stepped forward and hurled their only spears. On the far bank, shields were lifted in unison and the spears clattered harmlessly into the water. Braint bit Gwyddhien's hand. The tall warrior grimaced and held on tighter. "Don't throw your life away. Look at them laughing. They're trying to draw you out."

There was a need for action, for Braint and for everyone else. Breaca lifted two spears from the turf close by. To Braint, she said, "Can you hit the mark nine times out of nine?" She knew the answer.

The girl spat. Her eyes blazed. "Twelve out of twelve."

"Then take your spear and help me. But swear first you won't try to go out to him. He's dying. We can only make it sooner and mark him for the goddess. Will you swear?"

The girl swore on Briga, her namesake; an unbreakable oath. Gwyddhien released her. Breaca took her to stand at the reach of the furthest javelins and said, "Call his name."

The Coritani youth was the son of the man who had killed her mother, the man who had been Breaca's first kill. She had known it since he first came to Mona and, even so, had chosen him for the honour guard for his skills with the spear and his horsemanship. His name was Helovar. When Braint called it, he raised his eyes from the grass as a drunk man might, hearing voices in the night. At the second call, he found the source and, understanding, pushed himself up to kneeling. Two spears took him full in the chest, piercing the boiled leather jerkin. The small sound of his dying was lost in the roll of the river. The Romans cheered. The sky whickered again. A century of javelins grew around the fallen body. Three of them skidded forward to within a spear's length of Breaca's feet. She lifted the nearest, thinking to throw it back, but the shaft behind the tip was of soft iron and had folded over even as the thing gouged the earth. Without thinking, she broke the haft and put the iron in her saddlebag to melt and re-work later. Deep in her heart she was still a smith, her father's daughter.

At her side, Braint stared through silent, streaming tears. Breaca said, "He died bravely."

"He died for no reason."

"So you will not follow him. You can kill better than that." She turned to her other side, to Caradoc. "We can't stand long against this."

"I know." He, too, knew the need for action. He was leaning down from his saddle to speak to the Catuvellauni youth who was his runner. "Send word down the line that it is death to approach the boulders. We should lose no more warriors for the sake of it. Braint has shown what to do. Follow her lead if those you value lie dying."

Like Braint, the youth was weeping openly. He turned his face up to the man who was his god and had been infallible. "If they can reach us, we can reach them, too. We can throw better than them. We should be fighting back."

"No. We are too few and we have only one spear each. They should be saved for better use at another time. Pass the word."

The youth turned and ran. Breaca watched for those

who believed they could gain in reputation by daring what Caradoc of the Three Tribes and the Warrior of Mona would not, but the winnowing death of the javelins had been too cold, too heartless, and it was clear that those against whom they fought lacked any honour. Near the boulders, warriors moved back a pace save for those few who could hit the mark reliably, who gave death to their friends.

On the far side, bundles of javelins were once again passed forward through the ranks and distributed. The legionaries waited, and watched lifeblood leak from the dead. The Atrebatan traitor spoke to the commander and his word was passed forward. A thousand eyes turned on Caradoc and Breaca and the knot of their honour guards standing beneath the trees. Men spat and anointed their javelins, saying the names of those they hoped to kill. Breaca watched them, unmoved. The fire of Mona burned low within her, dulled by hate and the horror at wasted life.

A horn brayed reedily from the back of the ranks and a half-century of men converged on the boulders that Caradoc had scattered by the ford, hoisting their shields as cover. Beneath their shelter, bareheaded, unarmoured men locked oak staves under the rocks and began to roll them towards the river.

Breaca felt a passing warmth on her right side and turned. Dubornos pushed his heavyset skewbald up beside the grey mare. Breaca said, "I know. We should leave. In half a day, the slaves will have broached the ford. If we are standing here when they cross, we are dead."

He nodded assent. The singer in him brought peace when the warrior would only have brought war. In this, he was like Venutios and as valued. He said, "You have done what you can. We were only here to buy time for the runners to reach the tribes and the warriors to reach Togodubnos at the sea-river, not to defeat two legions."

"I know. And we have achieved that much. I think Togodubnos is ready." Breaca pointed through the trees to where a woman in the yellow cloak of the Trinovantes leaned against a yew. A foundering horse steamed at her side. Caradoc was already with her, listening. He looked up as Breaca approached and said, sourly, "We've found our missing legions. The Second and Ninth landed with their auxiliaries and cohorts on the far south coast. They're marching north now."

Breaca nodded. It was what she would have done. "Then we should leave and join Togodubnos before they come at our backs."

"We will do. The tribes are massing on the sea-river. Togodubnos has gathered all who are coming. He's destroyed the bridges and burned the boats but he has a guide who knows the route waiting to take us across. We must be there before nightfall to cross at low tide. If it comes and we're not there, she'll go alone."

Ardacos joined them, his face taut with the need to fight. He said, "What if the Romans follow us across? There are traitors all through the ranks of the Atrebates who will lead them in our wake. The river is only a barrier to those who do not know its ways."

The messenger shook her head. "There are none here who will tell them. Those who know the path across and wish to live are with Togodubnos. The rest are with Briga."

The group stood silent for a moment, acknowledging the dead.

Thinking forward to the battle ahead, Breaca asked, "What tribes are already there, in what numbers?"

"The Silures and the Durotriges have sent what warriors they can spare. In all, they make five thousand. The Coritani have sent one thousand and Venutios of the Brigantes, lately of Mona, has brought just over that number of his own followers."

Venutios, who had been Warrior and who, the day after he ceased to be so, had sat under a tree in the company of his successor with the burden of his new life clear in his eyes. Breaca asked, "Cartimandua has sent nothing?" The messenger shook her head. At her side, Caradoc grimaced.

"It is said she favours Rome," he said.

Breaca said, "Because you do not."

He shrugged. His eyes held hers, acknowledging nothing. She had never heard his side of the winter spent in the north with Cartimandua. It seemed unlikely she ever would. Passing over it, he said, "Every able-bodied warrior from the Trinovantes has answered the call. Last night, the warriors and dreamers of the Eceni joined them. They are not counted but my brother believes he has over twenty thousand spears, including the three thousand who wait here."

"And the Dobunni?" asked Breaca. "Has Beduoc joined us?"

The Trinovantian messenger spat. "Beduoc sent a sheaf of threshed corn back with the runners. Word has it he has thrown his weight again behind Berikos and Rome."

"Berikos is in exile."

"Not anymore." The messenger shook her head. "He journeyed to Rome requesting aid and Claudius has granted his wish. Berikos has returned to his people with the

Second and Ninth at his back to change the minds of those who would oppose him. For their part in his return, Berikos has granted the Romans corn and firewood in unlimited quantities. It is said that Beduoc has promised the same if they cross the sea-river and enter Dobunni lands."

"Where are the legions now?"

Caradoc said, "They have circled the forest-marsh between the downs and are marching north. They will be at the southern bank of the sea-river within two days at the outside. If we can't stop them, they'll cross and march on the dun. If they take it and the ports it protects, the tribes of the east are finished, and possibly all the tribes of the land."

He spoke into silence. It was not news. They had lived with this knowledge since before the Sun Hound's death. At times—when Amminios had gone to Gaul and not returned; when Berikos had been defeated and they had heard—wrongly—that he was dead—it had seemed possible they might avoid it, but they had never believed it for long.

Breaca stared out across the river, contemplating the chance of defeating four legions massed in one place. Rain smeared the sky above the Roman lines. Javelins fell sporadically when one of the defenders lost patience and moved forward. The slaves had rolled eight of the boulders into the river.

Caradoc, mounting, began to signal his runners. To Breaca and the waiting warriors of Mona, he said, "We have to hold them until nightfall. If we leave in daylight, they will see us and follow too closely. The boulders will not hold them that long. We must find something else."

The answer was obvious once the question was clear. It was without honour, but honour had been left behind when

Chanos died. Breaca raised her arm and grey cloaks began to weave through the trees towards her. "We have a dozen slingers," she said. "They can be protected by shields as the men are on the other side. If they concentrate on those without armour—the ones doing the work—they can slow them. If we can delay until dark we'll have a full night to withdraw. But they must not know we have gone."

"They won't." Airmid was there, speaking with the authority of one to whom the gods have spoken. "If the warriors of Mona can hold the river, Caradoc's people must see to the deception. Each one should light at least two campfires so that it seems as if we remain. Those who know the land best should stay until midnight, to make songs and let it be known we are girding ourselves for tomorrow's battle. The rest can ride for the sea-river and safety."

CHAPTER 27

At the eel-spate, the fires burned their lies through the night. The sea-river kept its secrets from those who would follow and held safe those whose lives depended on it. Under cover of darkness, three thousand warriors, with their horses and hounds, left one for the other, following the one guide left alive on the southern side, who led them across a low-tide swamp that promised a sucking, sodden death for any traveller who did not know the route. Long after midnight, they reached the broad river plain with its low hills and sparse scrub, readily cleared, that Togodubnos had chosen as his battleground. Fires in their thousands glimmered low in the night. Warriors in their tens of thousands slept beside them, waiting to make war on the invader in the morning. The incomers were greeted quietly, fed, and shown places to sleep—in huts for the leaders and dreamers who wished to use them, in the open for the rest. The Romans, left behind at the eel-river ford, did not notice their loss.

Breaca had chosen to sleep in the open. She woke the following dawn to the sounds and sights of twenty thousand preparing for battle. The hum of voices wrapped her like bee-flight in summer. Rising, she went in search of Macha, who had care of Hail, and found her in the nearest of the dreamers' huts, located by the smell of sage-smoke and hawthorn. Cygfa, the hound bitch bred by Odras, lay on the threshold. Since Bán's death, she had never been far from Macha. Hail lay at her side, stretched flat in the sun. Breaca knelt by his head.

"Will he live?"

"I believe so. He is strong for his years and Airmid stopped the bleeding early."

"Will he be able to hunt without a leg?"

"It has been known."

Macha had changed since Eburovic's death and her own spear-wound, but not in the ways that mattered to those who cared for her. She stood in the hut doorway, a tall, regal woman, made doubly so by the torc of the Eceni, held in waiting for the day when Breaca was no longer Warrior of the gods' isle and could return to her people as leader. Beneath the torc, on a neck-cord of silver, Macha wore the whole body of a wren with its wings spread as if in flight, and beneath those the front feet of a she-bear with the claws sheathed in copper wrapped her waist. Never had Breaca been shown so clearly the sources of Macha's power. They would have welcomed her on Mona and Maroc would have been her junior.

Hail lay sleeping in the sun at her feet, now curled like a whelp. Only by looking closely could Breaca see that his left foreleg was gone. A memory slid past her guard of Bán and the care he had taken when the hound was a whelp and close to death with the flux. She had not thought herself living in a golden age then, nor known that it might end so easily. She dug her fingers in the coarse grizzle of the great hound's mane as she did when they were going hunting and spoke his name, as Bán would have done. He slumbered on, unmoving. Breaca looked up.

"Why won't he wake?"

"We gave him poppy so that we could cut the leg away without pain. He will wake by noon."

"We will be fighting then. He will try to join us. You mustn't let him."

"He is bound to Airmid. She held his dream while we cut the leg. He will stay with her." Macha knelt at his other side. A shaft of morning sun made light of her years, skinning away the austerity of the elder. She smiled, and was the caring voice at the hearth, the caress in the dark night, loved as a second mother.

Cradling the hound's head on her knees, Macha said, "Your feathers have multiplied."

"These?" Breaca touched a fingertip to the fresh kill-feathers at her temples. The quills were golden, dyed with wild garlic, signifying Roman dead. They rattled as she shook her head. "The honour guard make them each night around the fires. They feel it a dishonour if I don't wear them. They will make no difference in what is to come."

"They make a difference to those who follow you, and not just the spears of Mona. There is no-one here who has killed as many Romans as you have. It gives the rest something to aim for." A hand reached out and smoothed Breaca's face, as her father had done once, long ago, after the first killing. "Why does it hurt so?"

It should not have been so clear. If Macha could see it, others would too. Breaca said, "They broke the honour of a challenge and then they threw unarmoured slaves into battle, not caring how many died." It had hurt all of them, killing men forced to work. Breaca had thought of Iccius. Others had kin who had been stolen by slavers.

Macha, understanding, asked, "How many died?"

"We killed nearly fifty before nightfall for the loss of one slinger."

"You did what was necessary."

"We still killed them. And then we abandoned the field of battle." That, too, had hurt. "Already they are celebrating the defeat of Caradoc."

"You knew you would never hold them at the eel-spate. It was always too small and you too few."

"I know. It still sits badly—a warrior should not leave the field before the battle is over."

Macha smiled, becoming the elder again. "You brought the battle with you. They will follow. There is nowhere else to cross but here. And you will not leave here unless it is won."

"True. And I think we can win, if the gods are with us."

Around them, all the warriors who had answered Togodubnos's call to arms prepared for war. They seemed as numerous as the Romans, too many to count, but in the coming battle, leadership would count for more than numbers. Before she slept, Breaca had been to the Eceni fires and spoken with Gunovic and the other spear-leaders; as they had against Berikos, they would unite with the spears of Mona and follow her lead. Only one man had been missing whom she had expected to find. To Macha, she said, "Why is 'Tagos not here?"

"Silla bore him a child, a daughter, on the day the runners came with the call to war. The infant died in her first day. 'Tagos was heartbroken; he had thought to be a father if he could not be a warrior. He has stayed to comfort Silla."

"Or to be comforted by her?" Breaca had not known that Silla had a liking for 'Tagos. Had the girl lived, Breaca would have been her aunt. If she died, today, or any other day, the girl would have ruled the Eceni after Silla. Breaca was not certain she wanted 'Tagos's child to rule anything. She looked at Macha and saw the same echoed in her eyes.

Macha said, "They comfort each other, I think. It makes no difference to the outcome of the battle. 'Tagos is neither warrior nor dreamer and we have enough of both here not to need an extra voice around the fire. And here is one who wishes to meet you—" She stepped out of the doorway. From within came the meaty smell of pine torches soaked in bear's fat. A tall youth with tail feathers of the grey falcon in his hair stepped into the light, blinking.

"Efnís!" They embraced. "It's good to see you." Breaca stepped back to look at him. "You have a new dreaming."

"It came with the last moon." He was shyly pleased. Only one dreamer in thousands dreamed with the falcon. His face had grown stronger for it.

Breaca had found a cache of freshly buried gold and silver coins when they made their first ambush. One of them bore the mark of a falcon. By chance, she had kept it. She tipped it from her pouch and gave it to him. "You should come to Mona. There is so much to learn."

"I will. When this is over."

She left him with Macha and Maroc, planning the means by which the dreamers could call on the gods to aid the battle. Everywhere else, as far as the eye could see, men and women in their thousands tied up their hair and wove in the kill-feathers, and painted fresh marks on their shields and on the shoulders of their horses that the gods and their friends might recognize them in the chaos of the killing field. Children raced between the fires, carrying messages and paints and whetstones and all the other necessary precursors to warfare that a warrior might need but might not wish to carry. Most of the children were within a year of their long-nights and had begged for a chance to fight in the battle. It would not be allowed, but they were permitted instead to help, to see how the kill-feathers were woven, to hear the songs and the prayers and to learn all that they could of courage and strategy from the example of their elders. In the battle, they would carry water to those resting behind the active lines. In this lay their best hope of honour and fame. Each of them knew, had heard in long tales by firelight, of how Breaca, Warrior of Mona, had won her spear in true battle at the age of twelve. A great many twelve-year-olds had set their hearts on achieving the same, or besting it, in the days to come.

From Macha's hut, Breaca walked the horse lines in search of the grey mare. On leaving the eel-spate, the battle mount had not only carried Breaca but had taken Hail across her withers—a weight half as great as a man—and still raced through the night to safety. Even as they ran, it had been clear that she was lame. At Togodubnos's encampment, Breaca had called for torches and had found the mare's tendons bowed out and hot to the touch on both front legs. She had spent time standing with the beast in a small tributary of the river, but the damage was greater than cold water alone could cure. Now, walking along the rows of waiting horses, Breaca found Airmid there ahead of her, wrapping shaved willow around the affected limbs. She crouched down to feel the damage. Her palm came away steaming.

Airmid said, "She won't be fit to ride today."

"Will she ever?"

"I don't know."

"Will she lose the foal?" The mare was four months' pregnant and the foal would have been the greatest battle horse Mona had ever seen.

"I don't think so, but we can't be sure. She needs rest and good food and she will get that only if the Romans are driven out."

"We will do it."

"Good." Airmid stood, pushing her hair out of her eyes. There was a brief, awkward pause. They never said goodbye on the day of battle; it had been so since the first fight against Amminios and this was not the day to break with tradition. Breaca stood still, filled with the need to hold the moment. Around them the noise of the camp rose to a peak as the preparations for battle neared completion. Close by, Ardacos marshalled a handful of children, giving lessons on safety and the need of warriors for water; further back, Cumal kicked a campfire into smouldering ash and lifted a cooking pot clear. Gwyddhien waited at a discreet distance, not for Breaca.

Airmid said, "I dreamed a snake with the head of a spear that killed an eagle. It pierced the body beneath the left wing, taking out the heart. You should remember it."

"I will do. Thank you."

They embraced in silence, nothing left to be said. Braint met Breaca as she walked away. The girl shone like a newly honed blade. She said, "Gunovic wants you. He has a new horse."

Breaca grinned. "Gunovic always has new horses." She remembered a message given earlier. "You should go to see Macha. She has the skull of a wildcat. If you meet her at the dreamers' hut, she will give it to you."

"Thank you. I will." The wildcat was Braint's dream; even without the skull, one could see it. They, too, embraced. The girl said, "Go safely."

"You, too."

Breaca's throat was cramped from too many unspoken partings. She walked upriver in search of Gunovic. For years, he had been telling her to train a new battle mount and she had not, feeling it a slight on the grey mare and arrogance before the gods. It did not surprise her that he had done it instead.

She found him in the upper reaches of the stream, cooling his hands in preparation for a day of fighting. Two horses grazed nearby, one a grey so pale as to be almost white, the other an ugly, big-boned brown colt with a coat already thick for winter and a nose that curved outwards, like a bear's. The smith splashed out of the water, grinning, and made a sweeping presentation of his gift. The grey was his and had been so for years. He would not offer her that. She stared at the brown horse and then at him.

"Gunovic, that's a bear, not a war-horse. It would be good for drawing a cart but it's not going to be useful in battle. In any case, I don't ride horses that have feet wider than mine are long."

"He has feet no bigger than your mare's. It's the hair about them makes them seem big. Get up on him and I'll race you to the tree and back. Then see if you want him."

They raced. Breaca won, or the horse did; she had put little effort into it. They tried out with shield and spear and sword. The bear-horse did not anticipate her movements as the grey mare had done but he was fast and turned well and knew what he was supposed to do. She dismounted and checked his teeth and found he was just four years old. She frowned, thinking.

"You've been south of the sea-river seeing to the defences or bargaining with the Atrebates for more than half the time since he first had a bit in his mouth. Who else has trained him?"

"Macha. She bred him from one of Eburovic's mares."

Breaca bit her lip. It could have been no-one else. "He's good."

"He's the best. With him, you can defeat the Romans."

He was the third one to say so. Breaca made an inward sign to Nemain that she not take the words as presumption and turned her new mount towards the river in search of Caradoc.

Caradoc was not hard to find once she knew what to look for. He had abandoned the white of the Ordovices in favour of the multicoloured cloak of the hero Cassivellaunos, newly made for him by the weavers of the Catuvellauni to include the colours of each tribe that had joined them. It drew eyes wherever he rode. Breaca had been offered the same and had declined it, keeping to the grey of Mona and the bloodred mark of the serpent-spear. Her hair was banner enough; in the sun it burned like living fire and the wind was rising. Come the battle, charging the enemy, it would fly like a flag.

She rode down towards the water's edge on fresh green turf with blackberry bushes in full fruit to one side. They should have been removed but had been left with their fruit intact as an offering to the gods of harvest. By chance, they marked the first fording place along the sea-river, too far inland for the Roman ships to venture, but not so far that a bridge could not be thrown across with ease, or javelins reach the defending lines.

Togodubnos had worked on the south side for some time, cutting trees to deny cover and firewood to the enemy and digging pits which he covered in brush to confuse the cavalry. He had destroyed the bridges that existed and burned those boats that were not brought across. A handful of charred and broken skeletons smoked fitfully on the southern shore. On the day before they arrived, he had made a ceremony with the dreamers and had cast into the river a fine bronze shield, worked at both ends with the shape of a horse, in offering to Nemain that she remember they held the water sacred and did not fight across it to dishonour her, but rather to ask her aid in defending their land.

Breaca joined Caradoc by the ford.

"Breaca, welcome." He turned, sharply alert, like a hound on the morning of a hunt. Everything about him had sharpened. The culmination of his life was upon him, and possibly his death. She had never considered the possibility that he might die, but now he grinned and, perversely, her mind made of him a grinning corpse, the skull flayed to whiteness, the teeth smashed back to the roots, the gold hair dulled to mud. The thought stalled her, twisting her gut as nothing else had done. Had Airmid been there, she could have said if it was a true vision. Lacking her, Breaca could only wait until it passed. She felt sick.

Caradoc's grin faded. His eyes searched her face. "You should wear a helmet," he said, having access to her mind. The wind lifted his own uncovered hair.

"As you do?" It came out more archly than it should have done. "If the gods wish us dead, a finger's breadth of iron will not stop it. In the meantime, it is better for you and I to be seen by those who follow."

"Oh, I think we will be seen." Humour had always been a shield for him, an automatic defence. He rallied it now, studying her horse with open curiosity. "You think the Romans will fear you more if you ride a bear?"

She, too, could hide behind mockery. "We could race to the trees and back," she offered. "I'll wager my shield against yours that an Eceni bear-horse can outrun a Roman cavalry mount."

"Really?" They had never raced. From the first winter amongst the Eceni through the competitions of Mona to the games at his father's funeral they had avoided it. On Mona, on the night of the choosing, they had competed against the gods and the dreamers but not each other. He tilted his head, considering, and she saw the humour wane. "Maybe not. My father taught me never to bet against certainties. And the time for racing may be over—now and for all time." He jutted his chin towards the river and said softly, "The enemy are here."

She had heard them all morning, the second noise behind the haze. Now she looked out across the river to the reality that the business of her own camp had hidden. The sight was not as awe-inspiring as she had feared; on the far bank, the standards of two legions had been raised but barely a single century of men stood ready. Behind them, a rippling snake of polished armour wound back to the east. The sound of horns and marching feet carried faintly.

Breaca studied the standards more closely. "Still only the Fourteenth and Twentieth," she said. "They have marched since dawn, if not before it. They will fight with less sleep than us."

Caradoc nodded, his horse sleek beside hers. "They are alone. And this time we outnumber them." It was what mattered most.

"Not for long." Togodubnos rode up to Caradoc's right side. "Sentius Saturninus is marching north at the head of the Second and Ninth. If we can defeat these two today, we will have as many again to contend with tomorrow, possibly sooner than that."

Togodubnos had aged in the month since the meeting on the salt marsh. The weight of invasion dragged at his eyes as if he carried the fears for all their deaths. Behind him, an argument reached its climax and a single warrior of the Trinovantes broke from a knot of others, followed by a straight-backed child on a small bay pony. As they neared, Breaca saw that the warrior was a woman and in a condition that should have kept her from battle.

She would have spoken out but she saw Caradoc's face and the curt shake of his head. Togodubnos turned and it was clear that his burden was not all caused by Rome. He made the formal introduction sketchily, as if time did not allow for anything more. "You know my son Cunomar, and

Odras, his mother. She has come to fight the invaders who would defile her homeland." He smiled, wearily. "I find that I can command ten thousand spears but not one woman."

"You should visit the Ordovices," said Caradoc, dryly. "You would not even try."

The woman rode close to him and, as Caradoc leaned over to kiss her, it was evident that the spark that had lived between them in a calf fair so many years ago did so still. Breaca thought briefly of Cartimandua of the Brigantes who favoured Rome because Caradoc did not, and a woman of the Ordovices who had given him a daughter, and wondered if either of them had seen him in the presence of Odras.

Caradoc was speaking. ". . . wise choice for one carrying an unborn child?"

Odras's head was up. He was not the first to ask that question. "The wisest of all. There are five months yet to go before I give birth. I do not risk the child. And I would have my daughter live free of the Roman yoke—or not at all."

She was the first one to acknowledge aloud that they might not win. All three heard it and let it pass.

To his brother, Togodubnos said, "You always said she could ride better than any of the men. Five of her cousins ride as members of my honour guard. She has vowed to out-fight them today and prove it."

"Good." Smiling, Caradoc spun his horse. To Odras, he said, "I will lead the Ordovices and the Catuvellauni on the left flank. If you find the battle too quiet in the centre with my brother, you are welcome to join me." He reached down to lay a hand on Cunomar's shoulder. "You would be better with Macha and Maroc." He was careful to avoid reference to children. "They will guide your part in the battle." The child had his mother's wide brown eyes. He looked up into the face of his uncle, the hero of three tribes, and nodded. He was not yet a warrior, but his heart was set on fame.

The morning came together with the certainty of a dream. Cunomar was taken back to the reserve lines to join the other children. Odras joined Togodubnos and sat her horse in the front line by the blackberry bushes with the greater mass of the Trinovantes and the small delegations from the Coritani and the Cornovii bunched behind them. Breaca rode upstream to the right flank, leading the Eceni and the warriors of Mona. Caradoc blew his horn to call the Catuvellauni, the Ordovices, the Durotriges and the Silures into a mass on the left, facing the stronger right flank of the enemy. Venutios brought his black-cloaked Brigantes to join the left wing with Breaca and she was glad. Waiting mounted at the head of them, she eased the serpent-blade in its sheath and began the inner search that would kindle the fires of certainty, seeking beyond herself for the thoughts of the dreamers to help her. For the first time in her adult life, her palm throbbed as it had done after the death of her mother.

On the far bank, horns howled in staccato rhythms. Men shouted and blocks of legionaries wheeled. The first cohorts of the XIVth and XXth legions ranged themselves in ordered lines as they had done at a narrower sea-river and, almost unobserved, the battle began.

CHAPTER 28

The ground vibrated to the rhythms of war. The Crow
smelled blood and wanted to join. Bán spoke to him, quiet
words of calm, and they were within sight of the wounded
at the back of the battle lines before he realized he was
speaking Gaulish; that in this place, at this time, his own
tongue had deserted him. He searched inside, for the shade
of Iccius or his father, for the memory of the elder grandmother, for any sign that what he did was wrong. He had
searched in the same way in Germany when word had first
come that Caligula had died under a hail of knives and that
Claudius, made emperor by the Praetorian Guard, planned
to continue with the invasion.

Later, as feuding and revolt threatened to topple the
new incumbent, Bán had grown complacent, believing that
the Senate was weak and, lacking the driving vision of a
Caesar or an Alexander, would never set its heart on conquest. Then in early summer the orders had come to muster
for war and the Ala V Gallorum had ridden east to join the
Legio II Augusta north of Argentorate, and then up to

the channel port of Juliobona and the ships that lay idle at the river mouth, awaiting final orders.

It was a long wait. In the early days Bán had ridden the Crow through the trees to the Gaulish shrine of Cernunnos, where the antlered god of the Gauls stood carved on a single massive slab of granite, holding court among the beasts of the forest. He had brought bread and a new horn-handled knife and left them beneath the stone together with his request for guidance. In the silence afterwards, he had feared that Nemain had deserted him for his duplicity and had spent a night alone under the full moon, praying for her return. When she did not come, he had taken an offering to the shrine of Jupiter Optimus Maximus, the soldiers' god, and left it on a pile of others. He did not make a living sacrifice—his gods would not thank him for spilling another's blood—but he left half of his saved pay and, later, took the bulk of the rest down to the water and gave it to Manannan, god of the sea.

For days his own voice echoed, hollowly forlorn, asking for help and none came. Corvus, who knew him best, had no answers but care and the logic of the legionary. He had spoken of it one night over wine and roast quail. The bronze Horus looked down on them, keeper of memories.

"You are one of us now. You have taken the soldier's oath, which is binding beyond all others. If the gods wished you to break that, they would never have let you take it in the first place."

Bán tilted his wine until the surface became a mirror, reflecting the lamps. Circular pools of light splashed away into the dark. His eyes were wide and fathomless. "Would you fight against your mother's people?" he asked at last.

"I did—in Pannonia. Those were my grandmother's people. They are our allies now."

"Will the Eceni ever be allies of Rome?"

"If they have any sense. If you read Caesar, it was a leader of the Ceni Magni who paid him homage when he invaded and was granted trade rights in return. If you allow for poor translation, the Eceni and the Ceni Magni could be one."

"They will not be left with trade rights now. Aulus Plautius has been promised the governorship of all Britannia."

"As Galba was governor of Upper Germany. It did not make Civilis's people into slaves and the Chatti still run free. These things have their limits. If the Eceni do not fight, they will not be enslaved, nor their lands occupied. Rome has no quarrel with your people."

"The Eceni will fight."

"How can you be sure?"

"They are steeped in the legend of Cassivellaunos and the many-coloured cloak. If Togodubnos and his brother call the tribes of the east to war, the Eceni will not hold back."

"Even after the death of Breaca and your parents?"

"Even so."

"If Caradoc and Togodubnos are both there, you will have your chance for vengeance against the sons of the Sun Hound."

"I know. Perhaps that's why I must go."

They sat in silence. The hour was late. Beyond the walls of Corvus's quarters, the world slept. The lamps ran out of oil one by one until the last guttered alone against the dark. Corvus reached his hand over Bán's. "If the wine has given no answers, the night will have fewer still. We should sleep."

The hand beneath his turned over and the smile was one he knew, stretching past the confusion. Bán said "Just sleep?" and the lamp guttered out before Corvus could answer, and they chose not to relight it but to fumble their way to bed and beyond in the sympathetic dark.

They slept in the end and woke with nothing resolved. Nothing could ever be resolved, Bán had realized that. He lived as two people: one was a shadow, living in the past, the other loved and lived and had taken oaths that bound him to the present. He would learn to live, in the end, with his duality, or he would die.

Bán had slept better in the nights after that, if not as well as he might, and when the order to embark had finally come he had taken ship with the rest, guiding the Crow up the gangway and into the hold, promising him a short crossing and good weather.

He had lied about both; the crossing had been hell and had lasted from before dawn until after midnight. For nearly a full day, Bán stood on deck, retching violently and wishing he were dead. They had been backing against the tide, the rowers exhausted and the sea fighting their every move, when the shooting star crossed their bows, showing the way to land. He had given thanks to Nemain, whose night it was, and to Jupiter, who ruled the heavens, for sending so clear a sign. Later, after they had landed, he had heard that Civilis and Rufus and the men of the XXth and XIVth who had sailed from the mouth of the Rhine had crossed in half a morning and landed in warm sunshine to no opposition. In the south, the Ala V Gallorum spent two days under the command of Vespasian, legate of the IInd Augusta, subduing

Vectis, the island that lay off the coast and was supposed already to have spoken for Rome. After that, they had marched for eight days without break to reach the sea-river where the tribes were massing in defence. Rumour had it that Togodubnos and Caradoc had raised a confederacy greater than the one that had fought against Caesar. The gossip did not take the trouble to name the tribes involved but in his heart Bán knew the Eceni would be there. He spoke to the Crow in Gaulish and reminded himself he was Roman. It sat less easily in his soul than it had done.

A horn wailed at the head of the column. The cavalry drew neatly to a halt. To their left, the first cohort of the Legio II Augusta did likewise. Further commands dispersed them, the cavalry to the right, the legionaries of the first two cohorts to pitch their tents out of sight of the wounded and prepare for battle. Others, further back, were sent out in armed parties of eight to forage for wood. The centuries to the rear, under the command of an engineer, began to dig fresh latrines; the eye-pricking stench of those further forward was only partially smothered by the gore of battle. The cavalry were signalled to rest their horses and await further orders.

Bán threaded the Crow carefully between chopped tree stumps, wary of traps. Ahead of him, Civilis held his cohort of Batavians grouped and ready; each alternate man mounted, those between walking forward on foot, scouring the ground ahead for pits and spikes and sharpened stones. Bán skirted a knee-deep pit marked with fragments of white bone. Close to it, it became clear that the markers were parts of a skull, cracked like an eggshell; the Batavians had never let go of their tribal roots.

Civilis sat his horse ahead of the others, watching the river. He went bareheaded after the manner of his people and his weapons were barely Roman. The spear on his arm would have done credit to a smith of the Eceni. He saw Bán coming and waved him up. "Where's Corvus?"

"With the standards. Aulus Plautius has called a command meeting."

"Bastard." The German made a gesture that would have got him flogged were it seen by a higher rank. "He lost Rufus, did you hear?"

"Lost him? How?"

"Sent him out on a foray, undermanned and underarmed." His voice became effetely nasal. " 'The barbarians don't have the stomach for battle. They scatter their crops and run at the sight of a real army.' " He spat with venom, his voice dropping back a register. "Ignorant Latin bastard."

"I'm sorry." Bán clasped the arm of his friend. A small, hidden part of him exulted at the defeat of Rome. The greater part shied at the memories of the bodies they had found of Atrebates along the route. All had been men known to be loyal to Berikos, working as spies amongst the Trinovantes and their allies; each one had been found with his throat cut and the mark of the sun hound carved on his chest.

Bán had despised Berikos as a weak-willed traitor but had not realized he was so hated by the Trinovantes. He wondered, then, if they mutilated the warriors whose land it was, what they might do to the Gauls, Batavians and Romans who had no right to set foot on it at all. He imagined Rufus dying the dreamer's death and the thought made him ill.

"Did they find his body afterwards?" he asked.

"Skewered to a tree with his balls in his mouth and the hell-mark of the barbarians cut into his chest." Civilis had been weeping; it showed in his eyes. "The fools sent out half a cohort in tens and twenties before they realized they were facing more than a handful of armed fanatics."

"They'll know it now." Bán looked across the river. Warriors in uncountable numbers fought at the water's edge, or took time further back to rest from recent fighting. Cloaks in colours he had never seen and whose meaning he had long forgotten mingled with the white of the Ordovices, the iron grey of Mona and the hated yellow of the Trinovantes. With a jolt, he saw that the western flank, beyond the grey, was solidly blue, the colour of the sky after rain. Pain crushed his chest, sucking his breath away. A moment later, he was made whole by the sight of one man with harvest-bright hair and a cloak of many colours who rode a flashy bay horse into the river and drew the other colours after him.

Civilis was looking where his eyes had been. He said carefully, "They are your people?"

"Yes. The ones in blue." Bán was distant. The world had moved back a pace. Iccius was close to him for the first time since Amminios died. His father stood nearby, smiling. He could see through them both only with difficulty. To Civilis, he said, "The yellow are the Trinovantes, except the one in the patchwork cloak. That's Caradoc. The black-haired giant in the yellow cloak with the sun hound on his shield is Togodubnos. If we kill them both, we have ripped out the beating heart of the Trinovantes. Our way will be clear to the dun."

"Good. Then I think the Batavian horse warriors should

be the ones to do the ripping. We have a score to settle with those two and it would sit badly if they were to be killed by someone else before we got there."

Across the river, the patch-cloaked figure of Caradoc backed his horse out of the water and rode along the bank. Bán narrowed his eyes, seeing a thing and not believing it and then finding it was true. Carefully he said, "I can tell you who killed Rufus. Caradoc is riding his horse."

"I know. He will die on my spear and his skull will adorn my belt even as his soul serves as slave to Rufus in the lands of the gods." Civilis sounded too much like the Chatti. Grinning, he looked out across the water and sucked his breath through his teeth, speculatively. "That river," he said, to no-one in particular. "Would you say it runs slower or faster than the Rhine?"

The push came in the late afternoon and was executed in classic style. Two cohorts of the IXth joined with fresh, unwearied men of the XIVth and XXth at the river's edge and made a concerted effort to take the ford. In iron ranks, they stepped forward through the water, shields linked in an unyielding line. Warriors and legionaries fell in their dozens and were trampled into the riverbed. The bank on the far side, long since churned to red-stained slurry, began to slide out into the river, flushed by the flowing lifeblood.

The warriors of the Trinovantes took the brunt of the attack, hurling themselves in waves against the rock of Roman shields. The defenders had seen the two new legions and knew what they meant. It had not noticeably affected their courage. When the horns urged fresh cohorts into the line, extending it downstream into the deeper water, Caradoc led the mass of Catuvellauni and all the warriors of the eastern flank into the river to hold them. War horns brayed. Warriors howled their death-songs. Horses and hounds fought to kill. Legionaries screamed in triumph and in death. The crescendo of war rose to a climax and stayed there, painfully. When it could get no louder, when the horns were impossible to hear and commands were relayed solely by the waving of the standards, when every warrior of Togodubnos's confederacy was committed to the river, Aulus Plautius, commander of the invasion forces, issued his second command.

The Batavians, as they had prayed, were the linchpin. Civilis had been given a woman of the Atrebates to lead him. Bán was seconded as interpreter. It was his first foray into battle for Rome and Corvus was nowhere near. He felt the absence as he might know the loss of a tooth, a nagging gap that came back whenever there was quiet.

There was no quiet once the signal came. The Atrebatan led them east along the riverbank, past the stumps of felled trees and into thorn-scrub that would have flayed the horses' legs had the woman not known the route through. They rode in single file in silence—a full cohort of Batavians and one erstwhile Eceni warrior, now a citizen of Rome. The river bent to the north. They followed it round. The havoc of battle boiled behind them, the noise becoming no less with the distance.

"Here." The woman pointed. "It widens and the flow is slower. Also, they will not see you. Go well and kill the Sun Hound's whelps."

Bán found himself redundant. Civilis had no need of an interpreter. The woman's words could not have been more clear had she spoken in German. Joyfully, the Batavian hummed his war-song. Already he was counting the dead he would send after Rufus to be his servants in the other world. He turned in his saddle to check his weapons. His men did the same. The woman grinned and dissolved into the scrub.

"Here." Civilis passed Bán a length of linen bandage. "Tie your sword in or you'll lose it."

"Thank you." Bán watched a man looping the linen round his sword-hilt and then through his girth straps and copied him. Coming from the Rhine—and hating it—he had never asked the Crow to swim. The horse stared at the water and snored a warning.

Civilis dismounted. His horse, knowing what was coming, edged towards the water. He turned in the saddle, grinning. "Think you can do it?"

"Of course." Caradoc was on the far bank; his warriors would be the first to face them. Nothing mattered but that Bán should be there to witness his death; it was part of the promise to Iccius and his father. And he was not going to be outdone by a German. He slid down from the saddle and tightened the girth. The Crow looked at him sideways, showing the white of his eye.

Men gathered in groups of ten along the water's edge. Civilis raised his arm and dropped it, sharply. "Let's go."

In the last moment before he entered the water, Bán remembered Breaca and the river race. The river was warm and tasted of blood. It embraced him, womblike, and sucked him down. He sank and felt the Crow's feet churn past his head and pushed himself upwards again. Somewhere, deep in his ears, he heard his mother singing. He broached the surface. The Crow swam with bared teeth. Foam fell from his muzzle and was swept away in strings on the current. Bán held on to his neck-strap and kicked with his outside leg. The far bank rose up to meet them.

"Mount. Don't talk. Draw your weapon and follow me."

Civilis was a changed man. His hair streamed down his back, held away from his face by the war knot above the right ear. He rode low in the saddle with his spear-tip trailing on the ground. The Batavian horses prowled like hounds. Crow danced on hooftip, snorting. Bán swore in three languages and calmed him. They followed the riverbank round the corner and emerged in sight of the battle. A thousand enemy warriors faced away from them, presenting their backs for the kill. Civilis fixed a linen strip to his spear-haft and raised it. At the command post on the opposite side, a standard dipped and waved and tilted twice to the west in reply. Civilis waved acknowledgement and turned to his men. The signal needed no translation; the legions at the ford were losing their battle but the IInd had crossed the river upstream and was in place in the west; it was the duty of the Batavians to draw as much attention away from them as possible.

Those were the orders but their hearts took it further. Beyond duty, the Batavians had a score to settle with Caradoc and the man rode in the van of the enemy, separated from the rearward lines by a thousand warriors or more. Whatever the courage and fighting skills of the Batavians, if they attacked from behind they would never see their prey; they needed a means to draw him round. Civilis's smile was savage. He gave the hand signals they had agreed upon and added one that was new. Grinning, the men of his cohort swung away from the river towards the reserve lines of the enemy. In horror, Bán grabbed at Civilis as he went past.

"You can't mean that." His words were lost in the chaos. The Batavian bent and put his mouth to his ear.

"It's necessary. If you can't stomach it, go back. We don't need you."

"No, I'm staying. But I'll not do that."

"Suit yourself." He was already gone, racing his mount to the horse lines. Bán watched until the killing began and then, retching, forced the Crow forward to join the rear of the milling cavalry. He had come to kill warriors, to avenge the deaths of his kin; nothing on earth would persuade him to take his revenge on their mounts.

The Batavians had no such scruples. A horse, when wounded, screams louder than any man. Forty horses with their tendons cut, their guts opened and their flanks carved to the bone screamed above the thunder of battle. Those not wounded panicked and broke their tethers. Some were unhobbled and able to run. The remainder broke their legs trying to do so and added to the noise. It would have been impossible not to hear it, not to feel sick at the sound. Bán leaned weakly on the Crow's neck and spewed his guts on the ground. Even the Romans, labouring in the lines, paused to listen.

The effect on the defenders was shattering. First in ones and twos and then in hundreds, the mass of Silures, Durotriges and Ordovices, and finally Caradoc and his Catuvellauni, turned towards the sounds of slaughter coming from behind their lines. They hesitated, caught between the need to hold the ford and the equal need to meet the fresh invasion.

A cry went up in a different note. There were mares among the injured and some of them were pregnant. A

Batavian warrior galloped the length of the horse lines with his spear held aloft, an unborn foal writhing mutely on the haft-head. He could have done no more damage if the dying beast had been a child. Calling down vengeance and death, the warriors of four tribes and a great wedge of the Trinovantes abandoned the battle at the river and kicked their battle mounts at the new enemy. The noise of their howling drowned that of the dying horses.

The Batavians numbered five hundred, a full cohort. The Britons outnumbered them hundreds to one. Caradoc pushed through, surrounded by the small knot of white-cloaked Ordovices that formed his honour guard, all picked from among his daughter's relatives. Half of them were women and all had given birth to at least one child. The dead foal became their standard, stolen and desecrated by the enemy—an act of sacrilege for which there could only be one answer. They cut through until they reached it and took alive the man who had borne it aloft. His death, impaled on his own spear, was slower than any on the field that day and clearly visible to the invaders. The Batavians, seeing it, fought with the ferocity of cornered bears; the horse guard could have done no better. Still, they fell like dead trees in a storm. Two hundred and thirty Batavian warriors died in less time than they had taken to cross the river. The remainder, led by Civilis, fought a bloody retreat back to the water. There, seventy of them formed a rearguard while the rest gathered in groups to swim across.

Bán was amongst the last to leave. The Crow fought him all the way to the water. The colt had smelled the death of other horses and become impossible to handle, killing indiscriminately. At least one Batavian had died under the flailing feet before the rest learned that the safe place to be was behind him or far to the side. Even at the end, with the madness abating, none of them would swim beside him. Bán used the flat of his sword on the colt's flanks and forced him into the water. The current caught them and spun them downstream. The horse struggled, thrashed and surged forward. Bán swam at his side, holding his sword in his right hand, letting the water wash it clean of blood and his own vomit and the screaming horror of sacrilege. The slaughter of the horses had numbed him to everything that had followed. He had killed his own kind and knew nothing of it. He had not seen Caradoc, except as a swirling mess of colour enclosed in a ring of lethal, screaming white. He had seen his enemy kill, but had not seen him die. His ghosts told him he had failed.

On the far bank, a Batavian hand thrust Bán into the saddle and the Crow, without intervention from its rider, followed Civilis as he led them back to their place in the lines. From there, dizzily, Bán made his way across the field behind the resting men of the XIVth to join the Ala V Gallorum who had gathered near the standard. Aulus Plautius was within sight, and Sentius Saturninus, who had led the southern landings. The legates and senior tribunes of each legion were gathered about them. Corvus sat his horse at the head of the cavalry, waiting. His face was pinched and white. They saluted, each according to his rank.

"You're alive," said Corvus.

"It seems so."

"Caradoc lives."

"I know. Civilis killed the horses."

"It happens in war."

"It should not. It goes against the gods."

"Then the gods have spoken to tell us so. Look."

The battlefield spread out before them like a drawing in sand. Bán had eyes only for the eastern side, where half a cohort of Batavians lay dead, their bodies already stripped of armour and weapons. One man stood rigidly upright, his helmet on the ground before him. From this distance, it was not possible to see if he still lived. A second, denser straggle of bodies was piled at the river's edge where the rearguard had given their lives for their brothers. Bán reeled at the scale of the slaughter.

"We failed. I'm sorry."

"No. You were only the diversion. It is the Second that has failed. They were a full legion and they should have broken through while you held the attention of Caradoc and his warriors."

"What happened?"

"The Eceni and the warriors of Mona hold the western flank. They are as many as a legion, and as solid. Vespasian has failed."

"The Eceni?" The words rang hollow in his ears. The rest washed over him, devoid of all meaning.

"Yes. I'm sorry. You should look, Bán. You can't change it by hiding your eyes."

Bán did not want to look. From the first sight of blue cloaks, his mind had erased for him the possibility of Eceni warriors killing and being killed, of Eceni dead left afterwards for the scavengers, of himself meeting a known face in battle. It took as great an effort of will as he had ever known to turn his head to the west, to look in detail at the upper fording place where the men of the IInd had crossed to the northern bank.

It was further away than he had imagined. At this distance, the thread of the river became a spill of molten iron in the low evening light. Figures massed and came apart and it was impossible to tell man from woman or adult from child. Only the legions were clear from their helmets and shields, and the solid wall of warriors that opposed them from their flowing cloaks—iron grey for Mona, blue for the Eceni and green striped with black for the Coritani. They fought as one body and the leading cohorts broke against them as a wave breaks on a cliff, losing men and making no headway. Then, as they watched, a mass of warriors in gorse-flower yellow galloped along the riverbank to fall on the legion from the rear.

"Gods, that's Togodubnos. He'll go through them like a knife."

"No. They have seen him. Look."

The IInd were seasoned fighters. Even as the first high note of the horn floated up above the battle, those watching saw the shimmer and break as every alternate man stepped out of the fighting line and turned back-to-back with his comrades to face the new enemy. It was a beautiful manoeuvre, executed well; shields linked and came up like the scales on a snake, swords and helmets dipped and flashed, and the new line took the shock of Togodubnos's attack and held against it, shrinking only slightly in length as the living stepped sideways to close the gaps left by the dead. The yellow-cloaked warriors fought in tight formation and the mark of the sun hound, yellow on white, showed even to those on the far side of the river. The losses were greater amongst the legionaries than the warriors.

Bán said, "Togodubnos won't let up. They will carve them to pieces unless Plautius sends them reinforcements."

"Which is why he is doing so."

Even as they spoke, a standard swung from left to right and dipped down to the river. The four cohorts of the IXth that it commanded had been waiting for just such a signal. They surged forward to the water in a single block, crossing shoulder-deep to come up on the band of Trinovantes from behind. The warriors, finding themselves assailed from two sides by infantry, galloped along the riverbank, outpacing the enemy with ease.

The legionaries did not follow; their orders were otherwise. The ranks of the IInd stood ahead of them, every man exhausted. The IXth were fresh and eager to prove themselves. They formed rows behind their comrades and clashed their swords on their shields in readiness. Horns howled throughout the length of the IInd legion. To a man, the cohorts facing the bulk of the Eceni disengaged, stepped back and spread apart, each legionary a spear's length from his neighbour. The horn sounded a second time and— raggedly, because manoeuvres executed in the push of battle rarely acquire the polish of the parade ground and the Eceni gave no quarter—the men of the IXth moved through the gaps between the lines to take up the van, closing ranks again in tight fighting formation. Behind them, the spent and battle-weary men of the IInd retreated in ordered blocks back to the river and began to cross in safety.

The fresh cohorts were outnumbered as greatly as those they were relieving, and the warriors they opposed had scented victory and drew strength from it. The fighting resumed with renewed ferocity. The band of Trinovantes that had attacked the rear circled back and came in along the riverbank, a wedge of yellow in a sea of grey and blue. A century of the IXth wheeled sideways to cut them off. The rest held their lines steady until the IInd had safely crossed, and began a slow-stepped retreat.

Bán bit back on his knuckles. Pride and terror warred within him. "They're still losing. The Eceni will not be beaten. The last of the Ninth to hold the bank will die as the Batavians did. Plautius will lose five hundred more men to no purpose."

"I don't think so. He has half a legion yet that are not committed to the fight. Watch. They're going in now."

The standard swung again and the remaining five cohorts crossed in the wake of their comrades to take the Trinovantes once again from behind. This time, half of the mounted warriors turned to face them and give battle.

"Gods, has Togodubnos lost his mind? They should run as they did before."

"Where to? They're surrounded. Hosidius Geta is the centurion of the first cohort. He's been fighting against mounted warriors for years. He won't let them go."

The moves had been practised often. The two lines of the IXth met at the ends, enclosing the knot of yellow cloaks as an oyster round a seething pearl. The yellow cloaks spun their mounts, seeking an exit that did not exist. Togodubnos yelled above the noise of battle and the sounds of killing changed as the Trinovantes made a circle facing outwards and began their death-songs, knowing they were doomed.

Corvus tapped a single finger tautly on the pommel of his saddle. "Now if Caradoc has a mind to try to save his brother, we may have just turned the battle."

Sickly, Bán said, "Here he comes."

On the edge of their vision, as if ordered by his words, a spear-head of white with a corn-gold tip hurled itself towards the IXth. The legion saw them coming and their commanders had time to prepare their orders. The Ordovices met no resistance. Like a doorway, two blocks of men swung apart to let the galloping warriors through and, like an iron gate, they closed smoothly behind them.

Pandemonium reigned amongst the trapped warriors as yellow cloaks mixed with white and a single multicoloured patchwork worn by a man on a shining bay cavalry horse. The ranks of the IXth closed tightly and did not give them time to form into fighting packs. The warriors abandoned their fighting formation and faced about in ones and twos, each taking care for a shield-mate but no more. The sound of the death-songs grew louder.

"That's it." Corvus bounced his closed fist on his pommel. "We've got them."

"Ardacos! There!"

Breaca forced the bear-horse forward, slashing at the white, unprotected face of the legionary who threatened Ardacos. The small man threw up his shield and the stabbing gladius slewed sideways even as the one who had thrust it died. The body was held upright for a while, caught between two others, living, until they too died and the three toppled together, leaking blood and body fluids, onto the churned and ruined turf. Their existence was forgotten long before their bodies fell; it was not a battle that gave time to the individual, to honour the courage of the foe, or the endless acts of selfless valour of those who fought side by side, saving, again and again, the lives of their shield-mates. It was a battle in which one killed, endlessly, on foot and on horseback, using spear and blade and shield-edge and bare hands if necessary. All day Breaca kept her knot of honour guard around her and they threw themselves into the thickest part of the fighting, at times on horseback, cutting off islands of legionaries to circle them, killing, as otters kill salmon, working from the outer rim inwards; at other times they dismounted and held a line on foot, leaving their horses with the best of the children, oath-sworn to mount and ride to safety if the battle overwhelmed the warriors.

Through it all, the battle anger raged in Breaca, spreading out over her warriors and those of the Eceni as it had done since morning, since the first clash at the ford when the two legions had surged forward and the warriors of the defending side had ridden to meet them. It had held through noon when the two armies parted under the high sun and the river had run with blood in the space between them, but only lightly so that it was possible still to see the green-brown weed and the shoals of silvery fish that flashed beneath the surface. It had held after that when the hard-ridden horse from the south had been seen to join the legions, its rider borne forward on a wave of enthusiasm to reach the commander, and the news of reinforcements, of the two missing legions, spread down from him to the ranks. Even then the fire of Mona had held and had carried them into a new charge and another so that still the warriors of the right flank believed in ultimate victory.

The certainty lived in Breaca as a thing apart, sustained, she believed, by the dreamers. She could feel Airmid, as if she fought at her shoulder, with Macha and Maroc behind, two bears linked in defence of their land. Luain mac Calma was everywhere, adding the sharpness of vision that was the heron's, and Efnís circled above, a grey broad-arrowed falcon seeking the kill. All of them kindled the blaze of the gods' fire and kept it burning in the souls of those who fought, that they might not know fear or desperation in the face of overwhelming numbers.

Only once had Breaca lost the feel of that. She had been on foot, braced against the onslaught of the IInd legion, when the unborn foal had been raised by the Batavian murderers on the far side of the battlefield and word had passed, like fire in ripe corn, of the sacrilege. She was caught at the edge of the river and could not reach the Batavians but she had killed instead their Roman allies, alone and recklessly, lacking the surety of Mona's fire but consumed only with a desperate grief that had pushed her far into the enemy lines, until Ardacos and Gwyddhien and Braint had dragged her back out to the safe place where the children brought water and had made her stop and drink and take thought for Mona and the greater good. But the IInd legion had crossed the river and for a while it was all any of them could do to survive. Later, word had come from the water-children that the slaughtered mare had been a bay, not a grey, and the knowledge had burned in Breaca; a small thing to be treasured through the carnage, adding to the greater exultation when the IInd were forced into retreat.

That had been an age away, part of her distant past. In between lay the red haze of slaughter. In the battle lines, she knew only the killing, the watch and strike at bared heads or limbs, the wrench of the bear-horse beneath her as it fought with her and for her, killing as she killed, to live, to make a space in front of her that Ardacos and

Braint, Gwyddhien and Dubornos might also live, to keep the stabbing blades away from Gunovic, who fought now on her right, his grey horse made russet with drying blood, his hammer breaking helmets as a stone breaks eggs and his sword severing limbs from the living. It was good, when she had time to think of it, to fight with Gunovic. He had slowed in the past years, but he still fought as savagely as he had ever done. Since the Roman reinforcements had come, he had taken to wielding his smith's hammer in his left hand instead of a shield, saying he could kill twice as many that way. Both of them knew he would die for it. Neither had said so; the choice was his own. Breaca killed that he might live and trusted him to kill for her in return, and for Ardacos who rode on her left, her shield side, fighting to protect her from thrown javelins and unseen blades. He had claimed and lost three shields and was fighting now with a legionary scutum, square-edged and curved for infantry, not cavalry. A gladius flashed up towards him and he beat it down with his own blade, leaving the kill for Braint, who gasped thanks and set up another for him in return. In a craziness of changing patterns, in a whirl of improvisation and invention that went beyond all of Mona's training, beyond even the battle against Berikos, the honour guard of Mona killed for each other, and for those beyond; and in the back of her mind, in the threads of her soul, Breaca killed also for Caradoc, who was bound to her by the bright weave of Mona and who, somewhere on the battlefield, was facing his death, or believed it so. In her mind, he grinned and became a grinning skull and the wrench in her gut set fresh fire to the anger and the loathing and the blaze of it burned more fiercely through her and those around her so that, after a moment, there was space to breathe and to look.

Breaca killed the man in front of her and let the bear-horse rise to smash the face of his shield-mate. In that moment, lifted high above the fray, she could see the greater plan of battle. She knew the Roman standards; their images were carved on her soul. The IInd legion was gone, called back beyond the safety of the river. The fresh men of the IXth held firm, fighting on two fronts, and, in their centre, a sea of iron encased a clustered bud of yellow. A dark head showed, towering above the others, and another harvest-pale with a multicoloured cloak beneath.

Caradoc.

The bear-horse dropped to the ground again and already the battle had passed them by; Venutios had led his Brigantes in a charge that cut across the warriors of Mona, pushing the legion back. A child of ten came running with water, risking bare feet on naked blades and the hacking spite of the dying. He was not Cunomar, but he was as strong and as agile and he had the sense to keep clear of the worst danger. With a smile that shone pride, he handed Breaca the jug. Remembering to smile back, she drank and passed the jug to Gwyddhien. The tide of battle swept onward, allowing those who had fought to rest and those who had rested to rejoin the fighting. It had been so since morning, but now Caradoc was trapped.

"The legions have taken Togodubnos and Caradoc." Breaca stood on her saddle to see.

"I saw it. Come down." Ardacos pulled at her sleeve, wary of hurled javelins or slingers amongst the enemy. "If they can't fight out, we can't get in. If they're hit, we'll hear soon enough."

They heard it immediately. *Togodubnos is down!* The word flew through the ranks ahead in half a dozen tongues, cheering the Romans and devastating the Brigantes who battled against them. *Togodubnos is injured by the river and Caradoc is trapped with him.*

Among the warriors of Mona, Gwyddhien shouted it first, as a question, and then others in confirmation. In her mind, Breaca re-drew the pattern of the battlefield: the solid block of Romans retreating now in the face of the Brigantes, and the ring of legionaries by the river, eight deep in places, that encircled the beleaguered Trinovantes. They were in a dip, at a place where the ground sloped unevenly towards the water. Bushes and uncleared scrub disrupted the Roman encirclement and there was a place on the far western edge where the ranks of the legion thinned to barely two men deep. Behind that, the land sloped up into a small hill. Breaca prayed to Briga, whose presence filled the air around her. In answer, she remembered Airmid's dream.

The Warrior's horn sprang to her hand and bellowed above the noise of battle. Breaca rose in her saddle and held her shield above her head where the serpent-spear could be clearly seen. Her voice carried high above the rest. "Mona and the serpent-spear, to me!" Her honour guard massed around her, then the loose warriors not caught in the thick of the fighting. Others backed away, still killing. She had fifty, a hundred, two hundred, enough. She turned the bear-horse to her right, to the north, away from the thick of the fighting. At her back, the pulse of battle shifted and quickened.

They were five hundred at most, riding against two thousand. Breaca led them at a gallop round the back of the small hillock west of the main battleground. The fighting had not passed this way before; on the cold northern side, their hooves printed tracks on undamaged turf. At the far side they paused, taking breath out of sight of the battle, and Ardacos squirmed to the top of the hillock, returning in moments to report that the ring of the legions was the same, but that more Trinovantes had died. He had not seen Caradoc.

Breaca gave her commands. The five hundred were of Mona; they trusted their Warrior and they had practised together for this. Briga was with them, and the dreamers. The battle rage burned, encasing them all, as it had at the first. With quiet efficiency, they made a long, waiting line, two and three abreast, and their horses tensed, prick-eared, as they might at the start of a race. Along the full length, warriors regripped their shields and brought their blades to the level. At the fore, Breaca raised the serpent-blade and put the bull-horn to her lips. It was not the first time since Mona that she had blown it, but it was the first with the fire raging pure and undimmed inside her. Her whole body shook to the beat of her heart, with pride and with passionate hatred of the enemy, with the fierce exultation of battle. She took a breath and gave everything to the sounding of the horn. In deafening purity, the blast rang the length of the battlefield and beyond, to the realms of the gods. The bear-horse leaped like a deer from standing start to racing gallop and the horses of Mona thundered behind, following the banner of radiant copper that marked their Warrior above all those in the field. As they rounded the hill, they made a writhing snake with the bear-horse racing in front, an ugly, perfect, lethal serpent's head—Airmid's dream, made real by Nemain's will, to send all of Rome to Briga.

Breaca set her blade in a perfect line with her arm and, this once, freed by the gods from the burden of the greater conflict, made by them their willing hammer of retribution, she howled the battle cry that was her brother's name.

From nowhere, screaming, red-haired, flaming death fell on the men of the IXth legion and those closest turned in terror, exposing their backs to the warriors trapped in the circle. In the moment of impact, the Trinovantes threw themselves on the inner ring of men as the snake-head of Mona smashed in from the outside. Caught between, the shell of iron shattered, pouring yellow cloaks like pus from a fresh-lanced wound. Romans died in their hundreds and lay as broken toys.

Breaca found Caradoc near the centre, surrounded by his knot of Ordovices. The multicoloured cloak lay on the ground at his horse's feet, covering a body. The battle had moved away from them, forced down to the water by Venutios's Brigantes and the greater mass of Mona, pursuing victory to its certain end. The Romans were running for the river with the warriors riding them down from behind. Those who died in the last moment of the battle did so with spears in their backs or sword-cuts to the spine. Of the ring that had surrounded the Trinovantes, none were left alive.

In the space where they had been, Caradoc slid down from his horse. Clotting blood glued his hands to the reins so that he had to struggle to free them. Blood crusted the left half of his face from a wound on the scalp. His eyes were rawly bloodshot, full of dust and the debris of other men's dying. Stiffly, as if everything ached, he knelt by his cloak and the body beneath it. Breaca dropped to the ground beside him. The blaze of battle had died, leaving her light-headed and hollow. To think required an effort of will, like walking through snow, but she had known before they ever stopped fighting that Caradoc was alive, that he had dropped his cloak to the ground and for whom. Reaching out, she touched the corner of the coloured weave.

"Togodubnos?" she asked.

"Yes." Caradoc nodded, pain and exhaustion plain in his face. He let her draw back the corner of his cloak. Beneath it, his brother lay still, his face white and pinched with pain, lacking the peace of the newly dead. Breaca put a hand to his neck and felt the faintest flutter of a pulse.

"He's still alive."

"I know. But he will die soon. See . . ." He drew the cloak further down, past the shoulder, so that she could see what he had already known. The haft of the javelin that had hit him had been broken off. The head lived in the space between Togodubnos's right armpit and his breastbone. It was a miracle that he had survived so long.

"Here." Ardacos was there, leading a spare horse. He had fought at her side all day. She owed him her life too many times to count, and he owed her likewise. He, too, knelt on the smashed turf and laid a hand on Togodubnos's neck. "We should get him to the dreamers. If he's to die, it should not be here. The Romans think they have lost and we have won. It will be good if they think our victory unmarred by death."

"They are right. Don't let this change it." The wounded man opened his eyes. He set his teeth and pushed himself half to sitting. "I can ride. Get me on a horse. I must be seen to leave the field alive. After that, you can give me to the dreamers."

"They've done it, they've routed the Ninth. And Caradoc lives. I think his brother also. He's riding from the field. It's over for now. It's too close to night to try again. They have won, at least for today."

Bán found he had not taken a breath and did so, heavily. For a moment, all about him did the same. Then the roar from the defending warriors reached them, as deafening as any in the battle. It began as inchoate cheering and resolved, presently, into a chant, a single word repeated over and over in triumph, in celebration, in challenge.

"What are they saying?" Vespasian was closest to them, the legate of the IInd, who had seen his men forced into humiliating retreat at the river. "You, Corvus, you know their language. What are they saying?"

Corvus's hands, gripping the pommel of his saddle, were bone white. With his eyes still on the enemy, he said, "*Boudeg,* I think. It means 'Bringer of Victory.' It is an accolade reserved for the greatest of warriors. It will be Caradoc, or Togodubnos. Or both; it could be for them both."

"No." Bán stared unseeing at the heaving mass of blue and grey that had been his people. The noise broke over him in oceanic waves and he wished himself drowned. "It's not Caradoc. He was lost. They're celebrating the warrior who rescued him." He turned to Vespasian, who was watching him keenly. "The charge from the west was led by a woman, the Warrior of Mona. The name they are calling is *Boudica.* She Who Brings Victory."

CHAPTER 29

The hut in which they laid Togodubnos was little more than a windbreak with a roof, set far behind the battle lines. Pyres burned at all quarters; their light flickering through the wall slats cast more shadows than the torches within. Sage-smoke sweetened the air, smothering the twin corruptions of battle-sweat and impending death. Togodubnos lay stripped to the waist, sweating in the cool air. The javelin head remained in place, black against the livid skin. It was clear even to those without skill in healing that to remove it would kill him faster than anything and that, while he lived, his pain would not be less with it gone. Cunomar stood beside the bier, holding his father's hand. The child had been near the horse lines when the Batavians attacked and had seen his father's second mount maimed and slain. He had not spoken since, except once to confirm that he knew his mother was dead.

At dusk, when it was clear the Romans would not attack again that day, Odras's body had been recovered from the tight knot of yellow cloaks lying dead by the river. Of the seven members of the royal household who had ridden into battle that morning, only Togodubnos was left alive and that only barely. Throughout the camp, word had spread of his dying. Because it mattered that the enemy continue to believe him to be alive, and because they had, after it all, won a victory against overwhelming odds that would be sung of by the winter fires for generations, the warriors celebrated the day's triumph with fires and songs and ale. The sound filled the quiet spaces within the hut as the rush of a river soothes the soul but does not interfere with necessary conversation.

"They will not leave just for this. They will attack again tomorrow, and tomorrow, until we have driven them back to the sea." Togodubnos spoke through tight teeth, harbouring his breath and his pain. His life drained with each heartbeat and he had more things to say than he could manage in the time allowed him. He grasped his brother's hand. "You must hold the people together. Caesar won in Gaul because the tribes fought among themselves. We have lost the Dobunni and the Atrebates. We cannot afford to lose—"

"I know. It will be done. Keep your strength. We have talked of this before." Caradoc spoke lightly. His face was still. His free hand twisted in the folds of his cloak, out of sight beneath the death bier, the knuckles yellow-white with the pressure. Only Breaca, standing closest, could see it.

"Good. Can you—" Togodubnos stopped, brought short by pain. Those around waited while he struggled. He abandoned the sentence. His lips formed a different word. "Luain?"

"I'm here." Luain mac Calma wore the entire tanned skin of a heron. The grey wings grew from his shoulders so that it seemed surprising he had not yet taken flight. The head and the killing beak hung down his chest. The eyes had been replaced by amber beads that took on life in the smoke. He moved behind the dying man and laid his long fingers on his temples. Silently, he began the invocation to Briga that she might keep safe the soul of one killed in battle. Macha, Maroc, Efnís and Airmid joined him. In the known history of the Trinovantes, there had never been more dreamers present at a death.

Togodubnos opened his eyes. "I don't want a tomb like my father's . . . just the fire."

"It is ready. We have built a pyre for you over the small stream that leads into the great river. You will rest on a place where fire meets water and earth meets sky. It could not be done better. Briga awaits you. You will go to her armed and armoured with horse and harness and all the food we can give."

"And Odras?"

"Odras awaits you also. She lies ready on the pyre."

"Thank you." Sweat slicked his face. His breath ran ragged and then seemed not to run at all. They thought he had passed beyond speech but after a while he opened his eyes and rolled his head to the side and smiled at the child holding his left hand. "Cunomar . . . stay with Caradoc, your uncle. He will love you as a son."

Caradoc said, "He already does."

The boy ignored them both. He stared past his father to the space beyond the fire where the door-skin hung open. Only here was there a gap in those watching, left clear for the departing spirit that it might find its way to freedom without hindrance of the living. With caution, and surprised delight, the boy said, "Mother?"

Crouching to child height, Caradoc said, "Cunomar, my son, your mother was the best of warriors. She gave her life for—" But Airmid touched his arm to stop him, and Togodubnos, lifting his head, smiled as if the sun had shown its face in darkness. "Odras . . . you came." His head fell back on the rolled blanket behind him. His mouth moved without sound, in greeting and in love. He listened awhile as questions were answered and then turned to his son, smiling through tears. "Cunomar, we will wait for you at the river."

He died as the last words reached the living. The child nodded, pleased, not understanding, and then broke into violent weeping as the death became clear. The adults, meeting eyes, honoured the departing spirits and did not speak.

They burned Togodubnos's body with Odras's on the waiting pyre. On this side of the river, wood was plentiful, augmented by the forest of logs floated across from the other bank in advance of the battle. All round the camp, victory fires and death pyres were as one; another would not arouse suspicion amongst the Romans. A black-haired giant amongst the Trinovantes had already been chosen to wear the helmet and bear a shield similar to that of the dead man. For the benefit of those who may have watched, he led the songs for the parting dead and then others for victory over the enemy. The greater mass of warriors joined for a while and then separated, to sit at their own fires or to sleep.

"You should sleep."

"I don't think so. Tomorrow I may sleep for ever. Why lose the night now?"

"Then you should eat, at least. You cannot fight on an empty stomach."

"I'm not hungry." Breaca had thought to walk the river-bank alone but Caradoc had joined her. They were the only ones left standing. The dreamers had withdrawn to their meeting place, promising an intervention from the gods in the morning if one could be found. Braint, Dubornos and Gunovic had retired, taking Cunomar with them and vouching their lives for his safety. If Togodubnos had spoken the truth, the boy would die; the dead cannot wait long for the living, but those left uncursed would see he did not die needlessly or for lack of care. The remaining warriors had left in ones and twos, rolling in blankets by the fires. On both sides of the river, campfires were banked to last the night. The wind had dropped and a thin mist obscured the moon and stars. The river ripped and spun, made turbulent by the piles of bodies logged beneath the surface.

They walked in silence, having nothing to say. Caradoc had set aside his mail shirt and the hero's cloak. He wore the colours of the Ordovices with a plain tunic beneath. It suited him better. Breaca had removed her mail but nothing else.

She stepped over a fallen warrior and bent to check the certainty of death. Long, tawny hair entangled her hand. She smoothed it away to reveal a woman's face, marred by the stabbing blow that had carved beneath one cheekbone and on into the skull, baring bone and teeth in its path. The lifeless hand still grasped her spear. The point was buried halfway up the haft in the groin of a Roman legionary.

Caradoc said, "That's Cerin." She had been one of the thirty on the night of the choosing. He could not have forgotten. He knelt at her side.

Breaca nodded, remembering. "She ducked to get the spear low beneath his armour. The man to his right drove his blade in when she dropped her guard."

"She took one with her. That is what counts."

"She took many more than that. She has fought them from the day they first landed. She killed three in the ambush yesterday alone. I thought she knew their ways better than that."

Breaca wrenched the spear clear of the body and laid it along the warrior's side. A grey cloak lay trampled in the mud behind her. Together, they freed it and wrapped her in it, laying her straight with her head to the west, to the night and to Briga. Breaca made the invocation for the battle-fallen dead. Caradoc retrieved her shield and washed it clean in the river, laying bare the mark of the serpent-spear painted in red on black. With respect, he laid it beneath her head. The warriors of Mona had fought like wolves to hold the river and turn back the onslaught of the IInd. "I'm sorry," he said. "She was a good friend."

"They are all friends and we are all sorry. We will be more so tomorrow if we cannot do better than this." Breaca was tired and had seen too many die who mattered to take the trouble to soften the words for the living. The fires of her soul were extinguished, and the battle rage and the certainty of victory. She could fight another day and others after that if she lived beyond it, but she was no longer sure she could win. Her consolation was that the legions, sleeping beside poor fires and knowing defeat, would feel worse.

Caradoc rose when she did and followed her away from the river. "We will do better tomorrow," he said. "And you should still eat."

"Later. After we've checked the horses."

The bear-horse was closest. They found him well tended and eating hay. Nearby, a gaggle of Eceni children slept with their grooming wads close at hand in the way warriors sleep by their blades. A dozen armed warriors stood watch in case the Batavians attacked again. Greetings were made in silence, not to wake the children.

Towards the end of the lines, they passed a pied mare, resting one hind foot. The sign of the serpent-spear had been painted in red on the black hide of one shoulder. It was beginning to fade, but not so much that it could not be seen. Breaca said, "Your cavalry mount was lame. I saw it as we rode in. You will need a new horse for tomorrow. This one was Cerin's second string. It would suit you well but we should find you some harness. Hers was destroyed when——"

"No." He took her arm. "Breaca, stop. I have another horse set by and the harness is ready. If I need one after that, I will take this one with pleasure, but for now you have to stop. If nothing else, you must drink water. It drains out of you as you fight and one never drinks enough on a battle-field to put it back."

She had drunk each time the children had offered and they had offered each time she had rested. Even so, it was never enough to replace what was lost in the wild heat of battle and, faster, from the wounds. She had not thought about it in the time since the last fighting; the exhaustion had left her light-headed and immune to pain. Reminded, she found she was parched; her tongue was a tab of dried leather and her voice rasped her throat like a file. Reluctantly, she nodded. "You may be——"

She stopped. All he had done was tilt his head. He was

standing beside her in a sliver of firelight. His eyes were the same colour as the river water, and his hair took on the light of the fire. He raised one brow. "I may be right?"

He knew her too well, and she him. The barriers between them, carefully tended, had gone. Crowding memories stabbed at her guts.

"No. Thank you." She removed her arm carefully from his and began to walk towards the hut that had been set aside for her. Caradoc followed in the space where Hail should have been. They stopped together at the door of the hut and it seemed likely he might try to follow her in.

She turned, blocking his way. " 'Tagos used to run at my heels like this. I had not thought it of you."

"No?" His eyes searched her face. The dry, half-hidden amusement was gone and she found she preferred it present. It was easier to deal with the humour than the caring. He said, "You saved my life and those of my friends. Am I not entitled to some concern?"

"But I did not save Odras for you. I'm sorry." Pain made her bitter. "Nor did I care for your daughter's mother. Did she live through the day?"

"Ah." He gnawed on a lower lip. It was the only time she had seen him uncertain. He stepped past her to lift the door-skin and peered inside. "Do you have water in there?"

"I don't know."

"Then the answer is no. Breaca, come away." He took her arm in a way that would have been difficult to escape with dignity. "It's dark in there and the smoke has stolen all the air. It's a good night. The mist is not cold, and you will be better outside."

She allowed him to guide her, lacking the will to fight,

He led her past his brother's pyre to a place far beyond it where a solitary campfire burned under a beech tree. A jug of water stood on a flat stone and a wrapped bundle held cheese and cold meat and malted barley in separate bowls. The smells rose with the smoke, clearing the dregs of battle. Hunger exploded within her, and a raging thirst. Caradoc released her arm and laid his cloak on the ground. A bear-skin beneath it promised more comfort for the sleeper. "My fire," he said simply. "I would be honoured if you would join me."

She sat, quickly, while she had control of her limbs. He passed her water and meat and watched her drink and eat without comment. When it was clear there would be enough for two, he sat opposite and joined her, breaking the cheese between his palms and sharing the crumbled chunks across the fire. When they were done, he leaned back against the tree and they sat together in silence.

"Airmid is still alive," he said at length. "That must be good."

"It is." She had been bound to Airmid long before Mona and the thread that linked them ran deeper than all the rest. It had stretched but not broken through the day. She knew without question that if Airmid had died she would have known it, that she would have lost all control and gone where neither Ardacos nor Braint could bring her back. "If she were not, I would be dead," she said.

"I know."

He laid a branch on the fire, old and dry and padded with lichen, flammable as summer grass. Fresh flames plumed around it. He watched her through them. "Cwmfen remains in the lands of the Ordovices with Cygfa, our daughter, and her newborn son. She did not ride out with the warriors of the war hammer when they answered Togodubnos's call."

She was too tired to be shocked or angry, and she no longer had a right to know of his life, as she had once believed she did. Equally, he had no right to burden her with details; it broke the bounds of their accord. Stiffly, she said, "I didn't know you had a son."

"I don't." He smiled. "The child's father rides now in my honour guard. I have sworn to protect his life with mine. Today, you saved it for me."

"I see." The branch cracked in the heat of the fire. The food warmed her belly. Other things stirred within her, unexpected and dangerous. The closeness of him traced lightly on her skin, melting her bones. Carefully she said, "You had spent too many months in the lands of the Catuvellauni?"

"And she knew that my heart lay elsewhere."

The stirrings stopped, plunged in cold. Dry-throated, she said, "Odras. I am so sorry. If I had known sooner that she was in danger—"

"Not Odras. She was always pledged to Togodubnos, from before we were grown. We were friends; she was the sister I never had. She was never a lover."

"But you would have liked her to have been."

"Maybe, when I was much younger, but she didn't want it. She was very kind, but very certain. Such a thing must come from both, or it is worthless. You know that."

She looked up, sharply. The change was in his voice and in the luminous, firelit stare of his eyes. He said it again, to remove all doubt. "The need must be from both, Breaca. It is not enough if the heart of one lies elsewhere. You do know that."

"Yes." Her throat was still too dry. She felt as she did in moments of mortal danger, when time slowed and a heartbeat dragged for eternity. She could have reached through the fire and touched him. He could have done the same. Neither of them moved.

"Cerin was Ardacos's lover," she said. "It's why I went to look for her. I knew where she fell. He is caring for Cunomar and can't go alone. Also, I think he doesn't wish to weaken himself for tomorrow. I would have asked Airmid but she can't leave the dreamers on a night when they are calling the gods for the sake of the people—" She was talking to fill the space. She stopped. He said nothing. The space between them stretched beyond endurance.

"Caradoc—"

He dragged his cloak away from the bear-skin. The pelt was amber in the light. "The bear has room for two," he offered, and he was shy suddenly, like a child. "If you were to come to it, I would know that the need was felt by us both."

She was standing, not able to go closer, held by an impossibility of longing. "Do you not know it already? How could you not? Have you forgotten Mona?"

"No, how could I? But I have also not forgotten my father's grave mound, nor a certain hillside overlooking the Atrebates. You are quite terrifying when you're angry." He smiled, lamely, only half serious. "And, besides, Airmid hates me. How could I offend Maroc's favoured dreamer?"

"Airmid?" The shock of laughter let her move. She stood and stepped round the fire. "She doesn't hate you. Airmid has been telling me for years that the gods cast you and me together for a purpose. I thought she was saying it because it was what I wanted to hear."

"And was it?"

"Oh, yes." She reached down and touched his palm, and his fingers closed on hers. Lightning sparked up her arm, stealing her breath. "From the beginning, yes."

"Then it is good we know now, when it is not too late."

The death and terror of the day were gone. His smile was the grin of a youth in a river, challenging the gods. It caught her heart and lifted it into the sway of the gods; it flayed her skin from her body so that every nerve ending ached for him; it shattered the last boundaries of her self-imposed restraint as the first floods of spring break a child's dam of sticks and straw, sweeping it into oblivion.

Trembling, she reached out and traced the line of his lips with her finger, prolonging the moment, holding an eternity of joy at her fingertips as she had held an eternity of death on the battlefield. He reached up and caught her wrist and turned it round and kissed the soft skin on the inside, where the pulse raced to a new rhythm that changed as his lips pressed onto her and then the soft tug of his teeth and she laced her fingers through the gold silk of his hair and down to his neck and his shoulder until, wrapping close, they slid down onto the bear-skin. The night was warm. The pelt beneath them was soft and safe.

In all ways and none was it as she had imagined. He was skilled, but not with her; she was used to other rhythms. They struggled to lose their clothing and keep their privacy in a place that was within earshot of every man, woman and child left alive on the north side of the sea-river. Both had seen the frantic couplings of other warriors brought together after battle by the shared intimacy of imminent death; they had a need not to feel themselves the same. The gods smiled and sent the mist to wrap them close and shut out the world. Later, with the mist still dense, the world could have crept up to watch and they would not have known it.

Breaca had no wish to sleep. Fog swirled round them, thick with the colours of the fire. She lay with him under the cloak, wrapped in the musk of his sex and hers, exploring. She found and counted the scars on his body, naming the weapon and the angle of each and the mistakes he had made in letting them through. He acknowledged the errors and did the same for her, ending at last on the serpent-spear set in ink in the skin of her forearm. He traced it with his forefinger, raising the hairs on her spine. "You did not have this when I met you first, nor on the night of the choosing."

"No. Maroc did it on Mona after I became Warrior. He had a dream and said I should bear the sign where it could be seen even without my shield. He would not say the content of the dream."

"It is everyone's battle mark now, did you know? I saw warriors painting it on shields around the fires last night; the mark of certain victory. We will fight with its protection tomorrow—today." They had forgotten the war. It came back, crushing the joy. His eyes clouded. "Don't let them kill you."

"I hadn't planned on it."

"Unless they kill Airmid." He was only half joking.

"Or you." His hand was still on her arm, covering the dream-mark. She had already searched him and found no inked mark; she had not expected to. She said, "You have no dream, no sign on your shield. How can the warrior of the

Three Tribes have no dream?" She had always wanted to ask it and had not had the right; only close kin or lovers could ask such a thing. The knowledge that she could do so freely melted her again and she leaned in and kissed him. With her breath part of his, he said, "My dream is the eagle."

"Of course." She should have known that. It ran through the core of his being. She remembered the soaring triumph she had felt when she had thought the eagle might be her dreaming. Holding him close, she said, "Your father would have been pleased."

"My father did not believe in dreams. You forget, he came to Luain very late in life. He forbade its use while I was still within his reach. When I was beyond it, it was too late. Amminios had heard of it and made it a weapon."

Horrified, she remembered. "His men bore the mark of the war eagle."

"Yes. If you had felt for your brother as I felt for mine and knew his hired killers sported the mark of your dream, would you want to paint it on your shield? Besides, we have no need of it now." He rose up on one elbow and reached for her, trailing his fingers through her hair. "Boudica. Bringer of Victory." He gave it the cadence of a singer, so that she was already a hero, with the tale of her charge sung beside the fire, and then said it again, differently— "Boudica"—in a way that made it a private thing to keep between them.

She frowned at the presumption before the gods and he grinned, wiping the creases from her forehead with the ball of his thumb before leaning back and pulling his shield from the weapons pile behind the tree. "See, it is all of us, not just the few." The shield was bull's hide on willow and could take an axe-blow without breaking. In the day, it had been white. Now the serpent-spear stood out in red on grey, exactly as it did on hers.

He smiled wryly as he had done before, knowing the places in her that hurt, and the reasons. "I asked one of your people to paint it for me this evening. If we are to win, we must fight under one dream, not many. If we are to die, I would as soon die under your mark as mine."

"Caradoc—" It was a gift, made before they had come together and greater for that. She could not speak. She pulled him close, covering her loss, and let him know how he had touched her.

A while later, with the length of him still inside her, she said, "Our son when we have him, will he be allowed to have his own dream?"

He arced back, astonished. "Really? Can you tell so soon?"

"No. But Airmid told me years ago. I would like to believe her."

He crowed, softly triumphant. "Then we should find a name, something for him to be proud of; one of those who died most bravely in yesterday's battle."

"Or who will die in today's." She was sober. The time for fighting was coming and one death, at least, had been foretold. The first fingers of dawn drained the colour from the night. The fog thickened with the coming day. She stroked his hair from his brow, kissed it and pushed herself out from under the cloak. Standing, she said, "He has a name already. It came to Airmid in the dream that told of his conception."

His face became still, his eyes wide and fixed. "Mine?"

"No. If I am alive to bear the child, you will be alive to rear him."

If. Nothing is certain but that some will live and some will die. The best of dreams shows only one path among many. Maroc had said that. She did not feel it necessary to tell him.

They were sliding into the mail shirts and strapping on their sword belts when he grasped her wrist and turned her to face him. "Who is it, Breaca? What name has Airmid given him?" *Whose life is already forfeit to the gods?*

"Cunomar."

The hounds gave first warning of the attack. Those at the furthest western edge of the encampment bayed as if hunting and were echoed soon by the rest. Waking warriors, caught dressing or voiding their bowels, rushed to arm and harness their horses. Breaca, who was saddling the bear-horse, mounted and looked over a sea of sleep-racked heads. The fog was thicker than it had been. To the east it hung sickly pink, defying the dawn. The west still lay in darkness. A hundred fires stuttered at the furthest margins of the camp, rosy pinpricks in the fog. Beyond them, in the scrub and sparse trees, a shadowed line obscured the ground. The bear-horse cocked his ears and whinnied. Far away, a filly answered.

"That's Roman."

"It can't be." Caradoc was mounted beside her on a horse that had been a gift from Gunovic. His new mount rolled its head at the feel of a strange hand on the bit. He peered to where she pointed. "We set sentries."

"We should have put dogs. In this fog, you could walk up to a man to cut his throat and he would not see you. Gods—" A fire flared on the edge of the camp as a warrior struggled to hold her baying hound. For a moment the fog cleared and Breaca could see clearly the lines of armour sparking in the light, unending lines stretching sideways and back. Terror flushed her, cold as ice.

"It *is* the Romans. A legion at least. They've forded the river higher up and come down in the dark, under cover of the fog."

The Warrior's horn hung from her saddle. Without thinking, she raised it to her lips. The high, clear notes soared across the campsite. The Romans abandoned their secrecy. A hundred legionary horns brayed an echo to hers. As the noise died away, five thousand legionaries clashed their swords on their shields and shouted in deafening synchrony. If Camul himself had sent thunder to mark the onset of battle, it could not have been louder. It was said afterwards that a dozen warriors died in fright at the sound.

Carnage began in the west and crept forward like ice across still water. There was no time to range in ordered battle lines. Those who were ready mounted and searched for others in the fog. Those still asleep—and they were many—dressed with a haste that left much undone. Half of the warriors who rode into battle that day did so bareback and lacking at least one weapon. Most of them died.

The honour guards of all the tribes were sharpest and most ready. Even before they reached the battle, Breaca and Caradoc were surrounded by grey- and white-cloaked warriors. Others joined as they rode. Togodubnos's followers among the Trinovantes still fought with the image of the sun hound on their shields. The remainder, grey cloaks and blue, green-striped Coritani, Durotriges, Silures—all bore the serpent-spear, freshly painted in colours that matched their cloaks. *For what good it will do them.* In the ravening fog, Breaca saw her dream become nightmare. Nausea tightened her hands on the reins. The bear-horse tossed its head as it ran.

"The dreamers . . ." Dubornos pushed his horse up to hers. He was grey with sleep, his voice hoarse from a day of battle. "They think they can hold a line. They want us to support them."

It was madness. The whole world was madness. Breaca turned her horse where he pointed and the honour guard turned with her. "Where?"

"By Togodubnos's pyre. The fire is still burning."

Earth met water, fire met sky. The pyre was as big as it had been the night before. Someone had taken it upon himself to keep it well fed and it shone through the fog as a beacon for a final stand—or a miracle. Those who believed they could call on the gods to protect them stood in a half-moon before the fire with Macha and Airmid at the apex and Maroc and Luain mac Calma at either end. Gunovic stood with Macha and the hound bitch, Cygfa. Ardacos, Braint, Gwyddhien and Cumal stood behind him with Cunomar on his pony between them. Seeing the child there, Breaca knew they would die; the gods and his father had said so.

Hail stood behind Airmid, steady on three legs. He greeted Breaca joyfully, as he had once greeted Bán, and she returned it in kind; his heart was great and he deserved her love. Airmid turned with her own greeting. She knew where Breaca had been and what she had done with the night and was glad. The firm, beloved hand clasped hers. The face turned up to hers for the kiss bore a landscape of unbearable grief and was still beautiful. "You came. Thank you. If we are to die, I would be in this company."

She would not weep on the day of battle. She could not. "Have the gods said we must die?"

"Some of us must." Airmid's voice carried the certainty of the dream-given. "But if you live to bear the child, Caradoc will live to rear him. I swear it."

If.

Caradoc was at the far end of the line with Maroc, almost out of sight. Others, seeing that a stand would be made here, were joining them. They were pitifully few. Breaca estimated a bare thousand, to hold a legion. They had done it before, but the pulse of battle had been with them; it ran against them now. She sensed death more surely than she had ever felt it. She looked down and found Airmid still watching.

"Are dreams so certain?" she asked.

"Some of them."

"Can you turn the legions back?"

"No. But Macha has dreamed that we can hold them long enough."

"Long enough for what? There is no-one to help us."

"We don't know. It will be shown us."

The first wave of warriors died in their hearing. More joined their stand by the pyre. They were fifteen hundred and growing. The fog swirled too thickly to be sure of numbers. Ahead, out in the white, the line of legionaries moved forward as if drawn by plough horses, slowly but without a break, each man safe behind his shield, each stabbing in the small space between. They lost one for every twenty warriors killed. Small numbers of Roman cavalry—not the wild Batavian horsemen of the cohorts or their Gaulish auxiliary comrades—covered the margins, preventing an attack from

the rear. Their control was terrifying. To ride within sight of
battle and not to kill spoke of discipline beyond imagining.

We are mounted; they are mostly on foot. If we can rout their cav-
alry, we can break them.

Breaca turned to Airmid. "We need to scatter the horses if we are to stand a chance with the infantry."

"Macha's dream is that we will hold them. The means
will be shown us." The dreamer was unnaturally calm. Faith
expunged fear.

Dubornos appeared by their side. To Breaca, he said, "I
have been to the far ends of the line. We are two thousand
and rising. Still not enough. They will not have sent less
than five thousand."

"I know. Airmid, if the gods want us to fight they will
have to show us——" The wind freshened, blowing from the
north. Flames billowed from the fire. Hail ducked flat to the
ground. The bear-horse flinched sideways in a haze of
singed hair. All the way down the line, warriors fought for
control of their mounts. Comprehension blistered the walls
of her mind.

"The fire——we can use the fire against them. See——"
Breaca was already cutting a length of her cloak. She carried
three spears now; weapons, once scarce, were plentiful. She
bound the cloak strip round the head of her spear, just
behind the haft. "Efnís!" He stood four dreamers up the
line. "Have you the bear's grease and pine resin?"

He was running before she completed her sentence. A
score of smoke-stained children scampered in his wake; he
had always been good with the young. When he came back
bearing the torch pitch, warriors in their hundreds were binding their spears. More children and the younger warriors

fetched beakers and jugs—no-one would drink that day, or if they did, it would be at the battle's end. The vessels were filled with cloth and grease and all things flammable. Children tied leather thongs about the handles and necks so they could be swung and thrown further. Each one saw in the weapons a chance for honour and a song told at firelight. Not one expected to come out alive.

Caradoc pushed his horse up on her left. His presence filled her. The serpent-spear brooch she had given him a lifetime ago flashed silver at his shoulder, the love tokens of red horsehair renewed for all to see. Pain jagged and caught in her throat. "Caradoc, I—"

"I know." He kissed her. "So do I. Here." He had found a cache of spears, some of them Roman, taken from the dead Batavians. They rattled to the ground between them. His colour-patched cloak lay across his saddle in fraying strips and he was already ripping the spare. She swallowed her soul and began to bind the spear-hafts. She said, "We should aim for the horses. If we can break the cavalry, we can attack the lines at the end."

"Until they send the reserves across the river to cut us off."

"Don't ask for what has not yet happened."

The river lay to their left. Breaca felt it through the fog, pricking her skin, promising danger. It would not be long.

They were ready. The Roman line had slowed, snagged on a knot of death-sworn Trinovantes. Their death-songs filled the mist, full of hatred. The warriors of the sun hound no longer fought for the protection of their land, but to avenge the death of Togodubnos. Breaca cursed. "They sell their lives too cheaply. When the legions break us, they will march straight for the dun and the slaughter will be terrible. They must know that, surely."

Caradoc looked at her as he had done once in the night, his soul on his face. His hand grasped hers. "Breaca? *When?* Not *if?* What do you know?"

"What?" She was distracted by the fire. The wind spiralled inside it like a summer dust storm. Flames lifted in a wash of red light. The elder grandmother stood within them, perversely opaque and bigger than she should have been. Around her, the warriors of the ancestors painted the serpent-spear in blue woad on their arms. Every one of them bore the same mark but the leader, who bore the hare. Above, in a blue sky, the eagles circled, ready to kill. The elder grandmother pointed a bone-thin finger through the fire. *They are learning, but not fast enough. These are the last. After them, there will be no more.*

Her own voice, younger, said, *These are only the men. There must be women and children. If they live, then the people live with them.*

The grandmother cocked her head sideways. *That is up to you.*

Her head spun. She felt ill. She grabbed at Caradoc's cloak because she could not see him clearly.

"The children—the children must live." She turned to her other side. Airmid was watching, alert for the voice of the gods. "Airmid—tell Macha, Luain, Maroc, all of them. We are not here to hold a line to stop the invasion, only to hold them back long enough for the children to escape. These are the warriors of the future. They must not die here."

The grandmother occupied her head. In a parody of her own voice, she said, *That is not enough. There must be those old enough to carry their ways, their dreams and their tales. How else does a people know itself?*

Aloud she said, "We cannot run. Warriors cannot flee the field of battle."

Then you can die for nothing and the people with you. For all time. You are the last who can fight.

It was sacrilege, the ultimate negation of the warrior. Pain knifed through her heart. For a moment, she believed she had been hit and her battles were over. She saw Caradoc's face and knew tearing regret. Airmid slapped her, sharply.

"Breaca! Speak to me. What have you seen?"

"We have to leave. We must all go, warriors as well as children. This is not the time and the place—not the right way to fight them." She swallowed on ashes, and the words scalded her tongue. In anguish, she said, "The warriors of the sun hound are enough to hold the line. Those of the serpent-spear must go. We have to live to fight again or the whole land is lost."

"What?"

"Are you sure?"

She was Warrior of Mona, she was Boudica, Bringer of Victory, and she was asking for retreat. All around, she felt the pressure of their resistance. Only Ardacos was with her. He knew the mistakes of the ancestors better than any, and trusted her above all others. "The Warrior is right. The battle is lost, but not the war. The children must live and enough of us to show them how to follow the gods." He looked round into the mist. "How do we find a way out?"

Nobody answered. All waited for Breaca's word. Caradoc's eyes, holding hers, were a broad and turbulent sea. Breaca felt herself drown in them, felt the tides of his spirit search the corners of her being. In gratitude, she showed him the elder grandmother and all her acid laughter and felt the bedrock of his understanding. To the others, he said, "We're surrounded by marsh and the fog is a gift of the gods to conceal us. If we can't see beyond the ends of our spears, neither can they. If those of us who stay here make enough noise, they will not see you go."

He clasped Airmid's arm as he had once clasped Odras's. Foolish that it had ever seemed greater than friendship. "Go," he said. "Breaca's right. There is nothing to be won here but a hero's death and that for nothing if everyone dies. Leave now and take the children. I will see that the line holds strong. The legions will pay dearly for each step forward." Turning to his other side, he gave Dubornos the warrior's salute, the first time he had done so. "You must go with them. The dreamers need a warrior's protection. Sing of us later."

Dubornos's smile shone in the mist. A childhood of enmity lifted from his shoulders. He made the singer's salutation of greatest honour, his eyes wet. "The song is already made."

"No."

"I won't leave you."

Airmid and Breaca spoke together. Airmid's voice, pitched higher, was best heard. "Caradoc, you can't stay. If Breaca lives, you must live. The dream does not lie. And this is your land. Only you can lead the way out. Go now with the others. The dreamers will hold the line. It is what we have lived for."

"What?" Breaca laughed, loosely and out of control. "Airmid, are you mad? What will you do? Throw pitchers of fire at the legions?"

"Macha dreamed the line and there were dreamers in it."

"Which ones?"

They argued against each other, against the dream, against time. The songs of the fighting Trinovantes became weaker, became the animal screams of the wounded and dying. Breaca read the pain of betrayal in the faces around her. The Boudica should not desert the site of her victory, even in the face of certain defeat. Shutting her ears to the cackle of the elder grandmother, she raised her voice to carry and said, "I will not leave this place unless every warrior who bears the serpent-spear rides with me—and their dreamers. If so much as one stays, we all stay."

That settled it for them. More than one would stay, given the chance. The warriors smiled their thanks, raised their weapons and turned to face the enemy. The plan died as it had been born.

"*No!* You will go when and where you are told. Do you think this fog is an accident? *Do you?*"

It was Macha who spoke, standing in the centre of the line of dreamers, her back to the fire so that the light flared red around her and her shadow swayed and swooped across them all. Her voice was god-given, penetrating far beyond the walls of fog. "In the time of Caesar, Onomaris and all the dreamers called on Manannan, god of the sea, for aid. The gods heard their plea and gave the storm that wrecked the invaders' ships. So again have we called on Briga and Nemain to aid their people and they have granted us this fog. What worth is it if we do not use it as they have told us?"

Caradoc said, "We will use the fog to fight."

Anger raised Macha higher. Her voice flayed him, and the warriors who had nodded agreement.

"Against four legions who have broached the river? I think not. You will use it to buy yourselves honour and glory and an easy death. What do you care for those left alive in a land without leaders, without dreamers, without warriors to carry the battle? You are selfish beyond all who have gone before. The gods will abandon you in death." To Breaca, in a voice of utter contempt, she said, "The elder grandmother gave the last strength of her life to bring you a dream of untold power. It is your choice alone if you cast it aside. Do not expect her thanks when you meet her in the lands of death."

She stepped away from the fire. The flames guttered and sank. The fog wavered and the Romans, seeing them, cheered. They were a dozen spear-throws away and the Trinovantes who held them could be counted in spare hundreds, not thousands.

Breaca stepped into the place before the fire. She felt the wall of heat behind her and heard the sucked-in breaths of those around. Ardacos raised his stolen shield as a mirror and she saw herself reflected in the boss, red-haired against a red fire with red fog around. She felt cold, and torn by the lash of Macha's tongue. She raised her shield and shored up her voice as Maroc had once taught her, that she might carry the authority of the Warrior.

"Macha is right," she said clearly. "The gods must be heard. We will go as she has asked. All who bear the serpent-spear will take the horses and the children. Those of the sun hound will stay and fight. Caradoc will lead those who are leaving."

The pyre hissed as if devouring new wood. The fog swirled and hid the battle lines. The gods could not have spoken more clearly. A long, moaning sigh swept the waiting defenders, like the first harbingers of mourning. Breaca felt the weight of their resistance lift.

She was alone and very cold. Caradoc gripped her wrist as he had in the night and, leaning down from his horse, pressed his lips to her head. Breaca would have spoken, but the words would not come. He nodded, grim-faced and silent, and turned his horse to the north. Every warrior who bore her mark turned to follow. Within a hundred heart-beats, the exodus had started. Silent, wide-eyed children were grasped and lifted onto saddles, their voices like reeds in the fog, asking if they were being taken to the fighting. Spare horses were untethered and took dreamers or children, two or three at a time. In the line of the dreamers, men and women took their leave. Of the Eceni, only Macha stayed, and Gunovic. Luain mac Calma had parted swiftly from them both and rode near the front with Caradoc. All that needed to be said between them had been spoken in the night, knowing what was to come. All who mattered had known, it seemed, but Breaca. The knowledge was a knife that scored at the rawness of her heart. She pushed the bear-horse forward to Macha. "How long have you known?" she asked.

Macha was no longer angry. Her eyes carried a peace they had not known since Eburovic's death. Her face was Bán's, lacking only his constant wonder at the world. Smiling, she said, "A while ago, uncertainly. It became clear in the night."

"Why didn't you tell me?"

"Would you have listened? I know what it takes for a warrior to leave the battlefield. It had to come from the gods for you to believe it." The bear-horse nuzzled Macha's neck. She soothed his muzzle, absently, and lifted her hands to the torc of the Eceni, as if the horse had reminded her of its presence. Drawing it off, she held it out. "This is yours as it was your mother's before you. Wear it with pride and when the day comes that you are free of your duty to Mona and can return to the Eceni, rule them well and with love, as she did."

Once, Breaca had thought of the torc as a living thing, a snake of gold in the hands of the elder grandmother. Now the fog folded around it, a cushion of white, and the band lay like a woven corn-crown in the centre of it. Bending, she let Macha fit it round her neck. The sense of her mother, briefly, was overwhelming. Macha saw it and smiled. "You will do as well as she, if the gods allow it."

Pain rose and set in Breaca's throat. "You are Eceni, both of you. You don't need to stay. Please come with us."

Macha shook her head. "We can't. Who do you think is holding the fog?"

The wrongness of it ached, and the calm acceptance. Desperately, Breaca said, "Our gods are not Roman gods. They don't demand the death of their people as the price of their gifts."

"A life freely given is not payment. One must stay to hold the fog, just as Onomaris walked into the sea to hold the storm in Caesar's time. It is the way."

"Someone else can do it." Breaca turned and found a face she knew; the sole dreamer of the Trinovantes stood not far from the pyre, her mouth moving in invocations to the gods. "Lanis is staying," she said. "She can hold the fog, surely?"

"No. I raised it. It is mine to hold."

"Then I won't leave. The children are safe. I'll stay. Ardacos, too." He was hovering nearby, his hand on the bridle of a child's pony. Breaca would have signalled but Macha restrained her.

"Breaca, no. Do you still not understand? This is not about *these* children alone. It is about you and Caradoc and the child you carry from last night and the others not yet conceived. It's about Airmid and Braint, Dubornos and Efnís, Gwyddhien and Ardacos and the others who will rear and teach them. Between you, all of you, you carry the seeds of the future. If you live through today there is hope that everything we are, everything we have—the dreaming, the gods, the songs of past and present—can survive. Without that, Rome will destroy everything until our children and our children's children will know as little of us as we know of the ancestors—less because the dreams will have gone. It will be as if we were never here."

"That could never happen."

"It can. If you don't leave now, it will. Even so, nothing is certain." Macha was serious now, not angry, but insistent. "Swear to me that you will fight them, in every way you can. That you will listen to the gods for guidance and follow the dreaming. That you will teach your children likewise."

Breaca laid her hand on the hilt of her sword. "I swear."

The mist held them close. To the north, it swallowed children in bites of ten and a dozen; dreamers and hard-faced warriors followed. Caradoc led them, far away at the front. Gwyddhien, Dubornos and Braint waited, gauging the distance to the Romans. Airmid was last, leading the grey battle mare. Hail ran at her heels. Gunovic stood at Breaca's bridle, talking to her horse. She gave him the warrior's salute. "Thank you for the bear-horse. He is the best I've ever ridden."

He grinned, a great bear of a man, who had taught her what it meant to race with an open heart and fight to win. He said, "He will sire better if you put him to your grey mare— but only if you leave now and give him the chance. I would hate the Romans to reap the fruits of four years' work."

"I'm going." Unforgivable on the field of battle, she was weeping. She reached down for Macha's arm. "We will sing of you every winter for a thousand generations. Don't let them take you living, either of you."

"It won't happen. Now go."

She turned the horse away. To her left, the last of Togodubnos's honour guard died and the legionary line moved onward, swords clashing on shields, boots churning the ground. They were blind in the fog and came slowly, testing each step with care. Breaca pushed her horse to a trot. Airmid waited for her with the grey battle mare.

Breaca said, "Can she run?"

"Yes, if you don't load her. Come on, we must hurry— Gods! Cunomar, no—"

Braint had been given charge of the child. His father's prophecy had been forgotten, or was being ignored, and, alone of those on the field who bore the sun hound, he was being made to leave. He had refused at first then suddenly relented and had followed the young warrior sullenly past his father's pyre. At its furthest margin, while she bent to lay her fire-spears on the ground, he wrenched himself loose, turned and, pulling a burning brand from the fire's edge, kicked his pony past the others and into the fog.

The death-song of the sun hound carried in high treble,

losing no force with the distance. As it reached a peak, red flame stained the fog. A horse screamed in terror. Men howled in surprise, cascading into panic. A child died on a dozen swords. Macha sang the invocation to Briga clearly, so that it carried through the fog: the sound of a wren at dawn's first light. The hound bitch, Cygfa, joined, raising her muzzle in the damp air. Beside them, Gunovic swung his hammer and laid the first of his fire-spears in the pyre.

Breaca found herself at the back of a silent string of warriors. Known faces wavered in the mist ahead of her: Airmid and Gwyddhien, Ardacos and Braint, Dubornos and Efnís, Luain, come back to see that they had all left, half of the honour guard from Mona, a sea of blue-cloaked Eceni. She hefted her shield and held it to the sky. Closed fists were raised around her. Airmid pointed along the path through the marshes to where Caradoc led the way to freedom.

"We must go."

At the pyre, the first clash of warriors masked the noise of their leaving.

EPILOGUE

Macha.

She was there, far more clearly than she had ever been in the visions. Bán could see her, standing with Gunovic the travelling smith, and a hound bitch he did not recognize; with Togodubnos and Odras and a child who bore the blond hair of one and the wide brown eyes of the other and who sat a small grey pony, smiling his battle challenge. She was there in spirit, as Bán had seen her these past six years, and yet her body, newly dead, lay charred and smoking on the remains of the pyre. The hammer blow that had killed her was clear on her head, the silver wren sagging in molten waves across her breast. Gunovic, whose hammer, in mercy, had made the blow and whose hands, in honour and grief, had lain her on the pyre with the hound bitch at her side, had died nearby on the swords of a dozen legionaries and had sent twice as many, maybe more, to the other world ahead of him. These, too, Bán could see, but more dimly, more wraith-like, as he had once seen his mother and his sister, believing both dead when one, at least, had still been alive.

The knowledge of his error and its magnitude came to Bán slowly and against great resistance. He had not taken part in the systematic slaughter that was the battle of the second morning; that had been reserved for the IInd legion, a gift from Aulus Plautius to their commander Vespasian to assuage the humiliation of the first day's defeat. The auxiliaries, Bán among them, had been called across the river later as the fog began to lift, to scour the battlefield for wounded, to slay any of the enemy that might lie feigning death and to ferry the wounded legionaries back across the water to the ministrations of Theophilus and his helpers. From the first, passing through the fallen lines of Trinovantian dead, the auxiliaries had found the shields bearing the newly painted serpent-spear and had remarked on it—the Gauls, too, had their ancestors and knew of their marks. Bán alone had been silent, shielding his mind from his heart's fear, from the terror that had touched him on a hillside the day before when a red-haired warrior had led the charge in the rescue of Caradoc and Togodubnos.

Only when he found the pyre, when he knelt, retching, in the acrid smoke of his mother's body, when he looked at what had so recently been alive and now lay, stripped of half its flesh, in the embers, when he raised his head and saw his mother's soul shining and radiant before him—only then did the shields disintegrate and the truth flood in.

"*Macha!*"

He called her name and received no answer. In the silence of the passing ghosts, Bán wept as he had never wept in his life. Pain unmatched tore through him, the storm of the gods, wrenching his soul from its moorings. Corvus was forgotten and all that he stood for. Death was his best and only hope, his deliverance. The knife at his belt bore the mark of the falcon god, Horus. It had been a gift from Corvus early in their days together, a promise and an offer that neither had expected to be fulfilled. Bán's fingers closed on it as if they belonged only there. Sweetly, it sang from its sheath and he swept it, point first, towards his breast. The pain was dull and hard but not deathly, the pain of impact as an iron knife blade strikes a medallion of solid gold and does not penetrate. His fingers, numbed, sprang open and his mother's shade reached down to sweep the weapon from his grasp. Even in the confines of Amminios's slave-boat, he had not known her so close, or so real. Looking up, he read only contempt in her eyes. His soul cried to hers. "Mother! I want to join you."

You cannot.

"Why?"

That is for you to find. You are forsaken. The gods condemn you to life.

She left him to join her people and Bán was not one of them. One by one, he watched as the dead of two days' battles—Eceni, Trinovantes, Brigantes, Votadini, Coritani, Catuvellauni, Silures, Ordovices—filed across the river into the care of their gods. Their names came to him, and their titles, their loves and their deeds, each one etched on his mind as on marble. At the end there was emptiness and the knowledge that the one who, next to his mother, he sought most had not passed him by. Macha had waited at the side, alone. She smiled at him, coldly, and nodded. "Breaca lives," she said. "Your sister is Boudica, Bringer of Victory. With Caradoc she cares for the children. Remember that."

The green and gold fields of the other world beckoned.

Macha turned and walked into the haze. The last Bán saw of his mother was the flat rejection of her back and the wren that circled over her, singing.

AUTHOR'S NOTE

The peoples of the late pre-Roman Iron Age in Britain did not maintain written records of their histories, dreams or oral teachings. We have no contemporary records save those written by the enemy—Rome—with all the political, cultural and social bias that implies. Of the woman we know as Boudica, very little is known beyond her role in the events leading up to and during the revolt of A.D. 60–61 as recorded by Tacitus. Of the preceding years, particularly the events surrounding the Claudian invasion, we have only the incomplete histories of Cassius Dio, written nearly two centuries later. Concerning her early life there is no written record, and thus everything contained in these pages—the people, their life and their dreams—is a fiction. As far as is possible, I have woven my imaginings within a framework of contemporary archaeological theory, but it must be stressed that this interpretation of the jigsaw of pottery fragments, midden debris, experimental archaeology and numismatic theory is entirely my own.

A little more is known of Boudica's contemporaries:

Cunobelin and his three sons are mentioned in the classical sources, and some details may be inferred from the existence and spread of the coins of the time, although only with due reservations. Most is known about Caradoc/Caratacos and he was undoubtedly a charismatic and intelligent war leader. Graham Webster states, "If Cunobeline [*sic*] can be said to have been the first British Statesman, Caratacus [*sic*] was certainly the first great British Commander."[1]

Others for whom we have credible authority are Berikos (Verica), Beduoc, Cartimandua of the Brigantes (her name means "sleek pony"), her consort Venutios and her charioteer Vellocatos.

On the continent, Julius Civilis was known to command a cohort of Batavian auxiliaries and claimed during a later revolt to have known, and consider himself a friend of, the future emperor Vespasian. My assumption that they met during the invasion of A.D. 43 is entirely unfounded but is not, I think, unreasonable.

The tribe who occupied the lands immediately to the west of the Eceni are currently known as the Corieltauvi. However, after due consideration, it seems that for the reader unfamiliar with local archaeology this name is too readily confused with the Catuvellauni, who lay to their south, and so, for purely editorial reasons, I have reverted to their former title, the Coritani.

With respect to the Roman aspects of the narrative, the sources are many and varied. In researching the character of Gaius/Caligula and the events in the winter of A.D. 39/40, I have chosen to accept the interpretation of Anthony Barrett in his book *Caligula—The Corruption of*

Power, particularly with respect to the events surrounding the "surrender" of Amminios.

The character of Corvus is entirely fictional but his military career is based loosely on that of Atatinus Modestus, a commander cited by John Spaul in his book *Ala*,[2] whose career began in Augustan times in the Ala II Gallorum and went on to sixteen years in the Legio X Gemina.

Finally, on the Roman side, I have followed Webster's depiction of Galba as L. Sulpicius Galba in the light of Suetonius's contention that he did not take on the name Servius until he took the throne in the year of the four emperors.

Details of the invasion itself remain a source of contention amongst professional archaeologists. Dio outlines two battles, both taking place at a river, but does not give us either the exact number of legions which took part or the geographical location of the landings, both of which are vital to an understanding of the events of this period. From a study of military records in the post-invasion period, it is generally accepted that four legions, plus their attendant auxiliaries and cohorts, took part—a total of around forty thousand armed men, twice as many as Caesar brought in 55 and 54 B.C. Best estimates suggest that a thousand ships would be required to transport them from the continent—nearly ten times as many as took part in the Spanish Armada.

At the time of writing, two schools of thought exist concerning the site of the landings. The first is that they landed at Richborough in Kent (the geography of the coastline was somewhat different from that which exists today) and marched west to meet the native forces, first at the

Medway and then at the Thames. This theory is backed by the fact that the landing site is a six-hour sail from Boulogne—the shortest possible route—and archaeological evidence of Roman military activity, which has been fixed at around the time of the invasion. This landing site has the advantage of being close to the Thames and Trinovantian territory, both of vital strategic importance.

The second theory has the invaders landing on the south coast at or near Fishbourne—this being supported by the fact that the Roman excuse for invasion was to return Berikos (Verica) of the Atrebates to his home kingdom. This gives the invasion the advantage of a landing in friendly territory and access to food, water and fuel while establishing bases. Against this is the fact that the crossing from Boulogne takes twenty hours and must run against two tides.

For the novelist who is required to build a fictional reality, it was always going to be necessary to choose one or other theory, until a paper published by E. W. Black,[3] examining other classical sources, proposed a third theory—that two separate landings took place, one at each location. We are unlikely ever to resolve this but, given the logistical nightmare of landing a thousand ships at any single location, this third theory makes more sense than either of the other two and is the option I have chosen. You, of course, are free to imagine your own alternative, as with all the rest.

1 Graham Webster, *The Roman Invasion of Britain* (Routledge, 1999).

2 John E. H. Spaul, *Ala. The Auxiliary Cavalry Units of the Pre-Diocletianic Imperial Roman Army* (Nectoreca Press, 1984, 2000).

3 E. W. Black, "Sentius Saturninus and the Invasion of Britain," *Britannia* 31 (2000), 1–10.

NAMES AND THEIR PRONUNCIATION

This is a complex field, not least because we are dealing by and large with a language that no longer exists. Clearly the inhabitants of tribal Britain in the first century A.D. did not speak English in any form—that came later, with the Anglo-Saxon invasions of the Dark Ages. Instead, two forms of early Gaelic were spoken: In the early fourth century B.C., "q-Celtic" spread from Ireland to the Isle of Man and Scotland, evolving into the Gaelic of today. The other form, "p Celtic," was spoken in the south and east and gave rise over time to the Brythonic languages of Welsh, Cornish and Breton.

Some characters of Boudica's time had names already in place and it was simply a question of choosing which form to use. In the list below, characters whose names are recorded in history have an asterisk.

As for the fictional characters, there are records of Gaulish names and it is therefore possible to choose those consistent with the period. However, for ease of reading in the modern world, I have incorporated some contemporary Welsh and Irish names as well.

The names below are spelled phonetically, the sound correspondences for the vowel sounds followed by an approximation of how to pronounce each name. In each case, there is equal stress on all syllables.

Breaca: \brā-a-kə\. \brā\ = the *a* of "prey"; \a\ = the *a* of "mat"; \kə\ = the *u* of "cut." Bray-a-ku.

Ban: \bän\. \bän\ = the *a* of "farther." Ban.

Macha: \ma- kə\. \ma\ = the *a* of "mat"; \kə\ = the *u* of "cut." Ma-ku.

Eburovic: \i-bŭr-ə-vik\. \i\ = the *i* of "tip"; \bŭr\ = the *oo* of "wood"; \ə\ = the *u* of "cut"; \vik\ = the *i* of "victim." I-boor-u-vik.

Sinochos: \sĩn-ə-kəs\. \sin\ = the *i* of "sign"; \ə\ = the *u* of "cut"; \kəs\ = the *u* of "cut." Sign-u-kus.

Arosted: \a-rôs-təd\. \a\ = the *a* of "mat"; \rôs\ = the *aw* of "law"; \təd\ = the *u* of "cut." A-raws-tud.

Gunovic: \gün-ə-vik\. \gün\ = the *u* of "flu"; \ə\ = the *u* of "cut"; \vik\ = the *i* of "victim." Goon-u-vik.

Dubornus: \düb-ər-nəs\. \düb\ = the *u* of "flu"; \ər\ = the *u* of "cut"; \nəs\ = the *u* of "cut." Doo-bur-nus.

Cunobelin: \kün-ô-bel-in\. \kün\ = the *u* of "flu"; \ô\ = the *aw* of "law"; \bəl\ = the *u* of "cut"; \in\ = the *i* of "tip." Koon-aw-bul-in.

Togodubnos: \tō-gə-dəb-nəs\. \tō\ = the *o* of "toga"; \gə\ = the *u* of "cut"; \dəb\ = the *u* of "cut"; \nəs\ = the *u* of "cut." Toe-gu-dub-nus.

Amminios: \a-min-ē-əs\. \a\ = the *a* of "mat"; \min\ = the *i* of "tip"; \ē\ = the *e* of "me"; \əs\ = the *u* of "cut." A-min-ee-us.

Efnis: \ef-nēsh\. \ef \ = the *ef* of "effervescent"; \nēsh\ = the *e* of "me" and the \sh\ of "shy." Ef-neesh.

Iccius: \i-kē-əs\. \i \ = the *i* of "tip"; \kē\ = the *e* of "me"; \əs\ = the *u* of "cut." I-kee-us.

Ardacos: \ar-dak-əs\. \ar\ = the *a* of "mat"; \dak\ = the *a* of "mat"; \əs\ = the *u* of "us." Ar-dack-us.

Gwyddhien: \gwith-ē-ən\. \gwith\ = the *gw* of "Gwynneth"; \i\ = the *i* of "pith"; \th\ = the *th* of "thin"; \ē\ = the *e* of "me"; \ən\ = the *u* of "cut." Gwith-ee-un.

Braint: \brānt\. \brā\ = the *a* of "fade." Braynt.

Cunomar: \kün-ô-mär\. \kün\ = the *u* of "flu"; \ô\ = the *aw* of "law"; \mär\ = the *a* of "farther." Koon-aw-mar.

BIBLIOGRAPHY

Barrett, Anthony, *Caligula—The Corruption of Power* (Routledge, 1993).

Campbell, Brian, *The Roman Army 31 B.C.—A.D. 337* (Routledge, 1994).

Cheeseman, G. L., *The Auxilia of the Roman Imperial Army* (Ares Publishers Inc., 1975).

Crummy, Philip, *City of Victory: The Story of Colchester—Britain's First Roman Town* (Colchester Archaeological Trust, 1977).

Cunliffe, Barry, *The Ancient Celts* (Oxford University Press, 1997).

Dixon, Karen R., and Southern, Pat, *The Roman Cavalry* (Routledge, 1997).

Gilliver, C. M., *The Roman Art of War* (Tempus Publishing Ltd., 1999).

Goldsworthy, Adrian Keith, *The Roman Army at War, 100 B.C.—A.D. 200* (Oxford University Press, 1996).

Hyland, Ann, *Training the Roman Cavalry* (Alan Sutton Publishing Ltd., 1993).

Le Bohec, Yann, *The Imperial Roman Army* (B. T. Batsford Ltd., 1994).

MacKillip, James, *The Dictionary of Celtic Mythology* (Oxford University Press, 1998).

Ó hÓgain, Dáithí, *Celtic Warriors. The Armies of One of the First Great Peoples in Europe* (Pegasus Publications Ltd., 1999).

Peddie, John, *The Roman War Machine* (Alan Sutton Publishing Ltd., 1994).

Rees, Alwyn and Brinley, *Celtic Heritage. Ancient Tradition in Ireland and Wales* (Thames & Hudson Ltd., 1961).

Salway, Peter, *A History of Roman Britain* (Oxford University Press, 1993).

Shirley, Elizabeth, *Building a Roman Legionary Fortress* (Tempus Publishing Ltd., 2001).

Spaul, John E. H., *Ala. The Auxiliary Cavalry Units of the Pre-Diocletaianic Imperial Roman Army* (Nectoreca Press, 1984, revised edition, 2000).

——, *Cohors. The Evidence for and a Short History of the Auxiliary Infantry Units of the Imperial Roman Army* (BAR International Series 841, 2000).

Webster, Graham, *The Roman Invasion of Britain* (Routledge, 1999).

——, *Rome against Caratacus. The Roman Campaigns in Britain A.D. 48–58* (Routledge, 1993).

——, *Boudica, the British Revolt against Rome A.D. 60* (Routledge, 1993).

——, *The Roman Imperial Army* (A & C Black, 1997).

Woolf, Greg, *Becoming Roman. The Origins of Provincial Civilisation in Gaul* (Cambridge University Press, 1998).

Woolliscroft, D. I., *Roman Military Signalling* (Tempus, 2001).

ABOUT THE AUTHOR

Manda Scott is a veterinary surgeon, writer and climber. Known primarily as a crime writer, her first novel, *Hen's Teeth*, was shortlisted for the Orange Prize. Her subsequent novels are *Night Mares*, *Stronger than Death* and *No Good Deed*, for which she was hailed by the *Times* of London as "one of Britain's most important crime writers." Born and educated in Scotland, she now lives in Suffolk.

Don't miss *Dreaming the Bull*, the next book in the Boudica series

Dreaming the Bull continues the story of Breaca—acclaimed as bringer of victory to her people—and her half-brother, Bán, now an officer in the Roman cavalry. Each stands on either side in a brutal war of attrition between the occupying army and the defeated tribes, each determined to see the other dead. Caught in the middle are Cunomar and Graine, son and daughter of two of the greatest warriors their world has ever seen. While in the heart of Rome, the Emperor Claudius and his implacable wife hold lives in their hands.

Knopf Canada